By
FRANK SWINNERTON

HARVEST COMEDY

HARVEST COMEDY

A Dramatic Chronicle

by

FRANK SWINNERTON

*"We are betrayed by what
is false within."*

DOUBLEDAY, DORAN & COMPANY, INC.

Garden City 1938 *New York*

PRINTED AT THE *Country Life Press*, GARDEN CITY, N. Y., U. S. A.

Contents

v

CONTENTS

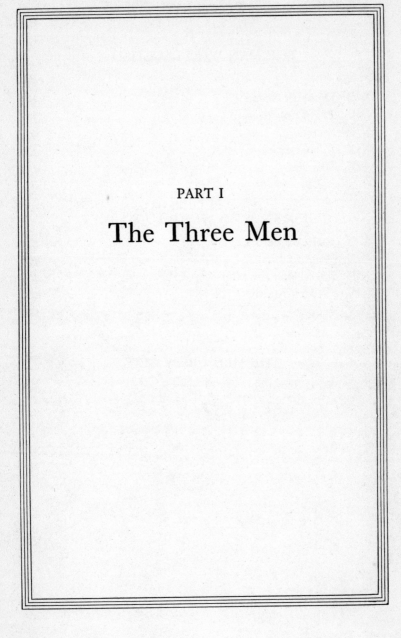

PART I

The Three Men

CHAPTER I

The Cap and the Baby

EVERY DAY, wet or fine, you can see walking along the broad promenade which runs from Brighton to Shoreham-by-Sea three elderly men. They all walk alone, and as they pass they give no sign of recognition; yet each must be perfectly familiar with the appearance of the other two. Moreover, the lives of all three, as the following story will show, have astonishingly crossed at different points during the last fifty years, and each has consciously or unconsciously affected the fate of the others in that period. It will be the same to the end. Do the three men know this? By the closest scrutiny you could not determine.

The first of them, and the portliest, is about sixty-five years of age. He has what is called a full face, displeasingly reddened by wind and sun, and decidedly flabby at the collar. His mouth, clearly visible below a thick grey moustache, takes a downward curve at each corner; his eyes are a glassy, haughty steel-grey. Some might imagine him a bully, others a heavy drinker; still others would look vaguely after him, wondering why it is that in spite of rather florid clothes he gives an impression of being short of money—a dealer in post-dated cheques and other financial ingenuities. A glance cannot penetrate to a man's pockets; but the questing thought behind such a glance often enough jumps to unwarranted conclusions. This pedestrian, whose name is Whistler—Robert Whistler—looks straight before him as he walks. You might think he did this to discourage duns or newspaper men. He is tall and stoutly built. He occasionally, when the breeze is still, smokes a cigar; and even this indulgence suggests a defiant ostentation of temporary plenty. Head up, mouth pompous, eyes hard, he progresses along the wide promenade at a slow pace, and never looks behind him or at the sea or at the flying traffic along the roadway.

The second of these elderly men is short, spare, clean-shaven, and of restless mien. His face constantly turns from side to side as he either dawdles or tip-taps in quick spasms of movement approaching a trot. One has no time to see the colour of his eyes; his lips, which are thin, occasionally part for an instant in a thoughtful, sneering smile which is no smile at all; he is past at once, or his shoulder is towards an observer, or, as if he prided himself upon a power to snap impressions, he has looked away again in a flash. Very often he glances back in a way which suggests that somebody —perhaps a ghost—has touched him startlingly upon the arm. In all weathers he wears a round hard felt hat, a tightly-buttoned single-breasted black overcoat, trim shoes; and he carries a carefully-rolled, undistinguished umbrella. There is something funereal about his garb; his face might be that of a solicitor, or an actor who has specialised in small parts such as those of men-servants, clerks, or detectives. His name is Richard Furness Firth.

The third man you would hardly notice at all in a first encounter, or even a second or a third. At a fourth, let us say, you might think to yourself: 'I've seen somebody rather like this chap . . . somewhere. Where was it? Shop, office, street? Gone!' But you would not feel sure about that until you had met him in the same circumstances day after day for quite three weeks. Then you would recognise him, look out for him, observe his unfailingly pleasant expression, and remember him for ever. He is not very tall, not very thin or fat, not very well-dressed or ill-dressed. He usually wears either an unobtrusive grey or an unobtrusive brown suit; his hat is a plain soft felt; he carries a cheap walking-stick. He walks just as everybody else seems to walk—you would not identify his moving legs among a hundred others. Not until you speak to him, or he speaks to you, is it apparent that perhaps, after all, he may be a little remarkable. But he would never agree that he is remarkable. Any such suggestion would make him laugh. 'Good heavens, no!' he would deprecatingly murmur. 'I'm the most ordinary man in the world.' What an old-fashioned thing to say in such self-important times as ours!

As I have mentioned, these three men may be seen every day walking within sound and sight of the green waters at Brighton. In no other seaside town in England—perhaps in the world—could they behave as they do; for Brighton is unique. To some a detestable place, to others (and Richard Jefferies was among them) it has peculiar brilliance. Certainly it is not as polyglot as Nice, that corner of earth common to men and women of every country; but one may meet here in an hour more extraordinary people than one would find in the same period in any but the greatest cities. Old actors, Judges of the High Court, jockeys and exquisites rub shoulders with retired clergymen and builders, elderly ladies with waddling goggle-eyed Pekinese, budding architects, holiday-making publicans and small tobacconists and clerks and shop-assistants. Dogs in dozens, wilfully ignoring every notice regulating their conduct, frequent the town, bark at the waves, walk on forbidden grass, and laugh at every peppered door-step. Rich men, very poor men, pampered ladies from the half-world, old spinsters very thriftily wearing still the smart garments of the 'eighties, downy boys, little film-fed virgins pathetically ugly in the latest boldness, and an immense assembly of the respectable (as of the Chosen), show every tolerance of one another and astonishing absence of social vanity. Brighton is a democratic town. In the summer, young people think it gay; at other seasons the elderly, who are residents, find it tonic. Our promenading men are but three out of many thousands who may live in Brighton to the age of a hundred years or more and die uncelebrated by obituary notices.

Occasionally the third of them, once identified, may be glimpsed during the day in a busy inland street. Then he is no longer alone, or if he is alone he waits meditatively outside a shop, leaning upon his stick and scanning the passers-by. That is truly one of the most interesting occupations in the world; but it is not for every taste or for every hour. And as a rule the three appear upon the sea-front only in the late afternoon, after teatime. Then Robert Whistler crosses from some distant spot in the direction of Shoreham, and slowly and haughtily strides towards the Aquarium and the Palace Pier. Then the dapper-stepping Furness Firth magically enters the promenade from a point near Ship Street, and slips and dawdles westward. Then William Harvest comes from nowhere at all, and goes either west or east (sometimes along the new undercliff-road towards Newhaven) apparently as his immediate impulse dictates. Backwards and forwards they pass, Furness Firth making the return journey between Ship Street and the Shoreham boat pool fully three times while Whistler manages it but twice (that considerable speed may be the reason of Firth's thin, leathery body, which is so restless and insatiable), and William Harvest travels hardly once there and back or at most inconspicuously one-and-a-half times, with an omnibus journey to bring him comfortably home. There is no doubt that Furness Firth sees Whistler every day; he sees everything and would relish every outward sign of inner disharmony. One suspects that Whistler is aware of Firth, if only as a passing shadow. It is possible—not probable—that neither consciously identifies William Harvest.

This has been going on for several years. Of course, in Spring and Summer, and in early Autumn, when evenings are comparatively long, large numbers of other pedestrians use this great promenade at the same moment. This would explain any lack of specific—of what may be called historical—recognition. But upon bleak and wet days, in Winter darkness and high winds when spray sweeps the pavement and clouds shut out every seaward prospect, our three strangers are unfailingly present. They pass; they never nod; they never perceptibly shun; their unconsciousness of one another is—or seems to be—perfect. The sea rolls; the figures come and go; and that is all.

II

It was not so formerly.

Fifty years ago, the county town of Moreton (anciently Moreton Lovell, and well-placed within twenty miles of the south coast of England) gathered itself, in the main, about two thoroughfares. One of these, Queen Street, was long and narrow and straggling; the other had once been a fine market place but had been transformed by certain demolitions into a short and very striking High

Street. The two intersected at right angles just where it had been thought proper a century earlier to set up the statue of a man in a wig. Moreton was not and is not a lively town; but liveliness is relative, and in those days it was livelier by far than its intimidatingly dull neighbours. For one thing, a grand agricultural show was held there every Summer; and, for another, in Winter travelling companies used sometimes to occupy the dingy theatre in Spenlove Row, and tread cautiously upon its dubious planking. That did not happen often. Political meetings took place at intervals in this same theatre; the not yet enterprising county newspaper was produced from a shaky building in a side street; in the Town Hall magistrates sat regularly to judge transgressors; and nearly nine thousand inhabitants managed to make a living out of agriculture, dairy produce, some brewing, fruit farming, retail trade, wealthy residents, Summer visitors in pursuit of milk, country butter and picnics; and in fact a host of activities which were all the time progressing with hardly perceptible steadiness to ruin. Owing, moreover, to the presence of a capable vicar, the local church was a respected and well-supported organism; and owing to collaboration between the vicar and a more than competent headmaster—Mr Otway—the Church School was better than most of its kind. The half-dozen intelligent people in Moreton delightedly believed that boys and girls who wished to learn anything at school could do so here. That may have been true; unfortunately none wished to learn anything, and the intelligent, as usual, were self-deceived.

The school of which we are speaking was an ugly dark grey stone single-storied building which stood remotely behind the ugly dark grey stone church of Moreton. It was shut off from the town, first of all by the church, and then by Daddy Griffin's large, square, red brick house, which had been in existence for nearly two hundred years. And it was reached from elsewhere by a flagged passage running between the cemetery and the high brick wall of Daddy's long garden. Indeed, the height of that wall was Daddy Griffin's retort to boys of an older generation, who had often enough shinned over its length to steal fruit; but its effect, coupled with that of tombstones visibly crumbling amid the cemetery's rank grass, was intensely gloomy. All men who passed through the alley were made to think of imprisonment, death, and decay; and as dusk fell no sensitive person made the hasty journey without feelings of almost uncontrollable terror.

On an evening early in November something more than fifty years ago, at a little after five o'clock, small knots of boys, released from lessons, were gathering in the school porch. A few of the brisker lads—those who fly effortlessly and thoughtlessly through the air like stones from a catapult—had already raced homeward in a cluster through the darkness; two or three, whose fonder and unoccupied mothers had come to fetch them, were sedately marching off under convoy; but one, a particularly small boy without escort and without comrades, loitered hesitantly within range of the vestibule lamp; looking with apprehensiveness along that dark alley leading towards the town. One could not, in so mystifying a flicker of light, see much of his face, save that it was round and large-eyed, or of his person, except that it was thin and small; but he was evidently not a coward, for he set his teeth and clenched his fists, and so perhaps he had an excuse for present irresolution. Moreover, at last he grew so bold, or so desperate, that he began to canter along between the high wall and the cemetery railings. Alas, the evening was extremely cold; and such heavy black clouds hung low in the sky that it was as if a velvet curtain hid all from those large, darkness-blinded eyes. In spite of the boy's every effort to still them, his teeth chattered. His feet were numb. Try as he would, keeping for safety as close as possible to the wall, he could not run at more than a snail's pace.

This was not surprising, for he was small and by no means muscular. And he was hardly more than half-way down the passage when the whisper of very fleet tiptoeing steps sounded of a sudden close upon his heels. Even as the little boy flinched, a rough hand caught the back of his neck and drove his head with stunning force against the wall, while another hand, equally rough, seized and tore off his cap. What then happened, the victim was no longer alert enough to discover. There was a windy rushing, a scuffling noise; two shadows much bigger than himself, and to a little boy in such a mood altogether terrific, passed at top speed; and everything was again dark. The very earth seemed charged with silence.

Dazed and cowed, Willy Harvest put a hand to his cheek and felt the sticky blood running there. He was so frightened at this that if his throat had been less dry he would have screamed again and again. Then a noisy troop of other little boys came bunching along the passage, kicking sparks with their iron-shod boots, and charging each other amid uproarious laughter. He was again knocked to the wall, but this time without malevolence; and, more by instinct than reason, although he was thankful for their protection, he joined the band, trotting blindly in a clatter for safety and the lights of the High Street. Only when he reached that haven, and when the other boys had galloped off in their several directions, did Willy realise that he had lost his cap. His blood froze.

III

At this same moment, in a house a mile out of the town, a baby was born. To her father, an unnecessary baby, an interruption, a threat; otherwise to her mother, who was a foreigner in a strange and still unfriendly land. The father, as was to be expected, was absent from home at the time; for his interests (he was a man of means and hobbies) called him often to London. Only the doctor, the nurse, and her mother took any interest in the baby, who as soon as she had welcomed the world fell fast asleep and thus early in life began to manage her own affairs.

'Will *you* tell Mr Manning, doctor?' asked the nurse, some time later.

Doctor Hodge scowled.

'How the devil am I to tell him?' he grumbled. 'I don't know where he is.'

'He's in London,' said the nurse.

Doctor Hodge struck his head with the knuckles of one hand.

'Bravo!' he muttered, sardonically. He shot a malevolent glance at the nurse. ' "Godfrey, England" will find him.' He was a thin, very tall man with a dry, grey, clean-shaven face and a sarcastic manner; and many of his remarks were unintelligible.

'No,' said the nurse. 'I think it's "George".'

'In fact, it's "Gilbert",' retorted Doctor Hodge. 'Well, I shan't telegraph. She's all right. Both all right. Why worry the man?'

'He'll be anxious,' remarked the nurse, who was washing the baby.

'As my foot,' said Doctor Hodge, whose keen eye was upon the mother.

The nurse, well used to the doctor, said no more. She was a professional midwife, and looked as if she had never been worried by anything in the whole of her fifty years. Clean, rosy, and grey-haired, she managed mothers and babies as if they had been rational beings. But she made no effort to manage—or even to understand—Doctor Hodge, who was a god, and a god who conversed with himself alone.

'I expect the cook's got a fuller address,' she said, as if to some third person.

Doctor Hodge laughed. At least, he wheezed, and two slight sounds, like clucks, occurred somewhere in his head. His thin mouth remained closed. Presently it was drawn to one side.

'He ought to register the child's birth,' he mused.

'That's what *I* thought,' observed the nurse.

'D'you know what her name's to be?'

'Minna.'

'Good God! It's the name of a fish!'

There came a protesting groan from the bed. As Doctor Hodge stooped over his patient he saw that her eyes were open—great globes in the dark hollows which her sufferings had created.

'Everything's satisfactory,' he said, reassuringly. 'You can sleep in peace.'

The mother spoke with difficulty.

'My baby,' she cried. 'That baby's name.'

'Nothing to worry about,' said the doctor. He was brisk. 'She's splendid.'

'A lovely little girl,' cooed the nurse, also reassuring. But the mother's heavy head rolled slowly from side to side. They had not understood her intention. She tried again.

'But that baby's name. It was my mother's. It shall be hers.'

'Well, it's a handicap,' muttered the doctor to himself. Aloud, he said: 'Of course it shall. And your mother will be as pleased as Punch with her namesake.'

Two tears formed in the large eyes. The patient did not answer. These cold English could comprehend nothing. The baby's grandmother was already dead.

IV

Because he heightened his wall it must not be supposed that Daddy Griffin was cantankerous. On the contrary, he was almost good-natured and frequently good-humoured. As a young man he had inherited house property in Moreton, and continuous thrift exercised since then for forty years had made him rich enough for every need. He was a busybody. He wrote letters to the Chalkshire 'Gazette' upon all kinds of subjects, from the desecration of the Sabbath to an old bone found in a gravel-pit (but, while the bone interested him, in expressing zeal for the Sabbath he indulged a private humour); and some of his letters—perhaps thirty per cent of them—were printed. He was not a Christian, and liked to shock the conventional by praise of Tom Paine, Charles Darwin, Thomas Henry Huxley, and Charles Bradlaugh. He detested Mr Gladstone. He never went to the theatre or read a novel. And although largely ignorant of the dead languages he had what was locally regarded as a curious obsession—the study of antiquity. He also loved his garden. This fact schoolboys could not understand; and a state of mutual malice existed accordingly.

Now it was Daddy Griffin's habit to take a brief stroll after his five o'clock tea; and that is why he discovered little Willy Harvest groping about in the passage under the wall, grizzling quietly to himself and every now and then leaning in despair against the cemetery railings. Because he recognised Willy as a boy (like some other elderly men he was highly sentimental about little girls),

Daddy Griffin was at first inclined to pass without comment. He changed his intention.

'Well, what is it?' he demanded, in a frighteningly snappy voice.

Willy was much too much alarmed to answer. Driven by panic, he almost nerved himself to run away.

'What? What? Your cap? Why couldn't you say so?' It was a one-sided conversation. 'Where? Who did it? Boys? Ah, boys! They've thrown it into the cemetery.'

Willy shuddered.

'Depend upon it!' snapped Daddy Griffin. 'Always do. Who were the boys? Don't know? Oh, that sorter thing's no good. Not with me. *You* know who they were. Eh? Speak up. It's no good telling *me* lies.'

He towered above Willy. He looked fully ten feet high. But he was not tall enough to see over his own wall.

'You'd better get another. What? Got no money? Who's your father? What? Got no father? What's your name? What? What? Can't hear! What!' He gave a jump as he heard Willy's name. For an instant his questions ceased. Then, much more quietly, he said: 'Oh, well, you come with me. What's that?' The quietness did not last. 'Why not? Why, you young fool, I'm taking you to get a new one!'

'Mother won't *let* me have a new one!' shouted Willy in desperation. And as Daddy Griffin ferociously exclaimed, he added: 'We can't *afford* it!'

That shrill voice—it was almost a scream—had a peculiar effect upon Daddy Griffin. Perhaps it alarmed him, or, by its passionate veracity, reached his understanding. He again spoke with less exuberance.

'D'you know who I am, child? I'm Mr Griffin. I'll *give* you a new cap.'

'Mother wouldn't let me take it,' cried Willy, having found his voice. 'I'm not to.'

'What d'you mean, "not to"? Don't be so damned silly. Not anything? Why, the woman's an idiot. A new cap! At your age I'd have jumped at it. Do you suppose you're any better than I am?'

This unanswerable question destroyed Willy's courage. Fortunately for him their colloquy was at this point interrupted. There were steps at the far end of the passage. A low voice, urgent and plaintive, pierced the air.

'Willy! Are you there, Willy?' Darkness still, but unmistakably a woman's voice. 'Willy!'

It was Mrs Harvest, anxious lest some terrible accident should have befallen her son; and Willy, deserting Daddy Griffin, ran up to her with a wild cry, hugging her arm, weeping, and beginning to stammer an explanation of his lateness and his plight. Daddy followed, at his snappiest:

'Good evening, madam. This young duffer's lost his cap. Won't say who snatched it; and won't let me give him a new one. Ridiculous. I tell you this, madam; you're bringing up this child to be a failure in life. A failure. The way to get on is to grab, tell tales, and keep your cap in your hand.'

'Thank you, sir,' answered Mrs Harvest. From the subdued respectfulness of her tone, Daddy Griffin recognised that she was a stubborn woman of refinement. 'I'm sure you've been very kind to him.'

'Not at all.' Daddy Griffin could not restrain his tongue. 'Can't get a word out of him.'

'He's very shy.'

'Stubborn.'

'Oh, no, sir. Some of the other boys are very rough.'

'They're boys, madam. That's enough. Savages. And they've thrown his cap away. He'll never find it. Absurd to look for it.'

'He shall have a new cap.'

'They'll snatch that, too.'

'I shall write to his teacher.'

'What good will that do? *He* can't do anything. If he tries, they'll pinch the child black and blue for "telling". Fatal. Fatal. But however, that's as may be. *I'll* buy him a new cap.'

'No. Thank you.' Ah, that was much too brusque! Hastily, she softened her words, although the tone had been sweet. 'You're very kind.'

Daddy Griffin opened his eyes in the darkness; for naturally he had observed the significant pauses between the sentences. Damn it, this woman—this *tender, gentle* woman, he sneered to himself —was unlike the ordinary women of Moreton. They'd have cringed avidly. This one was something of a lady. Poor, proud, absurd. What was she like? A woman of no size, Daddy Griffin could be sure of that; and soft-voiced enough to be attractive; but in this inky evening, although his eyes were very sharp, he could not distinguish her features.

'Why not?' he masterfully demanded. 'Any reason?' There was no answer; and Daddy, thinking he had gained an advantage, pressed it. 'He says you can't afford it.'

The quiet voice, nevertheless, answered with calm:

'He ought not to have said that. Fortunately it's not true.'

Daddy Griffin swallowed an exclamation. 'Good God!' he thought. 'What hoity-toity independence!' Obvious enough that she was threadbarely poor; people of means have less idiotic vanity. They take what they can get; and grin behind their hands.

'Well, I'm put in my place,' he grumbled. 'What?'

He heard her sharply indrawn breath.

'Oh, no, no! Thank you. Indeed I'm grateful. Very grateful. Come, Willy.'

What! Going? Daddy Griffin hesitated. His hand was in his pocket. Damn it, he couldn't see the wretched child's fist; impossible to slip anything into it! Besides, they were already moving away. He was baulked; and so, as usual in such circumstances, fell back upon gruffness. Touching his hat, therefore, he said 'Good evening' as boldly and abruptly as he could, so as to suggest boundless contempt, and strode off, leaving the field to the unworldly Harvests. Damn! He'd been snubbed! Treble damn! His tail was between his legs! Fifty-fold damn! He'd been caught without an answer!

v

After the darkness of the early evening, every black cloud passed away, and a full moon flooded the earth with light. Moreton put up its shutters and drew its blinds upon deserted streets. In all the homes, whether they were small or great, behind or above shops or in dignified detachment or at a distance from the heart of the town, fires glowed and tables were laid for a meal of some kind. Out at the Mannings', that new mother of German birth had fallen fast asleep, with her daughter—also sleeping—at rest in a cradle near by; at the Firths', young Dick Firth had sleeked himself and was ready to go to choir practice; at the Whistlers', over the grocers' shop kept by his father, Bobby was annoying the cat by pinching its tail and cuffing its head; and at the top of a house overlooking the High Street, Mrs Harvest was putting so neat a patch in one knee of Willy's knickerbockers that few but the maliciously minute would ever know it was there.

As she artfully stitched, she bent her head over her work; and in the soft yellow lamplight one could see that her hair had once been golden, although its colour now was lustreless and slightly greyed. She had very serious small lips, pursed together. A not very large nose just caught the lamp's beam. She was still in her fragile smallness rather unnoticeably pretty, and her present devoted pose, so rigid and so intent, held a pathetic grace of which she was unaware.

Near her, raised slightly by a tiny home-made hassock, Willy, aged not quite seven years, sat up to the table, reading a book by R. M. Ballantyne called 'The Coral Island'; and in this attitude of similar intentness it was made clear that he strongly resembled his mother in feature and character. He too was fair, but darker than his mother, and the hand supporting his head was very small, though browned and scratched. His forehead was hidden by a fringe of thick, well-brushed hair; and the chief difference between the boy and his mother lay in their expressions. She was always thinking of the past, so that even when she smiled a ghost seemed to stand before her; he, with no past to think of, had an innocently trusting welcome for the future. Both had clear brown eyes which held nothing furtive; in both the same weakness might be guessed, a passion for the steadfast endurance of pain.

The room on this Autumn night was silent, not very warm, and very barely furnished. A table (at which they sat by lamplight), three chairs, a square of old carpet, and a small bureau represented nearly all that was movable in it, and each of these objects, if one looked a little closely, revealed an imperfection. The bureau had a broken leg; the table at one corner was balanced upon a tiny block of wood; the carpet had more than once been scrupulously darned. None the less, the room was orderly, and it was not cheerless. Two pictures only decorated the walls, both of them slightly pallid water-colours the execution of which fell short of absolute proficiency. There was no photograph or portrait of any kind; and while Mrs Harvest's widowhood was indubitably authentic (for her husband's death was matter of familiar half-forgotten knowledge among the town gossips) nobody had ever seen any memento of that lost partner in her possession.

A short distance away, at the other end of this elongated square, the High Street, in the big old house against the garden wall of which Willy Harvest's face had earlier been dashed (the bruise by this time was blue, and the cut a dark ridge across his cheek), Daddy Griffin was seated at dinner.

His room was quite unlike Mrs Harvest's, for its ceiling, dimmed with smoke and cobwebs, was half as high again. The room was more than twice as large. Giant mahogany bookcases stood against one of the walls; against another a colossal mahogany sideboard was reared; in the third wall a monumental fireplace contrasted strongly with the meagre fire burning within the bars; while heavy velvet curtains which had once been green and which were now a brownish grey had been drawn across both windows overlooking the street. Everything in the room was tarnished and smeared and dusty with neglect; but in the half-light it all gave off a dull glow of aged splendour, from the fireplace with its lambent reflections to the books in their grand cases and the armchairs in their covers of faded velvet.

Daddy Griffin had one guest for dinner, his near neighbour, Doctor Hodge; and the two of them at this instant, while Willy and his mother bent together under the pale ray of their oil lamp, were just as absorbedly engaged in the practice of a great mystery. They were tasting a claret of which Daddy with reason thought well. It was a Léoville-Poyferré of 1864, not too full, and yet of so velvet a subtlety that both men, reflecting, simultaneously remembered vineyards in the sun, the uselessness of human effort, and a chiaro-

scuro of old sins and sorrows; while at another level of consciousness they experienced exultant optimism concerning the remote
future and at still another the most perfect present tranquillity of
spirit they had ever known.

'Hm,' sighed Doctor Hodge, still in reverie.

'A wine, eh?' asked his host, not troubling to assume an air of
nonchalance.

'A wine.'

No more. They nodded with profound understanding. Both
recognised that in so far as Moreton had any right to claim culture
or taste the claim rested upon themselves. Great men. Great men.
Men possessing depths of comprehension unknown to a herd lacking palate. That was what they thought. They thought further: it
takes quality to appreciate quality. They did not at once remember
that this is the stock consolation of the unsuccessful.

It was at such moments that Daddy Griffin liked in secret to
dwell, purring, upon his numerous but not innumerable benefactions. Recollections of them made him feel a good fellow, generous,
affable, and a gentleman. A gentleman: the word, Daddy felt, was
losing its meaning. Words, he continued silently to think, were
always losing their meaning, and disintegrating; but never dying,
and always in time reforming at a distance after each apparent
fatality. Like quicksilver. The miracle of language, he permitted
himself to say (still without saying anything at all), ever de-
teriorating, degenerating, depauperating, like an old family, and
finding new blood by marriage with coarser stock. The miracle
. . . Aye . . . Aye . . . In one aspect, though one might dread a
progressive decay, life was perpetual miracle. 'My God!' said Daddy,
under his breath. 'I'm inspired. I *know!*'

Vinous thoughts, these; daylight would efface them.

Both proud fellows were tall and lean, Daddy Griffin being much
the taller and because of his age and baggy clothes seeming much
the more emaciated. But this was their only resemblance. Doctor
Hodge, never affected by wine to any contemplation of the miraculous, had a keen Scottish face with a long thin nose and very bright
dark eyes set fairly close together. He might have acted as flattered
model, a few years later, for the original drawings of Sherlock

Holmes. But Daddy Griffin, though lost in his old clothes, had a plump, sagging face, a straggly grey moustache and beard, fang-like yellow teeth, and justifiably a greater air of always having indulged himself. The link between the two, apart from a common pleasure in wine, was interest in history and archæology; but both were gossips, and both loved humane wisdom and the exchange of relevant anecdote.

The doctor, indeed, was a man of excessively dry humour, quite content to keep his own jokes to himself. A cool customer. A reflective, silent fellow who sometimes, when he was alone, sat and laughed until the tears began to trickle down his cheeks. A bachelor who had discouraged the boldest mothers and the archest misses of his day. Where Daddy was abrupt, coarse, touchy, mentally bold but timid in action, the doctor had no daring, was interested in making simple people well again, and busied himself to obtain specialist treatment of all illnesses beyond reach of his own skill. He had neither money nor personal ambition. What he expected from life, otherwise than a day-by-day relish of experience and some eventual general recognition of his disinterestedness, could not be seen. The truth was, he expected nothing. It was enough, for him, to live usefully.

'Know a woman named Harvest, doctor?' asked Daddy, after sipping once more, sniffing his wine, and voluptuously closing his eyes. He spoke carelessly, with haste, as if he hoped to startle the doctor into candour.

'No.' It was the serious, obstinate murmur of a connoisseur who rejects an irrelevance.

Daddy persisted. There was a gleam in his eye.

'Think! You know everybody. Some sort of a lady.'

The doctor, shaking his head, set down his glass and pondered. Not only upon the question: quite as much upon its cause and object. That was his way; that was what made him seem sometimes rather slow. Then he frowned.

'Yes,' he said, deliberately. 'I do. She has a boy. Both very small. They don't trouble *me* much.'

'They're both healthy, then. That's something. What? I say that's something. Who is she?'

The doctor saw that Daddy's great hand was across his mouth, caressing both his moustache and his beard. The hand remained there, masking his face. Ah, thought the doctor; this was no idle question, and Daddy was seriously interested. What then? He said:

'She's the widow—I understand—I have been told—of James or John Harvest——'

Daddy interrupted with great vehemence.

'Jim. He was no good. Shot himself in a hurry, in case somebody helped him out of a mess.'

'The vairrdict, according to my recollection, was "accident",' said the doctor, leaning well back in his chair, with his head against the back of it, and steadily contemplating Daddy. Less a doctor, you would have thought, than a judge. The pose made him appear cadaverous.

'I know. But he shot himself out of vanity. Rather than take any help.' Daddy's excitement was undisguised. His fiery colour could not be hidden. 'It was a mania with him. A mania.'

Nevertheless, pursing his lips in the exasperating Scottish fashion, the doctor persisted:

'Uh-hm. I would have said there was a doubt.'

'She got any money?' demanded Daddy, impatiently brushing ignorance aside.

'Unless she's a miser, no. One wouldn't like to say definitely that she's not a miser. But probability's against it. At least, so I think. She lodges in two rooms. She and the boy.' Concealing great curiosity under deliberate slowness, the doctor drawled: 'That all happened just as I came to live here. I had nothing to do with it, pairrsonally. I'd re-e-ally forgotten the details.' He was unrewarded; Daddy only glared into the distance of memory. 'Somebody, I seem to recollect, persuaded him, or was said to have persuaded him, out of his little bit of money. Was that it? I entirely disremember.'

'That I can't say. He hadn't got any money. She's got nothing, then?'

'She's a dressmaker. You wouldn't suppose anybody would do such work as a hobby. At least, I would not. Genteel drudgery.

Would *you* stitch hour by hour? Ah, that reminds me——' The doctor broke off, made an entry in a small notebook, and sipped again at his claret. 'I can put some work in her way,' he explained. 'Baby clothes.'

'Good man!' Daddy at once appropriated credit for the kind thought. 'Glad I mentioned her. Yes, Jim Harvest was a fool—a long-headed, soft-boned, obstinate fool. I knew him. Knew all about him, too. But I didn't know he had a boy.'

'About six or seven years of age.'

'Yes, I've seen him. Tonight. A midget. And her. Another midget. Didn't know they lived in Moreton. Didn't know anything about her, who she was, what she did, or anything. Barely knew he was married.'

'But she gave evidence at the inquest, didn't she?'

'I don't know. I was away. I didn't want to be mixed up in it.'

'Were you?'

Daddy scowled.

'I've never seen her or heard of her. I didn't read the report of the inquest. Wouldn't. Shows you how quiet she is. What's she like?'

The doctor shrugged.

'As you've just said, quiet.' The words were dragged from him. Yes, but why 'wouldn't'? he asked himself. 'Independent. Skilful.'

'In other words, a fool. No doing anything for her.'

There was a long pause, during which Daddy Griffin twice swept his hand embracingly down his beard. He was very thoughtful. His cunning eyes evaded every inquiring glance of the doctor's; and the doctor, his head now sunk upon his breast, and his arm extended at full length, so that only the tips of his fingers caressed the stem of the wineglass, vainly cudgelled his memory for a clue to Daddy's agitated concern with the Harvests. Presently Daddy said:

'She'll ruin that boy. Make him like herself. Like his father.'

The doctor, reflectively smiling as the wine ran in his veins, answered:

'Well, I pity all lonely children.'

And Daddy, with raucous rallying, almost shouted:

'You don't! You never pitied anybody, you devil. It's I who've got the soft heart.'

The doctor smiled again. He had many secret opinions. They bred wisdom.

VI

It was not until nearly midnight, after Doctor Hodge had gone home, that Daddy Griffin strolled in his garden. He always took three strolls every day; the first after breakfast, when he went briskly round the town and kept in touch with its activities; the second after tea, when he passed the school and on light evenings walked the lanes reflecting upon Mediterranean civilisations; the third last thing at night, when he smoked a final pipe in the garden and addressed himself to the mysteries of the universe. If it was wet, he stood in the doorway, watching the rain and hearing the trees shiver. Then he felt himself become slim and young again, and at the same time, so elastic is thought, very old indeed, a believer in classic myth, and ready to die in his sleep.

But tonight, as it was fine, and the moon high in the sky, he took his old-fashioned lantern out of doors to shine in the thickets at concealed cats or other less likely interlopers. He felt no religious fervour or readiness for death in any form. On the contrary, he was gaily benign, expected to live for ever, and would have shied a stone from his rockery at any cat with the delighted certainty of missing his aim. It was now obvious that the frost would be severe; and Daddy was muffled to the ears and wore an old deerstalker hat. Upon his hands were thick woollen mittens which left his fingers free but kept his wrists warm.

He walked all round the garden, sniffing the frosty air as if it had been wine. The moon seemed very high above him in a far distant sable sky. Its whiteness yellowed the light of his lantern, so that he was quite ashamed of so trivial a contrivance. It bleached the grass, and caused Daddy to cast a squat black shadow there, as if some close-following grimalkin hung ever at his heels.

'Like shadows we are; and like shadows we depart.' The memory made Daddy Griffin shiver. 'Damned queer shadows, too!' Tonight they were so strong that they seemed to have substance and personality of their own. As strong as those poisoned draughts of memory which the mind repels until such a night makes them irresistible. Well, the follies of man and the immensities of the universe were old themes with Daddy, especially under the moon. He would have none of them. 'None! None! None, I say!' he suddenly shouted. . . . The noise of his cry came crackling back at him from the garden wall. His first thought was that it must have been heard all over Moreton, so still and frosty was the night.

Presently Daddy filled and lighted his pipe; and as the smoke drifted from its bowl the scent of tobacco was sweet in turn to his nostrils. That earlier mood gave way to one of calm, of content. It was a good world. Big and large, a good, comfortable world; at peace. The silence, so absolute that his steps audibly rustled the grass, was as effective as a covering wing. At peace. Plenty of money; in England, despite every threat of violence and distress, plenty of good, quiet, orderly, and not too industrious people; plenty of books to read in an infinity of sweet leisure; and nothing for Daddy to do but enjoy in tranquillity, and with an easy conscience arising from the continued practice of good works, the rest of his life. . . .

'The rest . . . enjoy . . .' Yes, but 'the rest'—eh? That suggested a limit, a set span. . . . 'I hear Time's wingèd chariot drawing near.' Damn! Any suggestion of limit was horror-striking. Especially after a cheery evening. He had had a couple of glasses of port. Sixty-five: how many more? Time he made a will and prepared his bed. Old, sinful, decrepit . . . A thousand ills he had done the world and his fellow-creatures, a million unexpiated sins mocked his contentment. He was old; he was—he must be—dying. Nonsense! You only died if you lost the wish to live. By God, he'd never lose his wish to live!

Suddenly Daddy Griffin paused in that ruminative walk. A small object lay near the edge of his lawn, like a tortoise. He approached, shining the yellow light of his lantern directly upon the object. Then his mouth spread in a slow smile. The subject of mortality, already slipping, slipped altogether from his mind; for he knew at once that his supposed tortoise must be the missing cap.

'By Jove, Jim's boy,' thought Daddy Griffin. He forgot everything for a few moments, lost in a tumult of memory. When he was again sensible of the garden and the night, he heard himself chuckling as he exclaimed: 'Whoever threw this aimed high. And to no good purpose.'

He stooped to pick up the cap. The whole episode of Willy Harvest was revivified by its presence.

CHAPTER II

The Pool

LATE IN THE SECOND SUMMER following the events just described, in a stuffy schoolroom filled with mote-laden sunbeams and an odour combining traces of salutary carbolic with the heat of bodies and dirty clothes, Willy Harvest sat snugly among forty other small fellows of his own age. He was so used to the room and its accompaniments that he was unaware of them; and his mind was gradually sinking to a state of afternoon stupor which was partly agreeable and partly loathsome. He was in his chosen place, about half-way between the top and bottom of the class; for thus early in life Willy had made a crucial discovery. It was that model scholars expose themselves to disconcerting questions and extra tasks, while dunces, unless they are good at games, receive anxiously indignant supervision from their masters. When one is both quick and lazy, mediocrity has its charms.

But the teacher of his class, by name Mr Stitch, was a zealot. Willy cared little for him. He was a tall, very young man with a ginger moustache, a polypoid nose, a recessive chin, and a throaty voice, who had come unhealthily from a London slum, wore a red tie, and took himself seriously. He took everything seriously; and as he surveyed the glistening faces before him Mr Stitch's dreams were all active ones. Nothing except passivity tired him. He wanted these boys of his, so young, so unformed, to be the most intelligent in England, all alike eager for knowledge, prizes, and power. They were to astonish the examiners in every subject. They were to grow into efficient, fine citizens, free men, noble ratepayers, and enthusiasts like himself.

'If you'll *work*,' he said—he had a passion for that horrible word

24

—'there's nothing you can't do.' He wanted to add: 'Look at me! Look at what I've done by determination, in spite of a boyhood of bread and dripping, tea, and sickliness'; but he checked himself, condensed his aside into a single coughing clearance of the throat, and continued: 'I don't say you'll all be famous. Great. Rich. But think of your fathers and mothers! Think how proud the town will be of you! Think of the credit you'll do *me!* I want every one of you——'

His glance roved among them, fanatically flashing and inspiring. For a moment he really saw these boys as instruments of destiny. They seemed to him to be like the morning stars singing together.

In the mass they looked, certainly, rather like a choir; for all their mouths were open. But it was a very hot day. The dirty little hands were extended (that was by Mr Stitch's instruction, so that they might be kept from other activity) palms downward upon the long inkwell-dotted desks, so much carved with initials, and so much a part, in memory, of school life that they are credited for ever with some of the sacred charm of the antique. Mr Stitch's spirit mounted. He felt very proud of his pupils. Poor, dirty, and ill-favoured as some of them were, he saw them all as examination-passers and diploma-snatchers; himself as headmaster, of this or some kindred school, busy with papers, kindly and keen, whose books—the Stitch Method—marked a revolution in educational theory. 'The man I want to see is Stitch.' 'There he is!' 'What, *the* Mr Stitch? This is indeed an honour.' 'Rise, Sir William.' . . . All reverently struggling to their feet . . . 'Bravo! Bravo!' For him the sunbeams were moted with a thousand confusing delights. And indeed if the schoolmaster may not have his dreams he might be as comfortable in Hell.

But in the midst of ecstasy Mr Stitch stopped. He glared.

'Willy Harvest!' he shouted. 'Willy Harvest! Stand up! This instant!'

To an accompaniment of general tittering and stir, Willy was nudged into wakefulness and prodded to his feet. He blinked, still in confusion. Alas, poor child, he had not realised that in order to escape Mr Stitch's notice at this exalted moment it was necessary to keep awake. Had his lips been parted, had his countenance worn an expression of stupid solemnity, he could have dreamed unchecked. But under such a glance, full of flame and fanaticism, a single pair of closed eyes must appear an enormity; and Willy's slumber had betrayed him.

Fatal error! He had become conspicuous.

II

To explain:

Willy Harvest at this time was almost nine years old; and the whole of his life had been spent in Moreton. Every shop-window in the town was familiar to him, and all the scribblings on the pediment of the wigged statue; all the broken places in the kerbstones, all the odd trees which somehow survived in unexpected corners, and all the short cuts and secret wonders such as grotesque knockers on some of the oldest doors and polished brass pots in the cottage casements. He knew by sight and name every boy in his class at school; and in the whole town knew about six grown-up people who said 'Hullo' if they saw him. But he had no general acquaintance. He had never been in the theatre, had never seen a painting of the smallest merit, had never heard anybody make a speech or play an instrument really well, and had never seen anybody dance except, once, a Jack-in-the-Green, and, once, a travelling bear; both of them kindred in style. He was poor and under-fed. He could not ask schoolboys to his home, and therefore was forced to refuse the invitations of those whose mothers were willing to receive 'some nice, well-behaved friend'. He rarely had new clothes, and what he had were home-made. The gift of a penny was such an event that it took him half-an-hour to spend it, and the offer of a ride in a milk-cart moved him almost to tears. For the most part he lived in his own inventions, and would have been 'old-fashioned' if he had not steered his path by the stars.

This was largely due to the influence of his mother. She had been the only child of elderly parents of rather faded gentility, and had been solitary enough before her marriage. When that marriage had been ended by violence she was left friendless and alone, so stricken that if it had not been necessary to work for Willy's sake she might have lost altogether the determination to live. But to friendlessness had been added reserve. She shrank from notice, and even when she had no work to do she spent much time in sitting deep in thought, or re-reading one of the books which remained in her possession through every trial. From her Willy had imitated silence and a reflective idleness; from somebody else, unknown, he had inherited a light heart. He adored his mother, and always accompanied her when she took work home to a customer. Upon the return journey, they walked arm in arm, slowly, Willy chattering and his mother proudly silent. She thought Willy perfect, but fortunately did not let him know this, for fear of spoiling perfection.

Willy had thus more character than the other boys in his class. He knew less evil than some of them, but he already had great shrewdness which he used for the purpose of avoiding effort. Not a wholly admirable character. No ambition to speak of; none of that desire to excel which carries men to high position in the world; but, on the contrary, as we have seen, a tendency to sleep when he should be up and doing. Hence the *débâcle* of this afternoon; other *débâcles* followed throughout his life.

III

Later, in the playground after school, two boys of a higher class than Willy's were amusing themselves with a ferocious kind of Touch. The boys were very nearly at the head of the school, both reputed to be clever, and both upon the point of graduation to what is called the School of Life. The education of one of them was finished: in three or four months he was to go into his father's business, and if he would stay there was already assured of prosperity, in the Moreton sense, for the rest of his life. The extent of the further education of the other was undecided; three men—his father, the vicar, and the headmaster—still very earnestly debated the problem.

But neither boy at this moment thought of school or career. Both ran in and out among their loitering or sportive fellows, and violently used the less wary of them as buffers or obstructions. Bigger boys might retaliate with kicks, and expect thereafter to be safe; but small fry were less lucky and more than one of them, including the crestfallen Willy Harvest, was sent spinning. Bruises were cheap that day.

As for Bobby Whistler and Dick Firth, their rough play ended in Dick being tripped and flung down upon the hard asphalt, from which he arose in a state of hysterical fury. Tearful, breathing very fast, and with a red spot in each white cheek, he sought madly to wrestle with Bobby and repay him for animal mauling with a rain of fierce, venomous, stinging punches. His smile had become a grimace; his features were so sharpened with anger that Bobby, scenting risk to a large, sensitive stomach, lost his nerve and fled. He went like the wind, Dick seething at his heels; while other boys forsook their own games and watched the runners out of sight.

Not until he was safe in the High Street did Bobby slacken speed; and then, breathing hard, but with a beam of triumph in his eye, he looked back. Dick, blown and resentful, was several yards behind; and upon Bobby's pause he drew level. Their shoulders bumped together. A glance of familiar hostility passed, such as two biting horses might give one another, treacherous and threatening. But the fight was not continued. In common with other friends, and some lovers, Bobby and Dick under the stimulus of an audience might taunt and spar and maul; but they never fought when alone. Then the dislike underlying their friendship merely estranged them.

It was so now.

'Comin' out tonight?' Bobby casually asked.

'No.' Dick shook his head. He was still trembling.

'Where going?'

Dick did not answer. He swallowed, and looked quickly over his shoulder, as if to discover whether anybody was within earshot. Nobody was near. Far behind them, groups of other boys and girls returning home from school split into parties of two or three and dispersed. But if Dick had been about to confide in his friend he changed his mind. A faint smile played upon his thin lips. The glancing swiftness of his grey eyes made him resemble a woman, but a sly woman. He seemed all nerves, and beside Bobby, who was so large, his fairness, his thinness and slightness, and his almost white eyelashes heightened an air of malicious delicacy.

Tired at last of waiting, Bobby repeated his question, rather bullyingly; and thereby did himself no good, for Dick coolly said:

'Stopping indoors.' It was an obvious lie, accompanied by a flicker of the lashes suggestive of scorn.

'You're not!' cried Bobby, incredulously.

'Yes, I am.'

'You're not!'

'I am, I tell you.' It was both cold and final. Dick moved away.

'Here! Dick! Dick, I got something to——'

There was no pause in Dick's movement. He feigned deafness. Soon he was out of sight, turning off through a little passage beside the bootshop twenty yards away, and so home.

Bobby saw him go, scowlingly ruminated, and at last, in a bad temper, crossed the street and passed through his father's big dark shop, which smelt of raisins, cheese, sawdust, candied peel, coffee, and tea. He did not observe his father, a long man in a white apron, stooping over the counter and writing something in a huge book. He did not sniff the assembled familiar odours of the shop. He did not glance towards that darker section of it which went right back into remoteness, where hams hung and bottles were racked and tins of corned beef were as thick as Autumn leaves after frost and rain. These affairs did not interest him; he was used to them. He was deeply, gloomily suspicious.

By the time Bobby had ascended the uncarpeted stairs and entered the stuffy room in which the Whistlers took their meals sullenness had descended upon him. Never, through long suppression, a cheerful boy, he was much more sensitive than he allowed anybody to guess. Also, he was deeply attached to Dick Firth, rather as a slow-witted man may be to a flirt; for Dick thought quickly and was incalculable, while Bobby's thoughts were as four-square as bricks. He was both wounded and puzzled. Nor did the atmosphere of his home lift any load from his heart; for at a moment when even furious reproof would have been welcome his entry seemed to be entirely unremarked and he felt, without knowing it, that, a nonentity, he was allowed there upon sufferance alone.

Mrs Whistler, indeed, hearing the tramp of heavy feet, was ready to protest at the sawdust he had brought from the shop, at his dirtiness, his lateness, and the wrongness of the place to which he had pitched his satchel; but her interest was concentrated upon two young women who were whispering together over the way. The half-familiar faces of these two young women, mysteriously intent, were very near one another, and what was said must have been well worth hearing; for as they parted the more communicative put a hand upon her friend's wrist—a warning to caution! But nothing could be heard; nothing could be guessed. They turned away, looked back, nodded meaningly, and disappeared; their secret still unrevealed to the watcher.

'Bother!' Mrs Whistler passed two quick hands down the face of her black silk skirt in a gesture of annoyance. She did not frown; she merely looked disagreeable and disapproving. The bold would have said 'queenly'. The irreverent, that she was rather like a well-fed cat. The truth is that she loved sleekly watching her fellow-creatures; and as she brushed dark coarse hair close back over her head and had a high-cheeked face with broad jaws and steel-coloured eyes and a curious long nose she gave the impression of being an outstanding mouser. Little happened in the street below that she did not see; and little happened in Moreton of which she did not presently hear what she so expressively called the ins and outs. She knew at first-hand how people paid their grocers' bills, whether slowly or with ungenteel quickness, reluctantly or with scraping; and as all must eat to live and as every man and woman can be cruelly judged by the test of money (possession of it, manner of spending it, honesty concerning it, and so on), she had an exacter mundane knowledge of the Moretonians than anybody else in the town.

Bobby feared and disliked his mother. Though he tried daily to outwit her, he never succeeded in doing so. And upon this afternoon his first impulse was to move as quietly as possible out of her sight across the room, sombrely vulgar with its mahogany and steel and plush, to the fireplace; where, flanked by giant vases full of rustling dried grass, he stood looking into a big, gilt-framed mirror. Bobby stared, however, not at himself or the reflection of browned walls or grass or pictures of angels and cattle, but at his mother, whose movements he could observantly follow without her knowledge. She was getting up from her chair—an immense figure of pale majesty—and making a stately progress to the door. How silent she was! If he had not seen her, he would not have known that she had moved. But it was teatime, and nobody but herself could unlock the canister. . . . Already, by her absence, the room seemed lighter and less thunder-ridden.

Still gazing idly in the mirror, Bobby then saw something which caused him to wheel about. It was a small disc, lying under the chair she had just left. In an instant he had charged across the room upon tiptoe, stooped, picked up the disc, and put it in his pocket; and then—like lightning—had resumed his stand by the fireplace as if nothing in the world had happened. Two rows of strong teeth showed in a grin that made him appear for once a happy boy. But again, as he stretched to his full height and threw back his shoulders, his hands all the while in his pockets, he changed to a young fellow of much more than his fourteen years. He might have been twenty, a big awkward youth with well-marked features, black brows, smallish eyes, and—like Mrs Whistler—broad high cheekbones. His brain began to click like a turnstile. What could he not do with this gloriously achieved shilling!

IV

Meanwhile Dick Firth, still faintly smiling and a little breathless, had passed upon his way through the court beside the bootshop. It led from the High Street to that small, almost equally old square in which he lived with his father and mother, and it hid him immediately from any but particular observation. Here not more than a couple of dozen houses surrounded a space of which the centre was a patch of very green grass. To reach the houses one trod upon flags set among cobbles; and each house had railings before it and two or three whitened or reddened steps up to the front door. In one of the houses Dick had been born.

He was pleased with himself for snubbing Bobby. Well pleased. Bobby was a brute; and he was tired of Bobby. He wanted nobody hanging about him all the time, lumbering, pestering to know why and how. . . . It had all got to be explained and re-explained and accounted for. Oh, it made Dick so *tired!* He didn't want to explain. Besides, he couldn't. He was going again—tonight—just on the chance—along the green lanes and byways towards the back end of Royals. . . . You never knew—more might happen. More! Anything might happen. . . . He turned mechanically to mount the steps to his home, burning with curiosity and excitement.

Dick had learned secrecy at home; for his father, although a grumbler with an acid tongue, kept his own doings close, and his mother, although insatiably curious, was ordinarily silent. Dick's mother would look, look away again, and preserve for ever in her memory a photograph of what she had seen. She memorised every sound. And she never forgot. To see the three Firths (for Dick at one time resembled his father and at another his mother) sitting about a table talking—or in some mysterious way communicating, for at such times they hardly at all parted their lips—and peering together through eyes that were no more than shining slits, was to receive a curious impression of triunity. All three were pale and a little sandy—Mr Firth bearded and unusually narrow-headed for a musician. They looked as if they lived by nibbling biscuits; for they even carried food to their mouths in confidence, and their mouths were kept bafflingly—and politely—closed as they munched. All of them had an odd habit of giving the tips of their noses every so often two little quick upward rubs or flicks with the back of a fore-finger, as if to dislodge a fly or staunch an unseen dribble. None of them ever laughed out loud, but all three laughed huskily and furtively—the sound was like that of falling ashes—at the same time giving that nervous flick to the nose. It was only when all three laughed at once that the ritual became irresistibly grotesque.

Dick found his parents already seated at tea; and here, as in Bobby's case, there was no word of greeting. But Mr and Mrs Firth did not ignore their son; they looked him over, faintly smiling, from head to foot, and Mrs Firth at once knew that he had been fighting and had dirtied his stockings and chafed a small hole in his knickerbockers. His father missed this damage to clothing, but perceived that Dick's knuckles had bled, which he thought might make them stiff for piano practice later. . . .

Washing made the knuckles smart again, and Dick assumed his place at table with a slightly vengeful expression. He drew his knees together, kept the damaged hands out of sight, glanced first at his father and then at his mother, who passed him a cup of tea, and began to nibble. The silence was long. At last:

'Extraordinary as it may seem to you, Richard, your mother and I take an interest in your doings,' observed Mr Firth. 'We should be glad to hear of your scholastic triumphs.'

'Oh, there aren't any,' murmured Dick, drinking.

'Too bad,' sighed Mr Firth. 'An unfortunate day, I suppose.'

'No; just normal,' retorted Dick. He had the appearance of snubbing his father; but his manner was demure. He actually hinted that he could have boasted to others, but that at home there was no need to boast.

'Your talented teachers merely passive,' said Mr Firth. 'Like your mother and me?'

'I don't know,' answered Dick. He forgot his hands, and stretched one of them neatly towards the bread-and-butter plate.

'Somebody's hurt your knuckles,' remarked Mrs Firth.

'Perhaps hurt by them?' inquired Mr Firth. 'Careless boy.'

'I fell down,' Dick said.

'Truthful boy,' said Mr Firth, smiling. 'Truthful boy.' He hardly ever laughed. Instead, he sarcastically grumbled. He belittled everything and everybody, with a kind of venom. Kings, statesmen, revolutionaries, idealists, and pessimists all alike aroused his contempt. He saw faults only, and no compensations; a fact which was due to the working in his soul of thwarted ambition. Mr Firth had dreamed dreams. He had seen himself as a great composer and a great conductor of orchestras; and he remained organist at Moreton church and a teacher of the piano to little boys and girls who seemed unable to synchronise the movement of their two hands. He could not get his works performed or published. When, in the ugly grey stone church, he played Bach, nobody listened, although if he romped through Mendelssohn's familiar marches more than one of his patrons, recognising musical commonplaces, made silent clapping motions of the hands at a subsequent encounter. Though he walked through the town with his head loftily cocked upon one side (like a person listening forever to the masters), nobody stopped to be patronised. And so he was ever ready to make fun of Dick. This, he thought, was good training for the boy, who would find the world full of unappreciative dullards.

'I admit I was wrestling,' said Dick. 'But it was with Bob.'

'That rough boy,' observed his mother, gently. 'I wonder you make a friend of him.'

'He makes one of me,' said Dick, with a sour grimace.

'And thus can't be entirely stupid,' commented Mr Firth. 'Whatever he may seem.'

'A grocer's son,' whispered his wife. Mr Firth, in a sighing speech behind his hand, retorted:

'She reproaches me because I can't afford to send my son to a public school.'

'But fortunately he will be leaving school at the end of the year. I hope you'll gradually . . . graaaadually escape from him, dear boy,' said Mrs Firth.

'I think so, mother,' replied Dick, flicking the tip of his nose.

'Oddly enough'—it was one of Mr Firth's conversational gambits to say 'oddly enough' or 'extraordinary as it may seem'—'Mr Manning was in church this afternoon. I was playing some of the *"Wohltemperirte Klavier"*. Just for a little while I fancied he was listening to me——'

'And was he not?' asked Mrs Firth, obediently.

'My dear!' replied her husband. 'That man! He was examining, if you please, the brasses. Somebody had told him there was something good to be seen. He found there was nothing; or so he said. Absurd fellow. Full of opinions. He told me he had no ear for music. I had been wasting my time. He thought I'd been playing something of Stainer's!'

'But then he's really quite eccentric, darling,' said Mrs Firth.

'Quite, darling. And his house is as eccentric as himself. What goes on there—by common report——'

'Sh,' interrupted Mrs Firth.

Dick kept his eyes upon his plate. He tried to look unconcerned. But nothing more was said about Mr Manning and his house. The subject was shelved.

Nevertheless, Dick had formerly heard his father speak of the people at Royals as half-mad. Mr Manning crazy, and his wife German. Their cook a maniac. As for the place itself, it might for all the world be a lunatic asylum, as he had discovered by examination when summoned to tune a cracked old spinet that was not worth five pounds or five pence. The house was dark and disgusting, all the rooms having low ceilings and black beams, paved with bricks like a stable, and as ugly as sin. The spinet itself stood upon bricks and was rusty and rotted with damp. Mrs Manning speechless; a fat coarse child hanging on to her skirt; Mr Manning abrupt and rude, interrupting him as he spoke, and, without attending to Mr Firth's complaints of the spinet, going out and slamming the door behind him . . . Sly maids giggling, and the cook in the kitchen with the back door open, singing like the Salvation Army, enough to drive a musician as mad as herself. As he left, unescorted, Mr Firth—as if infected by the uncouthness of the establishment—had slammed the front door. Nobody had noticed.

'There's a parcel for you, darling,' presently said Mrs Firth. 'From Augeners.'

'Damn!' muttered Mr Firth. His nose reddened at the tip. He flicked it. Then, smiling gently at his wife, he added: 'You're always tactful, dearest.'

Dick hardly noticed what they were saying. He thought only of Royals.

v

And at Royals, three hours later, Minna Manning lay in her cot. She was supposed to be fast asleep, and she had shut her eyes firmly so as to go to sleep. But the rustlings of the evening

kept rousing her, and a slight breeze moved the window-blind in
sudden plunges of alarming noise. She lay quite still, her fingers
and toes curled, her tiny mouth like the tip of fragrant logan-
berry, her brow white and smooth, and her eyelashes very long
indeed.

Such thoughts as Minna had were very small, for she herself
was very small—not quite two years old—and she remembered
hardly anything besides the biscuits and milk which she had
eaten and drunk a little earlier, and the soft brown shrew which
had been running and sitting bright-eyed in the garden path an
hour before bedtime. But although not very much crossed her
mind at this moment she foreshadowed all that was to happen to
her throughout life by her silence and smiling patience in face of
sleeplessness. A call would have brought mama instantly to her
side. She did not call. A cry might perchance have brought the
ugly man who made faces at her; 'papa' they sometimes (never
intelligibly) called him. He was a stranger; she did not think of
him in any way unless he was before her, when she unwinkingly
observed his grimaces and then calmly removed her gaze to something less unpleasant. He used to say: 'Not a success,' and wander
out of the room snapping the fingers of both hands. If he had
ever done this to begin with, Minna might have found him
amusing; but she did not know how to refer to the matter, and
came to regard that performance as associated peculiarly with his
disappearance and her own disappointment.

In the next room, her mother was standing talking to Mrs
Harvest; and the two—both so fair, and one so sadly buxom
against the other's tiny slender melancholy—were bending over
a little dress which Mrs Harvest had just brought home for
Minna. Their heads were close, their eyes serious, their lips com-
pressed. It was a moment of great gravity. Mrs Manning unfolded
the frock and held it up before her by the shoulders, more un-
smiling than usual in her pleasure. Neither saw anything ridiculous
in so minute a piece of finery.

'Ye-e-es, ye-e-es,' Mrs Manning was saying, in her strange accent.
'It is good. I like it. But this light—the low ceiling, the small window—it is so dark I cannot see the colour.'

'I'm very sorry. I only finished this evening,' explained Mrs Harvest, apologetically, believing herself to be in some manner reproached for the late hour. 'So much smocking took me a long time.'

'Oh, ye-e-es, I know. Yes, I think not of this, but of you. Bringing it tonight, you see; when tomorrow would do.'

'But I'd promised for today.' Mrs Harvest's little brow puckered.

'You always keep them—eh?' Mrs Manning gave a friendly shrug and grimace. 'Not all do that here. You have been too kind. Did you come alone?'

'My little boy is in the garden. I told him to keep still—if he could.'

'He will not, eh?'

'I hope he will.' Mrs Harvest smiled. For an instant she looked almost mischievous. 'He's very good—as a rule.'

'You are fond of him? You love him?'

'What strange questions!' thought Mrs Harvest.

'He's all I have,' she said, in a wondering voice.

Mrs Manning acknowledged the confession with a pressure of her firm hand upon Mrs Harvest's arm.

'It is the same—with me,' she said, quickly. 'And you are lonely, too. Like me. It is terrible to be lonely. One is never happy.'

As they spoke, they had been moving imperceptibly towards the door, and Mrs Manning paused for a moment ere they descended the broad, shallow stairs to assure herself that Minna was asleep and at rest. She was deceived. Then they continued their way directly into the living-room below.

It was a very large room, with walls of coffee-coloured plaster, smoke-begrimed, a floor of deeply worn bricks, and an enormous old fireplace in which, on winter nights, giant logs would smoulder and flame. The implications of age lay heavy upon this room, which was essentially unchanged from what it had been in the days of Charles the First. Several doors led from it into other rooms, and one of these, which was open, revealed a fragment of the garden in twilight. They stepped over the threshold.

In the air it was much lighter than it had been within; for in spite of the first greying of twilight day was still luminous. If he had kept as still as his mother wished, Willy should have been visible. He was nowhere to be seen.

Even as the women took two or three steps forward, there came through the evening silence a loud scream, a crashing and tearing noise, as if the branch of a tree had snapped and fallen to earth, or as if giants were in combat; and an instant later something resembling the splash of a heavy body in water was heard. Both, crying out, began to run down the path towards the sounds; but Mrs Harvest was so frightened that she could hardly save herself from stumbling. 'My boy! My boy!' she said, over and over again. 'Oh, my little boy!' she felt as if she were dying.

And as they hastened they were almost bowled over by a galloping lumpish girl who fled wildly from the disturbance and in her panic roughly pushed past them.

'Grete! Grete! What has happened?' gasped Mrs Manning, in German.

The girl, with a smothered exclamation, ignored this cry, and disappeared into the house; while Mrs Harvest and Mrs Manning, more terrified than ever, struggled on.

'That is the girl. Minna's stupid nurse. Oh, she is mad!' cried Mrs Manning. 'I am sending her away.'

'But my boy!' exclaimed Mrs Harvest, at the same moment, not hearing or understanding what had been said. 'It was *his* voice!' She called frantically. 'Willy! Will! Where are you? Will!'

There was a swirling of water, more plunging, more tearing of bushes. Silence.

'Will!' cried Mrs Harvest. 'Will!'

Her voice echoed through the air. And from somewhere not very far away there came an answering 'Coo-ee'. It was small and shrill, and very plaintive.

'He's alive! He's safe!' stammered Mrs Harvest, almost falling; while her companion uttered a deep sigh. 'Oh, thank God!'

The dusk was now all about them, deeper and darker than it had been because of the heavy overhanging foliage. They were blinded by the shadows and their bewilderment. But they heard a second hail; and a moment later both descried a small figure in the distance.

Willy, left alone in the garden at Royals, remained standing very still, as his mother had suggested. He put his hands in his pockets, screwed up his eyes, and contemplated the lavender bushes. Twelve, thirteen, fourteen of them . . . But after a time he looked very longingly to the ground beyond these bushes, where trees shed occasional slow leaves and thick undergrowth promised impenetrable cover for bushrangers and other likely bandits. He took a few steps towards adventure, returned, glanced at the silent house, waited with less patience, and at last dawdled his way down through the immense garden in the direction of that mysterious shadow.

It really was an immense garden, and largely in a rough unculti-vated state. And at Willy's home there was no garden: two rooms upon a second floor, and the rest forbidden territory. Therefore the garden at Royals, which had no palpable limits, no walls or neat lawns or flower-beds, but ran to wilderness and the unknown, was at one glance a combination of the Sahara and the Brazilian jungle, the Prairie, the Rockies, and the Australian Bush. It was the very island upon which the Swiss Family Robinson was cast, but free from all human bores. Every turn revealed new vistas, new hiding-places, new incomparable scenic effects for play. Never a grown-up; never a check . . . The bushes grew thickly, the leafy boughs hung so low as nearly to meet the topmost wealth of the bushes. From the earth arose a lovely scent of old leaves and departing heat; a long trail of ants travelled with determina-tion over miles of mountainous country; invisible birds whirred from shelter to shelter. Presently even a stream, running low indeed, but between grass-green banks and into the heart of a little wood . . . Anything might be made to happen here, from a grateful lion to hostile Red Indians. Hark!

At a sound, remembering every lesson of the pathfinders, Willy flung himself with reasonable silentness into the long grass, his heart beating quickly, and his spirits exalted. He kept perfectly still, listening with his ear to the ground. Nothing followed. He lay amid the whispering silence of the evening. There was opportunity for a secret voice to tremble through his consciousness; and the voice, he thought, said plainly: 'Waugh! It is good! The paleface knows the secrets of the forest!' Ever more faintly, so that Willy strained to hear the dying fall, and yet pierced unerringly to the Red Man's honourable recognition of mastery: 'Great Big White War Chief!'

That was all. No more words came through the hush: Willy listened in vain for further compliment. But at least he had not been mistaken in his first leap at truth. There was other movement in the wood besides his own and that of the birds. Stealthy sounds arose which he heard only because he was listening for them. He raised his head and crawled forward, ready at a sound to drop once again into concealment. Yard by yard, listening, twisting and turning, avoiding every open space, unconsciously moving uphill and ever to the left of his starting-point, away from the stream, he crept in delight. His heart sang. Hark!

Something caused our hero to sink noiselessly into the long grass. He was hidden. Just so might a great snake have lain concealed. . . . A snake? His skin prickled at the thought. No snake. 'Oh, God, don't let a snake come!' Forget snakes. Forget . . . Hark again! A twig had cracked. There was a long silence. Listening hard, Willy heard a faint rustle a few yards ahead of him and to his right hand. He made a few more cautious movements, found his progress barred by a solid hedge with a road beyond it, then again by the sucker growths of a large beech-tree; and with an extraordinary thrill of excitement—his best yet—discovered a way to squeeze between these sucker growths and squat beneath their dense shadow as in a wigwam. And as he lay snug he almost cried out, for ahead of him, not ten feet away, there rose from cover the head and shoulders of another boy, bigger than himself, his back to Willy, and all his attention given to some sight at a lower level.

Presently the other boy, bent upon nearer approach to the object of his interest, took some further steps which carried him out of Willy's sight. Like a flash, Willy left his friendly beech, whipped across the intervening ground, discovered new if less ample shelter, and was in time to see the other boy pressing his arms to his sides as he hid behind a tree trunk. In the same moment Willy recognised the stranger as Dick Firth.

By now Willy knew what it was that so strongly aroused the curiosity of his old enemy, and he jumped with excitement. Standing upon the higher land he rediscovered his bearings; first a hint of the open garden, then a faint glimmer of that friendly streamlet, finally in an open space in the wood a fair-sized pool. The space, at the bottom of the rising ground occupied by both boys, was surrounded by trees, and to the naïve must have seemed completely secluded; for Grete, the uncouth nursemaid supposedly in charge of Minna, believing herself unobserved, was splashing half-naked in the pool. She was singing in a cracked ugly voice, and dancing clumsily, twirling her legs and grotesquely gambolling. Her dress had been cast aside, and lay by the edge of the pool, together with petticoat and blouse. To the knees and above her legs were bare; baggy pink drawers of flannelette and chemise of cotton were her only garments; her hair was tumbled; and to Willy, who had never seen a picture by Hogarth or Rowlandson, she looked like a witless being from another planet.

But it was different with Dick Firth, who watched with trembling intentness. One would have thought him entranced. He took another step forward, so that he stood with his right foot upon an exposed and twisted root which projected immediately over the edge of the pond. Then with both feet, as he precariously balanced himself. What he intended to do next was not clear; but Willy, visited at this moment by irresistible impulse, crept silently closer. With terrible swiftness he ran forward, let out a piercing scream, and threw himself flat upon his face behind a bush not two yards from Dick.

At that scream, Dick slipped, clutched frantically at a dead branch which snapped in his hand, caught again, lost his footing and hold, and fell headlong into the pool a dozen feet below. There was a succession of female squeals, a great splashing, a tearing of leaves and branches. A moment later, with loud panting,

Dick floundered out of the pool, struggled up through the tangled growth dripping with water, passed not more than a few inches away from a now conscience-stricken Willy, and crashed through shrubs and young trees and so, after wild rustlings, into the lane and away at top speed. Willy heard his running steps go echoing into the distance, until all sound of them was lost.

VII

'You did not see the man, eh?' questioned Mrs Manning. 'No? He was a thief?'

'I don't know,' answered Willy, looking innocently up into the lady's face with a rather puzzled air (for now that the excitement had passed he was uncertain of everything). 'I saw *some-body*.'

'You are not injured?'

'No, ma'am,' said Willy, truthfully; as his mother again put her hand quickly to his shoulder and his knee, to make sure for the fourth time that he had not been in the water.

'You saw a woman? A girl?'

'Yes.'

'They talked?'

'Oh, no.'

'What were you doing, Will?' This was from his mother.

'I was playing Indians.'

'What is that, Indians?' Mrs Manning was bewildered.

'Pretending I was a Red Indian. You see——'

'Will, what made you scream?'

'Well, I saw——'

'Yes, yes, yes; you saw?' Mrs Manning was very much agitated. 'That is what I want to know. You saw a man. What did he do? A big man? A little man?'

'Oh, rather small . . .'

'Did he run away? Did he fall in the water? Was he hurt? Who fell? Oh, dear me!'

'Did you see his face, Will? Did you know him?'

'I . . . I . . . Well, I . . . Yes, he fell . . . he ran away.
. . . I sort of saw . . . Oh, look there! What's that?'
He gave a little jump and pointed towards the house.
'Look! Look!'

At first it might have seemed to a pair of inquisitive elders
—or at least to Mrs Harvest—that this glimpse of Willy's was
imaginary, for their slower eyes missed what he had seen. Nevertheless, although the diversion came to him now as a godsend,
it was true that he had spied something in the distance which
moved. It was something small and white, apparently shapeless—
a tiny ghost—a blanched shadow—and it was immediately hidden
by the lavender bushes.

'Jesu!' With a faint scream, Mrs Manning left the others.
They heard her scream again upon a high note, but this time
not in terror; and a moment later they found her closely embracing a tiny girl, clothed only in her long nightdress, who
sat straight up in her mother's arms without a trace of fear.
Amid all the exclamations of horror natural to the moment, Mrs
Harvest slipped off her shawl and put it about the child's shoulders, while both mothers exchanged a melancholy glance in
which dread, sympathy, wonder, and condemnation of youthful
prankishness were communicated and reciprocated.

Minna, however, very fair and blue-eyed, ignored the anxious
scrutiny and exploring hands of fear. She looked calmly down
at Willy, sitting upright in the borrowed shawl as if she had been
a queen at her coronation. She had the air of possessing secret
and deeply amusing knowledge of all those before her; and
in fact, having made with success for the first time, unaided, a
very hazardous journey from her cot to the garden, was brimming with self-assurance. When she saw that Willy was returning
her interested gaze, she stretched out a hand.

'Boy,' said Minna, informatively and with recognition of essential difference.

The hand was vaguely scrabbled on Willy's hair.

'But what a bad *girl!*' protested her mother, holding Minna
tightly.

'No.' It was the gentlest of contradictions. 'Not a bad girl.'

'I do not know what you will become when you grow up,' grumbled Mrs Manning.

'A good girl,' remarked Minna, with every sign of confidence. Roguishly, she flung both her arms about her mother's neck, and rested, cheek to cheek, in safety. But she still pored upon Willy in the dusk, seriously, musingly, as if she wished to understand him, or as if she were determined to remember him for ever; and even when her mother turned to carry her to the house she looked back until nothing more could be seen.

CHAPTER III
Death Calls at Moreton

IT WAS A WINDY NIGHT in November rather more than five years later. The streets were deserted, for the wind was chill, and in those days, once work was done, few except young lovers ventured away from the fireside. Every lamp in Moreton, bullied by the wind's assaults, shone brightly at one moment and hardly at all at the next. Accumulations of dust and waste paper had been blown miraculously into a thousand corners, so that the flags and setts and cobbles of the town were as clean as if they had been lately scrubbed. A wanderer, raising his eyes, would have been charmed by the colours of drawn curtains and lowered blinds, nearly every one of which was illumined from within by the glow of an oil lamp, and by the mysterious shadows passing now and again across the lighted area. He would have dreamed of the warmth within, the cheer, the love and disinterestedness of sturdy English provincials. But he would also, perhaps, with a sinking of the heart, have realised how small a chance he had of penetrating these homes, from which strangers were excluded for ever by the English passion for privacy.

Our wanderer, craving company, might have found it in any of the seventeen public houses of Moreton; but these public houses were so dingy, so ill-lit, so much—saturated as they were with the odours of old pipes and old swipes—places where dull men sat and smoked and drank and spat the evening away, that his spirit might have broken before he had sampled more than two or three of them. Things were decidedly better at the one hotel of any size, a flat, stucco-fronted Georgian building, with

45

portico and white-washed door-step, which was called the Royal; but the Royal, standing well down the High Street, just before it narrowed, had a history and a character of its own, and shone like a beacon in the general darkness. There, under the management of Thomas Taplow, a rosy-gilled, sharp-eyed man of business, cheerfulness radiantly glowed amid well-cleaned gas globes, well-polished glasses, and the cordiality of a fire big enough to thaw even a modern misanthrope.

All sorts of people used the Royal; some few to stay in when they visited Moreton for business, and more for the sake of internal and external comfort. But it was the parlour, where the giant fire shed its glory, that drew the men of Moreton. Few women, it is true, and these of no great merit, would be seen there, for in the eighteen nineties the sex observed its old traditions; but among men, at night, if some were still 'Sir', some 'Mr Robinson' or 'Mr Harris', and others again 'Sam' or 'John' or 'Jubbs', the assemblage was free and unsullied by class doubts.

In this place, all that was done in Moreton was discussed. Sometimes monosyllabically, sometimes in detail, sometimes with hardly a word spoken. If you wanted to know a man's reputation in the town you had but to pronounce his name. If you wanted to hear the truth about any local happening of importance, you had but to hint a question. There you learnt all, from politics to rumours of war, from cattle-prices to current morals, from the difficulties of little Sims, the coal-merchant, who gave too much credit and exacted too little, to the superhuman squeezes inflicted by landlords, rate-collectors, and other land sharks. But at a first entrance it was possible to be deafened by the noise of these confidences in chorus, or choked by smoke, or horrified by the sight of happy men; and the queasy stayed away from the Royal.

The queasy included, for instance, Daddy Griffin, who in middle age had given up going there because he was too conscious of discriminating eyes. They included Mr Whistler, the grocer, long ago weaned from society by his wife, a water-drinker who hated the confidences of the bar as much as she loved those of the tea-table; the vicar, who was strict and who had not yet to beat up his congregation by brotherliness; Mr Firth, the organist, who, though he might have deemed a German Bier-Halle the home of musical taste, scorned the hooves of his fellows; and Mr Manning, of Royals. Mr Manning, arriving one night in company with a familiar, was greeted by devastating silence. One would have supposed him a detective. And in this atmosphere, with dry grimaces upon his face, he stayed no more than five minutes that seemed like an hour, left snapping his fingers, and never again ventured through the door. For the rest of the male population of Moreton, the parlour was a club.

And on this windy night in November, about seven o'clock, a small group was gathered about the end of a long table in the far corner of the room. Glasses stood before the group, and George, the waiter, with sharp ears jutting, busied himself at a handy distance. Four of the men listened intently, their heads together, while the fifth, speaking very low, and all the time allowing the gaze of his prominent grey eyes to roam in case eavesdroppers were abroad, was communicating something of breathless interest. He said:

'I shouldn't have paid any attention, only they were in the corner, see? They were right under my window. By the pillar-box. It's quiet and dark—we often get girls and boys there, and stir them on, too. But these weren't girls and boys. She kept quiet—didn't say much—but . . . sort of snivelling. I thought it was some trouble about rent or money or something, till I saw she was holding his hand. I couldn't hear what she said at first. I could hear him. He said "It's terrible. It's terrible. But what can *I* do?" So I took a look, see? I was—well, I was as near them as I am to George——'

'Sir?' said George, coming closer.

The whole party grinned at this interruption.

"He's not deaf, is he!' laughed the narrator. 'All right, George; never mind. Forgive you this time.' There was a slight delay, until George had sufficiently removed himself. Then the story was resumed. 'Well, as I was saying, I took a look. . . . There she was, had hold of his hand in both of hers—leaning up against him——'

'Come on, Tom. Out with it!' grumbled one of the listeners,

straightening a cramped back. 'Why, damn it, they've been there half-an-hour already.'

The narrator's face darkened. He was ruddy and full-lipped, and a mischievous smile constantly hovered upon his face. It was clear that he prided himself upon ability to tell a tale, and indeed he was a noted bamboozler of women.

'And she said: "She's seen. You know how she creeps about." And he said: "No, don't be silly. Well, what could she have seen?" And she said: "Oh, yes, she has," she said. "And I'm going." He said: "Don't do that," he said. "If you went, what should I do?" he said. And she said: "Come with me," she said. "It don't matter. Nothing matters," she said. "Only let's get away from her," she said. Wait a bit! I hadn't seen him up to then; but just when she said that he sort of groaned, and said: "Oh, my God, Sarah; I wish she was dead," he said. "I wish I'd got strength to kill her," he said——'

'Sarah!' murmured one of the others. 'Well, who was she?'

'Just coming, old impatience. . . . Well, when he hollered like that, I thought to myself "Oh, you bloodthirsty villain," I thought; and I saw his face. And who d'you think it was?'

'Monte Carlo Wells!' cried the most facetious of the group; but——

'Oh, Christ!' exclaimed the impatient listener, in disgust. 'He makes a three-volume novel of it!' The others crowded nearer. In another instant their curiosity would have been satisfied; but before the narrator could speak again there was the noise of somebody shoving violently against the door of the parlour, a blast of wind swept the place from end to end, and a man entered as if he fled in terror from the angry gale.

A young man, who might have been in his earliest twenties, this newcomer would have attracted attention anywhere merely by his size. He was both very tall and very broad, of that dark type, black-haired and black-browed, which normally is fresh-coloured. But as he strode forward, ignoring everybody and going straight to the bar as if he were a somnambulist, it was the strangely ashen whiteness of his face that impressed those who watched.

So far, the stranger had appeared not to see the group at the table; and they, upon their side, observed him with considerable interest, not only because he was clearly labouring under great excitement, but because he was known by sight to each member of the group. All stared as he lifted an unsteady hand and tossed off a glass of neat whisky, and then each glanced at his neighbour. Not a word was spoken; nevertheless every look, however guarded, was packed with judgments. In particular, the narrator of that story, as he devouringly contemplated the unhappy young man, showed glittering eyes in which the smile had been replaced by something like malignant avidity.

The silence continued. It was so persistent that the rattle of some falling cinders upon the iron fender was like that of a shower of stones. Everybody seemed to be watching the newcomer, his broad shoulders, his convulsive movements, the glistening of sweat upon his brow. Everybody was alert with curiosity. At last, as he called for a second drink, the young man himself became abruptly aware of the silence. He looked round, started a little, and after first averting his glance, looked again at one of the men in the group, at the same time nodding unwillingly and surlily. He turned his back once more, trying to conceal his agitation; and after another moment or so the watchers removed their gaze.

'Well, who was it?' sourly demanded the pessimist with the cramped back.

His narrator, recalled to a state of mind belonging to the past, vehemently hunched up his shoulders and pursed his lips in warning to silence.

'Sh!' It was a long-drawn hiss. 'Sh!'

All were startled.

'What, not *him*?' whispered another, in disappointment. This was an anti-climax.

'No, you fool!' whispered back the first. 'Shut up! I'll tell you later.'

'Seems as if *he'd* heard something,' grunted the pessimist, in a slow murmur. He drank from his glass.

'Something else,' explained the narrator. He knowingly gave a slight jerk of the head—the movement being less jovial than a wink, but equally significant. The smile returned to his face. It played in malice over every feature. Behind his hand, he said: 'And I could tell you something about that, too.'

'Oh, you're a bally marvel!' cried one who had not yet spoken. 'Here, I'm going home to my supper.' He rose decidedly to his feet. 'So long, boys. So long, George.'

There was a clatter of chairs, a shuffling of feet. The group dispersed. A moment later the wind swirled in at the opening door and was shut out again with a crash. The parlour of the Royal was almost empty. Only Bob Whistler remained standing at the bar, his fists clenched and a small speck of blood showing brightly upon his lower lip, where he had bitten it.

II

Not much more than a hundred yards away, in a room upon the second floor which commanded a view of the Royal, Willy Harvest and his mother were receiving a visit from Daddy Griffin. Because the ray of the lamp was so tiny, their room was in shadow; but a small fire glowed cheerfully in the grate, and during silences could be heard whispering to itself, while a new rug before the hearth reflected every flame and shone again with unfathomable richness.

Daddy Griffin, now over seventy, was almost unchanged. His beard had become green near the mouth and white elsewhere; he might have been slightly thinner than of old, and through dislike of new clothes a little shabbier, but he did not stoop and his movements were brisk. Mrs Harvest had grown younger; she no longer starved herself in order that Willy might eat his fill, and now knew what it was to laugh occasionally under the influence of her son's drolleries. Willy, if still meagre, was almost as tall as he would ever be. He looked thin but compact; and his round face—one of those faces which always look clean—was increasingly pleasant to see. Under his thick head of brown hair were two well-defined eyebrows, a pair of very bright brown eyes, an unremarkable nose, and a well-shaped mouth which smiled readily and

with charm. He was modest but self-confident, and his manners
were unobtrusively good. But Daddy Griffin would never have
dreamed of complimenting him upon either his looks or his manners, for Daddy did not believe in giving any encouragement to
vanity and, besides, had not noticed their improvement.

Daddy had been with the Harvests for a few minutes only.
He had cast aside his thick overcoat and his hat, and now sat up
to the table, opposite to Mrs Harvest (who was sewing) in great
fear lest the chair, which creaked, should one day fail him. He
made all sorts of grimaces as he sat there, blinking his eyes and
showing his yellow fangs and protruding his tongue in a very
uncouth manner which he unconsciously believed to resemble that
of Doctor Samuel Johnson. And he also rubbed together with
force his two red-mittened hands.

'By Jove,' he ejaculated. 'It's a cold night. What a clime—and
what a climb! "E" and "b." I was blown here. Now I'm blown,
myself. Blown sky high! You're lucky to be warm. Can't get
warm in *my* house. Obliged to come here for it.'

'Oh-ho!' protested Willy.

'You're never cold, you scoundrel!'

'In school I am,' Willy said. 'The thermometer there never gets
above zero.'

'Then it's broken. Like my nerve,' puffed Daddy.

'When did that break, Mr Griffin?' asked Willy.

'Years ago. When you refused a new cap of me. And your ma,
too.'

'I've forgotten that.'

'Well, Mrs Harvest; *you've* not forgotten. And I've never forgiven.'

'I'm sure it never troubled you at all,' remarked Willy's mother.
She had her head bent over her sewing.

Daddy grunted in pretended disagreement. His face was extraordinarily contorted.

'Why shouldn't you forgive?' asked Willy, as if that thought
had just occurred to him.

'Oh, pride,' answered Daddy, in a lofty way; 'pride.'

'I should get it over,' suggested Willy. 'It's easier.'

'Easy!' groaned Daddy. 'Listen to him! Both ways, listen to him! Hear him choose the easy way; and hear him laugh at pride. Young fool! Now I'm a good-natured fellow,' he continued, running his hands several times down his thinning white beard. 'Too good-natured, I sometimes think. And I've come tonight on a good errand. It's about you, you undeserving scamp. I've been talking to your headmaster. He says you'll be leaving him next year.'

'Hurray!' cried Willy.

'Ah, but wait! He thinks a lot of you. Strange! Wants *you* to be a schoolmaster, like himself. Matriculate; all sorts of high-flown nonsense. What?' Daddy, his eyes on Mrs Harvest, saw the start she gave. She was slightly paler, too.

'I won't,' said Willy. He stood very upright, the colour in his cheeks, and his eyes shining.

'What d'you mean? Don't be a fool, boy!'

'Will!' It was Mrs Harvest's gentle, pleading voice. There was an agitated silence.

'Don't you want to be a schoolmaster?'

'No.'

'Don't you want to be educated?'

'That's another matter. We can't afford it.'

'But I'm paying,' said Daddy, explosively. 'That's what I mean, you idiot!' Willy shook his head.

'I've had all this out with Mr Otway,' he said. They saw his little jaw set. 'I'm going to work as soon as I can leave school. Thank you all the same, Mr Griffin.'

'Will! Look ahead!' urged Mrs Harvest.

'I've looked.' The round face was flushed. The bright eyes sparkled.

'You've looked as far as tomorrow!' exclaimed Daddy. He was suddenly inspired. 'You're just mad to get away from school.'

'Well, that's true,' admitted Willy. 'They don't teach my sort of knowledge there.'

Daddy laughed a long, old man's falsetto laugh.

'*Your* sort of knowledge!' he jeered. 'Why, you might as well talk of a cat's sort of knowledge.'

'You could,' retorted Willy. 'At any rate, I hate theirs. Examination knowledge. It's all stupid rules; doing things this way because you're *told* to. I know exactly what I want to do. I want to be a journalist.'

'Good God!' ejaculated Daddy. 'Why, you'll never get anywhere!'

'You'll see,' was the calm retort. 'As far as a schoolmaster. And I want to help Mum now—as quick as I can.'

'Rot!' cried Daddy. He plunged as if he had been stabbed. Poison was working in his mind; the poison of memory; the recollection of another scene which had taken place in the too-present past. He snarled. 'You don't want to be tied to her apron-strings all your life, do you?'

Willy lost a little colour.

'No,' he said, coolly. 'I never have been. She's too good for that.'

'Too good, is she?' sneered Daddy. 'Mother's boy!' But Willy smiled.

'Do I do her credit?' he asked cheekily.

Daddy brought both his fists down upon the table in fury.

'Don't be saucy, boy!' he shouted. 'Can't you see I'm trying to make a man of you!' Malice made him add, tauntingly: 'Instead of a milksop!' He wanted to hurt, not only Willy, but his mother, to make them feel poor and helpless and silly. It had worked before; why not now?

Although Mrs Harvest was white under these savageries, she remained mute, and Willy seemed imperturbable. After all, he had known the brutal side of Daddy from the first moment of their acquaintance.

'I expect it seems silly to you,' he said, with exemplary patience. Who saw him tremble? Only his silent mother, who with swelling heart breathlessly watched the conflict of obstinacies.

'Extraordinary!' cried Daddy. 'Simply extraordinary!' Tone and manner were both contemptuous. But he was discomfited, and his truculence began to ooze away. He dissembled his feelings, pretending that his anger had been all the time a mock anger. And after an uncomfortable pause, he said:

'Then that's finished, is it?'

'Please,' answered Willy.

'You too, Mrs Harvest?'

She bent her head in agreement. Daddy glared at them both from beneath puckered brows.

'Oh, you encourage him,' he rumbled. 'You're in the whole business. I can't understand it. However, if you're bent on folly . . .' He admitted defeat. 'I've got no more to say. I'm certainly not going to beg. Why should I?' After malignant delay, during which all stared downward, heads throbbing and hearts beating fast, he pushed his defeat into limbo. 'To change the subject,' he said— and was savagely amused to see their relief—'to change the subject, I may say that I've discovered a relation.' The announcement seemed to give them nothing but pleasure. 'Yes, a relation. French. A comtesse.' He mouthed the word, smacking his gross lips in anticipation of their awe.

'What's a whongkess?' asked Willy.

'Well, a titled lady,' answered Daddy, taken aback by such ignorance. 'A countess.'

Mrs Harvest, because she had been so indignant, asked with placatory eagerness:

'Is she coming to stay with you?'

'Not she! Too grand!' But Daddy's bushy eyebrows had shot up. Eh? Eh? His attention had been successfully drawn. He began to beam and fidget. What if he asked her, eh? It would stir the tabbies. 'My cousin, the comtesse.' 'O-o-oh!' Why, there would be a riot; not merely because she was noble, but because she was French, and the *French* . . . What morals! 'Oh, she's too grand for me. Eh? I should have to refurnish my house.'

'Have it spring-cleaned,' suggested Willy. 'That's all it needs.'

'What d'you mean, boy!' Daddy, entirely distracted from his exasperation, became convulsed with laughter. 'My house is my house. You may think it dirty, and it is. What's the matter with dirt? Eh? Good old Doctor Johnson said he was no friend to clean linen; and he was a philosopher who lived to be—well, getting on.'

'The world's changed since then,' remarked Willy.

'What if it has? For the worse, I say. After all, Doctor Johnson went to school as long as he could. He only left because somebody gave him a pair of boots. He hadn't got his own precious system of knowledge.'

'Well, he's dead,' said Willy. 'For all that.'

It was an arresting thought to Daddy. Where had this child learnt to argue for himself?

'Here, I don't like you,' said Daddy. 'You talk too much.' He covered his mouth with his great hand, removing the hand only in order to say: 'And you're obstinate, too.' Willy smiled.

'I know,' he admitted. 'But you were going to tell us about the comtesse.'

'I wasn't. But I will. My father had a . . . harum-harum . . . had a half-sister, we'll say, who married a Frenchman. Not being given to boasting—none of the Griffins are that—she didn't boast of it; but apparently this Frenchman had a title. He's dead. She's dead. But her daughter's alive, and she's also married a title—or so I gather. And she's written me a wonderful copper-plate letter that I can hardly read—thin foreign notepaper—as slippery as jellied eels. . . . Found my address . . . Letters from my father to her mother . . . "Mong Cousang"—all the rest of it . . .' Daddy began to ramble.

'A nice surprise for you,' Mrs Harvest said.

Daddy's nose wrinkled.

'Ah,' he said. 'Yes; but I strongly suspect that my cousin wants to know if I've got any money——'

'But if she's a comtesse——' said Willy.

'Simple boy. Simple uneducated boy. Every Frenchman likes money. Every Frenchwoman stuffs her stockings—pardon me, madam—with sovereigns and francs and napoleons and farthings. And why not? There isn't a man or a woman alive who doesn't worship money——'

'*We* don't,' said Willy.

'Eh?' Daddy's jaw dropped. He stared at Willy. 'No, I don't think you do.' He sat silent for quite a minute, turning this odd and distasteful thought in his mind. 'But then you've never had any. Besides, there's something queer and cranky about you. You

don't want to get on. You don't want—oh, I'm not going to go
over it all again. I give you up!' He began to struggle out of his
chair. 'Here, I'm going. What with countesses—if she's a real
countess, and not a counterfeit, which is more than I'll guarantee
. . . What with foreign countesses and the wind and obstinate
little fools who spurn helping hands——'

'I didn't spurn it. I shook it,' cried Willy. 'It's most awfully,
awfully kind of you——'

'You shook your fist in my face, my good idiot.' Daddy rose to
his feet. 'You've got swelled head; that's what's the matter with
you. And nothing in it. Empty. You'll do no good in life, mark
my words. Die poor and neglected, after a life of misery. And all
deserved.'

'You're not angry with him,' pleaded Mrs Harvest, in sudden
fear, dropping her work and standing up with such an expression
of anxiety in her eyes that even a landlord might have relented.
'Oh, don't be angry with him! Or with me for not——'

'I'm furious!' roared Daddy. 'Furious! You've spoilt him. I'm
furious with both of you! Good night, my dears.'

He stamped down the stairs, leaving them with their arms
linked. The room must have become suddenly cold, for their teeth
were chattering as they heard the front door slam. But Daddy,
swearing his way through the darkness, shouted aloud in his
fury. And in the midst of fury came reflection, no more pleasant.
Yes, he had wanted to make a gesture; the gesture of a generous
old man. And they wouldn't have it! Damn them, they were implacable! No gestures. No gratitude for favours to come. When
nothing came, no sense of grievance. She knew something! She
wouldn't let him make any reparation. God! under that pretty air
of modesty she was as resolutely inert as a dead woman!

III

As the evening advanced, the force of the gale increased. You
would have thought that every tile and slate in Moreton must

have been stripped off, and every shallow-rooted elm in the neighbourhood torn from the earth. Daddy Griffin had reached home after considerable effort, and now sat in his front room, the thick velvet curtains drawn, his lamp alight, and the fire burning freely except when a great puff of smoke swept out from the chimney and darkened the atmosphere and caused Daddy to cough as if he would never have done coughing. Daddy dined alone. And after dinner he drank his usual two glasses of port. Then, pleasantly drowsy, with a book upon his knee, he listened to the wind, dreamed, awoke once and read a few lines, dozed, and listened again. All the storms he had known melted into this one, so that his mind was as often in the past as in the present. Gradually he knew little of the night.

He was roused from a web of dreams and words and sensations by a loud ringing of his front doorbell. That wheezy jangle ran through the old house like a gallop of ghosts. It caused Daddy's heart to beat rapidly, and his imagination to picture a dozen emergencies—the doctor, the comtesse, nay, Death himself come before his proper hour. And in such confusion he sat staring at the fire, hearing the wind in the chimney, and collecting his wits. Only after a moment or two, knowing well that his old servant, Anna, was fast asleep in the kitchen, beside a fire as ample as his own, and with a brain so much more dense that no call but that of the Judgment Day would ever awaken her, did Daddy draw himself slowly together. He rose to his feet, stretching as he stood upright with an ecstasy which almost sent him sackwise back into the chair from which he had risen. Taking a heavy candlestick from the sideboard, and lighting the candle by means of a spill of twisted paper which he took from among fifty others, he went cautiously out into the bleak wide hall to the front door. His patient caller had not rung again.

When first Daddy undrew the latch, his front door opened stiffly, with a cracking noise; but as soon as the door was open a blast of violent wind rushed in, blowing out the candle and making the pictures upon the wall—great engravings of pensive lassies and faithful dogs—clatter like clogs. But although blinded,

Daddy could faintly distinguish the shape of a man much smaller than himself, and it did not occur to him to feel afraid of his visitor.

'Who is it?' he shouted. 'What? What's that? Can't hear you. Come in!'

He pointed to the lighted room, battled with the wind, slammed the front door, and a little breathlessly shuffled back along the passage with something of the gait of an old sheep dog.

'Whew!' he whistled, as he recovered breath.

The room was full of smoke, and in the centre of it, holding his hat in his hand, was a young man who might have been about twenty. He was very slightly built, and—for an evening such as this—was astonishingly trim. Sandy, white-faced, his hair rather long and carefully-brushed, he at first bewildered Daddy, who felt that he half-recognised and half did not at all recognise the features and carriage of his visitor. A first glimpse was favourable —a long, sharply-pointed nose, demure presence, downcast but candidly appealing eyes, and, when he spoke, a little bubble of earnest foam at one corner of the small, thin-lipped mouth. Hm. Daddy was impressed.

'Sit down. Sit down,' he commanded, in his friendly, bullying way. 'And take off your coat. I'm all alone, dropping off to sleep. Why you want to come at this time on such a night, I don't know. But then I don't know you or your business. Or do I know you, after all? What? What? That's better. Draw up your chair. I'll keep mine where it is—it suits me so. Now, what can I do for you? Eh?'

While he spoke, he watched. He had had a long experience of men; and he prided himself upon an ability to read character. As the young man peeled off his coat and seated himself bolt upright in the indicated chair, Daddy saw him smile. Well, it was a small mouth, and the smile was tight-lipped; but Daddy was pleased because his visitor, if funereal, was very quiet and apparently accommodating. After the implacable Harvests, he needed the company of somebody who would be a little easy.

'I . . . I'm Richard Firth.' The voice was light—almost what Daddy styled a yappy voice, a Congregational pulpit voice. The stammered pronoun was not a real hesitation; many after-dinner speakers use it as an effective device.

'O-o-oh!' roared Daddy. 'Of course. I've seen you. I've seen you as one of these damned schoolboys. Eh? And your father—of course; of course. I don't know your mother. What's she like? *You're* like your father. I've known him for thirty years or more. Organist. Clever fellow. What?'

'I . . . I—really, sir, I hardly know how to describe my mother,' came the quiet, high-pitched voice.

'Don't try, then,' growled Daddy.

'She's a wonderful woman. I . . . I owe her a great deal. . . .' ('For God's sake!' thought Daddy.) 'Of course, she does a lot of church work.'

Why, the young devil talks like a parson! 'Cha-arch'! In spite of his wish to be polite, Daddy frowned, and took a peep at the clock upon the mantelpiece. A quarter to ten! Monstrous! And at that moment a vile puff of smoke rushed from the chimney and enveloped the visitor. How long before he retired, choked? How the wind roared! But as the smoke rose, Daddy could see Richard Firth unperturbed, thoughtful, submissive as ever. He was touched. He listened.

'Unpardonable, I know, that I should come so late,' continued the young man. 'I . . . I hesitated a great deal. But I felt . . . Excuse me, I . . . I knew you were a man of such experience, such learning . . .'

'Rubbish!' said Daddy.

'So kind, and so understanding,' insisted Dick Firth. 'I . . . I thought that perhaps when you knew why I'd come . . . It needed all my courage.'

'Oh, you've got courage, have you?'

'I'm here, Mr Griffin,' said Dick Firth, demurely. That faint smile passed across his face so quickly that Daddy could hardly be sure it had been there at all. This was damned interesting; and there was something *in* the fellow. Daddy had not been in the world for seventy-two years without learning that design may lurk in the apparently simple; and he liked to believe that still waters run deep . . . *very* deep. . . .

'Hm. That's true,' he agreed. 'But what I want to know is, why? The stuff about "learning"—all rot, you know.' Daddy grinned from ear to ear. He dragged his hand down his beard. 'I'm a plain man. A bit outspoken; but that's our English way.'

'I've read the contributions you sometimes send to "Notes and Queries", Mr Griffin. I know that you're an archæologist. I . . . I know that you're a man of liberal thought——'

The devil! Daddy scratched his head. He began to see his visitor in a decidedly amiable light.

'Besides,' said Dick Firth, as if upon impulse. 'I . . . I felt you'd *understand*. That's everything. Nothing else matters. Understanding . . . Mr Griffin, I want your advice. Your help, if you'll give it; but chiefly your advice. May I ask it?' He fixed his eyes upon Daddy, and really Daddy could not resist a sort of magnetism in them. They seemed to be blue, and they were eyes that followed one everywhere. Daddy wished he had foregone his second glass of port, wished he had not fallen asleep, wished he had not been tired and upset by his visit to the Harvests.

'Hm,' he muttered, his hand over his mouth. Anna fast asleep! Nobody! 'Hm.'

'As you know, my father is a poor man. Very poor. I won't say that life's been hard on him, or that people haven't been generous enough—whatever one may think. He doesn't complain. But he's poor. He did everything he could for me—rather more than he could afford. . . . I left school a little more than four years ago——'

Daddy jumped. Left school! Somebody else was just leaving school!

'You did, did you.'

'Mr Otway wanted me to be a schoolmaster——'

'Did he, by Jove!' Was that a lie? Or was it Otway's crotchet? You never could tell with these people.

'A-nd Mr Thorold, our rector . . . He thought, and I . . . I thought, I might be able to fit myself for the Church.' Daddy gave another jump, this time of complete incredulity. The Church? He'd not thought of that for Willy! Damn! It was just the place for a prig. 'But we came to feel—we both came to feel—that for me the

Church would be a mistake. I . . . I have an intense wish to do good in the world—intense. It's my one really great ambition. But, Mr Griffin, it's a narrow sphere. I . . . I can't, I simply *can't* accept the teaching of the Church——'

'Hm,' said Daddy, with a single grunt of laughter. His fangs showed. 'No more can I!'

'I . . . I knew that,' murmured Dick Firth.

Ah! It was first at this moment that Daddy wished he could pinch his weary head into life. It was half-numbed, fit only for the exquisite release of sleep.

'Oh, you did,' he answered, grimly.

'So—it was this Spring, sir—I considered everything fully and decided on a new direction. Because I've got gifts, Mr Griffin. I *know* I have. I *feel* them.' The magnetic eyes were again full of light by which Daddy felt himself paralysed. 'Finally I went into the editorial department of the "Gazette"——'

'Not a journalist!' groaned Daddy. 'What's come over the world?' He sank back in his chair, quite confounded; and he saw before him Willy Harvest, so rebellious, so like his—by Jove, there was a contrast here! Yes, there was a contrast between this chap and Willy; and the advantages were all on one side. Adaptability! You could help this chap: he'd be grateful for it. . . .

'Of course, I . . . I knew one couldn't expect much of a local paper, a county paper,' the voice continued. 'That didn't really interest me—the money side, I mean. I . . . I wanted experience. A stepping-stone to something—oh, very much bigger. As big as London, Mr Griffin. As big as politics, even. You see? But that's . . . Excuse me . . . I've had that experience. I've reported everything, from weddings and choir-outings to political addresses. You may even—naturally, without knowing it—you may even have read some of my——'

'I never read the paper.'

'But Mr Griffin, you're the largest shareholder.'

'It was a bad debt. I'm not rich on it,' growled Daddy. 'D'you know what the "Gazette" earns its shareholders?'

'As a matter of fact, I do,' said Dick. He smiled charmingly. 'I do,' he repeated. 'And that's——'

'I suppose you want to be editor,' sneered Daddy, into whose mind a certainty popped as he grasped the young man's method of introducing this subject.

'Oh, no!' It was a cry of repulsion. 'I wouldn't dream of it. To work in that box, to be eternally busy with little trivial things. Oh, no! Besides, my work outside has given me the *entrée* to all sorts of houses. I've got to know a number of most valuable people.' Daddy felt the fervour with which he spoke, especially when he added: 'And I wouldn't do anything to injure the present editor, who does his work *excellently* and is *exactly* suited. No, as far as my *work's* concerned, London's the only place. As soon as . . . But, Mr Griffin, about your shares——'

Daddy had sunk back again into his semi-stupor. Both his hands were now raised to his mouth, so that it was covered. He looked out from behind the hands as from behind a barricade. He was be-wildered and intimidated; but he was also impressed and charmed and—it was the only word—excited by this curious high-pitched eloquence, to him so alien and so persuasive.

'Do you want to buy them?' he grunted, without removing his hands.

'Pardon?' Dick Firth was at once all attention. But Daddy irri-tably shouted:

'I said "Do you want to buy them!"'

'No, sir,' answered Dick Firth, most demurely. 'But I think I might be able to find somebody—to persuade somebody—to do so.'

Daddy leapt upright in his chair; his hands, removed suddenly from his mouth, caught its two arms.

'What's this?' he asked, in a voice of thunder. Was this the 'ad-vice' the fellow had so obsequiously wanted?

'I . . . I happen to have made a friend,' murmured Dick. 'A wealthy man . . .'

Daddy saw that Dick's hands were no longer still. They roved, caressing his lips, his cheeks, and then coming together to clasp his knee as if in obedience to a command for repose. He noticed that Dick's eyes had become more candid than ever, but less fervent; they did not seek his own, but lay as it were quiet in his head,

'with never a corner for serpent sin'. A voice within his head cried:
'Yes, but what about Willy? You wanted to give him a hand. Put
him into the paper—leave him the shares.' Eh, that would be a
solution. No, by heaven! The child should taste an empty belly as
his father had done for the same defiance! Daddy loved money;
he had been affronted; he needed reassurance and profit.

'Who is this friend?' he asked, harshly.

'I can't tell you. At the moment.'

'Hm!' Daddy's grunt was loud. 'Huh!' It was ribald. 'Does he
exist?'

Dick smiled. The thin lips parted; his sharp teeth were revealed.
But his eyes were rapt. One would have said that he was a dreamer;
and it was this aspect of him that really affrighted Daddy and
fascinated him, for it was incomprehensible.

'Oh, yes, he exists. I'm not a fraud, Mr Griffin. Not even, I'm
afraid, very adroit. Of course, I . . . I've got some other plans,
too.' He grew confidential. 'You see, I'm hoping this friend of
mine, who's got a great deal of power, will help me to London. I
think he will. I don't want to go there as a beggar. I want to go
with something—call it power—behind me. It's the only way.'

Again Daddy was impressed. This was intelligence. This was
plan. He had never met a young man with such ambition; such
determination to use his opportunities. He liked that. If he himself
had had clear-cut schemes there'd have been nothing to stop him.
Nothing!

'Why can't your friend deal direct?' he asked.

'He doesn't know anything about it.'

'Doesn't know he's going to deal?'

'No.'

'Well, you've got a cheek!' Daddy could have struck his head
with impatient knuckles because the brain inside was so fogged
with age and port. 'Don't forget there's a certain amount of sentiment in holding shares in the local paper!'

'Which you never read.'

The impudent fellow! His cynical daring quite startled Daddy.
It was a long time before he said:

'How much?'

The answer was pat.

'Seven shillings.' Daddy bounded in his chair.

'Good heavens, no! Good heavens! Absurd! . . . Fifteen, per-haps!'

'My friend will probably offer five. He's a business man.'

'Well, I'm a business man, too.'

'That's why I offered seven,' observed Dick Firth, softly.

The little devil! The little devil! Daddy had a frightening sense of being helpless in the grasp of one who knew his weakness. He struggled. He heard himself shout:

'No! No, I don't want to sell! I *won't* sell!'

And all the time he knew that he was going to sell. He knew that he would ask ten and sell for seven-and-six. It was as clear to him as a decree of Fate. He was oppressed by a sense of old age, of weakness, of the need for protection against the ruthless per-suasiveness of his visitor, who could see him as the bluffer he was, who was determined where Daddy was weak. And he was fasci-nated. He thought to himself: 'My God, I pity any poor woman . . .'

'Thank you,' said Dick, as if he accepted the inevitable. 'Of course, I knew you might feel that.' He immediately rose, discreet and submissive, and began to don his overcoat. Daddy watched him, spellbound, knowing that this was not the end, knowing that like a woman his visitor would return, unfailingly, until he had his way. 'I . . . I envy you your books, Mr Griffin!' He indicated Daddy's loaded shelves. 'One of the difficulties I can't get over in Moreton is the lack of books. And another the cost of them. It's prohibitive.'

'Perhaps your friend would help you,' prompted Daddy, watch-ing him. 'Your wealthy friend.'

Dick Firth smiled, shaking his head. He was ready to go. Im-pulsively, it seemed, he said:

'I . . . I wonder if I might come and see you again one time, sir. Not about shares. Just as a booklover. A fellow-booklover . . .'

When he had gone, Daddy crept back to the smoky room, and to the sideboard, from which he took a decanter. Having mixed himself a stiff tonic, he sat again by the fire, listening to the wind in the chimney and seeing the puffs of smoke fly out into the air before him. He coughed slightly. He was shaken.

'Oh, but that fellow,' he exclaimed aloud. 'That fellow's dangerous!'

IV

As he left Daddy Griffin's house, Dick slightly shivered; but it was from excitement, and not from cold. He was burning. All the time he had been indoors it had been hard to restrain betraying movements of eagerness, and now that he was free he felt as if the excitement had been almost unbearable. He had never dreamed it would be so easy to play this old man by flattery, but he had learned a further lesson in the naïvetés of the human mind. Men were no different from women. Oh, he was a master! How deeply he despised the stupid!

Having impulsively hunched his shoulders and buried his hands in his overcoat pockets, he began to hurry—an odd, thin-legged figure darting in the shadows—alive with shrugs and secret nods of commendation, taking occasional sharply-drawn breaths of joy, of ecstasy, which narrowly parted his lips and admitted dagger-thrusts of chill air. How much he loved a secret! He had a thousand secrets, all locked within, nourishing his astuteness, consuming him with laughter. And yet, since secrets have their penalties, although he kept close to the dark shops for protection, he walked as apprehensively as a cat, every whisk of sound causing him to start and look back as if he feared danger from behind.

Of course he had not been truthful to Daddy. He had gone with definite instructions from his principal. His principal was Thomas Lott, then emerging as a man of affairs in this neighbourhood, one who had made money in a variety of ways and whose ambitions were known only to himself. He was planning to develop Seahampton into an urban property, a mass of rents for himself and quick profits for the companies he controlled. He wanted to become M.P., a social leader, a political influence; and he intended that one of his instruments for these purposes should be the county newspaper. It had power; it would be a plaything; and he wanted it. Naturally such matters were merely details in his greater aims, but he did not despise details; on the contrary he had time for innumerable details. And he was ready to use any agent.

Lott's house was one of those to which Dick had gained the *entrée*. He had done more than gain an *entrée* there; he had attracted Lott's personal notice. And Lott was using him. The scheme by which Dick's visit to Daddy had been dictated was Lott's. Lott had said: 'You can't lay it on too thick. He's old; he's vain; he's a provincial.' But Dick, having his own interests to serve, knew that he had well executed that scheme, and believed that he had taken still another step in the making of his fortune. He was triumphant. As he darted along he kept thinking to himself: 'I've got him. I know him. I know just what to do with him—so!'

In this mood of jubilance he did not dare to face the all-seeing eyes of his father and mother; and so, instead of going straight home, he made a *détour,* walking to the lower end of the High Street, down its narrower continuation to the railway-station, and by deserted side streets to the tail end of a long thoroughfare, the Causeway, which brought him back again to his father's house. In all this journey he saw only one person out of doors, a man making his way through the windy darkness to some distant uncomfortable bed. It seemed to Dick that when once this man had slammed a door the town would be deserted.

The impression was false. For as Dick, warmed through and through by triumph and his rapid passage of the night, came near home he received an unpleasant shock. There, standing with one great fist upon a railing in front of the house, was the tall figure of yet another late rover—ominously quiet, his shoulders broad and grimly bowed, looking to Dick's startled eye like some reincarnation of the executioner of Lille, and as dreadfully threatening as he. Unconsciously, Dick inhaled the bitter air so deeply that its coldness ran through him like a wound. He felt his stomach sink and his knees turn to water. He knew in a flash that Bob Whistler had learned a secret of dreadful moment to both of them, and the discovery was appalling. It instantly crushed his glee. He was like a rabbit with a dog at its heels.

At the encounter, nevertheless, he did his best to feign easy surprise.

'Hul-lo-o!' he cried, upon a rising, delighted note. 'I never expected to see *you*. How are you?'

Partly because he needed its support, and partly because his mood
dictated a furious passivity, Bob continued to stand with his thick
fingers grasping the rail. But he stared at Dick as if he saw something loathsome.

'Oh,' he drawled, slowly and contemptuously. 'You're there, are
you. You've come out of your hole. You bloody rotter.'

Even as his fear was confirmed, Dick caught the faint odour of
spirits, and his nose crinkled in distaste. Bob had been drinking.
He had a wild flicker of hope. Perhaps this was but drunken
humour. He must pretend! Pretend hard! It might be nothing;
how idiotic to jump like that! But drinking! Dick was consciously
sorry for that. 'Oh, dear,' he thought. 'I'm sorry for that. Sorry.'
Bob, he remembered, was not yet twenty; a boy. If at such an age
he drank—whatever the cause, a discovery, a misunderstanding—
(but how could he have found out? Impossible that he should!
And yet—why was he here? It was frightfully alarming. 'I'm all
nerves')—or, well, when worried, to put it no stronger—he might
later on . . . Dick was distressed at such an imagining of Bob's
fate. 'I'm so sorry,' he thought. 'It's *such* a pity!'

He clearly heard the words in his head, as if they had been spoken
to a third person; and was so far convinced by this hallucination
of liberty that he took satisfaction from them and pursed his lips
and slowly nodded his head in sympathetic condemnation. He was
a moralist. A moralist, and so sorry . . . But while he was being
consciously sorry he was watching Bob with a cat's eye, and subtler
thoughts than these were occupying his attention; for regret gave
him no present strength, and he was desperately uneasy. What did
Bob know? Had he seen Kitty? What had she said? Women
couldn't be trusted; they lost their nerve. Damn! He'd have managed everything for her. He'd *told* her he would! Somehow! And
now Bob— 'My God!' thought Dick. 'My God, I'm frightened!'

He swiftly calculated the distance to the front door. Too far for a single step; and though he might use his key he had no hope of entering. Before he could manage that he would be thrown aside, knocked down, kicked, wounded . . . He knew Bob in savagery; at all costs he must get the fellow away. Where? Lead him, with the pretence—the offer—of quiet talk, explanation . . . then . . . If he'd only be quiet! One could explain, deny . . . 'I absolutely deny. Is my word good enough for you, Bob?' Dick felt the sweat running down his back. He shuddered.

'Been here long?' he asked, in a friendly way.

'They said you were out,' observed Bob, with detached truculence. 'I didn't believe them. I said so. I said I didn't believe them.'

'Oh, Bob!' murmured Dick, reproachfully, edging nearer to the door. 'That wasn't kind!'

'Unkind, was it?' Bob sharply forsook the railing. 'You dirty beast! You foul cad!' His voice echoed like thunder in that closed space. It threatened to burst Dick's throbbing head. Dick thought his enemy was like Goliath, a huge figure of menace; but that thunderous echo was worse than everything. It made Dick cower and dart forward, frantically bent upon escape within doors. The dart was his salvation, for Bob's blow was mis-aimed. It no more than glanced the side of Dick's head, and sent him scrambling with frightful violence upon all fours. So great was the force behind the blow that Bob, carried off his balance, also fell sideways, tripping over his feet, while his hat rolled away out of sight and was lost. So, for a moment, both were on the ground and helpless. Bob, struggling to his knees, shuffled a few inches towards Dick and raised his fist murderously in the air. Dick, however, although dazed and jarred by the blow and the fall, recovered enough strength and presence of mind to roll swiftly over, scramble to his feet, and run. He had no time to slip within doors. He must fearfully do his best to escape. Both thus rushed out of the quiet square, into the High Street, and about the town.

As he fled, Dick heard stubborn panting behind him, and an occasional oath; but Bob did not shout. Thank God! And yet his silence was more terrifying still! Once Dick was nearly caught. He felt clawing fingers upon his shoulder, and screamed, as a hare screams when its strength is ebbing. But he dodged desperately;

the fingers were shaken off; a quick turn sent Bob staggering on, while Dick, doubling, gained a few precious yards. He heard Bob fall; and at a choice of unlighted turnings he darted into the deep doorway of a shop, held his sobbing breath, and cowered, listening. His heart sounded like a knocker wielded by an angry man. Surely Bob must hear it! He was hot and moist with sweat. 'Oh, God, oh, God,' he panted in an agony of terror. 'Help me! Help Thy servant!'

Nothing. There was no sound. He imagined Bob as also crouching, listening, panting. He knew Bob's frightful tenacity. Bob had waited for an hour this evening in the cold wind, determined to kill. He would wait as long again, listening relentlessly for the first betrayal of his quarry's whereabouts. Dick pictured him out there in the darkness, ready to leap.

Endless time passed. The wind rose again and came whipping round the corner like a thousand knives. It tore at him until the perspiration was like ice upon his body, and he crouched, shivering, in the darkness. He dared not move.

v

Doctor Hodge had said good night to himself. He had blown out his candle and settled his long thin head comfortably in the pillow. He had in careful thought gone back over the day—old Mrs Peddle, the Matty twins, a strange spinster with a hare lip and spasms, and a dozen others. Not an interesting day; a tiring day in which he had been all the time faintly exasperated by the uniform stupidity of his patients. He was not too well satisfied with himself, either; for he had felt from early morning a little queasy and irritable, which to such a conscientious man was matter for head-shaking. A doctor should never be out-of-sorts: that was his practical philosophy.

But now he was warm, his conscience clear, his mind sober; and a good night's rest, he thought, would—— Doctor Hodge's eyes were closed. The beautiful sensation of being unable to keep awake another instant was creeping stealthily over his faculties. He was nearly lost. But even as his first long slumberous breath was drawn —almost a snore—the night bell rang.

So precisely had Doctor Hodge accustomed himself to promptitude that sleepiness was at once banished. He jumped out of bed, struggled into his dressing-gown, and in less than thirty seconds had flung up the window. A violent gust of wind took his breath away, and passed, rattling the window as it careered onward.

'Doctor! Doctor!' A woman's voice. She stood below, bareheaded, bulky, unknown. She spoke in a screaming whisper. 'It's Mr Whistler. Oh, it's awful! He's had a fall. He's dead! For God's sake come now!'

'Go back. I'll come,' said the doctor, withdrawing from the window, slamming it down, and turning to find his matches. He was now wide awake; a man who had never dreamed of spending a night quietly in his bed. Indeed, he was already, in imagination, at Mr Whistler's side. Never in any serious sense a patient of his, the grocer had hardly occurred to Doctor Hodge as a potential subject for medical attention. No fat; eyes clear; abstemious; a good life enough. And a decent fellow, too; honest, narrow, not too bright . . . But a fall: how did that happen? Dead, was he? They'd see whether he was dead. If he was dead, there was no use of him going. Methodically the doctor dressed again, took clean collar and handkerchief from the top drawer of his chest, rapidly brushed his hair, donned overcoat and hat. . . . He was out and round in the wind-swept High Street within ten minutes of that unexpected summons.

What a cavern the shop seemed as he trod gingerly among its pitfalls in the candle-lit darkness. A smuggler's cave could not, in this light, have been stranger or more romantic. The air was heavy with the scent of spices and foodstuffs, heavy and at the same time subdued and enchanting, as if the East had a corner here. But the doctor was immediately alert, for they had lighted a lamp somewhere at the back of the shop, and its gleam sent a dozen thin fingers among the merchandise. Moving forward, he saw two women, one tall, broad-shouldered, and erect, standing motionless, the other kneeling and violently sobbing by that silent figure. The one standing was Mrs Whistler. She looked a giantess.

As it proved, they had been right. Whistler was dead. A moment's examination showed that there was no life in this body; and Doctor Hodge dropped the man's hand with an uncomfortable stir of the heart. Still upon one knee, he turned his gaze upwards and met the close scrutiny of Mrs Whistler. He could see only a distortion of her face in the rising beam of the glass-globed lamp; but he was impressed afresh by her immobility. She might have been a statue. Yet she was watching him intently; her eyes glittered.

The doctor shook his head.

'How did it happen?' he asked. 'I can't do anything for him.'

Mrs Whistler made no reply in words, but stooping swiftly, she knelt, and moved the lamp so that Doctor Hodge should be enabled to see her husband's head, where he had received injury. There was a sharp, deep cut in the forehead which had opened the flesh almost as far as Whistler's left temple; but what had caused death was not this cut. The man's neck was broken. Unconsciously the doctor drew breath and clucked his tongue. A shockingly violent fall had killed this fellow. He must have come down those stairs with a force and speed difficult to imagine.

'Good heavens!' muttered the doctor.

At last Mrs Whistler spoke.

'My son is out,' she whispered. 'My husband was angry with him for staying out so late. We thought we heard him; and my husband ran out of the bedroom with a candle. Just by the top of the stairs there's a roll of oilcloth that he'd been going to move away, and hadn't. He was going to lay it on the stairs, you see. I heard him fall. That's all I know, except that I got up and called him, and then lit the lamp and called Sarah—this is my maid. There was nobody at the door. It was latched on the inside. It must have been the wind misled us.'

'Is your boy not home yet?'

'No.'

'Where is he?'

'I don't know.'

'Well, we can't leave your husband here. He's dead. Until daylight I can't examine him properly; but he's past help.'

'Perhaps Mr Percy, next door, if he's awake——'

'You help me, doctor,' said the woman who had summoned him, and whose noisy sobbing—now checked—had formerly emphasised her mistress's tearless silence. 'Mrs Whistler's not able to do it.'

Mrs Whistler interrupted.

'Why do you say that, Sarah? You know I'm perfectly well able. I wouldn't touch him before the doctor came——'

What an even voice the woman had, thought the doctor. She looked strong enough to lift a horse. Lazy, perhaps. The voice was that of a sensual woman. It was all upon one dull collected note, but that was not the whole truth of it. Not a sign of grief. Impassively grim, like a figure of Justice. Probably suppressed, with hysteria to follow. But he'd have found it more tolerable if she'd had everything less pat.

'No, not now,' replied Sarah. 'You're not fit to carry him.' Her tone might have seemed savage if there had been any reason for bitterness between them. She was still drawing sobbing breaths, and of the two was the more plainly distressed. A much smaller woman, bowed, but in any case smaller.

'This boy of yours,' said the doctor, sharply. 'He's strong, isn't he?'

'Very strong,' said Mrs Whistler. He could have sworn that she smiled in the darkness. The impression irritated him to the verge of explosion. That and the confused snuffling of the other cowed woman. Damn the pair of them! They were all topsy-turvy.

'We'll wait a bit. You'd better have a chair, hadn't you; with all this strain. Would you like to go upstairs?'

The doctor knew that she had shaken her head. She said at once:

'I'll stay here. I prefer it. Sarah, get Doctor Hodge a chair from upstairs. And don't fall with it——'

Was that a sneering emphasis upon the word 'fall'? The doctor exploded.

'Good God, no——'

But Sarah, like a moth, had gone from their sight. Mrs Whistler, in the same tone—and he received the impression that she had purposely sent away the maid—continued:

'Doctor, will there have to be an inquest?'

The doctor grunted. He began to hate this woman.

'Yes. I'm sorry; but that's inescapable.'

'I was afraid of it.' Mrs Whistler seemed to be, not shocked or distressed, but deeply thoughtful, as if she were planning the immediate future. 'Oh, doctor,' she added a moment later, with similar calm. 'Do you think—I mean, its being an accident—will it make any difference to the insurance?'

She could not see the little nick between the doctor's eyes. So much the better. He answered, slightly pausing:

'It should not do so.' And as he said this he took a step away from the tranquil widow, almost as if he would leave her. A reproach rose to his tongue; according to his custom he suppressed it, shrugging his shoulders and sighing.

She made no further remark; and they heard Sarah, that unidentifiable quick-breathing shape in the darkness, tramping down the stairs with a heavy burden. She was bringing two chairs, one for each of them; and the heels of her slippers left her bare feet at every step, clop . . . clop . . . clop . . . At the same moment there was a knocking upon the outer door of the shop. Its handle squeaked. A wild gust of wind swept along the floor and made all shiver but the silent corpse. They heard somebody forcibly shut the door and bolt it. Then came the sound of slow steps across the boards of the shop. The shadow of a bulky form could be dimly seen, blacker than the gloom, and again haunted by a greater, blacker shadow as it came quite close to them and broke the rising light of the lamp.

The doctor had a half-glimpse of a young man's sweating face; and as he saw the dust upon the man's clothes, and saw that he had no hat, and heard his heavy breathing, was sufficiently mystified. But although unfamiliar with his features he knew that this was Bob Whistler, the dead man's son, who had returned home at last.

Bob, drawn by the light, approached and stared down speechlessly while they all three, standing still and breathless, closely watched him. They had unconsciously stepped back from the corpse, the chairs, unheeded, still grasped by Sarah; and so Bob, without warning, saw his father—white-faced but for the deep gash in his forehead—lying alone in the darkness, with shadows about him, as if he had been murdered. He gave an exclamation of horror, muttered something to himself, and leant helplessly against the shelves behind. They heard him begin to sob, saw him cover his eyes with his hands. The odour of spirits seemed to fill the air.

CHAPTER IV

The Arrival of Julie

AT THE AGE OF SIXTEEN one knows practically everything. Everything worth knowing, of course. And yet about ninety-five per cent of one's knowledge is inexpressible. It is not that one hasn't plenty of words—although at times the supply, or at least coherence, unaccountably fails—but that one's certainties outrun pettifogging data. Also, other people are very obtuse. Very obstinate. For example, there came moments when Minna could argue no longer with her father. She knew he was wrong, and evasive and bulging with dialectical red-herrings; but for some reason she could never bring his wrongness home to him. The ultimate retort always leapt to her mind five minutes too late for use.

Another thing. Minna, home from school for the Summer holidays, found that the garden was still shrinking. Not really shrinking, but growing smaller as she grew larger. And it was an extremely stupid place. It had no trim lawn for tennis or croquet, which she and her friends now played to perfection. It had no trim flower-beds. Its greenhouses were out of repair. It had no rosegarden, no yew parlour, and no winding paths. All it had was a sort of waste effect, with fruit trees, bushes, bare patches, and lots of uninteresting vegetables cropping up here and there in the general tangle. Some of her friends liked this; they said it was very quaint, and found the wood deliciously shady and the stream perfectly enchanting. That might be so. But these friends were not at Royals for long; and Minna, comparing the garden there with other gardens she knew, was quite ashamed of its baldness. She saw quaintness as disorder and decay. And it was clear that John Crooks, the one man of the establishment, had no time or inclina-

tion for proper gardening. If she said to him: 'Wouldn't it be nice
to have great beds of different flowers—one mass of lupins, or one
mass of dahlias, or one mass of lovely stocks—like they do in other
gardens,' he began to hobble away like a dwarf in a fairy tale; and
he made answer: 'Eh, Miss Minna, all them thingses costs money,
I reckon,' or 'Excuse me, Miss Minna, I think I hear cook
a-whistling for me.' And Minna was foiled.

'I'm continually *foiled,*' she said to herself. Her chin was set with
determination. Her clear blue eyes were dark with the same fixed-
ness. 'All right, my boy!' was her next exclamation. But whether
she was imaginarily addressing her father or John Crooks she was
not sure: perhaps they melted subtly into a single figure of exasperating manhood. 'When I'm home for *good,* we'll see!' Two
more years; and then, hair up, full length skirt, plenty of time for
everything, she would make a bee-line for change. Flowers everywhere. Daffs, tulips, and beloved wallflowers in the Spring; and
in the Summer masses of phlox, delphinium, roses, stocks, sweet
peas—all the gallimaufry. Colour! Colour! What a pity mother
wasn't interested in anything outside the house! Because of course,
otherwise, she was such a darling. . . .

Why did one say that? It was a disparagement. It implied that
she was *not* something else. Like 'honest'. A darling never affected
your self-esteem. Minna's quick mind ranged. She loved her mother,
but she never wished to argue with her. You just stopped, full of
compassion. As if you said 'Mustn't hurt her feelings.' And with
father you stopped because you were boiling. If he had not been
your father, you might have disliked him a little; but as it was you
merely avoided his bristly yellow hollow cheeks and long skinny
fingers, grew indignant, and presently, when he blinked and winked
and was charming, you forgot your annoyance and were very
slightly afraid of him.

No doubt was felt among the older girls, her friends, at school,
that all parents, in their different provoking ways, were born foilers.
'My dear! They live in the dark ages! They wouldn't *hear* of it!
As if—I mean—— Don't approve of girls thinking for themselves
. . . dancing with strange young men . . . smoking . . . using
powder . . . reading anything really *thrilling* . . . Oh, *they!*' Well,

as Minna had often explained, they truly belonged to a different order, a curious worn-out purblind half-asleep order; it was difficult to imagine that they had ever been young. Had they? Or just forgotten? Did all—would she—get crabbed, and censorious? Hideous! There was one comfort, the world was getting much better. Progress. Everybody more intelligent. More wide awake. Miss Heneage—— Father sneered when she said that. 'Well, Miss Heneage——' 'If you knew how I dislike that woman's name, Minna.' 'But she's wonderful! She's marvellous! What she doesn't know——' 'I wish I knew half as much,' sneered father. . . .

It used to seem an immense distance from Royals to Moreton; now it was nothing at all. You merely marched along the road for a quarter of an hour, under the shade of glorious chestnuts and oaks and beeches; and you were all at once in the High Street. En route you saw, it might be, a few farm carts with plodding, fly-beset horses, a milk-cart bright with yellow paint, a dashing little butcher's cart upon which young Wompas in his blue coat and striped apron was perched high above the tail of his scampering dappled pony. Clack-click-clack-clack went its hooves as all four legs twinkled in the sunlight. You snuffed up the scent of the leaves and fields, just as you were doing at this instant. And suddenly the road widened slightly and houses began; there was a little crowd of people, or there were trudging ones and twoes among whom, often enough, familiar faces could be recognised; and a moment afterwards the busy, dreary little town enveloped you. No great noise, but a movement; people still fully alive upon this hot, lovely day, and shopping and gossiping and holding prams containing the oddest assortment of fat babies . . . Bundled in like parcels, and red faces staring from the heap. Almost darlings, but in some way disquieting and repulsive, as if you could have altogether too much of a good thing. . . . And forgetting the fat babies, if you were frightfully lucky, walking into Moreton because you were so restless at home, you might meet somebody you really liked. . . .

Of course, for that, William had become a bit too much of a Young Man, which meant 'a stranger'. He had been Minna's best friend for as long as she could remember; one with whom she had had an ideally confident relationship. Not a nurse or a grown-up.

Not another girl. Reliable, understanding, always *there:* that was it. Something indescribable. But in the last few months he had changed, growing away from her. He seemed now—not always, not even often, but often enough to wound—to feel much too old to value her opinions. Minna resented that. Who wouldn't? It hurt.

Her politics were not his. He had become a determined Socialist, whereas all her girls had the utmost disdain for the horrible poor. Even for mere day-girls, who sort of belonged to the lower orders. He didn't share her detestation of the Boers and their abominable treacheries, or her passionate adoration of Robert Louis Stevenson. Sometimes she suspected that he thought her quite idiotic and was too kind or perhaps only too indifferent to say so; and once or twice, after what had been upon her part a fierce battle in which she had launched strong words against him, she had been so much oppressed by this notion that she had cried. Not while he was there. Ah, no! She would never do that; though as a little girl, she knew, she had often enough been comforted or had her tears dried by William after a fall or a rage. But such things belonged to the past; she didn't let anybody know now if she were unhappy or hurt. How extraordinary it was that you could feel such admiration and love and respect for somebody you disagreed with as much as she disagreed with William. She could not picture herself as ever convincing him of anything; but she could not bear to think of ever seriously quarrelling with him. . . .

He was good-looking. The girls all thought that. Rose Saunders had said 'Rather a nice type.' Not a type at all, of course; but Will. All the same, if not handsome, good-looking. Not more than that; but a something . . .

II

Minna's thoughts had travelled right into the ideal, and were among fairy princes, when her heart inexplicably gave a small jump and she stopped, bewildered. Then she laughed and ran forward. For there, not ten yards away from her as she walked dreaming, and looking intently into a shop-window like a starving street arab, stood the very person she had been thinking of. Not a fairy prince, but a friend; a young man in a dark tweed suit and a bowler hat, an unremarkable figure, but one she never saw without that lifting of the heart and a sense of ease and comfort exceeding any other she had ever known.

The young man was so deep in contemplation that when Minna took his arm in her light fingers it was quite a second before he could detach his mind from the great problem upon which it was engaged. But when, after faint bewilderment, he too had returned to earth, he accepted her presence as naturally as she had done his, just looking across his shoulder and straight into her eyes. He was very little taller than Minna, who for her years was of good height, and he was neither very broad nor very stout. His face was un-lined; his eyes, round which there were some small creases produced by laughter, were bright and quick; and his smile was both pleasant and mischievous. He had a frankness of air to match Minna's, and he seemed delighted to see her.

'That must have been your cue,' he said. 'I've got a heavy task on me, and you're just the person to share it.'

'Oh, but William! Cakes!' cried Minna, reproachfully. 'I thought it must be books at least. Or fossils. You were crouching so tiger-ishly. Don't you know that life is real, and life is earnest?'

'I do,' said he. 'But there's a time for everything; and cakes are just having their turn. Are you coming to tea with us?'

'If you ask me,' she replied, elated. 'I hadn't thought of any such luck. I came roving out, and—wallop!—here are you. How's your mama?'

'She's well. And she's having cakes for tea. She'll like them all the better if you've chosen them.'

Minna knew this was not true. She knew that Mrs Harvest idolised her son and regarded his choice of anything as incomparable. But she said:

'I must have been wafted here; I thought I'd walked.'

They both looked into the pastrycook's window, in which were all sorts of delights, from macaroons, and doughnuts, jam puffs, custard tarts, jam sandwiches, cream buns, ordinary buns, rock cakes, sponge cakes, chocolate éclairs, and cream cornets to such massive dark threats to digestion as genoa cakes, pound cakes, gingerbread, and hardbake. From the shop's doorway flowed a never-ending faint aroma of newly-baked bread and pastry; and all within was quiet and orderly, as if the very girls in the shop lived in a dream of delicate eating and were proud to display so many charming goodies. What a view those girls had from their warm dark retreat of tempted human beings outside the window in the scorching daylight!

'I say!' said Minna. She could have groaned with happiness. William, cakes, tea with Mrs Harvest! All was well in her world. 'They're all marvellous. I don't know what to suggest. I'm very fond of those with the cherries on top. Madelaines——'

'Six madelaines,' said William.

'And oh, William, those strawberry tarts! Have you got lots of money?'

'More than I know what to do with,' declared William. 'Five shillings. And thirteen of these cakes will only cost a shilling. Twenty-six . . . Seventy-two——'

'Yes, I'm beyond simple multiplication, thanks,' interrupted Minna—surprised by the agility of his mental arithmetic into a merely schoolgirl rejoinder. 'And it's not a choir treat.'

'Only you.'

'Well, those little scones are very filling. Only a ha'penny each. The rest's just greediness, you know. Your mama won't eat many cakes.'

'My mama will eat as many as you or I. My mama will put them away as if they were nonpareils.'

Remembering that little woman, so slender and unobtrusive, Minna was astonished.

'She won't! Will she really? Mother never will.'

'It's her birthday.'

'Oh, William! How beastly of me! I wonder, could we——' Minna felt her cheeks grow hot. Partly this embarrassment was caused by piercing self-reproach for ignorance of what closely affected those whom she complacently described as her friends, and partly by the sudden check she had to put upon her tongue. For she had been about to sponge thoughtlessly upon William— how often she had done it before!—as if they really dipped of right into the same pocket. 'Oh, it hurts me,' she stammered. The pain increased. She averted her head.

But William paid no attention. He said:

'She's terribly old, you know. Forty-seven!'

Overjoyed by a breakneck escape from pain, Minna exclaimed: 'What an age!' Then, resignedly: 'Well, I shall be nearly that in another thirty years.'

'And I shall be fifty-three!' said William. 'What a depressing thought!' They both sighed, unconsciously and for different reasons. He was the first to rally. 'However, we'll get her the cakes. They'll knock ten years off her age. Or double it. I forget which.'

'William, you're frightfully fond of her!' With a sudden emotional glimpse into her own old age, Minna was assailed by an extraordinary sense of loneliness and dejection. What if, then, there were no William, and no . . . no nobody? Old, all energy lost, every face and heart indifferent. This intense vision passed as quickly as it had come, and nobody but Minna would have guessed that it had ever been. Not even William.

Together, the two entered the baker's shop and stood waiting to make their purchases, all eyes and noses for the treasures displayed there. Indeed, the place so smelled of bakery and exquisite confections that Minna, excited and exalted, lost her years and felt half-way to a gingerbread Paradise. Her mind sometimes flew so fast that despair and jubilance had often been endured between two flickers of her eyelashes.

As they came out again into the sunlit street, and were alone, William said, as if he continued their former conversation:

'Would you like to take her some flowers?'

'Yes, please!' cried Minna, urgently. 'But I've got no money. You'll have to lend me some.'

'I've got plenty. I think I shall become a money-lender, grow a big nose, and die rich.'

Minna gave him a swift, half-serious glance.

'You'd soon shut up shop,' she said, warningly. The world became all at once full of black sharks. An instant later, she added: 'Some people *never* pay back. They feel it's beneath them.'

William shook his head. He was just as certain as she. He said:

'No, they just can't part with it. They feel "my need is greater than his".'

'Then they're greedy beasts. And mean.'

'Not at all. You don't know what it's like to have been poor. They're cautious. I'm just the same.'

It was the last sentence—the personal sentence—that caught Minna's attention.

'You're not. You're the honestest person I know. Scrupulously honest.'

'When it suits me. You haven't seen me tempted.'

'I never have. I should like to. Do you owe a lot of money, Will?' He laughed.

'Nobody's ever lent me any. Nobody would.'

'If they did, you'd pay it back. You'd always pay it back. So should I.'

'That's another kind of weakness, too.'

'Rubbish!' What more she might have said about that matter, which moved her much more than its importance or unlikelihood would justify, will never be known. Instead, she cried: 'Look at this girl coming towards us.'

'I've already done so,' observed William, with complete detachment. 'She's going to speak to you. She's going to ask you the way somewhere.'

'She's not!' Minna was caught. 'Is she? I believe she is. She's dreadfully shabby, poor thing. And yet, in a way, smart. It's the way she walks.'

'Probably because she's French. Is your French all about gardeners and pencils; or do you speak the language?'

'Golly, I hope *she* doesn't.' Minna was in a panic.

They had hardly uttered these breathless communications before the girl whom both had singled out from among the approaching pedestrians came directly towards them and addressed herself, in French, to Minna.

III

The entire scene took place in the High Street at its broadest part, some distance east of the bewigged statue, and east also of the cross turnings, along one of which Minna had come in entering the town. And although none of the actors in it was aware of observation—so engrossed were they all in their own concerns—it was watched by a fourth person who found it of the greatest interest, now and hereafter. Bob Whistler, stepping to the door of his shop, or rather of his mother's shop, to bow out a certain wealthy Mrs Carados, remained within sight and hearing of the assembly. The day was so fine and warm that he had allowed his door to stand wide open; there were no other customers; and because the High Street was brilliant with sunshine he lingered in the shadow, unseen. He might have been his mother over again.

He might have been his mother in this respect and in the matter of appearance; for he had her height and breadth and erect carriage. Like her he was dark, and smooth and black of hair; like hers his eyes were a steel-grey; and like her he had plump cheeks and high cheekbones. But where she was white he was tanned by the sun, and his teeth were bigger and more generous than hers. His mouth was less firm, his chin large and suggestively shapeless, and his jaw obstinate. He wore good clothes, and no white apron such as his father had always religiously tied about his waist; and if you had seen him away from his store you would have thought him—as he wished you to do—a man of business rather than a shopkeeper.

For some reason, whenever William Harvest came into view Bob always left off talking or looking at anything else. His lips parted as if his jaw had dropped; his eyes narrowed; fascinated, he stood very still, and watched. He felt no animus against William, but he was puzzled, curious, speculative. He had noticed two years earlier that wherever William might be his companion or companions laughed and looked happy. Why? It seemed strange that a man so comparatively small, so poor and of such parentage as William, should have so many friends.

Bob did not want friends. He had once had a friend, and the friend had proved a Judas. He had stolen Bob's girl, led her into mischief, and caused her to run away from Moreton. Nobody knew what had happened to her afterwards. As for Bob's friend, if he had been able to do so Bob would have killed him; but with the death of his father Bob had been forced to work night and day, a good cure for passion, and when that period had ended he had found he did not care so much for Kitty after all, and in fact was relieved to know that she would trouble him no more, the bitch. But what a friend! Bob was finished with friends. He trusted nobody.

None the less, he was interested in William Harvest; so that when, standing concealed in his doorway, he saw William and Minna meet and talk nonsense and enter the baker's shop together, his stare was that of a bull over a five-barred gate. It was the same old story—Harvest chattering, and the girls looking at him as if he was wonderful, and laughing . . . But perhaps he wasn't so very wonderful after all; only a fellow who'd got plenty to say for himself and nothing to do. Unlike Bob. 'I'm busy, you see. No time for women. Besides, I'm not a talker: I *do* things!' Harvest would never do anything. Yes, but just what was it? 'They never look at *me* like that!' . . .

Still gravely turning the problem in his mind, Bob waited for William and Minna to reappear; and while he waited he looked up and down the High Street (taking care that nobody should see him and suppose that trade was poor with him) at all the other people, assessing every one of them in his own terms of character and value and putting them all into his private categories. It was in this way that he noticed the figure of the girl in black.

A glance over his shoulder at the clock in the shop told Bob that she had arrived by a train reaching Moreton from London at ten minutes past three; but nothing told him where she was going. He saw that she was fairly tall and very dark; thought that she looked strangely smart for Moreton; admired that smartness, which stirred his interest and pride; and guessed from her demeanour that she was a puzzled stranger to the town. Something else, too, which he could not define, ran through his veins at sight of her.

He had half-determined to step out of doors and look critically in his own window, so that he might catch the girl's eye and if possible be the one to whom she applied for information, when William and Minna emerged from the pastrycook's and came laughingly towards him. They paused a moment immediately under his eye. He heard all they said: . . . shabby, French . . . How did the fellow know that? Probably wrong. Cocksure. There was nothing in that; you either knew, or you didn't. 'Why, I should make two of him,' thought Bob. 'Size, strength, everything else.' Still more secretly, he added: 'Brains included.'

Afterwards he returned through the shop to the little cubbyhole which he had installed behind it. The place was dark, hidden, and all-comprehensive. There, except when there was a rush of customers, or when somebody such as Mrs Carados seemed to be worth his personal attention, Bob spent his days. A shopman in a white overall moved about behind the counter, while a second man travailled in the half-light of yet more distant shelving. They were always busy, always doing something, whether it was packeting tea or cutting cheese or hammering butter or rearranging the stock. And it was Bob who told them what to do and saw that it was done. Was not that work justifying a reasonable self-esteem? 'I'm not a talker: I *do* things.' The phrase was often in his mind.

IV

As Minna had seen, the stranger was dressed very shabbily, in a rusty old black frock which, coupled with her sallow complexion and a similarly rusty black hat, gave an impression of dinginess. Her face was very thin, and she had a long thin nose of that Queen Elizabeth type which one considers distinguished or not according to taste in such matters. In repose, it was a slightly melancholy face, as if the girl had been disillusioned early in life. When she spoke, however, the prettiness of her mouth, and the expressiveness of the black eyes under her thin black eyebrows, quite changed its aspect. What had seemed at a first glance to be sallowness proved to be a creamy complexion deepened by the frowning hat; what had seemed a peakiness of chin was but the end of an oddly attractive pear-shaped face rather like that of a Madonna by Quentin Matsys. And yet not quite like that of a Madonna; for Madonnas tend to fixed placidity of countenance, and of that there was no sign in this girl. Furthermore, one at least of the beholders saw that her shoes and gloves were of good quality and perfect fit, and suspected that the same might be true of stockings well hidden under the neat amplitudes of that shabby black skirt.

The stranger carried a degenerate old bag, once black, which was about the size used by modern footballers for their kit, and which was cracking brownly here and there as if it might presently fall to pieces and precipitate its contents at the owner's feet. The handle had been roughly repaired with some wretched grey string; its catch was desperately strained by over-packing; and a piece of the same coarse grey string had been hopefully tied about the whole concern to hold it together. With the French, string is a great standby. And in this stranger, as Minna came presently to realise, French precision in important matters, such as the details of personal adornment, was united to French unconcern with the inessential, such as the fastening of bags.

'Excuse me,' said the young woman, in a manner anxiously courteous and in a voice so polite that Minna found it disappointingly flat. She spoke to Minna, and in French, as has been said; but Minna saw that she allowed herself a half-glance, so rapid as to be almost imperceptible, at William. 'Is it that you speak French, mademoiselle?' And when Minna, with misgiving, had admitted that she understood something, at least, of that mysterious tongue, she continued, gravely smiling: 'Monsieur Griffin; can you tell me where he lives?'

Minna was greatly embarrassed.

'Monsieur?' she stammered. The whole of the speech would have been intelligible to her if she had been able to follow the stranger's pronunciation of Daddy's surname. 'Monsieur?' She turned in despair to William; and William, whose mind skipped less than Minna's but ran more swiftly in a straight line, and whose memory in an instant embraced Daddy's nine-years-old revelation that he had a French cousin, a comtesse, had no difficulty. To Minna's astonishment he swung round, all alight, brandishing dangerously the precious bagful of cakes, and indicated Daddy's old house at the end of the High Street, beyond the statue and to the north of the church. Including Bob Whistler, four people followed the direction of that raised arm, and four people heard the rustle of that violently whirled paper bag.

'Monsieur Griffin,' said William, pronouncing the name so that Minna's mind was instantly cleared. Oh, clever William! What an idiot she had been! 'There, mademoiselle!' The stranger stepped close to him—so close, Minna thought!—and pointed her own slim hand. 'That large red house.' 'Ah,' agreed the stranger; 'that large red house.' 'Do you see?' 'But yes, monsieur.' It was a pretty scene. Minna saw William's smile turn to what she supposed he must think appropriate gravity as he continued: 'But Monsieur Griffin is old and very ill, mademoiselle. Very ill.' 'That is indeed terrible.' 'I am not sure that you will see him. . . . Perhaps you know that?'

Minna, standing aside from the duologue, was unconscious of her own emotions; she saw only the extraordinary changes of expression which accompanied every turn of this little talk. At the first instant she had been amusedly in fear lest the paper bag should split as mademoiselle's leather bag had done. But as the stranger pressed so close to William extraordinary perceptions flew like impulses through Minna's mind. She saw herself eliminated. She saw that the stranger's manner changed in a trice. It held nothing of the Quentin Matsys' Madonna, but everything of confident familiarity. As if they had met before; as if they would meet again. And William? Had she so quickly seen that he was charmed by her? Was the familiarity due to delight at hearing her own tongue? To amusement at his accent? Pleasure in his fluency? The stranger was smiling with self-assurance. There was in her air keen interest, appraisal, submissiveness, and a half-arch promise of better understanding which caused Minna's heart to sink. It was as if a cold wind had whipped icily through the Summer afternoon.

'Thank you, monsieur,' said the girl. Her eyebrows were a little raised, so that they gave her face a look of raillery, of experience. Minna thought: How black and thin they are! How broad and intelligent her forehead. I'm helpless. Her voice isn't flat any longer; but low and a little hoarse—very sweet, full of expression. What was she saying? 'I knew he was very old. I am his relation. But I have come from France. I have nowhere else to go.' A moment afterwards, in English, and with a different, serious smile, she said: 'Thank you, sir.'

There was a very slight pause, almost of intimacy, as if something further had to be said or as if silence itself, thus prolonged, said everything. The stranger then made William a little bow, swept Minna with the remains of her smile, and as they returned her salutes stepped off the pavement, carrying her shabby bag and walking to admiration upon the rough stones of the roadway. They watched her go. Minna's heart was like water.

CHAPTER V

Epilogue to Part I

THE LONG PINE-PANELLED ROOM behind the Royal Hotel, where societies met and socials were held, was being used as a Coroner's court, over which Mr Merrow, the leading solicitor in Moreton, presided. Only a few townsmen were present, and these were scattered among the chairs at one end of the room. The jury might all have been cousins, so much did they generally resemble each other; but Mr Merrow knew each one of them by name, and he knew, also, which of them were more stupid than the rest and more cantankerous. That is a great art. In watching his exercise of it, William learned much.

But William was always learning, because he was always interested in little things. Sitting at a side-table with his notebook open before him, he allowed his eyes to rove as his pencil traced its mystic shorthand characters. He saw how seriously the jurymen took their task, the little flickers of self-importance and nervousness that showed in their faces when they glanced at each other over some significant phrase, the way they fingered waistcoat buttons or rubbed their hands upon the knobs of chairs, and nodded or shook their heads. At the end of the room he recognised the usual attendants at such functions, the idlers, the inquisitives, the friends of those most involved. Nearer at hand, the police witnesses and the relatives of the dead, in black, awed and tearful, yet with pride in their concern in something which seemed to them of importance . . . Looking about the large room, and through the open windows of it, he saw the sunlight flooding a white-washed wall across the cobbled courtyard, disappearing, and brilliantly coming again; and he knew that out of doors white Spring clouds were passing quickly under a blue sky, a gusty breeze blowing to and fro, shadows rolling along the High Street, doors and shop-signs swinging, and the air full of enchanting echoes that made the heart rise. He longed to be there away from this gruesome feast.

He could see Doctor Hodge, who was impatient with the slowness of the proceedings, and whose answers, when he gave his evidence, were so dry as to seem hostile. William smiled within himself in sympathy with the doctor; for Doctor Hodge was growing no younger, and he suffered from a nervous irritability which made him sometimes irascible. But he had a regard for William, and always greeted him with irony in which esteem was flatteringly disguised. He liked William's colour, which was fresh, and his cheerful restraint, which impressed him. William liked the doctor's cramped kindness, and certain tricks of manner which give Scottish humour its own charm. Neither Doctor Hodge nor William, however, was expansive; and even when they met at Daddy's they had very little conversation together. The doctor was too tall and grave for William; and William, as yet, was too young for the doctor. Both were unambitious; both were more interested in others than in themselves.

Mr Merrow, the Coroner, was a smallish man with a grey beard and gold-rimmed glasses, very quiet in manner and very shrewd in estimate, excellent for this unspectacular and exacting job. William had no difficulty at all in hearing and reporting his lucid remarks. But William, while interested in detail, was not interested in the proceedings of a Coroner's court, which had been long overfamiliar to him. A man had been found drowned; and it was clear that he had walked, while drunk, into flood water, fallen, and been choked through his inability to rise. For the rest, the evidence consisted of repetitions and discrepancies so laborious that if Mr Merrow's skill had not been equal to his intelligence the whole of a beautiful day might have been spent in the pine-panelled room.

When the predictable verdict had been reached, William obtained certain particulars from the relatives and the police, and was about to quit the room when Doctor Hodge, who had been speaking to Mr Merrow, called him by name.

'Where are you going, William?' he asked, walking stiffly alongside. 'Not to Mr Griffin's, I suppose?'

William said:

'To the office, now. After lunch to a wedding. Then the Sports Ground for the Cup final. Then there's old Firth's organ recital at five. And at eight the Cricket Dinner.'

'Good heavens!' They had reached a door leading into the court-yard, and for the first time met the sunshine before passing again into the hotel on their way to the street. The air was so Spring-laden that William caught his breath. The doctor, who had no longer any interest in Springs and the hearts of young lovers, grumbled: 'Waste of time. Waste of time. Are ye fond of music?' William laughed.

'I shall be one of a dozen people in the church.'

'Ay. He's a strange, obstinate man. Does he do it, d'ye think, for the glory of God?'

'I think he does it for love.'

'Hm. Uh-hm. He would scratch out our very eyes for love. Well, I care only for the auld songs, such as "Robin Adair" and "The Wee Cooper o' Fife." But no doubt you've a better taste.'

'I'm bright with ignorance, doctor,' answered William, frankly. They were in the sunny High Street, and walking west, towards the church and Daddy's house. It was a day upon which the scent of Spring flowers seemed to fill the air, with a little dust to season the odours of Paradise. 'All the music I know I've heard my mother sing or Mrs Manning play on the spinet.'

'So. Mrs Manning, the poor body. It's an atrocious instrument, like a beginner at the banjo. And does the wee gurrrl play?'

'Oh, yes. Also on the spinet. And though I hate Mr Firth, which I shouldn't do, he plays very well, and what he plays is a revela-tion——'

The doctor reflectively interrupted.

'I don't know why one shouldn't hate him. He's a poor sort of a crack-brained, bitter creature. Now was it you or he who wrote a piece in the "Gazette" demanding a String Orchestra for the town? It was signed with some sort of ejut vanity about visions and per-ishing. That was never you, William? You're no perisher.'

'It was signed "Visionary". And that's old Firth. It's because he wants his own pieces played.'

'Unctuous fellow. He won't get that. And yet, you know, William, there's something to be said for bigots. They're horrible; but all we easy-going fellows wouldn't stir much, after all, if they didn't rouse us. We hit back. Or gradually we give in. We're impressed by their fanaticism. That's how history's made. Now, with Firth, could you persuade yourself there'd be one more—just one—to his recital today than there was three months ago?'

William was inexorable.

'No. Not one. Two fewer, in fact, because one of the old ladies who live over the chemist's is bed-ridden, and the other's staying at home to nurse her. But they were always deaf. Though they brought their ear-trumpets, they always thought he was playing Mendelssohn.'

'You scorn Mendelssohn, I see,' quietly remarked the doctor.

Snapped in an instant of priggishness, William brazened it out.

'Oh, I think you've got to scorn *somebody,* you know.'

'Ay, and be scorned. That's politics, my boy. That's not music. Taste changes, and Mendelssohn's in the doldrums. It's all this fellow, this Russian, Choswosky, or whatever the name is. Outlandish names. I was taken one day to hear a symphony of his. I thought it was a lot of whimpering. But when I tried to say so, my friends—oh, no, it was the latest. The Slav mind. I said "Are we to bow to a lot of Asiatics? Why, it will be the Africans next." There was trouble, I can tell you.' He smiled, with melancholy relish of himself as an *enfant terrible.* 'There's always enthusiasts, like Mr Firth, and obscurantists, like us.'

'Oh, speak for yourself, doctor!' laughed William.

The doctor's smile died.

'But, like young love, the enthusiasms pass. Choswosky will go the way of Mendelssohn. By the way, William, I rarely read the "Gazette". It's a poor paper, compared with "The Scotsman" or "The Glesky Herald". But that was a good bit about the auld women in the Crossgate. I went down there and had a look at them. It was very picturesque. Who wrote it?'

'I'm glad you liked it,' said William. He had reddened a little, with pleasure. 'Henderson put it in, but he jibbed.'

'Oh, but Henderson's a fool. Sucking that great pipe as if it was one of these damned comforters. You're observant, I think. That means *you're* not a fool. How's the French gurrl getting on with her English?'

Unconscious of the doctor's medical side-glance, William answered with eager enthusiasm:

'Splendidly. She's as quick as lightning.'

'Uh-hm. She does you credit, then. She's made a difference to the auld man. He was far gone last Winter. It's a wonderful change.'

'*She's* a wonderful *girl.*'

Doctor Hodge answered drily:

'Ay, at your age they're a wonderful sex. At mine they're a fanciful plague. All right, give us some more of those bits about the *auld* women, William. The auld are best. Goodbye!'

With a nod, he crossed the street, having said what after the nature of the man he had all along intended to say. William, left gazing bright-eyed after him, was in a tingle. Wonderful: was she not wonderful? Upon such a day as this, when one could hardly maintain sedate English dignity for the sweet Spring air and the swelling heart of exultant love, she seemed the most beautiful thing in the world.

II

Throughout that afternoon he thought of Julie. He thought of her while he lunched at home with his mother, and while he watched the excitement of a little wedding-party, and during the scramble of a local football match, and while he listened to Mr Firth's not quite excellent performance of a programme ranging from Pasquini to Stainer. At home he was silent, an unusual happening; with the result that his mother, too, fell silent, and when he left her sat thinking awhile, a little figure as fragile as she was fair, of her son who for a time was lost to her. She had too much dignity and courage to protest against his forsaking. But her afternoon, in any case a lonely one, ended sadly.

At the wedding there were perhaps twenty people, all very excited; and the bride, a plump girl with frizzy mouse-coloured hair and gooseberry eyes, smiled as if she would never leave off smiling, while the bridegroom, grey-lipped with agitation, was only happy when the service was over. Although a stranger, he then tremulously winked at William, who smiled back, relieved to find that the groom was a conscious martyr to publicity, and not a husband by capture. Everybody else was in boisterous high spirits, tittering jubilantly, fondling packets of rice from which each, in the end, hysterically showered the hero and heroine, wincing only at the discomforts of tight shoes or corsets, stiff collars and new bowler hats, and invincibly feather-headed. What an extraordinary ritual it was! thought William. The women loved it. They loved the excitement. All the men, although they grinned, were a little sheepish. . . . If Julie and he . . .

At the swift picture of himself in this bridegroom's place, with Julie beside him, William felt that he must suffocate, so thickly did his heart seem to beat in his throat. For a time he was quite blind.

Thereafter, at first unquiet, but latterly absorbed in the game, he stood for ninety minutes in the sun and the breeze while a score of sturdy young men rushed violently from end to end of a field, kicking, hacking, breathing hard, and with pathetic seriousness losing their heads whenever an open goal stretched wide before them. 'Shoot! Shoot!' yelled their partisans; and 'O-o-oh!' they groaned as the light ball flew high in the air or scuttered in futility over the grass. What drama! What ineptitude! The game epitomised the lives of all the players and all members of the crowd. So much energy, so much goodwill, so much worry and fuss; and in the end victory and defeat by a penalty goal awarded for some unintentional fault. William, deeply depressed, returned to the church in time for Mr Firth's organ recital. He felt sure, as if by revelation, that Julie would never marry him. Black, bitter thought!

An inquest, a marriage, a game; it did not strike William that he was skimming the cream of local life that day. But so it was; and he now with interest observed, scattered through the empty church in as many separate solitudes the thirty-one staunch patrons of Mr Firth's effort to establish music in an unmusical town. He knew them every one, from old Mrs Dorp with the tic to Colonel Wallis with the sunburned eyes. They sat under the high arches, in the curious filtering of dingy light which penetrated unbeautiful windows; and their dumb stoicism in face of physical discomfort equalled their creaking endurance of a programme defiantly rather than inspiringly played. Most of them were middle-aged and middle-class, in black, possibly mourning Queen Victoria, who had been dead so short a time that she still spiritually presided over each melancholy occasion in which the elderly took part. Most of them coughed until hard echoes travelled through the stagnant air. Most of them sat with blank faces. William, knowing that English people will submit to any sonorous music and offer it the tribute of solemnity, wondered what they were thinking about. It was not, certainly, any communication from the composer.

William himself, this afternoon, did not listen as devoutly as usual. He was thinking of Julie. She had changed his whole attitude to life. Before her coming he had been carefree; now he alternated between thrilling happiness and appalling despair. He did all his work for her eye, and—though his mother unconsciously learned it by heart—could not be sure that Julie had glanced at it. All the English she knew, he had taught her, explaining patiently the use of words, steering her past the pitfalls of 'ough', 'nice', and such moral terms as 'cricket' and 'sporting', and answering so many searching questions about English life that he was forced to abandon his own lazy acceptance of phenomena in order to satisfy her love of system. Daddy, amused, laughed after the fashion of a horse recognising friends in the next field; but William did not hear Daddy's laughter, or see his arch old eyes, or take his merry innuendoes. He was lost, drowned, enchanted.

And he had learned far, far more from Julie than he could ever teach her. His eyes, his heart, his mind, had all opened under the stimulus of love. She was never absent from his thoughts. He could see her—as tall as himself, slim, ever graceful, making no movement which was not perfectly in rhythm, walking with a grace such as no other girl in Moreton could match, sitting, standing, as if her body were forever under precise control; that was a revelation! Of her face he knew only that its shape, from the curved olive cheeks to the rather sharp chin, had exquisite beauty, and that the veiled eyes and demure mouth, ever promising secrets, smiles, tendernesses, sometimes drove him to distraction. What did she think? It was always withheld; a mystery, to be guessed at, but never to be certainly construed. She baffled him. Wonderful! Wonderful! How unlike Minna, whose mind he knew, and whose play of expression, so much quicker and more spontaneous, was in corresponding degree less alluring! The one still a child, the other not merely a woman but the incomprehensible feminine. Sitting in the dim church, with the celestial harmonies of Mozart for once as a background to emotion, William felt thankful to life for permitting him to love Julie while he was yet young enough to do it with rapture.

She did not laugh much. She had a way of turning laughter to that more subtle thing, the hidden smile. She said little; but she gave the impression of understanding all. Though in years she was younger than himself, she was immeasurably old in wisdom. Not cynical: wise. He felt that the questions she asked were crystallisations of thought, and she did not answer the flying questions he put in return. Though he was upon terms with her of frankness and apparent confidence, she had, and kept, a thousand secrets, being alternately very intimate and very remote from him hour by hour. But as love reconciled every enigma he came to persuade himself that she was right to be secret, right to baffle his questions, right to promise a smile when laughter would have been a disarming innocence; for these reserves did but heighten her charm and keep him guessing.

> Room after room,
> I hunt the house through
> We inhabit together.
> Heart, fear nothing, for, heart, thou shalt find her—
> Next time, herself!—not the trouble behind her . . .
>
> Yet the day wears,
> And door succeeds door;
> I try the fresh fortune—
> Range the wide house from the wing to the centre.
> Still the same chance! she goes out as I enter.
> Spend my whole day in the quest—who cares?

'Who cares?' He took courage from that certainty: 'Next time, *herself!*' He adored her.

Thus William, in church, while the organ played. The afternoon went, the dusk came, shadows cast beauty upon the scene.

III

As the last throbbing echoes still moved among the arches, unseen now in the gathering darkness, and as the coughing black figures rose stiffly from their chairs to straggle homeward along the twilit aisles, William continued for a little while to dream. And as he dreamed he turned his head, still thinking of Julie. He saw, at first, only the tall pillars of stone and the painful procession of ghosts, and in his mind's eye thirty-one lives brought together for an hour into the one common sensation; but then he felt his veins chill extraordinarily and immediately afterwards burn like fire as he peered at a shadow—was it hallucination? a dream?—which continued to stand as if looking fixedly at him from a pew not half-a-dozen yards away. No shadow; but a living figure, and as incredulity struggled vainly in William's mind, it in some way communicated interest and amusement in his stupefaction. No shadow; but Julie herself.

She must have entered the church so quietly, after he had taken his place, that he had not heard her. He, to whom the poet's 'My heart would hear her and beat, had it lain for a century dead' was a commonplace! She had not coughed or rustled or stirred. And he—insensible being!—had been so little alert that he had dreamed of her when he might have been at her side, relishing the less etherealised reality. Fool! Idiot! thought William, in fine indignation at his own blindness and deafness. Wretched whippersnapper! Well-punished sloth! He sprang up, and in a few steps was before her. Yes, she smiled! She seemed amused beyond expression at his belated discovery.

'You are at the last awake!' she whispered. Beautifully distinct, the words had a strangeness arising from her still foreign accent.

'No, no. Blind, deaf; but unwinking!' declared William, with a hand to his breast. Reproachfully, and very low indeed: 'How could you let me be so stupid! It was unkind.'

'I am unkind?' she asked, with tender archness.

'I thought so,' stammered William. 'I see you are not.'

She was dressed in grey; a dress entirely of her own making, which would have defied the hands of any other woman in Moreton. Her hat alone, which was of black, with a white wing feather, broke the shadowy monotone; and the impression created by this costume would have been one of mournful gravity if her carriage had been less elegant. As it was she suggested a demureness from which gaiety was not wholly absent.

'I came only a little while ago,' said Julie, still in a whisper. He saw the enchanting movement of her lips.

'Did you guess I was here?'

'Oh, no. I did not know how to pass the time.'

'If I'd thought you'd have cared for it, I'd have begged you to come.'

'Begged?' repeated Julie, with a droll glance which criticised his English powers of self-humiliation.

'Entreated,' breathlessly said William, thinking her merely perverse. His very tone, even now, was entreaty.

She said nothing, following from the corner of her eyes the interrupted progress of a bent old lady who had taken all this time to travel from her seat near the organ, and who now at last pushed open the inner door of the church and disappeared. When they were alone, she turned back to William. He saw her eyes gleam; as she led the way out of church the beautiful slenderness of her shoulders made him tremble; and in the porch, as she paused, her arm touched his, the scent of violets reached his nostrils, the intoxicating curve of her cheek was close to his eyes. Surely she could not so exert her power upon one to whom she was indifferent? He trembled again. If fear of her proud displeasure had not forbidden, he could so easily have embraced her that temptation was desperate. He dared not. His arms, moving impulsively, fell back to his sides. He could have groaned.

'So you would have entreated,' murmured Julie. 'That is very exceptional in you, in the English. It is very flattering, I think. But in that case I should not have come. I should have known that you wished to educate me.'

'To educate you! I?' Oh, but this really *must* be unkindness! Not? Of course not! 'No, it would have been selfishness,' William protested, trying in vain to recover some lightness of tone, though he hardly knew what he said. His voice was unsteady. 'Selfishness!'

'It was so *amusing* to see you there,' mused Julie, seeming not to notice his agitation. She rested her gloved hand upon his wrist. 'My dear William, so *amusing*. If you could have seen yourself. So sad, so drowsy, so lost to all the world.' Her face was puckered into a mime of melancholy. 'In this damp church, which all the time suggests that it is haunted by spiders! By cockroaches! By little devils of sins! And with those old . . . frumps!' She pronounced the word with consummate care. 'They are like witches!'

'But did you like the music?' begged William, imploring her with his eyes, which said: 'I love you. You are adorable. I am distracted.'

Julie had removed her hand. He was lost without it.

'No!' It was explosive. 'Never! Never! It was most *horrible*. That whine! That grind! That growl! Mon dieu, that wheezy *grognement!*' She shrugged her shoulders. Amusement returned. 'But *you,* my dear, *you* were so devout! That was such a revelation!'

'At least you were amused.' William was disappointed, charmed, bewildered. With a mind distraught he could only mutter.

Julie had stepped away from him. They stood beside one another in the dusk, at the top of the High Street, in which the lamps had just been lighted—odd little pools of yellow in the opal loveliness. And while they looked shop-windows also became sheets of light, and the light was reflected upon the pavements, so that shoppers were silhouetted as they stood poring upon what they would not buy. It was a picture of life and the passing day, exquisite enough to move any person quickly sensitive to the beauty of scene; and William, unsteady with feeling, was rapt into ecstasy. He was half-way to Heaven when Julie continued to speak.

'I know,' she said. 'But it is such a bore to be devout. I do not mean that you are a bore, William. I mean that it is a bore for me

to be so solemn, so serious, as the good folk here would have everybody. Do you understand?'

Could she be anything, anywhere, but the object of devotion?

'It is for you to be whatever you wish,' he stammered. 'The good
folk must go hungry.'

'They wish to force one by will, by prayer. It is a tyranny, which
I resist.'

'You resist irresistibly.'

'Perhaps. But it distresses me.'

'That's because your heart isn't stubborn, as you suppose; it's
excessively tender.'

'Charming.' She lightly glanced at him. 'But you know it is very
sad that what is good has such little attractiveness. William, I
think you are good.'

'You frighten me,' William said, with perfect truth.

'Yes.' She seemed not perfectly to hear what he said, for she
answered with preoccupation. 'Do you know what I think? I think
I must now go and buy some . . . some biscuits.' She looked
towards Whistlers'. 'Shall I?'

William was quite without resource. He could but answer,
breathlessly, eagerly:

'May I come with you?' His heart sank and soared again at her
abrupt change of mood.

'Let us go.' Julie began to walk away. Then stopped. 'Or do you
think Mr Whistler will be there? If so, perhaps I shall not.'

'Mr Whistler?' How incalculable she was. 'Why, does he bore
you? He's very good.'

Julie shrugged. She said:

'He is all *raight*. Is he good? I do not know. Do you like Mr
Whistler, William?'

It was William's turn to shrug. True, Robert Whistler had
been several times to Daddy's. Had he then bored her? What did
she wish to be told? Was she even listening?

'He's quite decent.'

'Decent: what is that?'

'*Un homme honnête.* The highest praise an Englishman can
give, you know.'

He barely caught a lightning glance from Julie's eyes. Her mouth was twisted awry. William expected some caustic remark upon the English to follow; but almost as if she mocked him, she said:

'He is big.'

'Very big,' agreed William. 'He is bigger than I am.'

'He is strong.'

'He has muscles of iron.'

'But you do not like him. You are jealous of him, perhaps.'

'Yes, I like him. Don't you?'

'I'm not sure,' said Julie, drawling the last word with a tantalising relish of doubt. 'I do not think he is as decent, perhaps, as you say. He has . . . oh, I do not know . . .'

They had reached Whistler's shop, and so had returned to the spot upon which they had first met. How much had happened in their relation since then! William remembered the afternoon so vividly that he turned to Julie, startled, to see whether they were sharing an emotion. She was smiling at him with such kindness that he caught his breath. But when he would have demanded what memory she retained of the meeting she was already entering the shop, where Robert Whistler stood as one expectant of her coming.

PART II

The One Who Stayed
At Home

CHAPTER VI

Motives

THE GREAT WORLD outside England was busy with Wars, Assassinations, and war-making Diplomacy. In England itself, as peace following the South African disillusion allowed men time to quarrel among themselves, there was bitter violence over the War Commission, Education Rates, and what was newly called Tariff Reform; and after a bad harvest there had been a Winter of general distress. But Moreton was hardly touched by outside events, and while some men were unemployed and some few argued and feared, ordinary men continued to pay their rent and rates, eat plenteous cheap food, and occupy themselves with their own concerns as if nothing mattered but what occurred within the borders of Chalkshire. If Joey Chamberlain's sharp English nose had not cropped up so often in the papers, and Mr Balfour's hands had been seen less often at the lapels of his coat, the seething England of which they read might as well have been China. Indeed, Moreton, basking in the sunshine, amid green meadows and ripening cornfields, was reluctant to follow the progress, even to realise the fact, of modern revolution; and its inhabitants slept, muttered that everything would right itself in time, and slept again.

Not all Moretonians were drowsy, certainly; for some of them were young and some of them had keen senses for any change in wind and weather, politics and society. Nor were those whom we have met in earlier pages of this story still in their old grooves. If we were to take a peep into the lives of these persons at a single moment in the high Summer of, say, 1904, we should find them all doing very different things in very different places. For example, Doctor Hodge, who now had his closed carriage, was sitting in it as he was carried between high green hedges towards a house three or four miles out of Moreton; and beside him upon the cushioned seat lay not only a copy of 'The Lancet' but a copy of 'The Autocar.' The doctor himself, apart from the fact that his hair was grizzled, looked exactly as he did at the birth of Minna Manning nearly twenty years earlier. Sceptical lines had deepened around his mouth, following a constant dry pressure of the lips; his eyes were rather deeper than they had been in his narrow head; but he was otherwise unchanged, for he had belonged since early manhood to the older generation, and the only difference was that whereas then he had looked a young forty he now looked an old forty.

Back in the town, in the shadow of his high garden wall, one of a generation still older, Daddy Griffin was fast asleep, well wrapped in rugs and with a shapeless cloth hat perched piratically upon his lolling head. To the drone of bees and hover-flies was added another low buzzing noise which came from between Daddy's parted lips; and anybody who had crept for the first time into that quiet garden, and seen the hollowness and pallor of Daddy's cheeks, would have known that this was a very old man indeed, heavy-lidded and shrunken, hardly living, and perpetually weary.

The long French windows of the room through which Daddy's chair had been wheeled to the garden were wide open; and while the furniture there was older than it had ever been the whole place had a new brightness. Jugs and bowls of flowers stood everywhere; fireirons shone; ancient chairs were covered with cretonne of a forceful pattern. And as one gazed upon this vigorous display the author of it came quickly from somewhere else in the house, stepped into the garden, took a businesslike peep at Daddy, and then returned to the bright room. She was no longer a stranger to the house, but looked every inch a chatelaine. Very self-assured, very chic in clothes that were far ahead of Moreton fashion, Julie Boucard looked as if in two years she had made herself mistress of Daddy's house and possibly of his affairs. As to that we shall learn more presently. It is enough now to picture her drawing her dark head to one side as she made sure that Daddy was shaded and well-wrapped, and then lightly and erectly wheeling, walking within, and with a touch placing a flower-bowl more precisely in the middle of the table. Having done this, she sat down with perfect grace in an armchair just inside the open windows, ate a chocolate, and began very scrupulously to polish her finger-nails.

Not half-a-mile away, in the dingy editorial offices of the 'Gazette', William Harvest was correcting some long galleys of proof which smelled strongly of printers' ink and were as damp to the touch as paper that has been wrapped round fresh fish. He was as nearly scowling as a young man could be to whom scowls were a physical impossibility; for it was a part of his work to make sense of the senseless and entertainment of the dull, and this, although an unrewarded task, was not an easy one. At intervals, his scrawling pen pierced the wet galley as if it had been a needle. The room was dark, and because of the working machines below it had a slight perpetual rumbling shudder such as one feels at the summit of Mount Vesuvius or at a point above the toiling screw of an ocean liner. And William, who felt delightfully busy, was smoking a pipe in that bliss-imparting state between the new and the foul, and with one hand rumpling his thick hair, and the other (except when correction was necessary) holding the galley aloft, he was ideally occupied. In the street below could be heard the clop-clop of horses' hooves and the innumerable murmurs of a Summer day; sunlight lessened the darkness of his room; the tapping of a typewriter elsewhere might have been the love signal of a wood-beetle in the building's timber frame; and the idle sailing of three or four flies above William's desk was like the movement of stars in a planetarium.

But as William ceased to read his galleys, which slowly sank to the desk when his arm fell, and as he relapsed into a brown study, the professional scowl disappeared from his brow and his delicious pipe no longer smoked. You would have supposed him transported to Elysium; but in fact his imagination had gone no farther than a garden half-a-mile away, and he dreamed he was in the shadow of Daddy's great wall, amid the scent of roses, no longer alone.

William's mother, half-a-mile in the opposite direction, was neither working nor dreaming. She was at home, and had seated

herself comfortably in her last birthday present at the shady front
window two floors above the High Street. Upon her knee was a
large scrap-album, in which had been pasted a number of William's miscellaneous contributions to the 'Gazette'. Some of them
were short, and some were long; some were neat descriptions of
local scenes, some leaderettes, some character studies of real or
imaginary people; but all were her favourites. Believing that she
read these papers with complete detachment, even with particular
severity, Mrs Harvest wore during the perusal an expression
altogether strange. Upon her little pale face sat a light which a
painter of story-pictures must have called 'A Letter from the
Dead'; she seemed to listen to celestial harmonies. From time to
time she gravely nodded approval of what she thus read for the
fiftieth time. Once her lips trembled and a tear or two made her
eyes brilliant, but the moment passed and she read sedately as
before, thinking her son inspired.

As for Minna Manning, she cultivated her garden. In an enormous sun hat and cotton dress, she clipped the departed blooms
from scabious and coreopsis, love-in-a-mist, rose, larkspur and
pink. Her great wooden trug-basket, borrowed from John Crooks,
was full of this sad wreckage, and her hands were brown and
slightly scratched from exposure to the sun and the thorns. In
spite of the afternoon heat, which Minna did not observe, she continued to work slowly and fairly methodically, stopping only from
time to time to exchange comments with her escort. The escort
consisted of one cat, large, male, and ginger, whose name was
Horace, and one robin rather the worse for wear. There was a
truce between members of the escort, partly because Horace was
fat, well-fed, and clumsy, but partly also because both had reliance
upon that British love of fair-play which Minna, being the daughter
of an Irish father and a German mother, exemplified.

The person we know who was farthest away from Moreton
was Dick Firth. He had been in London now for six active years;
and he was in a fair way to enjoy the success which he had long
craved. At this moment, however, he was not in London. On the
contrary, he was up to his neck in sea water off the north coast
of Devonshire. Rather nearer to the shore, and bobbing up and

down in shallower water, was a pale young woman with a small
nose and very light eyelashes, whose hair was entirely protected
from brine by a large cap or hat resembling the headdress favoured
by cooks. The young woman's face was turning blue, for she was
exposed to a strong wind and her bobbing did not involve a great
deal of personal exercise. She had already cast a glance or two
at Dick, whom she now addressed with some energy.

'Dick!' she screamed. 'Dick! I'm cold!'

'Darling!' cried Dick in return. His head only was visible above
the blue water. He watched her flounder towards the shore, the
long legs of her bathing pantaloons clinging to their slender contents and the frills and skirts belonging to the rest of her costume
trailing runnels of sea.

'Dick!' she cried again, slipping and tripping upon a hidden
rock. 'Ow!'

He swam slowly and easily towards the shore, and very soon,
lean and meagre as of old, rose from the shallows. His companion,
meanwhile, was ungracefully scampering flat-footed to their tent,
pausing only to make sure that Dick was following. As soon as he,
too, was on land, and safe, she disappeared within the tent.

It was Dick's turn to make that awkward ascent, which he did
to the accompaniment of a genial hum. He was well pleased with
himself. The sun shone, glittering upon the water; the breeze ran
pleasantly over his body. He smiled his demure smile, which was
so charming; and two or three times flicked the end of his nose, to
which a trickle from his head and brows was falling. And just in
that instant he had a sudden memory of Moreton and his boyhood,
the offices of the 'Gazette', Daddy Griffin's garden, Bob Whistler,
the High Street. By Jove! He could see them all, slowly dawdling
through life, stupid, agreeable . . . He stopped, his bathing costume as sleek as a seal's back. By Jingo! He had never answered
Daddy's last shakily pencilled letter. A mistake. Tut-tut-tut! Dick
was quite troubled; he found that after all the wind bit shrewdly
this afternoon.

'Dick!' came a plaintive voice from the tent. 'Come *on!*'

'Coming, darling,' he called. The faintest of frowns passed
briefly across his face.

II

Although she was not as young as she had been, Mrs Whistler remained, even in the new century, an impressive figure. She stood five feet ten inches, and her shoulders were broader than those of many men. But for all that she moved about the living rooms above the Whistler shop, and sometimes unexpectedly in the shop itself, without making a sound. Such excursions had latterly increased. She rarely, nowadays, went out of doors, and had done so little enough since her husband's death, not because she was home-ridden, but because as she grew older she grew more suspicious. If she went out, she did not know what advantage might not be taken of her absence.

Her husband, good honest fool, had been a plodder. Exact weight, exact change, and a calculation of profits in farthings were the foundations of his system. But for her he would have remained a little fellow, doling out grains and pennyweights, the servant of others, and a poor man. She could remember all, and smile and frown over it as she remembered. Every morning he had risen at the same moment, had opened his shop, had made it spick and span for the day. John, with a broom, and his lips pursed . . . And there, occupied with farthings and ounces and whatever wholesalers cared to offer him as bargains, he would have stayed. What a fool! Even when he had a boy to sweep the shop he had watched the boy over the tops of his spectacles in anxious supervision, his fingers twitching.

It had been she who had insisted upon better quality goods, removal to the High Street, credit accounts, and the establishment of sliding scales of prices. If the doctors did that sort of thing, why not the grocers? The rich paid for their privileges. And they liked obsequiousness so much that they troubled little about the bills which followed it. Also, Mrs Whistler had been in the habit of going through all the accounts and keeping her eye upon the debtors. She had the first intimation of money difficulties in any family in the neighbourhood, and acted accordingly, with never

a glimmer of mercy. She still so acted, for she was still the proprietor of the shop. Every order was passed by her before being
given. Although Bob looked big and solemn, and said 'I' to the
travellers, he had no power and would have none. Mrs Whistler
would never part with that. Sometimes, conscious of her power,
she sat alone grimly contemplating it as misers hug gold or as
other women play patience.

But she was older. She was sixty. Bob was her second child,
born four years after her marriage and two years after the birth
and death of her other son, Arthur. And while she had wanted the
first she had been indifferent to Bob from the moment she knew
he was coming. Ever since. Nowadays she took a little pride in
his appearance, which in largeness and strength resembled her
own; but she found him stupid and rough-mannered and untrust-
worthy. He had a likeness to his father, a sort of plodding half-
intelligent dullness, and a lack of judgment which caused Mrs
Whistler to shake her head. Thank heaven he could do nothing in-
dependently. When she thought of that she allowed herself the
pleasure of a cold smile. Her grey eyes glittered.

She had never had a young maid in the place; but always
women of sober middle-age. At first, charwomen; gradually, as the
business grew, maids. Never more than one at a time. But the older
women who were any good became impudent when they found
that other situations could be had, and the slatterns were discharged. Sarah, the quietest of them all, who had been with her
at the time of John Whistler's death, had gone long ago, and was
swallowed up in the world. Mrs Whistler heard nothing of her,
and thought nothing—whatever she might have done at the time.
A lot, then . . . There had been a dozen, two dozen, since
Sarah. The latest, and one of the worst, was just going. She did
not know it yet.

That was Mrs Whistler's way. The first thing her maid would
know of impending discharge was from an accidental glimpse of
her possible successor. Or else guesswork. It was the same with
the shopmen, of whom there were now two, with a couple of boys
for delivery. These fellows had no warning of her approach; they
only looked into her cold eyes and were stricken with terror. It

was the same with Bob, whom she had once caught neatly
modelling a toy boat when he should have been checking his
stock. Childish nonsense! If she did not know all that went on in
the shop, and what systematic pilfering Bob had developed cunning enough to hide, at least she ruled upon every floor of the
establishment, from cellar to attic. And so great was the effect of
dread upon these sweated underlings that they believed she could
see them as she slept.

Sleep she must have. Drowsiness always came upon her, now,
after the midday meal; and when she sat as of old at the window,
looking down at loiterers in the High Street and reading their
business by means of every gesture they made, her heavy lids
would close, her breathing would become audible, and for half-
an-hour she would be lost in a cloud of confused images. Only
Bob knew this; and she did not know that he knew it. She thought
him deceived; but he was not deceived, only under-rated. It was
during her half-hour of insensibility that his own mind roved unchecked and his own waking dreams, of which Mrs Whistler
guessed nothing, went farther and farther into the unknown.

As Mrs Whistler awoke, she was immediately alive to all that
was passing about her. There was no interval of drowsiness. She
opened her eyes and her mind was clear. That explains why, upon
this afternoon, she heard the creak of a board in her bedroom and
knew that somebody was there who had no business there. She
did not hesitate. Noiselessly, without appearing to creep, she went
across to the door and drew it open. There was no sound. But
kneeling at the chest of drawers beyond Mrs Whistler's lonely bed,
hands busy at the back of the bottom drawer, was the maid whom
she had determined to dismiss. A small woman, very dark and
wrinkled and much older than she admitted, this maid had from
the first been unsatisfactory; but she had not hitherto been dishonest. Now, quite feverishly, she was feeling for something
which she believed to be in that drawer. The door to the landing
stood ajar. But Mrs Whistler commanded both that by which
she had entered and that by which the maid had expected to
leave.

You have seen a cat watching a mouse as yet uncaught. It was this expression which glittered in the mistress's eyes. But she did and said nothing until Flora, apprehensively peeping across her shoulder, saw the appalling figure in the doorway and grew pale. Still neither spoke, but Flora sank back upon her heels, staring.

'I've lost the tea cosy, mem,' she faltered. There was no reply. 'I've looked everywhere for it, mem,' she added, in a high convincing voice of falsehood. But she slowly rose, with great difficulty, to her feet, and stood holding herself upright with the aid of the chest of drawers. Her trembling was visible.

'Did you think it was there?' asked Mrs Whistler, with contemptuous dryness.

'Well, I've looked——'

'Funny place for it to be, isn't it?' queried Mrs Whistler.

'It's . . . not there, mem.' Flora gulped. She seemed to be in a fainting state.

'Who told you that you could come into my bedroom? Who told you that you could rummage among my clothes?'

'I only thought——' began the wretched woman.

Mrs Whistler shook her head.

'You didn't find anything else, did you? Not what you were looking for?'

'I . . . I came for the tea cosy, mem. . . .'

'You did nothing of the sort. You came to try and find something else. What was it?' Mrs Whistler took one step towards her, and the effect of this action was so menacing that Flora's knees gave way. She almost fell.

'Nothing, mem!' she cried. 'Oh, nothing, mem.'

'Would you like me to send for the police?' asked Mrs Whistler, in her slow, quiet way. 'Perhaps they'd suggest something to you?'

Flora sank to her knees. She was grey with terror. With her last strength, she screamed and fell forward; and even then she might have lain untended if the sound of running steps upon the stairs had not preceded Bob's impetuous entry to the room. By the time he arrived, Mrs Whistler had flung the contents of the water bottle from the neighbouring washstand over the maid's face, and without effort had turned Flora on to her back. Bob arrived, therefore, to find his mother tending a woman in a fit; and she looked up at him with almost her usual calm deliberation as he blundered into the room.

'When I want you, I'll call you,' Mrs Whistler said.

'I thought you did call,' cried Bob.

His mother shook her head.

'Quite a mistake,' she murmured. 'You should have known better.'

III

Later in the day Bob and his mother had another exchange of conversation. It was after the shop was shut; and they were alone. While she sat in her chair by the window, he walked about the room, his chin upon his collar, his shoulders raised, and his hands in his pockets. She knew that he had something to say to her; but she gave him no help because it was a part of her method to intimidate by reserve. Nevertheless, she was curious. His behaviour was unusual; it suggested that whatever troubled him was of importance. Yes, he was slow.

'I don't know if you've heard about it,' he began. A feeble opening! Of course she had heard of anything that mattered to the business. 'But there's queer doings at Seahampton.'

'They've been building there for a year or two,' said his mother. 'Is that what you mean?'

'That's just it,' Bob remarked. 'They've been building quite a lot. Would you like to drive over there?'

'Why?' asked Mrs Whistler.

'I think it's a good opening.'

She was astonished at his temerity. Or she pretended to be astonished.

'You think *what?*' she coldly demanded.

'For a branch,' explained Bob. 'We could get a shop there and capture the trade.'

'How simple!' observed his mother. She looked out of the window. However, Bob also turned away. He instinctively went over to the fireplace, leaned his arm along the mantelpiece, and looked at his mother's reflection; so that he caught one stealthy glance from her before she had realised what he was doing. From that moment she kept her eyes averted.

Bob, biting his thumb, then said:

'I've been thinking about this, mother. I've set my heart on it. I've never said; but . . . well, my ambition's to have a chain of three shops, one here, one at Sandersfold, and one at Seahampton. Seahampton's new. I mean, of course it's old as a *place;* but it's being made new. I've been there a lot, on Sundays. I know all the shops. The people who've been there for the last twenty years are slow. They don't see the possibilities. At least, *I* don't think they do. And we can get a new shop in the centre of the town before anybody else seizes the chance. That's important. It's *most* important. You may think we're well enough where we are—well, we may be; but times are changing. Perhaps you don't realise it. You never get out. I do. And I hear things. Movements, and schemes, and what's happening in different places . . . At any rate, that's as may be. What I want to explain is that if we stay here, just jogging along as we've done since father's death, we're in danger——'

Three or four times during this halting speech, Bob could have been interrupted. His pauses had been long, for he was no orator, and he had committed certain *gaffes* of which his mother was not unaware. But she had endured everything until he came to the word 'danger', which she never could endure.

'Danger? From what?' As her anger increased, Mrs Whistler's tone became more coolly sarcastic.

'London,' said Bob.

'It's a big city, they tell me,' she retorted. 'And it must be full of fools. But it's seventy miles away. It won't move.'

'It's spreading,' Bob said. 'It's coming South. It's coming to Moreton. Yes it is. You know what I mean. The money's there; and it's the money that's coming. If we're not quick we shall be caught by it.'

'And then?'

'Outsold. A big shop opposite. Another next door. Cut prices. Competition crushed. It's happening all over the place.'

Mrs Whistler, accustomed to a small world of certainties, had no stomach for this rhetoric. She was contemptuous of it, and of her son.

'Travellers' tales,' she remarked. 'That's the stuff men talk standing at bars.'

'Bars!' Bob was furious. 'What do you mean, "bars"?'

'They seem to have done your business. They won't do mine.'

'I've heard it at no bars. I'm telling you the truth——'

'You're talking big. That's all.'

'Oh, I've got bigger ideas than that,' answered Bob, with something of her own insolent tenacity. He laughed.

'So had the frog,' said his mother.

It silenced him. She saw him clench his fists, jerk them both simultaneously before him, and resist an impulse to rush headlong from the room. When he spoke again his voice was hoarse. He was so much in earnest that it trembled.

'You don't suppose I want to stay here all my life! Screwed up in that desk; bowing to the ladies and gentlemen! You didn't want Dad to do all his own work and serve every Tom, Dick, and Harry with his hands twisting. You've often said you tried to stop that. And did stop it. Well, I don't want to do what he did. I want to go with the times. I want to make my own chain before the other people come and crush me with theirs. At my age, many a fellow has got out of the rut and made himself a fortune. I want to do that. Why can't I? There's no reason why I shouldn't. I've got the knowledge; I can buy and sell. And I want——'

As he grew eloquent, Mrs Whistler interrupted him.

'You won't make a fortune by opening a lot of tin-pot branches. Leave that to cleverer men. You'll do it by staying where you are and making a success of *this* place. Why don't you? Can't you? You're not doing it, you know.'

'I'm doing all you let me. God!' Having shouted at his mother, Bob stood glaring at her, rendered speechless by that implacable profile. Mrs Whistler contemptuously said:

'You say you've got big ideas. I wonder if they're really big. It isn't gas and boasting that count, you know; it's the way you use your opportunities. Your father used his, such as they were. He was careful. I saw to that. It was your father's ambition to make enough to retire on——.'

Bob swore. He rounded upon her. He shouted:

'I'm not old. I don't want to retire!'

Anger was useless; for Mrs Whistler merely spoke with a more acid distinctness.

'No. So I see. Apparently you want to ruin us both.'

'I don't!' shouted Bob. 'Not at all. You don't understand. Never have; never will.' He was quite beside himself, restlessly marching about the room, pushing chairs out of his way, stamping, and jerking his fist in the air with rage, all the time looking like a big schoolboy furious at a tormentor. The old floorboards shook, and ornaments tinkled at his ferociously heavy tread. 'You can't. You haven't even seen Seahampton for twenty years. If you saw it, you'd be surprised. New streets and new houses. Room for rows of big shops. A promenade. Big hotel——'

'All mushroom growth,' sneered Mrs Whistler. 'You'll see it tumble in five years.'

'Not at all. Not at all,' cried Bob, angrily. 'You wouldn't be so scornful if you'd seen it. You couldn't be. You sit at that window, thinking this High Street's the world. It isn't. It's the dead world. We're in a new century. Queen Victoria's dead; and England's waking up at last. Mother, don't you realise that it's now or never?'

For the first time during their interview, Mrs Whistler had moved impatiently. It was because he had attacked her habit of sitting at the window. He implied that she saw only what passed before her eyes. It was deadly insult. From that moment she ceased to snub him, but malignantly used her power.

'We haven't got the money,' she said.

'For this, we have. We've got money, and we've got credit. You think nothing of my brains; but other people do. I tell you I can do this thing. We've got plenty of money. Oh, mother!'

'No.'

'Well, we can get it. *I* can get it.' Bob was threatening her. 'Don't forget that.'

'What?'

'I can get the money on my own. On my own, d'you see?'

'Oh, are you leaving me?' she asked. 'I'm sorry for that.'

Bob wheeled round at the bitter taunt. He stared at her. He had flushed deeply.

'What d'you mean?' he demanded. Mrs Whistler's chin was a little higher. A faint smile played upon her lips.

'Didn't you hear what I said?'

'Yes, I heard. What did you mean?'

'Only that I'll have nothing to do with it. Only that this business is mine, Robert,' said his mother, whitely smiling. 'I've been hearing about *your* plans and *your* ambitions; but they don't concern me. If you want to make chains, that's your affair. Make them for yourself. And if you want to leave me, you can leave me. I can manage without you.'

'By God, you can't!' cried Bob, as one paralysed.

She continued to smile, and saw him blanch.

'Think it over,' she said, composedly. 'You've got swelled head. They've flattered you. It's their mistake, and yours. They don't know that you only do what you're told; but you ought to know it. That's enough; I don't want to hear any more about this nonsense. I've had a tiring day, what with Flora and you.' Indeed, she looked rather tired; but with boredom and distaste, not with agitation. Her smile had given place to an expression of dry displeasure.

'I can get the money from somewhere else,' declared Bob, but in a lower tone of bluster which showed his discomfiture.

'Get it,' answered she. 'And good luck to you. And before you go, hand me the "Gazette". It's on the table there. It'll be a change from looking out of the window.'

She held out a steady hand for the paper; and Bob was so confounded that as if he had been still a boy, and not a young man, he snatched it from its place and crammed it ferociously into her arms. His impulses were murderous. For an instant he stood glowering down at the averted head. Then he stamped from the room, beaten.

Mrs Whistler, who still needed no glasses for reading, smoothed the crumpled paper and opened it. She saw the headlines: 'MR

RICHARD FIRTH MARRIED IN LONDON. SON OF LOCAL MUSICIAN. PRETTY
CEREMONY.' Her eye skimmed the column. 'Son of Mr Gerald Firth
. . . some time a member of the staff of this paper . . . public
spirit . . . platform . . . publicity . . . bride is a London girl,
and only daughter and heiress . . .' She yawned. Somebody was
always getting married. Always bringing into the world children
who were as great fools as their fathers . . . That was the way
civilisation was carried on, for want of a better. As great fools as
their fathers, and as clumsily obstinate. But controllable. There
was nothing in all this. It would pass. She would have no more
trouble with Robert. He was over-excited. The flare-up had been
coming for some time. But it was now over.

IV

Bob, rushing blindly into the High Street, cannoned into young
William Harvest.

'Hullo, Whistler . . .' William would have passed; but Bob
impulsively caught his arm. It was a gesture of desperation for
which he could have given no excuse. He cried vehemently:

'Got five minutes? My God, I want to *talk* to somebody.'

The least demur would have sent him bitterly from William's
side; but there was no demur.

'I won't keep you——' Why, he heard his own voice; and it was
abject! This was what that old hag—that old curmudgeon—had
driven him to: while she sat there at the window sheathing her
claws like a great tabby. 'Hand me the "Gazette" '! He should have
choked her with it! Miser! Devil! With an attempt to simulate
coolness, he said as drawlingly as he could: 'Besides, I think you'd
. . . be interested.'

He breathed roughly, almost gasping; for his heart, beating so
fast, seemed ready to choke him. It was worse now—just as he'd
spoken, trying for self-control—than before. Well, he'd been carried beyond what he'd intended; ordinarily he'd never have
stopped anybody like this. Never. It was a humiliation. . . .
Harvest would think he was drunk, or trying to borrow—excuse

me, sir; just a minute, sir: it was exactly what beggars said as they
seized hold of you with a tale of misery. Now he had a sudden
inkling of what beggars felt; he'd never again brush them harshly
aside. Yes, but why beg? He'd changed his mind. He'd say: 'Oh,
I didn't mean that; pardon me. . . .' Walk away . . .

Too late! While Bob, torn with self-distrust, felt his inclination
for unbosoming wax and wane like the flame of a guttering wick,
William had turned, considerate, attentive, unbored, as if such a
request were the most natural thing in the world. God, he was
cool! How much had he understood? Or known previously? You
couldn't tell. He was short; his eyes hardly above the level of
Bob's shoulder. . . .

Together, as if by agreement, they continued at Bob's pace along
the south side of the High Street until farther progress was stayed
by the ugly old grey church of Moreton. Then they crossed the
sparrow-frequented open space before the church, went along
under Daddy's wall, past their one-time school, and out between
the hedges into the country. By chance, every step linked them
with old associations, and every association had its effect upon
their minds; for while they had not until recently been upon
familiar terms their lives had been spent unchangingly close at
hand, coloured with vision of the same people and social habits,
the same buildings, the same skies and sunsets; and in such a
moment as this the common past wove a thousand emotional
strands of which neither knew although both were simultaneously
influenced by them.

And Bob talked. Within ten minutes he had broken down his
natural reserve, forgotten his past contempts and more recent
jealousies, forgotten his seniority, which had meant less with every
year of manhood, and opened his heart as he had never before
opened it to any human being. He told William all he knew about
his mother and father, his father's death and his feelings at
stumbling upon that silent group around the body, the business,
the general situation of small businesses in country towns beset by
the ventures of new great combines of unlimited resource and
merciless ambition, and finally all about the late battle by which it
might have been proved that the Devil is a woman.

'You see?' he kept saying, at first imperiously, and then with appeal, and finally with the sense that he but exchanged thought with his silently attentive companion. 'You see? That's reasonable, isn't it? Of course, you've no idea what it's meant—living there, I mean. All the time; year after year; every hour. I ought to have got away long ago. But my father dying so suddenly. And I was only a kid. I mean, what could I have done? I'm an only child; I've always been treated as if I hadn't got a will of my own. I can remember thrashings because I'd tried to be clever and stand out for something or go my own way. I was told to shut up. *She* told me. You can't shake off that sort of thing, can you! And I couldn't walk out of the place. You see? Naturally, I thought the business would come to me. It *will* come to me. She's got nobody else. But my God! She may live twenty years.' He gave a bitter laugh. 'By that time it'll be too late. There won't be anything to save. . . .

'Well, what am I to do? I'd made up my mind to go to Lott. He's a business man, and he's got big schemes on. I expect you know all about them—over at Seahampton. He'll see it all right; don't you think he will? You don't? You do? Yes, but the thought came to me: suppose he doesn't? Suppose he listens—you know how he half-listens and takes everything in—with his wooden face; and makes a few notes; and then shakes his head.

'Or his fist,' put in William. 'I know it well.'

Bob stared. The fellow was smiling. But this was serious. Hadn't he understood?

'Well, where am I then? Or suppose he does it himself; just pick my brains, collars everything, and throws me over. That's what he did with Dick Firth; made him his catspaw, and then, when he'd got the nuts, put him in the street. You heard about that, didn't you?'

'It isn't absolutely the whole story. There was a loose nut somewhere.' Bob saw William glance aside at him, half-sympathetic, half-merry. He said, brusquely:

'I'm not surprised. Anyway, I don't mind about Dick, who's an absolute rotter. I'm thinking of myself. D'you see?' But having been so emphatic he grew a little afraid. Had he been too sharp?

He hastened to placate his listener. In a different, apologetic tone, he said: 'I can't help thinking of myself. It means everything to me. I know you understand that. You do, don't you? And you don't mind me speaking like this. . . . Well, now, suppose he lets me have the money—gives me a run—on his own terms; am I any better off than I am now? Exchange masters. Go on for a time; and it doesn't answer. Things are slow, or Lott gets tired, or there's trouble. It ends, and I'm thrown out for good. No money; nothing . . . I mean, if I quarrel with her, clear out, make a mess with Lott, and then there's another blank wall. . . .'

William did not reply; but the merriment had disappeared from his face. He did, then, appreciate the seriousness of the problem. Repeating the words 'and then there's another blank wall,' Bob fell silent. He was so moved that he felt as if his mouth were full of paste, and he trembled a good deal. He several times took a good long examining look at William, trying to read his thoughts or test his temper. He had too little skill. The face he saw was frank, pleasant, but as yet uncommunicative. Bob's lips parted; no speech followed. And yet there was much he had not said, much more he had still to say; for he had reached the crucial part of his confidence.

For a long time they marched along in silence. The sun was setting; a few small white cirrus clouds shone against the azure distance; full-throated skylarks climbed far and near. The road our two men trod was so dry that a white dust shot up at every step and powdered their legs. Everything upon the adjacent land was still, and the shadows of elms and stacks quietly lengthened as the sun sank. Already those white clouds, like minute islands in a fathomless lake, had been caught and gilded by valedictory beams; and a twilight darkness gathered immediately below the western brilliance. Perhaps unconsciously influenced by a sense of the passing day, the two travellers felt their hearts grow heavier.

v

Long afterwards, as it seemed, when the sun was gone and the clouds had changed again from gold to red and grey, Bob heard his companion begin to speak.

'I wish it was anybody but Lott,' said William, deliberately. 'Because Lott's a queer fish. I can't make him out. I've seen him plenty of times, and watched him, too; but I can't get at his mind. I'm afraid he'd let you down in the end.'

'People always let you down in the end,' replied Bob, with gloomy fatalism. He heard the gentle murmur:

'I hope not.' And he was instant and fierce in rejoinder.

'They do. It's my experience.' He could almost have said: *You* might! And such a notion did cross his mind, to be checked by a wholly reassuring glimpse of his confidant. This chap was sincere. He might be silly or stupid, but he was genuine. Bob would swear to it. 'Did you never have a friend who let you down? I did. A fellow I trusted—I thought the world of him; thought we . . . sort of blood brothers. My God, I shall never forget it. Why I trusted him, nobody knows. I suppose because I was a fool.'

'We're all fools,' William said.

'Yes, you realise that later.'

'Well, I know who your friend was,' added William, slowly and candidly. 'I don't know what he did. But you said a little while ago that Lott sent him off at a moment's notice. He did. That's quite a common thing. We're always expecting it to happen to ourselves. It's Lott's way of keeping discipline—by terror. Very demoralising, like conscience. You can see chaps crumbling under it. Firth didn't crumble; he looked after himself. In one way very rightly.'

'Hm. Did he? He *would*. What's he doing now?' asked Bob. Though it had gnawed in his mind, this was the first chance he had had of putting that question to anybody. He would have liked to hear that Dick Firth was in trouble for his pains, the clever devil!

No luck! Bob saw William shrug and smile; and heard him answer, with new animation:

'In London. All sorts of things. Speaking, writing, foraging. He's a busy man.'

'I bet he is.' Bob could not restrain a surge of hatred. Yes, but he was curious. He thought for a long time about Dick. 'You know him, do you?'

'I've seen him at the office. He was always a bit above me.'

Eh? What, brains or years? Dick would make rings round Harvest. Yes, the rotter! But he'd gone from there. London, was it . . . A busy man . . . Up to no good. Well, Bob never wanted to see his face again. But he often thought of him, sometimes with admiration. At that moment, on edge, he thought of him with a kind of sick venom. Memories came so insistently that Bob was quite absorbed in them. But presently—as if he could *not* understand a domestic tyranny—William asked:

'Don't you think you could persuade your mother? Bully her? Coax her into it?'

Damn! It was so futile that Bob felt irritated. The chap would never grasp things as they were. He moved his shoulders restlessly, ignoring the beauty of the greying meadows; and at last demanded:

'Could you persuade an elephant?'

William laughed.

'It has been done.'

'Or coax Mont Blanc?'

'That's more difficult.' Still he smiled. Bob cried:

'You don't see. She's worse than either. I'm frightened of her.'

He could tell that this blurted truth impressed his listener, who for a moment was silenced. At last:

'Couldn't she be made a little frightened of you?'

'Only by choking.' His hands rose before him, and were brought together with ferocious force. God! He could have crushed that thick white neck with such a grip! His feeling was so strong that his body shook.

Apparently Harvest was discouraged; for it was long before he tried again. He seemed to be thinking deeply.

'I suppose you've thought of speaking to Daddy?'

'Daddy?' That old man? Bob saw Daddy's hollow cheeks, heard his antique cackle. Well? He hesitated; a dozen reasons against it rose at once to his mind. Giving one that had not occurred to him, he answered at random: 'But he's practically a dead man.' His doubts continued.

'By no means,' said William. 'By no means.' He had recovered his lightness of tone, and his voice was laughing. 'He's old, and his body's feeble; but he's got a mania for helping people he likes——'

'Does he like me?'

What a quick movement Harvest gave to his hands. They were small hands; Bob saw them for the first time, and was struck by their white flicker in the dusk.

'I don't know. You ought to know. I expect he does. He's pleasant to you, isn't he?'

'I've known him damned *un*-pleasant.'

'That's his manner. He's brusque. But I'd trust him—over money —rather than Lott. He's an old rogue, but he's not a crook. And since Doctor Hodge took him off port, his head's often as clear as crystal.'

'Hm. Is it? I always feel he's laughing at me.'

'Perhaps he is. That's a good sign.' Bob frowned. 'And Julie,' continued William. 'Julie's making him younger every day——'

Bob interrupted.

'Well, you know why that is,' he said. 'She makes him think he'd have a chance if he was half his age. He's a rare old Blue-beard. She sized him up at once.'

'Oh, do you think she could?' It was dubious; almost a protest.

'You bet she did. They've got ways, you known. She has, any-way. Told me so.'

'Julie?'

What a lot of persuading the fellow needed!

'Yes!' laughed Bob. 'But Daddy's out of the question. Impos-sible.'

William sighed. When he spoke there was an edge in his tone. 'All right. Put it out of your head.'

But Bob had already done so. How far could he trust Harvest? He could still see his face, but only in profile, a white clear shape; the expression upon it was baffling. He could not be sure whether, living upon some high and mighty plane, Harvest thought himself entitled to despise him.

'I say,' he began. No; that wouldn't do. How stupid! He groaned. 'Look here, I want . . . Of course, it's awfully compli-cated.' His fists were clenched, his cheeks were warm. 'I mean . . . complicated,' he said again. That was where he was handicapped. Feeling things deeply, as he did. And not being naturally a talker. And feeling that Harvest, with all his goodwill, didn't properly —wasn't old enough, man of the world enough to—understand even what Bob could force himself to say. . . .

'It's certainly not simple,' admitted William, coolly enough. Yes, he could be cool. He had nothing to lose. 'Unless you take every risk. Then, perhaps, it's fatally simple.' He laughed slightly.

'Ah, but——' Bob threw away all caution. 'You don't under-stand. I haven't told you everything. There's a lot more. I've never told anybody what's at the back of it, because, well, it's not only my own affair.' Half-proud of his declared reticence, and yet greatly embarrassed, he was stammering; but Harvest seemed not to notice it. Harvest had given him one look, and then looked away. There was absolutely no knowing what he thought of anything under the sun. And yet it was impossible, now, to go back. If he couldn't be trusted—— Bob said: 'This is between ourselves, Harvest. A dead secret.'

'Certainly,' agreed William, in the most innocent way.

Well, they had got so far; and Bob realised that he was in a perspiration. He was in agony lest his companion should scoff or discourage. As for Harvest, he appeared to swing along without effort, his head up, his shoulders back, his heels firmly striking the road at every step. Bob stammered again.

'You may have seen something—guessed something. I don't know. I don't think so. I mean . . . At any rate, whether you have or haven't, I'll tell you. There's Julie——'

Dreading only interruption, he heard and saw nothing. He might have imagined an arrest and a sudden glance; but he did not do so. He thought all was as before; that as the shadows increased a weight of constraint which had lately oppressed him was a little lifted, so that he could speak more freely. And now that he had pledged himself he was able to continue, like a patient who has revealed his worst fear at the beginning of a consultation. He hurried on:

'In a sense, it's *all* her. You wouldn't understand what it means to me. And it's too long a story to tell. All about me. You've had enough of that. But up to a little while ago—perhaps you do the same—I went on day after day as a matter of course. Never bothered about the future. Yes, I did; a little. Now and then. But it's only in the last two years, since she came, that I've begun to take stock of *myself,* so to speak. You know, look inside, and weigh myself up. And last Winter, one evening when I was with her alone, she began talking rather seriously. Well, I don't know if she's ever done that with you; but it made an impression on me. Has she?'

There was a very long pause.

'What did she say?' asked William, at length, in the same cool voice as before.

Bob had thought so many things in the course of the pause that he was a little confused.

'Oh . . . oh, I know. She was talking about Doctor Hodge. He was with the old man. She said he was quite satisfied to potter along, doing his day's job, getting nowhere. She said she felt she wanted to go behind him and *push*. D'you see? I saw what she meant—at once. And it was after she'd said it that I began—in a way—to realise my own position. I thought: I wonder if she thinks that about me? You know, it was like lightning. Was it a hint: I suddenly thought: why, here I am, half-alive; but as to what's going to happen to me, and what I'm doing with my life, I haven't the least idea. Been taking it for granted. You know, the business, and all that. It made me think, I can tell you. D'you know that I've never had any proper wages? Just pocket money! Of course, I don't mind telling you that I've had a bit more that mother knows nothing about. Well, I couldn't have dressed as I do . . . But all the same, when I started thinking about Julie, and . . .

calculating the chances, I realised that unless I did something pretty big and pretty soon, I hadn't the smallest hope. With her, I mean. She's the sort that many a fellow would go after. Naturally, mother knows nothing about it all.'

'About what?' asked William, in a cold voice. 'Do you mean you're engaged to Julie?'

Why must he be so direct? It was almost like an accusation. Surely he knew that there were degrees in these things?

'Not exactly,' Bob said, out of breath again. 'Still, you know, I think she would. I mean, I haven't put it to her in so many words. How could I? With some, you could; but not with her—— She's self-possessed. It keeps your tongue still. But I've said one or two things. You know, as near as one can, about marriage, and branching out in business. Talked about it generally; said I wasn't satisfied to do the small, safe thing; saw my way, and so on. She's interested. Not just politely, but as if it mattered, rather. She knows what I mean. I'm sure of that.'

'Yes.' It was hardly a sound at all. Bob's memory summoned a picture of Julie's face, half-smiling, shrewdly attentive as he told the first wonders of his plans. It satisfied him. He was reassured. There was no possibility of mistake. The picture was instantly gone.

'But she'd got big ideas. Naturally, being a sort of aristocrat. She wouldn't like the thought of marrying anybody no class, or anybody who had to take everything from his mother——'

'Oh, but the French don't mind that,' said William, quickly. 'The whole family lives in a clump.'

'Ah, yes; but *my* mother!' cried Bob. 'Don't you see, she's a terror! Put yourself in my place. If I've got no position but what mother chooses to allow me, it's pretty humiliating for both of us, isn't it. You see what I mean, don't you. Julie's not a quiet little girl who takes what she's given.' He laughed slightly, almost complacently. 'She wouldn't suit me if she was. That's too easy. She's —well, you know Julie as well as I do. Almost as well as I do.'

'I thought I knew her,' murmured William Harvest.

'What?'

'You say she's got big ideas?'

'Haven't you noticed?'

'To me she's always seemed so perfectly simple.'

Robert brushed that aside.

'Ah, but you're—well, I mean, you're a youngster. She'd be different with you. More a sort of sister.'

'I see.' William's lips turned in a faint smile.

'Besides, you don't really know the game.'

Robert thought he saw his companion's brows fly up. But the reply he received was:

'Are you expert at it?'

'No, but I know something about women. They're all things to all men. They're tougher than we are.'

'Oh, heaven!' was what William said. Bob, encouraged by his apparent stupefaction, continued:

'I should think you'd be the sort of chap to worship a woman— when the time comes.'

'Should I?' William was walking quite dreamily along the road. A change from his former briskness! But they were dealing with very personal things, so this was not surprising. Bob thought he smiled to himself; it was difficult to imagine why. Perhaps some private thought? Inscrutable fellow!

'You don't really see what I mean about Julie. I don't say she's not simple. I think she is. I think she's wonderful——'

'Oh. Yes, I'm glad of that,' said William, gently.

'But I think she's all there,' explained Bob. 'That was what I meant. And I'll tell you something else. Of course it hasn't got anything to do with it—I mean, you'll see when I tell you. . . . Daddy's fearfully old, now. And Julie's his nearest relation. It's not unreasonable to suppose that she'll get all he leaves, is it? This is something quite apart from what we've been discussing. I mean, I hope I'm not the sort of fellow to go after a girl just because . . . But what I thought was, Julie having a bit of money—a *good* bit, because Daddy's a warm man—that would make everything a lot easier. For one thing, the old girl loves money. That's why she's kept me so short. Yes, but damn it, these old people are so bloody healthy. And Daddy hangs on to his own. He gets older and older, and as you say stronger and stronger. A little while ago it was all beef tea and slops; but since he's had his new teeth he puts away the breast of a chicken like a two-year-old. Hear him snapping it! And Hodge looks on, purring. What is he? Eighty-five? Eighty-six? He might live to be a hundred; at any rate, ninety. And I can't *wait* for that; because I want the money *now*. It's so important. My God, what a curse money is! I hate the stuff; and yet I admit I'd like to get hold of fifty thousand pounds. Even ten. I suppose I've rather addled things with mother by having this row with her.'

'You're in a mess,' remarked William.

'I am, aren't I,' agreed Bob. 'I hope you're not glad.'

'Oh, we're all in messes,' said William. 'Galore.'

Bob did not know whether that was an invitation or not. He had no time to leave the main theme.

'I've got all sorts of things worked out; but I'm checked. I'd go to the bank tomorrow; Perkin's a very decent chap, and he'd let me have every farthing I need. But if I went to Perkin he'd say: "What about *her?*" That would finish it. When I met you, I was beside myself. Felt I hadn't got a friend in the world. And I haven't, either.'

'Oh, come!' said William.

'It's true. I suppose I'm too exacting. Something, at any rate. My God, I hate the trade I'm in. Retail. You know, it's big figures that interest me. Planning. That's what I told Julie. But I want to be happy, too.'

'Yes,' answered William. 'Something we all want.'

'I suppose you do, too. It was a bit thick of me, nailing you like this tonight. But I've always thought you were the kind of chap who'd understand. And besides, talking about you with Julie——'

'Talking about me with Julie?' exclaimed William, sharply.

'Yes.' Bob hesitated. He said: 'She thinks a lot of you. Did from the first. You were the first person she spoke to in Moreton.'

'No,' corrected William. 'Minna Manning was the first.'

'Oh, well, Julie doesn't count her. She's a child. You were the first *man*. I say, old chap; don't be offended, but she worries about you.'

'That's very kind,' said William, coldly. Bob blundered on: his tongue was desperately loose.

'She's afraid you won't—you know, set the Thames on fire. It worries her. Well, I've got something the same idea. But I feel you're genuine. You know what I mean: reliable. I . . . sort of trust you. Of course I do: otherwise I couldn't have told you all I *have* done, could I!'

'No,' said William. 'You couldn't, could you.' Before Bob could be sure about his tone, William added: 'Then, if you talk things over with Julie, why not ask Julie's advice? About leaving your mother, going to Lott, waiting, and so on. If you're sure of her, and she's involved, it seems only right that she should have some say in it——'

'Good lord, no!' Bob felt a stab of consternation run through him. 'I say, you won't give her the least hint, will you! Of course you won't.'

'I shan't say a word,' said William. 'But it does affect her, doesn't it?'

'In a way. In a way. But not the way you think. Listen; I'll tell you something, Harvest. It's this. When you have anything to do with women, you've got to be very careful *what* you let them know, and *how,* and *when.* Always the *fait accompli. After.* Keep them busy catching up to your plans.'

'Marvellous!' William exclaimed. 'How's it done?'

Bob gave him a great slap on the shoulder. Then he dropped his voice to a hoarse whisper.

'Julie knows perfectly well about Daddy's money. Knows everything—I mean, about the use it would be to me, and all it stands for. But if I were to give her the smallest hint that I knew she'd ever thought of it, or that I'd ever thought of it, she'd go crazy. She'd never speak to me again. They call it "pride". It isn't. It's just that they like to wrap life up in petticoats as long as their own. Flannel petticoats.'

'Wonderful!' said William. 'They call it "pride", do they? It sounds to me like Psychology.'

'I don't know the proper name for it,' answered Robert. 'But I wasn't born yesterday. And I know Julie better than you do.

She's all there; but she's simple. In some things she's got to be kept in the dark, and in some others she's got to be rushed. Now, Julie . . .'

They were five miles from home, and it was very nearly dark. Stars were in the sky; the trees were blacker and closer about the lanes, as if they crowded together for the night; and the road dimmed before the travellers. Bob could not clearly see William's face; it was no more than a shadowed pallor somewhere to the right of his shoulder. But he continued to address his speech to that pallor, confident of sympathy. His heart felt warmer and warmer towards William, who in virtue of semi-invisibility became increasingly the perfect embodiment of understanding. His courage revived. His spirit mounted.

VI

Minna stood very quietly at the big gate in front of Royals. She could no longer see the road to Moreton; for while she waited at the gate the distance had first blurred and then, very gradually and beautifully, had crept closer and closer until nothing at all remained visible in that soft darkness. An owl's shrilly menacing cry from among the trees filled her with foreboding. And Minna, though the lighted windows of her home were within a hundred yards, ignored them, watching and listening as if her very breath were stilled in the effort.

A long time passed. A sense of solitariness caused her to shudder, but she did not move. At last she heard, faint in the night silence, the ring of very distant steps and a confused murmur of voices; and she knew that two men would presently pass the gate by which she stood. They would not be able to see her, because she wore a grey wrap reaching to her heels and was well-masked by the shadowed entrance; but as they came abreast of her she would learn if one of them had come this way with purpose. If William was not there, she could stay no longer, but must go back to the house with all hope for the evening abandoned. Meanwhile, sighing, she waited. The evening wind, still warm, and sweet with the perfume of roses, touched her cheeks and her parted lips as if in caress.

Tramp, tramp; they were striding in step. Two bold venturers marching about the lanes and rearranging the universe. Ah, but from the opposite direction to the one she scanned! Then her hope was vain! Wait! Wait! Listen! She strained her ears. One of the marchers talked and talked; but it was not he. Minna thought: what a deep grumbly voice the man has! It rolled upon the air like muffled drums—thud, grrrr; and if it were possible, as Miss Rapson always said, to assess character by voice alone, this was an enviable chance! What was the speaker like? Trying to divert her mind from its painful concentration upon a single theme, Minna guessed him to be a strong, humourless, conceited man with a long black Niagara moustache and a big watch-chain and a coif. Very fixed eyes, like a doll's, but duller—like a bridegroom in a rural photograph. 'You know my methods, Watson!' That awful boom! It was much nearer now. And yet not a boom, but a mere noise, as if he were talking into a jug or through a bandage. Louder, louder. Uninterrupted. A very common man, she thought. Perhaps honest—that was probable. But without poetry, without noble sensitiveness; or he could never, on such a night, under the stars and with the warm wind playing, have bawled so. Whisper, my man, whisper! He was married, of course. Apt in haranguing his wife—wahm, wahm, wahm. Domineering to his children. Tramp, tramp! The other voice said something brief. Oh, dear, too brief. She could not plainly hear the voice; yet the conviction that it was William's stirred her heart and brought a quick smile to her lips. They came nearer. Very near. There was no slackening of speed; they would pass in the darkness. In a moment they would be gone.

'I'll tell you something else about women,' boomed the talker, upon a note of egregious triumph. 'And that's that they'll swallow *any* compliment at a gulp——' Oh! The pompous! The odious! The mere! She strained her eyes to see him. Yes, a big man. But his companion was not; his companion was——

'William!' cried Minna, desperately. 'William!' Certainty stilled every doubt. She would have known him everywhere.

Both men stopped. So instant was the halt that somebody's feet scrabbled upon the roadway like those of a slipping horse. A voice —his voice—came like music through the darkness:

'Where are you, Minna?'

Hadn't she known? Oh, her heart was light enough now! She showed herself, a ghost in the darkness, invisible until she raised the white handkerchief which had been held tightly in her fingers. Then, like bobbing phantoms, they came towards her and were suddenly immense and palpable.

'You'd forgotten!' Minna said, reproachfully, to William. 'You'd never have come!'

'Oh, my aunt!' It was a gasp of unalloyed concern. 'Minna! This is terrible!'

Forgetting that he could not see what she did, Minna vigorously nodded.

'It is,' she implacably agreed. 'Intolerable. But you're forgiven. I can't see who's with you.'

'All my fault, Miss Manning,' growled the burly voice, in great good humour. Not a trace of shame! 'Robert Whistler. Excuse me. We've been for a long tramp. I persuaded him to come.'

Horror! This man? If the kind night hid Minna's disgust, she was still in a difficulty; for charity did not extend from the intolerable to the insufferable. Why, what on earth could William have to do with Robert Whistler? He was *utterly* mere!

'Good evening, Mr Whistler.' Then, severely: 'Mr Harvest promised to be here by eight o'clock.'

There was a murmur between the two men; some apologies, evidently, being made by Robert Whistler. William said:

'I say, isn't it a bit too late, now? I don't know what the time is. I'm so sorry, Minna. I'd better go on——'

'Don't be ridiculous!' Minna felt that she would die rather than let him go. Particularly to Robert Whistler! She put out her hand in the darkness and caught his arm. 'William, mother's expecting you.' Was there more she could do? Inhospitable—yes, but this wretched man—if he was William's friend. And William such a Socialist! She struggled to say: 'Perhaps Mr Whistler would come and explain to her?'

For a moment, because they both hesitated, Minna's heart sank. That moment seemed a long one. It gave time for the light play in her heart of every emotion between hope and despair. But William's new friend showed that he had sense. Even tact. He did not stammer; he quietly thanked Minna, and refused. And thus became in her eyes—and vocabulary—almost godlike. Finally he pressed William's shoulder with a firm hand of resolve.

'Good night, old chap. You've saved my life,' he said. 'I'll never forget it.' And then: 'It's very kind of you, Miss Manning. I appreciate it. If you knew everything you'd forgive us both. I'm sure Mr Harvest's better at explanation than I am. It takes me a whole evening, you see. And I . . . er . . . rather think . . . that *my* mother will be waiting. . . .'

He grasped William's elbow to emphasise the profoundly humorous meaning of his remark, and perhaps to stimulate his own courage; raised his hat, and turned away. A few steps sounded; a shadow moved; and night swallowed the interloper. Minna and William were alone in the darkness.

She slipped her hand familiarly within his arm, her cheek close to his shoulder.

'That wretched man! It's a pity you saved his life, William! However, he's better than I thought. William, I was afraid something had happened to you. Did you just forget?'

How low he spoke! How wearily and unsmilingly! No joggle of the arm; no tenderness. Just a flat:

'I forgot. I'm so sorry.'

Minna, still elated, said:

'But he made you.'

'He talked to me.'

She shook the arm she lightly held. It was rigid.

'Good heavens! Talked! I could hear him any distance away! Odious man! "Women will gulp *any* compliment"!'

'He's in trouble,' explained William.

'So you let him cling!' cried Minna. '*He'd* have no conscience.'

'I thought of you at first.'

'And then you were drowned.'

'Absorbed.'

'William! But you're easily interested, poor lamb!'

They were walking close together up the carriage-way to Royals, and the lighted lattice windows were before them in the darkness. Near the house the leaves of a golden privet caught the lamp's ray and shone again with breath-taking lustre. But Minna, who ordinarily would not have missed such beauty, was listening and thinking too intently to notice it.

'I'm sorry for him,' she heard William say, in a murmur almost inaudible. Minna was indignant.

'You're sorry for everyone—except yourself!' she exclaimed.

She felt a movement of his arm, as if he had shivered; and was filled with remorse.

'And I'm pestering you! Oh, my poor William, what an evening you must have had!'

'A bit tiring. What's the time?' asked William, in a brisker tone, as if her expressed pity had roused him to a show of present-mindedness. 'I'm sorry I forgot you, old girl. Isn't it too late for me to come in now? I feel it must be five minutes to midnight on Judgment Eve.'

So bitter was the tone that Minna was terrified.

'As tired as that?' she breathed. 'Something's the matter! William!'

'Nothing's the matter,' said William, firmly. 'Nothing that I can tell you.'

'*His* business?'

'Oh, yes.' It was weary enough. 'His business.'

A moment later they were indoors, dazzled by the light of the room, greeted by Mrs Manning's slow smile as she looked up from idle contemplation of the crochet which lay upon her knee.

'Weel-liam!' she said, in her slow, pleasant way. 'I had almost given up hope for you. Is Minna there? Minna, darling——'

Minna was standing back, looking at William. He was so pale that she thought he must be ill. His lips were dry, his eyes so drawn that they seemed to stare.

'He's had two hours or more of a politician, mother. That big young man, the grocer. Sit down, William. Two minutes of Mr Whistler makes me yawn——'

'Oh, but you're so impatient, Minna,' drawled her mother. 'She's like her father, William. As restless as he is. And so quick-tempered——' Mrs Manning had always spoken slowly, in a rich and painful voice; but by this time, owing to the fact that she was very ill, her slowness had become a drawl.

'There's some supper for you, William,' Minna said. 'I'll ask Rose to bring it in.'

That gave her a moment, which was very necessary; for the shock of realising that William was unhappy affected her so strongly that her teeth seemed ready to chatter. She was absent from the room for an instant only, and when she returned William was sitting near her mother, listening to the slow recital of a dream or some irrelevant adventure, abstractedly smiling as if nothing at all had happened. In shadow, and seated so that his hands were hidden, he might have been as debonair as usual. If Minna had not been strung by her vigil to heightened sensitiveness, she would have been deceived. She was not deceived.

She was familiar with every expression of William's face, from the gayest to the gravest; and she had never seen such pain about his lips as that first stupefying glimpse had revealed, or such alternate constraint and lethargy as there was in his present manner. Hesitating in the doorway, and watching him as he believed himself unobserved, she did not realise how fast her thoughts flew and how impetuously they tried to penetrate the infinities of her ignorance. A miracle only could have discovered the secret; and though Minna tiptoed to catch inspiration she was still baffled. What did she know, what *could* she know, of him, save—blindly—that he was William, the kind, the loving, for twenty years her dearest companion, sum of all the sympathy and strength of character she had ever experienced. Not once had he failed her. Not once, until tonight.

Minna was trembling. She had loved William all her life with the completest trust, proudly assured of his unshakable courage; and if he should be beaten she would be robbed at once of her last certainty. Now, if her nerves, her straining intelligence, her leaping, vehement guesses, told her the truth, he needed her help. How gladly Minna would have given it! Not even the fear of his displeasure, his dislike of demonstrative emotion, his self-protective ridicule, would have driven eagerness back into the warm heart from which it came. But she could not move. She was transfixed by an intuition so swift that it had passed before she had fully grasped its import. 'He won't tell me anything. Ever, as long as we're alive. I can't help him. I'm useless.'

So crushing was this realisation that the blood drained from Minna's cheeks. Her eyes shone. For a moment she was insensible to everything that happened about her.

CHAPTER VII
A Conflict of Ideals

THE CLOCK upon the mantelpiece struck seven, which meant that
the time was a quarter to ten. Pausing for a moment in her work
—she was dusting the front ground floor of Daddy's house, where
he kept his books, and where there was now such cheerful cleanliness that hands no longer blackened at a touch,—Julie moved
towards the window.

The High Street was almost deserted. An extremely old retriever
dog squatted outside the cornchandler's shop, and two or three
women with provision baskets dragged their long skirts over the
clean pavement; but the hour of general shopping had not begun.
And so, with the duster hanging from her half-raised hand, Julie
saw at a glance all that there was to be seen out of doors. A kind
of mocking melancholy was in her dark eyes, the whites of which
looked so delicately blue, and upon her thin lips, where promises
eternally hovered; and although she did not smile she seemed
every minute about to do so.

> *'Quand j'étais p'tit,*
> *Je n'étais pas grand;*
> *J'allais à l'écol'*
> *Comm' les p'tits enfants*
> *Mon pain dans ma poch' . . .'*

That she should now hum one of the little tunes that French
schoolchildren chant together was possibly, though not certainly,
a sign of abstraction. One never knew, with Julie, who might have
hummed as she fed a dog with poison or tortured a lover or suffered in herself an agony of incurable pain. The dark eyes, which
at first had been directed carelessly from point to point in the

139

scene, were narrowed into watchfulness. The thin lips straightened. The hand which held the duster sank very gradually, like a listless ensign, to her side.

Immediately afterwards, something happened which brought the promise of a smile again to Julie's lips. Her waning interest in the scene was revived, and with knuckles lightly pressed to her corseted waist she rather ironically gazed out of the window. Far down the High Street, upon its southern pavement, almost opposite the Royal Hotel, a single moving figure had appeared.

The figure was that of a slight, rather short man in his early twenties, plainly dressed and inconspicuous, who walked so quietly and quickly that his arms swung hardly at all. The young man advanced upon the High Street towards Julie. He passed the Bank and the linendrapers' double-fronted shop which showed all the new fashions of a season earlier. He was abreast of Miss Arnold's old red brick house (oddly plain amid the plate glass fronts of its neighbours), of Whistlers', of the pastrycook's, the stationer's . . . In a moment he would be almost level with the statue, would cross the street diagonally behind it to the north side, glancing towards Daddy's house and smiling, as he always did, although he never knew that she was there to see his greeting, and would then disappear. To work! Julie drily smiled. One knew well that his work was an unprofitable idleness, a dream, something—yes, something that did not in the least matter. Charming, kind, futile young man! So much understanding; and so little force of character! She shrugged impatiently. One could do nothing with such a nature...

Such thoughts were interrupted by a surprise. When the young man crossed the street he did it blindly, without raising his eye in salute to Daddy's house. His head was lowered. That was exceptional. It was inexplicable.

'A migraine.' There was a change in Julie's expression, from irony and impatience to concern, and then to a darkness which was almost cruelty. 'No; he is distrait. He obeys his mood—it is weakness. Always high or low. At this moment, dying. In an hour he will live again. I, too, am dying.' The duster was cast down. 'But I am strong. I do not yield. He loves me; he is an angel. But what levity! "We have nothing to eat; but never mind, there is th sun shining, and the birds are singing; and there is this charming poem I shall read to you. . . . So much better than bread." Mon dieu! How innocent! How careless! A feather!'

Her thoughts ceased to express themselves coherently, and went farther into nature. She imagined herself married to William, who, since he had grace and charm, was not displeasing to her. More than that, who was pleasing to her in relation to every lighter impulse of love. But she believed him incapable of transport. Kindness, that gift of the gods, he assuredly had; but passion, no. To one such as herself, an ogress (she thought), what a gentle, unsatisfying lover! Julie shook her head in decision. It was essential that she should have irresistible power over the senses of the man she married. It was equally essential, to her self-respect, that in marriage she should seem to retain a spiritual superiority, that she should as it were yield with exquisite reluctance to a coarser will. She now had, over William, the unearthly power conferred by his own reverence; but since he was as quick as a woman he would in time make full discovery of her mind, leaving her nakedly desirous. . . .

Good heavens! Julie's face grew haggard. It was fortunate for her that, as she stood tapping an impatient foot, with her back to the window and her arms challengingly folded, she spied in a recess at the nearer end of the mantelpiece a small paper bag of sweets. For the first time that morning the promised smile destroyed her gravity and triumphed over crisis.

II

Julie's childhood had been spent drably enough in the home of her maternal grandmother, who lived—a very small, meagre, chocolate-eyed woman in black with a many-wrinkled face and the thinnest white hair in the world—upon the outskirts of Lyons. There was no grandfather; he had died long, long ago, even before the Franco-Prussian War. It was a poor household, its food exclusively bread, soup, eggs, and home-grown vegetables, and was for the most part supported by irregular remittances from Paris, where Julie's seldom-seen mother lived in reputed affluence. She was a great lady, they said, the associate of ministers, wits, artists, and the like, who occasionally, in her preoccupation with weightier matters, forgot to send money to her beloved maman and her little daughter.

And then, one day when she was twelve, Julie had found her grandmother stiff and still in a chair, a truly shocking experience for one so young. The discovery had left its mark upon her mind to this day. But after a little confusion there had been some correspondence, and Julie, with everything arranged by a neighbour who did well out of the business, had left the hovel in order to venture alone to Paris. There—astonishingly—her mother lived alone in a small apartment near the markets, almost as poorly, it proved, as the grandmother had done; and for the most part supported by irregular remittances from somebody whom Julie did not see until much later, when she was fifteen. This was truly an illustration of the French saying, *plus ça change, plus c'est la même chose,* a fact which Julie did not fail to observe.

When the remittances came, there was jubilant feasting, with sweet white wine and chicken and beautiful cheeses; but between whiles there were long stretches of insufficiency, and sometimes whole days upon which Julie was forced to go hungry, cold, and miserable. As a rule she wore only such clothes as she and her mother could devise from the cast-off garments of others. They grew clever at the work, and in delving among the market stalls on Sunday mornings for what could be turned to account. It gradually occurred to Julie that neither her grandmother, who had worked incessantly, grumbling and groaning, nor her mother, who stayed in bed when she had no food and who was spendthrift when she had any money, had made the best of their lives. Neither could answer her practical questions but with rodomontade, excuse, vague reference to old splendour, pride, France, and the rewards of Eternity. And so the younger Boucard (her grandmother had been Madame Brisset), who was born observant and cool-headed, quite early determined that her own bid for fortune should be of a different order from theirs.

There had ever been, for maman—that dying, faded young

woman with the brusque manner of a spoilt favourite and the fantasy of deferred wealth—the English cousin. She had had the common French belief that all Englishmen and Americans are rich; and she had been convinced that the English cousin would prove to be a Crœsus. She used him relentlessly in obtaining credit or credence; she dreamed of him; but when she applied to him for help he remained obstinately silent, and his very silence gave him additional promise. She pretended that he wrote her the most charming letters, that he was full of business, that he was presently coming to Paris with a coach, lackeys, and money bags. The meals he would give them, the meals they would give him, were so superbly planned that in imagining them maman often felt she had already dined. She smacked her lips. Ah! Ah! Delicious! But Julie never felt that she had dined. She only felt hungrier than ever.

'My cousin, Monsieur Griffin, will give you a magnificent dot, *ma chérie*,' declared Madame Boucard, upon her deathbed. 'And will find you a husband with money and food in plenty.' 'My faith,' answered Julie; 'I shall have need of many meals!' 'In England,' added her mother, ignoring the interruption, 'such men abound.' Indeed, at this moment she saw a procession of them, long-visaged and with innumerable large teeth, all wealthy. . . . In her last days she composed a beautiful letter to the rich cousin. With how much conscious humbug it was impossible to say, she pressed it superbly into Julie's hands and bade her be of good cheer, for it was a talisman. Then her illness took a painful turn; she gave, either in confession or delirium, glimpses of her early life which the child never forgot; and when the end came Julie escaped the plans of her mother's erstwhile protector, strapped everything she owned into a single bag, and left her native land as resolutely as any younger son in a fairy tale. Fortune, she was confident, lay ahead.

Her first introduction to Daddy had been a blow. He had looked to be a dead man. She at once saw herself destitute in a strange land, helpless and starving once again. But she had found Daddy just strong enough to say that she might remain in his house. She had taken charge of the cooking. She had nursed him. And now, in Daddy's house, she breathed more freely than she had ever done. With the aid of one quiet middle-aged woman (Daddy's old housekeeper, Anna, had just found rest in the churchyard), she kept the place as sparkling as the age and unconcealable wear of most of the furniture in it allowed. For this work she received lodging and ample food, with occasional presents of money which were given by Daddy with fervent surreptitiousness. And she had expectations. Daddy liked to call her his niece, and to stroke her fingers, and as a great treat to be kissed by her upon his bald forehead. He sometimes stared hard at her, and nodded, with a grunt; which suggested that he made plans for her future. But what these could be, Julie could not discover; for although Daddy was quizzically, secretly, body-shakingly amused at the immaculate residence in his house of a beautiful young woman, he preserved silence as to every future prospect.

III

Having eaten abstemiously of the sweets, Julie hid them again—from herself. She resumed and finished her dusting, without again beckoning agitation by further intensive thought of William Harvest. Some thought she gave him, of course, but it was of that dismissive order which goes with a waved hand or a trifling cry of impatience. She went up to Daddy's room, where although, in the vain hope that she would treat him as a baby, he pretended each morning to be too feeble for the task, she made him wash his own face and hands. She then helped him out of bed, and while he grunted and panted his way into the day's clothes she threw back the bedding in fine disorder to air the mattress. Daddy refused altogether to have his mattress and bolster hung out of the window, French fashion; and not a window in the house could be opened while he was within sight or hearing.

At the end of the toilet came Daddy's first moment of happiness; for Julie then brushed and combed his hair, tweaked his beard, gave the top of his head a tap, and held a little mirror before him so that he could approve her handiwork. His second moment came when she gave him her arm to the door. How feebly the old man leaned upon it! He exaggerated the amount of help he needed.

And Julie showed that she knew he exaggerated. And Daddy sniggered and chuckled as they tottered along together, she so straight and slim, and he so bent; while he thought to himself what a fine piece of luck it was that he should have such an attractive cousin to support him in his old age. 'Why, I could almost envy myself,' he thought. 'But if I was forty years younger—ah, but then I shouldn't get any help! No, and I shouldn't ask it, either, he-he-he!' His chin sometimes, even now, almost managed to rest upon Julie's shoulder when they paused, but never quite.

Once Daddy was downstairs, Julie and Sarah—that was the maid-of-all-work—made his bed, swept and dusted his room, and allowed light and air to sweeten it. Usually he sat in the drawing-room which opened its French windows on to the garden; but today the weather was so warm that Daddy was steered straight into the garden and to his comfortable chair under the blue sky. There, well wrapped about with overcoat and rug, and wearing an old cloth hat which made him resemble a scarecrow, he basked in the morning sunshine with a book into which he never once peeped.

Instead of reading, he looked out over the ragged flower-beds, and slightly shook his head as if with incipient tic, while a thrust sang in the tree above, a chaffinch fearlessly hopped near his feet, and the lovely ripple of a wren's laughter rose above all the simple-minded chirruping of busy sparrows. Daddy never read now. He made a choice among his books, and sometimes called for a favourite; but when it was in his hand his eyes wandered, his mouth fell open, and presently the book slipped and tumbled to the ground. Then Daddy swore, and shouted screamingly for Julie, who left her work and brought a little table upon which the book might lie until he wanted it. She knew he would not lift it again. He only wanted her to wait upon him.

Leaving Daddy there, his head drooping towards his right shoulder, his eyes rather vacantly fixed as if he listened entranced to the beating of his own heart, and his yellow chin now visible through the thinned and straggling white beard, Julie returned to the house. It was half-past eleven. How restless she felt this morning! The glimpse of William's melancholy had stirred her mind. From the moiling depths arose memory of another face. It was not a picture;

a sense. Fancy, being seized, grew more and more active, rising quickly each instant until Julie's senses trembled with life. Ah! This was a different curiosity, a changed approach, as significant as it was rapid. What was *he* doing? No name, but *'he'*. Excitedly, she thought: *His* great strong hands and arms and shoulders could crush the breath out of her body. . . .

'Mon dieu!' She was stifling, struggling. The small teeth showed between her lips.

'Sarah!' she called. 'I am going out. To shop. Yes, to shop. What? some starch? Yes, yes. But, my dear Sarah, there is plenty of soap. We do not *eat* soap. At least, I do not! Very well. You will listen for Mr Griffin, won't you! Thanks.'

In ten minutes, with her head downcast and her face bafflingly demure, she left the house carrying a basket. How warm it was in the High Street! She must walk slowly, quietly, or she would grow moistly over-heated, as these poor souls were who trudged along pushing their ugly children in wheelbarrows or go-carts or whatever they called themselves. Red-faced, gauche, solemn. Their skirts sagged from the waist and the tails of them dipped awry. Their corsets creaked and bulged. They were bunched with too many clothes. They feared to show a morsel of stocking. Their heels were turned. They were slatternly hypocrites and slaves. How stupid. How flaccid, tasteless, cow-like! . . .

Calmly walking past the loiterers without appearing to notice them, Julie missed no single envious or sullen glance, no spark of admiration, no whisper, no averted head, no following eye as she crossed to the shady side of the street upon her high-heeled French shoes. It amused her to know that she attracted so much jealous attention. Dawdling a little, she allowed herself a rich sigh which filled her breast with exquisite lightness. A swift sidelong glance in the pastrycook's window; a touch to her hair . . . Then, very self-possessed, she stepped across the threshold of Whistlers'.

The shop was very dark, and it was crowded with goods. All along under the counter were square biscuit tins; above the counter and tucked into every corner of the busy shelving were tins and packets and little jars which glowed like rubies with re-flected light. And Julie, well used to the procedure of Whistlers',

waited at one side while a grand lady with a loud voice monopo-
lised the anxiously servile attention of an assistant, and while the
other assistant smacked and lashed in fury at a great butter-berg
behind the marble façade of the dairy counter. Smack, crash! went
his large pats; and two little girls stared at him as if their eyes
would pop right out of their heads in rapture.

The loud voice of the grand lady sounded like a foghorn voice
of a soap-box speaker. Two other women chatted in whispers as
they waited, so quietly that their lips hardly moved, and with
such mysteriousness that they heightened the air of exceptional
industry and suspense which today pervaded the shop. But where,
amid this conspiratorial constraint, was *he*? Julie's heart fell. She
was tempted to walk out again into the street.

Julie did not leave the shop. She would have done so if she had
not at that moment seen Robert Whistler hurrying—he, too, un-
wontedly, feverishly, alert!—from the remote darkness; and at
sight of him, although her heart did not quicken, some inner
tension relaxed. You have perhaps seen a cat's eyelids momentarily droop in recognition of a master or mistress? The softening
is gone again at once, and the coolness of apparent indifference is
restored; but feeling has been shown. It was so at this instant with
Julie, who could give or withhold encouragement at will. She
stood, nevertheless, as before, noticeably unaware of his nearness.
She regarded with irony the loud-voiced lady, who thought herself impressive and was in fact ridiculously self-important. Fat,
shapeless; one had no need of a cruel mind to know that she was
flabby with self-indulgence and ill-health. But Julie's mind held
great malice; she saw more than that, without remorse. The lady's
clothes, the lady's hair, the bags under the lady's eyes, were all
instantly comprehended. Smiling in secret, she passed to the
second of the two women who had been chatting; but found her
inquisitive and without interest, and after causing the woman to
lose countenance looked away again. The first woman now engaged Robert's attention.

'Aaaaand send me . . .' bawled the lady.

'No, two *ounces*,' whispered the woman, to Robert.

'Mon dieu!' thought Julie, with sharp impatience. Her foot

tapped the floor of the shop in a bitter tattoo. This place was be-witched! It had an atmosphere of disquiet which all, apparently, felt. What was wrong, with him, with everybody? He was hand-somer than ever today. A little pale; it suited him. But something harassed; not himself. Another person had looked so: had he and William quarrelled? Over her? Stupid. Yet amusing, perhaps. Wil-liam was absurd; it would not be he that quarrelled. . . . Her lip curled as she thought of William; and at that instant Robert looked at her—furtively. Not his old possessive yet entreating glance, which asked always if she understood his wish, loved him, permitted him to hope, while she ruthlessly answered yes or no at whim and laughed, relishing her power. Quite different. Dis-agreeably, it was a look of shame. What, had he fallen out of love? For a moment, a cruel desire to hurt him arose in her. With teeth set and lips pressed close, she became as hard as a stone. But under that air of harshness she was conscious of a loss of assurance in herself.

Robert was gone again. No greeting. No unseen signal of pleas-ure. It was incredible! There must be some reason. Not even a quarrel with William could explain such carriage. Julie grew more uneasy. What *was* the matter? Without moving her head, she em-braced more searchingly the occupants of the shop—the bawling lady, the whisperers, the two children, the servers; none of them could account for his agitated neglect to greet her. Stealthily, she scrutinised again the too-zealous assistants, who were ordinarily suave, patient, and leisurely; brisk only in an hour of extreme pres-sure. Did not they, too, show signs of quite exaggerated concentra-tion? Did not they ever and anon flick into the darkness, always to the same spot, a peculiar apprehensive inquiry?

At last, following one such peep as it flew, Julie fancied she saw something. She almost laughed. A ghost! She looked again and again, always from under her hat, through her lashes, without turning. No ghost, but a tall woman standing in the shadow. The dimness at first hid and then gradually revealed a dead white face which she would have recognised anywhere from its resemblance to his. His eyes, but colder, more malignant. His height and strength, but a greater impassivity. Julie was moved to intense interest. She had never before seen this woman. She now had a first chilling glimpse of her; and as if by magic there came a complete elucidation of the whole scene. More than the scene; a whole situation of the utmost importance. She grew very grave.

Gravity was still upon her as the two whispering women departed; and when Robert, forestalling the assistant who had served the two children, interposed his broad body between that mysterious watcher and herself she was so troubled that she treated him with alarming coldness. As if this drove him to desperation, Robert, in taking her order, seemed deaf and unable to concentrate. His hands were unsteady. He said, too loudly:

'Yes, madam; the three-and-ninepenny size?'

Imbecile! He was beside himself.

'Listen!' hissed Julie, warningly. Then she smiled at him.

The effect was instant. Such relief crossed his face that she could have laughed.

'I beg your pardon. Certainly, madam. . . .' Under his breath: 'Will you be at home tonight? May I come and see you? It's very important—very.'

Julie's heart leapt to rapid movement. Her coolness was less. But she allowed surprise to chill her tone, nevertheless.

'If you wish.' They said no more.

He was calmer thereafter, but still humble; she self-confident, thoughtful, disappointed, at the height of sensitiveness to all that was happening. When she looked again for that silent figure it had disappeared; and she saw the assistants exchange grins of relief. Then other customers entered; she received her parcels; and without any further exchange of speech she left the shop. Crossing the High Street with less verve than she had shown a quarter of an hour before, Julie entered Daddy's house absorbed in thought. She had received a shock which for some time paralysed her will.

IV

In deep abstraction, she went very quickly to her bedroom, tearing off hat and gloves and throwing them down upon the white counterpane as if they had been distasteful, and moving restlessly about the creaking boards. This shock—the discovery of Mrs Whistler, the lightning perception of a new and possibly craven Robert—filled her with consternation; for the kaleidoscope had turned and her life's pattern was suddenly awry. Less than two hours earlier, feeling secure, she had dismissed William with exasperation as a feather; now, inexplicably, she felt herself surrounded with uncertainty and was fighting against panic.

William could be delayed; but unlike one less quick he could not be cheated. If she played, she lost him. Under lightness, there might be steel. He had captured her fancy, her taste; and self-love sought a thousand ruses to keep a lover forever unsatisfied. Confronted, however, with the direct question, her judgment had seen no prospect in marriage with William but an unhappy one. Unpassionate, unpractical, unworldly fool! cried Julie's judgment. Well, there had seemed, an hour earlier, to be a plain alternative, prudent and satisfying, the thought of which had caused her blood to tingle. Safe, strong, within her powers. She had decided. But, immediately, she had encountered that white-faced woman, full of menace. She had seen *him* afraid. That was horrible! The swift, shocking thought came: William would not have been afraid. . . .

It maddened Julie. She drew one palm sharply across the other, as if to show that she was finished with all this. But if this were finished, what succeeded? She was terrified. Plunging with clenched fists about the room, she was shaken with unuttered screams.

Before luncheon, Julie was calm again. Nevertheless, as she sat alone at the table, while Daddy munched and mumbled at a little table beside his armchair, she was long silent. She was so long silent that Daddy tried to make a little conversation. He said:

'Is young William coming round today?'

Julie jumped at his tone and his theme. With suppressed exasperation she answered:

'I do not know. He is very stupid.'

Daddy grinned.

'I never noticed it,' he remarked. 'And I don't believe he is. Of course, I don't say he's a genius.'

'No, he is certainly not that,' said Julie. The old fool was exasperating her. He meant to do so. 'He is not even intelligent.'

'Oh, I thought you liked him,' teased Daddy. 'I do.'

'Yes, you are foolish, too,' she responded, in great irritation.

'A nice young lover,' Daddy said.

Julie could have screamed.

'A young spinster,' she snapped.

'Oh!' Daddy's brows went up. 'Then you don't want me to leave my money to him?'

She glared upon Daddy. There was no will: she had looked everywhere for one, and it did not exist. What would happen? If he were to die without making a will, how should one act? He was taunting her, twitting her!

'Nothing I say would affect you, my dear uncle,' she harshly asserted. 'I shall say nothing as to that.'

Daddy began to chuckle.

'You're right, of course!' he wheezed. 'Absolutely right!' When she spoke to him again he ignored her remark. She was alarmed. Her mind flew into suspicion, dread, plan.

William threatened her happiness, her independence, her very life. He must go. If he went, there would be no influence between Daddy and herself. She must somehow set Daddy against him. Impossible. Daddy loved William. No! She must bring William to withdraw. It would be almost cruelly easy; punishment to herself, but a clear course. He had the devil's pride; wound it, and he would trouble her no more.

She would insult him. Then a little feigned carelessness with Daddy; an occasional kiss, a fondled hand . . . He was the ruin of a sensual man; and with sensual men a young woman had limitless power to promise. . . . Dark thoughts closed Julie's eyes. She summoned knowledge of evil to her aid. From such a man as Daddy, given time, she would cozen the world.

So absorbed was Julie in fears and plans that Daddy, peeping inquisitively sideways, saw that her elbows rested upon the table, her chin pressed downwards into supporting hands, and her legs sprawled like those of a kitchen wench. Such relaxation in Julie was new to Daddy, an expert in women; and he nodded secretly to himself at a discovery relating not only to mood but to character, to breeding. 'Countess my eye!' His old eyes narrowed. He had no clue to her thoughts.

v

That afternoon the sunshine was so hot that even the old-fashioned cabbage roses in Daddy's garden hung their heads. Under the high wall's shadow, evening primroses bravely opened their yellow flowers; but elsewhere all passed from life to sleep. Daddy himself was dreaming in the garden. The sun had just caught one exposed hand, and was warming it.

Daddy was roused by something—he knew not what—which caused him to blink his eyes and clear his throat. Perhaps it was a choke. That was often the cause of his awaking, and a disagreeable one. He blinked again, listening; only the sparrows chirped as if they exchanged blithe monosyllabic comments upon the day. Damned sparrows! They knew he was helpless, the cads. Shoot them all! Damn that convolvulus! Nobody to dig it up, and it was strangling everything. Nobody cared. Should he call? Pooh, Julie would slyly cut off the visible growth with scissors and leave the villainous root. Sarah would tear at it and break it. The stuff would irk him, fidget him, all the afternoon. What was that? Eh? Somebody spoke. Somebody was sitting beside him.

'Hullo, you rascal!' cried Daddy, grinning from ear to ear as he recognised William Harvest. 'Look at that bellvine!' He pointed. 'Could you?' That was the boy! He watched William grub with his pocket knife, look about for a fork, find one where somebody had carelessly left it in the open, tear forth the ever-whitening strand of convolvulus root, and put it for safety in his pocket. 'Good! Thanks! Plenty more where that came from. By Jove, *you* look well enough! Where's Julie?'

'Upstairs, I'm told,' said William smacking his earthy hands together.

'Hm. "Resting", they call it. What *we* call a snooze, eh?'

'How are you?'

'Horrible. No sleep. I'd just dropped off now, I believe.' Daddy was desirous of pretending to William that he was ordinarily alert; but he did not know why he should, after all, pretend, so he added: 'Now or a bit earlier. Did you come to see me?'

William smiled.

'Both you and Julie,' he said.

'Hm. That means Julie. You couldn't say anything else. I know I've got no friends.' When Daddy saw that William continued to smile, he chuckled. 'Don't mind me, eh? I must croak a bit now and then. I'm old; that's the trouble with me. I don't *feel* old, and yet I *do,* if you know what I mean. At first, seeing you, I thought it was Hodge. Like a bad dream. He used to be my friend, but now he's my evil genius. But I mustn't say that. He's done marvels for me, you know. Marvels. I shall live to be a hundred.'

'I hope you will,' replied William.

'You've no reason to hope otherwise, I assure you.' Daddy peered at him. *He* didn't care, the fool! 'Needn't think you'll get a farthing!'

William shook his head in reproof.

'I'll try and bear it,' he said.

Daddy nodded. How was he to know that William, with an eye to the house, was not attending to him?

'You're cracked,' he muttered. 'A Christian, that's what you are. I've got no use for Christians. They're too pure. But I'll tell you something, William. Nobody there, is there? Money buys you a lot of fun; but it makes you suspicious. You think everybody's after it; and you're right. However, I like it. Damn it, why should the poor be the only people to get something for nothing? I'm the wicked landlord, you know. Me! When I've scrimped and saved for my old age. I used to do all my own sums—six shillings a week here, seven-and-six there; and tenants do their own repairs . . . It took me a couple of days a week to collect the rents. But I get Merrow to do that now, and I save on it, because he's not soft-hearted, like I used to be. Especially when the tenant was pretty, he-he! You could have done that job for me; and learnt a lot about human nature. But you're too uppish. I don't know what you think. Come now, what's your notion of things? I've always wondered what it is that keeps noble-minded young fellers like you going. Eh? What is it?'

'Wound up,' William said, promptly. Ah, for all his smile and his quick retort, the boy didn't, Daddy saw, look too blooming. Down in the mouth, eh? 'Can't stop.'

Daddy fell into a dream. He wanted to say: 'Your father stopped all right, the fool. He shot himself, you know. Did you know? Did you? By God, I'll *make* you say!' But he said nothing. His mouth fell open. He was an old man; too old to be any good.

'I've got no friends,' he said, presently. 'Though why I should tell you that, I don't know. It's a sort of boasting, isn't it? Don't believe what I said about the Christians. I like you; you don't like me. Well, not much, eh? Can't be expected at my age. You've come to see Julie. She's young.' He could not see what effect the words had upon his silent companion. This boy's face, bright, a little freckled, apparently open, hid everything. He was really what they called 'inscrutable'—much more so than the dark thin-faced fellers who baffled people because they were the same colour all over, and flat. Curiosity was too much for Daddy, so he plumped out the question: 'Now, between ourselves, what do you really think of Julie?'

'I think she's perfect,' answered William, with unreadable calm. 'Pchah! Would you trust her?'

'What with? I wouldn't trust her not to break a dozen hearts.' Daddy cackled.

'That means she won't break yours, you devil! Selfish little brute! No—she's not there, is she?—no, I meant——'

But before Daddy could explain the nature of his curiosity William's face lightened. Daddy, although he could see only what was before him, knew that Julie had come from the house. Eh? That was a give-away, wasn't it? That look? Daddy jumped slightly in his chair. A celestial thought occurred to him. It hammered at his old head. He trembled with sudden excitement. What? What? Messages seemed to rush upon him from nowhere. But when he looked again William had advanced to meet

Julie, and Daddy was as much alone in the garden as he would have been in the Sahara.

To a lover, she was delicious. As tenderly graceful as a thrush, and as gentle as a summer night. Merely to see her walk across the lawn was an enchantment; but close at hand the elegance of her corsage was irresistible. Into a cream-coloured cotton dress was woven a golden yellow pattern which caught the sun; and while the puffed sleeves of the dress were large, after the fashion of the day, they did not seem, as they would now do, grotesque. The line of her body, emphasised by severe corsets, was exquisite. Her skirt flowed as she walked; and at its edge her delicate shoes could be seen, with sometimes, if she quickly turned, the glimpse of a beautiful ankle. As for her face, with its smooth brow and straight nose, and the mysterious promise of her lips, it was this afternoon more than ever like that of a Madonna. But her greeting, perhaps, was hardly that of a saint.

'Ah, you two!' Julie said, banteringly. Having from a window seen them with their heads together, she had hurried. She now passed William with a cool half-smile, and went straight to Daddy, who kissed his hand to her in admiration. 'You are both such gossips, I think. You sit thinking evil and speaking good, like all the English.'

'How they misunderstand us!' exclaimed Daddy, still arch with his great idea. 'Foreigners. Two of the most innocent creatures in the world. At least, I'm innocent. I can't speak for William.'

'Oh! Oh! Oh!' Julie, full of quite another suspicion, pointed a derisive finger; and this gesture, with her cry of incredulity, made Daddy chuckle until he choked. He loved to be accused of wickedness. Well, perhaps the charge was true? He'd been a bit wild —how many years ago was it? Ay dear! Long before these children were born. Long before . . . His mind stopped. No more of that. Here he was, eating chicken with the best. Yes, but he felt lonely. What did these children care for him? Nothing. They ogled each other, and grew as sportive as lambs; but for him they cut no capers. He had to beg and fawn for everything. 'Oh, my God!' thought Daddy; 'is this what it comes to?' In the midst of his merriment and choking he was overwhelmed by a sense of helpless dependence upon the indifferent; and tears trickled unchecked out of his eyes and down his cheeks into the uncharted labyrinth of his white beard.

Julie was still apparently laughing at Daddy's delight in the charge of sin; it was William who wiped the tears away. And Daddy quickly repulsed the tender hand which humiliated him, and the big kerchief seized by William from Daddy's breast pocket.

'Go away, damn you!' he wailed. 'Can't an old man snivel if he wants to? You're the sort of busybody that stops a woman crying when she's happy. Here, give me that handkerchief. You're like a nursemaid blowing a child's nose.' He mopped his cheeks with the handkerchief. To Julie, he said: 'Now then, miss; what about tea for my friend?'

My friend! Julie's heart jumped. My friend! Father and son could not be more familiar . . . Consciousness of dreadful danger beset her.

'You want me to go, is that it?' she demanded, with an air of gaiety. 'So that you can tell your stories!' She made a brusque movement towards the house.

'Nonsense!' cried William, deceived. 'Julie!' He held out a detaining hand.

'Stories!' protested Daddy, waggling his eyebrows. 'He doesn't *know* one. He's barren. By the way, William, did I ever tell you——'

'Never,' said William, fretting with recognition of Julie's hostility. 'And you won't.'

Julie ignored him.

'Then it is because you were talking of *me*,' she cried. 'I shall *not* go.'

'Hopeless!' remarked Daddy, lifting the kerchief and letting it fall. 'What on earth should we be saying about you?'

'I am interested to know. You would both find something cruel, I am sure.'

'O-oh!' roared Daddy. 'Why, he was be-slabbering you!'

Ah! She had been right. Hardness settled in Julie's eyes. She braced herself.

'I said you were perfect,' said William, smiling, but with grave scrutiny.

'It's absolutely true,' Daddy blustered. 'He did. I told him *I* didn't. By Jove, no! But it was no good.'

The effect of these assurances was quite different from what either had intended. It was first of all a chill such as might have been caused by a cloud obscuring the afternoon sun. Then:

'So that is what you say.' Julie did not smile at all. Her face became as still as marble, her eyes sombre. 'I wonder why. You have some motive.'

'Only the truth,' declared William, gallantly.

'I do not believe you. My dear William, you are either very innocent or very malicious.'

'Malicious?' exclaimed William, crimsoning.

'Here, I say, Julie!' bleated Daddy. 'Can't you take a joke. I say——'

'Please!' She silenced them both. Continuing to William, she said coolly: 'I prefer that you do not speak of me.' Her voice failed. Hardly audibly, she with an effort completed the sentence she had begun. 'What you say is neither interesting nor true.' At last, in a whisper to be heard only by William: 'Bon dieu, voulez-vous me quitter et que je ne vous voie plus.'

There was silence in Daddy's garden. A long glance passed between Julie and William; upon his part bewildered, tragic, but without entreaty—because what she said but confirmed sentence of death; on hers reluctant, disquieted, almost hateful. At length she turned away, frowningly embarrassed, as if the exchange had shamed her, and went quickly into the house and up to her room. William grew pale. He did not hear Daddy's demands for explanation.

VI

The church clock was striking nine. The house was in darkness, upstairs curtains drawn, the interior black; but out of doors daylight had not yet disappeared, the street lamps shone yellowly, and in the dusk an occasional dark figure could be seen crossing the High Street or passing briskly down its length. At the big window of Daddy's study upon the ground floor, where the book-cases stood in dimmed splendour, and where the old clock ticked in the silence, Julie waited for Robert Whistler.

She sat in an ordinary chair in the shadow of the curtain; and as she sat her mind endlessly travelled the day's journey of perplexity and trouble. Trembling, and with tightly clasped hands, with an ear strained for any noise within the house, and her eyes tired with the greyness without, she felt that she could again and again have screamed with impatience at the slowness of time. She had been sitting here for an hour; and the striking clock came at the farther end of an eternity. 'Oh! Oh! Oh!' She could keep still no longer; but must rise and move about the room, whatever the consequences.

What was that! A shadow passed under the window. It was he. She had almost missed him. He had turned quickly from the passage beside the house, and his faint tapping at the front door, in its secrecy and its urgency, set her pulses racing. She stood for an instant with both hands at her throat, and felt there the throbbing of her heart.

Then, like a cat, she left her place, crept to the front door, admitted him to the darkness.

'Julie!' It was eager—but more than eager. Triumphant. Her quick ear heard the triumph; and immediately every instinct of caution was aroused.

'Sh! Sh!' It was imperious. What a fool she had been to give him the rendezvous! He took it, of course, as a confession; and the dark house . . . As it was! Had she no pride to lose? Julie's heart sank.

She shut the door again with such extraordinary care that the latch made no noise; and as she turned away from it she stumbled against Robert, who in the darkness caught her elbows and would have held her close in his arms; a gesture which carried her sense of peril to extremity. The fool! No, it was she who was the fool, to give him such encouragement. What else had she to expect? She shuddered.

'No, no. Please.' Freeing herself, Julie led the way to the

study, shut that door, so that they seemed alone in the dark house; and immediately moved away from him, her heart beating so fiercely that she found it difficult to breathe without sobbing.

Neither spoke. Robert, as if nonplussed by the manner of his reception, stood looking at her. He was tongue-tied. Alone in the twilight, they were still undeclared lovers, but for want of words only, or that essential community of impulse which would have eased all. Failure threatened. Both were at a loss. At last Julie, with a great effort, and in a voice that seemed to herself to be strange and very weak, said:

'You wanted to see me.' Still Robert did not speak. 'Didn't you?' she asked, with increasing dryness.

'Yes.' It was hoarse; equally unfamiliar. 'Yes, I did.'

'Well?' She was calmer already. He was not so triumphant. He was as timid as she. She had it in her power to give or withhold everything. 'Shall I light the lamp?'

'No.'

'You prefer——'

'I want to talk to you. I want to tell you everything.'

She saw him move his arms helplessly and look away.

'Is it disagreeable?'

'Some of it. Not all, I . . . I hope.'

Julie, with her back to the window, smiled. She could permit herself an unseen tenderness of glance.

'Tell me the less disagreeable part first,' she said. It was as if she teased him; although, indeed, if she played it was still with a heart that beat stiflingly.

Robert remained silent for a moment. Then he said:

'The less disagreeable part you know, I think. It's—well, it's that I'm in love with you.'

Julie's eyes closed. Her lips were stiff. She trembled.

'I think,' she murmured, 'I think I shall sit down.'

She sank into a chair; and Robert, moving quickly to her side, sought to take her in his arms. But he was awkward, his arms unsteady, and as her head flew aside he kissed but the nape of her neck. When he swore, she laughed, made a movement of protest, yielded tenderly, and at last, pushing him away, rose to her feet and again laughing was enveloped in the embrace she had so often and so eagerly imagined.

'Oh! Oh! Oh!' she murmured in a thick voice of happiness. 'So rough! My darling, you hurt me. Yes, you do.' But the protest was not unkind; for fever ran in her veins, and though she chided she quietly laughed and turned her head away from his wolfish kiss with an exultation which she did not try to hide. 'Ah, but you are too strong, my darling! You frighten me quite.'

'Do I?' He was breathless, masterful. 'Why?'

'Oh, no, no! That is a question you must *not* put——'

'But I put it,' he insisted.

'You said this was the *less* disagreeable——'

'I asked you why I frightened you,' said Robert. She heard his voice tremble. He, too, was trembling, this strong man! 'Eh? Tell me!' She pressed away from him, relaxed, whipped herself free; and although he sought her in the deeper darkness of the room he was soon constrained to stop his pursuit. She heard him breathing hard and quickly.

'Now listen!' whispered Julie. She had her hands to her hair, but she watched him closely, ready to fly again if he approached. 'You must be very good—and very quiet!'

'By Jove, yes!' Robert stood quite still. 'But will you come to me?'

'Perhaps. Wait. First tell me the disagreeable . . .'

'I want to be near you when I do that.'

'How unfortunate!' She laughed again, knowing well that it would bring him again to her side. 'Silence! Silence! Listen!' They stood straining their ears to hear nothing but the ticking of the clock and the sharper tick of the watch in Robert's pocket. The conspirators! Their hearts beat rapidly; dry-throated, thrilling, their sense of being alone together in the silent house was heightened until it drew them once again vehemently into each other's arms.

CHAPTER VIII

A New Path

LONDON. William Harvest, passenger from Moreton to the unknown, stood up as his train crossed the Thames at Vauxhall. It was an instinctive act of homage, and as he was alone in the grit-fouled railway compartment none but himself knew how much this apparently unemotional young man was affected by his arrival at the centre of the world. He had never previously seen the river as it was now, in twilight, at the beginning of a great adventure, when all he knew and loved lay behind, and he, sick at heart, but resolute for change, was adrift; and the effect of the flowing water, dark, but gleaming in the dusk and speckled with lights and shadows, was overwhelming.

> *There is a tide in the affairs of men*
> *Which, taken at the flood, leads on . . .*

In this case, to what? William, cold with suspense, stared down at the river as if he sought instant answer to that unanswerable question.

What *did* lie ahead? He was altogether too vague about himself even to suppose a precise future. He knew only that as he reached the heart of the city every extravagance came closer, leaving illimitable space beyond for farther dreams. Though all became gloomy as a vast roof slid over the scene, his eyes were still filled with the vision, which he never forgot, of black barges sliding through the current, and giant buildings mysteriously rising upon every hand. London. An ugly name, a mumble; but from China to Peru, and from Archangel to the English provinces, a magic and a potent word, beautiful for its associations.

A moment later William heard the hissing of the tireless engine and the clatter of a thousand echoes. He stepped from the train and saw and smelt and listened to the activities of a great railway terminus. First of all, the vaulted roof from which every noise returned and travelled, billowing, into oblivion; smoke darkened it, and more smoke rose without end to gather aloft in perpetual fog. Below, busy porters, knots of passengers and their waiting friends, dim lights, and an activity to which he was unaccustomed. Everywhere grime, dinginess, creeping mist as the evening fell, and a sense of the common acceptance of miracle. It was stupendous! Moreton, already far behind, became a speck at the back of memory.

Carrying his small portmanteau, which no porter thought well to wrest from the hand of a young man whose clothes were rurally shabby and whose air of independence, though mild, was plain, William trod the long platform at Victoria as if he thought it holy ground, which, at the moment, he did. And as he moved forth, conscious as a true journalist should be of his assault upon a stronghold of the established, he paused to look admiringly at that miraculous engine and the grave middle-aged man who had brought his train safely to journey's end.

William would not and did not show the awe he felt at sight of a better man than himself, but he smiled from his groundling level, as cats do at kings; and the engine-driver, calmly regarding the universe from the height of his cab, and with dignity wiping his oily hands upon an oilier rag, gave the friendly but quizzical admirer a slight nod of encouragement. As if he said: 'Welcome to London, young shaver. Keep your head, as I do; and you'll come to no harm.' And William's smile said: 'Thank you for your help and good wishes. I respect you. If I could promise to keep my head, I would do so. But you, for all your skill and nerve, have a straighter line than I to follow. All the same, of course . . .' Not because he understood what was in William's mind, but because he was attracted to the young man's candid face, the engine-driver, who was of stern mould, permitted himself some relaxation of severity; and, this exchange of greetings accomplished, our traveller stepped out into the town and lost, if not his head, at least his bearings.

But William had been exhilarated by the driver's kindness, which he considered a satisfactory omen. He was also pleased at being allowed to carry his own bag, just as a semi-linguistic English visitor to France is gratified when waiters or concierges allow him to speak French, and for the same reason, which is that bluff has prevailed over the scepticism of a whole order. He believed the bag, which contained a suit, two shirts, two night-shirts, eleven collars, several pairs of socks, some handkerchiefs, and some damnably darned underclothing, together with thirteen lucky books that might as well have been left at home, was a light one. It seemed so for fully five minutes, after which it moved as steadily against him as the pointing finger upon an oculist's test card. And he was bent upon avoiding all touts, pickpockets, confidence men, thimbleriggers, and ladies of ease. He also meant to discover for himself a cheap, respectable hotel, to have a good meal and his first pipe in London. Afterwards, there would follow an exploratory ramble by night through what the local journalist in him insisted upon calling the hub of the universe, the capital of the British Empire, the world of Charles Dickens, and the focal point of the Press of Two Hemispheres. He stood outside Victoria Station in a mood to accept the editorship of 'The Times' if it should be offered to him that night. There would be no haggling over salary.

In all directions the traffic of London took its then unregulated way. Horse-drawn omnibuses and hansom cabs, horse-drawn drays and vans and growlers, barrows pushed by hand, and a sprinkling of motors, some of them lamentably derelict, made chaos of the roads; while foot-passengers, rebellious then as now, strolled and darted at will, as they do in 1937, to the danger of all parties, including themselves. The street lamps, although so much brighter than those at home, illumined the thoroughfares and the crowds less than they romanticised them; and William, as he turned westward, towards Belgravia, where the press was

diminished, saw trees and the pale smoke-hazed sky, heard more
faintly the thunderous din of vehicles, and was

> *like one within a dream, who dreams*
> *That he is dreaming.*

He walked smiling among strangers; and they, so far from recognising his delight, or thinking to themselves that this was a young
hero freshly arrived to conquer the town, hurried past, assuming
that he was as they were, indifferent to the fate of mankind. The
assumption did William injustice. He did not inordinately love
his fellow-creatures; but he liked them and was interested in them.
But then he was not yet a sophisticated burgess; only a stranger
from the country, taking his first solitary walk in modern Babylon.

The bag grew heavier, until William's arm ached; and as he
grew hungry his heart began to ache, too. Melancholy thoughts
of Julie crept into his mind, coloured by all the incredulity of
the defeated lover. Nothing, however, could altogether cool his
exulting sense of adventure.

II

He was awakened very early the next morning by a delivery
of coal at his hotel; and from a dream of avalanches stirred to
find his blanket upon the floor, crusted grime—darkening the
darkness—upon the outside of his window, his head aching, and in
his ears, behind a racket of coal and dust, already, at that time of
day, the unmistakable roar—such as one hears in a seashell—of
the old London traffic. He lay blissfully absorbing sensations, jumping at the louder crashes, but enduring them with fortitude because, like the odours of Paris or the taste of garlic, they surpassed expectation. It was six o'clock.

William was as near heartbroken as one who is not a coward
can be. He had been disappointed in a deep, tender, but not passionate love which had absorbed all his faculties. From wisdom,
not from infirmity, he had decided to leave Moreton, find work in
London, and make a new path for himself. Only two people

guessed anything of the truth—his mother and Minna—and they guessed it because their knowledge of William was derived from love as true as his own; but neither had revealed her knowledge. They loved him; they did not underrate, as others might have done, certain qualities, of quickness, artfulness, and resource, which would have been more conspicuous to the world if he had been less honest. It is a mistake to suppose that the honest are inevitably dull; some of them are merely guilty of lifelong paradox.

Three hours after he had been aroused by what sounded like the destruction of London by dynamite, while the early flocks of clerks, typists, and office-boys—due at nine o'clock—were scrambling to be punctual, William had breakfasted and, with the day before him, was encountering that stampede. It stupefied him. He was scared by all the faces of these troglodytes; for it was the first time he had seen them in such concourse. At Moreton, people took half-an-hour to dawdle the length of the High Street, and they marked down the exhibits in the shop-windows as children pore upon the treasures of a detailed drawing; here, the pace, which never slackened, was fifty times as rapid. Nobody, not even the girls, stayed to look at the shops; if they glanced aside at the windows it was with a white preoccupation which betrayed no interest whatever in display. All rushed along, heads down, like hounds upon a hot scent. Some of them carried newspapers, others what were called 'lahbry books', others little leather bags or small parcels which might possibly contain luncheon sandwiches. But all were pale; all stared at the pavement. To a young man who hoped to become a recorder of human affairs, the spectacle was entrancing. William in five minutes quadrupled his knowledge of manners.

And as he walked eastward the first rush subsided, to be succeeded in twenty minutes by another, of fortunate persons who were due to reach work at half-past nine. William stood in the Strand, east of Charing Cross, and watched them pass. He saw that they showed less frenzy than their nine o'clock brethren. They were better dressed. They looked as if some, at least, had found time to breakfast and brush their coats and shoes, instead

of leaping straight from sleep to clothes, and from toilet to train.
He was delighted with his own observation. The article which all
provincial journalists prepare to write after a few hours in London took shape in his mind. He called it: 'What's the Hurry?'
But he knew what the hurry was. He knew why it was greater at
nine o'clock than it would be at ten. A quietly-burning pity for
those who must work in order not to starve oppressed him.

William's course still lay eastward; and as he came to the
first of the Strand churches his attention grew still keener.
Fleet Street lay just ahead. As if one whispered 'Mecca'. Not for
nothing had he filled many leisure hours with intensive study of
Sell's 'Directory of the World's Press'; in this morning freshness
of learning he could have passed an examination in the contents
of that great book. The towns of England, their populations and
their morning, evening, and weekly newspapers, were as much in
his familiar possession as the form of horses must be to a racing
tipster. Like Sherlock Holmes, he could distinguish a fragment of
'The Leeds Mercury' from a fragment of 'The Western Morning
News'. Nay, he could identify a journal from its very ends as they
stuck out of a postal wrapper, from its correspondence column or
its fudge. Farther than that, few men could go. And all the
newspapers, from A to Z, had offices in or near Fleet Street. The
Magic Circle!

At first, if his spirits had been less high, William might have
been disappointed in the Street, which was narrow, architecturally
commonplace, and smoke-ridden. He was not disappointed. A
bazaar in Baghdad or an alley in Pekin could not have pleased
him more. Not Venice or the Golden Horn, Pompeii or the
Pyramids would have meant as much. The green omnibuses
struggled along, road sweepers leapt dexterously with their shovels
and brushes under the nose of any trotting horse. Fruit-laden
barrows pushed by seedy individuals littered the gutters; errand
boys dawdled, whistling; and there was a curious stir and idle
alertness upon the pavements which promised a million columns
of expert print. What if everything was dingy? What if errand
boys slouched? William was used to boys quite as slow; and the
office of the 'Gazette' at home could meet all Fleet Street upon

terms of equal squalor. He glanced into doorways, grimy alleys, at the historic names over the shop-fronts—Posts, Guardians, Leaders, Telegraphs, and Observers were upon every hand. An extraordinary emotion seized him. 'Non angli, sed angeli.' This was not Fleet Street, but Paradise. 'J'y suis, j'y reste'; it was a resolve. They couldn't keep him out of it.

III

The secretary of the Institute of Journalists (William had been an Associate Member of this body for fully two years) recalled him from dreamland to the factual universe. The secretary was a bearded man of middle-age, with a mild demeanour and a slow tongue, whose judgment William saw indicated by a manner of deep melancholy. There was no jar at the encounter, for if William's manners were good they were at least equalled by the manners of his host. But a strange discomfort spread through him as the interview began. It came from the abdomen, to which his heart seemed gradually to retire, as upon its last defences. And Mr Spruce, the secretary, shook his middle-aged head. His glasses, slightly awry upon the bridge of his nose, picked up a reflection of sunlight from a framed portrait over his fireplace.

'I'm not going to discourage you,' he said. 'I hope I'm not. But you know you weren't so badly off at Moreton. Cosy job. You could have stayed there all your life.'

'That was the trouble,' William answered, smiling ruefully.

'You thought you'd storm Fleet Street,' mourned Mr Spruce. 'And it cannot—it simply *cannot*—be done.'

'That *is* a little discouraging. I must mention it,' urged William. The smile still existed. He was aware of an answering gleam behind those big spectacles.

'Unfortunately, young men don't know when they're well off,' suggested Mr Spruce.

William could not immediately answer that observation. Presently, he said:

'Perhaps they know when they've got to make a move. Just as

chicks do when they break the eggs. Or caterpillars when they
make the chrysalis. I think I ought to tell you that I wanted to get
away from Moreton.' He was slightly embarrassed in saying that.

'Nothing wrong, I hope?' Mr Spruce said. He did not seem at all
impertinent; only kind.

Wrong? The question brought everything back in tumult to
William's mind—that summer afternoon, Julie in her cream
dress with the golden design, Daddy's chair, the convolvulus,
what he thought the death of all his hope. He did not, he could
not, speak for a moment.

'I wasn't happy at Moreton,' he replied.

Mr Spruce said no more about that.

'I'll tell you how it is,' he continued. 'Young men come to
London from all over the country. They think they're going to get
sub-editorial jobs on the big dailies——'

'Oh, no,' murmured William.

'That's what they think underneath. On top, they're too
shrewd or too timid to be so confident. Now, I'm not speaking
of you. Let's be impersonal: I want you to understand the position.
I see you're intelligent. You're more sensitive than most. These
fellows come to town. They come to me, or they go to editors:
"What can you do?" "Oh, anything. Everything. I can do *your*
job, if it comes to that." "Thanks, but I'm keeping my job."
"Perhaps there's another job?" "No, and there's fifty youngsters
just as good as you waiting for a chance." That's the sort of conversation that takes place. Sometimes not spoken, you see.'

'Well, my heart's in my boots,' said William.

'I wonder if it'll stay there,' grunted Mr Spruce. He waited for
an answer, but none came but a discouraged smile. 'Now, look
here. I'll give you some advice. You've come to London. You'd
best look out for a job in the suburbs. That's a beginning, you
see. Better than hanging about waiting and eating your heart out.
Have you got any money?'

'No. Five pounds.'

'Nothing to fall back on? What about "The Balham Eagle"?
They want a reporter-sub. Thirty-five shillings a week. Decent
fellow, Hubble; he runs the paper himself, treats his boys well.

You'd have useful experience. And you'd be able to keep your eye on the Street.'

William was silent. He was disappointed, but not crestfallen. If his heart had been in his boots or his belly it was beginning to ascend. He did not for a moment underestimate the kindliness of the advice, and he even had a glimpse of its wisdom.

'Yes,' he said. 'Thank you. I'll try that. Shall I go at once, and ask for Mr Hubble?'

'I'll telephone him. Wait a minute.' Mr Spruce rose and went out of the room, leaving William to stare unseeing at the walls before him. How shabby his hat looked! This was worse than anything. High hopes, clichés about stoppings and stayings; and now the truth. He wasn't to set the Thames on fire. Julie—oh damn! his eyes were smarting. . . . Yes, it was no good; *he* was no good; and she'd seen it. That was bitter! Big enough in his mother's eyes . . . He'd go back to the hotel and get his famous book of cuttings—his samples! Wouldn't be able to stay at the hotel—it was too dear—but if he got the job would have to find a lodging near it. Julie was in Daddy's house, as he'd so often seen her. Julie——

'Oh damn! Oh damn!' William gritted his teeth. It was funny that this should have swept over him at such a moment. Thought he'd managed to cauterise it. Fool! You didn't cure the love of a lifetime by running away from it. . . . No good. He saw himself for ever as a shabby hack. To the end of his days . . .

'Now, Hubble will see you,' interrupted a voice which made William jump. He looked up into the kind face of Mr Spruce. 'He's well-disposed to you. I think it'll be all right. If not, come and see me again, will you? Come in any case. I'd like to know how you get on.'

It was sincere; the handclasp was warm and unhasting, the eyes behind the spectacles medical in reassuringness. William was himself again. In two minute, his spirits soaring, he was en route for Balham. 'The Balham Eagle.' That sounded lofty enough for any purpose.

IV

Though lofty in name, and perhaps in aim, the paper had its offices in a back street. They might have been the dwelling-place of a jobbing printer; but within doors there was an order and dignity greatly surpassing that to which William had been used. He was attended to instantly, found himself in the presence of his new employer, and in ten minutes was out of the place again bound for the house in which he was henceforward to lodge. Mr Hubble saw to that. Mr Hubble, small, pink, and fatherly, with a foam of white whisker about his cheeks, concealed under the appearance of a member of the Pickwick Club shrewdness which William would remember all his life. Mr Hubble saw him, sized him up, adopted him.

'You'll suit me,' he purred. 'I'm easy to get on with. So are you. Balham's a healthy place. Don't despise it. There's plenty to do here, and lots to learn. Always remember, you don't want to be a soldier of fortune.' (He said 'sholjer'.) 'You want to be a soldier of life. Have you read Dickens? The Master! We've got a Dickens Society here—you'll make friends there. Dozens of friends everywhere. But first, lodgings. If you go to Mrs Dooms—don't let the name worry you; I send all the nice people to her. She's the widow of an old employee—if you go there, you'll be handy and comfortable. Now goodbye. Come Monday. Plenty to do. 'Voir.'

As he left the office, William laughed until the tears leapt to his eyes. He had already plenty to tell his mother in his daily report. But more was to follow. The house to which he was directed was one of a hundred similar houses built in a single straight line about the year 1860. All the houses looked alike; all were of dun-coloured bricks with facings of plaster, all had large porticoes, ten steps up to the front door, basements, iron railings, and a look of paintless misery. Within doors all the rooms were large, the stairs innumerable, the light bad, the wallpaper soiled, the furniture disheartening. But Mrs Dooms, the landlandy of number 65, was brisk and business-like. She was not more than fifty; she had coal-black hair, a faint moustache, and eyes as bright as those of a gipsy. As a young woman she had probably been of very striking appearance; now, because she had lost a front tooth, she drew her lips close.

'If Mr Ubble sent you here,' she said, 'that's enough for me. If the room suits.'

'Oh. Oh, yes,' William agreed, politely. 'The room will do splendidly.' He was thinking to himself: 'If this woman belongs to any county but Chalkshire, I'll eat my shabby hat and buy a new one.'

'It's not a mansion, of course.' Mrs Dooms looked around her with a severe expression, as if she saw the room's every defect. But the room, in fact, was very neat and clean, with a small black iron bedstead in the corner and a small yellow chest of drawers in the window. It had no texts upon the walls, but a couple of quite excellent lithographs, and there were three strips of carpet upon the floor which looked perfectly agreeable. 'The furniture's odds and ends,' continued Mrs Dooms. 'But the place is quiet. And it's clean—I can promise you that.'

'It's all that matters,' William assured her, thinking: 'Chalkshire! That soft roll of the "r"; that gentle "quoiet" and "quoite"! She's from within ten miles of Moreton. Who's lonely?' He was aroused by something more individual.

'And nobody's died here. That's a thing I always used to ask when I first came to London: Pardon me, but has anybody ever died here? I've got a prejudice about that. I expect you have, too.'

'I've never thought about it,' acknowledged William. 'But I've never been away from home before. I suppose people have got to die somewhere.'

'Well, if anybody's died, I should feel they was always looking at me.'

'Oh,' said William, interestedly. 'Do you believe in ghosts?'

'Goce?' repeated Mrs Dooms. 'What, walking about, d'you mean? No, it's not so much goce as the shivers. I like *live* people.'

'But do you like *people*?'

'Depends. If Mr Ubble sends 'em, I do.'

Could there have been a pleasanter compliment? William glanced aside at his landlady. Although her lips met tightly, the rolling black eyes were peculiarly innocent and cordial.

'Well,' he said frankly. 'London's supposed to be a rather unkind place to strangers; but I think that can't be true. I'm sure I shall be happy here.'

Mrs Dooms raised a hand.

'London's full of people who ain't Londoners,' she said. 'Some of 'em ain't even English. You find all sorts here, and form your opinions from what you meet. Where might you be from, if you don't object to me asking?'

'I'm from Chalkshire. From Moreton.' William smiled as he observed the effect of his words. It was tremendous.

'Well!' exclaimed Mrs Dooms. 'Well, well, well! But I'm not reely surprised. I knew you wasn't North Country, because you're not bumptious. Anybody from up North has to tell you so at once, and say what's wrong with you, too; which I always think's cheek. But fancy you being from Moreton. I'm from Sandersfold.'

'If you'd been from farther away than that, I should have had to eat my hat,' cried William.

'What, could you tell?' Mrs Dooms was delighted. 'Then I haven't lost the old ways. But I've been in London twenty years, now. See, what's your name again? Arvest? I don't seem to recollect it; but then I never knew anybody in Moreton, reely. Used to go there, you know. Used to read the old "Gazette" every week; and still do, sometimes.'

'I worked in the "Gazette" office,' William said. He had already taken a great liking to his landlady, and it grew with every moment of their talk.

'Oh-o-oh!' It was a long-drawn echoing sound, by no means a monosyllable. 'That's where my husband was till he came to London. He was a comp-positor, a very deep-thinking man. He used to go into the "Gazette" every day; but he had a row with somebody there—somebody who's dead now, so we won't blame him —and came to work for Mr Ubble. But he caught a cold, and it settled on his lungs; and I lost him. It was Mr Ubble who arranged all about this house, building society and all. He's a kind gentleman. Very kind. I shall have paid it off in another ten years, and make my living, too. I owe him a lot.'

'Do you have many lodgers?' asked William.

'They come and go. I've got my first floor let steady—it's the best in the house. An ole—well, elderly—gentleman that Mr Ubble recommended. Not on a paper, but in the City. A Mr Marsh; very nice' (that was indulgently, rather pityingly said, as if Mrs Dooms did not utter a second clause beginning with the word 'but'). 'And second-floor front a young gentleman, a clurk. Now there's you. Nearly full up. I could let my ground floor, only we use the back room as a dining-room, and just at present my niece sleeps in the front. But any time your ma came to London, it would be quite easy to make it specially nice for her. Have you got a ma? And a pa?'

'Ma, but no pa,' admitted William. 'Pa died when I was a baby.'

'What, did your ma bring you up, then? Very sad. She's sorry to let you go, ain't she? Come to seek your fortune. Oh, you'll find it, I've no doubt. A quick young gentleman like you. The gentleman next to you, the clurk; his name's Mr Bryant. He's very nice, and very kind; but essentric. Always being funny: d'you know what I mean?'

'Jocular,' suggested William.

'Yes.'

'Rather depressing?'

Mrs Dooms sighed.

'No,' she said, thoughtfully. 'Just queer. Kitty—that's my husband's niece who lives with me—she gets tired of it. Well, Mr Arvest, as we're confidential, she can't stick him. I think it's because she thinks he's a bit sweet on her. Well, whether he is or he isn't, he's a gentleman. You'll see. He's essentric.'

'I hope he's quiet.'

'Oh, you won't have no bother. Everybody in this road's very respectable. And that means quiet.'

'Not sly?' asked William.

Mrs Dooms's face wrinkled into a very mischievous smile, but her lips were not parted.

'Ah, that's telling,' she said, demurely. 'But there's no slyness in this house. No, that I'll swear. We're all good here.'

'It's a boast!' objected William.

'Poor but honest,' Mrs Dooms insisted. 'You'll see.'

With that, and a sharp friendly nod, she backed out of the room; while William, happy and amused, looked from his window down into the dishevelled grass plot which lay two-and-a-half storeys below. Some clothes were hanging out on the line; and as he gazed down he saw a young woman come out to take them indoors. Simultaneously, another young woman appeared from the next house, bent upon a similar errand.

'Why, the district is crowded with young women!' thought William, misogynistically.

But as the thought was then so depressing to him he turned from the window and prepared to leave the house. The sooner he brought his bag from the hotel the better. He would then be settled in. Still happy, he ran down the stairs; and as he reached the foot of the last flight he heard the door of a room to his left quietly closed.

CHAPTER IX

Troubles Never Come Singly

IN THE EARLY MORNING, exactly four months later, silent darkness hung over Moreton. Swiftly-moving clouds were passing across the sky, and a little chill rain spattered the pavements. The street lamps had been extinguished; the draughty wind swooped at every corner and particularly along the passage—which was like a funnel—between Daddy's home and the church. Julie, cloaked and shivering, slipped out of the front door of the house, stood still while a milkman's cart clattered at the cross-roads, and then, pulling the door to, heard the latch click behind her. How cold the wind! How low, at this hour before the dawn, was her heart! The latch's click was like a threat. She half-ran over the space before the church and to the corner of the cross-roads. Another blast of wind swirled about her. She saw the dreary endlessness of this road which led under sodden trees to the sea. Her teeth were chattering.

A few early cyclists pedalled past, most of them coming towards the town, but one or two going away from it upon their own errands. Julie heard the men greet each other by crying a Christian name, and knew they must all be casting sour, uncordial, peasant-like glances at her. She wished herself invisible. But they were like shadows in the morning darkness, and she hoped, she believed, that for them she too, hurrying with averted head, was but a shadow. The bitter wind! The misery of the morning! Presently, when she was clear of the last fingers of the town, she drew aside into the hedge, waiting, hearing her breath come quickly, and seeing it before her in little frozen clouds. Almost as soon as she had stopped walking, the sound of a horse's hooves roused dismal echoes in the lane; and from the town behind her came a hooded rickety cab which had a hollow rattle upon the rough road. Julie shuddered.

The cab stopped abreast of her. She saw the old bottle-nosed driver in his heavy coat, smelled the familiar smell of the spirit-less horse, which never lifted its ears but trotted like a mechanical toy; and as the door of the cab was opened from within she stepped forward. From the cab jumped a burly man, also heavily overcoated, who caught her arm, assisted her into the vehicle, and slammed the door. She heard a cry of command, and as the horse again moved forward she was jerked back against the seat and then, by ricochet, into the arms of her companion. His warm lips were upon her cold cheeks. Shuddering again, violently, Julie clung to her cavalier, pressing her forehead to his breast and shivering as if she would never be able to recover from the bitter dampness of the day and the bitter trepidation of her heart.

'I say!' exclaimed Bob, with boyish clumsiness. 'We've done it marvellously! Haven't we! Don't you think so?' In his excitement he shook her until her teeth chattered. 'Nobody saw you? I don't think anybody saw *me*—or heard me, either. I was up at five. Crept about. Made myself a cup of tea. Did you manage?'

How stiff Julie's mouth felt!

'I think nobody saw me,' she whispered. 'Some men, perhaps. I don't know.' As if she had 'managed'! When she had been too agitated to eat or drink! Within his embrace she felt the warmth slowly creeping through her numbed body, and tears filled her eyes. She could not raise her head, but longed only for love and protection. 'I'm so cold, I can't speak.'

Bob groaned indulgently.

'Oh! Poor old woman! Never mind, you'll soon feel better!' What! That was the way in which Englishmen spoke to horses. They had no emotions. They were not lovers. Whatever her need, she must not expect tenderness from Robert, for Robert had no tenderness. What then? A quickly-spent animal amorousness; then nothing, the morning paper, goodbye, love forgotten . . . heigh-ho! . . . Robert looked out of the cab windows, first upon this side and then upon that, while the cab jolted and rattled upon its naked wheels along the ill-surfaced road. He turned back with a smile. Julie, watching him from the corners of her eyes, saw it all and gauged his mood of satisfaction. Complacency! He was almost whistling! Insensitive! A hard cheerfulness! . . . 'Just passed Royals. Where the Mannings live. They don't *know!*'

'Yes?' Julie spoke with consciously repressive irritability. She would have liked to make him sensible of her discontent. And of her malaise. Could he be so dense? Or was this but the Englishman's resolute refusal to exhibit his feelings? The movement of the cab made her so sick that she did not know how she would endure the journey to Sandersfold.

But Robert seemed deaf to tones. To him, this was but part of the game. An early morning drive, the church, the return; it was his notion of romance. Julie, piercing with venom to the truth, moved her head in distaste; but still Robert was cheerfully unconscious.

'I didn't see the old lady last night.' He was rambling on, really to give her courage. 'Just as well, I think. Don't you think so? By Jove, if she could see me now!' He did then, at last, whistle slightly, under his breath, a gay tune.

'Robert! Don't!' She could have screamed as at a slate pencil. 'That row!'

'I say! Aren't you well, darling?'

'My dear Robert, I cannot keep my head up!' She struggled to free herself from his arms, and for a moment sat upright, desiring to awaken his tenderness, his sweet love. But although he embraced her, as she wished, Robert's words were directed to reassurance, of which she stood in less need.

'Poor old woman.' Again. Maddening. Even *he* could not miss her leap of exasperation. 'I'm sorry. I'm stupid. Doing my best, you know. Eh? You'll be better when it's over. I say, it's all going to turn out excellently. I'm sure it is. We shall be neatly settled in when it happens. Just right.'

'I wonder,' she groaned, looking far into the spiritual future.

'It is, I tell you. I've got everything fixed. Everything. Everything.'

'Yes.'

'Of course, I know it's not *perfect,* darling. . . .'

That was not an apology; it was almost a charge of fussiness. Well, he was a man, and saw things so. He was well content; he thought she should be the same. As his lips pursed themselves for another tune, he remembered her protest, smiled again, and gave her a warm, domestic hug. Julie was outraged at his lack of finesse; he already took her for a matron. His cheerfulness was intolerable. This was not the moment for it. She said, in a tone of exasperation:

'You have the ring?'

'Of course I have. Ring and the witnesses. This old cabby's one.'

'Mon dieu!' She struggled afresh. 'He? Oh, but that I will *not* have! He is a rascal, a toper! He'll talk. A toper's always a gossip. My dear Robert!'

He was impervious.

'Sh! You needn't be afraid. I've known old Dottle since I was a kid. His nose is nothing to go by. Indigestion. He's as sober as a judge. Besides, what does it matter? It's only a signature. And in a week or two, once the agreement's through . . .'

Julie could bear it no longer. She began to scold.

'I don't *like* him, Robert. I can't *stand* him. This filthy cab! It drives me mad! It makes me ill. Don't you see!' The cab lurched. 'It's frightful!' Another lurch. A ghastly feeling of nausea. She lost her head. 'Oh! Oh! Make him stop! Make him stop! Robert, for God's sake!'

Robert, seeing her livid, took fright and shouted from the window. But the old driver, who was deaf, answered with a wave of his whip, and expertly caused the lash to whistle around his nag's drooping ears. The horse, startled at such a noise, swerved and began to run faster and faster. In vain did Robert shout. At last, in spite of the swaying and pitching that followed, he stood up, forced open the door, pulled at the driver's sleeve, and thereby caused such an abrupt check that Julie was flung with violence against the side of the cab. That shock gave the last touch to her discomfort, and she was seized with desperate and uncontrollable sickness.

Her wedding morning! She wished that she were dead.

II

It was broad daylight, and the weather almost fair, by the time Robert re-entered the shop. He had observed the same precautions upon the return as upon the outward journey; and when once Julie had alighted from the cab he deliberately ordered old Dottle to drive him to the railway station. From the station, pretending that he had been out on business, he sauntered back to the shop, stepped over the threshold prepared, as he thought, for any emergency, and saw Parks and Mercer, the two assistants, briskly engaged in weighing tea and pounding butter. He hung his hat up quickly, dived into the little cubby-hole which he used as an office, and after smoothing his hair pretended to resume the study of his accounts. That was all right. A bit of a strain.

Robert relaxed. He was elated. It had satisfied his notion of the unconventional to ride off with his bride. Not a coach, and not at night, with galloping horses; but in the dawn, a ceremony in a dim church, all shadows and melancholy echoes over a dropped book or a kicked stool, and slight nervousness lest something untoward—the appearance, for instance, of his mother! Gosh; that made him flinch!—should happen at the last moment. Nothing had happened. Julie was relieved, satisfied. He thought, satisfied; at any rate relieved from fear. All was well. All was better than well. Bravo!

But Robert did not for long remain delighted with an easy success. While he still glanced at his reflection in the window of his cage, and gave the young husband and father, as it were, a congratulatory nod, his eyes fell upon a piece of paper which stood propped up against his inkwell.

'I want to see you,' he read. There was no signature; but the writing was his mother's. Robert felt himself turn cold within.

It seemed an hour before he could rouse himself from the stupor of dismay into which those words plunged him. In that time he was bludgeoned by all his past angers and failures and terrors. The fine plans he had made for deceiving his mother wilted into mere half-hearted stratagems and left him defenceless. At last, as one who awakens from heavy sleep still struggling with the ultimate horrors of nightmare, he sighed heavily. He gave a dull grunt that was nearly a groan. He could not sit still, but drummed his desk with the fingers of both hands. Then, with one hand, he struck short blows upon the desk. There followed a silence in which he thought he felt the skin pressing upon his cheekbones. As if he were shrinking! Presently, with a show of resolution, he rose to his feet, taking the note in his hands. Better get it over.

Something else immediately occurred to alarm Robert afresh; for just as he caught sight of a gleam of wintry sun upon the windows of the boot-shop opposite, Parks, the rosy-faced assistant with the black hair, called out to him:

'Oh, Mr Robert. I forgot. Letter for you. Came quarter of an hour ago.'

A letter? How lucky that he had told the men to keep any letters for him. She'd open anything. Ah, delivered by hand. From the Bank. He opened it without suspicion.

DEAR MR WHISTLER,
  I shall be glad if you will give me a call this morning.
                              Yours faithfully,
                              H. F. PERKIN, Manager

Hm. Short and sweet. Not peremptory, was it? He was in demand today. First his mother, then this. Of course, the two summonses couldn't be connected. Couldn't they? Any hitch was impossible. Eh? Damn it, there was *always* a chance of a hitch. Bank managers had power; but not unlimited power. Robert was worried. *Was* there any connection? Oh, God! He was getting into a funk! That damned tyrannic old hag's note had upset him. . . . Should he see Perkin first? Or his mother? 'For God's sake, make up your mind!' . . .

Never had the journey upstairs seemed longer. It was as long as the journey at school, to the headmaster, years ago, from the classroom at the back of the building, when one was sent for caning. . . . The same sick dread, concealed under an air of bravado . . .

He found his mother in the living-room, sitting at the big table, her back to the fireplace, with a number of papers before her and a pen in her hand. Although she, who heard everything, must have heard his heavy steps upon the stairs, she did not look up at his entry, but methodically added some comment to whatever it was that she had been writing. Robert could not see what this was, although he tried to do so. Ignored, he stood just within the room, trying to seem preoccupied, impatiently self-confident, like a busy man interrupted for a bagatelle; but his mother's delayed attention, as usual, had its full effect upon him, so that he looked as he felt.

Robert's one advantage was his height, which enabled him to survey her from above. There was a large area of silver, invisible when she stood, in his mother's closely-brushed hair; and this sent its message to his judgment. White. Thinning. Two swollen pouches, also, under the eyes. 'By Jove,' thought Robert, with returning presence of mind; 'she's ageing! She's old! She's ill! I've only got to hold on!' But when he saw the line of her mouth, he trembled. This was to be a row; and in a row his mother held the advantage.

She was dressed, as usual, in black. Strangers supposed that she continued to mourn her husband, but in truth she wore black as the outward sign of respectability. Mrs Whistler, though upon her own terms, was a God-fearing woman. The breadth of her shoulders was remarkable, but owing to the sedentary life she led she was steadily fattening. Unseen, there was a progressive deterioration of the heart. That was why Robert saw the white chin spread more amply upon the high, stiff, lace-edged collar of her close-fitting bodice. That was why he realised that she had begun to age. Her wrists, too, were thicker; and her plump, short, wide-tipped fingers had some of the disgusting pallor of silkworms.

Only when Mrs Whistler was satisfied with the composition in front of her did she raise her head; and when she looked at Robert it was with an expression of contempt which suggested that she knew everything he had done.

'Nearly ten o'clock,' she remarked, drily.

'Yes.' Robert was defiant. He leaned back against the door. 'Yes, it is.'

'You were out a long time. I put that note on your desk before eight.'

'I had some business,' Robert said.

'I know,' answered his mother, contemptuously hard-eyed. 'You've had a lot of business these last few weeks. Some of it's kept you out all night.'

Robert, although he started at the disclosure, and lost a little colour, did not answer. His mother continued:

'I wonder you can afford it.'

'You ought to know,' answered Robert. His jaw was set, to give the appearance of immovable strength; for which he received a warning glance from his mother. She at once retorted:

'I don't think you *can* afford it. But you were always stupid.'

'I've managed this business since father died, anyway,' growled Robert.

'Have you?' She stared at him so very steadily that Robert's eyes fell. 'You've been neglecting it lately. Going after a Frenchwoman, they tell me.'

Robert was stung. He left the door and came nearer to the table.

'That's *my* business,' he said, fiercely. 'It's got nothing to do with you. Or with your spies, either.'

'She's out for all she can get. She'll make a fool of you.'

Robert's indignation gave way to triumph. He looked down at his mother with, for the first time, an expression of scorn. She knew nothing, then, of his morning errand. She was bluffing. It was upon the tip of his tongue to say: 'It may interest you to know that I married her this morning, and for a reason that would wipe your eye.'

'You know a lot,' he said, tauntingly.

Mrs Whistler's face showed no sense of repulse; but the direction of her attack was instantly diverted. She said:

'Well, we'll get back to business. Very important business.'

'Your own or mine?' asked Robert. Oh, they were enemies; and while he was afraid of her he was determined not to show his fear if only he could conceal it.

'I shouldn't talk like that if I were you,' advised his mother. 'It's foolish. You weren't here when I wanted you. You haven't been here, when I've wanted you, for the last two or three months. It's been a pity, for your own sake.'

His own sake? Robert's heart leapt. She was threatening him!

'I've been here all the time the shop's been open. Practically all the time. The stocks are all clear. The books are all clear. Everything's in order. What I do after the shop's closed is my own affair,' he said. Less coolly, and more frantically, than he wished. His mind tried to deceive his ears, which recorded a faltering betrayal of the heroic words.

'What you've been doing has been in *my* time,' said his mother, showing a slight anger.

'No,' answered Robert, defiantly.

'What you've been doing—and what you've been trying to do— is something you've no right to do.'

'Oh,' cried Robert, in a loud voice of bravado. 'What's that? Eh? Let's have it!'

'You know, and I know.' She spoke very distinctly, and stared at him with a glance of steel. 'Make no mistake about that.' Her voice changed. It became soft, and menacing. She said: 'See, you had a letter this morning from Perkin, didn't you?'

Christ! She'd found out! Robert's heart for an instant stopped beating. Although he clenched his teeth, he could hardly prevent himself from crying aloud in horror.

'Didn't you?' repeated his mother, ferociously. She continued to stare at Robert's ashen face, and at the sweat that had started upon his forehead. 'Of course you did. I've stopped that.'

Robert could not speak. He tried several times to do so, and moistened his lips; but no speech followed. He was appalled. His mind fumbled desperately.

After a time, his mother continued:

'I noticed you were out a great deal; and that gave me a chance to do something I've had in my mind for some little while. It was the clothes, Robert. The clothes and the boots. Of course I liked you to look smart; but I felt you had too many in your cupboard——'

'My God!' exclaimed Robert. 'So that's what you do!'

'And handkerchiefs, Robert. Some of them silk. Very smart indeed, I thought. So I've had an auditor on the books—not Greenbank (he's too old), but a London man. Privately. He's been here with me in the evenings—while you were out courting, you see. He's found a number of strange things in the books. I've got a list of them here. Very interesting. He thought you could explain them. I didn't. But I thought *I* could explain them. They'd put you in prison for quite a while, Robert.'

One of the white hands was extended to a folded paper in the scattered pile. Robert watched the hand as if it had been a deadly snake. He was very pale, and stared, fascinated, at the hand and the paper. He had never been so much afraid.

'Only a copy, of course,' explained Mrs Whistler. 'You've been helping yourself, it seems. Liberally. Not very cleverly, of course. That I shouldn't expect. But in the last five years you've had a good deal of money. It comes to a good deal, I say. I don't know what you've done with all of it, but apparently what I've given you hasn't been enough for your private expenses.'

She waited for an answer. After a long pause:

'No,' said Robert, hoarsely. 'No, it hasn't.'

'You've got grand ideas. And instead of telling me it wasn't enough, you went another way to work.' There was silence. Mrs Whistler said again: 'Instead of speaking to me, you dipped your fingers in the till, like a pickpocket.'

'What of it?' cried Robert. 'What are you threatening me with?'

'Listen, Robert. I'm saying that you stole, instead of speaking to me.'

'What's the good of speaking to you?' demanded Robert. 'What's ever been the good of speaking to you?'

'Have you ever tried it?'

'Lots of times.'

'That's a lie, Robert. You preferred to steal. It's your bad nature. Your bad nature.'

Robert shouted:

'It's not. It's your fault. You say I've never spoken to you. Well, I'll speak to you now. I'll tell you that you're a skinflint and a curmudgeon. I'll tell you that while you sit here getting fat and old I do all the work and get nothing out of it. I'm wasting my life. I'm sick to death of it. Sick to death of it!'

He turned, and was upon his way to the door when his mother, still quiet, said:

'Robert, you're a thief.'

That stopped him. In a fury, he shouted:

'That's a lie. You're the thief. You've stolen my business!'

'Robert, you're a cheat and a liar.'

'Prosecute me, then. See what a character you'll get.'

'You may bluster, my son. Bluster and brag and thieve—sure marks of the coward.'

Robert's pallor turned to a flame of red.

'Coward?' he screamed. He was quite beside himself. 'That's enough. I'll stand no more. I'm going. Christ, do whatever you like with the business! Do whatever you damned well like! Ruin it!' He thumped the table. His voice was shrill. 'But as for me, I'm done with you!'

'Go and see what Mr Perkin says, Robert. He'll tell you something.'

He was out, trembling, upon the landing. 'I *will* go!' he shouted back from the other side of the slammed door. Fury carried him half-way down the stairs; but there he was caught by misgiving. 'Oh, my God! What shall I do?' He put a weary hand to his brow, struggling to think. His hat and coat were below; he must get them at once and walk straight out of the place. For good. For ever. His head was high with anger; but already a chill began to steal upon his bowels.

III

Still in passion, Robert presently found himself standing within the doors of the Bank, where he thought both inquisitive counter-clerks looked at him with sneering glumness. It was strange how irresistibly his anger, so much mingled with mortification, now forced him into imperious rudeness and ill-manners. He walked restlessly in the confined space of the Bank, while the Manager

was being told of his presence; and as he glared at the man who
was left in charge his thoughts churned to a fever of apprehensiveness. The counter was very broad, and the clerk seemed to dodge
away from Robert behind a laden desk, peeping at him between
ledgers, and saying with every glance: He's been found out. Found
out. Found out. His mother, the bitch, caught him with his fingers
in the till like a pickpocket, trying to cheat the Bank. Cheat the
Bank. A liar, a cheat, a thief, a coward. He's got a nasty hour in
front of him. . . .

Summoned at last within, Robert strode past his escort into the
Manager's small dark office at the back of the building, which his
big body filled. He had that advantage, at least, of size and manner;
for Mr Perkin was a small and meagre man, with a goatlike voice,
and side-whiskers upon his pinched face so long and straggly that
they hung like grizzled stalactites from his ears. Mr Perkin had a
way, also, of darting mousy glances in all directions, as if he feared
eavesdroppers or burglars; and he was always drawing his lips together in small spasms through some nervous habit which suggested a constantly reinforced impulse to caution. But he was a
clear-sighted and honourable man, who kept many secrets as safe
in his head as they have been in the Bank's strong room.

'Er, good morning, Mr Whistler.' Mr Perkin rose immediately
upon Robert's entrance, nervously rubbing his clean-shaven chin.
'You had my note . . . my note?'

'Well,' retorted Robert, with the truculence of doubt. 'Here I
am.' He scowled fiercely at Mr Perkin, feeling that here at least
he had a man to deal with, and a man whose neck he could wring
with ease. 'I had it ten minutes ago.'

'Thank you.' Mr Perkin fumbled with his papers. 'Will you sit
down, Mr Whistler?' He followed Robert by seating himself. Then
he leant forward, clasping his hands in front of his chest. His
manner was earnest. 'Yes, I wished . . . wished *very much* to see
you.' Robert waited grimly. With a sharp preliminary intake of
breath, which was audible, Mr Perkin began: 'Mr Whistler, when
you proposed to the Bank to . . . to advance money for your
branch at Seahampton, I was very glad. I was glad to see your
enterprise. I liked your father very much; and I've advised your

mother fairly often as to her investments. I thought everything would be quite simple.'

'Isn't it?' asked Robert, defiantly.

'Perhaps not *quite* as simple. Mr Whistler, you gave me to understand, I think, that the business here was your own.'

Robert felt sick.

'When?' he asked, brazenly. 'When did I do that?'

'Throughout.' Mr Perkin shot a sudden glance, and stiffened. Robert knew that he was receiving a warning; but he could not check his immediate retort, which was already upon his lips, or control his mood of desperation, which was robbing him of his senses.

'Well?'

'You realise that I have a responsibility to the Bank.'

'I see,' said Robert. 'But I don't know what you mean.'

Mr Perkin paused and looked directly at Robert in such a way that Robert's nerves were slightly calmed. For Mr Perkin's expression seemed to say to him: 'Look here, my boy; bluff's no good. You're talking to a man of experience. Are you going to spoil your chances by insulting me? In that case, you can go at once. Or are you going to help us both by controlling yourself?' While his face remained pinched and sallow, and his voice goatlike, he impressed Robert by his gentle fearlessness. He said:

'Don't you?'

'I gave you all the relevant figures.'

'Yes, but Mr Whistler, Mrs Whistler informs me that . . . that she knows nothing of any branch.'

'That's not true.'

'And that the business *here* is solely and entirely hers.'

'You mean you won't lend the money,' cried Robert, in sudden passion. 'In that case, please say so at once.'

Mr Perkin held up a hand.

'You're not helping me very much, are you, Mr Whistler? Think! We're now asked, not to give extended credit to an old-established and prosperous business, but to finance an entirely novel and really very speculative enterprise. A different thing altogether. You do see that, don't you?'

Robert was stupefied. Also, he was disarmed by Mr Perkin's sweetness. He had no reply ready but a reference to honour.

'You've got my word. You can have my bond.' The words sank dead in a terrible silence. Mr Perkin had again interlocked his fingers, and he looked lugubriously down at them, so that Robert was maddened by hopelessness. Of course his word was no good: he'd been caught cheating! He cried vehemently: 'Are you backing out? Refusing?' He thumped the Manager's desk with a furious clenched fist. 'If so, for God's sake tell me at once. Mr Perkin, this means everything to me. I've been absolutely depending on you. If you let me down, I don't know what I shall do. All this time— my God! What are you saying to me?'

Mr Perkin, nodding mildly, said:

'Of course, I wish you'd told me all the facts at the beginning. But we won't speak of that. Instead, will you please tell me if you have any security—any *other* security—to offer?'

'My word's not good enough, then?' demanded Robert. 'No, I see it's not.'

'I think I ought to tell you—*à propos*—that Mrs Whistler, who called upon me at home last evening, informs me that ... that ...' (Mr Perkin had much difficulty in finding a phrase) 'that she is dispensing with your services immediately.'

Robert's agitated movements ceased. He sat aghast.

'She told you that *last night?*' he asked, in a suddenly lowered tone.

'Last night,' repeated Mr Perkin, looking wistful.

Good God! It was incredible. Last night? Wait a bit. Wait a bit. Robert sat silent, turning the matter in his mind, hearing again almost all the exchanges between his mother and himself. The row. Had she engineered it? If she had, then he had made a fool of himself; for if she had told him to go she *must* have compensated him. He could have sued her. The old devil! He'd got nothing. By God, she'd goaded him, cheated him. She'd done it deliberately.

'Did she tell you why?'

Mr Perkin's eyebrows shot up in gentle protest.

'Oh, Mr Whistler! She was speaking to me in confidence.'

Robert was ferociously calm. He said:

'Yes, but don't you see, Mr Perkin, that if she gave you a reason, it might be slanderous?'

Mr Perkin took another hasty glance across the desk.

'You mustn't think of me as unfriendly to you, Mr Whistler.'

Robert sat back in his chair.

'What was the reason, Mr Perkin?'

'Oh, dear, Mr Whistler; you are asking *me* questions, you know!' A nervous smile flitted across Mr Perkin's face. 'It was I who asked *you* a question, if you remember.'

Robert thought. He did not think with fluency at any time; but now, when he was so much troubled in mind, he could only overcome confusion by being more than ordinarily slow. He *must* be calm. He *must* be resourceful. His aim had been to buy a freehold in Seahampton, stock a shop there, and, upon money borrowed on the strength of a good name in Moreton, to make himself independent of his mother. His love affair, culminating that morning in a marriage precipitated by Julie's pregnancy, had taken him much from home. Hence his mother's opportunity. If, at a crucial moment, he had not relaxed vigilance, this could not have happened. Hell!

But he had been asked for security. In that respect, his position —hadn't it?—had been strengthened by his marriage. When Julie told Daddy; or if Daddy died . . . like all desperate men, he caught at straws. And as probability was strengthened by desire he took a risk.

'Well, Mr Perkin,' he said, greatly sobered. 'There'd be the mortgage on the shop. And for the loan I suppose a guarantee from Mr Griffin would be enough.'

'Oh, yes. Oh, yes. If Mr Griffin . . . That would be . . . Naturally I should wish . . .'

'Of course. I'll see him. I'm sure I can get it. I've good reason. Very good reason.' Robert almost added: 'the truth is, I married his niece this morning—an heiress, you understand.' But he checked that impulse to blab. In a moment, as his mind returned from dreams, he said: 'What I should like to know is, did my mother make any complaint about me?'

Mr Perkin jumped.

'Oh, no, Mr Whistler. None.'

Robert grunted. Damn her! She was too clever. Or was Perkin politely lying? He persisted:

'But she put you against me.'

'No. I can't say that. Except, of course, that she . . . she was dispensing . . .' Mr Perkin lowered his voice. 'I admit that—well, one doesn't "dispense", you know . . . as a rule without some disagreement. Some disagreeable circumstance.' He hesitated, thought, hesitated again, and at length, very kindly and gently, asked: 'Is it really true, Mr Whistler, that you aren't aware . . . Excuse me, I . . . dear me, this is very difficult and perplexing. I think we're slightly at cross purposes. I see that I must be . . . Mr Whistler, did you not *know* that you were leaving your mother?'

Robert shrugged.

'I gave you my word, not until this morning. Of course, I meant to leave her—when the new shop was launched. That was part of my own plan. Not hers. I knew nothing whatever about "dispensing". In fact it's a damned lie. I've walked out. No "dispensing" at all. Good God, no. There's just been a row. I—well, I won't talk about that. My mother's a very peculiar woman, Mr Perkin. I regard the business as mine. It was my father's; and since he died I've run it. I've managed it for practically nothing. Pocket money, and precious little of that. Naturally, thinking it was my own— enjoyment deferred. My God, it's awful! When I think of it, it makes me mad. You see, my mother, some time before father died, made him transfer the business to her. There was a deed. I don't know why it was done. Perhaps to escape the Estates Duty. May have been to keep me from messing it up. Anyway, she's right: nominally, it's hers. But she can't manage the business. She thinks she can, but she can't. It's absurd. Part of my scheme was to show her that. I wanted to teach her a lesson. That's one reason why I'm opening at Seahampton. You see . . .' His voice tailed off, be- cause when he used the words 'I'm opening' his heart turned cold again.

'Yes,' murmured Mr Perkin, reflectively. 'Yes. It's clear that you're not in her confidence.'

Disturbed in his own bitter reverie, Robert started. He cried:

'What? Nor is she in mine.'

Mr Perkin seemed to be pressing the tips of his fingers into his little mouth.

'No, Mr Whistler. Quite. Quite.' He was buried in thought. At last he looked up. 'I . . . I . . . really think I must. It's a matter . . . I don't think it was said in strict confidence. It must surely be quite an open secret. Yes. I think I must. Mr Whistler, then you don't really know that your mother has *sold* the business?'

Robert stared at Mr Perkin. He could not speak. He felt himself grow smaller and smaller as he sat in the chair facing that insignificant little man, whose eyes darted at him and darted away again, mouse-like, full of kindness, curiosity, and embarrassed triumph.

'Is that true?' he groaned, with a great effort.

Mr Perkin nodded his head, and now looked resolutely at his hands, which lay flat upon the desk before him, the fingers all close together, so that they looked like a pair of small pink fish.

'To a big firm. The London Supply Company.'

Robert said:

'Chain stores. My God!' Then, wildly, leaping to his feet in a frenzy of realisation: 'My God, she's done me! Oh, the bitch! I could kill her.'

IV

Impossible to go now to Julie. Robert lurched from the Bank, a prey to every doubt his brain could suggest. Wherever he looked, he saw a blank wall. No money, little credit, married and with a child coming, his plans ruined . . . If he had obeyed the voice of savagery, he would have returned to the shop, stamped up the stairs, and seized any weapon that offered to batter the head of the devil who had brought this upon him. He could not obey. He found reasons against returning for another row. No, he had said he was going, and he'd gone. Of course, he'd done that with an object; but she had beaten him. She'd used his own communication of the danger of the chain store to beat him.

'The old devil!' thought Robert. 'She'll get all the money!'

He was walking fast towards the station as he left the Bank, because that was in the opposite direction to the shop. It was his object to put distance between himself and the temptation to murder. No, no, murder—killing—was impossible. They hanged one for killing. Extenuating circumstances. But a woman. No, he must get away. Away . . .

As he approached the station it was just after eleven. The London train was in, and a trickle of passengers had emerged into the station yard. Robert saw the figures and stupidly noted the facts of the train and its load. He would have passed on, if the leading passenger had not reached the entrance just as he drew level with it. Something, a familiarity in the bearing, in the features of this man, who was of his own age, caused Bob to hesitate. The man hesitated similarly; a thin fair man with a pale face which had grown plumper in the cheek than Nature intended.

'Why, Bob!' he impulsively cried, and put out his hand, at the same time sweetly smiling.

Robert knew him. Robert knew him only too well, the little swine; with his fat cheeks. His instinct was to thrust the fellow aside; but somehow memory had so far to go, and the old grievance was now so faint and distant, that he lost the momentum in repulse which his pace would have given him. He faltered. Though dislike and distrust were strong in his mind, he was at the same time so conscious of curiosity and old attachment, his need for some human company, that . . .

'I don't want to talk to you,' he cried, brusquely, and made as if to move past.

Dick Firth looked hurt. He caught Bob's elbow very quickly, before it was too late.

'Oh, my dear Bob,' he pleaded, in his light, ingratiating voice. 'Can't we let bygones be bygones? We're not as young as we were——'

'I don't know what you mean,' interrupted Robert, grimly. 'All I know is——'

Dick entreated.

'Everything happened such a long time ago.' In a breaking tone, he added: 'Bob! We were such friends!'

That was true. It was poignantly true; and it brought them both to a full stop.

'Whose fault?' demanded Robert, hoarsely, looking down at Dick with almost piteous discomfort.

'I know. I know. The fault was mine. But my dear chap, be merciful! Show your magnanimity!'

'. . . my pride,' Robert said, in an undertone. But he had weakened; and Dick had gained an advantage.

'I . . . I behaved abominably, Bob. Abominably!' What a voice! What emphasis! 'I . . . I've regretted it a thousand times. I wanted to write to you. I tried. But that's so difficult, when one's in the wrong. Besides, what can one say? I've suffered a great deal, Bob; thinking of you, and thinking of that poor girl. That *poor* girl! Bob, we're great brutes when passion has hold on us.' He shook his head. Tears were in his eyes. 'Do you see anything of her now? No? I was afraid not. I don't. I lost sight of her. I . . . I've tried *every* means, since. I have, really. *Every* means. So that I could *try* to make some reparation. . . .'

Robert looked down at Dick's secret face. Dick spoke with such an air of urgent sincerity that what he said seemed to be true. And yet . . . It was certain that she had left the town. He sounded genuine. It was all old now. Old and half-forgotten. Almost quite forgotten. Only an old smart of wounded . . . pride. It wouldn't have done. She'd never match Julie. Why keep up the old feud?

'I'd have killed you if I'd caught you that night,' he said.

A shadow crossed Dick's face.

'You'd have hanged for it, dear boy,' he said, quietly. Then: 'How are you? What are you doing now? Isn't there some place——'

'Oh, I've got something more serious to trouble me now,' Robert began. 'Not more serious, perhaps, than I thought it then; but more serious to me *now*.'

'I see what you mean, Robert. I see. I'm so sorry,' murmured Dick, nodding his head wisely and rather like a toy mandarin. 'I . . . I wonder if I could help at all. Bob, why shouldn't we—I mean, have a talk. A quiet talk. Like old times. I . . . I . . . I'm just down here for the day to see my parents, and one or two people. But I'd love to have a talk. Isn't there somewhere we could go?'

Robert hesitated. Then he threw in his hand. His present need was so great. His memory was blurred. Dick was such an ingenious chap; he'd always liked and admired him, until that . . . He glanced back, and across the street.

'There's the Royal,' he said. 'Nobody there at this time of day.'

'Oh.' It was now Dick who hesitated. 'As you know, I . . . I'm not a drinker. But, however, yes, yes, why not the Royal?'

'You can have a ginger ale,' suggested Robert, with a great sense of irony.

'That's exactly what I shall do,' agreed Dick. 'Oh, my dear chap, I'm so glad to see you!' He caught at Robert's elbow as they crossed the street. 'So glad we can have a talk as we used to do in the old days.'

'Good old days, eh?' said Robert.

'By George, yes, Bob. One's rushed off one's feet these days.'

'Busy, eh?'

They had reached the Royal and entered it between the two tubbed evergreens. It was very cheerful; the fire glowed. And there was nobody in the room, so that both newcomers were content. Bob ordered drinks, which were brought over to a table in the far corner. There, in the quietness, not face to face, but rather side to side at a corner of the table, the reconciled friends bent together over their glasses.

'Oh, dear, yes, busy,' sighed Dick. 'Good gracious, I hardly know where to turn. I'm doing such a variety of things. Newspapers, publicity, speaking . . . But don't let's talk about me, Bob. It's about *you* I want to hear. *Your* troubles. Mine are very—well, my dear Robert, they boil down to this. I'm trying to do too much. Too many irons, too many activities. If you know what I mean, Robert, I . . . I'm too successful.'

'By God,' muttered Robert. 'I wish *I* were.'

'Let's hear all about it.' Dick ceaselessly took in all the signs communicated by Robert's air—his good physique, his present pallor under sunburn, the fear at the back of his eyes, the slightly trembling hands. He saw him toss off his whisky, and when this

happened he gave an imperceptible shake to his head. But although
he saw so much, the expression of interest, of sympathy, never left
his face. 'What, is it a love affair? By the way, Bob.' He glanced
stealthily and suspiciously over his shoulder, fearing an eaves-
dropper. 'You know—just for one moment going back—it's my
last word—I . . . I don't think I did you such a *very* bad turn. . . .
You know?' His fingers, so thin and delicate, clasped the glass of
ginger ale. 'I think she was just a little—just a very little *easy*.
You'd have had trouble later, I think. I mean . . . Well, that's all
I was going to say. We won't speak of it again. Tell me all about
yourself. What *is* this great trouble? I might be able to help you,
you know. Bob, I don't want to boast; but I . . . I can pull a few
strings, my friend.'

Robert raised a forefinger which only George, the waiter, saw;
and George went to the bar for a second whisky. Robert was thinking to himself: 'My God, he's fallen in my way. He's been sent by
Fate.' He said:

'Strings, eh? Well that's just what I need. I'll tell you.'

v

While her husband had these three interviews, which all together
changed the face of his life, Julie, having reached Daddy's house,
resumed her daily routine as if no interruption in it had occurred.
The moment she entered the house, using her door-key, she smelled
such an exquisite odour of fried bacon that—hungrily faint as she
was—she felt her mouth water. Her eyes glistened. Slipping off her
new ring as if it burnt her, and concealing it in her purse with the
certificate, she did not trouble to go upstairs to remove cloak and
hat, but flung them carelessly aside in the hall and ran at once to
the kitchen, where the table was laid for two. A great sizzling noise
came from the grate, where Sarah, the maid, stood with the handle
of a frying-pan in her left hand and an active fork in her right.

'Oh, Sarah, what an *angel* you are!' cried Julie. She could say no
more, because she had taken a ravenous bite from a slice of bread
which lay, ready cut, upon her plate. Presently, still munching, she

said: 'Mon dieu! How I was frozen and famished!' She had already
moved to the fire for warmth, and stood before it, toasting first one
foot and then the other, sniffing the bacon and eating the bread,
while Sarah, who had not spoken at all, momentarily forsook her
cooking and in silence poured a hospitable cup of coffee.

Julie had just dipped a corner of her bread in the spattering fat,
but when the cup was offered she let the bread rest in the pan and
drank a little coffee, grimacing as she tasted it. Excellent woman,
Sarah supplied a liquor which was hot and which contained perceptible grounds, but which remained fatally dual. In French, aloud
but to herself, Julie exclaimed: 'How perfectly horrible! And yet,
all the same, how delicious!' She hastily recovered her bread and
ate with redoubled relish. Across her mind flashed a memorandum:
'She must never again make the coffee!' But nothing could check
her high spirits, for by this time all trace of misery but the dark
shadows under her eyes had disappeared. She was another girl.
Her smile mocked, her chin was tilted; she could have teased Sarah
to tears.

'I shall buy you a present, Sarah. A bed-jacket. A flannel night-
dress. A hot-water bottle. Some wine. Nothing but that will show
how thankful I am to you for this.'

Sarah said nothing, but shook her head in grave disclaimer. Julie
continued:

'You say "no"; but I shall do it. You do not like my choice of
gifts, perhaps. What, then, shall I buy? A hat? No: in Moreton a
hat is a farce. It is something a horse should eat. Some gloves?
Ye-es; gloves are possible—but only possible. Shoes are not; you
have small feet, spoiled with too much standing. Stockings, che-
mises, pantaloons, no. Those you must buy yourself, for I will take
no responsibility for them. . . . You have no lover, Sarah? Have
you a husband, perhaps? Had you one? You wear no ring. You
have no visitor—except that old woman, Flora.' She pouted, looking
as old as possible in imitation of the visitor. 'But you are not quite
an old maid, I think. . . . There is something. Something in the
face . . .'

Sarah sat opposite, lugubrious but attentive to these observations
and inquiries. But she did not respond to them. Julie's self-correc-

tions were all made at the bidding of her own quick judgment. To save time and trouble they always breakfasted thus, because while Julie's other meals were taken with Daddy, Daddy lay late in the mornings; but whatever talk occurred between them was supported entirely by Julie, who triumphed if she caught a slight nod or faint shake of the head in reply to point-blank questioning.

'Talking to you is like saying one's prayers, Sarah. One feels sure that one's prayers are heard; but it seems that they are never attended to. I ask if you have a husband or lover, and although such a thing is life itself you do not answer. Yet I have heard you speak. However, if that is your nature, it is a very discreet one. . . . And it must be admitted that you yourself never ask inconvenient questions. . . .'

Sarah, who was now perhaps forty-five, and thus (in Julie's eyes) past the age at which lovers were a credit, was small and thin, with a narrow face suggestive of much suffering. Tears might have worn those hollows in her cheeks. She was dark, though not as dark as her mistress. Her curiously broad forehead gave her an appearance of thoughtfulness; but her manner was morose, and she was so monosyllabic that everybody, Julie included, was prevented from discovering just how great or small her intelligence was. Not even Grimaud, the slave of Athos, said less than Sarah. When she was in a room where conversation was proceeding, she anticipated every wish of the diners and seemed, without listening, to follow whatever was said; but never, by any change of face, did she indicate interest in the conversation. On the contrary, she looked implacably stony. In another society she would have been thought 'deep' and rather disagreeable; in present-day literary circles, gaining credit for disdain of the common, she might have been venerated as the most superior of all, to whom, as to Ben Jonson, nothing insipid must be repeated. But Julie liked her. She treated Sarah with a one-sided cameraderie. However, she did not confide in her.

Accordingly Sarah had not been told beforehand of this morning's doings, and she was told nothing now. She could sit facing the bride, and did so, hearing all that was said, storing words and expressions in her memory, and perhaps guessing a thousand things by means of her unseen, unerring register; but if she knew much more than Julie supposed she gave no sign of it, but listened close-lipped to every word. Only when Julie, having finished, lay back carelessly in her chair, had Sarah any remark to offer. She then said:

'He was asking for you.'

'Mon dieu. And you never told me!' Julie's basking mood of satisfaction, which had succeeded that of gratitude, was abandoned. She jumped to her feet. 'Oh, that was not right, Sarah. That old man should be considered, you know. It is important. To *me,* it is most important of all . . . now.' She rubbed her hands upon her napkin. 'I go this instant. Poor uncle!'

Unheeding the dry look which made Sarah more expressively inexpressive than ever, Julie dived from the room. She would have run up the stairs if her heart had allowed; and she was soon in Daddy's bedroom upon the first floor, at the back of the house, overlooking the garden.

She found the old man lying upon his back, both arms outside the blankets, and his beard spreading whitely upon the turned-down sheet. He was quite cosy, and was staring up at the ceiling as if he traced there a table of his remoter doings. No sign of death or the loss of faculties did he give; for at sight of Julie his mouth stretched wide in a grin which displayed his gums and made him look as healthy as a baby. She might well have expected to see the first signs of new teeth growing in that rosy cavern.

'Ah, my dear uncle!' cried Julie. 'That stupid Sarah. She has just told me you wanted me. I am desolated. Mind you, it was kind of her—to me—because only when I had eaten my breakfast, my last mouthful, the last drop of coffee——'

'Doesn't matter,' mumbled Daddy. 'I only asked where you were. You look well this morning. Where were you?'

'Oh, I overslept, you know,' explained Julie. 'That Sarah let me sleep on. She didn't wake me. The clock strikes, and I don't get up. So there it is. Now, what are you going to have for breakfast this morning, uncle?'

'A good look at you,' grinned Daddy. 'That's a feast!'

'I'm afraid that's not qua-aite enough, you know,' teased Julie, who always used rather more of an accent in speaking to Daddy than she did with others. She now spoke, indeed, when she pleased, quite ordinary English, with a minimum of foreign intonation. 'It would be like lentils or oatmeal—crowded to begin with, and then nothing at all. You know?'

'What's Hodge say?'

'He says bread and milk.'

'Huh! Sop!'

'Or you could have porridge.'

'Huh! Skilly! What they give our noble convicts. Just why they should be so pampered I don't know. I'd give them all my toast crusts to mumble!'

'Oh, but uncle, the birds get them. . . .'

'Damn the birds. Damn them. The dear little birds. They had my best plums this Summer. They had my best strawberries. My best cherries. The tits had my peas and the blackbirds and missel-thrushes my fruit. Hear them laughing!'

'Well, you should have a proper gardener.'

'I'm too poor. You don't know how poor I am. When I did my own gardening . . . It wasn't so then.'

'But you are old, uncle. You can't dig and put traps for the birds now. The mice ate the strawberries. We should have several cats.'

'Cats!' shrieked Daddy. 'I can't stand cats. Hate 'em. Why, they'd dig the whole place to bits. Moroll-moroll-miau-moroll! No, we'll have no cats. Not while I'm alive. Well, now, Julie, I'll have some eggs—some nicely, lightly-boiled eggs. You know how you do them. And some nice thin bread and butter, with the crust off. Eh? And a cup of tea. Strong. Eh?' He drew in his breath with a loud watery noise of anticipation. 'And then we'll have our talk.'

'Our talk?' cried Julie. 'Why, that would interrupt my house-work. Who would then cook your lunch? You are to have some beautiful boiled chicken today—so beautiful! So tender! And creamed potatoes.'

'I want *new* potatoes!' cried Daddy. 'My own potatoes.'

Julie shrugged her shoulders.

'That is impossible,' she said, with great definiteness. 'There are none. They have died.'

'Well, then, I want young William to come and cheer me up.'

At this unexpected demand, Julie's glance darkened. He had been silent about William for so long that she had hoped William was forgotten. Wrong! This was just an old man's fancy, perhaps?

'You know perfectly well he is in London,' she objected. 'And can't possibly be here.'

'But I want him back. I want to see you looking happy again.'

'Me?' She was really astonished. 'But my dear uncle, William is nothing to me. Nothing. Nothing.'

'They always say that,' chuckled Daddy. 'Always. The more they say it . . .' He grinned from ear to ear. He winked with both eyes. His meaning was not merely obvious, it was outrageous; and Julie grew alarmed.

'But you know perfectly well that he comes and goes. He has his own peculiar way of doing things. It is nothing to me. He goes to London to edit some paper. He leaves you. He leaves his mother. He is indifferent to you both. Just as I am indifferent to him. He is a good fellow, but nothing.' Her tone was one of languid protest. Daddy grinned again, to Julie's dismay. 'You have the most extronnary ideas, uncle. I merely tell you that you over-estimate that young man. He amuses you by his rudeness. Me he annoys. He is tiresome. He is both dull and frivolous.'

'Got a lot of ideas about him, haven't you!' chuckled Daddy.

Julie stopped speaking. She had been exasperated with the old man; and he thought she pined for William! That exasperated her the more. She designed to belittle William; she only fixed Daddy's thoughts upon the absent.

'I shall get your breakfast,' she said, briskly. 'So no more just now.'

With that, she turned about and left him. But she was in considerable perplexity, none the less. This whim had been unexpected. What did it mean?

VI

Partly because she did everything to discourage it, the subject did not recur during the day. Daddy dozed all the afternoon in his chair by the fire; and Julie was busy with her own business. After tea, Sarah went out for an hour, and Daddy and Julie played cribbage for a while. But Julie's mind was elsewhere, and she made so many mistakes in the scoring that Daddy, who loved to win, lost his temper and swept card and box to the floor. By this time Julie had lost her spirits again, so that she began to cry, and left him alone; whereupon Daddy rang his bell like a muffin-man, brought her back in a rage, and provoked her to a scolding match.

It ended, as usual, in reconciliation; but Julie was very subdued as she helped him to bed, and Daddy, once between the sheets, would not let her go, but made her sit with him by candlelight, holding his hand. Julie obeyed him with constraint; and she felt so melancholy that while she sat there, and Daddy talked to himself, she could feel the tears every now and again tickling her cheeks and running down to her chin. She did not dare to wipe them away, in case he should suppose her weeping to be due to love of William.

So preoccupied was Julie that she did not hear what Daddy was saying, and she was recalled to attention by a severe shaking of her hand. Daddy, speaking in a very low voice, was repeating a former remark.

'I say that a young man doesn't realise the consequences of his actions,' Daddy was mumbling. 'And I don't know if it's ever struck you, my dear, that there's an odd thing that doesn't get realised. It's this. Young people cry out about old people, and vice versa. But the young people have never been old; whereas the old people were all young once. Got that?'

'When?' asked Julie, dully.

'Why, when they were young, silly! I know I'm old. I get older every day—and when I say older I don't mean only a day older, but older in every way.'

'Yes, that's true,' Julie murmured, listlessly, but with a stirring of hope. 'Yes.'

'It's not true!' snapped Daddy. 'I only said it to see if you were listening. Why, d'ye think I'm a maudlin old dotard, then? I'm nothing of the kind. I sit here thinking of all sorts of things.'

'I'm sure you do,' agreed Julie, trying to release her hand.

'About you, you know.' She sighed wearily. So this teasing was to begin again! Oh, she was bored with it! 'Of course I'm not going to die yet. But I'd like to see you comfortably settled before I go.'

'You would?' Julie became instantly alive. Ah! Ah! Was this . . . was this the opening she had sought? Could she speak to him of Robert? Their love, their difficulties? Not the child, naturally; but, very guardedly, their need . . . Yes, it was the appointed moment. Thus, preparing itself in secret, did every circumstance lend its aid to true lovers! Smiling, she looked aside at the shadowy face. 'Then you would——' But Daddy was not listening. Before she could say another word, he had begun a long speech.

'I'll tell you something, Julie. Hold still. Can you hear me? I've never told it to anybody. Anybody.' He paused, collecting his thoughts. 'A long, long time ago—shall I tell you?' He grunted doubtfully; but Julie still wore her smile, and he was misled by it. She felt her hand pressed by his bony fingers. . . . 'Well, mind you, I wasn't a boy any longer. That you'll see. I was over the hot days when no man's merciful or a Christian or even a civilised creature. I was old enough to know better. Fell in love. Me! Yes, and with a married woman. She lived over at Sandersfold. It's all right: she's dead now. I'd got house-property there, and she and her husband lived in one of my houses. I sold it afterwards. I used to see her, but not him. He was some sort of a clerk on the railway, I think. I can't recollect if it was railway. Savage little fellow: quietly savage. But he had to travel about. Left his wife a good deal. She was lovely, and I was . . . well, I was fairly near; and constant. I suppose like a bee to honey. For a long time she'd have nothing to do with me; but I was always artful. I got her in the end. . . .'

There was a long pause while Daddy remembered his triumph. He resumed:

'Well, now, that went on a long time. Then she wouldn't have anything more to do with me. Going to have a child. Got respectable. Frightened. I said it was my child; she'd never admit it. Said it was his. Well, when I began to think about it, I felt disgusted at the thought that she'd been carrying on with both of us at the same time. I told her she was no better than a harlot. But I suppose I was only angry. . . .'

'You *must* have been angry,' agreed Julie, in a dry voice. 'That poor woman!' Her tone was like the hiss of a snake. She was coldly scornful; and thereby provoked a retort.

'Trust a woman to take a woman's side,' grumbled Daddy. 'You don't understand my feelings. Well, we quarrelled. Parted. She left the house and moved away. I sold the place—couldn't bear to go there again, so you can see I was fairly deep in it.' He grunted complacently. 'I never heard from her again. Never saw her again.'

'How interesting,' sneered Julie. 'You were indeed unfortunate.'

'Wait a bit. Wait a bit,' said Daddy. 'That's only chapter one. Chapter two began fourteen years later, when the husband suddenly turns up here, in this house, with a boy. Mother's dead. The father knows nothing about me—I mean, as far as his wife's concerned—and thinks her a paragon; but comes to me for old time's sake because his son's a clever boy (so he says) who wants to go in for architecture, and will I use my influence. I thought "Why the hell should I use my influence?" but all the time I was looking at that boy and trying to make up my mind whether the other fellow or myself was his father. He was like his mother. I made up my mind to help him. I thought: "Why, this child may be my own boy." So I helped him. But he was ungrateful.'

'He di'n' do what you told him,' Julie suggested.

'Pretended to, as long as he wanted help. Then he threw me over. It's the way of the world. Kick away the ladder; spurn the hand . . . He got married when he was twenty-one, the fool. He got married to some little girl I'd never heard of. Came out by chance—"By the way, I'm married." I said I wouldn't have any more to do with him for that. . . .'

'You are a cruel man!' murmured Julie, looking at him with dislike.

'A devil gets hold of me. Well, I didn't have any more to do with him. I'd said I wouldn't, and I didn't. He got married; and then.

after a year or two, he lost his little bit of money. Oh, that made a difference. He sang smaller. He tried to see me. I wouldn't see him. He shot himself. At least, they said he didn't—brought it in an accident—even Hodge says he didn't; but I know he did. I'm sure he did it to spite me. Well, that was the end of him. I'd washed my hands of him, and I never bothered any more. Why should I? But one day, as I was going along the passage towards the school, I found a child who'd had his hat thrown over my wall. He was grizzling in the darkness. I stopped. "What's the matter?" I said—you know my way; it makes some people think I'm unkind, though I'm not. "What's your name?" I said. Well, to cut a long story short, I found he was the grandson of my old flame. Perhaps my own! It's a thing I can never be sure about. I wish I could. But at any rate now you know why I think such a lot of William.'

'My God!' whispered Julie, in consternation. Her head whirled. 'But he has no claim on you!'

Daddy relinquished her hand. She was alone in the candlelight.

'Nor have you,' he said, at once. 'You're no relation of mine at all. There's nothing in all that. It's a yarn of your grandmother's—your great-grandmother's. Your mother told you the story, because she believed it; but it was all lies. I looked into it at the time—French solicitors—and there wasn't a word of truth in it. Your mother wrote to me when she was hard-up, claiming relationship. I sent her something from time to time. Not always. But my father never had any sisters or half-sisters or anything else. The woman was his landlady's daughter, I believe. Of course, it amused me to boast about a French countess. But she was no countess——'

'Oh!' cried Julie, in warm protest. 'Excuse me. Not a countess, it may be; but of noble family——'

'Not a bit of it. Not a word of truth in it. All a yarn.'

'What ridiculous nonsense! Our family is ancient.'

'The oldest family in the world.'

'My dear uncle!'

'All lies,' declared Daddy, slapping the bed with his old hand and cackling away to himself. 'I've sometimes laughed here till I've cried. You coming here to your loving cousin!'

'This is abominable!' cried Julie. 'Abominable!'

'Oh, *you* weren't to blame, of course. I *know* you believed it all right.'

'But it is true! You *know* it is true. My family does not invent such tales!'

He was laughing still; and as if to prove that he had accurately recorded the effect of his own laughter he wiped the tears from his cheeks with the back of a tremulous hand.

'All rubbish,' he insisted, with a falsetto hoo-hoo-hoo of old man's merriment.

'Oh, but my uncle!' Julie rose in a passion from her place beside the bed. 'You are insulting me. You behave monstrously. I listened to your revolting story of that seduction and that murder; they were not to do with me. I was disgusted. I hated it. But this! It is a bad joke! You say it all to break my heart.'

'No. No, I don't.'

'You do. You cannot dare to persist in it.'

'I love to see you cross.'

'I am not cross. I am furious. I shall leave you.'

Daddy's laugh became a chuckle again. He said, blandly:

'No you won't. Got nowhere to go.'

'I have, thank God. At once!'

Daddy shook his head from side to side in the pillow.

"You won't. And I'll tell you why. I gave you a home. Didn't I? It was a good bargain. On both sides a good bargain. You were starving. You were penniless. . . . Don't forget! Besides, I'm very old. You'll stay on to the last.'

'I am going!' She stamped, and went to the door. Daddy was no longer laughing.

'Don't go!' he begged. 'Listen to what I've done for you.'

'You've done nothing.'

'I've made a will. Made it three months ago. Four months ago. Going to listen?'

Julie hesitated, swallowing her anger. She hated him. She hated him for cruelty, for affront, for this final dreadful power over her. If she left him she would lose all. He would be as vile to her as to that other.

'You think I am to be *bought!*' she exclaimed.

'I've left you something.'

'You suppose that affects me? A woman of the noblesse?'

'Oh, no. Oh, no.' He was chuckling again, with irony. 'But I want to tell you about it. Come back. I can only see your shadow on the wall; it looks frightful. Come back to me here.' Julie reluctantly returned, standing in angry hauteur at the foot of the bed; and Daddy continued speaking. 'Yes,' he said. 'I've left you a little dot. Two hundred and fifty pounds. It's a fortune. You like that, don't you? That makes you smile, eh? Well, you've been a good girl. A good girl. And if you're clever you'll do better yet. . . .'

Two hundred and fifty pounds. Disgraceful! It was nothing! She was stupefied with indignation. For two hundred and fifty pounds she had spent these years of labour, this time of slavery— yes, slavery—to a beastly old man. A miser. A murderer . . . seducer . . . Hush! What was he saying? He was still chuckling. He spoke so low that she could hardly hear. What?

'You see, I've left everything else to William. My grandson—if he is my grandson. I owe him that. Owe his father. Owe his mother. But William's mad about you. He's broken his heart over you. However, you're mad about him, too, so all's well. You marry William. You get the lot. Simple! Aren't I a generous uncle?'

At last Julie could recover from the suffocating amazement which had kept her silent through this enormity. She screamed. She screamed again, spurring fury as with a bugle. She wildly shouted:

'You old brute! You old brute! You old brute! I loathe him and you. To suffer all these years for this! Abominable. It cannot be so. I shall not agree. I shall protest the will. You——' Indignation forced her into her own language. She shook both fists in the air, then one at Daddy while the other was knuckled into her waist as her body swayed in fury. The violent shadows of her arms peopled the four walls with a hundred spectres, and the walls threw back the screaming incoherence of her cries until it seemed as if the closed room itself must burst. Then, because he still cackled uproariously as one diverted to ecstasy by the sight of a virago, she shrieked epithets ever more shrilly. 'You are a brute! Blackguard! *Crapule! Salaud!*' There would have been no end to her abuse if the door behind her had not opened unheard, to admit Doctor Hodge.

So unexpected was the interruption that Julie at first glared at the doctor in bewilderment, her mouth wide open; and as, amid Daddy's horrid laughter, she saw him gravely and contemptuously frowning at such hysterical rage, she was checked in mid-flight. Incapable of immediate recovery, she continued for a moment to shout—some account of what had happened, and some complaint to the doctor of Daddy's conduct—and at last, silenced, shrugging her shoulders with the utmost violence, she swept past him to the door. It was because of this discomfiture that she ran into Sarah, who was upon the landing not a yard from the room; but she was too much excited to notice what then happened, and pushed Sarah to the wall in her flight downstairs.

Only when she had reached the old man's study did Julie feel alone and free to yield afresh to her angry disappointment; and her first impulse was to destroy everything she could lift and cast to the floor. A table-vase, books, an odd tumbler, were all hurled, crashing, into the fireplace. But when she had stormily cried for a few minutes passion slackened and sanity began to reassert itself. She was not less angry than she had been; but she was no longer lost to self-control. She threw herself down in a chair and stretched her arms straight out across the great table, grasping the table-cloth in handfuls and shaking it as she might have shaken the shoulders of a wicked child.

'What am I going to do?' she demanded, of the air. 'Bah! Two hundred and fifty pounds! They give such sums to housemaids! Whereas I——' She struck her breast. It was ridiculous! Outrageous! And Robert, what would he say? What expectation had he? Certainly, of a fortune. The child—poverty—uncertainty . . . Her position with him would instantly be worsened. He would forever be able to scorn her as portionless. A beggar. That was intolerable. 'Mon dieu, something must be done. At once. This moment. I have sworn it, I . . . But what?'

A faint noise, stealthy and at first inexplicable, caught Julie's ear. It was the squeaky slipping of a moist hand upon the china door-knob. Somebody was there. Almost screaming again, she shrank back, trying to hide, and staring at the door. It began slowly to open. To her horror, an arm appeared, followed by a cautiously intruded body, and at last the entire figure of a bulky man who painstakingly sought to glide unnoticed within. Robert! He must have entered the house, as he had often done before, by the door in the garden wall. But while, in her recognition of him, Julie leapt exultantly to her feet, she did not then move forward, but stood with both hands suddenly to her throat, breathing fast, her eyes dilated. For Robert, very pale, his hat at an angle of neglect, wore upon his face an expression of such imbecile solemnity that it did not need the reek of spirits to tell her what had happened to him.

CHAPTER X
Twenty-six Hours

WILLIAM HARVEST, seated at his table by the window, the lamp-light concentrated upon his paper by means of a cardboard shade which darkened the room, threw down his pen. He gave a shout of rage, and laughed silently until he was almost convulsed. Ten o'clock at night; and Bryant, in the next room, was declaiming something in a voice that rasped the hearer's stomach. Bryant's dramatic society, dominated as such assemblies are by a clique, refused him great parts; and when he sighed for Catiline or Prospero fobbed him off with footmen. Hence, in compensation, the practice of discordant noise, like the outcry of hungry oxen, and the incessant learning of tragic poetry, night and day. Of Bryant, Kitty briefly said: 'He's potty.' William, more merciful, called him 'a genius *manqué*.' 'What's *that*?' asked Kitty. 'Potty,' explained William. All the same, the fellow was a nuisance. His ululation rose higher and higher. William, ignoring a derelict fire, rushed head-long from his own room to Bryant's.

Bryant, before a fine blaze, and under the flare of two whistling gas jets, stood admiring his reflection in a mirror. His arm was lifted, his mouth was wide open; he looked like a modernised Charles the Second. He had the same height, blackness, seamed cheeks, and glowing eyes as Charles; but no spaniel. His hair was worn long and brushed back over a bald crown; his chin, though shaven daily, was like a thunder-cloud. By day he was a publishers' clerk, and by night a dreamer of dramatic dreams in which he heard the rapture of an ecstatic multitude. Voices called him by name. Agitated men said: 'It's a miracle. A miracle. Such acting! Seven calls, and more to come! Go on, man. Go on; it's *you* they want. Nobody else, now! . . .' Famous in a night . . . He

209

glowered for a moment at William, before declaiming in a moderated tone:

> '*And thou art welcome, aged man,*
>   *Aye, ten times welcome to Maid Marian. . . .*
> *My Robin stirs: I must sing him asleep.*'

'That's no lullaby!' announced William, with scorn. 'It's an alarum and an excursion.'

The reciter's tone dwindled to a mellow self-indulgence.

'Oh. Oh, sorry, old chap. Could you hear me?' It fell lower still, to a whisper. 'As a matter of fact, I've only just got going, you know. Working up. Up. Up. First piano, then allargando, gradually crescendo, then diminuendo, a dying fall. . . . "Oh, it came o'er my ear like the sweet sound that breathes upon a bank of violets. . . ." Are you working? You oughtn't to do it. Bad. Bad for the eyes, the mind. Look here, I'm sorry. I say, Harvest, old chap, what d'you think of this——'

'Stop!' cried William, brutally. 'What do you suppose Ben Jonson or Marlowe would have done if you'd interrupted their work?'

'Eh?' Bryant looked confused. 'Oh. Oh, but they're different. I mean, they were geniuses, dramatists. Rather different to journalists, you know, my dear boy.'

'They'd have killed you,' William said, with threatening coldness.

Byrant started.

'But you wouldn't do anything like that, would you? Of course, I know it would make good copy, and all that; but think of the disgrace to Mother Dooms! All sorts of journalistic riff-raff on the doorstep. Poor little Kitty interviewed. Besides, they'd hang you, I should think. They might not. You'd find a way of wriggling out of it, I daresay, you know, old chap.'

'I shouldn't be here. I should let myself down a rope into the back garden, walk round, and find you lying in the road. No marks. Deceased was off his rocker; presumed he overbalanced.'

Byrant looked frightened. He turned so that the gaslight caught his eyes and made them luminous, as a dog's eyes are luminous in a sudden beam. The trick was familiar. 'Wonderful eyes!' strangers thought. 'There's genius there!'

'But the police are jolly smart, sometimes, old boy. They'd ferret out the rubbing of your rope on the windowsill. And where you kicked the wall on your way down.'

'Well, I should write my own story,' declared William. 'Splendid advertisement.' He was unimpressed by the lustrous eyes. Bryant considered the matter, and changed the subject.

'I say, what are you doing tonight, old chap?' he demanded. 'Coming up West?'

That was Bryant's notion of life, to go to the West End and sit in a brasserie drinking lager and watching the people. What people! Bounding boys, fallen women, paint, raffishness, an atmosphere thick with smoke and suggestiveness. In such surroundings he felt as if he floated in a beautiful haze of not too dangerous sophistication.

'No, I'm working,' said William. 'But *you* can go up West. In fact I wish you would.'

The eyes were switched off. Bryant's eagerness changed to dolour. His voice dropped.

'Too damned lonely. Too damned expensive. Besides, old man, between ourselves, and not to go an inch farther, I'm no man for the birds. I'm fastidious. And the same with drinks. I can't stand sin. I want quietness. An armchair, a fire, a loving little wife to take my boots off and hear my lines . . . "But now I am cabin'd, cribb'd, confined, bound in to saucy doubts and fears." . . . Shut that door, will you? Oh, don't go. Listen. The Thespians have cast me for the butler in "Dandy Dick". Well, damme, the fellow only fusses and fumbles his aitches. They cold-shoulder me. It's not only the Thespians. Our little Kitty's shoulder must be frozen, she turns it such a lot. Why, at the Thespians the girls call me "Bogey Man" and the fellows "Chirrup". Can you explain that?'

'Only by saying that women are realists and men ironists,' suggested William, edging to the door again.

The eyes became luminous once more.

'Now is that kind, Harvest? I ask you, is it human? Humanity. Humanity. That's what we want. Joey always tells the novelists so.

"Write us something human," he says; "and we'll publish it like shots," he says. "And sell it like hot cakes." Of course, they only sniff and snigger. Half of them don't know what "human" means——'

'What does it mean?' asked William.

'Well, it means kindness, and pity, and gentleness, and love!' cried Bryant.

William shook his head.

'Oh, no, it doesn't,' he objected. 'It's got to involve hardness and knavery and a lot of other dirt. And blether, too, if it comes to that. Blether, my boy. You know what I mean, don't you.'

Byrant answered, with dignity:

'I knew what you'd say. Of course, you know, I see plenty of your type in office hours, old chap. All cynical disbelievers. They stamp in as if they owned the business. But they creep out again with parcels under their arms. Not so big. One man looked at me the other day, and snarled: "Where the carcase is, the crows will gather." Now what did he mean, d'you think? Another one said: "You're the devil of a time a-dying, Charlie." Naturally, I made no reply. I couldn't call up anything crushing. But I say, Harvest, don't you think it's a bit thick about the butler in "Dandy Dick"?'

'Damnable. They ought to give you the ranting, laughing, bawling villains. You bawl——'

'Good gracious, what a word, my dear What's-your-name! You've got no ear. D'you think my voice is more resonant that it was?'

'By twenty foghorns.'

'Good. I know that at bottom you're sincere. You've got your own crude way of saying things; but one day you'll be human. A nice little wife, old chap, would humanise you. Do you see what I mean?'

'Go West, young man!' retorted William. He withdrew.

But his hope of peace was vain; for when, re-entering his own room, William slammed the door as fervently as Nora does in 'The Doll's House', he was greeted with a faint squeal and a rustle. In his absence the room had been invaded.

Kitty, who had been curiously examining the manuscript upon the table, whisked round, facing him. She had been caught.

'Good heavens!' exclaimed William, aware, however, in the same instant that his neglected fire had been stirred to brilliance. 'This place is becoming a Hell on earth!'

'Sh!' She put a finger to her lips. 'You'll get me into trouble if you don't mind!'

'Why should I mind?' demanded William.

'No, you wouldn't care,' grumbled Kitty, 'I know that.' She moved calmly from her place, and squeezed round beside the table in order to peep out of the window, down at somebody who was in the next door garden with a lantern. 'What's that fellow doing?'

After investigation from the other side of the table William said:

'Burying his bones.'

'Nonsense. Dogs don't carry lanterns, silly!'

'Human bones. Human bones.'

'How do *you* know?'

'I make it my business to know a great deal. It's useful to me in my profession.'

'Profession!' jeered Kitty, with a darting glance of bright scorn.

'And I've seen him there before. I watch him night after night, digging little holes, sprinkling in a little lime, and burying a bone.'

'Oh, you're a proper sleuth. My word, I'm getting fat!' She squeezed her way out of the corner again. 'I wonder you don't take up private detective work. Like Sherlock Hollums.'

'Too busy. As you see, I'm working this evening.' That was very sarcastically spoken. 'I've just persuaded Mr Bryant to go up West for an hour, so that I can work. He didn't—and doesn't—want to go alone.'

Kitty, still facing the window, looked at William over her shoulder. She was short, and because the light was shaded he could not clearly see her face, but only the lower half of her left arm, including the hand, with a part of her dress below the waist.

'Meaning?' she asked, drily.

William, backing slightly from the desk, jerked his thumb past his right ear in friendly dismissal. Kitty rebelliously did not move.

'Work,' remarked William. 'W-o-r-k. Elementary, my dear Watson. As for poor Bryant——'

'Is he going now? I don't want to run into him. Let's wait a minute and see if he goes.' She stood in the shadow, while William crossed the room to the fire, standing with his back to it and putting his hands despairingly in his trousers pockets. 'He says his poitry to me till I could box his ears. You know, I can't stand that fellow. Always bringing me chocolates and books. Trying to improve me, I suppose.'

'With chocolates?' asked William. 'Impossible.'

'No, books, silly. Browning and Shakespeare. Poitry. I can't read it. Besides, I don't want to be improved. I suppose you think I ought to.'

'What, go West with him?'

'No. Want to be different.' As, smiling, he did not answer, she continued: 'I don't think people *ought* to try and make themselves different. Improve themselves. It's not natural. If they're not ladies, they're not.'

Humouring her, William said:

'The leopard and her spots. How would you define a lady?'

'Well, for one thing, a lady stares at you. Other people don't: they're too polite.'

William laughed.

'Splendid. Do you stare? I always forget.'

Kitty came out from her place in the shadow. Her quick ears had caught the sound of Bryant's steps, first as he passed the door, and then as he began to patter down the stairs. She and William were alone upon that floor of the house. When she heard the dull thump of the front door she knew that Bryant would be absent for quite two hours. She was now quietly nearer to William, who could see the silhouette of her round face and plump shoulders, and the light, trim body which moved as quickly as that of a squirrel at play. He always thought of her as resembling a squirrel; for although Kitty was a very pretty young woman—a sort of mature child—with big round bluish eyes, a small, babyish nose, much fair, wavy hair, and a rather generous, soft-lipped mouth, she worked hard and with expert rapidity, and could by no means be considered a goose.

'I'd like to slap your face,' Kitty said, pleasantly. 'Do I stare, indeed!' She was now staring meditatively at him, biting her under-lip. But when William silently laughed she swung past him with what was half a challenge and half a movement of petulance. 'He's gone,' she said. 'Master Billy Bryant. I bet he's left his gas alight. Flaring.' Since that provoked no rejoinder, she added, carelessly: 'Mr Finch is out for the evening.'

'I'm the only worker, then,' said William, with a side-glance at his paper.

'You think a lot of your work, don't you?'

'It's my bread and butter.'

'This isn't. It's a tale. All about some black-eyed girl. What do *you* know about girls?'

'Nothing,' said William, blandly. 'I make it up.'

'Pity you don't find out a bit more, isn't it? With your nose to your pen all the time.'

'Not *all* the time,' protested William.

'Pretty well. I suppose you've never been in love, Mr Harvest.'

'Not often,' admitted William, quiet under her gaze.

'Once?'

'Once,' said William.

'She got black eyes?'

'When I'd done with her.'

'Ph! You wouldn't give anybody black eyes. Fits, perhaps.'

William sighed.

'I think I should always suffer in silence,' he said.

There was a pause of perhaps ten seconds.

'I'm worrying you, I know,' said Kitty. 'You'd rather I went, wouldn't you.' But although she moved she did not prepare to go. Instead, she closely examined one of her finger-nails, her head bent and her body relaxed.

'I'm always pleased to see you,' was William's first ambiguous rejoinder. 'But for this particular kind of work——'

She flung up her head.

'Work!' she cried, with an affectation of jeering scorn. 'More like waste of time, to me.'

'But you're not a reader,' suggested William, mildly. 'Even of poitry.'

Her scorn shone. It as quickly subsided. You would have thought her meekness itself as she said:

'I expect you think I'm stupid.'

'Far from it. *Far* from it. Oh, the reverse.'

Kitty, realising that he laughed at her, smothered a smile of gratification. But self-pity persisted.

'I suppose I *am* stupid. Not clever, like you. . . . But I'm lonely and cross this evening.' She took a step towards the door.

William sighed again, very quietly.

'What's made you cross? Headache?'

Kitty raised her head and looked over at the window.

'Why don't you draw your blind?' she demanded. Then: 'I wonder if that fellow's still burying his bones.' She came lightly back across the room, passing close to William, and went to the window. 'He's gone,' she explained, after peering below; and with that she whisked the dark curtain half-way across the window with a jerk of her arm. 'There, that's better. I put some oil on the rod the other day, so's to make the rings slide easier. You might remember that another time.'

'I will,' promised William, sighing. How pretty she was; and how destructive of time!

'And your fire, too. You don't seem to know how to make yourself *cosy* in here!' She pushed him aside, and in spite of his effort to be first in the task stirred his fire afresh. 'Don't want you to freeze altogether, cold-blooded as you are.' She straightened herself and stood, the top of her head barely upon a level with his shoulder, with a sudden mischievous smile twisting her lips and bulging her eyes. 'Eh?'

'You take my character away,' said William, stooping to her. 'But you make me very comfortable.'

The smile was shot with electricity at the nearness of his face. She seemed to lose her breath.

'Oh, well,' said Kitty; 'I can't stay listening to *your* chatter. I've got wo-o-ork to do!'

Laughing as she pompously mouthed that fatal word, she raised her hand, gave him a light blow on the cheek, ran to the door, and slammed it after her. William, as he started forward, heard the key turned in the lock from outside.

II

Next morning, descending late to the grim room upon the ground floor in which Mrs Dooms and her lodgers ate a common breakfast, he found a letter upon his plate at the table. He was the last to come down, and Mr Finch, the cadaverous man with a chestnut wig, who acted as bookkeeper to a firm of City tailors, was almost ready to depart. Not so Bryant, who dallied over his tea reading a book. Mrs Dooms embraced the tea cosy, while at William's entry Kitty slipped out to bring his piece of smoked haddock from the kitchen. She did not glance at him as she passed; and upon her return set down the plate without a word. William, hailing the party with a smiling nod, took up his letter. The others watched. He saw the Moreton postmark.

'Not either of your usuals,' Mrs Dooms said, candidly admitting her interest in all correspondence.

'So I see,' agreed William, tearing open the envelope.

The letter was from Doctor Hodge; and it read:

DEAR WILLIAM,

I think the old man is very near his last call. Please come down as soon after you get this as possible. N.B. You are an interested party.

Yours,
J. M. H.

William re-folded the letter, and—without knowing what he did —methodically restored it to its envelope. Still unconscious of observation, he sighed. His table-companions exchanged glances of dismay. They, too, sighed.

William was the only person in this house who received letters; and some of these, the ones in long envelopes, were considerately hidden by Kitty until William had left the house. He wondered, finding them at night in his bedroom, why rejecting editors so uniformly missed the post; but Kitty took pride in the uncensored residue, which at times she was able to arrange beside his plate in various fantastic shapes for the envy of the unlettered.

Not one of these solitaries would have steamed open an envelope or prigged its contents once they were available; but to all of them a letter was a mystery, to be fingered and microscopically examined until the owner's arrival. Then, while he read his mail, all breathlessly watched William's frank and impenetrable face. When, as now, he sighed, they felt themselves participants in drama. At any hint that his letter this morning spoke familiarly of death, they would excitedly have trembled, for they saw death as the climax to drama. 'Man dead. Woman dead. Dramatic story.' . . .

But William thought: 'Daddy's dying.' That old shrunken man with his wispy whiskers as pale as the very sheet beside them; his cheeks hollow, and his eyes shut until some impulse forced him fleetingly to open them, was at last to loosen his tight grasp on will. He had lived long—too long. Far better to die briskly, in the heat and midst of living, so that your death struck a blow at all who knew you, than to be as Daddy had been for weeks past, the merest simulacrum of a man, waiting for the end. . . . William desired never to be old. Old age was the intolerable state when one's look at every face was supplicatory. 'Do you love me still? How can you love me? I have lost charm and quickness and the power to give. Do I bore you? In that case I'm so defiantly sorry for being alive after my sweetness has passed. I'm so indignant at finding myself, unloved, in your debt; pleading for kindness, insisting upon a gratitude that has been long weary. . . .' One's labour in vain. One's hope gone. Longing only for oblivion . . .

It was no wonder that at this point in his reflections William abruptly pushed away his plate, drank off a cup of bitter tea as if it had been hemlock, and left them all with a preoccupied glance and a word of apology.

They watched him go, every eyebrow raised. In a group they were like patient dumb animals.

'Oh, dear,' murmured Mrs Dooms. 'Oh, dear. It's bad news!' She rolled her head from side to side. 'I didn't like to *say* any-

thing; but I *thought* that letter was an omen. It was so *thin*. And
the writing so ugly—a sort of scribble. And I could tell from the
way he *looked!* Oh, I wonder what it is!'

Kitty jumped briskly up from her chair, as if she felt that somebody must keep her nerve.

'Here you are. Time you went, Mr Bryant. There's the school
bell.'

As the others loitered gloomily in the dark room, she whirled
to the door and, while William still mounted the stairs, was upon
her way to the kitchen with dirty plates. But if she hoped to overtake him her hope was vain; and William, high above, was too
much concerned with his unhappy thoughts to look back. 'You are
an interested party': the thrifty Scot! 'An interested party': the
loathsome words raised a picture of expectant relatives at the bedside. Relatives! His mouth flew open at a horrified intake of breath.
Good God, Julie!

William's head was for some time in a state of considerable confusion. When, therefore, he ran downstairs again, wearing his
overcoat, and carrying a little leather case which at this time he
affected for the transport of papers, he did not see Kitty until
she stepped from the lobby's shadow. It was a dark house.

Kitty's mind also was full; but of one thing only. Her eyes
were used to the dim light. Her hand was ready for his passing
arm.

'Bad news?' she whispered. 'Or good?'

There was an instant's pause.

'I don't know,' answered William, hurriedly, brusquely, hardly
glancing at her. And with that ambiguity he left the house, not
dreaming in his preoccupation that the reply had been as disconcerting as a blow.

III

Robert Whistler also had a letter that morning. He, too, after
reading it, would have put it in his pocket; but he was not quick
enough to do so unobserved, which meant that he lost his opportunity. Julie held out her hand for the letter, not entreatingly or

commandingly, but with an expression of confident interest. And Robert, again too slow, obeyed her gesture before realising what the sequel would be.

They were at breakfast in a back room over the shop in Seahampton, where the paint was all white and the curtains were of a really delicious white spotted muslin which Julie had found in London at the time of their settlement. Because this room faced south, it had a brightness and cheerfulness lacking in the bedroom; but unluckily, at Seahampton, the prevailing wind is from the south-west, and it brings rain, which the rather porous bricks used for building Robert's premises could not entirely resist. A great damp stain accordingly browned the pretty wallpaper, which for a couple of yards was badly cockled. This unsightliness perpetually caught the eye, like a stage corpse which the actors are determined not to see; and to Julie it appeared always to be growing larger, as the first clouds do upon a day doomed to bad weather. Apart from this stain the room was delightful; but because of it the breakfasters felt ominous discomfort.

Julie knew all about the letter, because it had been delivered to herself by the postman. The postman, in fact, had handed her the entire mail; but, as this consisted otherwise of bills, she had given the letter pride of place at the head of the pile. Thereafter she had observed its fortune; Robert's first careless fumble, the jump he gave at identification of the writer, and presently his falling face as he mastered its contents. Bad news indeed! Notably bad news.

Julie was dressed this morning in a trim frock of blue cotton, over which she wore a large white pinafore. She looked, as usual, as if all she wore were new. It was not. Their daughter, Rachel, in a high chair, sat as it were under Julie's lee; and Robert had a whole side of the table to himself. The bills he did not trouble to open; the letter caused him to stick his thumbnail between his teeth in gloomy perplexity. But he would not have allowed Julie to read it if she had not held out her hand. Then, indeed, after a first instinctive resistance, he pushed the letter beyond her hand, with a gesture of petulant desperation, as if he said: 'Here, see what *you* can make of it. It's time *you* did something. . . .' And he would immediately have snatched the letter again if Julie had permitted, being so exasperated that when Rachel, following imitatively the gestures of her parents, also held out a hand for it, he aimed a fruitless smack at Rachel's tiny fingers.

'Ah! ah!' cried Rachel, jerking herself back out of reach. 'Naughty daddy!'

'You keep your hands to yourself!' cried Robert, harshly.

Rachel subsided in her chair, looking ruefully at her two hands and twisting her fingers together, half-inclined to cry at his frightening fierceness, but bravely deciding not to cry. She looked at him from under her brows with droll and intimidated gravity.

Julie read the letter, stretching her unoccupied hand reassuringly towards Rachel; but the movement was inattentive, for her mind was given to adult concerns.

DEAR ROBERT [she read].

I have had no reply to my letter of the thirteenth, and I must say I am very disappointed both at receiving no reply and at the accounts which you at last sent me, many weeks late, showing the state of affairs up to the end of August, which should have been your peak month. My dear chap, you will really have to do something, for my friends are pressing me and I find it more and more difficult to stave them off! You will admit that I have been very patient, and things cannot go on like this. *Please let me hear from you without fail* by return, *to say what you propose to do about the matter.*

Yours sincerely,
R. F. FIRTH.

Only when she had twice read this through did Julie restore it to Robert's impatient hand. As she did so, she said:

'Well, what are you going to do?' The pupils of her eyes had grown so large that they almost obliterated the iris. Her cheeks had become faintly grey.

Robert moodily re-read the letter, which he then put in his pocket—too late to avoid this inquisition. He sighed heavily, as William had done, but with more explosive force than William. He sat back in his chair and put his clenched fists with difficulty into his trousers pockets. His chin was obstinately thrust forward. But he said nothing until his wife repeated her question with increased shrillness.

'I don't know,' he stubbornly answered. 'Take no notice.'

'You carn' do that.'

'Can't I?'

'Is it true?' Again she had to put the question twice—fiercely. 'Robert!'

Robert growled.

'I don't know what you're talking about. You know as well as I do that he found the money. I had no money. You had no money.'

She rolled her shoulders in an exaggeration of impatience.

'Oh, mon dieu; yes, of course I know that. But this other letter: did you receive it? The accounts: *are* they as bad as he says?'

'You know they are.'

Julie gave a high-pitched cry of protest.

'I know *nothing*. Nothing, nothing, nothing. How could I know? You have said to me that trade is not good. Well, is it to get better? Is it to get worse? Don't be so stupid! We cannot ignore the letter, as if nothing happened, I suppose?'

Robert stared sourly at the great stain in the wallpaper; but he did not see it. He was only troubled by a monstrous cloud of threat.

'Well, I owe Dick Firth three thousand pounds; and I owe two hundred pounds for stock. If we were sold up we might get a hundred for the lot,' he said, in an angry, defiant voice, as if Julie were responsible for every misfortune.

'But my God, Robert, that is desperate. It is fantastic. Absurd. It carn' be true. It——'

'You've read the letter,' said Robert, scowling down at the table.

'But you haven' had all that money.'

'I owe it, anyway. No, of course I haven't had it.' He jerked himself upright in his chair, took his fists from his pockets, and brought them down together upon the table. At each sentence, each separate clause, he again beat the table, thump, thump. 'What d'you think I've had? I've had nothing for myself, except the worry.

Nothing but worry . . . But Dick offered to help. He bought the freehold of this place, paid for all the decoration, advanced the money for some of the stock, and the shelving, and all that; led me into all the advertising and circulars and sandwichmen, the grand opening that was such a frost. You know all that. You knew it; you know it. He said it was "modern methods". Modern quackery!'

Julie, still grey, shrugged her shoulders immoderately, with impatience of his futile bitterness.

'Yes; but you agreed, my dear Robert, di'n't you? You di'n't refuse?'

'No,' Robert said, quietly. 'I didn't refuse. You kept on urging me not to refuse.'

'I?' She gave a gasp. Her black brows shot up; her eyes shone. 'Oh, then it is *I* who have done all this!'

As she stared, his head was turned away; but they both frowned heavily, and both were pale.

'You've done more than that,' Robert said at last. 'You've done your share to make things impossible.'

'Three thousand pounds. My God!' Julie folded her napkin with unsteady hands.

Savagely, he shouted:

'Oh, you knew all about it. Why play the innocent? You've known all the time that the shop wasn't paying. I've told you over and over again to be careful, to go slow——'

'Yes? I have *been* careful.'

'Not too careful with Mrs Powder-Clay,' growled Robert.

'That aw . . . ful woman!' Julie's shoulders were up to her ears; her face was contorted in an extraordinary grimace. 'She behaved as if I was a slave. She stared at my dress, my shoes——'

'Or Mrs Barrett or Mrs Peto. *They* didn't insult you.'

'Hoh! Shopkeepers!' she cried. 'Leedle English creeping spying puritans! How did I offend them? They came to call on me—yes; I called on them. Very English. But they are not ladies; they bore me; I am at arms'-length with them. Hoh! How wicked!'

'You wouldn't go to church.'

'Good heavens, Robert! Would *you*?'

'Or chapel. Or mothers' meeting. Or anything. Certainly I'd have gone. You know perfectly well how important it is in a small place like this. Church to please the good class people; chapel for the locals. I told you that. I explained. Yet you put all their backs up by strolling about in smart clothes——'

Julie, in despair, raised her eyes to the white ceiling.

'Smart clothes! Oh, it is my fault!' she exclaimed. 'My fault entirely. I have driven everybody from your shop. I am not a dowdy prying old maid. I am French. I made you borrow the money. I made you start here. I married you. I had that expensive baby——'

From irony she was ascending to declamation, when Robert interrupted. He shouted:

'Shut up, Julie! Talking rot! Working yourself up like that! Rubbish!'

'You accuse me! That is what you say!'

'It isn't. Nobody can say I'm not just. I don't say it's all your fault. No! There's much more. We're in the wrong street, for one thing—it's full of debts and derelicts. We did several things wrong——'

'*You* did nothing wrong!' cried Julie, scornfully. 'That *could* not be!'

'Oh, yes, I did! But you've helped to make things worse.' He again thumped the table at each accusation. 'You've offended people. You've dressed too well and made us live too well and turned your nose up at decent people because they were tradesmen. As *we* are. You spent too much on furnishing. You've made the place look like a palace, and——'

'Look!' commanded Julie, turning swiftly and pointing at the great unforgotten stain upon the wall. 'A palace!'

'Not economising,' said Robert, refusing to look. 'Dolling up the child. Spending. Spend, spend . . . It's not all you. Not by any means. But as we're talking about it I may as well say what's in my mind——'

'Oh, certainly,' agreed Julie, with vehement politeness. 'Every word, please. Every villain thought.'

'And there's no need for you to get huffy because you don't like the truth.'

'The truth!' she exclaimed, laughing. 'It is exquisite! I love to hear it. From my husband, who begged me to look smart, to give the place chic; who said he will not do this and will not do that because it would show the grovelling spirit. You remember, perhaps? No?' She laughed again at Robert's dogged face. 'But you at least were always right. You at least have repaid some of your debt, surely?'

Robert scrambled to his feet, and began to walk about the room. Countercharges irked him.

'Oh, the devil!' he cried. 'That's Dick Firth all over. My dear friend. Eager to help me for old times' sake, when we were boys together. But he's got no money himself. Oh, no. Only a big house at Ealing, and a rich wife, and a father-in-law who's made a fortune in tin. No money; but he'll get it for me. From friends. Other friends. Stiff friends. Marvellous what a lot of friends he has! They're all himself. So I'm paying him on a mortgage for the shops; and interest first on the original loan of a thousand and then on another loan borrowed to repay the first loan, and presently, I suppose, another loan to repay that, until I'm swamped with loans. First it's seven per cent—very friendly and reasonable —for a year. Then, oh, things don't look as good; the people—his friends—will have to call in their money; but never mind, he can get somebody else—another friend—to come to the rescue, only the interest will be fifteen per cent for six months. And then— well, when you're desperate you don't look so close. That's what I've been paying—up to the end of June. Fifteen per cent—extension after extension. What else could I have done? I'd have paid thirty, forty, fifty, to carry on. But what with bad trade and bad debts I've missed some payments; the principal's long overdue; and he's worried. Worried to death. Patiently worried to death. "Yours sincerely." Not "your old pal, Dick"; but "R. F. Firth." "Yours sincerely." See the difference? Well, let him worry. He's already had about four hundred pounds out of me, one way and another.'

Julie gave a cry of horror.

'Robert! Good heavens, it's monstrous!'

'And I still owe him the whole three thousand!' shouted Robert, blaming her, but torturing himself. 'See? Three thousand! That's the way to get rich!'

She could not scream; but, wringing her hands, demanded hoarsely:

'But how, what have we done to get this great burden? How could it have happened?'

'I'll tell you how. Because when you've got no money you're at the mercy of people who have. Because you can't start a business without capital. Because when you do start you find that you've got to buy everything brand new, from stock to delivery barrows—everything, baskets, scales, window-blinds, cash books, string—God! the whole shoot! You've got to print your invoices and your leaflets. You've got to lay in a lot of useless, experimental stock. In a new town, with a new business—people coming from everywhere, all over the country, and wanting what they're used to —you've got to gamble. You feel big. You order big. Of course you make mistakes. I'm human, aren't I? I've got stuff I shall never sell; stuff you'll never use up. . . . And if you can't pay cash you lose your discounts. And if you *pay* cash, you've got to borrow it from somebody. And if you borrow it you've got to pay it back in so long, and pay interest at so much a year or so much a month; and if you can't pay your interest you've got to promise to pay more interest; and if in the end you can't pay that they sell you up and put you in the street for being poor. And that's the end of *you* as a shopkeeper. My God, since I've been here I've learnt a lot.' He gave a shout of laughter. 'And keeping it to myself, to save you. While you couldn't be bothered to be polite to people because they're not ladies. . . . Good God, was there ever such rubbish!'

Though still pale, though still trembling with the agitated contemplation of disaster, Julie shrugged at his return to herself as the villain. It was significant, a fixed, self-excusing idea. All knowledge of him began to crystallise in her brain. He was a fool. What was to be done?

'This Firth,' she said, abruptly. 'Perhaps he is *still* your friend. . . .'

Robert swept round upon her.

'Still harping on that? Have you ever done business with a friend? I have. I've done business with a mother. It's expensive. Dick Firth's got about as much feeling in his soul as a fish has in its slimy body. He's a clever, treacherous devil. Why I let him get round me that day I can't imagine. But I've remembered a lot since. Why, when we were youngsters together——' Robert stopped dead. One would have said that something had robbed him of breath. He looked sharply at his wife. Then his tongue, either because he wished to injure Julie or because it was loosened by despair, hurried him onward. 'Women and business—they're the test. I'll tell you. I used to know a girl—long before I met you. I was very fond of her—she was a little thing. Different to you. A *little*—— Well, what did Dick do? My dear friend, you know. He met her; nothing doing. But somehow, maybe because he knew the game, he got hold of her, spun a tale—he's always got a tale —put her in the family way; and when I found it out—by God, I nearly killed him. But he'd packed her off somewhere. As for Dick, he was as sweet and smarmy as ever, "Oh, *Robert!*"—church, hymns, good works . . . She went; he stayed. Nobody knew. But I knew. Yet because *we* were in a hole, and I didn't know what would happen to *you*, I——'

Julie interrupted.

'Hoh! Of course you were the honest, honest man!' She had stored his reminiscence with lightning speed. It would never be forgotten. But her face expressed nothing but impatience of his long-winded diversion. 'There is no need to tell me of it. But something is happening *now*, my dear Robert. Remember! Unless you do something, we shall be in the street—no home—starving. Rachel and I, both!'

'Oh, it's the same for me!' cried Robert, furiously, startled into arrogance by her contempt for his old love-story. 'I need food, just as you do!'

'That is why you should cease rambling, and blaming me; and should make *some plan!*' said Julie, with a cold look.

Robert was amazed. An angry retort was upon his tongue. But fury gradually died in him. He said, at first rather sulkily:

'Let him make me a bankrupt. He'll get nothing. And he knows it. He won't let it come to that. Oh, no.' After a pause: 'That's the worst of starting afresh in a new town. If I'd been able to carry out my original plan and run this place from Moreton, things would have been very different. I could have halved the expenses.'

'But my dear bo-o-oy, you are *not* at Moreton. Not. What is the use of this "if it had been *so* . . ."!' She mimicked him.

Robert, far away, muttered:

'Damn that old devil! I could strangle her! She's got the throat for it!'

Silence.

'You must go to see her,' said Julie, with decision.

'I'd sooner starve.'

"Yes, they are big words. The fact is less pleasant.'

'So's the fact of seeing her. You don't understand.'

'I shall go to see uncle. We will both go.'

Robert thought: 'Well, why not? Even two-fifty would be something. We could live on it for a year!' His eyes narrowed. She'd messed that. When he'd thought her so shrewd. What a revelation!

'Last time I heard of him he was pretty bad.'

Julie, unconscious of his thoughts, flashed:

'It was I who told you. It was from Sarah, the good Sarah, I heard it. Robert, there is something which suggests itself to me. It is that I go to see your mother. That I take Rachel.'

Robert felt his heart leap pounding in his breast.

'My God, don't you dare!' he vehemently cried. 'I'd kill you if you did! Rachel—why, she'd shut her fingers in the door. If you think you can play Little Lord Fauntleroy with her, you're wrong. She's not that sort.'

'Mm? Why does she not love you?' asked Julie, ignoring his command. Robert said:

'Because she recognises a will as strong as her own.'

The faintest of smiles hovered upon Julie's lips. At the same moment she realised for the first time that Rachel, who had been affrighted by the raised voices, was crying, her tiny body jerking with sobs.

'What, my little one; have they made thee weep!' she said, in a softer voice, as she bent over the child. Rachel, still afraid, drew back into her chair, the great black eyes bathed in tears; and it was a moment before Julie remembered her real preoccupation. 'But Robert, what are you going to do about this Firth, your friend?'

Her voice echoed. Taking advantage of her concern with Rachel, Robert had escaped.

IV

There the old man lay, exactly as William had pictured him. He might have been already dead, for the grey Autumn light shadowed his face as it shadowed the faces of all who were present. They were all grey, from Doctor Hodge, who grew parchment-like and more remotely concerned than ever with some inner ironic melancholy, to the middle-aged sensible nurse who wore a grey dress, and the small quiet man, with a pointed grey beard and gold-rimmed glasses, whom William well knew to be Mr Merrow, the solicitor. They were grey and attentive; so that William had the sense of entering a room full of shades, all waiting for death to add one to their number. Julie, to his relief, was not present; and neither he nor any of the others realised that, as she ushered William into the room, Sarah entered it behind him and remained. She stood, silent and unobserved, just inside the door, her eyes cast down, a pale, tired little woman whose humility, although it was extreme, did not cringe. She was dressed in black, and her shoulders were so bowed that nobody could have guessed the great strength which lay in them.

Faint movements of Daddy's hand as it flickered upon the coverlet drew the eyes of all. His eyelids twitched, but did not open. These futile motions were signs of some still active inclination for life, and before ceasing they persisted for several seconds. There was then a ring at the doorbell, and Sarah slipped out to answer it, while William, dreading that Julie must now appear, moved back into the darkest corner, to be the last person she would see upon entry. It was not Julie, however, who next came into the room, but Richard Firth, who stood like a mute in the doorway looking at them all through his long fair eyelashes with a dim ingratiating smile upon his lips. His thin body was made to seem thinner by the long black coat which he wore, and by the tall stiff collar which swallowed his neck. Nobody spoke; but Sarah, re-entering, silently closed the door and stayed before it. When they had taken their eyes from Richard, Doctor Hodge with a murmur stepped sharply to the bedside. In the instant during which their attention had been distracted, Daddy had died. The hand lay still upon the coverlet where it had just restlessly moved.

A moment later, it was as if Daddy had been dead for years. No shock was apparently felt by any of them at his passing; and only William was conscious of any emotion, even of relief. The others were discreet; they lowered their voices, they turned away, they moved instinctively towards the door. But for them all Daddy was now nothing but a recollection. Covered with a sheet, his body lingered. When that was gone, he would, for all his many years of life, be forgotten. . . .

Presently, shuffling down the stairs under the leadership of Mr Merrow, William found himself joined by Dick, who pressed his arm in a half-timid, half-familiar greeting.

'How are *you?*' came the soft voice. 'What an age since we met. You're still here, then, in Moreton. But not, I think, still on the "Gazette".'

'No, I'm in London,' William agreed, looking round with a smile into those curious screened eyes. They were pale, and in this light rather greenish, and behind those fair fringes they communicated nothing but the sense that their owner kept his own counsel. William, vaguely remarking this, did not realise how extraordinarily these eyes could change, or how magnetic they could be, and if he had been told of this he would have scoffed. Nevertheless, he was interested. He had always been interested by Dick Firth, whom he had known for a time in the 'Gazette' office; and was amused by his demureness, attracted in spite of inexplicable doubt by what he thought a rather effeminate charm. So his smile, if reserved, was genuine. Dick warmly responded:

'Really. Really. In London. Oh, but we must meet sometime. Are you on a London paper? I . . . I've quite lost sight of you. Unintentionally. I try very hard. But I . . . I'm so busy.' It was deprecating. His lids were lowered, and his hands slightly swam before his breast.

'I see all sorts of accounts of *your* activity,' William remarked, perhaps a little archly.

Dick looked pleased.

'Well, that's something, isn't it. You can tell how . . . I . . . I mean . . .' A vagueness came into his speech. William knew that his attention must have been distracted. So much the better. They were entering Daddy's big study upon the ground floor; and this room, for William, was so crowded with memories of Julie that he was thankful to escape attention. The long curtains, the heavy shelves, the big fireplace, they were all, seemingly, unchanged, unchangeable. Nothing had been altered. Here she had sat and moved, the one truly living thing in the household; and as he looked towards the window he imagined her there, a light figure amid the ancient furnishings, like a first Spring flower colouring wintry soil. He heard her voice, with its foreign intonation and the irresistible little mispronouncings, saw the turns of her head, the mocking lips, forever promising a smile and forever tantalising his expectation, re-created the magic of her personality as only one could do in whom love still lingered. . . . And his heartbeat quickened. But Dick, who remembered nothing of this because he had never seen Julie in Moreton, and at the time of their meetings elsewhere had found her sallow, tiresome, unattractively heavy with child, listened with attention to Mr Merrow; and Mr Merrow, as brisk as a conjurer, held a paper which he had taken from his breast pocket.

'I needn't keep you long,' Mr Merrow said. He wore a well-fitting frock-coat, which as it was of good cloth made him look very trim. His hands were white. He was precise. He looked at them shrewdly, with unwarmed benevolence, over his gold-rimmed spectacles; and nobody could have doubted either his kindness or the fact that it would be followed by a statement of account. 'But I thought you'd like to know that you both benefit under the will. You, Mr Firth, of course get the lion's share. That's because he owed so much to your advice over investments.'

'I . . . I'm glad I was of use,' stammered Dick. A faint colour touched his cheeks; his lips were pursed, and the muscles about them stiffened as if he repressed a deeper smile, perhaps of delight. 'So glad.' Then: 'May one ask . . . if you have any idea . . .'

'About fourteen thousand pounds for you. You're probably familiar with the amounts of his holdings. Not as much as that for you, Harvest. . . .'

What a subtle difference of tone! William looked vaguely at Mr Merrow, whose words he had heard without understanding them. He had been thinking of Julie. Both Dick and Mr Merrow, accordingly, were impressed by his inscrutable silence, and felt secret admiration of him as one able to conceal his thoughts. They marvelled. Had he expected more? Anything at all? Impossible to tell! Mr Merrow continued:

'You are the residuary legatee; but in the last three years he'd sold most of his house-property and invested under Mr Firth's advice. There are some old cottages that might fetch perhaps seven or eight hundred pounds. And this house; with everything in it. But that's complicated by the stipulation that you're not to sell it. Well, but I can let for you at once, on a five or seven years' lease; so it's a good investment. We can talk about that later. Both of you. Naturally. This is quite informal. Hardly, perhaps . . .' He swept them both with a glance, looking for criticism of his taste. 'I just thought you'd like to know where you stood.'

There was a gentle sigh.

'Oh, yes, thanks,' Dick murmured in a kind of ecstasy. He seemed to glow. He kept his hands down to his sides, closely gripped, with the thumbs turned inwards. Fourteen thousand pounds! It was wonderful. It was a fortune. It was a tribute. And a . . . a reward!

'There are no other legacies.'

Silence followed.

'No other?' William, hitherto only half-conscious, and quite lulled by Mr Merrow's voice into a stupid vagueness of mind, at length awoke. 'But Julie—Miss—Mrs Whistler,' he cried, abruptly. 'Mr Griffin's niece——'

The trim frock-coated figure was unchanged. The face above it was expressionless. Mr Merrow's eyes blinked once. Suavely, he replied:

'They quarrelled, if you remember. Even so, she was never . . . She had only a small legacy at any time. . . .'

William was dumbfounded. His mind flew back to that still figure upstairs. No explanation. No kindness. A deliberate and uncharitable neglect of Julie. What ingratitude!

'Do you mean that he changed his will?'

'Oh, yes, several times.' Mr Merrow did not intend that William should learn of his own losses. He had conscious considerateness. After all, where ignorance is bliss . . . 'There have been three wills. He changed his mind a lot in the last five years. Quite sound mind, you understand; but relaxed. Full of whim. And this is the last of them. It was made not very long ago; it doesn't mention Mrs Whistler at all.'

There was another silence.

'I . . . I say, *what* hard lines!' at last murmured Dick, in a regretful voice that was like a prolonged sigh. 'It seems hardly . . . mm . . .'

William, caught by the sighing tone, turned full upon Dick in candid explanation. He was quite animated, and for the first time felt a warm heart towards the chief inheritor. He cried:

'She did *everything* for him.'

'Too bad,' agreed Dick, nodding sympathetically. 'Of course, I . . . Well, that's what these . . . But it really is a little unfortunate; when I'm afraid they're rather badly off. Poor Robert!' He put a hand consolingly upon William's arm, his smile charmingly intimate. 'You know, I . . . I do wish we could do something about it. You and I . . . Perhaps we could. D'you think? Some little . . . However . . . Of course, you know that Robert has a business at Seahampton. . . .'

'Yes, I know. I haven't been there,' meditated William. He thought: 'And I'm not going. But I shall have to go.' To Dick, aloud, he added: 'Yes. Yes. Of course we'll do something.'

'Very kind,' remarked Mr Merrow. 'But perhaps . . .' He was faintly quizzical, thinking of Daddy's humours, slightly (to himself) ridiculing the fastidious humanitarianism of these young legatees.

'You're his friend, I think?' said Dick, impulsively, to William. He seemed to have been struck by an impression, and it was because of this that he ignored the solicitor's deprecating speech. 'I mean, his *real* friend. Excuse me, my dear fellow. I was going to say that I've known Bob for so many years—much longer, naturally, than you can have done. We were inseparable.'

'I remember,' remarked William, with unexpected dryness. Well, he had been struck by a note of unction; and his mind had flown back to an old episode, when he had lost his cap. . . . He *did* remember.

Dick resumed:

'Quite inseparable. Until . . . We went different ways. I branched out. He stayed at home. Just that, of course. He stayed at home. I lost touch. Until three or four years ago, when I was able to help him a little——'

'Ah!' cried William. '*You* helped him! Yes, I wondered——'

They had forgotten Mr Merrow, who stood folding his papers and looking quietly from one to the other. But Mr Merrow had by no means forgotten himself.

'Is there anything else I can tell you at this moment?' he asked, with a slightly reproachful sternness. 'You'll both be hearing from me in the course of a few days; and any instructions . . .' He went to the door. 'I shall wish you good afternoon.' He was through the doorway; and William could see, without, the weary visage of Sarah, who waited in the hall. Had the door been altogether closed? 'Oh, Harvest.' Mr Merrow invited William, by a jerk of his head, to join him outside the room. In a lower voice, he said: 'The tenant for this place. It's Mrs Whistler senior who wants it.'

William, glancing past Mr Merrow, saw Sarah's white face in

silhouette: how strained it seemed! She was listening intently to the murmured conversation.

'Mrs Whistler senior wants to *live* here?' he asked, doubtfully. 'Well, I suppose that's possible——'

'At any rate, you wouldn't mind if she looked the place over? Say one day next week?'

'What do you say to that, Sarah?' William saw that Sarah was biting her lip with what appeared to be nervous excitement. 'You'll be here, won't you?'

Sarah nodded. Her face glowed. 'Poor woman!' thought William. 'She's had the rottenest time of anybody!'

'You must be very tired,' he said with his friendly smile.

He saw the gleam of Sarah's teeth in an answering smile.

'Never tired,' she said.

'You're marvellous!' William assured her. 'I was *born* tired.' Indeed, at this moment he could have yawned again and again, so much did the day's events destroy his nervous strength. When Mr Merrow had gone, he continued speaking to her. 'Sarah, did you hear what he's just told us?' Sarah nodded. 'All of it?' She nodded again. 'It's bad. You were fond of Miss Julie, weren't you? She was kind? And Mr Whistler: you liked him?' She nodded with energy in reply to each question. 'I shan't take my share. I shall hand it over to her.'

'No,' said Sarah.

'What? Why not?'

'Mother's rich. Got ten thousand pounds.'

Astonished at her tight-lipped loquacity, William said:

'Yes, but *they've* not got it. Some quarrel. Do you know all about it? The dickens you do!' A thought struck him. 'About Miss Julie's quarrel? About me? Gosh, I believe you do! I hope you don't know *too* much, Sarah.'

Sarah jerked her head towards the study door.

'Listening,' she warned.

William, thus directed, could also see a faint shadow moving upon the wallpaper just within the room; and without more ado he rejoined Dick Firth, whom he found apparently examining with scrupulous care one of Daddy's books. Sarah vanished. She had heard all she wanted to hear.

v

After dark, with the blinds of the lonely house drawn, Sarah Tweed rested in her kitchen, knowing that Daddy lay dead upstairs, but in no way terrified at the knowledge. It is true that she heard every creak that ran through the ancient boards as they settled for the night; and perhaps imagined movements across the empty rooms. But she did not stir, and her heart beat no faster than usual. She sat quite still, listening. She was waiting for a particular sound.

At last it came; a step upon the garden path, followed by a slight finger-nail tapping at her door. Somebody had used the door opening from the school passage—that same door which Robert, unaware that Sarah could hear his every movement, had often used in visiting Julie—and was at the back of the house. At once Sarah left her chair to admit the caller. The chill night air caught her face, and a woman much smaller than herself came from the darkness into the kitchen.

'Here I am,' said the stranger, breathlessly. 'I see he's gone.'

Sarah nodded. Her visitor, smiling timidly, took off her black heavily-braided cape, and hung it over a chair, but did not attempt to remove a black bonnet which pressed down upon her crisp grey hair, and so sat down, looking as if she must be ready at the slightest sound to make an escape. She was very wizened, a tiny wiry woman, with a face greatly wrinkled with innumerable anxieties. But as she sat opposite to Sarah at the kitchen table there was such a likeness in the secret way they turned their heads that nobody could have doubted a relationship between them. In fact, this was Sarah's mother, not Flora Tweed, but Flora Bright, owing to a second unfortunate marriage.

'Nobody here, then?' whispered Mrs Bright. 'I didn't know. Was it bad, at the end? Mr Harvest come? I saw him last week; of course, he doesn't know me.'

'He's nice,' Sarah said. It was her mother's turn to nod. Sarah then said: 'Some news.'

'News?' urgently repeated Mrs Bright, who still whispered, from long habit, although she knew they were alone. As she nodded, the shadow of her bonnet danced along the dresser shelf and into the dimness of the outer light. 'What, of *her?*'

'She wants to live here.'

'Sal!' It was awed. Mrs Bright shuddered. She added: 'I saw her yesterday. She's still there, at Mrs Fisher's. They were coming out. I don't like the look of her; no I don't. So changed.'

'Old,' added Sarah.

'Ill,' mouthed Mrs Bright. 'Suffering. For her sins, I suppose.'

'She still got it, d'you think?'

The mother shrugged her shoulders.

'All her furniture's at Mrs Fisher's. The girl there says she keeps the chest locked.'

Sarah nodded.

'I'd like that,' she said, reflectively. 'Wouldn't mind anything, if I had it.'

Mrs Bright pursed her lips and drew them, so pursed, to one side. Thus did she signify her sense of the difficulties lying ahead. She did not make any other response, because she could not think of anything helpful to say; and after a considerate silence she let her anxious eyes seek relief in a tour of the tea-table. When she saw that a pot of plum jam had been specially opened, a few of the lines nearest her eyes slightly deepened in a smile of joy at the provision of her favourite conserve. Motherly gratitude, a detestation of the gum-wounding sharp pips to be found in strawberry and raspberry jams, anticipatory pleasure, and memory of former jousts with plum jam were all indicated in that smile. But all she said, as she jerked her head at the bright new pot, was:

'Whistlers'?'

'No, Supply,' was Sarah's dry answer. That was a reminder that Whistlers' shop had changed hands. The goods now sold in it came as far as possible from a single central organization. Old-fashioned brands were being replaced by others which had been produced in quantity. The new were cheaper; they lacked idiosyncrasy. And having scored this point over her mother, who acknowledged a wound by raising both hands at once from her knees, Sarah gave ear to the first trifling whistle of a kettle about to boil, and began serious operations by warming the teapot. Her mother apologetically said:

'That's me. I always forget. Don't seem right, the old names going. All the old ways. Specially Whistlers'.'

At a memory which those words lanced, Sarah put down the teapot so abruptly that it clattered. She had grown very pale. It seemed for a moment as if she must collapse into a chair. But, quickly recovering herself, she continued to prepare the tea as if nothing had happened and with such apparent calm that Mrs Bright remained unconscious of all embarrassment.

VI

Travelling back from Moreton by the train reaching Victoria shortly after eleven o'clock, William fell fast asleep in his corner, and did not awaken until the door of the compartment was flung open by a noisy porter. Even then he was hardly awake, for the day had been a trying one. He had ended it, as he thought, by putting in an hour at the 'Gazette' office writing a special memoir of Daddy for the mid-week issue. 'Want to do the old man well,' the editor said; 'you've got a light touch for that sort of thing.' 'Hm,' William had retorted; 'I heard nothing of that when I worked here.' 'Oh, no,' answered the editor; 'doesn't do. Man gets swelled head. More wages.' 'You damned capitalists!' objected William. And the editor: 'Who, I? God! I'm a wage slave myself! Wish I could get to London.' William could re-picture the scene as he walked home from the tram-stop, the editor puffing very professionally at a big curly pipe, and thinking himself important, and shining with the manly cynicism of the half-baked. Still smiling, he unlocked the door of Mrs Dooms's house.

'All in. Put out gas,' read the note by his candlestick on the hall table. Kitty had added: 'Supper in the dining-room.' Bless the child! What a good girl she was! Supper was what he needed!

He bolted the front door and tip-toed into the back room, where a peep of gas and a dying fire accompanied a half-covered table upon which bread, cheese, butter, a bottle of ale, and some ragged celery had been spread for his cheer. It was neat and clean, and the room was warm. What luck! . . .

Why was it that chaps in tinpot newspaper offices were such frightful men-of-the-world? So knowing? So damned silly! Why, under their veneer of sophistication, were so many rank-and-file journalists callow? Boys in beards. Children who quaffed beer and talked big and dragged their unlaughing laughter into groans of disillusion . . . A problem for William as he crunched his celery. The real journalists, the men who wrote the real papers with real brains, were not so. They were not cynical, but experienced. They knew what went on in the great world and were not shocked or shaken by it. Theirs was not a vocabulary of clichés, but a flexible language suited to the rapid expression of thought. . . . He came to the conclusion—but he was very tired—that he himself, like the rest, was always pitching the note too high, into insincerity— avoiding the common—making a show of a little knowledge—trying to impress; while the real men, given confidence by their knowledge, cared less to impose than to communicate. Was that only the contrast of youth and age? What rot; it was the contrast of congenital inefficiency and class. . . . 'Gosh!' thought William. 'There I go; "the real men"! Why not "big"? The big blokes . . . important people . . . Journalese! What a lingo!'

This was his last conscious thought. His hand, in the fingers of which was a small piece of bread, fell to the tablecloth; the bread tumbled away, and the hand sank to his knee. His head drooped, lower and lower. He was asleep; while the fire died and the yellow and blue gas flame continually trembled in the globe above him, and chill air crept from the corners of the room and under the door and in at the window-sashes. There was silence, except for William's soft breathing.

It was then that the door began slowly to open, without sound; but William knew nothing of it. He was dreaming confusedly of all the people he had seen that day, from Mrs Dooms and Kitty and Bryant and Finch to the group by Daddy's bedside, Sarah, his mother and Minna, the editor of the 'Gazette' at Moreton, the noisy porter at Victoria; and particularly of Dick Firth and his pleasant manner. . . . And into this dream Julie came, looking sternly at William and saying 'I loved you; but you're no good, as I soon found out. . . .' She took a great deal of money from him and seemed then to relent; but carried a candle and whispered in his ear 'Darling! Darling! You poor darling; you're tired out and cold and your hair wants cutting. . . .' And as he slipped gradually from sleep to wakefulness the voice continued: 'I'd do it myself with a basin; but you're such a pet. . . .' Hands and arms were warmly about him; his head rested upon the softest sweetest pillow he had ever known. . . .

Shaking his head as a dog shakes his whole body, William sat up. 'Good heavens!' he muttered. 'Idiot. Fast asleep. That beer's flat. Ugh. Horrid.' He gave a huge sigh. 'Hm. I must get to bed.'

But something caused him to look over his shoulder; and there he saw Kitty, standing watching him, smiling.

'Hullo!' William would have risen, but she pressed him back in his chair.

'Did you hear me?' she asked, as he struggled round. Her hair was loose; and her eyes shone. Though she wore a blue woollen dressing-gown it was awry at the throat and the high-necked night-dress could be seen within it. 'Hear what I said?' She was laughing. Her cheeks were flushed. How pretty she was!

'Did you say something about cutting my hair?' William felt at the nape of his neck; true, a haircut was overdue. 'Here, but you said something else, didn't you?'

Kitty laughed outright.

'Ah, but you didn't hear that!' she said. 'Too much of a gentle-man.'

They spoke, both of them, in undertones, as was fitting at such an hour, when the household was asleep; but the softness of their speech had subtly another effect also, of a shared privacy, which one of the two, at least, did not intend.

'I'm not sure that I did,' said William. 'Did I?'

She had seated herself upon the arm of a big leather-covered chair half behind William; and if he had been more wide-awake he would have seen that she was shivering as much from excitement as from cold.

'I've been waiting for you,' Kitty said. 'Listening. Everybody else in bed . . . You were so beastly this morning. I wanted to know if your news was good or bad.' Even the memory of their last brusque encounter brought tears to her eyes; and William caught in a flash, perhaps in the movement of a swollen cheek, something which told him she had cried a great deal. What! He was filled with concern.

'Good? Bad? Oh, Kitty!' he protested. 'I don't remember anything about it. *Was* I beastly? I'm so sorry. When I was going?'

'You were *horrid,*' she said, in a broken voice. Immediately, though she smiled, her face puckered; and as the tears welled again to her eyes she bent her head to hide their flow, hesitated, and then like a child took two steps forward and in another instant had pressed herself against William, his head to her breast, her arms around his shoulders. William, no longer confused, but in a kind of acute pleasurable consternation, started. What was this? She loved him. Was there triumph in his heart? None! What of Julie? As he uncontrollably moved, she slipped to his knee, within his arms, closer, closer, not laughingly, temptingly, but with desperation; and as he embraced her William could feel that she was violently sobbing.

'Why, why, poor old girl!' murmured William, astounded. 'Here, you'll hurt yourself! I'd no idea—never *meant* to be beastly. Good heavens, no! I shouldn't dream . . . Kitty, you know that!'

Kitty's wet cheek was pressed hard against his. She was still crying, but she was laughing as well, in a state close to hysteria.

'It's not you at all,' she whisperingly sobbed, withdrew her cheek, and, laughing, pressed it again to his. 'It's me. It's *me*. Being silly.'

'Yes,' he agreed, in the same secret murmur. 'Yes, it's you, being silly.'

' 'Tisn't!' The word was spoken right into his ear. 'It's you being beastly.'

William was fully awake, and his memory was as active as his sense of the present and its implications. He, too, slightly trembled. How easy! How easy! With what temptation he was faced! This was but the end of all that had been developing in the last few weeks. But what did *he* want? For time to clear his head, he prevaricated.

'Both of us being silly,' he murmured in return, sweetly, kindly, without passion; although his heart was beginning to beat fast and his throat to grow dry. 'How's that?'

'No.' She but clung the closer to him, all softness except for the firm arms which brought her heart against his breast. The sobs ran less violently through her body. In a moment she withdrew her face, so that the tears dried upon his cheek, and glanced sharply towards her knees, from which the dressing-gown was falling away. William, following her glance, was amused; and she, knowing that he smiled, smiled too.

'Not to look,' she said; and sighed heavily. Then she laughed whisperingly, shuddered, turned her cheek back to his with arch shyness. And as she did that, recovering, she released her right arm, and drew the dressing-gown together again. 'Let me go.'

The instruction was certainly not genuine.

'Oh, I thought you were cold,' William said.

'What?' It was a tender murmur. Then: 'No, I'm burning. Feel.' She bared her arm, and put it to his lips. What could William do? Hadn't she wished that? But the arm was cold, and she withdrew it with a shiver. 'I don't know what you think of me. . . .'

'What d'you suppose?'

'I was worried about you. I didn't mean this. William——'

'You meant this,' William said, coolly. He was not cool.

'I didn't.' She pushed herself free, but did not go. 'Did *you?*' Her eyes were veiled; he knew that through her lashes she was watching him.

'I was asleep,' he answered; and saw her lips tremble. 'I dreamt it.'

'You didn't!'

'I did.'

Her mood changed from one of teased incredulity to despair. She whispered:

'You don't want me.'

'Desperately.'

'You don't.' A sob checked her. The last words, spoken so low and cryingly as to be barely audible, were the confession: 'Not like I want you.'

William thought his heart stopped beating altogether. He could not speak. At last, unsteadily, he said:

'Yes. Much more. Oh, much!' And when she shook her head: 'Rot. You know nothing about it. Nothing at all. Look here, I think we'd better get married, you know.'

She started; he felt the tremor run through her body. But she did not smile. Instead, she turned her head sharply away from him, so that until he used a little force he could not look into her shining eyes. She shivered again. The room was growing very cold. As he kissed her lips he found them frozen. But an instant later she began quietly to laugh like a child, trembling and high-spirited; and in this new mood threw her arms about his neck and gave him kiss for kiss with such ardour that his blood mounted in tumult.

CHAPTER XI

Mrs Whistler Goes Visiting

UNHURRIED, Mrs Whistler walked from her lodging, which was at some distance from the High Street, and approached the house in which Daddy Griffin had lived for so many years. She gave the impression of walking slowly because she was aware of her own dignity; but in fact she could no longer walk very fast. She had aged greatly in the last few years. She had grown stouter, and her face with its broad high cheekbones was apt to take on something of the bruised appearance of a pomegranate. One of her hands was swollen; she became, although as yet she was unaware of it, each week more sluggish and less inclined for effort. But for thirty years she had coveted Daddy Griffin's house; and now, for the first time in all that period, she was to be within it.

This prospect excited her very much. Like other elderly women in Moreton, Mrs Whistler had known something of Daddy's life. She had given him that interest which the consciously virtuous take in those of the other sex who are said to be irresistible; and while speaking very contemptuously of Daddy she always grew alert if he came into view, and closely followed him with her glance until he had passed from sight. His every betraying gesture—the adroit hands, his habit of caressing his beard and grinning when he looked at girls, the impertinent assurance of his address, the stiffening of his slightly bowed legs, and a sort of uneasy boredom in the presence of men—was evident to Mrs Whistler. She never saw that other men despised him; for such understanding would have needed a larger range of vision than hers, and an ability to stare comprehendingly at more than one person at a time. But what she could see she could recognise. Just how Mrs Whistler recorded her certainties was not clear; unlike those who are the slaves of

244

their vocabularies she did not think in words. Nevertheless she
knew much about Daddy; and she was desperately curious to see
his house—to know more and more and more about him, the dirty
beast. . . .

There was bright sunshine this afternoon; but it would soon be
gone, for the year was declining, and by the time the children came
out of school it would be very nearly dusk. They would rush headlong through the passage between the cemetery and the high wall
of the house, the smaller and weaker of them glad to get into the
High Street before darkness fell. There would be some shouting
and tumbling; but in five minutes all would be quiet and the school
locked up for the day. And Mrs Whistler wished by that time to
have made up her mind which rooms of Daddy's house she would
use for her own purposes. He, she understood, had preferred a
bedroom at the back. But while that room was certainly quieter
than the others it only overlooked the garden, and nothing could
be seen from its window—'nothing' being, of course, 'nobody'—so
Mrs Whistler was in secret quite determined to have the front
rooms for her own use.

Some, she knew, might think the house too big for one woman.
It was nothing of the kind. Although tall, it was by no means large
—seven rooms at most; and if she could find a suitable maid she
could live alone cheaply and in comfort, surrounded by her own
furniture, sitting at the windows, well content for many years to
come with tranquil solitude. A few of those whom she needed
could call and drink tea with her and tell their tales; those whom
she did not need could stay away. And she was ready, she had told
Mr Merrow, to sign an agreement for any term of years that was
wished, provided the rent was satisfactory. 'Seven, ten, fourteen . . .'
she had said, with that cold air of contempt which she favoured.
'Of course I must have an option of renewal.' Mr Merrow's odd
non-committal thoughtfulness in response—as he silently estimated
Mrs Whistler's age—had made no impression at all upon her. Why
should it do so?

Slowly she walked along, very upright, dressed as usual in black,
with a black imitation ostrich feather in her hat and black silken
embroidery upon her mantle. Nothing escaped her attention, from

the sidelong peeps of nursery-girls pushing prams to the muddy face of a child playing in the gutter before his mother's front door. She looked up and down the High Street, when she reached it, turning aside as ridiculous a curious misgiving lest she had already lost familiarity with this little world. Certainly there were some changes; other shops besides Whistlers' had varied their styles; nothing stood still. But that faintly chill draught of doubt was at once checked. Oh, she'd missed the High Street—that was natural. She'd soon get back to it. From the doorstep of Daddy's house, to which she had a key, she surveyed the scene. Like old times. Exactly the same. It was the sunshine that made it all look a little shabby. . . .

The house, once the front door was shut again, was beautifully quiet; but dark. She had not realised that it would be so dark. Paint was sombre; the doors were all closed; some heavy curtains draped them. And coming from the sunshine . . . There were no windows at all in the wall overlooking the churchyard. They all looked due east or west. This front room, where the old man's lumbering books still shed their musty odour, was particularly dark. It was those curtains. They were of plush, not velvet; and the colour in them had deepened to a sort of chocolate. Otherwise the place was light enough. She switched the curtains as far back along their antique pole as they would go; and the noise was like that one hears as an anchor is dropped. That was better! The High Street lay before her. She could see right down it, even beyond the point at which the street narrowed. Excellent. It seemed odd to see the statue at the cross-roads from this angle; and there was just this fact against the vista, that one saw everything sideways and at a distance. The goings and comings were all a little removed, instead of being, as they had been from the first floor window above the shop, immediately under her eye. . . .

Books did not interest Mrs Whistler. She hardly glanced at Daddy's pride, so jealously gathered and ranged in the great shelves. They would go, like all this furniture. She would see that the ceilings and walls were done before she signed anything. Her own big sideboard would do very well against the north wall, and her own carpet would just about fit. There was nothing more here to delay her. It was quite a relief to escape the musty smell of leather. As to the back room, which she next entered, that was lighter; but it was only half-furnished. An ugly wallpaper like a print dress, a table, a chair or two. The room had never been used. Trust a man! The garden—she was not interested. It looked very tangled from this window: she would probably be able to rent it to somebody. . . . What about that door down the short flight of steps?

Opening the door, Mrs Whistler found herself in the room which had been transformed by Julie into a sun-parlour; and through the French windows she could see the garden more immediately than before. But here there were holland blinds, which were lowered; and it was not until she had sent the blind up with a great flacking of tassels against the window-panes that the visitor could see an array of light, bright cretonnes, a white satin-faced wallpaper ornamented with small roses climbing an invisible trellis, and the pale blue and white carpet with a wandering pattern of pink and green ribbons and flowers. When she did see them—and the thin gilt-framed amorous prints set sparsely amid those climbing roses—she uttered one word of comment—'Ridiculous!'—and walked heavily out of the room again.

Ridiculous; and also, at a glance, wanton. The girl—Robert—the old goat . . . Like father, like son. Two fools. The father whimpering after a servant; the son after an old goat's drab . . . French . . . The other a pinched slut . . . But she hadn't been deceived. She'd known everything. . . .

The silent stairs were a strain to Mrs Whistler, who put a hand to the stair-rail as she mounted. This was a longer flight than she really liked. However, the house was an old one, and one must expect some inconveniences. The stairs were rather steep. But the rail was solid enough. When she had reached the small landing at the head of the stairs, and before she mounted the three further steps to the main landing which ran from the front of the house to the back, she looked down the stairs. A long flight. And those three extra steps were very awkward. She must be careful of them. Stairs were dangerous. But no doubt . . . She pushed open the door of the front room, entered, and was immediately entranced.

Here, owing to the fact that Mrs Whistler was at a familiar height above the street, she could really enjoy her old pleasure in the High Street. The different angle, she knew, would soon seem right, and the range was much greater than it had ever been from the room above the shop. Very good. Very good indeed. This should be, not her bedroom, but her sitting-room. She would have her own chair here by the window; long side curtains but no short lace ones; the old mirror and vases upon the mantelpiece. A work-table. No bed, of course. A new carpet—perhaps young Harvest would sell this one, which was very well. . . .

He'd probably be glad of the money. Both very poor; and the mother far below Mrs Whistler's dress-making requirements . . . Feckless people . . . Very good for children's frocks, they said. You could buy them ready-made. Why spoil children? There would be a sale, she expected. But anything she wanted . . . This carpet, for example; it was good, very little worn. The dressing-table looked solid. She didn't want the bed. The pictures only if they were cheap. Not even then. But the room was very well, very well. And the window just what she had hoped. The window, the newspaper, her work—she'd find plenty of occupation. She would sit down now for just a moment; the stairs had been a little trying. She must get her breath. Once she was in, she would not need to race about, and she would soon get used to the stairs. It was what you were *used* to. All the same, the flight was long and steep. A good job she didn't wear high heels. They might catch.

Mrs Whistler spent rather more time than she had intended at the window of her new sitting-room; and out of doors the light became slightly glaring as the sun, in sinking, caught bright ornaments and upper windows and every excrescence and turned all to a stream of gold. She felt that her eyes were tired by so much light; and when she went into what had been Daddy's bedroom at the back of the house she was really dazzled by the fiery blaze which assailed the window. Whoever was in charge of the place had shown gross carelessness in leaving the blinds of this room undrawn, and everything exposed to the sun. . . . But the room, in this brilliant light, had its interest. It had been his. The bedroom.

Mrs Whistler's lip curled. With great fastidiousness she touched the bedrail, standing for a moment and staring at the dust-sheet which had been drawn over mattress and folded blankets. At last, holding herself very erect in conscious distaste, she threw open the door of the wardrobe. Good gracious, his clothes were still there!

How strange a shock the sight of them gave her! They seemed to retain something of the old man's very look. Coats and waist-coats and trousers and elastic-sided boots, exactly as he had worn them. As *he* . . . More than that, they recalled the time when she, too, had had a man's clothes to dispose of after death. That had been done. Done quickly . . . Memories rolled upon her mind like thunder.

Giving no other outward sign of agitation, Mrs Whistler hastily pushed to the door of the wardrobe and turned the key in the lock. She then reversed her position and again stood looking at the bed in which Daddy had died. The sun shone directly upon her, pick-ing out the silk ornaments upon her mantle, moulding her face afresh by emphasising anew the high cheekbones and the gross, spreading chin, and giving a peculiar glitter to the coldness of her eyes. She was almost blinded by its blaze.

Well, there was one more upward flight of stairs. Should she mount it? No, the upper rooms were of less account. They would be small. No doubt a maid had used one of them. *She* the other. Mrs Whistler's lips pursed themselves in what was apparently a smile, malicious and inscrutable. *She*. Robert's wife. Somebody else's darling first. Her mind roved. No doubt that ridiculous room below was her doing. From what she had heard, there was the same sort of rubbish at Seahampton. At any rate, there was no need to climb stairs in order to see what she had made of her own bed-room. When the rooms were empty . . .

Hm! Coming from the fiercely sunlit bedroom, and closing the door behind her, Mrs Whistler could see nothing at all. It was pitch dark. She was forced to stand still for a moment upon the landing, while her heart thumped aloud and her eyes played tricks by dazing her with shooting flashes of strange colours, orange and green and red and purple; and her white hands groped a little feebly before

her breast for some substantial contact. It was the effect of the
sun, of course; but the house was too dark, anyway. There should
be——

Was that a slight noise in the darkness? She began to make her
way forward with the aid of a hand against the wall; and as she
went the black nothing by which she was surrounded grew less
impenetrable. There were shadows. She could see a greyness above,
and the line of the stair-rail, and, somewhere to her right a long
and sombre mass which she had noticed earlier as a heavy velvet
curtain beside the front room door. When drawn, that curtain
must exclude all draught and sound from within the house; but
now it was bunched back into the corner—almost filling the corner.
Her eyes grew more used to the dimness, and she thought: Curtains, yes; but here—it would never do. *Somehow* there must be
more light on the stairs. More light; or she might have an accident. . . .

It seemed to Mrs Whistler, as she cautiously reached the head
of the stairs leading back to the lower floor, that there was more
light below, which caused the darkness about her to be greater
again; and in pausing at that moment she looked up towards the
roof, thinking that if a skylight could be cut in it this whole landing, and indeed the whole house, would be much lighter. Why was
there not one already? Was there one? Was it, for example, covered
with a blind or board—for some purpose? She could not tell without climbing to the upper landing. And she was too tired to do
that. . . .

'I'm upset,' Mrs Whistler said distinctly, without, however, moving her lips. She did not say what had upset her. It was the sight
of those clothes in the wardrobe.

It was strange that old Griffin should have lived so long in this
house without accident. In the darkness. She must remember to
make a point of this. A skylight. 'There's one thing, Mr Merrow.
A skylight is most necessary. As it is, the darkness, and those stairs
with the sharp turn . . . Positively dangerous . . .' She held the
stair-rail with her plump white hand. 'Positively dangerous,' she
repeated, with a sort of unction. 'One might miss one's step;
and——'

Just as, in imagination, she said that to Mr Merrow, Mrs Whistler unquestionably heard a slight rustling noise. It might have been a sigh or the merest movement of a hand against silk. Few but herself would have caught the sound; and it came, she thought, from just behind her, in the denser shadow, where the heavy curtain seemed almost to swell and billow into life. She looked over her shoulder. Her right foot was suspended in the very act of stepping down to the next stair. She had one hand upon the stair-rail and the other half raised in the air, and as she turned the entire weight of her body rested upon the left foot, which was a traitor. In the gloom she could discern, or so she believed, a small pallor that might be a human face. But everything happened in a single instant—the glance up to the roof, the step downward, the sense that there had been a rustle, the turn of her head. Before any other impression had time to enter that slow mind she received a heavy blow upon the back of her neck, and, propelled by some unseen, incalculable force, her feet muffled in her long skirts and petticoats, she pitched terribly down the length of that steep unlighted staircase. At the foot of it, where faint light, penetrating the glass upper half of the front door, reached so far, she lay as if she were nothing but a bundle of old clothes.

II

'Nobody could call William a dressy man,' remarked Minna; 'but it strikes me that his coat's been ardently brushed this morning.'

'Very true,' agreed William. 'I was coming to see my mama. And to see you, too, of course.'

'Too great a compliment,' sighed Minna. 'Very charming, all the same.'

However, honesty, which was William's ruin, led him to add:

'The truth is, Kitty came after me.'

'Oh, Kitty.' Minna might as well have said: 'Oh, a black beetle.' Her fair head was turned aside with a quick movement. She was still not old enough to conceal impulse.

But William, absorbed, and not observing the tone or the hardly perceptible jerk, continued:

'Kitty caught me by the tails. There was I, short of time for the train; but she said "If you're going to Moreton, you've got to look tidy; or else your mother will think we don't look after you."'

'That wouldn't have mattered,' said Minna, coolly. 'But *does* she look after you?'

'As a cat a kitten,' laughed William. Mrs Harvest—the conversation was taking place in her sitting-room, where she and Minna and William lunched elegantly under the shining faces of those two pallid water-colours which she had painted before her marriage—smiled gently.

'Poor Kitty!' she said. 'It's cruel to call her a cat. Such a little one! And she's very kind.'

'She sounds officious,' added Minna, briskly. Minna had never seen Kitty. But how jealous she was of any woman!

'Oh, she is,' agreed William. 'Not a doubt of it.'

Although he was so ready to speak gaily upon this very subject, however, another emotion constrained his merriment. He had not as yet told his two loved ones that he was going to marry Kitty. Nevertheless, he was in high spirits.

'I do better than poor Bryant,' he explained. 'Kitty's merciless. Got a hard heart.'

'Perhaps she's cruel to be kind,' suggested Mrs Harvest, who believed that all women were as good as herself.

'Well,' said William; 'no. She's like a Miss Muffet who can't get away.' It was necessary for him to speak of Kitty, however laughingly. 'And Bryant doesn't know he's a spider.'

'Silly creature!' said Minna, outspoken. Yes, but why did William talk so much about this girl? There was something. Something troubling. She felt her heart beating more quickly.

William shook his head, smiling. Minna only frowned, pretending that she was not interested in the subject of their talk, which in fact engrossed her. She was now twenty. Her long fair hair was wound about her head in plaits as tight as she could contrive to make them; her blue eyes and what she called dairymaid cheeks were full of expression which changed every instant in response to the eager movement of her thoughts and her mood; and she was extraordinarily pretty, though as yet too immature to be beauti- ful. She was of good height, slim and full of grace; and sometimes her heart so burned and brimmed with tenderness for those whom she loved that the emotion was well-nigh unbearable. But nobody except herself knew of this; and even now, when she was stirred with fear of Kitty, all that her friends could see was that gravity was struggling in her mind with happiness.

Fear of Kitty! Yes, she was deeply alarmed!

'I think she'll relent,' added Mrs Harvest.

'Hm,' grunted William. 'Well . . .' Oddly enough, he could not bring himself to say 'she's going to marry me.' He thought: 'Funny! I can't move my tongue!'

Minna saw his lips part, and saw him swallow slightly. She looked away again at once, and so she never forgot the expression which was upon William's face at that moment.

They said no more then; but when, later, they walked to Royals so that William should visit Minna's mother, the subject recurred.

At first setting out, the two passed straight up the High Street; and they were abreast of what had been Whistlers' shop at the moment when Mrs Whistler was arriving at Daddy's house. They saw her actually upon the doorstep, and the door opening as she turned the key.

'My tenant,' remarked William, with a jerk of the head. 'Pro- spective, of course.'

Minna, who might have followed that indication, looked instead at William's face, and she was rewarded by seeing a little unex- pected play there. First the smile: it was at his own pleasantry. Then a frown. Then an inexplicable expression which was like a pallor. Lastly a thoughtful reserve such as was well-known to her. All together, these changes were so baffling that her heart sank. And at last, after plotting and planning the speech for a quarter of a mile or more, Minna sprang a question upon him.

'William,' she said, breathlessly. 'Are you unhappy?'

At once, with an air of surprise, William answered:

'Far from it!'

'No!' she protested. 'I meant, *really*.' She was imploring him.

That was so obvious that it became extravagant, which Minna had by no means intended. Oh, God! How silly one sounded when one was sincere!

'Do you want me to say I am?' asked William, his smile broadening. He gave her the old teasing look, full of sweetness, which had been familiar for nearly twenty years. It was the look of a loving, indulgent, protective senior; not condescending, but such a glance as took one's breath away and at the same time made one feel hopeless. A terrible expression! 'I believe you do. Sobs, tears——'

'Don't be ridiculous!' expostulated Minna, with the greatest heat. Sentimentality punctured! 'As if I were a baby!' She showed her indignation by walking faster along the road under the bare elms and chestnuts with raised chin and averted head. How perfectly William knew the signs! How instantly he abandoned laughter and grew serious! He took her arm; and they proceeded together in the glitter of Autumn sunshine, which this afternoon was so strong as to be dazzling.

'Well, old girl,' he said. 'I'm in a muddle. Look at that squirrel up there. His tail's like a feather! He's gone. I've got a lot on my hands and in my eyes and under my waistcoat. And I don't know what to do about everything. See? Just apply your mind to it. Tell me what *you'd* do. Squirrel's coming with us, d'you see? There's mother, for one thing. Quite well, not very ancient, but no occupation. She's used to Moreton—and comfortable here; but I know in my bones (because she doesn't mention it) that she thinks she'd like to come to London to be with me. A splendid idea; but no good.'

'You don't want her there?' asked Minna. 'William, you don't mean you're less fond of her!'

'I'm differently fond of her.'

'More coldly?'

'No. More oldly. I think I know what's best for both of us.'

'That's nothing new. There's a sort of awful——' Minna stopped. Then she continued: 'It's rather exasperating, as a matter of fact.'

William shook her arm.

'Silence!' he cried. 'Or at least, wait a bit! Then you ought to see the hovels Daddy's bequeathed to me. Quite unfit for habitation; and I've got no money to put them right. I'm stuck. *Several* other things. A strong-willed man would take decisions about them, cut here, thrust there. I only maunder. What d'you say to all this?'

'First of all,' said Minna, 'that you've got a very strong will indeed. No need to worry about that. But, about the hovels, how many of them are there?'

'Five. Five old cottages down by the river. Picturesque. Artists paint 'em in what we journalists call a riot of hollyhocks, sunflowers, and lush grass; pink, cobalt, emerald, and gold. All in bad repair. No drains; damp; shocking. Roofs gone, walls cracked. As an honest man—if I'm an honest man—I ought to pull them down. But the poor wretches who pig there are desperate in case I turn them out.' His eyes were directed towards the squirrel, which leapt from branch to branch with exquisite lightness and as if with humour. As tantalising as truth!

'Wicked old man!' thought Minna, aloud. 'Do you think he did it on purpose?'

Caught unawares by this beam of light, William gasped.

'What, to ruin me? No, to bring me up against my own principles? The Socialist Slum-owner? I say! It's not impossible, you know.' He thoughtfully added: 'The only thing is, that I wonder if he was ingenious enough.'

'Wasn't he very malicious?'

'The *will* was. But not towards me. He may have thought it was a good joke on me. Perhaps it is. That's another possibility. More likely. I suppose I could sell the hovels, and get rid of them at once. I could give them to the poor piggers. But if I can get a mortgage on Daddy's old house—which I can't sell—you'll find me robbing Mother Whistler to pay for renovating the hovels! I'm going to see Mr Merrow about it immediately after tea.'

'And not coming back to us? It's a blow!'

'You see? I'm so sorry. Lost in good works and high finance, I affront my friends.'

'Not affront. Crush and bludgeon. Go your capitalistic way.'

'Do you envy me?'

'Only in being a man. You *are* able to do something: I'm *not*.

And really, you know, it's awfully interesting to have such problems. And to solve them.'

'Which I don't do.'

'You will, silly. You're very resourceful. But about those others, William——'

'Forget them. What about yours? How about *your* mother?'

Now they had come to a really acute problem, and both knew that it was acute. For Mrs Manning, in the last few years, had grown much more than quiet, and her lassitude had become marked enough to impress even her husband. At first she had been disinclined for effort; then she had spent a great deal of time working quietly before the fire or in the sunshine, according to the season, on the fine crochet which was her pastime; and Minna at last had noticed that the crochet was often untouched as it lay in the listless fingers. When this had gone on for a season, she had told her father; and in spite of his incredulous indifference she had gained permission to ask Doctor Hodge to stroll out to Royals one evening. Subsequently, armed with his word that the trouble might be serious, she had done much, with William's help, to obtain the necessary medical opinion and even the periodical observation of a specialist. And now, it appeared, the doctors thought a nurse should be always in the house, which in itself was a warning so plain that it signalled Danger.

'Father's coming down. He says I'm to do what's necessary; but not to spend too much money, as he's not a millionaire. Such affectation! But Doctor Hodge and Doctor Brewster will both come while he's here; and they'll tell him the truth.'

'You think she's much worse?' asked William.

'Oh, she is!' cried Minna, shuddering. 'Will, I'm horribly frightened!' Her head was bowed now, and her fists clenched. William said:

'I'll come back after seeing Merrow.'

'I'm so stupid and useless!' she exclaimed, chokingly. 'I can't do *anything*. Nothing for her; nothing for you. Nothing!' She was crying.

William was aghast.

'Minna! Minna! You're helping me all the time. Always. Why,

good heavens, just now—— When I've been saddling you with all
that's on my mind——'

'No.' It was mournful.

'But I assure you——'

'Not everything!' cried Minna, piercingly. 'Not the *chief* thing!'

William dropped her arm as if it burned him. 'Good God!' he
thought. Aloud, he exclaimed:

'Look! There's Royals. And the squirrel's ahead. I'll race you
both to the gate.'

He was off, and in spite of Minna's fleetness he had an easy victory. The squirrel was left far behind; and Minna, distracted
momentarily by defeat, was explanatory.

'I'm out of practice,' she panted. 'And you took me by surprise.
And you forget I'm not a kid any more.'

'Don't be conventional!' answered William. They were off the
road now, and in the drive leading to the house. He added: 'You're
losing your speed. You want to pull yourself up. And don't forget
for a minute that you're the best friend I've got.'

The final words, very quickly spoken, were so unexpected that
Minna felt her heart, the beat of which was already accelerated as
a result of the run, leap and swell until it filled her breast. She
would have spoken, but she could not bring herself to do so. If
she could but have wept in his arms!

It was after a pause, and in a dry voice, that she at last spoke.

'You wouldn't say that to please me. . . . No, of course not. And
you don't think I'm stupid?'

'Idiotic,' said William.

Her spirits mounted.

'Don't be absurd. You ought to be abjectly grateful!'

They were almost at the front door of the house; and before
them were the latticed windows which always, from without,
looked so dark because they were so old, and from within looked
so clear, as if they increased the radiance of the garden. A moment
later they were indoors, and there Minna felt at once as if she were
liberated from constraint. Her heart grew lighter. She smiled again.

The room, in spite of its great size, was comfortably warm, with
big logs quietly burning upon the hearth, reflected lights glowing

upon the tiled floor and many-hued rugs, the polished handles of
the oaken dresser gleaming like flames. Both Minna and William
were to remember it as long as they lived.

'Oh, how I miss you, Will!' cried Minna, boldly. 'When you've
seen mother, will you tell me honestly what you think? Doctor
Hodge only jokes Scottishly, and slips in questions that frighten
me—about where father is, and when will he be home, and . . . He
wants to see father *soon*. I do wish father would stay at home, instead of raking these insanitary shops for bargains and treasures
that I feel all the time may give him some frightful Eastern disease. . . .'

'Is he in London? I might hurry him down.'

'He wrote from Marseilles. Do you think he could help you over
your hovels?'

'Oh, no. I can manage everything if only it will keep still. Unfortunately nothing keeps still. I'm like the toper in the reeling
room, trying to catch the bed as it whizzes past.'

'I'll keep still, William,' said Minna, quickly.

'You least of all. You're growing out of my reach.'

'I?' She was thunderstruck. How extraordinary everything was!
'I can't understand it! I thought . . . You've just said I'm a help
to you.'

'It's true. But at this instant . . .' Minna saw him flush. 'At this
instant I'm trying to tell you something. Something you may not
very much . . . Hullo! What does *he* want?'

Minna turned, and also stared as William was doing out of the
latticed window. Fierily outlined by the burning sunlight was a boy
in uniform, who arrived that instant at the house and rang im-
portantly at the hanging bell.

'Will!' It was a cry of extreme alarm.

Perhaps it was William who opened the telegram; perhaps he
only took it from Minna's trembling fingers after she had torn the
envelope. But he understood its meaning sooner than she did.

The telegram was from Mr Manning's valet; and it read:

MR MANNING UNWELL IN NURSING HOME FIVE HUNDRED B CROM-
WELL ROAD CAN YOU COME RATHER URGENT.

Rather urgent . . . Unwell . . . Impossible to mistake the purpose of such tactful understatement! Impossible not to translate the terms into Dying and Desperate! For one moment William's arms were about Minna, and her head was against his. She shivered terribly; freed herself; and stood, trembling, waiting for him to tell her what should be done.

If only everything would keep still! If only . . .

III

It was an hour before William and Mr Merrow, having briefly spoken together about repairs to those five cottages, went to Daddy's old house. Mr Merrow, who liked William, was helpful and ready to advise; but he thought the young man a little quixotic.

'The mistake you're making, Harvest,' he said—they were still in his threadbare office among the black boxes—'if you'll allow me to say so, is that you think the cottagers feel your own sensitiveness to discomfort.'

'And the mistake *you're* making,' retorted William, with a dry glance of humour, 'is that you think I'm concerned with anything at all but my own discomfort. I just can't accept responsibility for those places as they are.'

'Pho!' exclaimed Mr Merrow, stroking his little beard. 'Very creditable.'

His sarcasm was appropriate. So trim a little man, who knew all bad things about the town, and a few good ones, could be nothing but calm before every infamy.

'But we must hurry, I think,' said William, sitting forward in his chair with an eye to the fading light, 'if we're still to catch Mrs Whistler at the house. I'd like to see her, and settle. Once that's done, we can make a start. And I must be back at Royals very quickly; for I'm taking Miss Manning to London this evening. By the six train.'

The solicitor reached for his sleek hat.

'Your mother is going to Royals?' he said.

'I shall call for her on my way, take her in a cab, and use the cab back to the station.'

'Take care not to pay twice for the double journey,' remarked Mr Merrow.

It was twilight by the time they reached the street. The sun had gone, and a clear sky promised frost for the following morning. There was even a noticeable chill in the air. But with lights already visible in many of the shop-windows the High Street was at its best. One saw the breadth of the street, and the flat Georgian fronts of several of the buildings, the warmth and kindness of the upper rooms, the epitomised tranquillity of England; and, over all, the darkening, unclouded heaven, as yet without stars. It was beautiful.

'And yet——' said Mr Merrow, half to himself. He was not insensible to beauty. It amused him to see William's lifted head and the clear eyes that sought every gleam and shadow which gave loveliness to the whole. And yet he remembered Cowper's line: 'God made the country, and man made the town'; and he wondered, as he had often done before, whether the beauty-lovers were not, after all, deceived. Mr Merrow, respectable, long married, a Churchman who had laid up for himself riches upon earth, knew a number of the secrets of those less scrupulous than he, most of them nasty; and some of the nastiest of them related to Daddy Griffin, and some to Mrs Whistler, whom they were to see in a moment. So, upon consideration, he did not finish his speech, just as, also upon consideration, he kept the secrets to himself. The church in front of them looked very black. 'Has it ever occurred to you to remark that not more than a dozen people in this town have any idea why that statue stands there?' Mr Merrow asked William, pointing to the effigy of the man in a wig. 'Or who the man is? And what he did? Do you suppose anybody thinks of it as anything but a landmark?'

'You might say the same of nine tenths of the statues in England,' answered William. 'They're only perches for the birds. Great cotes would be more useful.'

'I suggested some years ago that it should be removed, and a seat placed there for elderly people.'

'I remember. There was a row.'

'Pure conservatism. I even had an anonymous letter. But I know who wrote it; and I gave her a fright.' Mr Merrow suffered William to receive a glimpse of his secret hardness, the cruelty underlying his calm. He shook a little with silent, malicious laughter. 'One must deal quickly and harshly with anonymous letters,' he added, as if in apology. They crossed the street. 'Well, here we are.'

Daddy's house rose steeply before them, richly dark in the dusky light. It looked as if it were deserted.

'She's gone,' exclaimed William.

'I think not. She was to call on me afterwards; and we haven't passed her. Probably poking in cupboards.'

Mr Merrow produced from his pocket a key to the front door; but before using it he rang the bell, and they heard its hollow noise echoing through the silent house. Then the two of them entered, Mr Merrow punctiliously brushing his shoes upon the mat.

'It's extremely dark,' he said. His voice had dropped. 'Is the maid not here?'

'Is anybody there?' cried William, when he had shut the door. There was no answer. They both smiled broadly at the continuing sound of his voice in that steep well of a house. The place hummed as a room does long after a tuning-fork has been struck.

'You should have been in the choir,' muttered Mr Merrow. He added: 'I'm afraid you're right, after all. Is there no gas in this place?'

William struck a match. A big candle stood, as it had always done in Daddy's day, upon the gigantic racked piece of furniture which reared itself just within the doorway, and he lighted this. But the wick was long and obdurate, and for a moment they were in a darkness blacker than before. Only when the flame rose at last, and William held the candlestick aloft, thereby distorting all the shadows and giving the gaunt hall the look of a vault, did they both at once see the curious large mass, apparently of clothing, which lay at the foot of the stairs some yards away.

'Good heavens!' exclaimed Mr Merrow, who was the nearer to it. 'What on earth's that?' He stepped back, almost into William's arms. Then he moved forward, William, close behind him, holding the candlestick aloft. Before William could see what the object was, Mr Merrow had recognised it. 'Dear, dear!' he cried, in a tone of amazement. 'Dear, dear!'

As for William, he felt his heart plunge. For a moment he was overcome with a sensation of sickness. But he conquered that first recoil; and while his heart beat rapidly and the multitudinous nervous reactions to shock drove him almost to hysteria he forced himself to remain cool, to set the candle upon a neighbouring chair, to kneel by the dead woman's side. The light caught those staring eyes in the livid face with horrible effect.

'Dear, dear!' repeated Mr Merrow. 'A doctor . . . William, you're younger than I. . . .'

William groped in the black mantle for Mrs Whistler's wrist.

'No doctor,' he said, under his breath. 'No doctor's going to cure this.' His eye swept into the darkness as he imagined the stumble, the clutching hands, the descent to death. He shuddered. In a cry of sudden temper, born of agitation, he burst out: 'Damn! Why isn't Sarah here? What's come to her?'

Mr Merrow stood erect again, dusting his hands together and looking down at the body. His shadow was rigid.

'No doctor could cure, certainly. But a doctor must be summoned.' Then: 'What a coincidence!' he muttered. 'Eh? I suppose it *is* a coincidence?'

William, still kneeling, started. He looked up, and Mr Merrow saw his face illumined.

'Suppose?' William was puzzled. 'Coincidence? Ah, I'd forgotten——'

'You remember that her husband . . . I suppose, in his case, it *was* a fall?'

'It's legendary to me.' They both nodded, and the shadows twitched. Then William impetuously cried: 'Yes, but Sarah ought to have been there. She ought to be here now. Where is she?' His voice again rang through the house: 'Sarah! Sarah!' It was in vain. 'It's very extraordinary,' exclaimed William.

As William spoke they heard a key turning in the lock of the front door; and both, with the violent turn of conspirators discovered, swung round to observe the entry of a newcomer. Because the light out of doors was still pale they could recognise Sarah long before she saw them. She looked very small, very meagre. A small and shrinking figure, clad in a tightly-fitting short coat and a full thick skirt which made her appear like a silhouette in black paper. She came in secretly, as if upon tip-toe.

'Sarah!'

At first a silence, as if she had been seized by terror. Still with the door open, she peered towards the flame of the candle and the black group in the shadows. At last:

'Yes, sir.' It sounded quite composed. Sarah quietly shut the door after her and was lost to view. She came nearer, very slowly indeed; and as the candlelight caught her they heard her draw breath with a hiss. But she did not scream or start. She only, at length, stooped a little over the dead woman, staring into her face, as if she saw it for the first time.

'It's Mrs Whistler,' whispered Sarah.

William saw that she herself was as pale as death, and that her hands, in one of which she held what might have been a packet of tea or sugar, trembled very much. Her whole body trembled. He heard her teeth chatter. The candle threw its beam up and sharply shadowed her face, giving a hawklike line to the nose and emphasising two cruel lines which ran from each nostril to the corners of her mouth. She seemed to grin. And for William the light did something more. Sarah was stooping, and he was kneeling; the flame was below the level of his eyes and almost upon a level with Sarah's breast. Pinned there to her blouse, invisible until in stooping she displaced the front of her jacket, was a small cheap brooch of which the design, in red stones, represented two hearts joined and as it were made one by means of a gold ring in which some initials were twined. 'S' was one of them; he could not, in that hasty, inattentive glance, recognise the other.

'She's dead, isn't she?' asked Sarah, in a murmur.

'She's dead,' replied William, in the same quiet tone. 'But she's not cold yet. Where *were* you?'

There was a pause. At last:

'At tea with my mother, sir,' explained Sarah, hardly opening her lips, not turning to him as she spoke, but staring whitely at the corpse. 'I didn't think necessary to wait upon *her*. She must have fell.'

'Like her husband,' said Mr Merrow, looking sharply at her.

The lines running to Sarah's mouth tightened. Her lips were pressed together. They parted only in order to answer:

'That I couldn't say, sir.'

'You remember Mr Whistler, don't you? Jack Whistler? Oh, no; I'd forgotten you're a comparative newcomer to the town. . . .'

Jack! William saw Sarah's hands move. The packet she had been holding fell to the ground. She seemed to breathe deeply and painfully, and as she straightened herself she swayed backwards and forwards as if she must fall. Suddenly her forearm went up to her face, and she began broken-heartedly to sob aloud.

'Oh! Oh! Oh, if I'd only been there! If I'd only been there! She'd never have done it! Never, she wouldn't! She *couldn't* have! She *couldn't!*'

Her sobs turned to laughter, the laughter again to rending sobs; and before they could save her she had turned away and thrown herself upon the floor, pounding it with clenched fists and crying frantically in the intervals of wild screaming.

IV

Robert Whistler was up in the white, lace-curtained drawing-room above his shop when the news reached him. After shutting the shop he was sitting in an armchair reading that morning's newspaper; and he had reached in it an account of a charitable meeting, held in London, which had been addressed on the previous day by Mr Richard Firth. An appeal for funds for a good object. A good object. With mocking savagery, Robert mouthed the words attributed in the report to Mr Firth, good will, deserving, more fortunate, less fortunate, ladies and gentlemen, my friends, our duty to God and man . . . And as he finished saying the words through for the second time, goading himself, he madly flung the newspaper to the ground. Anger caused him to leap to his feet and pace the room.

'Dick Firth!' he growled. 'Dick Firth! Our duty to God and man!'
Fury spurred him to still greater vehemence. He stamped more
loudly. He stamped both feet upon the newspaper, battering it.
He narrowly escaped stamping on Rachel's doll, Eva, which lay
upon the floor near the fender with its eyes closed and its flaxen
curls in a frizz. He saw in a mist of excitement the white satinate
walls of the room and Julie's gilt-framed pictures, which seemed
to swim together and move about him like fog-banks. The mist
came closer, threatening him. Shaking his fists in the air, he bel-
lowed oaths and abuse as loudly as his voice would ring, until the
voice cracked and grew hoarse and his throat was sore. He mingled
his mother and Dick, the two vile causes of his distresses, in common denunciation. They were responsible for his every ill. His
misery, his poverty, his humiliation. A mother and a friend. A
leech and a bloodsucker. Two foully-begotten devils from Hell;
two loathsome ravenous ruining fiends who had plotted apart to
destroy him . . .

'But they *shan't!*' shouted Robert. 'By God, they shan't!' And,
louder again: 'I say they shan't do it!'

He went back through all the stages of his misfortunes, and
traced each to one of these two malignant forces. First his mother,
always bullyingly cruel to him as a boy—brutal, brutal, like a brazen-
faced monster—a Minotaur; his father, harsh, indifferent, frightened of his mother and in nervous fussiness pettily fault-finding;
Dick Firth, pretending loyalty, turning against him, spying, lying,
smarming and smiling, stealing and ruining that young girl, escap-
ing him that night, going by stealth to London and growing rich
by God knew what subterfuges and scandals—good will, our duty
to God and man—faugh! . . . His own scheme for wealth and
leisure, for the life of ease and gentility which he had desired, which
he still desired, to build upon bigger business and grander range;
Julie—by God, but for Julie all this need never have happened!
She was another of them! She'd tempted him (he could see that
now), fired him, first roused his enthusiasm and then his desire—
the way women worked! But for her, he'd . . . 'Julie!' It was a
scornful cry, as if he answered one who had named her as one of
his boons. 'Julie! Ah!' He laughed when he thought of her, and

when he recalled, in a flood of memories, all the extravagance for which she had been responsible, all the penury she had caused by her behaviour in Seahampton; but the laughter was unamused, strident, and shamed. . . .

And Dick again. He had wanted to pass. Dick had stopped him. 'Can't we be friends, Bob? let bygones be bygones?' 'No,' he'd said. He'd pushed past. The fellow had clung, pleading. . . . And his mother. His mother, sitting aloft and still bullying as she had always done. Creeping. Prying. His mother selling the business. His mother *discharging* him—God, how that rankled! She'd have had to come on her knees to him; only, the old vixen, she'd cheated him after all by selling the business. . . . Dick getting Daddy Griffin's money. Julie's money, by rights. Julie's money—even the paltry two hundred and fifty pounds the old Shylock had promised had been swallowed by that dirty swine. . . .

The Judas! The Judas! His *friend!*

'My *friend,* d'you see!' shouted Robert, ferociously. 'It's a wonderful word, is that!'

Stooping, he picked the battered newspaper up again and straightened it with blows from his trembling hand. Yes, he had been right! Dick had begun his speech with the words 'My Friends'! Not 'Ladies and Gentlemen': he had apologised for it—saying he couldn't call them that. *Laughter.* No, 'My Friends!' Yes, he'd suck them dry, all right! He'd pick their pockets! His friends! Friends and allies. He'd got a thousand friends—all like himself. And Bob had none!

No friends. Not a friend in the world. Young Harvest—yes, but Julie had kept him from writing to Harvest or seeing him. She had taken a dislike to Harvest. He was no good, she said. 'Don't have anything to do with him.' He, like the rest, was treacherous. . . . Where was the evidence? 'I know.' No evidence at all! The one friend he'd had, she'd turned him against. . . . The one friend! Young Harvest. Yes, but she'd said . . . What had she said? Something—— Robert could not remember what it was. He couldn't remember, d'you see. . . . Perhaps if he had another whisky he'd remember. . . .

Yes, but he'd had one glass. Or was it two? Or three? Well, he couldn't remember that, either. Never mind. Julie grudged him a drink. She mustn't know he'd had it. She was so quick to notice. . . . Too quick, Bob thought. It was possible to be over-quick about a thing of that sort. Of course, she was quite right, in principle. In principle. Yes, nobody agreed more strongly than Robert that drinking *too much* of anything was bad for a man. Nobody. But he didn't drink too much. Just a glass or two now and again. A refresher. You needed it after a hard day. . . . And to drink nothing at all was priggish. He was no prig.

No! He was not a prig. He was opposed to drinking too much. But moderation . . . moderation in all things was his motto. He was moderate. A glass of whisky, a pipe—a man. A man, d'you see? But Dick Firth wasn't a man. No! He didn't drink, didn't smoke. . . . What did he do?

Robert enumerated some of the things that Dick Firth might be called. All were revolting, a fact which relieved his feelings a great deal. Having helped himself to another glass of whisky, and returned the bottle to the sideboard in case Julie, when she came back into the room, should notice that he had had anything to drink, he felt his parched tongue refreshed and his brain on fire with wisdom and eloquence. Wisdom, understanding, courage. He was better. Calmer.

'The pair of them!' he cried, throwing himself back into his chair. 'The bloody swine. The one a dirty swine; the other a dirtier swine. And I'm not afraid of either of them. I never *have* been afraid of either of them. How I used to stand up to her! Look her straight in the face . . . Nobody else ever did that, I swear. But I was never afraid of anybody. That's one thing that can be said of me—never afraid of *anybody*. I don't care who it was. . . .'

One day the tide would turn. He'd get a bit of his own back. If he could cut all this stuff at Seahampton, and get back to Moreton, where he was *known*. They'd come flocking. The moment the name of Whistler went up again all the old people would come back—why, it's like old times! Glad to see you, Mr Whistler! Why did you ever go away? These nasty wholesale stores! Of course, he knew the trade there. He knew just what they wanted, and how, and why. Well, he'd grown up to it, you see. He knew the ins and outs, the people, the *feel* of the place. . . . If ne could get back to Moreton, he'd snap his fingers at Seahampton.

The place was no good. And the situation was no good. A bad spot, bad trade, bad beginning, everything bad . . . Back in Moreton he could manage Julie. He could make her see reason; make his strength felt. Get her away from the kid; give her an interest in the *business*. That was the thing. Sometimes she was too pernickety—sulky, greedy—a man had something else to do, besides love-making. . . . All very well for her; but she didn't realise . . . All high-handed; black looks all day long . . . Sometimes she seemed almost to blame him for her own troubles. . . . She'd have to learn to be content with what she got. It would all be different if only he could get back to Moreton.

Yes, but how was he to do it? How was he to stave off Dick Firth?

'By God!' cried Robert. 'I wish the old bitch was dead!'

He lay back in the chair, his broad shoulders back against its cushioned ease and his legs stretched straight out before him. And as he was quieter his thoughts grew quieter and still further quietened him; and presently his eyes closed and his mouth opened, and he fell asleep. He did not snore, but his breath came thickly; and to anybody who saw him now, with the vitality gone from his great body, it would have been apparent that the ruffled hair was greying above his ears, and that his cheeks were a little swollen under the eyes and near the chin, and that his mouth, thus relaxed, looked pathetically unformed, as if it were still the mouth of a boy. He looked weary and discouraged, much older, and yet at the same time so much as he had looked while still at school that he was plainly the boy who had wrestled with Dick Firth in the playground and afterwards found and pocketed his mother's dropped shilling. And as he slept he dreamed of old days.

It was to a sleeping Robert that Julie, unchanged since we last saw her, presently returned, and she came into the room with all her old assured carriage and beautiful swiftness. But she was not alone. With her was Mr Merrow, who, trim and sleek, stood glancing about the room with such a faint smile of comprehension that he seemed stoically to regard the over-familiar. First of all, Mr Merrow smelt the whisky. His first thought thereafter was that Robert was drunk and in a loggish stupor. But when, at Julie's sharp call, the sleeper awoke and jumped upright and then, in a kind of flurry, to his feet, flushed and explanatory of his doze, Mr Merrow realised that he had made a mistake. This man was not drunk, but exhausted. Robert's eyes, it is true, were bloodshot; but—after a little drink and a little nap—he was still quite sober.

Sober enough, indeed, to imagine Mr Merrow no friend. A look of suspicion came instantly into the bloodshot eyes. Mr Merrow rightly guessed that Robert believed him guilty of coming to try and collect a debt. That was untrue. He had come briskly to announce an inheritance and acquire a client. To put an end to all apprehensiveness, he said:

'I've some bad news for you, Whistler. It may be a shock. But I've come straight out to tell you that your mother's met with an accident this afternoon.'

'Hey?' roared Robert, his face one mass of lighted surprise. 'What's that? Accident? An accident? What's she done? D'you mean she's dead?'

The relief to him was so great that as the little solicitor nodded in discreet promise and commiseration he plunged clumsily forward, first upon the crumpled and disregarded newspaper, and then, in avoiding the paper, upon Rachel's recumbent doll. The doll, squeezed about the middle, squeaked a faint 'mama'; and that tiny voice, so inappropriate to the scene, was too much for Robert. He fell back into the armchair from which he had sprung. 'Ha ha ha ha!' he laughed, in a voice of thunder. 'Ha ha ha ha ha ha!' The room shook with his tumultuous merriment. '*Ma-ma,* d'you see! Damned funny—with *her* . . . Ha ha ha ha ha ha!' As he laughed the tears coursed down his cheeks. Mr Merrow had never previously seen such savage glee.

PART THREE

The Good Girl

CHAPTER XII

Memory and Meeting

THE AGE WE HAVE REACHED is always the age of wisdom; and in after years Minna Manning saw this whole period of her life with a ridicule which made her eyes smart while she still laughed at an idiot who was, was not, could not have been, and must have been herself. Memory picked out scenes or emotions, re-created them at something more than life size and life heat, and as quickly substituted others equally eager, pleasant and unpleasant, as memory is apt to do for all impulsive people. But judgment, which is sagacity, forces the honest to admit that they have formerly been extravagant; and since Minna had the capacity to learn by experience she cooled as the years passed. In those days she was not cool.

In one vision she saw an immense auditorium, and simultaneously felt the rustle and fervour of a great assembly and heard a remote, clear voice riding upon bellows of responsive emotion to the farthest corners of the hall. The speaker, a small woman, apparently composed but quick with intelligence, turned like a little doll in this direction and that, not gesticulating, but by force of character giving poignancy to her speech. Light poured upon her from above. The words she spoke—now long forgotten by Minna—seemed like flashes of fire; and under their force the crowd stirred with excitement. Everywhere hung purple, green, and white ribbons, banners, and sashes. All was hot and exalted, fiery, as if the general enthusiasm lifted each woman present right out of dullness and made her a flame. In her own breast a heart throbbed loudly—or she thought it must have done, for it threatened to burst—and to her cheeks rose an uncontrollable warmth. She felt gloriously in the march of progress, and ready for every sacrifice to the cause of innumerable sisters. Beside her, before her, behind her, women as excited as herself laughed and rippled with indignation and resolve. And while Aunt Katherine, dimly seen as one jet and silver vivacity in the brilliant collection of people upon the platform, sat waving a sheet of paper, Cousin Ruth in an earlier row of seats turned round, her face gravely alight, beaming with exaltation. Wonderful! Wonderful! At that moment Minna knew that she adored the great Mrs Fawcett. She thought her nothing less than a queen. She, too, waved her handkerchief. She, too, cheered; joining those of the others—the young and the enthusiastic—who stood up in their places to pay homage. . . .

Back again went Minna's memory to her old room—her own room—at Royals. She had loved that—defensively, because she was proud of it and because disapproval of it implied disapproval of her sensitive self. Bookshelves stood in the corner, filled with volumes of the Temple Classics bound in green lambskin, volumes of the Temple Shakespeare bound in crimson leather, and other books such as the original green 'Earthwork out of Tuscany', a 'Golden Treasury' in sedate blue, some little dark Stevensons, 'Aurora Leigh', a complete Tennyson in green, and a blue pocket edition of Henry James's 'Portrait of a Lady' in three volumes. She had the books still; but not the room. Never again the room, or the old joy; the nightingale in the wood, mother, William . . . Never, never again.

Its walls were distempered in green as pale as the young leaves of lily-of-the-valley, and they were decorated with small reproductions of 'The Fighting Téméraire', Whistler's Mother, Vermeer's 'Girl with the Necklace', and the head and shoulders of Botticelli's Venus. A green arty basin and ewer rested upon a wooden washstand which had been enamelled white by ardent, unexpert hands; and rush mats lay upon the richly genuine oaken floor. Minna had tried to put some tiles in the hearth and up beside the fireplace, but the attempt had been a failure—no William to help her, of course—and they all looked irritatingly crooked. One had always to brush aside a little shame of them, and pretend that they looked the better for being rather amateurish. . . .

How sensitive! How juvenile! This was where the eyes began to smart; but Minna did not fly from memory. She knew that if she did this it would be always lurking, ready to slip discomfitingly into her mind whenever she was unhappy. And yet, when she remembered her enthusiasms, her arrogances, her sappish greennesses, she was ready to weep—not in regret, not in self-love, but with exasperation at the waste of so much strength in absurdity. Why must Nature always so exploit youth? Why torment, spoil, discard so cruelly? That was an old passionate demand. She had made it with half her thwarted generation. Too stern, she had burned her verses. She had torn up most of her feebly amateurish drawings (which nowadays would have seemed to be in the very van of art); and she no longer played upon the spinet or the violin, but only, when nobody was near, very quietly, doubtfully, upon the piano. Neither Aunt Katherine nor Ruth had an ear. She met none, among so many who thought of concerts as social occasions or exhibitions of virtuosity, who cared to listen to schoolgirl reveries. And her favourite authors had ceased to be, very simply, Kipling, Stevenson, Conan Doyle, Dante, Louisa Alcott, Charles Lamb, Omar Khayyam, and Anthony Hope. They had become—well, some conglomeration equally absurd, it may be? That was the worst of destructiveness; it left one not a leg to stand on. Ridicule was one's only consolation! One drawing which she had not destroyed was of William. Its edge still showed two inches of a jagged tear, but no more. She had fiercely begun to rend, had hesitated, wept . . . The drawing was to be found, somewhere. (She well knew where.) She had not seen it for an age. Nor that of her mother. Put them away, quite away, far below present thoughts!

Minna had dropped William. It had been easy, once her mother was dead and she had gone to live with her father's sister. William, after all, was tied by his work—and his wife. 'His wife': never 'Kitty'. And Minna was caught up in a new kind of society, very different from the solitude of Royals. She, in majestic Kensington, could not be supposed able to find time for—no longer Balham or Brixton, but another district unknown to her. . . . It could be explained in several ways. One of them was that she had grown out of the old dependence.

She had seen him once, a year afterwards, walking along Kensington High Street with his wife; the wife clinging to his arm, a little soft doll-faced girl without character. A doll, a doll, a dolt! But although, afterwards, Minna had cried in earnest and with deep bewilderment, she had instinctively shrunk back in her aunt's brougham as it passed the pair. How poor they had looked! Not poor; but . . . insignificant. That, in William, belying her impressions of twenty years, had been the worst shock of all. *Rangé*. Not the shabbiness of disregard; but the shabbiness of acceptance. Who did not shrink from a hero dwarfed by time and situation?

In the hour of Minna's double bereavement William had done everything for her, as a matter of course, until Aunt Katherine, coming upon the scene, had ousted him. Minna had acquiesced in that. Shameful! She had been listless, broken-hearted, furious in the midst of her pain at his ridiculous marriage. Having sullenly accepted his aid, she had allowed her aunt to suspect him—no, no, she had not understood that! Not until much later, when it was altogether too late—of peculiar designs. Either of marriage or of some confidence trick. Her aunt had been rude; William, unused to suspicion, dry; there had been no apology or explanation. And William, having scrupulously completed his task, leaving Aunt Katherine disconcerted, had allowed himself to be dropped. Quite readily, easily, resolutely, in spite of the effort she had made to disguise her feeling. His fault was bitter pride.

It was not that Aunt Katherine, either, was a snob. However much she might suspect William of furthering his own ends ('After all, he's a man; and no man's innocent,' she said, when rudeness had been too much for Minna. 'I know what I'm doing. I'm saving *you,* my dear.'), she did not despise him. No, the trouble was that she was devoted to a Cause. The Cause of Woman! The sister of Minna's father, long a widow with only one child—Ruth—rich and friendless, she thought in terms of committees and propaganda. She was short and thin, with coarse brown hair which quickly became untidy, stern blue eyes, a quick, damning temper, a soft heart, a stiff collar, no judgment, and something of her brother's fanaticism (which, in his case given to antiques, had left Minna with a load of junk, a mortgaged home, and a microscopic income); and she believed in manipulating men for her own ends. She made them work for her. The weak acquiesced and soon betrayed; the unscrupulous pretended support, accepted hospitality, laughed, and cynically deceived; the righteous, who shared her love of committees, seemed to Minna at first angels, then zealots, and at last insufferable bores.

Of course the greatest contrast of all, for Minna, was the change from country life, the garden, solitude, and an over-simple mental life in which impulsive tastes were allowed to seem God-sent and William was half-divine, to town life, a Cause, a cousin of almost her own age, constant society, the discovery of men and women of gifts and education far exceeding her own, taste as a social fashion, and William as an inconspicuous nobody who scribbled for a negligible Press. The sense of contrast had at first caused Minna to feel very gauche, naïve, stupid, and a cause of half-hidden sniggers; but in three months embarrassment had disappeared and she was already able to distinguish those whom she liked from those whom she did not like at all. She knew the clichés of the set, had a sufficient smattering of knowledge of new books and plays to serve every turn, and could hide most other ignorances behind a smile. So much was easy. She knew enough of the Cause to share her cousin's enthusiasm for it; she grew used to the brougham, to dinner-parties, dances, public meetings, telephones, motor-cars, and noise; and William, William's mother, the High Street of Moreton, the sombre agedness of Royals, and the pleasures of her old life receded into the distance. For a time, they faded. Other figures, and her new home, came closer. They possessed her.

That was the only excuse which Minna, plying backwards and forwards in time, could afterwards find for herself. She had been possessed by the new life, elated, carried into a kind of delirium. For there was then a kind of delirium in England, and all sorts of changes in manners and morals were beginning to be seen. Things which would have been thought natural in the year of Minna's birth, and shocking at the turn of the century, were again becoming natural and even rather timid by the hour of her entry upon life. A new vitality had invaded the political world with the tremendous surge of Liberal ideas and the split of the Conservative party. The feminist movement was growing with extraordinary speed. The streets were changing; men and women, if not changing, were at least throwing off cloaks and opening windows; and a sense of Progress was in the air. Very intoxicating for a young woman fresh from Moreton. Very exhilarating for a growing mind. Very dangerous, it may be, for one whose love had been thought of little account by William Harvest.

II

Aunt Katherine's forehead was larger at the top than at the bottom, near the eyes. I am not phrenologist enough to know what this means, whether it is a sign of combativeness or reason or good memory or merely an accident of formation; but as she strained every hair back from the forehead it seems clear that she either was proud of her intellectual appearance or knew nothing about it. Almost certainly the former. The hair was crisp and unruly; and Aunt Katherine did not help to keep it tidy by a habit she had, when in company, of resting her right elbow upon the table and the tip of one forefinger to her brow just at the point of its greatest width. Then her blue eyes shone; the finger or the elbow sometimes slipped; she attained, during dinner, when her thin cheeks flushed a little, a wild look which made those who disliked her a trifle ribald. They pretended that her glass had been filled too often. Nothing of the kind was true.

She had begun life with plenty of money derived from investments in gilt-edged securities and gas companies, and she had married a man wealthy with the wealth of bank shares and a nice packet of stock in a firm of great importers. Her husband had not greatly cared for her, but he had soon died, leaving Aunt Katherine with a fortune of three thousand pounds a year, a baby three or four years of age, a sense of fortunate escape, and not very much to do except spend her money and bring up her child. Aunt Katherine, being bodily meagre and active, requiring but five hours' sleep in twenty-four, and having a mind which travelled with velocity in only one direction at a time, soon began to look about her for further occupation.

She decided very soon to bring up her daughter as one of the best-educated women of the age, sent her to a college at Cambridge, and by degrees—through association with those who were bent upon raising the status of women in England—began to concern herself with the feminist movement. Owing to her money, her enthusiasm, and her nineteen-hour day, she lent great aid to this movement; but owing to her quarrelsomeness and her un-timely determination to carry in committee decisions which wiser members of the party knew to be futile she was less popular than she might have been with her co-workers. Recognising the un-popularity, she found an explanation for it in the stupidity of others, and laboured the more furiously to get her own way. She developed a habit of snapping. She rose to go. She threatened resignation. In the end, to the general disappointment, she did not fulfil her threat, and indeed had never purposed doing so; but as she was very simple she did not in the least understand herself or her own motives and objects.

Between Aunt Katherine and her brother, Minna's father, there had been a sarcastic affection, he looking upon her as an opinionated fool, and she upon him as a clever waster; between Aunt Katherine and her sister-in-law, Minna's mother, there was no affection at all. That, upon Katherine Telway's side, was due to an absence of heart; and upon Mrs Manning's side to inability to like those whom she found dislikable. Minna, less disillusioned than her mother, and with a strain of the Irish in her, had always found her aunt amusing; and for some time she believed that the apparent absence of heart was merely a peculiarity of manner.

As to Ruth, that highly-rarefied product of feminist education, Minna throughout felt differently. She began by admiring her without hesitation. Ruth, who was almost a foot taller than her mother (very nearly as tall as Minna herself), was darker, rather beautiful in the brunette style which sometimes runs to a downy shadow at the extremes of the upper lip, carnelian-eyed, flat-breasted, and very self-assured. Minna, conscious of her own pink cheeks and Gretchen-like hair, had first of all been attracted by her cousin's darkness and crisp confidence; and as Ruth was older in age by three years and in maturity by half-a-dozen she had unquestionable claims to leadership. However, she did not press them. On the contrary, she seemed to take a really affectionate interest in her cousin, and was even more active than Aunt Katherine in adopting Minna as an inmate of the large Kensington house. It took Minna a considerable time to understand Ruth's character; and in fact she never did properly understand it.

That was a curious household. A butler who looked like a slightly over-ripe tomato managed everything below stairs; two maids assisted him to wait at table; all was decorous and without noise. Minna, used to waiting upon herself and her mother, at first found the insistent presence of servants at mealtimes a menace to privacy; but she soon discovered that Ruth and Aunt Katherine ignored the servants, ate hardly anything of what had been cooked for them, and at all times talked without the smallest constraint. The servants heard all, seemed to hear only when they were personally addressed, and gathered up the plates without any sign of human disappointment at untouched food. The mistresses continued talking, while Minna, more sensitive than they, felt troubled at the unfriendly atmosphere. Following their style as far as temperament allowed, she still could not fail to recognise rudiments of human nature in Hallows, the butler, and the two maids, Doris and Mabel; and it surprised her to find in due course that the servants, grateful, it appeared, for such unwonted courtesy as she showed them, responded by the only means in their power. They pressed her to take more of their mistress's food and drink, of which they reserved her the tit-bits; they looked carefully and lavishly after the fire in her bedroom; they smiled with real affection when greeting her. Nevertheless, she would sometimes have welcomed a loud bang, the sight of Hallows sliding down the stair-rails, or the sound of laughter and singing from any part of the house. All she heard, unless there was a party, was the crisp speech of Ruth and the high-pitched murmur of Aunt Katherine, the ticking of old clocks in the silence, the crushed, demure whispers of Doris and Mabel, the hoarser inquiries of Hallows as he stooped with bottle or decanter.

In the evenings the place would often wake up a good deal; for Aunt Katherine gave parties for the benefit of the Cause and sometimes Ruth's friends would be assembled. Were they friends? Minna did not know. They were at any rate young; and for a time Minna liked meeting them. There were tall young clean-shaven men with longish fair hair and solemn expressions, and there was a small, quick man with a tiny black moustache and a plump rosy-gilled face and a very quick tongue, and there were several other men who were slow, not too humorous, and heavy-eyed. Minna noticed how the shirt fronts of these older men bulged, and how, when they rose to their feet, they touched the table with the tips of their fingers as if they were going to respond to toasts of the British Empire; and she preferred the younger men. In particular, she preferred the small quick man with the rosy gills and the black moustache. He was full of vitality; his eyes moved rapidly and his parted lips never betrayed what his real thoughts were; and she thought he was honest. His name was Bernard Mather. But Ruth at last gently warned her against this man, as a confirmed humorist; and from the day of that warning he was asked no more to the parties, came seldom to call, and at last disappeared altogether.

That was something else for Minna to discover, the ebb and flow of friendship in this circle. The women were more or less constant —Ruth's friends Clara Blake and Margery Stafford, for example, were very staunch, and even when she snapped at them through dinner Aunt Katherine liked to keep in touch with her fellow-workers—but the men passed on. They came; they spoke, it may be, at a meeting or two; and either reneged or were dropped or retired to a smiling distance. Why was that? Minna never knew. She marvelled, instead, at the extraordinary range of her cousin's acquaintance. She envied her freedom from self-consciousness and doubt. Politics, personalities, literature, art, all were familiar to her. She could speak of Tintoretto, Bach, Dante, Colet, Crom-well, Spinoza, Disraeli, Spurgeon, Wolsey, and a hundred living persons with the same assurance. She gave the impression of know-ing all that had ever been written or said about most other sub-jects under the sun, from the Pyramids to the Soane Museum. She

spoke briefly, stared, smiled; and all the men were very polite to
her. How impressed they must be! thought Minna. Perhaps that
was it; *too* impressed? Why, what an odious thought! It implied—— Minna checked herself. 'I'm not only an idiot, but a disagreeable idiot,' she said severely. All the same, she was perplexed.
For Ruth never listened to music, never pored upon a picture,
never suffered herself to be moved to ecstasy by a poem. Of course
not; she had no need. . . . 'One mustn't be sentimental, Minna:
that's Victorian. We're finished, thank goodness, with Vic-
torianism.' And if there was one thing truer of Ruth than another
it was that she was deeply sincere.

If you said that she knew too much and that men were too much
impressed by her knowledge to enjoy her company, you implied—
in your nastily sentimental way—that you supposed Ruth to be
disappointed of a sweetheart. That, clearly, was not the case. She
one day said in her downright way that the thought of being
married was abhorrent to her. 'Sex, and all that,' she had called it.
'Quite intolerable.'

Poor Minna (the day was early in her residence in Kensington)
had been taken aback.

'Wouldn't you like to have a baby?' she had asked, in return.

'Good heavens, no!' Ruth had cried, as if scandalised. 'What on
earth should I do with it?' Minna, seeing the faintly flushed cheek,
had smiled. Ruth had added: 'One needn't, of course, marry to
do that. It's a convention. I should like to break down all such
conventions. There's no reason why a woman should be tied for
life to somebody unutterably gross merely because she wants a
child.'

'Are men so gross?' asked Minna. She had known hardly more
than her fastidious father and William. But Ruth, instead of
answering that question, had continued to answer the former one:

'You think I'm unnatural, extraordinary? I'm not. I'm only not
sentimental. There are many women like me; there will be more.
We want to be something more than breeding machines.'

How far, thought Minna, her cousin had gone from naïveté!

'Then you don't believe in anything as mindless as love?' Minna
asked; 'I mean, between men and women.'

'I see I shall have to lend you "Man and Superman",' replied Ruth, smiling. 'It's a simple lesson in biology.'

'Yes, of course I know nothing about biology.'

'You should know more.'

How strange that every word of that conversation, and every glance of Ruth's dark, polished eyes, should now return so vividly! No contempt, no repressiveness in her manner; but a superiority, a lofty certainty. How did one un-learn certainty? And why? Was it by growth, or by lost confidence in oneself? Such a funny consternation, too. And 'somebody unutterably gross': in retrospect, how timid that seemed! Poor Ruth! Oh, dear, dear, poor everybody!

III

In the end something happened; and that also was a memory. First of all a very mild morning at the beginning of February, with soft rain and rushing clouds, an April day quite two months before its time. Minna, as she lay in bed, heard a pair of blackened Cockney sparrows chirping on her windowsill, and in imagination fled instantly back to the garden at home, and the flaccid sweet-smelling muddy earth and the chorus of birds which she knew must be busy there. That caused her heart to feel very large and cold, and then brought the walls of her second floor room forbiddingly close. She was a child again, with William—whom she no longer loved—close at hand, and her mother sitting in the shade, and limitless green all about them in pale sunshine; the thrushes very blithe, and a robin perching on the handle of William's spade as soon as he relinquished it in order to pick her up after a tumble. Resting against his shoulder as he knelt, his arm about her, she had watched the bright-eyed bird. . . .

She remembered Aunt Katherine entering the drawing-room later upon this Spring-like February day, and in her high-pitched voice crying triumphantly: 'Well, *that's* settled, thank goodness. We've got our M.P. coming to dinner tonight after all.'

'What, Sir Somebody Something?'

'No, child; certainly not! *That* old curmudgeon! Why, he's a furious Anti. Women's place is in the Ark. I wouldn't have him at my table. And he wouldn't dare to sit there, either, for fear of poison. He thinks I'm a Borgia. Oh, if I could, I'd break every window in his house and every bone in his body, and then singe his whiskers till he howled. No, there's a new young Liberal M.P. who's going to speak for us on Thursday. A coming man, and a fine speaker. At least, *I* think he is. You may not agree. Who cares? *Quite* satisfactory. *Perfectly* manageable. However, you'll see him tonight for yourself.'

No more. She had swept to her place at the table and turned over a sheaf of paper which lay there. Always a sheaf of papers. The agenda, even if the papers were blank. Bending over it, she looked like a parrot in a wig.

By evening Minna had forgotten what had been said, and, having come downstairs early, had been very quickly joined by Bernard Mather, whom she liked, as others did, because he made everybody laugh. A nice cosy, rosy, much-shaven little man with a droll mouth, eyes like boot-buttons, and a funny little flick of black moustache upon his upper lip. He joked and moved his head as if he had a rapid, happy mind; and something that perhaps only *sounded* like wit came from him in a voice as neat as his mouth. It was very entertaining.

Minna supposed Mather to be cosy and rosy and neat and trim all through; and the truth is that, like others, she under-rated him. He was a barrister who, being young, had as yet no briefs. He knew the law. He had some eye for character. His knowledge of what went on in the world—by which is meant, of course, that part of the world which is gossiped about by middle-class people —was equally compounded of penetration and hearsay. And he was no fool. He was to play a bigger part hereafter in this same world than Minna could have imagined; and, pleasantly, quietly, without expectation of reward, he was in love with his companion. At all times this unobtrusive kind of love makes for agreeable relationship. It demands nothing save tolerance.

As they stood as far as possible from the hot fire and the big series of gas jets under round globes which lighted the room, Mather had done his best to stay at her side, alone, in defiance of every effort made by others to detach him; and as neither he nor Minna knew anything beforehand about that night's visitors he had amused her with irreverent analysis of the arrivals. He knew all about them, and little of it was good. This one was a mutton-head, and that a careerist; another was full of money and a fourth of impudence. And at last he had drawn his breath with a slight hiss.

'Ah!' That had been the comment Minna heard. It was almost too full of meanings.

'Well?' she asked, with ridicule, looking towards the door.

She had there seen a not very tall man, young or youngish, fair, and very graceful. A slight figure which struck her—not quite convincingly—as familiar. His face was long and pale (the cheeks a little full, as if newly so); his lips were thin, and were drawn back from small, very white teeth, so that his expression suggested ingratiating innocence and at the same time a faint, unreadable mockery. But what impressed Minna most of all was the remarkable colour and quality of his eyes, which instantly met hers. Very strange eyes indeed. Not bright, but piercing. She was aware of a shock of interest for which, perhaps, Mather's hiss of recognition had in part prepared her.

'You like him?' asked Mather, in a whisper. 'I see you do. You feel you *must,* eh?'

'Not sure, yet,' laughed Minna, with such an arch half-glance that she did not notice how Mather's manner had changed from vivacity to the caution of a fighter. 'You haven't said who he is.'

Mather, smiling again, said in a ventriloquial murmur, as if he spoke behind his hand:

'He's a remarkable man. You can put it in capitals. It's like that.'

'You're teasing me.'

'I'm telling you the truth. He's what used to be called a carpet-bagger. Yes, that's a very good name for him, in all its implications. He got himself adopted two years ago in a hurry as Liberal candidate for some wretched constituency that was on the swing. He scraped home without a re-count; but only just. Like others in this extraordinary Parliament, he was washed in on the wave of hysteria——'

Minna laughed outright at the distaste of his tone.

'The deluge is after us. What a shocking Tory you are!' she cried. He nodded.

'Yes, I'm a Tory. What else is left for self-respect?'

'Progress! The vote!'

'Sh! You'll get the vote, and it won't do you any good. Democracy's doomed.'

'It's never been tried.'

'Read Aristotle!'

'Oh, heavens! Everybody tells me to read something——'

'The Tory party's the only party for a gentleman. We may have lost the land, and we certainly lost the last election. But we've still got the Peers and the Principles.'

'The vested interests. Imperialism.'

'What's wrong with Imperialism? At least it's not truckling to the mob. Its motto—the motto of real government—is *noblesse oblige*. But you'll hear less and less of that as these mountebanks dig the country's grave.'

'Are you serious, Mr Mather?'

'No,' he answered, smiling again very charmingly. 'The Tories are duffers. And yet what I say is true.'

'You've still not finished with the visitor.'

Mather shrugged. He must have seen that this, and nothing else, was her real interest. People, not Politics! If she had been less pretty he would have considered her brainless. Deceived, however, as young men in love often are, he continued to speak above her comprehension.

'Well, he's hardly begun, himself. Comparatively speaking. He's a journalist, an orator, a financier. He's an earnest Liberal. A tee-totaller. An opportunist, they say. Somehow—and I can't tell you how—he's made a lot of money. I hear he's bought some papers and a bookshop at bargain prices, which shows that he's either a genius or a fool. He'll use 'em; or they'll break him. Very ambitious, not too scrupulous, and a good speaker. Dangerous.'

'To whom?' asked Minna, who had observed the stranger's proper respect to Aunt Katherine, his suave attentiveness to Ruth, and his admirably calm response to the too fawning approach of

another man, evidently bent upon gaining his favourable attention. 'To whom dangerous?'

'To everything,' answered Mather, with a dark look. 'To everybody. To you, to me——'

'You just mean he's a Radical?'

'Is that what they call them?' retorted Mather. He sighed. 'If
so, it's a euphemism.' He ruffled his short black hair with a gesture
of rueful perplexity. Into his quick-glancing black eyes came a droll
misery, which resembled the world-weary expression of a tired
monkey. 'No, it's not his politics I mind. He'll change them with
the winds of fortune. That's what's the trouble with him. He's—
well, I've said it already.'

'You're terribly vague!' laughed Minna, quite bewildered.

'Am I? It's my vice. But *he's* not!" declared Mather. 'Oh, dear,
no! Nothing like it!'

Aunt Katherine, completing her introductions, rather fussily
sought her niece in the withdrawn coolness of that pleasant tête-
à-tête. She was closely accompanied by the fair, smooth-headed,
ingratiating stranger.

'Mr Mather you know,' she abruptly said, with a scowl at the
fainéant. 'Minna, this is Mr Furness Firth. A pillar of strength,
my dear. *Such* a comfort! My niece, Miss Manning.'

'Of Moreton,' murmured the stranger, his hand outstretched.
His voice was low, slightly feminine, almost caressing. 'I . . . I
know you already, Miss Manning. From afar. I . . . I've often
seen you . . . at home. Dick Firth. You don't remember, of
course.'

Minna heard Mather sigh. She herself was looking directly at
the newcomer's penetrating eyes, which were gleamingly grey by
a conjunction of blue and yellow; and in doing this she quite
omitted to reply in words to his speech of greeting.

CHAPTER XIII

Morning of a Man in Love

AT THE WESTERN END of London, at Ealing, in a fair-sized smart red brick house with four bay windows, a broad door between the lower ones, and an assembly of evergreen shrubs between the house and the trim road, Dick Firth lay fast asleep. Not for Dick the doctrine of 'early to rise'; for the London he now pursued was a London of actively late night hours, nine o'clock breakfast gong, and a ten o'clock start for business. He was plumper in both cheek and body than he had been as a boy; but even now his head was racked with schemes, and in his dream he was upon the point of bringing off another great manœuvre to his own advantage.

The last few years had been years of unhindered success. Nothing had come amiss to him, from public speaking in good and Liberal causes to press publicity, the organisation of bazaars, journalism, and ingenious finance. He was always a step or two ahead of his immediate object, could think of several different things at a time, and did not scamp detail. Of these abilities the successful man must be an infallible master; and Dick was moving upward and onward, pushing through the crowd like a spearhead, not only by his own volition but with the willing help of those who by a kind of mass humility yield place to the man who knows his way to the front.

Now his foot was almost safely within political circles of importance. He was there regarded—so experienced are politicians in the practicalities of their craft—as useful and easily rewarded or rewardable. His wife's money, Daddy Griffin's legacy, his odd undefined connection with the Press, the great electoral upheaval of two years before, which had given him another opportunity of serving his country, had all worked for good; and, waking or sleeping, Dick supped the greatness of his future. In slumber his lips were pressed together in a pinched, secret smile; the long light eyelashes seemed to quiver; he looked as one shamming sleep, like a human Brer Fox.

His pale wife, whose face resembled solid milk, lay beside him, fragilely fair; the corners of her lips pathetically turned down and her eyelids as grey as those of a very young sick child; her gold hair, of which there was so little, loose upon the pillow, like a little girl's. She might just have fallen asleep after hours of wakefulness; she might almost, but for the rise and fall of her white breast, have been dead. Sometimes she wished that she were indeed dead. The children were in another room, at the back of the house, far from their preoccupied parents, and as silent as newborn kittens; and the pretty nurse had gone for good.

Presently Dick awoke. But he did not at once open his eyes, for there was always a delicious passage between dream and waking which yielded him valuable ideas, and, knowing this, he prolonged it. His mind was then at its most rapid, and before he allowed the light to disturb him he passed many secrets in review. He saw how he must contrive this and that, see one man, write to a dozen others, refuse, accept, watch these stocks or those, promise his wife that thing, exact another from her, placate somebody else, frown here and smile there in the plenitude of his growing power. The broadest smile of which he was capable at last parted his lips —it was a sweet, odd smile, when it came—and he peeped with whimsical demureness through those long lashes. Light shone in at the sides of the cream blinds, and the bedroom was touched with the hue of dusky old gold. How quiet it was! Ah, but he was happy. He had never been so happy.

The room was a large, square one, and all the furniture in it was of inlaid mahogany—a wedding present from Eileen's half-opulent insufferable father—while all the decorations were in Eileen's taste, conventionally refined, as if it had been filleted. Dick's glance moved to Eileen herself, so milk-white that the lace-edged pillow upon which her head rested was greyed in contrast.

The smile did not pass as he familiarly saw the pale lips, the slender neck, and the revealed softness of her breast; rather it was intensified, but not lovingly. He knew her too well to love her at all; her suburban gentility, her one-syllabled thoughts, the insipid movements of her body, the little cravings of a passion as fragile as a baby's search for its mother's nipple, the so easily penetrable disguises of her mood, the childish reserves and pruderies which she believed to become a lady, her essential nervous fear of him, were all established knowledges in Dick's mind. But he did not dislike her. She was obedient and long-suffering. She did not whimper. There was in her just that amount of character, and no more. Having granted to him in early days every tepid freedom of her mind and body, she had owed him ever since, in return, nearly all the fragile interest she had in life. She was still fascinated, and was still proud of his success, which she thought she had foreseen and aided. And she was a devoted mother to his three children, who were all girls, all flaxen, all apparently (for he saw little of them) as uninteresting as their mother. They absorbed her. If she would only not insist upon sharing his bed, she and he might very pleasantly drift along for the rest of their lives without conflict. She insisted. It was a mistake. Because of course that insistence hampered him and aroused resentment, without achieving its object. She had never had any brains. These thoughts were hidden in Dick's mind as he glanced at his wife; they were expressed in the stiffening of his smile. Junket was feeble stuff. As a diet it resembled wedded life with Eileen.

In a moment Dick slipped stealthily over to his other side, away from his wife. Although he measured her so ruthlessly, he did not under-estimate her penetration into one part of his life. Loving him—nay, cloying him with that tiny adhesive voluptuousness of hers—she showed uncanny quickness in detecting his inclination towards another woman. Infallible! It really was an extra sense, an intuition reared upon Dick knew not what sign in himself of either dawning excitement or instinctive withdrawal. Except in the matter of casual amours, where feeling was unaroused, he had never yet quite succeeded in deceiving her. Though she might know nothing of the woman, she had from the first no doubt of

her existence. And Dick, exasperated and maliciously amused by
the instant anxious whiteness and pertinacity of her attention to
him in these crises, wished with all his heart that in the present case
she should suspect nothing. Sometimes, in the past, when indulgence would have been dangerous, discovery, he knew, had
saved him. But not now. Not now. This was different. *Somehow,*
she must be deceived. How?

The smile passed altogether from his lips. He grew very silent
indeed.

II

Two hours later Dick was in the West End, at his new offices,
which were in a turning off Drury Lane. The offices occupied the
whole of a big grey brick building with perpetually dirty small-
paned upper windows and an imposing entrance; and upon a
highly-polished brass plate beside the door one read the name
DUCKETT & Co. A few books, one or two of them novels, but the
majority texts and primers, lay upon a sloping board in a small
shop-window; while in a frame beside the door was padlocked a
copy of one of the firm's periodicals. Everything select and full of
dignity; books and periodical alike newly dusted and very ugly, as
if Ducketts' had long carelessly prospered without competition;
was there also an odour of decay?

Ducketts', which Mather had belittlingly described to Minna as
'some papers and a bookshop', were Dick's latest investment, his
newest toy. They were publishers; and the branch of their business
with which Dick was most immediately concerned consisted of
two successful periodicals and a sickly failure. The successes were
a respectable weekly newspaper called 'The Retail Shopkeeper'
and a more than respectable monthly temperance journal called
'Wise Cheer'; the non-success was another weekly which advo-
cated, in addition to temperance, the end of spiritual sloth, Imperialism, and slums. It bore upon its cover the effigy of a State
trumpeter, and was called 'England, Awake!' But England, so
far, had not stirred.

Dick pushed his way through a swing-door and across a large

open space in the middle of which a girl, a heavy brunette, sat typing at a desk. In passing, he smiled at this girl; but because, like others in the firm, she feared that the new proprietor might reorganise her job out of existence, she did not return his smile and instead typed more fixedly. Dick understood. That preoccupied smile of his alarmed all employees; and he savoured his knowledge anew, as he did every morning, in passing through the clerks' office to his own room at the back of the building. They were scared into busyness; and he was a master. Though the days of slavery were past one could still taste the grandeurs of power and feel an ever-renewed ichor running in one's veins.

A fire was alight in Dick's room and the windows commanded the view of a grim wall and a miraculous solitary plane-tree standing in the middle of an empty yard. Here Mr Joseph Duckett, now deceased, the former proprietor of the business, had sat in stingy benevolence for thirty years; here Dick would sit for as long as it suited him to do so and no longer. The great secret of life was that one must use possessions for one's ends, and not as ends in themselves. That was a profundity. Meanwhile his letters, his telephone, the nervous agitation of his staff, the pleasant noise of hidden London, and the music of his own thoughts gave Dick such crowing pleasure that he felt as gay as a kitten with a ball of wool. The Spring! Or Love! Was that it? Sh-sh-sh! He withdrew his head into his shoulders. Never weight an emotion with a name! Never breathe the word 'love' lest it be overheard and its secrecy destroyed! It was Spring—Spring only. In reality, he was taut with triumph.

Well, why should he not feel triumphant? He was thirty-five. He had started with nothing; and by energy and shrewdness—these were his own words—he had first of all obtained experience; then, coming to London with his aim clear and a job in his pocket, he had so pulled strings that he had advanced with great speed. Women had been kind; marriage had helped him; some foresight into the growth of publicity as a force had seemed inspired; Daddy Griffin's legacy had given him for the first time substantial capital of his own; he was now in Parliament; he had this business— mortgaged, it is true, but at his command—and these papers, which

were to mean so much to his further advancement, a wide acquaintance, some power, more to follow, the world before him.
By the time he was fifty he might be in the Cabinet, a millionaire,
decidedly an influence upon his age. Already, the people here
cringed to him. Others should imitate them. More and more.
More.

'Dear God!' he suddenly prayed, closing his eyes and growing
rapt. 'May I never abuse my power! May I employ it only for
good!'

. . . In the midst of his successes, Furness Firth remained a
man of strong faith, humble before the Source of all Good, and
deeply recognizant of the Aid vouchsafed to him in Full
Measure. . . .

Thereafter, sighing faintly, as if he emerged from a trance, Dick
seated himself at his desk. He had just drawn forward the small
pile of personally-addressed letters which lay there when a tall
man of his own age came into the room and stood respectfully
waiting. What now? Dick peeped first through his eyelashes, and
saw that his visitor was Bryant, the gloomy fellow with the lined,
dirty-looking cheeks of an old actor, and assumed his gentlest
manner. This was the two-pound-a-week starveling who had the
whole book business at his fingers' ends.

'Good morning, Bryant,' he said, mildly. 'Yes?'

Bryant responded. One saw him this morning as Hamlet.
'Whether 'tis nobler in the mind to suffer——'

'Good morning, sir!' What a sepulchral voice! It vibrated. It
caused vibrations. The room clattered as with castanets, and the
voice so filled it that a shudder ran down Dick's spine. On no
account would he consider an increase in Bryant's salary. No, no,
a thousand times. To have to work for ever through a bassoon
would be intolerable! Bryant, unaware of these swift reactions, so
different from anything he could conceive, maintained his progress: 'I thought I should let you know that Chivers, who's on the
till, had a fit half-an-hour ago. I sent him home with Banks as
escort.'

'Dear me!' said Dick, completely surprised. He stared. Bryant's face was drawn, his mouth pompous, his Adam's apple groping about his neck like a marble on a bagatelle board. 'I . . . I . . . Is he subject to fits?'

You have seen strong men upon the stage who confess disaster by shaking their heads because the dramatist has not given them a line.

'I'm afraid he is.'

'Is it seasonal? It's . . . it's a beautiful day.'

Bryant remained grave. He had become a family physician.

'I think not, sir. A beautiful day, yes; but the fit was genuine. Otherwise, I assure you, I should have kept him here.' The voice, though still resonant, was lowered.

Dick thought for a moment.

'Do you want to discharge him?'

Astonishment stopped the Adam's apple. Bryant's eyes were cast aloft, and were caught by the light.

'Oh, no, sir,' he boomed. But he was now diminished to the rank of a butler.

'Then why——' Dick picked up a letter. Sonorities chilled him. 'Oh, sack him, Bryant. It will prevent the others from having fits.'

Bryant was torn between embarrassment and a Florence Nightingale love of suffering humanity.

'This is quite exceptional,' he said. 'Poor little beggar. Excuse me, sir; but I really came to suggest that he should have a fortnight's holiday.'

'A fortnight's holiday!' Dick was electrified. 'Nonsense! We should have an epidemic of fits. Get rid of him. Then he'll have as long a holiday as he wants.'

'I'm sorry I mentioned it, sir,' said Bryant, brought by such sharpness to the place of a schoolboy before the headmaster, and much alarmed. 'He's a good worker.'

'Of course you mentioned it!' cried Dick, with temper. His pale cheeks had flushed. He looked straight at Bryant, his thin lips set and his eyes like those of a cat at a mousehole. 'Of course you mentioned it.'

'I hope you'll reconsider that, sir,' said Bryant. He was no longer an actor, but an awkwardly dishevelled man in fear. Dick saw **it** all. Play-acting. Booming about humanitarianism. Collapsing. What a fool! He began to open his letters, as a sign that the interview bored him. But the first letter he read caught his attention. Oh, J. B. Good man! It looked—— What was this deflated tragedian saying? 'You see my responsibility, sir. I shouldn't be able to look the boy in the face. I meant to help him; and if I . . . He's about the keenest worker we've got; and keenness isn't a quality you generally get for fifteen shillings a week——'

Everything was preposterous. Why lose one's temper? This man was a mere gargoyle. Dick smiled.

'Eh?' he asked, abstractedly, in a different tone. He was so elated by what he had just read that his irritability passed. 'Oh, well, I'll see him myself when he's better. I . . . I feel I ought to, poor little chap. And we'll have a chat later. All right, Bryant.'

Bryant amazedly withdrew, to spend the rest of the morning in a quarrel between terror and self-praise for heroism; and when he had gone Dick looked steadily at the closed door. The smile passed as it had come, and was replaced by a frown. He mustn't be troubled like this. He must get a good manager to keep the staff in hand. Bryant was no good. Afraid of responsibility. Bryant would have to go. However—

Dear F. [read Dick].

The man you want is named Harvest. Wm. ditto. He's had good country and suburban experience, and for a year he's been on 'The Shocker', where he's out of place and gives joy to nobody. (Burton's a brute, anyway). In the last 3 months he's written a regular feature in 'The Torch', under signature 'Mr Edwards', after Sam Johnson's non-philosophic friend. Pretty good. Neat, nice humour, and not costive. The man's got sense, which is what you want. He's about 30. Nice chap. Modest. Lives in your neighbourhood. I should have a look at him.

Yours,

J. B.

Really excited, Dick rang the bell for his secretary. J. B., as he was called (his name was John Brainerd Satterthwat), was a very experienced journalist indeed. He praised rarely. His manner was laconic. Such detail as he had accorded William Harvest was testimony of great worth, and Dick's estimate of his fellow-townsman flew in pursuit of J. B.'s. How interesting! What luck! Oh, but this was indeed a *simplification!*

'Miss Neilson, I want a copy of Boswell's "Johnson" from stock. And send out for the last half-dozen numbers of "The Torch": it's a threepenny paper. Come straight back.' He was alight with zest.

But when Miss Neilson returned with the book he was using the telephone, holding it to his ear with one hand while, very awkwardly, he unfolded a letter with the other. He was talking to his broker, nodding, snapping out prices, glancing at the newly-opened letter, tossing it aside, opening another, and sometimes snatching a pencil to make a note upon a small desk pad. He was the picture, Miss Neilson thought, of a busy business man—very like her imagination of a Napoleon of finance—and she waited in patience, mechanically recording what his instructions to the broker were, but not thinking for a moment of turning them to her own account. How could she have done so? She had no money at all but her weekly salary, and sixteen pounds in the Post Office Savings Bank.

Miss Neilson did not realise that Dick was watching her as he spoke and wrote and read, but in spite of his other activities he could see her quite well. She was a tall girl with a sallowly dark face which would have seemed expressionless if two well-developed eyebrows had not given it a sulky cast; and as Dick had perceived instantly at their first interview wrinkles were already showing in her porridge-coloured neck. She had large, ringless hands of good shape which suggested that she might be in the habit of playing some musical instrument, and she was dressed a little mannishly. But her hair was abundant and soft, her eyes were liquid, and as she drooped, resting the Boswell upon the edge of her employer's desk, there was nothing masculine in her figure or her carriage. Dick therefore motioned to her to sit down, put the last-unfolded letter (from which a scent smote the air) quickly into his outer pocket, and, as he listened to what was said to him on the telephone, held out J. B.'s letter, marking the name 'Edwards' with his thumbnail, and pointed to the Boswell. That was enough. By the time his talk was ended she had found the first of several references to Oliver Edwards, and as a boy then brought copies of 'The Torch' Dick was able instantly to dictate his letter.

Having begun to do this, he glanced at a page of the open book, carefully read one article in 'The Torch' and skimmed another, and from time to time, as will be seen, interrupted himself.

'My dear Harvest,' he said.

'I have often remembered that melancholy day at Moreton and my promise to get into touch with you. Alas! the weeks pass so quickly with me that I am at odds with many such promises. Mea culpa! But now circumstances have arisen in which a meeting between us might be mutually advantageous. . . . Miss Neilson, I . . . I wonder if you'd mind giving me your opinion of Mr Bryant?'

Miss Neilson, having begun to write that sentence in shorthand, flushed. She turned her liquid eyes to Dick, and was guarded.

'He's very trustworthy, Mr Firth,' she said, shutting her mouth.

'But brains, Miss Neilson.' How softly he spoke! 'Brains.'

'He acts,' she answered. But whether she meant that as testimony to Bryant's intellect or not Dick could not gather.

'Yes, perpetually.'

'He's started a society for the staff.'

Dick, jumping for an explanation of her demeanour, asked: 'Do you belong to it?'

She chilled. Clearly, it was a sore point. Oh, didn't Dick know the heart-burnings there could be in any such society! None of them fitted to assume strange rôles; all immediately in rivalry . . .

'I think it's silly,' she said. 'I like to go to a good theatre and see good actors. Not this.'

'Mr Bryant doesn't agree?'

'Obviously not. He's mad on it. But then he's acting all the time. It's funny.' A little excitement showed in her manner. Well, there were younger girls in the firm. . . . She recovered in time to say with what seemed to Dick to be amusing detachment: 'He's liked.'

'But not by you.'

Miss Neilson was terrified.

'Oh, I like him all right,' she said. 'Very well. Only not——' A slight greyness in her cheeks showed that she had paled.

'Yes,' agreed Dick, thinking to himself: 'Not his preference for others.' Aloud, he said: 'You *play,* don't you? What; the 'cello?'

Miss Neilson's eyes glowed.

'Did somebody tell you?' she asked.

'I don't need people to tell me everything, Miss Neilson,' said Dick, with his odd smile. 'I . . . I can see for myself.' He looked closely at her, and saw that under his glance she grew confused. Laughing within, he resumed his dictation:

'I wonder whether you could call upon me here one afternoon? Say on Thursday, at 3? If this is not convenient, please make your own suggestion. I cannot refrain from telling you how excellent I think your "Edwardian" contributions to "The Torch" are. Mr Edwards has long been my favorite minor character in biography, and that cheerfulness of yours, which, like his, "was always breaking in", is irresistible. The articles are full of *sense.* I have followed you now for some weeks, always with delight, and feel that many other readers must have done the same. Congratulations, my dear fellow. Yours very sincerely. And now, Miss Neilson,' concluded Dick, 'you won't, of course, tell anybody that I asked you about Mr Bryant. You see, I . . . I'm going to rely on you a great deal in my work here.'

She was breathless.

'Yes, Mr Firth.'

'I . . . I shan't be here all the time. You'll have to be my memory and my conscience.'

'Yes, Mr Firth.'

'And if you'll run away now and type that we'll get it off at once. Send it by hand care of "The Torch". And if Mr Harvest rings up be very nice to him and make an appointment for *any* afternoon, because—well, you understand, I . . . I have a use for him.' His eyes gleamed very brightly. They seemed to shine straight into

Miss Neilson's being and leave her trembling. 'When you've done that we'll deal very quickly with the rest of the post. D'you see? Everything?'

'Yes, Mr Firth.'

She went away, greatly excited; and Dick, following in thought, wondered if he had done right to dazzle her with so bright a prospect. Would she do? Willing enough, and conscientious, and careless of hours; but heavy. Camel feet. No verve. Never had a lover; great capacity for rather soggy feeling; lonely tears and a sense of having been thwarted by life . . . Eh, dear, dear—he drew his breath hissingly—that was a sure accompaniment of camel feet. But I say! It was a line. A *line*. Never call them, stupidly, 'unwanted women': it suggested something left over after the charity bazaar. 'Superfluous' was just as humiliating. But if one were 'frustrated' that meant, surely, that one was superior to one's lot. Too good for it. No scope. 'I say! I say!' exclaimed Dick aloud in delight; 'that's really most excellent! Too Good for Life; the Tradegy of the Frustrated Woman!' He scribbled the words, not upon his little pad, but in a waistcoat-pocket notebook.

In high spirits—and forgetful of the derisory phrase 'too good for life'—he began to open the rest of his letters. Damn! there was another from Cicely. She must be stopped, the fool: this was the third, though he had ignored the others. It was indecent that a woman of her age should not take a dismissal. She wasn't a child. And it had happened before, with Barrett, with Penge. . . . Idiot! Ah, Lady Penwyn: 'So delightful . . . charmed . . . most interesting people, and you would adorn . . . next Tuesday week . . .' I say, Lady *Penwyn!* He's arrived all right. Dick gave no further present thought to Bryant or to his secretary or his journalistic plots and slogans; he was in the *haut monde,* and was at once farsightedly busy with still greater schemes.

III

However, as the hour advanced and he felt the approach of midday, Dick forgot even Lady Penwyn in a single intense preoccupa-

tion. At half-past twelve Miss Neilson would not have recognised
him; for the excitement he had shown after reading J. B.'s letter
was nothing to what he now felt. He was quite transfigured, glowing as with white heat. Not one of our friends, not Bob Whistler,
not William Harvest, not Mr Merrow, not Daddy Griffin, nor old
Mr and Mrs Firth themselves had ever seen him thus.

He appeared to grow taller; his expression was exalted; he
moved about the room, white-handed, with long, noiseless strides.
Sometimes the hands were clasped next to his bitten underlip,
sometimes they were extended before him as if he conducted an
orchestra; but they were never still, and were full of expression.
And at last, still with those noiseless strides, he walked out of the
building into the musty sunshine of Drury Lane and Long Acre,
and made his way westward so quickly that his shadow was as
fleeting as that of an April cloud. The stumps and baskets, the
tissued boxes and rolling apples of Covent Garden were passed
unseen; the offices of many of those new rivals of his, the publishers, were left behind as if they had not existed; and he was at
length beyond Piccadilly Circus, behind Piccadilly itself, and in a
soberly chic restaurant there, groomed anew, smouldering, apparently cool and debonair. What capacity he had for hiding his
thoughts!

The place was decorated throughout in pale blue and old gold;
and it was very discreet, and very silent, as a restaurant should be.
The waiters had all the easy hauteurs of an ideal *corps diplo-
matique,* and the *maître d'hôtel* with whom Dick consulted was as
tall, lean, long-fingered, sphinx-like, and indulgently courteous as
a prince in 'The Arabian Nights Entertainments.' He did not
speak; he inclined his head. And what his private thoughts might
have been no English sporty boy, all muffler and tweeds, could
have imagined. That they were voluptuous thoughts of beautiful
women was not impossible. That he cared for gold and precious
stones was not improbable. That he took personal interest in food
or tips was inconceivable. But his aloofness did not prevent him
from communicating by changes of expression his approval or
doubt of whatever Dick remarked in both menu and wine-list;
and it must be said for Dick as host that the *maître d'hôtel's* final

inclination was not merely one of the head. It was an acknowledgment of mastery.

Dick then, having critically inspected the table reserved for him, returned to the shaded vestibule, consulted one of the long mirrors in which its beauties were multitudinously and duskily reflected, straightened his tie, questioned his own half-closed eyes, and waited. He no longer moved about or gesticulated.

First among his guests came Mrs Perse, the black-browed, red-lipped, *soignée* widow who was everybody's confidant and above suspicion of anything but remunerative social journalism. Her history, a sad one, was half-understood by a small circle, and the source of her income was rarely suspected; for those were days when women journalists were a minority and social news was a treat. She was no Suffragist; a practical butterfly, rather, who knew much more than she ever told about the strange world of intrigue in which she lived and had not to pretend to familiarity with those whom she had never met. Her defect was that she was vain enough to tell a man what she had seen in his face, and this, while it was sometimes accounted a compliment, at other times estranged a friend.

Minna Manning was but an instant after Mrs Perse, and by contrast with her was a rosebud next to an amaryllis; the rest of the party were the Furies (both of them novelists, she popular, he creeping with the aid of microscopic sales into lists of approved virtuosi) and old Boonge, the Etonian bore for whom all found excuses because he was aristocratically connected and jocular. 'Oh, it's very clear,' whispered Mrs Perse richly in Dick's ear as they moved in a bunch to their table; 'very clear, my dear man, who the heroine of your party is.' 'I . . . I thought it was you, my dear madam,' retorted Dick, with an enigmatic glance. 'Was I wrong?' Their eyes met. Nothing betrayed him. He was as arch as his friend, and as cool. He hardly looked at Minna. But when he did so his eye flew all over her in thrilling ecstasy.

She was at his left hand during the meal, and he divided attention between her and Sylvia Furie, who looked like one's notion of a brownie, with straight lank hair, cut in what later fashion was to call a bob, and a thin, half-ecstatic and half-pinched *café au lait* face devoid of all feeling. Nobody without a magic ear could have detected the difference of his tone whenever he spoke to right or left, and nobody ungifted in sight could have caught the fire of his eyes, or the way in which they rested, as swift as those of a cat, upon Minna's hand, her wrist, her cheek, the enchanting sweetness of her neck. But to himself Dick was all the time breathing prayers of thankfulness for the vouchsafed miracle of this blessed day, when the sun shone so warmly, and Spring was in the air, and hearts were warm and light, and he was with his dear love, free, it might be, in a little while, to walk by her side through the parks and watch her smile and see the sunshine catch her eyes and pierce the shadow of that big hat until her every secret was granted to him. He would have given much—all—to take that tender hand, to dismiss these others, and then, with confident ardour, savouring to the last the exquisite reluctances of her pride, to make her triumphantly his own. Instinctively his arms curved for the embrace; his body tingled; he was forced to veil his eyes lest imagination should be seen fierily at work within them. He was quite breathless.

They talked, of course. He flattered Sylvia Furie, who was so avid of flattery that she must be dosed with it; he chaffed old Boonge, with his red face and white moustache and stupid arch smile and anecdotes of Eton in the 'sixties; he steered among the advantages and dangers of exchange with Mrs Perse, seeking and giving unobtrusively news of the paragraphable great, learning much more than he gave from his companions and storing everything busily in his intricate and wonderful memory. And all the time, within, he was trembling at Minna's nearness, and treasuring her laughter, with each flying glance endeavouring to read the elusive candours of her eyes and carry further joy to his fainting heart, at every turn with the greatest guile pretending to all these others that he was but the agreeable host, while he sought to charm her into the knowledge that everything was for her, from the blush roses upon the table to the little strawberries which seemed so miraculously to have made their appearance in Springtime at his behest.

'You're a magician,' Minna said, at the strawberries.

'Magician!' exclaimed old Boonge. 'He's a bally Prime Minister!'

'And a gossip!' cried Mrs Perse.

'They tell me you publish books, too, Firth,' drawled blond, calculating Harold Furie, whose thoughts were supposed to float high above commerce.

'Only good ones!' laughed Dick. 'Thank you, ladies and gentlemen; thank you.' He pretended that he was about to make a speech. 'I . . . I . . .'

'By the way, what sort of M.P. does Asquith make?' demanded Boonge. 'I thought he'd got his quietus over the Licensing Bill.'

'Sh-sh-sh!' Mrs Perse put a hand upon Mr Boonge's arm. 'Don't start him on temperance. Look, he's drinking water himself; while we're——'

'Good God, so he is!' ejaculated Boonge, goggling.

Dick pledged them with his glass of water.

'The best wine of all!' he said, for a moment serious. Then, quickly: 'But I . . . I'm no bigot. Among friends.' They were all his friends. 'You know, when I was in my constituency before the Election, I . . . I went to a big dinner there, and sat next to the chairman of the local Temperance Association. Champagne was served; I refused. My neighbour *didn't*. I said to him: "I say, I . . . I thought you were a teetotaller." He said: "So I am. But this is *free!*"'

'All alike!' roared Boonge in his hoarse, porty voice. 'Never did *me* any harm. Warms the blood. I never have a cold. Besides, I enjoy it. There was a feller——'

'Mr Firth,' murmured Sylvia Furie, approaching Dick's ear: he thought he heard her bones rattle. 'I wonder if you'd be interested in seeing Harold's new novel. *I* think it's quite the best thing he's done—*absolutely* first-rate; but Melvilles, who published the last, are no good at all. I want him to leave them. I was wondering . . .'

Dick saw the anxious depths of her eyes below the smiling polish of their surface. He read the message cruelly enough. Did she take him for a simpleton?

'Of course, I . . . I should be charmed——'

'Dick Firth!' called Mrs Perse, from the foot of the table. 'Stop this man from telling this other man a story he doesn't want to hear, and tell me if Lloyd George and Asquith are on speaking terms. And who the old lady is who always shouts "Cad!" when Ll. G. is speaking. And whether John Burns really did say the Thames was Liquid Istry . . . And . . .'

'Oh, my dear Agatha!' sighed Dick, peeping through his lashes. 'I . . . I'm a very humble camp-follower. I don't know these great people. I . . . I pass them cringingly in the House. I . . . I sometimes get a nod from an Under-Secretary; but, as to the leaders, they're far above me. Even my vote isn't really valuable to them: they've got so many others in their pockets.'

'Are they rude?' asked Minna, with incredulity.

'Say Olympian,' he begged, turning quickly, and smiling with her —their eyes so close, her mouth so enchantingly within a few inches of his eager lips that in spite of everything he could not repress the signs of his longing. 'They have weighty affairs to think of. The back-bencher belongs to a lower order. He only represents his constituents.'

'But his voice is heard in the land?'

'Very rarely. Too rarely. His constituents, yes; his local paper, yes; but in the House—— However, there are rocks ahead. Ministries always decline in power. There will be trouble. Misfortune is a great chastener of pride.'

'Remind them of it in your papers!' cried Mrs Perse, boldly. She brightly stared.

Dick sent her a glance of warning; but she was triumphantly immune. She could read his mind.

'Thank heaven not all women are clever!' murmured Dick, under his breath.

'Ah,' said Sylvia Furie, wrinkling her nose. 'But it's the stupid ones who are dangerous.'

'There are none here,' Dick assured her. 'Yet I'm afraid!'

Minna laughed aloud. It was as if a wren sang.

'Beware of auntie's meeting tonight!' she said.

Boonge, a little late, guffawed. He looked with old-manly familiarity towards a pretty girl into Minna's eyes.

'What's that?' he laughed. 'A meeting. Are they *all* stupid? What?'

Mrs Furie grimaced again.

'Stupid *men* aren't dangerous,' she said, as if it were an epigram. 'They're only stupid.'

'What do you think, Miss Manning?' asked Boonge. 'Are men stupid?'

Minna, who saw that all were listening with strange faces, coloured slightly.

'They've made a horrid muddle of the world,' she hesitated. 'And most of them are very good-natured.'

'I breathe again!' cried Mrs Perse. 'Nobody could call *me* good-natured.'

'I was just going to,' sneered Furie.

'But I don't quite see——' began Boonge.

'That's why you're such a darling!' declared Agatha Perse.

And at last the luncheon was at an end, and the Furies had gone back to Dulwich to write novels, and old Boonge had taken his way to his club in Pall Mall, and Mrs Perse, who was in fact very good-natured indeed, showed kindness by staying with them long enough to protect Minna from any air of intrigue, and they were upon their sauntering way into Hyde Park and Kensington Gardens. The air was like wine, and very intoxicating. The Spring flowers were as yellow and as blue as sunshine and the soft breeze could make them. A few riders were in the Row. Some ducks paddled, quacking sotto voce, near the edge of the Serpentine, eyeing three little girls who had brought them bread and were choosing the visibly weakest for their benefactions. The two walked side by side along near the water, Minna carefree, Dick suffering her to be some quarter of an inch in advance of him so that he could always look aside and observe what her lips and chin and eyes would betray in response to his every adventurous word.

'You liked Agatha Perse?' he asked.

'A little afraid of her, I think,' mused Minna, smiling. 'She makes me realise my own——'

'What?' pressed Dick, bending close, touching her arm, as if inadvertently, for an instant. He could not control himself; for when she smiled he was on fire. 'But you're wrong to make any comparison. Poor dear, she's one of the frustrated women of our time.

Frustrated. Frustrated. There are so many; and I'm so sorry for them. They've started with high qualities and objects; and when they were young they've dreamed dreams and seen visions and had high hopes—as . . . as we all do. And as the years pass they don't realise their dreams, and the visions fade, and the hopes perish. Having too fine natures for the rough and tumble of life, too little alloy, they become failures——'

'Is that because they're too good?' asked Minna, in doubt.

'Because they're too good.'

'And because . . .' She looked adorably puzzled, still smiling, with the white teeth showing between her parted lips. 'And not because they aren't good enough?'

'Too fine.'

'Mrs Perse?' It was an incredulous sigh.

'Tell me what troubles you.'

'So much assurance. Such quickness in seeing and despising what they think callow. Such sophistication——'

'My dear. Forgive them. These women are unhappy.'

'That may be. You still say it's because they're too fine to be happy?'

'Ah, not all of them. That I allow. Some are unhappy—many of them—because they've never really *lived* at all.'

'Lived?' Again that incredulous sigh. He saw her brows rise. Eagerly he fell into dithyramb:

'Haven't known love and rapture. Haven't . . . *fulfilled* themselves.' Did she understand his meaning through the veil of his speech? Did she? Still a child, lovely, innocent . . . 'I see them everywhere. Frustrated. Poor Agatha! In her heart, how she must envy you!'

'Me?' It is difficult for the untrained mind to observe at once a change in argument. Minna smiled at the thought that Mrs Perse should envy her. Dick watched with adoring eyes, in which, nevertheless, there were a hundred urgent questions. Had he deceived her? Could she read, could she in any degree appreciate, the strength of his feelings? His hunger, his shocked, suddenly uprearing sense of the waste of so much energy, now and in the past, upon unworthiness and folly? His indifference to Agatha Perse,

to his wife, to a dozen other charmers to whom he had given himself in his quest for the ideal? Was she, as her ingenuous air suggested, blind to his burning eagerness? Her eyes were so clear:
what lay behind them? He was desperately tormented. Minna said:
'I don't know why she should envy *me*. She's so obviously—I should
have thought—what she wants to be.'

'And you're not?' His voice caressed her.

'And I'm not,' answered Minna, candidly. 'But then I don't *know*
what I want to be.'

'You're enchanting,' said Dick, in a whisper.

As if she had not heard—and perhaps indeed she had not heard
—she impulsively added:

'Even about things very close to me.'

'Such as?' For she had stopped, her eyes darkened, and her lips
drooping.

'Well, Mr Firth,' said Minna, after a pause, 'I'm beginning to
think I don't care as much as I ought to do about the Vote. As the
sort of end of existence, I mean. Isn't that terrible! As if a kind
of hedonism——'

'Kept breaking in?' Dick's heart leapt. How sweetly and naïvely
she betrayed herself! 'Perhaps that's because you're beginning to
care more for something . . . for something more personal? I
. . . I wonder if I dare whisper to you that I . . . I'm as wicked
as you are?'

'About the Vote?' She looked straight at him, as if she were
startled.

'I think it's nonsense.'

'Oh!' cried Minna, in horror. She flushed. 'You're a traitor!
Poor Aunt Katherine!'

At once—seeing that she really had been unprepared for his
swiftly-uttered confession—Dick was all fears.

'Sh-sh!' He laid a hand upon her elbow, at once removing it.
'You mustn't betray me. I . . . I thought we were comrades. . . .
I thought I could trust you. If you were to tell your aunt she would
detest me for ever after. She would forbid me the house. I should
never see *you* again.'

'Yes, she'd punish you,' observed Minna, with an air of pleasure.

Dick shivered. Was the sun obscured? Its reflections were still upon the water.

'I should die of chagrin. Oh, dear me, don't misunderstand. I've been a loyal supporter. I . . . I still am.'

'You said it was nonsense.'

'Believing as I do that the Vote is profoundly useless——'

'Oh! Oh! But you were elected by votes, Mr Firth!'

'Then haven't I *reason* to know what nonsense it is? The manipulation, the promises . . . I have a loathing for the chicane of politics. I'm an idealist, Miss Manning. It's the Cause I care for—the Cause of Humanity; not the pencil cross you put for a man you don't know and a policy you don't understand. I want to leave the world a little better than I found it. I want to get rid of politics. I want Justice and Mercy and Love to rule; not Expediency. I want to recover the Garden of Eden!'

'Wouldn't that be a little primitive, Mr Firth?'

'At least, in such a garden, it wouldn't be so difficult to be good,' said Dick, quickly.

She laughed outright at the change from eloquence to policy.

'Do you find it so difficult, Mr Firth?'

She was demure. He thought her a temptress. If they had been alone, Dick would have said in heat, 'With you, impossible.' But they were not alone. Many others, likewise rejoicing in the Spring, were close at hand and observant. Relief was out of the question. He said gravely:

'Only fools find it easy, Miss Manning. Or the dead.' And then, still with purpose: 'I . . . I'm afraid I . . . never have done so.'

They were silent for a moment, he watching her to see the effect of his words, she walking onward, apparently unaware of his scrutiny. Experienced as he was, Dick had been forced to take what he found in his ascending path; and because of the directness which drew him to Minna he could not read her mind. It was too simple. The quivering lashes, the fluctuations of coldness and radiance, the uncontrollable movement of shoulder or hand, the betraying lips which in other women had made easily readable the progress of his siege, were here all absent. She belonged, he told himself, to a naturally virginal order of women. He respected her the more. Yet she had a heart. She was alive. She could be passionate. If she loved him she would in the end, not in simulated capitulation, but by a gesture quite natural to herself, give him the message for which he waited. But not yet. He might have to wait for months. He might fail. No. Not now. At last Minna continued:

'What was that you were saying a little while ago about frustration?'

Dick received a shock. He had spoken of love, rapture, fulfilment. He had spoken to prepare in her mind—as associated with himself—the conception of passionate love. What had she understood? All? Nothing?

'The Movement's full of such women,' he said, eagerly. 'Some of them diverted into it by a noble resolve that others should have a better chance than they. Some merely embittered against a state of things that could allow their potentialities to be wasted. But others, outside the Movement, women for whom a cause of any kind is not a rallying-point but a further irony, women born to go alone through life, keeping up an air of indifference——'

'Mrs Perse?'

Again she made him feel that he had been rhetorical. It was, he knew, a danger. But was her insistence upon Agatha Perse a form of jealousy, akin to his wife's extra sense? Dick's brow wrinkled as his mind, slowed and confused by perplexity, strove to adjust itself. No, no. Minna was smiling broadly, innocently, and looking straight into his face as she would look into the face of a friend. She was blithely teasing. He stammered:

'Well, Mrs Perse . . . Mrs Perse will serve as an instance. Oh, you don't understand her. You think she's hard and self-satisfied.'

'That *wasn't* what I meant.'

His thoughts hastened to Agatha. What had fixed her in this child's thoughts as an antitype? The cosmetics, the cigarette-dried voice, the perhaps too obvious care for an appearance of physical perfection?

'She has the look, I know, of somebody . . .' He hesitated again. Minna took up the definition.

'No, the manner,' she said. 'Of somebody very experienced.'

'Ah, the manner.' He was relieved. 'Yes. But her experience hasn't been what you think. At least . . . She's had a sad story. Let me tell you. I . . . I heard it by accident, long ago.' Was Minna listening? She was intent. 'She married a man who . . . who drank. That was why she told me. You saw today that I'm a water-drinker. Well, he treated her shamefully. Shamefully. In the end she had to leave him. Now he's shut away somewhere—for his own good—has been for years; and she . . . there she is, alone —worse than alone—with the terror, the *terror* that he may be released, that he may at any moment appear, demanding money and a home, that he may live another twenty years and keep her in suspense. What a bitter experience! You may think she's had lovers. It's possible. But if she has, could you blame her? Would you say that an unhappily-married person—man or woman—is never to love again?' His voice trembled. 'That would be hard indeed. I'm sure you're not hard.'

'I hope I'm not hard,' said Minna.

'You couldn't be. I know you couldn't. You're all sweetness. Then consider this poor woman. I think, personally, that her sophistication's a veneer. I think she's unhappy. Pretending to be hard and cold because if she didn't do that she would go to pieces. You see what I mean. The thought that she's carrying it off with an air's her salvation. I think she knows she hasn't been treated fairly by life. That's what I mean by frustrate. Not knowing *happiness*. Not daring to take *risks*. Not living to the fullest *extent*——'

'Who does that?' asked Minna, unexpectedly. But his answer was pat.

'The courageous woman.'

She thought for a moment; then shook her head.

'You're very brave yourself,' he urged. 'Very brave indeed.'

'I'm nothing of the kind. Anybody can look brave when she knows nobody will harm her.'

'When she knows——'

'Who would? I walk a lot about London—everywhere. I know there's a policeman, or respect for order, or real chivalry, down every street.'

'*You* will never be frustrate,' declared Dick. 'You're young; but you're obviously made for a life full of joy. Full of action, and love, and beauty——'

'You're praising me at least twenty years too early, Mr Firth.'

' "And this I cannot praise, I . . ." ' The words of a poem leapt to his lips, and he dared not complete the line. 'May I be there, at the end of twenty years, to remind you of the prophecy, Miss Manning.'

Minna was smiling at him, very kindly, but without the smallest consciousness.

How maddeningly lovely she was! She walked with a grace and ease proper to the frankness he so adored in her. She was tall enough to be his peer, and her fairness had retained in London a fresh beauty rare in the women he knew, who lived upon their nerves and grew haggard in preserving their own secrets. Her short, straight nose and wide brow, the so easily parted lips and clear eyes, were all precious delights to him. She had the expression which comes only to the faces of those who have quick minds and merry hearts. Each instant he loved her more hotly, more ardently; so that it was with difficulty that he prevented himself from trying to touch, to hold, to embrace her. Each instant she tantalised him anew by a thousand sealed promises. Upon this Spring day, under the sun, with the water beside which they walked rippling and glittering almost to their feet, he forgot everything in the world except Minna—his wife, his work, his plans, his ambition. They were afar, negligible, beneath contempt. He remembered only, very breathlessly, in the midst of rapture, that he must not too hastily alarm her into realisation of his ultimate object.

CHAPTER XIV

Hearts Do Not Break

LUNCHEON WAS ALWAYS a dull meal in Kensington. It was the merest pecking at food, with indifferently cold water to drink; and there were never any guests. For one thing, Aunt Katherine was often in a hurry between committees or meetings, and sat at table with her hat on, pushing it awry, as she pushed her hair awry, by resting a forefinger high up on her forehead and slipping.

'You must try and recover your enthusiasm, child,' she said to Minna. 'I've noticed you're very luke warm. Remember, it's on behalf of you and those like you that we are working; for your children and grandchildren——'

'My children and grandchildren,' thought Minna, who had addressed several hundred envelopes that morning because Aunt Katherine regarded this as an economy. 'Doesn't it seem funny to speak of them *en masse*. As if they were sacks of flour!' Aloud, she said: 'I know it must disappoint you.'

'Oh, it doesn't disappoint *me*. I saw at once that you had a shifty eye. Well, what I mean, of course your eye's not at all shifty, dear, or for that matter anything but the eye of a Manning. Eagle-like. But you haven't been properly educated. And the truth is I'm too busy to educate you.'

'You *are* busy, aren't you, auntie.'

'It's something terrible. And Ruth's busy, too.'

'You're both busy; and both very kind. And of course I love helping you.'

'No instinct for the Cause. Governed entirely by personal feeling. That's your mother, of course. Your father had no personal feeling for anybody except himself. Your mother had no intellect.'

312

'A very warm heart,' declared Minna.

'That's just what I say. Heart and intellect are mutually exclusive. I'm all brains. Brains and business. Whether I'm the better off for that I can't tell you; but at least I'm a fighter, and not a slug. Now, Ruth, what about the sixteenth? I'm very anxious that the wives of all the M.P.'s should support us. If they don't——' She ground her teeth.

Ruth smiled coolly, not quite amused, but tolerant.

'Mother, we've got seventeen coming. Several have declined for one reason or another. One's having a baby, but offers to come——'

'Ridiculous creature!' snorted Aunt Katherine. 'As if we wanted such a sight!'

'Offers to come later, when the baby's weaned.'

'Good heavens! Weeks ahead. Probably months. And the woman must be a complete idiot if she thinks we can put off our meeting to suit *her* convenience.'

'I think she meant to show sympathy, mother. Obviously she can't come now. The offer's a sort of gesture.'

'A rude gesture?' Aunt Katherine, who had picked up some notes for a speech, had not perfectly heard Ruth's explanation. She said: 'Maybe. Oh, I'm too busy to argue. These wretched notes of mine are undecipherable. Minna, you write a good round hand; if you really wanted to be useful you could do a lot more secretarial work——'

'Oh, auntie! My envelopes! When you know you prefer to do everything yourself!'

'Well, that's because I know it will be done properly. Or at least, as I like it; which perhaps isn't the same thing. As for your envelopes, two of the last lot came back. Wrongly addressed. Or perhaps the people were dead—I forget. I once had a girl who addressed Lady Skipton as "Mrs Skipton Bart": a perfect chump. I told her so. I had to get rid of her. She grizzled, and said *I* was a *frump*, which I'm not. I suppose just because it rhymed. That cured me.'

'If there's anything I *can* do, auntie——'

'No, child. I don't want unwilling service. Go your pleasure-loving way. It's bad enough to have to beat up the men, half of whom want our support at elections and will sneak out of their bargains on the smallest pretext. I never had much use for men; but for pitiful back-sliding our so-called male supporters take the cake. Abominable! Women are the only honest sex; and *they're* as spiteful as toads as soon as one pushes them out of the limelight.'

Ruth, patiently waiting for Aunt Katherine's breath to fail, continued her record.

'Young Mrs Ferrall is going to America.'

'A milksop. They'll have nothing to do with her. They've got real women of their own.'

'And Mrs Firth won't come, mother. She's curt. She doesn't give a reason.'

'Mrs Firth? Who's she?'

'Mrs Furness——'

'What, the wife of our Galahad? Why won't she come? What's the matter with her? It can't be a baby, because he's much too busy in good works to bother about trifles. I never knew a man so devoted to causes. But perhaps he's a domestic bully. Such things happen—with men. There's a masterful look in his eyes. Gimlets; no, icicles! Don't tell me *she's* a back-slider!'

'I've never seen her, mother; and you know as much about her as I do——'

The voices faded into an alarming greyness. Minna, who had been enjoying the rapid and incalculable movement of her aunt's tongue, sat quite still. A numbness as of paralysis had seized her limbs. His wife. It was all she had understood.

In a moment the blood began to creep back into her cheeks, which grew hotter and hotter until they burned, and then, under the intense effort of self-control, it ebbed. She became very pale. Her knees, hidden beneath the table, trembled violently, and her heart, ice-cold, sank deep in her body. His wife. In that instant of horror she felt that she had died and seen from afar the worthlessness of life and her own doom to a sterile eternity of suffering.

'Nonsense, child! I haven't even seen the woman's letter. Oh, she writes like a cretin! What vulgar notepaper! Here, take it back!'

Engrossed, the two others paid no need to Minna.

II

For those who do not cry out at the approach of pain its blow strikes inward, deeper and deeper, until it reaches the heart. Minna, defenceless, made no sound. She did not even sigh. But she heard no more of the conversation until, it seemed, long afterwards, when gradually, as if she had fainted, there reached through her darkened hearing what were recognisable as familiar discords of controversy, and she returned with shivering reluctance to the common scene. A moment later she moved, and found that her hands hurt very much because they were tightly clasped together, grinding bone against bone. She drew them apart, sitting in her place and strangely smiling. Then, aware that her aunt and cousin were completely absorbed in discussion, she rose with stealth from the table and left them. Her going was unperceived; in this house of preoccupation all her emotions were unperceived; she despairingly knew that she was without friends and frighteningly alone.

It was a relief to be gone from the trouble of those busy tongues; but once in her room after an endless journey up the silent stairs, having closed the door and turned the key in the lock, Minna did not cry. Pain had struck too deep to allow of such release. She stood with her back against the door, her hand still upon the key, her head lowered, her chin resting upon her breast; and a witness without knowledge of what had happened would have supposed her merely deep in perplexing thoughts. Alas, poor child, she had received news to stir the mind to tempest; and immeasurable knowledges and self-knowledges revealed themselves as if by flashes of forked lightning to her tormented understanding.

His wife. His love. Not for herself; for another. And yet, until that hour, she had had no doubt of his true love, or of her own, or of their fortune together. His wife. He had loved before. He loved now. Somewhere in London, at home, perhaps with children, was his wife, who knew his mind and possessed his heart. At this moment they might be together and, if they were together, in accord. That was her understanding of marriage, that it was in truth a

common fulfilment. It was so that she had imagined their life together. Hope died.

How unbelievable, said her heart, that he should ever have looked
and spoken to another woman with just such ardour as of late he
had shown to herself. Their happy meetings. Glance to glance,
recognition for recognition; strange identity of being, pressed home
at every quick turn of circumstance. How glad and proud and certain she had been of his love! It had brought so much joy into
her life that she had felt laughing humility at such exaggeration of
her virtue. At least, she had thought, it is beautiful of him to think
me what I am not! At least, in this miracle, the glory of his love
is made manifest! And now derisive denial had been given to every
fond assumption. Oh, the folly was not to be believed, or the shame.
If she believed it she must die.

Words spoken aforetime in her ear, so meaningly, so caressingly,
swept back into consciousness and rearranged themselves from
chaos into a positive message. Doubt sprang to Minna's mind,
clearer and clearer. How could he so have abused her? It was unjust. It was cruel. Her spirit fainted. But then, how, in the alternative, could he have whispered: 'You must never—never on any
account, whatever the temptation—fall in love with me; for although I seem to woo I may not do so, and my seeming lies wholly
in your foolish imagination'? And yet he had not so whispered; he
had wooed. Consciously? Consciously. Reaching back into limitless
treasure she brought to attention a score of sayings, ambiguous
now, and seen to be of doubtful coin, but at the time of storage
warranted to be the pure gold of communication. You and I, you
and I in common candour, speaking truthfully to one another
because we are in love and because those who are in love exchange
secrets in their idlest talk, was the burden of all these sayings.
Some were from long ago; others, dearer yet, were of later coin-
age. Each had carried the same message, the same assurance. What
had she understood from them? Not, certainly, that he amused
himself by deceiving a foolish girl, so mad with vanity that she
imagined a suitor in every cavalier, or so gullible that she read a
profession of love into every compliment.

This was the second time. First William; now . . . She shuddered.

Then: there had been no crime, no lie. None at all. 'Would you say that an unhappily-married person—man or woman—has no right to love again?' 'He *does* love me! He *does!* He does!' The echoes of her cry went rolling through shame, dispersing it and bringing pride again to her aid. Had she not every testimony but open confession that it was so? But how did that translate this horror into joy? Suppose he loved her; suppose he had wooed in spite of every caution, every constraint; suppose his marriage a misery. What then?

His career. Did not that, to a man bent upon the heights—and such heights—mean all? She groped among flashing threats, and was bewildered.

It was the end. Clearly, it was the end. She had received a mortal wound; and the blame lay with herself alone. Dick must be absolved. He was at once absolved. He had said, he had done—nothing. She had imagined. That was the answer, the truth. Never! Whatever had been done had been done deliberately. He had a man's mind; the baffling mind of a man! He had loved her and he had shown his love. With what object? What had he planned? 'Oh, God! Oh, God! I shall go mad!'

She was alone. She was in love. For the second time. The other had been the love of a child; this was the love of a woman. She could feel, and could fiercely welcome, his passionate desire for her, his hands upon hers, his lips upon her lips, his body against her body. Oh, God! If she were never to know his love! If he should go from her in silence!

Stumbling forward to the bed, she flung herself down beside it and threw her arms forward upon the coverlet. Her body was shaken with sobs so anguished that in terror lest they should be heard below she was forced to stifle them at last by dragging at the coverlet and pressing it with convulsive hands suffocatingly to her mouth.

More than two hours afterwards, Minna crept again down the
stale mustard-coloured and thickly carpeted stairs to the ground
floor. She had lain in stupor after the sobs had ceased; and on
recovering awareness of her surroundings and the inescapable con-
tacts of the evening she had started to her feet in a fright. Nobody
must know of her pain. Tonight—— He might be at the house!
Hastily she bathed her face and resolved that she would go out of
doors. There she could breathe; the fresh air would do her good;
perhaps nobody would see her; she could think, plan, resolve.
That was why, with light steps and without noise, she fled down
the stairs. Nobody was there. She had escaped! No! For as she
reached the ground floor she heard Ruth, whose eye must have
been caught by a passing shadow upon the yellow wall of the staircase, summoning her to the little parlour at the back of the house.

This room, fortunately, she felt, was ill-lighted (it was because
of that fact and the existence at the turn of the stairs of a frosted
window with red and blue side-panes that Minna's shadow had
been visible); and Ruth was standing by the empty fireplace with
a small crystal-glass bottle in her hands.

'D'you think you can open this for me?' asked Ruth, thrusting
the bottle forward. She was in a new dress of old gold, and as her
hair had been carefully done she looked unusually smart. 'Your
fingers are stronger than mine.'

It was untrue. Ruth had very strong fingers; but they were already aching, and as defeat was unpalatable to her she wished
some other person to experience similar discomfort. Minna, knowing hopelessly that her fingers would be soft and unsteady, took
the fragile bottle and tried to loosen its stopper. In vain.

'A bother, isn't it!' exclaimed Ruth, with raised, impatient hands
watching her cousin's effort. 'Aach!' It was an irritated cry. 'The
thing's bewitched!'

Again Minna struggled with the tiny, obstinate stopper. And as,
trembling, she strained to move it, the whole bottle flew from her

fingers, struck the sharp corner of the fender, and broke, scattering its contents over Ruth's ankles, shoes, and the lower part of her new dress, where they made dark dreadful spreading stains. At once the room was filled with a strong perfume of violets, for the bottle had contained scent; and both girls were momentarily choked by its pungency.

'Oh, your dress!' Minna was horrified.

'Dear me! How clumsy you are!' cried Ruth, impetuously. Her tongue clucked. 'I couldn't have done worse myself!'

The humiliation of this accident and Ruth's cry of impatience were more than Minna could endure that day. Overcome with distress, she began speechlessly to cry, her face puckered and the big tears standing upon her cheeks before they tumbled.

Ruth, who had also received a shock, and who nervously detested an open display of weakness, stared in astonishment.

'Good heavens!' she exclaimed, in her crisp way. 'Fancy crying about a thing like that! Minna! Dear me, my shoes! However, it can't be helped. I don't expect they'll suffer really. Come, Minna, don't be an idiot. What on earth's the matter with you?'

How could Minna tell her? How could she speak, or even think, the words: 'I'm broken-hearted. I don't know what I'm saying or doing'?

'It's only that I'm a complete idiot. It's awful!' She stamped her foot, still crying. 'It's *awful!*'

'Well, I know. But crying's no good. If it had been *I* who'd done it——'

'But you *wouldn't* have done it!' protested Minna, in the loud voice of a weeping, agonised child. 'Don't you see! You *couldn't.*'

Ruth shrugged. Her expression was cool and puzzled. So was her voice. She had a curiously scholastic air.

'There's no need to get into a state. Aren't you well? You look rather suspicious. Perhaps you're run down.' Her voice quickened and roughened. 'It's not the amount of *work* you've been doing.'

Weary though she was, Minna's heart jumped; and with her heart jumped a thought: Ruth disliked and despised her. The certainty of another failure was overwhelming. What misery! What a day of fate and humiliation! Drearily she groaned:

'I'm sorry, Ruth. I think I must be the stupidest person alive.'

Ruth answered:

'Not at all. At least, you needn't be. It's really only rather inconsiderate of you. Not blameworthy. One can't help one's nature. Though I must admit I don't understand it. When you can see how much mother and I have to do.'

Yes, Minna could see that. She had long seen it.

'But then you're so awfully self-sufficient.'

Ruth uttered a brisk sound that was meant for laughter.

'Self-sufficient! On the contrary, we're only too anxious for your help.' As an afterthought, following a keen glance, she added in a much more gentle tone: 'I think you must know that. And for your happiness, too. That above everything.'

Minna said subduedly:

'I know it. I'm sure of it.' But there forced themselves from her lips other words which confessed the pain in her heart. 'And yet I can't *feel* it.'

'Minna!' cried Ruth, severely. 'That's ungrateful!'

'It's not meant so.'

'But still!' She began to look more and more sharply at Minna. More and more like a headmistress reasoning with an obstinately backward child. 'You've got some ridiculous idea in your head. Surely you're happy here? Aren't you? I mean, you seem so. I know I'm busy, and sometimes impatient. But we've given you interests, new friends. What more do you want?' There was no answer. For a moment Minna could not speak. 'You've been crying, haven't you? Before this. Not just now. I remember you were quiet at lunch. Mother spoke a little frankly. But that's her way. She's thoughtless. She didn't mean, of course, to be unkind.'

Mother! Minna would have given the world to be able to seek her own mother's arms. But her mother was dead. This questioning and analysis was like an icy wind to her loving heart.

'Oh, no, no!' she protested, shivering. 'You're both very, very kind.'

'I hope so. No, it's yourself. Something in yourself.'

'Yes.' Minna nodded gravely.

'What you need is the determination to pull yourself together.'

'I do indeed,' said Minna, immediately impressed by a truth which she could grasp.

Ruth improved upon her success. She pursued:

'I wonder you don't take up a course of reading, Minna. Solid reading.'

'I?' stammered Minna, as one in a dream. 'Is that what *you* do when you're unhappy?'

'John Stuart Mill, or somebody. You need to *train* your mind, you know. Not just let it stray. It's the absence of training that makes you so wayward and unbalanced——'

'Unbalanced?' exclaimed Minna, as if she had been struck a blow. 'Ruth!' For a moment she could say no more. Then, in anger, she cried: 'Oh, but John Stuart Mill—no! I don't want to be like him——'

Ruth in turn became imperious.

'Why not, pray?'

'He's so dull. So priggish.'

'Nonsense! That shows your ignorance. It's idiotic to be so complacent. But if Mill's too abstruse for you, you could read somebody else good. I meant as a discipline. Something that will fit you to re-shape the world. Women have a great part to play in the future. When we sit in Parliament we shall have enormous influence on social legislation; and——'

Minna despairingly interrupted.

'But Ruth, dear! I don't propose to sit in Parliament. I'm not interested in re-shaping the world. I should think it impertinence.'

Ruth ejaculated something.

'Impertinence! Really, Minna!'

But Minna was not to be checked.

'You say I'm ignorant. I know it. I don't pretend otherwise. But can't you see that not all women want to boss the world? I don't want to. I only want . . .' She faltered. The ridiculous tears had sprung again to her eyes. 'I only want to make others—my immediate beloveds—happy, in a home—quiet, good. . . . It's such a simple thing. It's useful. And yet . . . and yet, oh, dear me! I'll never be able to do it as long as I live. I'm in despair. I know I'm all faults. I know *you* just despise me. But Ruth! we can't be all alike. And

if . . . if you lecture me any more I'm afraid I shall scream——'
She stopped. She was at the verge of hysteria.

Ruth's head had been flung up during this speech. Her cheeks
had mantled. Her manner was at once indignant and accusing.

'Yes,' she cried quickly, vehemently, in a voice that trembled with
suppressed excitement. 'Yes, you're a traitor. I know that. I've long
known it. You would betray your own sex with a very easy conscience. I've seen you ridiculing me to stupid, ignorant men, getting into corners with them and laughing at me——'

'Never!' cried Minna, astounded. 'Never once!'

The denial was brushed aside.

'But you're making a mistake. You're falling into their ways,
fawning on them, trying to be as *they* wish you to be. I've seen that.
Your dress, your manner, your attitude. You don't see how humiliating it is. You don't realise how, though they laugh and flatter,
they despise you. You're not fastidious. You belong to the prostitute
type. For you, sex is everything. Instead of fighting to save women
from being in eternal subjection to men you're perpetuating our
servitude and making it more and more difficult for us to get our
rights. You're a *real* traitor; one who lives at the heart of the Movement—very near the heart—and is all the time treacherous to it,
seeking to destroy it, ridiculing it, betraying it——'

She stopped as suddenly as she had begun. Minna, stupefied,
caught at the back of a chair, stared hollow-eyed at her accuser,
and wonderingly repeated the only two words she had understood,
the charge against her:

'Prostitute. Sex. Ruth!'

They stood looking at one another, both apparently frozen, but
both hot and terribly excited at the unexpected conflict between
them. For Minna, the words used by her cousin would have been
horrible if they had been applied to another woman: in relation to
herself they were at first so abominable that she thought Ruth must
have gone mad. But in the silence succeeding her cry of protest
there followed a blow greater than any coming from outside—the
blow of self-suspicion. What if that charge were true? The thought
was like a thunderclap.

At last, by a great effort, Ruth recovered something like normal

composure, and stirred, breathing quickly. With the blood, however, still bright in her cheeks, and her eyes hard and minatory,
she said:

'I'm sorry, Minna. I oughtn't to have said that. It was rhetorical
and absurd. It was unpardonable.'

But Minna answered in a low voice:

'It was something you'd really felt about me.'

'No!' cried Ruth. 'I didn't really feel it. I was angry.'

'Yes, you were angry. You're still angry. But that's when truth
comes out. Behind everything else—the kindness and the con-
descension—you've thought that. You think it still.'

Ruth fretted with denial.

'I lost my temper. I'm on edge. I assure you I don't think it.' She
took a step forward, her hand entreatingly outstretched. Minna
could see the ugly flush in her cheeks, and the parting of her thin
lips, which showed two large eye-teeth. 'Please forgive me for saying such a thing. If you knew everything——'

Contrite words. But Minna heard them unconvinced. She was
still stabbing herself with suspicion. She had hoped to be wife,
mother, *châtelaine:* had she only dressed a steamy voluptuousness
in the innocence of a household pinafore? She said brusquely:

'Oh, of course I forgive you. But *why* do you think sex is everything to me? *Why* do you think I belong to the prostitute type?
I want to know that. It's very important, you see, to me.'

Ruth blanched. When they were bitterly spoken by another she
could not stomach her own words.

'Minna, please!' she began. And, at a shaken head: 'Oh, you're
merciless. As hard as stone.'

'But I *want* to *know!*' cried Minna, in a hysterical voice. 'There
must be some foundation, or you wouldn't think it. Can't you
understand? You don't think it of other women. Why of me?'

'Hush, Minna! Somebody will hear you. You're hysterical. I was
excited——'

Excited! Ruth excited! But why? What sudden hatred had
moved her to make this charge? Was it jealousy? Some vileness
behind that chilly mask of virtue?

'You won't tell me,' Minna said, more quietly. 'Perhaps you can't.

I understand that. Very well. It may be true. I can't say. I hope it's not. I hope it's something you've distorted from dislike of me. But if it is, it's so horrible that you ought to *pity*——'

It was Ruth who screamed: a hard, choking sound as dry as a cough.

'Minna, I don't dislike you. I love you. You *must* believe that. You *must*. I can only tell you—no, I can't even do that. I'm bitterly ashamed of myself.' She spoke desperately, an old maid in a fluster. All composure was stripped from her. The colour in her cheeks had grown patchy, and her mouth, spoiled by public speaking, gaped loose as if all muscular control had lapsed.

Minna, shuddering, stepped backwards, away from her cousin; and in doing this she trod upon a fragment of the broken bottle. It split beneath her heel. The perfume seemed at that instant to rise more strongly than ever to her nostrils. Struck by a sudden, inescapable thought, she looked from the broken bottle to Ruth.

'Ah!' she exclaimed, breathlessly and with deep reflectiveness. 'I *wonder!* I *wonder* if sex is as little to you as you pretend!'

Ruth did not answer. She disdained to answer. She stood as she had done earlier, with her head thrown back and her eyes dark with impenetrable hardness. No longer did her mouth gape. And Minna, turning abruptly lest her over-charged feelings should again betray her into the terrible sobbing of the afternoon, ran quickly out of the room. She did not know where to go, once she was in the hall; but as she had all this time been dressed for walking, and as she caught sight of herself now in a mirror, wearing hat and coat, she turned mechanically to the right, going out of the house and slamming the front door impetuously behind her.

IV

Once in the street she strode with rapid steps in she knew not what direction. She saw before her only the alternate blaze and darkness of enlightenment and disgust. Faces meant nothing, voices meant nothing. With her head in the air and her eyes starry with anger, she hastened as one possessed. Useless, unbalanced, a prostitute: if that were the opinion others held, what wonder that Dick had scornfully and safely and cynically wooed her! She was distraught.

What was she to do? High-spirited, modest, and innocent, she had suffered more intensely than she knew from William's old indifference to her. It had undermined self-confidence. She had suffered from the repressive humour of her father and from solitude at Royals during the last two or three years of her mother's life, when her school friends had separated and William had been in London. She had suffered deeply, but unawares, from the dismissal of William by her aunt and from her own unimportance in Aunt Katherine's home. And from immersion in a cause which none of her early training had taught her to value. And now, as blitheness returned and the younger men of her aunt's gatherings found her amusing and charming, she had flowered into radiance and fallen headlong into love. If that love were to be disappointed, what was left to her?

Long afterwards, having walked until she was tired, and having without intent to do so crossed the Thames by Hammersmith Bridge and followed the broad road from its further end, she found herself upon an open space which proved to be Barnes Common. Here, first conscious of her escape, she saw the last fire of the sun and felt the rising breeze of early Autumn and was transported by a sense of liberty. She sat down upon a seat, watching some ragamuffin children who ran to and fro upon the grass, and a poor woman in black who seemed to be with the children, and the passing omnibuses and carts and carriages upon the polished wheels of which the sunshine made a perpetual flutter of brilliance.

She sat for what seemed a long time, until her thoughts had all fallen asleep and left her to the sequel of what was very nearly apathy. It was seven o'clock before she looked at her watch and struggled unwillingly to her feet. How they dragged! She did not want to go back to her aunt's house. She had quarrelled bitterly with Ruth. She had never quarrelled with anybody before: it was a horrible sensation. She would not know how to meet Ruth again. She wished she had not said that to Ruth: she had been angry; and now she was ashamed. If she had not said that, she would have minded less. But if she did not return to Aunt Katherine's, where could she go? She was friendless and without refuge. Her feet were like lead. But they were not more leaden than her heart.

Slowly, step by step, she paid for the impulsive energy of her outward flight. The houses grew darker in the extending shadows, and the heat of the pavement died. Tired to exhaustion, she re-crossed the river, which was beginning to run like quicksilver where the reflections ended and the water was no longer coloured by the sun. A few people had gathered to watch small boats which had appeared in the late afternoon. They stood in little black knots, with their shadows behind them, quite absorbed in what they saw; and Minna, appreciating their intentness and the beauty of the knots and shadows, was stirred to a fleeting smile.

'They're onlookers,' she thought, quickly. 'It's not bad. They'd think nothing of me.'

v

Only when she saw Hallows's face did Minna remember that her aunt had a party that night. He was very excited, and his tomato-red cheeks were redder than usual and his hands, which shook a great deal when he had to serve a number of guests, were already quivering. His watery eyes watered; his flabby lips yawned open. 'It's all right, Hallows!' feebly murmured Minna, pushing past him as he stepped back from the front door. 'I'd forgotten.' He still remembered his duty: 'Sh-shall I send Doris, miss? She's in the dining-room.' Minna shouted 'No, thanks,' over her shoulder; and ran upstairs as if she were not at all weary. Thoughts were erased by the need for rapid action.

But time passed. She was late. She could hear nothing in her room, which was upon the second floor; but she knew that the visitors must have arrived as she dressed. Her fingers became stupid; and although, after a very hot bath, she felt less bruised and listless than before, she was still, when it came to the brushing and coiling of her hair, unable for any length of time to keep her arms raised. Listening, guessing, with hairpins between her teeth, she glanced again and again at the mantelpiece clock which she could not see. The meal must be served; it must have begun! Still she was not ready. . . .

At last she slipped into the dining-room, and at her entrance the solid noise of talk was like an explosion. She heard, as yet, no separate words. Yes, there they were, the old familiars: 'Lloyd George', 'Mrs Pankhurst', 'the Lords', spoken from the other end of the table by her aunt or some other; nearer at hand, where voices were less shrill and the talk was less fanatic, she caught no distinguished names but only the dropped tones of confidential communication. Even Ruth, conversing with Mr Isaacs, a middle-aged banker, seemed subdued.

But what a large party! Counting herself as one of them, there were eight people down each side of the table; and as the lighting was by means of heavily shaded candles which illumined hands and silver and the little dishes of almonds and sweetmeats scattered upon the cloth she was unobserved to the last. She could see the backs of those nearest, and Aunt Katherine at the head, her hand fumbling in her frizzy hair, her mouth open as she screeched about 'this man Asquith . . . Meeting . . . and the Lords,' and told how she had said to somebody: 'Why, you don't understand your own stupid policy!' and to somebody else: 'Political leaders are always quite five years behind the rank and file!' It was what she always said. She repeated her own effective retorts until they were flabby. And the men upon either side of her listened as ever with respect, rather solemnly, but with occasional bays of agreement. . . . Poor woodenheads!

Aunt Katherine, engrossed in her own perpetual tirade, did not see Minna. Ruth, at this end of the table, felt her presence, gave one glance, and with the appearance of being unmoved continued to listen to her tonsured neighbour, presumably talking of deposits and credits and the financial genius of the Rothschilds. Hallows and the maids were at the sideboard, and Hallows moved forward to lift Minna's chair. And in a flash she was in her place, so swiftly and quietly that only the two between whom she was to sit knew that she had arrived. Though still blinded and deafened as a

stranger coming into established company must be, she knew that
one of her neighbours was Bernard Mather; the other—her heart
stood still—was Dick.

First, the shock of nearness to him was like a streak of lightning.
She must keep all her secrets. Then a thought almost equally quick
discovered that her situation at table, between two known friends,
one of them obviously the partner in supposed traitorous ridicule,
had been Ruth's *amende*. The third thought, which lagged, was of
the kindness of both men, who drew no attention to her, but whispered brief greeting, smiled, and at once behaved as if she had been
all the time in her place. Normally she would have taken this for
granted; tonight she was more sensitive. Nobody could have seen,
unless it were Mather, that she drew herself a little away from
Dick. Nobody, although in her throat a nerve fluttered, could have
heard how quickly her heart was beating. How still she must sit
during this ordeal!

Bernard Mather, shortly afterwards freed by his other neighbour
(while Dick was held by the hostess, in deep red that clashed with
the flush in her cheeks), said in a low tone:

'I was afraid you were ill. I looked for you frantically before
dinner. The sands are running out.'

'*I* was out, *too*. But what sands do you mean?' asked Minna, in
the same tone.

'I daren't tell you, in case I'm overheard. I had such short notice
of this party. An hour. Does that suggest anything? I remark,
however, that I shall fight for you to the bitter cognac.'

An hour: the implication was clear. But she shook her head.

'Fight with whom? You're very cryptic.'

'My rival at your other side.'

Minna felt her shoulders grow rigid as she struggled to remain
apparently detached. She said:

'You must excuse me if I seem to gobble my dinner. I'm famished.'

'As you gobble, do you think I can safely tell you what I think
of my rival?'

Again the shaken head. This time very quick and decided.

'No.'

'Does that mean you don't want to hear? Or has he ears at all angles, like a wall?'

'It would be very bad manners.'

'How prudish! As if those would stand in my way.'

'And dangerous, too. I'm certain it's nothing good.'

'It's appalling. I've learnt a lot. If I were to tell you half, you'd ask me to change places with you.' He glanced aside at the woman upon his right, whose horse-face was filled with conversational concern at something she was hearing from another. 'Worse than I thought.'

'I don't believe it.' Minna's eyes sparkled.

'I was afraid of that.' For an instant she saw the little rosy-gilled face stiffen, and the mischief die from Mather's funny little lips, which were as quick and clean as the edges of a buttonhole or the lids of an eye. 'You won't let me warn you. I wish you would.'

Warn? He was grave. Minna's heartbeat was faster yet.

'I'm so tired of lectures,' she murmured. 'I improve as fast as I can.'

'Poor child! Are they so many? But this one's different. It's a mother's cry to her whelp.'

'I think you're the boy who says "wolf",' she answered. 'It's a bad habit.'

'No. You're quite wrong. I wouldn't put out a hand to save most people from going into the lion's jaws. But a friend's a different matter.'

'I'm glad to have a friend,' said Minna. She smiled, a little tremulously; and although she could not know how dark and sad her glance at him had been she could not miss the emotion that leapt to his eyes.

'To the death——' he gallantly began. But at that instant another voice, in her other ear, destroyed the happiness of the exchange. She did not realise how quickly she turned, or with what apprehensiveness. Mather did. The other voice, soft and lingering, said:

'I . . . I *hoped* you'd be here tonight. But when this place was left empty I . . . I thought you must be away. Have you been away? And are you well? You look wonderful.' She saw Dick swiftly run his eyes round the other faces at the table before bringing them back in delight to herself; and as she answered him she, too, embraced the other diners. He was right: they did not look well. Their mouths were all open: one surprised them in inelegance, and Ruth, at the foot of the table, looking haggard and colourless, was a death's head. Minna realised with compunction, from that single glance, which destroyed every trace of anger, how much Ruth, as well as herself, had suffered this day. Poor woman! Already their relationship had changed again, so that it was Minna who soared high into pity. Dick continued: 'I . . . I've been away, in my constituency. Working very hard. I only came back this evening, bent on being here. . . .'

'Then we're lucky to get you,' said Minna, conventional, as most people are, less from native stupidity than from politeness and because if they spoke out what is in their hearts it would stop every dinner-party in Kensington and elsewhere. 'Were you there long?'

'A week too long. A week. Opening bazaars. Working Men's Clubs. No intoxicants, of course. Darts and draughts. I send them some books from the office. And I've been seeing the men who run the local committees. One tests opinion that way, you know.'

She was watching his lips with a kind of fixity. Did they lie? That they could lie easily and suavely to Aunt Katherine she knew. She did not like that. She hated it. Oh, she did not understand him at all. He was a stranger. When emotion ebbed, or when it lived on in one or other only, men and women were all strangers. Sometimes enemies. It was different when hearts were warmed and tender, drunk with the same nectar. Then, for a time, strangers kissed. But only for a time. It was thus with Dick and herself, who because they were lost among other people, and because of this terrible new barrier between them, were as cold as fish. At this moment they were complete strangers.

'And do you think of something new to say each time you open a bazaar?' she asked, as if she were indeed a stranger. Dick's lashes quivered as he smiled.

'D'you know, I . . . I'm afraid I do,' he answered, confidentially. 'It's my—you've noticed it for yourself—you've more than once checked me, or it, in full flight—my tendency to be eloquent on small provocation. . . .' He was smiling more deeply. 'Don't you recognise it? . . . Minna? . . . I think you do. That . . . that bad habit of mine. Do you?'

Minna felt that as she watched his lips her blood quickened and her heart grew larger and larger. But he, too, was watching; and his eyes, bent in turn upon Minna's lips, had a purpose no less anxious than her own.

'Have I checked you?' she said, breathlessly.

'Enchantingly,' he answered. His smiling eyes were giving themselves to her in full confidence. The eyes of a lover. As they had been. As she had pictured them to herself that afternoon. A lover! His voice again caressed her. 'Nobody else has ever checked me as charmingly—or as firmly—as you do. Whenever I feel myself rising to rhetoric——'

Rhetoric! That was the word used by Ruth not three hours before. After she had charged Minna with being so horrible that in the act of remembering the word Minna grew hot. Rhetoric! It was her enemy.

'You think of me.' She completed his sentence as he had wished, smiling proudly back, steel unconsciously mingled with her tenderness. 'It's often done.'

Dick's brows jumped, and remained aloft.

'Oh, I do that *much* more often. The rhetoric's only an occasional lapse, I hope. I . . . I don't know why one should ever be rhetorical; and yet in its proper place, on a platform, it's what few modern speakers allow themselves. You're perfectly right, of course, to loathe it when it interrupts a conversation. But you don't need to be told that, I'm sure.'

'Does your wife go with you on these trips?' asked Minna, inwardly trembling. She thought he started. He certainly looked, steel for steel, into her smiling eyes. What a change of manner!

'Good heavens, no!' he muttered, shortly. 'She stays at home. Always has done.'

'You'll get into trouble with Aunt Katherine if you speak as if she were in place there,' said Minna. 'Because you know Aunt Katherine doesn't think women's place is the home.'

He had recovered.

'I . . . I can't answer that. I . . . I'm sitting next to her.' He gave a slight grimace. 'One's tongue-tied, to say the least of it.' Then, to Minna's astonishment, he brought his face boldly close to hers and said in a very low voice: 'I should like you to meet my wife. Then you'd understand.'

Minna felt as though she were suffocating. She bent her head. She tried with all her might to restrain the question which he was inviting her to put. Forcing her to put.

'I should be very interested,' she answered, with difficulty.

'She would like you very much.'

'I should probably like *her* very much.'

'That's as may be. At least you'd understand how little she means to me.'

Hardly audibly, Minna whispered:

'I should be sorry to do that.'

He was looking at her, she knew, closely, closely and mercilessly; and the blood was rising fast until she thought she could feel it suffusing her cheeks and even her shoulders. . . .

'Mr Firth!' cried Aunt Katherine, in her snapping voice. 'I know you're not in favour of the Militants. Nor am I. I detest them; they take no notice of me. But nobody can deny——'

Minna leaned back in her chair as he turned reluctantly away. She was trembling. She did not know that having slightly flushed, she had grown pale. She knew only that she had become sightless, that she must at all costs keep very still and not speak again or let Dick speak again of his wife, and that she was in deadly danger of open betrayal to Dick's contempt, if indeed his last speeches, insolent as they might be under their entreaty, had not shown that the betrayal had been made. Fatal folly! Why had she—except through irresistible folly—challenged him?

'Has he?' asked a gnat-like voice in Minna's other ear.

'Please don't,' she implored, in a whisper. She did not look up, but stirred for safety towards her friend. 'Don't torment me.'

'Never, except for your pleasure. But what shall I speak of?'

'I can't suggest anything. But please *speak!*'

'Has he told you about his wife?' asked Mather, with a malicious glance. 'Or shall I——'

Minna's courage returned in time to steel her nerves against this fresh assault.

'I expect he would like *you* to do that,' she answered, with spirit. 'And *you* would *certainly* like to do it, wouldn't you! But you're playing with fire, you know. You'd far better tell me something about yourself.'

'Oho!' Mather was taken aback. His mouth, like Gibbon's, was a small round hole in the centre of his face. His tongue was as quick as an ant-eater's, and his eyes were as black as those of a pink shrimp. But he was all good-nature. 'Would you really like it? Nothing, I need hardly say, could be more congenial to me. I was born of rich but honest parents—but I fear it's a long story to tell between the meat and the savoury. It would need a lifetime.'

'That's longer than I can spare,' said Minna. She did not know how she kept her teeth from chattering.

'I was afraid you'd insist on abridgement. Elegant extracts. Let me see. A moment ago I was trying to be topical.'

'I thought, slanderous.'

'Oh, well, what's said in one ear has certain privileges. It goes out at the other. And what I wanted to tell you is really much more scandalous and pathological than anything in *my* life. Practically, that's been free from scandal.'

'But then it's been free from temptation. It's been a private life.'

'You taunt me——' began Mather.

As he would have proceeded, however, Minna sharply drew her breath; for a hand had touched her other bare elbow—a hand cool, steady, and fleeting, like that of a nurse.

'What . . . what were we speaking about?' asked Dick, from her left side, in his soft voice, which was like the murmur of doves. Ah, he lied! She knew him guilty of every treachery. She despised him. The echo of what they had been speaking about must still be in his head. It was of her life, and his life; the impudent pretence that he had forgotten was as offensive to her understanding as it was cruel to her love. He too well knew his power.

'It was something . . . of no importance to you, I think,' answered Minna. She could not meet his piercing glance. She could not move. She was paralysed, but with a burning heart. By a desperate effort she tried to break the spell he was weaving about her. She said, in a clear voice which others could overhear: 'However, let's forget it. I'm very curious to know what you say to your committee when they object to a vote you've given in the House.'

'Bravo!' whispered Mather, in her other ear. 'A good gambit. His votes are a disgrace.'

Dick gave no sign of trouble or amusement. He remained suavely as before.

'Well,' he murmured; and then observed the evident attention of those across the table. With one quick glance at Minna, which might have been of reproach or admiration, he threw himself to the greedy listeners who thanked God for a diversion from their own conversational darning. He changed the pitch of his voice from what was confidential to what was coolly contemptuous. 'Well, I . . . I say something like this: You, gentlemen, from this favoured, almost Olympian distance, naturally can see only too clearly, and at once, frailties in the government which we, confused by our nearer view of difficulties——' But Aunt Katherine interrupted.

'Mr Firth,' she said, peremptorily, for the whole table to hear. 'Listen!' She was not going to let such a chit as Minna direct the conversation. And she was not interested in whatever excuses he might give to a committee of men. 'That's all very well for a committee. Committees are the time-servers of privilege. I have trouble enough, myself, with such dunderheads. But we're *not* a committee. And I think it's very ridiculous that your wife won't sit on our platform. Processions I can excuse. Some people can't walk; they have weak legs. And our skirts are a nuisance, collecting dust and dirt and tram-tickets, and so on. But a platform's different. Every woman with a brain in her head ought to sit on it——'

Minna leaned back in her chair again, half-listening, half in reverie. The particular had become the general. Rhetoric had supervened. For that time she was saved.

CHAPTER XV

A Tide in the Affairs of Women

FOR THAT TIME; but not for long. There was now no escape. She had taken care to be alone with him no more on that night at her aunt's house or for several days afterwards. Because he then gave her no peace, but appeared wherever she went, increasingly importunate, she next asked an old school friend with a house in Devonshire to support her awhile in the country. It had been a failure. Immured for a week with a strange countrified woman absorbed in a tweedy husband and two children, she had realised what a thin link old fellowship had been; and as her heartache proved unendurable she had answered his long letter. Pretences were down; he was full of protestation. Within a fortnight Minna was back in London: there, in the roar of those Suffragette days, when the House of Commons was raided by women and her world was in ferment, she was at his mercy.

Now, after three weeks more of pursuit and agony, with November darkening into December, she had been able to fight no longer. It was evening, and everything out of doors upon a windy, rainy day was black as night. She sat alone, furred and shrinking, in a railway carriage at Paddington. Some luggage was in the rack above her head, and she could hear and see porters trundling their barrows forward along the platform, and the echoing misty roof of the station, and a group of people at the lighted bookstall. But nothing more. Something was happening to her, she knew; something from which there was no escape; but its direction was wholly in Dick's hands and she seemed to be without will of her own. She had no thoughts; only the groping obedience of an hypnotic.

That Dick was near, she was assured. That was all. A quarter of an hour earlier she had chosen journals almost at random from a newsboy with a wicker tray, and these remained, unread, in her listless hands. They would serve, perhaps, in emergency to conceal her face from anybody inquisitive enough to peer in at the window. And at last, because she remembered that Dick had spoken of it as his property, and newly a great success, she raised one of these journals, which bore in bold capitals across its cover the name 'England', and held it before her eyes. But not to read. She only recalled Dick's pride in the paper's progress, and felt that as she was now to be his for ever she must take interest in everything of concern to him. Everything. Did young wives feel as much discomfort as she? They could not do so: for them the unknown future was unclouded. Minna shivered. She pulled the window up, and was safe in the warm carriage.

Phrases turned themselves slowly over in her head, echoes of former thoughts. They were heavy with a kind of stupidity. Waiting for the divorce . . . for months . . . seeing nobody except Dick . . . That she understood, and did not dread. How much easier everything would be, Dick said, when all was over and they were married, after months of delay. People, he had told her, soon forgot. No, they didn't forget; they pretended to forget. There was polish in their greetings; but contempt lurked, a vile respectable distaste for anything that had once been queer, unctuous relish of another's soiled virtue. . . . It wasn't going to be pleasant, Dick said. Did he know it better than she? And yet, once their love had been granted and his insistence upon a clear issue justified, what alternative was there? Her scruples, he swore, were Victorian. Was she prepared to be governed by fear? No, no; she had not heard all the talk of women's rights for nothing. It would be disagreeable for him, he said; but for her as well, hidden quietly away . . . 'What's become of Waring?' Raised eyebrows, shrugs, little laughs . . . Soon they would not ask. His wife would be her enemy. *She* would not spare her. And yet, for all that, it was Dick's wife who was to be pitied: she must once have loved him, and she was losing all.

Minna let the paper drop, and stared sightlessly out of the window at moving figures on the platform. Oh, God, the suspense!

If ten minutes were a martyrdom, what of the months ahead? It would not be long before the train started. Then Dick might— or might not—join her. He liked to do whatever was unexpected, mysterious. In that, she told herself, he was a boy—it was a part of his charm—although sometimes he was not a boy but somebody old and frighteningly *rusé,* and sometimes, however gentle, so urgently amorous that she had no defence against him but that of obvious distaste. Would distaste avail her now? How much of it, if Ruth were right, was a sham? What would happen to them both? He spoke of having to resign his seat in Parliament, and of a bad advertisement and difficult times; but always, in the end, smilingly, when her anxiety had become intense, of the world well lost and of their happy future. The months would be blotted out; and the past. She believed that was his sincere opinion. He loved her. And memory was short, he said. Was it so short?

'I'm rambling!' cried Minna, sitting bolt upright. She was angry with herself, and threw the papers impatiently on to the seat opposite. Wretched things! It was their weight that depressed her. Let them go. At all costs, having given her word, she must not break it through misgiving. She looked with determination out of the carriage window, trying to concentrate only upon the moment. People were moving quickly now. Those who wished to ride in the front of the train were hurrying. They were people of all sorts, men in great overcoats, men in top hats, one man in week-end tweeds; but all were men. They made Minna feel lonely.

Suddenly she shrank back into the corner of the carriage, turning her face right away from the window as she might have done to avoid a blow. A man had passed. He was not walking fast, but slowly, and with his head a little lowered in thought, so that a single glance had given the clear picture of a face and character. A round, fresh-coloured, thoughtful face, half-smiling; a character better known to her than any other. William! An extraordinary shock ran through Minna's body. It was like nothing she had ever experienced before, and was as if she had fallen from a great height into icy water. She whipped off her gloves and pressed cold hands to her burning cheeks. William! Years were obliterated. She was a child again.

She stood up. The train began to glide from the platform; and as it did so she pulled the window down, to assure herself that after all he was not still on the platform. No. He must be somewhere in the train, which he had caught in spite of that unhurried step. He had not seen her. He never saw anything. The idiot! William! It was just like him. He saw things with his mind; not with his eyes. What would he think of her? If they could have spoken! No, no, no; thank God he had been blind!

Greatly agitated, she shut the window again, fell back into her seat, resumed her gloves, and tried to see the world outside. Since it was represented by nothing but blackness speckled with small, disembodied lights she saw only her own face colourlessly reflected in the glass and was appalled by its expression of misery. The corners of her lips were turned down and the lips themselves looked swollen; her eyes stared tragically from dark hollows beneath a shadowed brow; her cheeks were pinched and without beauty; was this the picture of a woman hastening to love?

Bitterness deepened. Pretending in vain that the glimpse she had had of William had not troubled her soul, she used her handkerchief to wipe those terrible eyes, coughed a little, and picked up the copy of 'England' which was at the top of her discarded pile of newspapers.

II

It was no good. Minna's eyes smarted, and she could not read. When every word ran swiftly into a general blur she threw the paper once again to the opposite seat, from which it fell sprawling to the floor of the carriage. Such a longing for past days filled her that she pressed the back of one hand to her forehead to shut the light from her face, and would have cried if she had not striven indignantly and successfully against this weakness. She did not cry. The tears filled her eyes; she would not yield to them.

The better to resist their importunity she stooped to pick up the sprawling copy of 'England'; but in doing so she received another shock. For across the middle opening of a paper, exposed by its fall, was a double-page article with a big heading: 'ARE WE

ALL PEERS HERE? by WILLIAM HARVEST', and as in panic she hastily turned that page she saw on another, framed with a thin black line, the words 'ENGLAND, a Weekly Journal for Men of Goodwill. Edited by William Harvest'. Edited. Then he was everywhere! The paper flew convulsively from her hands into the farthest corner of the carriage.

Not only was Minna's repressed excitement doubled by her discovery, but she was humiliated. She had known nothing of this. She had the sense of having been purposely ignored. What did it mean? Dick was her lover, William her oldest friend. Any association between them was of urgent interest to herself. They should have known it. How? They should have known! cried her anger. But the association itself was inconceivable, monstrous. Monstrous. Why, how monstrous? She felt quite sick. Sick with —was it jealousy? Terror? Shame? Love? In anger she thought, of Dick: 'He despises me! Loves and despises, as men do!' What a farce, their supplication!

Were Dick and Will, in any true sense, friends? She could not believe it. The mere assumption caused indignant tumult in her mind. How *could* they be friends? Two men, so different, so . . . But they were closely working together. William was on the train. He might with Dick's acquiescence be going to the house to which she was being taken. In an hour she might be confronted with him there. Forced to spend an evening . . . enduring the past . . . secretly justifying the present in his eyes. The thought was horrible.

But William was no longer her friend.

'He is! He is!' cried Minna, vehemently. 'He's my *best*——'

And then she stopped; for what she had been going to say was not true. How frantically stupid she felt! She had been brought abruptly into contact with her own unreason. Long ago, when she was somebody else, she had thought to love William all her life, and he had thought her a child. How loyal and hopeless she had then felt! And, at his marriage, how angry! And again, creeping through her anger, what an impulse to despise! He had seemed reduced in importance, a small man with burdens, already a failure; beneath the courtesies of the shrewd, narrow minds about

her . . . She had been treacherous to him. Oh, base, base, un-
conscionably base! Minna could no longer resist her tears, which
rolled down her cheeks unchecked.

Long afterwards, it seemed, she realised that Dick did not know,
and had no reason to suppose, that she and William were friends.
He had been away from Moreton for over sixteen years. If he
had seen her in the town before leaving it he must have seen her
as a child; and of late William had been seldom with her. She
had not really recognised Dick that first night at Aunt Katherine's.
He could not have told anybody—least of all William—his secret
. . . *their* secret. How unjust she had been to him!

Full of self-reproach, Minna recovered the paper and began to
read William's article about the House of Lords and its enmity
to the people of England. She was still staring at it—for she could
comprehend nothing but the separate words—and recalling the
sound of William's low voice, which was deeper than Dick's and
less full of sibilants, when the train stopped again in the darkness.
She did not move. She was in a dream. But there came a loud rapping upon the window-pane; and outside she could see a shadowy
figure; and while she continued senselessly to sit in her corner
a porter threw open the door of her carriage. She had arrived.

Exhausted by the journey, she stepped to the platform, where
the same draughty wind was swirling a few leaves over a glistening,
rain-moist surface. That shadowy figure, which she recognised now
as Dick's, slipped away and was lost; while Minna, following her
porter through the damp air, clutched the paper to her breast as
if she would never part with it. The big collar of a fur coat was
turned up about her cheeks; except by somebody closely observant
she could never, in the dim station lights, have been recognised;
and the small knot of people ahead of her had dispersed by the
time she passed the barrier. Only in the station yard, where there
were cabs, did she think she heard once more that familiar voice.
Then all was swallowed in night.

She next found herself alone in an automobile, the porter gone,
and everything done without stir. The car was cold, and perhaps
from excitement she shivered a little, her teeth chattering as she
peered through the glass before her, trying to see what kind of

man the chauffeur was. She could not distinguish. And when they had gone a little way along a dark road the car stopped and waited. Rain purred against the glass; only a black curtain of nothingness responded to her effort to stare out of the window. In a moment that same shadowy figure which she had seen upon the platform appeared again; the door opened; Dick stepped in; and they were off again. Dick laughed and threw his arm about her, burying his face within her fur collar and kissing her neck.

'Darling!' he cried. 'You darling! How lovely and warm you are! Are you cold? You were alone all the way. I . . . I know. I couldn't come to you. The most absurd mischance. One of my editors was on the train. I'd forgotten all about it. I . . . I saw him on the platform at Paddington, and hid. He dawdled. Oh, how I cursed him! And then, of course, I . . . I couldn't come and find you.' He laughed again, in high glee. 'But here I am; and it's all for the best. I know you've missed me. I feel it.'

'Need you have hidden?' asked Minna, drily. Why should he have hidden? He, so adroit!

'Well, *dearest!* I naturally didn't want to advertise *too* grossly. Remember, a *little* advertisement——'

She could not see Dick's face. He pressed it archly against hers, whispering endearments and promises and grumbles as he kissed her cheek again and again. Not her lips, which she denied. His arms were possessive. But he released her for a moment as the car swerved to overtake a horse cab which was jogging up the hill. There was a flash of yellow lamps, and the faint glimpse of a moving piebald rump, and the cab was left behind, a bell upon the horse's collar still feebly tinkling.

'That was he!' cried Dick, craning to look back through the little window behind their heads. 'Somebody's lent him a cottage right at the top of the hill. *Our* hill.'

'Oh, are we on a hill?' said Minna, in the same dry voice.

'Yes, indeed. A considerable hill. Almost at the top. A beautiful outlook over the river.'

'That will be lovely,' said she, straining for animation.

'Winter past, Spring here——'

'Then the ordeal,' groaned Minna. 'The divorce.'

'Er—yes,' answered Dick. 'This fellow's wife's ill. I didn't know about it; but somebody's provided the cottage. Well, I know who it is, too; but that's another story, as Kipling says. If I'd known before, I'd have arranged not to have him in the neighbourhood. However, you won't see him at all.'

'No,' said Minna, drawing her breath quickly. 'No, I shan't see him at all.'

'I . . . I think better not,' confirmed Dick; and fell silent.

Very soon afterwards the car stopped again; and Minna, stiffly alighting from it with the aid of Dick's arm, could hear the wind busy in large shrubs and feel its chill flounderings upon her face. She saw a light in a porch, and then an opening door which allowed another rich glow of light to pave their pathway; and as they entered the house together, Dick still holding her arm, she smelled warmth and comfort. Her spirit rose. Nevertheless, as she exchanged a glance with the maid, a woman ten years older than herself with a sleek, secret white face in which a long pointed nose was the most noticeable feature, the reassurance she had felt was diminished. This was no friend, but a callous and watchful dweller below stairs.

Dick said something which Minna did not hear. The door slammed in the wind; and the maid reopened it to admit the chauffeur. Minna, meanwhile, moved farther into the house, and as, from that shadow, she looked back across her shoulder she saw at the illumined door a scene which she never afterwards forgot. First of all, when the maid took a bag from the man, she had another glimpse of her face, which although it was set in a smile looked malicious and as if normally it would be a little sullen. That made Minna's heart sink deeper. Then, as she turned once again for support towards Dick, who was behind her and almost directly under the light, she caught his reflection in a large mirror upon the other side of the hall. She saw simultaneously the curious behaviour of the chauffeur, who glanced straight at herself in the shadow and immediately afterwards with an odd sidelong confidence at Dick. His face, like the maid's, was expressionless, a plump, dark, clean-shaven, unrecognisable face which was only revealed when he took off his peaked cap. But his eyes moved furtively in search of Dick's, and the muscles about his mouth were drawn into something that resembled a faint smile. Heightened sensitiveness made her either see or imagine that a message passed between them, familiar on the man's part and on Dick's so quickly impatient that she thought his head was warningly shaken. Then, still clutching her paper, she followed the maid upstairs.

III

The room in which Minna found herself was a small one, and a small bright fire had been lighted in it to welcome her. Its chief furnishings were a dressing-table fussed with little muslin hangings and ribbons in pale blue, a large wardrobe the door of which contained a full-length mirror, a divan with two or three cushions upon it, and a low armchair. Long lace curtains covered the single window, and a light blind had been drawn down behind them. A pale blue carpet and a fleecy rug, some pallid watercolours of river and meadow scenes in gold frames, and a small bureau completed the decoration. It was a man's perfunctory notion of a woman's boudoir, and a failure.

'Hot water there, madam. I shall bring your other luggage.' Although the maid spoke civilly she did not raise her eyes until she had reached the door. Then, indeed, she undisguisedly shot a quick, dry glance of curiosity at her new mistress.

'Thank you.' Minna, still wearing her fur coat, which she had unfastened, made no attempt to slip it off, but fell into deep, troubled thought.

She was alone. Why had the chauffeur given that unspoken message to Dick? Although the wind stirred the leaves outside, how oppressively and expectantly silent the house was. She could hear nothing. Was the maid still outside the door, listening? What lay beyond that other door? She crossed the room, and opened it. There, half-illumined by a single gas jet and the flames of another bright coal fire, was a large bedroom in which the walls were white and the hangings were all of flowered chintz. The room seemed to be repeated over and over again in two or three large mirrors. A florid picture of naked lovers embracing was before her; so much more than suggestive that Minna shut the door again as quickly and silently as she had opened it. Her heart was beating in her throat. She stood rigid in the boudoir, thinking.

'Well?' she said to herself, at last, in a thin voice that was hardly more than a contemptuous whisper. 'What else did you expect? You fool!'

Without realising what she did, she struggled out of her coat and moved away to the fire, her foot resting upon the low brass fender, an unsteady hand upon the mantelpiece. The picture, the servants, the blue ribbons, her own horror, what did they mean? Her mouth felt dry, and her tongue swollen. Her mind flew impotently among terrors.

Some impulse quite independent of conscious purpose led her to go next to the dressing-table, where under a feeble lamp there was a small looking-glass; and in this glass she surveyed herself. But all was shadowed and distorted there. She saw nothing but two eyes staring back into her own from a white, desperate face; and that vision, proving her fear, heightened it. Before she could do more, the maid was back in the room with her dressing-case, and until the maid had gone Minna, watching in the mirror that black and white flitting figure, tried to seem occupied at the table with her own concerns. She continued there, indeed, after the door had closed, and at last opened its top drawer, intending to put therein her gloves and handbag; only, however, to have her attention caught by the fact that the sheet of white paper which had been used as a lining to the drawer was soiled.

'That's also very odd,' Minna said aloud, in the same thin voice as before. She did not know she had spoken.

She drew out the soiled paper and crushed it in her hands. There remained behind, at the back of the drawers, a little roll of what appeared to be fluffy dust, the sight of which, following so closely upon that of the soiled paper, affected her strangely. How did such dust come there? This wasn't an hotel. The room was supposedly a boudoir, lovingly prepared for herself; and the furniture had been—or so Dick had said—newly bought. It was extraordinary. Fierce with suspicion, she began with feverish hands to open all the drawers, and because her roughness was excessive they resisted a little in turn. In each, the lining paper was quite clean. The bottom drawer, however, after opening for a few inches, refused to budge farther in spite of Minna's every effort. She pushed and dragged in vain.

When at last, by removing the drawer above, she reached what was causing the stoppage, it proved to be a flimsy illustrated periodical for women, printed in French, and called 'La Femme Soignée'; and this carried her disquiet to new heights. Was the paper the slit-eyed maid's? What a peculiar thing for such a person to read. Why had the paper in the top drawer been soiled? The soiling had been—yes it was!—reddish. Unquestionably some red powder had been spilt and smeared there. Rouge. Ah! Ah! The knowledge came like lightning into Minna's head: 'This isn't new. He's had another woman here.' The blood rushed to her cheeks and drained away, leaving them livid. She cast the French paper back into the drawer, which she pushed vehemently to, and stood erect again, panting, her hands tightly clasped before her breast, as if she had been trapped. She *felt* trapped. The maid's face, the chauffeur's glance, which had been an insolent appraisement of herself; Dick's impatience of that familiarity; all were irresistibly explained.

IV

Still shaken by these successive blows of discovery, Minna heard with hysterical shrinking the noise of an arch tap at the door leading from the bedroom; and at her faint call Dick himself appeared. He had the air of tip-toeing. His face, so fair and palely-lashed and demurely eager, was full of mischievous, confident smiles, which came and went upon his lips and brightened his eyes, giving him at the same time a look of consciously irresistible charm. Bitter at heart, alarmed, with little frantic tremors of fear running through her body, she still could not fail to pay that charm the tribute of a white smile. Her pulse quickened at his coming.

'Well?' whispered Dick. 'A-are you all right? Do you like your nest? I . . . I'm so sorry she's put no flowers. It's an oversight. I asked at once; and I've read a lecture. But chrysanthemums were all she could get, and chrysanthemums aren't suited to boudoirs. They smell of death, she says. Not very bridal, eh? Bridal! My God, I can hardly believe you're here at last. How I've planned and longed and suffered!' He came close, and put his arms about Minna's shoulders, and she prayed that he might not notice that she shuddered. 'You're rather pale, darling.' His soft voice was in her ear, his fair cheek so close to her own. 'You're cold, I expect. But that's the journey, you know. You'll soon be warm here, and happy. Always happy. Happier and happier. You and I alone. Oh, my beauty, my pretty one!' He drew aside the edge of her bodice to kiss the warm neck, and as she shrank his lips felt like knives upon her flesh. 'There! If I dared! Minna!' He approached his un-satisfied mouth to hers; and Minna, meeting his eyes so directly, saw that the smile remained as arch as before and yet that fire lay behind the smile and burned it to a frightening compulsion. Struggling for time, or for reassurance, or for some clear message from her own heart, she yielded her lips at last, and felt how urgently his arms grasped her, and how possessively his body pressed against hers; but she did not kiss, and at the instant of release looked back into those piercing eyes with almost wonder-ing detachment. The eyes contracted. He understood her. But as if he ignored a contrary mood he continued breathlessly: 'Oh, my dearest, how much I love you! My queen! My rose! My jewel!'

Still Minna did not speak. He slowly relaxed his embrace and freed her, laughing teasingly, as if he taunted her for unnecessary alarms, holding her hand, but at the same time allowing steel to show through his laughter, in proof that to love was added in him extraordinary passion for dominance.

'There!' he sighed. 'You're tired. Wait till you've had some din-ner. Some wine. That shyness will pass. You'll grow so bold, so beautifully and wonderfully bold. . . . Oh, my darling, I . . . I——'

He would again have embraced her; but Minna put her other hand upon his, so that his hand was imprisoned.

'Dick,' she said. 'I don't like your maid.'

Dick laughed. She saw his sharp teeth, his little pointed tongue. His brows rose very high.

'Why,' he teased, 'she's not beautiful, I know. Nor radiant. But she's tremendously discreet. If she's not as you want her, teach her. She'll learn. Plenty of time. By the way'—his eyes roved— 'oughtn't she to have . . .'

'I don't like your chauffeur, either,' said Minna, pretending to smile.

A little droll look of ostentatious patience came into his face.

'Darling! I'm very sorry for that. I've had him for a couple of years, and he's never let me down. But you like *me*, don't you? A little? A very, very little?' He spoke to a child. 'I thought you did. Listen, I love you——'

'Has he been here all that time?'

'Here? What d'you mean? This place is *yours*, darling. It's for *you*.' He seemed incredulous of her doubt. 'It's for our love.'

Minna delayed an instant. At last she said:

'And yet you've had another woman here.'

She felt him give a little start—the faintest movement of that hand which was between hers—but his face betrayed nothing. He still smiled. His expression was cloudless.

'Why, my own, dearest!' he protested, with wide-open eyes. 'What a notion! Really, you're unkind. How could I possibly dishonour you when I love you so much! Darling, you're tired. It's wrong of me to keep you standing. I ought to have realised. Look, sit in this armchair.' He drew her towards the fire, tenderly smiling. 'Sit there; I can feel how cold your hands are. You're naturally a little . . . but I assure you there's nothing to fear. Nothing. You understand me? Look, I'll stir the fire. Let's change your shoes. You sit here very quietly and cosily——'

'No!' she cried. 'I shan't change my shoes. I want to talk to you.'

'But later——'

'Dick!' Minna spoke so distinctly that he looked in alarm, first across his shoulder to the door, and then, with a finger raised to his lips, at herself. She continued in a lower tone, but still with firmness: 'You *must* tell me. You *must* be honest. We can't begin our life like this——'

'It'll all seem so different in an hour, dearest,' he whispered. 'In two or three hours. Listen——'

'You remember that, in the car, I spoke of your divorce. I suppose you *are* sure that your wife will divorce you?'

It was a tone so new that he was forced to attend. He looked at her very closely, withdrawing slightly, so that they were quite apart. That had its object, perhaps. It did a little frighten her.

'I can't understand what you mean, dear. I thought it was all——'

'She does know about us, doesn't she?'

'No.' Dick shook his head. 'No, she doesn't—yet.'

'I thought you'd told her.'

'No.' He continued to use that odd, scrutinising look, which was a weapon to threaten displeasure.

'Isn't that . . . rather strange?'

'Why? Don't you trust me?' He changed again, laughing tenderly. 'Oho-ho-ho! You alarmed me, darling. I . . . I thought—just for a moment—you were serious. You see, things a-aren't quite as simple . . . To you, of course——'

'To me?' Minna smiled again. How cold her heart felt! He was not the man she loved, but a stranger hard put to it to keep his temper. She could tell that his gay manner had become set. His teeth showed in a smile; but he was watching her. He could be cruel.

'They're over-simple.' Ah, this was counter-attack. 'I give you what I've never given anybody else—my love. Does it content you? By no means. You ask questions. You make stipulations——'

'I ask that your love should be honest.'

'Well?' He turned upon her. 'I swear it's that. Why, if my wife discovers——'

'Discovers! Good God!' cried Minna. She half-rose from her chair. 'I understand!'

'Before my plans are ready!'

'Your plans! What are your plans!'

'For you. For me. Darling! Oh, you're difficult. My God, how you torment me! Don't you realise what a temptation you are? Here am I, poor flesh and blood; and you're like marble! I'm on fire; and you ask questions; you demand and threaten; and I can't do as I'd like and crush you until you're helpless. I can't, because I want you to go all the way with me, kiss for kiss, joy for joy. Why, how absurd it is that when we've come so far, when we're here together, and I'm a lover, you should be asking questions that a father would have put fifty years ago. "What are your plans?" You aren't a fool. You know why you've come here, and what I want—what we both want—and you ask questions! Well, I give it up! Minna!' He was close beside her, his arms like steel about her shoulders and his lips savagely upon her neck and throat. 'Minna, dearest, give me some comfort! Say you're only tired and cold and panic-stricken. It's not you that resists me like this.'

'I don't resist you,' said Minna, slowly.

'You're like a corpse!'

'I feel like a corpse.'

His mood changed once more. He released her, jumped to his feet, and struck his hands together.

'What a brute I am! I've been tormenting you as much as you torment me. Oh, don't think I don't understand, darling. I do. Perfectly. But you jump to conclusions. Wrong ones. I wanted to have these first wonderful days together, quite unspoiled.'

'I'd rather you had shortened the time of waiting.'

He did not understand her.

'Won't you leave all this till afterwards?'

'I see,' said Minna.

'And then!' He laughed again, with exultation. 'Then we'll see whether you're as cold as you pretend; whether you distrust me and resist me . . . and *faire la morte*. . . . Oh, I swear I'll *make* you love me as I love you! Well, is it a bargain?' He took her hand, and tried to draw her to him; and when she neither resisted nor yielded but suffered him indeed to find her a corpse, he at once let her go. While their cheeks were so near to one another, Minna asked:

'To let my questions go unanswered?'

He said, from a foot away:

'I've answered them.'

'Yes, I think you have,' she said, in a tone of despair.

'I'd answer them for ever.'

'I'll think of some fresh ones.'

'You will? Splendid! I know the answer to them all.'

Boldly and possessively, he stared at her, his eyes half-closed and his lips parted in a curious intense smile that was like a grimace; and when Minna laughed at him in bitter derision he misunderstood her laughter, came again, kissed her, and held her at arm's length in order to examine the effects of his impudent boast. Whether he was then baffled or not by her glance she could not tell—her heart was too full—but she smiled darkly back until the grimace faded from his mouth and his hands dropped to his sides. She heard him sigh. At last:

'I . . . I wish I knew what it was,' said Dick. 'You won't tell me. Something. I knew in the car. Nobody's been speaking to you?'

What a confession of perplexity! Minna was moved by it.

'Nobody,' she answered. Yes, he was alarmed. He was to be pitied.

'Not telling you anything about me?' pressed Dick.

'Who could have done so?'

'No. That's *it*. You know, you make me . . . unhappy.' Insincerity had crept back into his voice with that last word. He had been going to use another. It was spoken with an air of too great frankness. 'I thought I'd done everything to please you. I . . . I *will* do anything, you know.'

If his power had not been lost he would have charmed her.

'You *could* have done everything,' answered Minna, with unsteady lips.

'I still can,' he declared. 'I'm sure of it. Darling, give me time. Trust me. Believe in me. I . . . I think if I were sure you loved me I'd move the world.' She saw that he was still trying to discover the origins of her change to him. 'I've never felt that about any other woman. This is my hour! . . . I . . . I thought it was.' When she did not answer, he took a step or two about the room. She heard his tongue clicked against the roof of his mouth. She saw how his eye roved in search of explanations. At last he went to the bedroom door, and looked back at Minna. 'I'm going to change now. Discussion to be resumed—after dinner. Is that so?'

'It certainly isn't quite finished,' replied Minna.

And when he had gone she continued to contemplate the door behind which he had disappeared, and to imagine him passing through that loathsome room on his way to another room of his own. Her heart was like water. She had no plan. She knew nothing of what was going on in her own mind. But after she had been for a few minutes alone she shuddered very deeply, her teeth so chattering that it was a little while before she could still them.

She trusted him no longer. Even his assurances, so far from convincing her, had but changed fear to heartsickness. How he misread her! He had not told his wife—he would not do so; that was clear. He was relying with assurance upon her own malleability —and the impossibility of escape. She was here, with him, far from help, committed. He was only so far committed as he wished. Protestations were contemptuous lies. How he must despise her! Oh, he knew his strength. Had he not reason for assurance? He knew. . . . If she had not found that paper. If she had not seen that interchange of glances with the chauffeur. If she had not . . . William! Oh, God, it was William! A sob shook her. She had seen William. William, whom she trusted. William, whom she loved. Through all her confusion Minna knew quite surely, as if by revelation, that this had been a dreadful madness, and that there would never in her life be a man to answer her soul as he did.

She darted to the divan upon which her coat lay, slipped the coat on in frantic haste. Then, stepping to the door, she listened. All was still. In an instant she was out upon the stairs, silently closing the door of the little room behind her and standing breathless as she tried to place the risks of discovery. It was light here; she could be seen. But as soon as she had left the landing she was a shadow among shadows visible only to one who should detect a movement there. Stopping, she listened again, crept farther down the stairs, farther, reached the hall, came abreast of the doorway of a lighted room and saw that the room was empty, and reached the front door without a sound. The porch light had been extinguished; and as she opened the door a terrifying wind swept about her ankles and made the inner gas hiss. But she was at once out of the house, holding the latch until the last second so that its click should not immediately arouse pursuit. It was very dark now, black and moonless, with pitchy clouds crowding the sky; not a light to be seen anywhere. Rain was being swept in gusts before a rising wind; and as she reached the gateway and felt liberty at hand Minna was seized with frightful panic. What if she were caught! What would they do to her! Like a deer, she ran wildly from captivity. But she ran lightly and noiselessly. They could hear no step. She kept as close as she could to the sombre hedge. They would never see her. She ran up the hill and not down it. They would never imagine such a possibility. And as she ran, and her teeth chattered and her knees trembled, she was crying to herself, with rain and tears indistinguishably wet upon her cheeks: 'William! William! William!' as if that talismanic name would carry her through every danger to a sure haven.

PART IV

The Man Who Laughed

CHAPTER XVI

Domestic Scene

IN LONDON, if you wish to drop your friends, you move into the next parish and never set eyes upon them again. That is, unless you travel a thousand miles or so away from home, to Cannes or Semmering or Amalfi, when you are liable to have a surprise in the lounge of your hotel. And the explanation of both circumstances lies in the fact that all animals use familiar paths, even ruts, which you leave by going into the next parish, but resume when you visit the common resorts of your kind.

This was what happened to Minna Manning, who travelled from one rut, in Moreton, to another, in Kensington; who as soon as she left Kensington ran again at once into William Harvest; and who as soon as she took a little flat close to the Harvests' home in Highgate Village was safer from such Kensingtonians as Aunt Katherine, her cousin Ruth, and their associates, and from that highwayman of wider range, Richard Firth, than she would have been in Timbuctoo. Because their lives were public, or semi-public, Minna could follow by means of the Press all that they did; she, being inconspicuous, might almost, as far as they were concerned, have been dead, or married.

From the November evening when, flying through wind and rain from Dick's arms, she came unbidden to the dark old cottage in Berkshire, until the time, three years later, at which our story is continued, she had attached herself to William and Kitty Harvest. She did this without the smallest difficulty; and, as will be seen, with benefit to all parties. But she often recalled that night of tortured growth; for upon it she had become a woman.

Her first hasty fumbling at the door of the cottage, which lay back from the road in the middle of a little copse, had been that

355

of frantic hysteria. She had missed William's lodging, run wildly against a fence some hundreds of yards farther up the hill, and only when numb with cold and despair had she caught the faint hopeful glimmer of a light among the leafless trees. Meanwhile her coat was sodden and heavy-weighted with rain, and wind had tangled her hair, and her feet and legs were plastered with mud; so that when she reached her haven she looked as desperate as she felt and was plainly at the limit of endurance.

At first she thought her rapping unheard. Then the movement of a candle within the cottage intensified her dread lest this place, which she had thought to be sanctuary, should prove a final calamity of the night. And ultimately, with the opening of the door—when she had prayed for William himself—by a woman whom she did not recognise, fear caused her stammered, shivering inquiry for Will to be almost unintelligible.

What happened after that was so unexpected, and yet as she found so characteristic of the Harvests, that she always laughed when she remembered it. The little woman raised her candle high; and Minna saw behind it some soft hay-coloured hair and a clear forehead, but nothing else at all. The light was cast flickeringly upon her own face. There was a terrible pause. Then she heard, in a tone of relief:

'Oo, I know who *you* are! Thought it was bears. Come in. I'm Kitty—Will's wife, you know. Good gracious, what a night! Can you see? Mind that pram—blessed thing's always in the way; there's nowhere else to keep it, and besides, as you can imagine, we didn't really *expect* a visitor on a night like this. All the nicer. Shut the door, will you? B-r-r-rh!'

The door was shut, and they were alone with the candle. Minna's hand was taken in a little warm clasp of work-hardened fingers. She was frozen. What kindness! What lovely friendliness! In her present mood it was overwhelming. With chattering teeth, she felt herself drawn cautiously forward past sombre obstacles until she was blinded by the light of a scene so entrancingly domestic that at sight of it she began quietly but hysterically to laugh, still clutching Kitty's talismanic hand for fear the vision should fade. Before her at a white-clothed table sat William, newly washed and brushed, eating a solitary dinner of which the savouriness taught her instantly that she was famished. His mother was erect in a low chair beside the fire, and upon her lap, cosy in a nightgown and blanket, with a new bright toy in his hand, reclined a round-faced two-year-old child who like his father was attentive to all that happened while he was awake. The room was small and warm and mellowly lamp-lit. And it seemed to Minna that from this room and this household, by some alchemy of the spirit, every terror, otherwise running madly and homelessly in the wintry storm, was excluded.

She turned again with loving gratitude to Kitty, so tiny and plump and kind, who was beside her. She saw, well below the level of her own, two large, childish, gooseberry-like, mischievous eyes, and, beneath them, a short, rather jaunty nose and a pretty, smiling mouth; and then she saw William himself rise as easily as if they had parted a week earlier and she had just stepped in from over the way. With his leisurely smile, saying nothing, he came across the room, felt her wet coat, unbuttoned it, and, as he had often done throughout her life, took it off. His glance went to Minna's draggled skirt and then aslant to Kitty; and Kitty at once, without another word, clasped Minna's arm to lead her away. Master Roland Harvest, at the same instant, as cordial as his parents, waved his bright toy and jubilantly hailed her; while Mrs Harvest, in spite of her burden, half-rose, one hand freely outstretched in sympathy. Minna exclaimed: 'Oh, how kind you are! How sweet you *all* are!' adding fervently: 'This is an ark!' To her happy surprise, they laughed aloud, so that she, too, laughed; and William responded: 'So far, so good. Mrs Noah, take your dove upstairs and give her some dry clothes. Or else she'll catch a cold and pass it round; and that's the last thing we want. Then she can have some supper.' It seemed to Minna greeting from Paradise.

Blessed warmth and borrowed clothes and hot food followed; and, as she thankfully ate with William, and recovered her heart, she racked her brains for some not too dangerous explanation of her presence. In vain, and, as it proved, unnecessarily. For as soon as she left off eating, and drew her breath to speak, Master

Roland, until he was removed to bed by his granny, called out, or William drily offered her bread or beer, or Kitty at the same moment began talking; until it really seemed that they were the most delightfully incurious people in England. One would have supposed them only glad that she should have come when enough food for all was in the house and when they had room for a guest and time to relish her company. What a relief! Minna sat smiling, altogether radiant, thinking: 'I'm safe. I've fallen on my feet. They're my friends.'

Even when the two other women were gone to prepare a bed, and she was alone with William, she could for a long while say nothing. She had been drawn to the fire and placed in one arm-chair, while William sat in the other; and the fire was very bright and everything was divinely still; and after William had lighted his pipe and made a few communications—still as if a former talk were familiarly resumed—about Moreton, and Kitty, and Roland, Minna fell into a reverie in which she refused admittance to the more frightening experiences of the evening. She roused herself ten minutes afterwards, still looking at the fire, to say:

'Will, it's terribly difficult to say anything. You've been—all of you—angelic. I don't know what you think of me—now. Is it very bad? Or what you thought, before. When mother died. There isn't any excuse. There couldn't be. You've always been my friend, and I knew it just as much then as I do now, at this minute, when I can hardly keep from crying; but I was angry with you. Because you got married without telling me you were going to. It was only silly wounded vanity. Nothing else. Nothing at all. It wasn't, I mean——'

Embarrassed the more by his silence, she turned her head to look at William. He sat back in his chair. His pipe was held in his hand. His eyes were fast shut.

'Did you hear me, William?' asked Minna.

There was no answer. For an instant Minna felt the blood run to her cheeks. Such indifference, now, killed her. Then she rested her head against the shoulder of her chair. He was asleep. And how tired he looked! How drawn! Once his eyes were closed one could see the physical weariness hidden by his waking expression. He had heard not a word of what she had said. He wasn't interested in it. He already knew everything about her. Maddening! And yet, tonight, what a consolation! William! Old William! Her lips trembled. A little quiver of blissful laughter shook her and released the tears.

II

Now, at Highgate, three years afterwards, she was alone in a flat which she ran for the most part herself; and the others were close at hand, two doors away, all of them her friends. Master Roland, aged five, was included in the number, and so was Rosie, surnamed The Podge, who had been born within three months of that night in the cottage; but of the whole family of Harvests Minna was most thankful for Kitty.

It was Kitty who ran everything, from the home to her mother-in-law. She had very little æsthetic taste, and the house furnishings were only beautiful by chance; she never read a book that was not what she called 'a tale'; she did not know, as of course everybody in Kensington at that time did, the differences between Bergson and Berenson; the Bachs; Ibsen, Nietzsche, Eucken, and Shaw; Piero della Francesca and Puvis de Chavannes; Steinlen and Epstein; or Wordsworth and Harmsworth; but Minna, who had smattered a good deal in these important affairs, found that Kitty had other wisdoms of greater value to her circle.

She could, for instance, keep house to a marvel, and knew how to make everybody around her happy, including the children. She adored William, and never wearied him. She knew a cheat when she saw one, and a busybody; and could put either of them to the door without a scene. She was as naïve as a child; and when a lesser character would have railed at circumstance she quietly and cheerfully handled disaster as an inevitable discipline. And she never, in any emergency, lied. These were salutary discoveries for Minna, who admired Kitty the more as every day produced some further proof of her sagacity, and compared herself at first ruefully and then emulatively with one who in Kensington would have been ignored as too uninformed to be worth a courtesy.

Perhaps Minna's admiration was given because although she had sojourned in Kensington she had not been born there. Perhaps she was the more ready to admire from gratitude, because she had learned to know Kitty in an hour of great discomfiture. But at need she could always prove her case for Kitty's genius by reference, not to herself, but to Mrs Harvest, who in Moreton had been gentle, amiable, and negative, and who from the moment of William's marriage might miserably have faded from life, her occupation gone. Now she was full of resource, and proudly devoted to William's children. Her interests had expanded. She no longer brooded over a collection of press-cuttings, but read widely, kept a keen eye upon England's political leaders (to whom she drafted stern letters of reproof that were never sent), and pitted her will against Roland's, sometimes scoring an ingenious victory over him. When she did this she was grotesquely triumphant.

The one member of the family whose feelings Minna could not read was William; and William baffled her quite completely. Having seen him asleep that night, with all the vivacity drained from his face, she believed him to be sick at heart, and possessed of many secrets; but if he had secrets he was not the man to proclaim them, and he did not share them with Minna. He wanted— or seemed to want—nothing that she could give him; neither love nor help nor express sympathy. Yet what Minna needed now, especially from William, and what she had needed all her life and would need as long as she lived, was the self-justification that comes of conscious power to grant, to bestow. How jealously William guarded that power in himself!

III

Minna had other friends in Highgate, besides the Harvests; but they were friends in a different sense. She also read a great deal, from Shakespeare to Graham Wallas, and from Madame de Sévigné to William James, and without a qualm threw over several of her old favourites, who had lost pace with the times and ceased to minister to her critical romanticism. She visited a number of people whom she could help, martyred herself by sewing and making for the poor and sick, as well as for her friend The Podge; and pottered with the others in the Harvests' quarter-acre of garden, which had fleeting moments of brilliance in consequence. In this way she grew from twenty-two to twenty-five; and at twenty-five was decidedly more at peace with herself, as well as more beautiful to the eye, than she had ever been before. She grew in other ways. She even had some ideas of her own which were not contemptible.

It was William who noticed these ideas. He noticed everything. He strolled hardly-seen into a room, looked round it, and strolled out again, having made up his mind about everybody present. But he said nothing about any of them until he was asked to do so, when he would sometimes, by his comment, rouse obstinate resistance in Minna, as well as smiling dissent in Kitty, and by his unshakeable certainty reduce them to rear-guard insults. 'He's nothing but an old egg,' Kitty once said. 'You're no chick, yourself, my girl,' replied William, calmly. 'Deplorable!' cried Minna. 'I'm in this difficulty,' said William; 'that I get no peace. My house is a nest of ideas and obstinacies.' 'I know whose the obstinacies are,' reported Kitty; 'the ideas must be yours, Minna.' 'Right,' agreed William. That was how Minna learned that William had noticed her ideas.

Yes, but did he respect them? She believed not. Further, although she loved William, and knew that she loved William, beyond all other men, and sometimes wished most selfishly that Roland and The Podge had been her children, and not Kitty's, she felt free to observe deteriorations in William's character. 'He's not *serious*,' she thought. 'Now I know I'm not serious, myself; and that's regrettable. But in his case it's criminal. I shall speak to him about it.'

She did so. They were gardening one Saturday afternoon; and William, who did not know that he had streaked his face with earth and therefore made himself delectable to the female eye, was sitting light upon the edge of an upturned box which had contained plants. He had loaded a pipe and had been overtaken by thought. Minna, burdened by a smaller box, full of little dark blue lobelias, arrived in gloves and an old coat, rather breathless, to find him idle; and, as those who garden in common suppose themselves to be doing all the work, she sprang to the conclusion that William was slacking. After a scathing stare, therefore, of which he was unconscious:

'Finished?' asked Minna, with irony.

William returned to the immediate.

'Yes,' he placidly answered; and fumbled in his pocket for matches.

'What about these?' She indicated her late burden.

'They're superfluous.'

'After I've lugged them all this way?'

William grinned.

'Ah, that's a common mistake,' he remarked. 'You say "We've got these; we *must* use them." The artist knows when to stop.'

He was rewarded with a great shrug.

'What an artist!' cried Minna. 'You're always stopping.'

'The supreme art is, never to begin.'

Minna eyed him with only half-smiling reproach.

'You're not serious enough, Will. I've thought it for months; and now I shall say it.'

'In the fulness of time truth outs. How much more serious do you want me to be? As serious as John Morley or Samuel Smiles?'

'I should like you to be as serious as Beethoven.'

'Good heavens!'

She brushed aside his ridicule. She said:

'Why not? It's no want of talent; it's criminal want of trying. When I read your paper I always feel it's entertaining but not solid enough. You need solidity to *impress* people.'

'What people?' asked William.

That was disconcerting; for Minna, somewhere at the back of thought, although she felt a contempt for Aunt Katherine and her kind, wanted William to dazzle Kensington. She said:

'Intelligent people.'

William grinned again.

'Ah, you want me to be a charlatan.'

'I don't!' cried Minna, violently. 'Only to do yourself justice!'

'It's one way to success. If you impress too many people you're called a prostitute.'

Minna blinked at that word, which had bitter memories; and William was quick to seize his advantage.

'Some of our readers aren't fools,' he continued; 'whatever the rest may be. Bishops, doctors, Members of Parliament, barristers, and other journalists, for example. Is it nothing to amuse and irritate such men? I'd rather do it than be a frog ridiculously swelling to make himself as big as . . . Beethoven.'

'It's not I who call you a frog!' interposed Minna, warmly. 'Nor yet a prostitute.'

'Of course not. You're too nice. But I'm proud of my paper, you know. I've raised its circulation from seven thousand to eighty thousand. In another couple of years it may be a quarter of a million.'

Minna stood obstinately before him, her knuckles resting upon her hips.

'What of that?' she demanded, in scorn. 'Who cares if it's a million?'

William's eyebrows lifted.

'Well,' he said, as if reasonably; 'it's success. My proprietor, Mr Firth, grows rich. He grows famous and influential. He's pleased with me. And as I have a small commission on sales I'm able to buy a new pair of pantaloons for my son Roland and may one day send him to school. Consequently, being more serious than myself, he may be Prime Minister, or play cricket for England against Australia. Higher, he can't go. Meanwhile it's true that I'm not as rich as my proprietor; but owing to modern methods of multiplication and distribution—you know how far we are in advance of the backward ages—see Mr Firth's speech last week to the News Hounds' Benevolent Society—the man who *produces* the goods never does make as much as the man who *sells* the goods. He's the artist, delighting in his own handiwork.'

'Horribly cynical!' protested Minna. 'I don't want you to be loathsomely rich. I want you to be, like your proprietor, a power in the land.'

'To cut a figure. That's all. I shan't do it.'

'Hopeless!' stamped Minna. 'And immoral. You just hand the world over to the exploiter. Can't you see that? It's irresponsible. Of course, I know *I'm* not serious.'

It was an afterthought. William grinned maliciously, and retorted:

'However, you had a bad quarter of an hour with your aunt. She taught you to exact seriousness from others.'

'From nobody but you,' answered Minna, firmly. 'And then only because——' But William raised a quelling hand.

'It's moral exploitation,' he said. 'Half the mediocrities alive—I don't mean you, darling—are badgering people who've got gifts to pull their social and political chestnuts out of the fire. They can't do anything themselves; so they get parasitically busy on others. "You ought to do this or that, for your soul's good." Oh, I hate it. I much prefer the honest exploiter. At least he's not self-righteous.'

'So that's what you think of Aunt Katherine,' murmured Minna, reflectively. 'Self-righteous.'

'Aunt Katherine?' His surprise was unfeigned. 'No, no! I wasn't thinking of *her*. She's doing her own little best. She's as active and practical as a man of business. But you're taking a high moral line, which I hate. I feel that high-liners are only inferior people on stilts—living above themselves. Now Firth runs his businesses to make money. He's an honest exploiter. He took a chance with me, and handed over a failure. He told me the exact truth, and offered a six months' certainty with the probability of the sack at the end of it. Don't you think that showed decency? I was half out of a job; Kitty and Roly and mother on my hands; and no prospects. I also took a chance. It was very lucky for all of us. And he's been generous——'

'Really generous?' asked Minna, her heart beating a little faster.

'I think so. I like him, you know; up to a point.'

'To a point, yes. You despise him.'

'I despise nobody.'

'Yes, you do. High-liners. Me, for example.'

William smiled, shaking his head, not looking up.

'Not even you,' he affectionately contradicted. 'And if I despised the high-liners it would be because my line's even higher than theirs, and doubly self-righteous. I say, that's a terrible thought! Well, we won't go into it——'

'Oh, yes!' pleaded Minna. 'This is just what I want to go into.'

'But it's a philosophy—an irrational philosophy—and that means it's indefensible.'

'You don't trust me!'

'As a sister. As my truest friend.'

'William! You want to make me cry!'

'I want to make you patient. Let me tell you about Firth.'

'I know it all.'

William smiled. Then he said, good-humouredly:

'Well, I don't. He's very quick, and extraordinarily approachable. He sees what he wants, and goes for it; and he can say "yes" and "no" and take the consequences. Great qualities, all of them. When you said I despised him, I think you meant that he didn't come up to my angelic standard of public morals.'

'Public?' breathed Minna. She was thoughtful. Certainly there was a contrast between Dick and Will. Will had an incorrigible naïveté. 'I thought you had no standard of public morals.'

'Oh, yes, I have. But if you're travelling as fast as Firth you've got to skip some parts of the copybook. You adjust yourself to expectations—in advance. That's the larger tact. You protect yourself with ambiguities. Your opponents are always after you with what you said five years before, with distortions of what you did say and inventions of what you didn't; and you *must* protect yourself. If you don't, you're outwitted. You disappear. But Firth's a born politician.'

'Yes,' Minna said, nodding. 'He's a born politician. An exploiter. He sees what he wants, and he goes for it. I don't admire any of those things.'

'My slower pace upsets you; but you scorn the express.'

Minna sighed.

'You're a devil's advocate,' she said, sadly. 'I look on you as virtue, and I want you to be triumphant—visibly—over the Firths. Over Dick Firth. Will, how far do you think he'll rise?'

William was silent for a moment. Then he said, with a slight lift of the shoulders:

'How can I say? Probably until he cracks. Well, until he's found out.'

'You think he'll be found out?'

'I think so. But oh, golly! just as a spectacle—I don't want to be farther in it than I am—public life's engrossing. A kaleidoscope. Much more. Always shifting and recomposing in wonderful new patterns, like a novel by Henry James, but much bigger and richer than a novel by Henry James.'

'But isn't it full of humbug?'

'Yes, of course; but it's a terrific series of tests, too. Sooner or later it finds every flaw. It's a fearful strain on the heroic. On what you might call principle. And Firth's got everything—everything —except principle. That's what will stop him. That's what, for me, makes him in a way exciting.'

'Oh, you're fascinated by him!' murmured Minna, impatiently.

'Do him justice!' pleaded William. 'He's got lots of good qualities. He can be very kind, from simple affection. Do you know what he's done for his father? That old boy who plays the organ at Moreton. He's written a lot of banal music, without a note of distinction in it—about as serious as Beethoven, and nothing else —what you'd like *me* to be—and he's never been able to get it published. But Firth's worked a miracle—by paying for it so secretly that the old boy suspects nothing, and thinks he's beaten down the barriers at last. He's beside himself with triumph. He's written me a long letter about the rigours of prejudice against original work, and the persecution of the provincial; and how in the end even vested interests have to yield to the pressure of reality —it would be noble stuff if it weren't humbug. . . . And Dick's trying to get some of the orchestral music publicly performed. He's pushed his way now into a musical set; and he'll probably manage it, in the same way, by paying golden goblins at the back door. By the Winter there'll be a recital of old Firth's works in a West End hall, packed with nobs and friends and hirelings, and every corner stuffed with suborned pressmen who'll try and scrape notices into their papers while the subs aren't looking.'

'Disgusting!' interposed Minna. 'Dishonest. And a special puff will follow, I suppose, in "England".'

'Ah, no,' answered William, with a smile. 'There we draw the necessary line. That will be Dick Firth's Waterloo.'

'You couldn't refuse him,' she scornfully said. 'How could you?'

'I've got a will of adamant.' He was grinning at her; but under Minna's candid eye and grimace of disbelief he confessed. 'It won't be easy, I admit. Sooner or later, in fact, we're bound to fight over what he wants put in the paper and what I won't let him put there. It's the roseleaf under the seventeenth mattress. He's tried already—often. Puffs of his friends and his companies, for example. I've said "no", on the ground that we're building up a sale and a reputation for disinterestedness. Hitherto he's given way.'

Though William laughed, and spoke lightly, Minna was conscious of great alarm.

'But if he insists?' she asked.

'I shall refuse.'

'But if he still insists?'

'He'll have to get another editor.'

Oh, God! She was so disturbed that she shivered.

'Be awfully careful, Will,' she whispered. 'If you quarrelled——' She meant: 'He'd be pitiless. You'd be in the street. Every hand against you!' She could see the two men—Dick smiling, with his lips drawn back from those sharp teeth and his eyes fanatically fixed; William also smiling, but with closed lips, a little pale, resolute, with hopeless courage. The one would have the power, and would use it without scruple; the other . . . the other would not yield an inch, but he would be defeated.

The more she imagined the outcome of such conflict the more terrified she grew; and at last she was forced to take two or three agitated steps away from him across the garden, her fists clenched. Ought she not to tell all she knew? It was impossible. She dared not risk the loss of his respect. He was blind!

But William continued to sit upon his box. He looked after her. As if he had read her vision he equably answered:

'Don't be afraid. Or melodramatic. It takes a lot to surprise me.'

'Not surprise,' tragically murmured Minna, turning back and

facing him once more. 'Not outwit. But *beat. Beat.*' She struck one hand hard upon the other. 'Don't you see?' Oh, the fool! He didn't realise how much she knew, and how much more she had guessed. Deep, deep down into Dick Firth's nature, which she had well conned for three years. William was too good to know the evil of another's heart.

'It's a daily risk,' said William. He was still smiling at her, very affectionately. 'No greater now than it was three years ago. Less, in fact. I'm protected by success—the mere vulgar success you despise so much.'

He gibed in vain.

'I wish you were independent. Safe.' She was terribly in earnest. But William shook his head.

'I can't be that. But there's no need to be in a funk the whole time, old girl. I've got another two years on my contract. And then —who knows?—I may be . . .' His voice died.

'You may be *what?*' asked Minna, breathlessly.

They heard Kitty's voice calling them both to tea. They saw her standing at the head of some steps which led from the house to the garden.

'Oh, I may be back in Moreton in one of my own slum cottages,' said William.

With a shrug of despair Minna walked beside him to the house. She must stir him to alarm, quicken his apprehensiveness until it ran with her own! Oh, he was impossible! One could not move him! Glancing aside in terror, she thought of Kitty, of his love, his folly——

'You probably don't know that your face is covered with mud!' she said, savagely. 'It looks *awful!*'

But that was not what she meant. Nor, perhaps, did William misunderstand her.

IV

Minna had learned to be afraid. Although many people spend their lives from childhood to the coffin in being afraid—of grown-ups, poverty, responsibility, disease, and extinction—it was a new sensation to her; and when she slipped back through her life with memories as fleet and piercing as a Fly-Catcher's darts she knew that the reason for this absence of fear could be found in William's protectiveness. He had let nothing harm her. She had thought him invulnerable. But now, when so much had happened to them both in which circumstance had outweighed determination, she saw him fighting unarmed against a thousand perils.

Here was the whole fabric of a family life—Kitty's, the children's, Mrs Harvest's, and in some sense her own—reared upon the one base of William's expectation of continued income; and William's expectation in turn rested upon the character of a man of whom William himself had just said that he lacked principle. The phrase had been a beam of light to her. It was startling. Frightening. She had had experience of Dick Firth which caused the sound of his name still to chill her bowels. She did not *know* him, for nobody knew him; yet with that flight of fear to the very extremity of imagined disaster she pictured Dick suddenly malignant, snarling, ruthless. . . .

William would not run away, as she had done. He could not do so. For William there was no William. How helpless, how useless she was! As she entered the room in which tea had been laid Minna's heart was so heavy that she could not at first bring herself to smile at the assembled family. She took her seat at the table in silence.

'Were you scolding William?' Kitty asked. She had been busy with the children, and was now half-hidden behind a big tea-tray loaded with cups and jugs and a horrible cosy that resembled a bad dream. A faint flush was in her cheeks which Minna had noticed there once or twice before, and her voice was slightly hoarse. But she seemed unperturbed.

'I began to,' sighed Minna. 'I tried in a gentle sisterly way— you know how one does——'

'He's provoking,' agreed Kitty.

'To hint a fault.' Minna was rueful. It was she who had been corrected! And now she was in alarm. With distressed laughter she added: 'Either I'm idiotic or William's as slippery as a fish. We wandered on to a dozen other things. Exasperatingly. I didn't do much scolding. I only made myself cross. And—I've just remembered—we didn't, after all, plant the lobelias.'

'He gets the best of us,' observed Kitty, looking into the tea-pot.

'I wish he would, of everybody else,' said Minna, thinking of Dick Firth.

'He will,' answered Kitty. She never wavered. 'He's as artful as a wagon-load of monkeys. And so are *you,* my girl,' she added, taking Rosie's fingers from the sugar-bowl. 'What with one and another of them, I feel like a fly in a spider's web—perfectly giddy.'

Minna thought that she shared Kitty's confusion.

'*I* feel as if he'd shouted me into a panic,' she complained. 'My mind's bruised all over.'

'And he just laughs,' said Kitty. 'Sneers, rather.'

'Children! Children!' protested Mrs Harvest. 'Don't forget you're speaking of my son! A fish, a spider, a bruiser, who shouts and sneers! We all know he's a monster; but——'

'"I believe they talked of me; for they laughed consumedly",' quoted William Harvest, as he joined his family.

CHAPTER XVII

Five Conversations

IN A ROOM upon the first floor of that building near Drury Lane where the dusty upper windows contrasted so strongly with the spruceness of the entrance, William Harvest occupied his editorial chair. It was a large room, so sparsely furnished that it looked much larger than it was; and William's desk, quite dwarfed, stood in the middle of the room, sideways to the light. Before it was a deep armchair expressly intended to reassure visitors and make them confidential. And at a little distance, under the window, was another, smaller desk, at present unoccupied. No pictures hung upon the grey distempered walls; slate-coloured linoleum covered the floor; and only a single large square of blue, very hard-wearing cord carpet broke the dullness of the place and saved it from looking as chill as perpetual November.

You would have thought at first that William was doing nothing, for his chair was tilted back, his hands were clasped behind his head, he smoked a pipe from which thin spirals of smoke rose at idle intervals, and his gaze was as expressionless as that of a Chinaman. But he was not at all like a Chinaman. His colour was fresh; his well-cut hair and firm eyebrows were of a chestnut colour, his nose was a little blunt and not quite straight, and his wide mouth and round chin encouraged friendliness in others. His lips were tightly pressed together, in spite of the emergent pipe. They were uncurved, but not thin. The lines running from the base of his nose to the corner of his mouth were deep, as the result of a frequent quiet smile; and when he smiled his cheeks puffed into benevolent plumpnesses of the size of crab-apples. At this moment he was unemotionally regarding another man, three or four years younger than himself, who stood very erect (in order

371

to make the most of a slim height of five feet three) and who nipped between his finger and thumb a printer's long galley-proof, the end of which trailed upon the floor.

This young man was very different from William, in character and mien. You could not look at him without slight unrest of mind; for his face was as lean and sharp as that of a wolf. He had a very pointed nose and a small, bitter chin, restless grey eyes, a tiny mouth, and a black moustache like a Devil's coach horse. And as he stood he fidgeted a good deal, from impatience. His name was Milton; and while, nominally, he was the assistant editor of William's paper, 'England', he was in reality Richard Firth's jackal.

'Well, it's such a chance,' Milton was saying in a high-pitched, assertive voice. 'Surely it's better to come out strong on one side or the other. Either side. Make oneself *felt*. All this eternal sitting on the fence bores me to tears. Here's Firth apparently waiting to go for the Government over Ulster, and on the platform at any rate fighting tooth and nail over Tariff Reform; and yet you're printing stuff—good stuff, I admit—about the down-and-outs as if they mattered more than the big political issues. They don't. Who cares a damn about a lot of wastrels? They'd be better dead. I think you're missing a terrific opportunity of jumping to a million.'

'I am,' said William. 'Or dropping to ten. D'you say we're ignoring these other things?'

'Not ignoring, no. Treating them almost casually as minor.'

William nodded. He did not argue with Milton.

'Does Ulster worry *you?*' he asked.

'Depends what you mean by worry,' replied Milton, forking through his long black hair with uneasy fingers. 'It's revolution. Not a joke. But what I'm thinking of is the dramatic interest. I mean, surely it's the whole object of modern journalism to keep the public sizzling.'

'You'll get on, Milton,' said William.

'I mean to,' answered Milton, with a sparkle. Oh, yes, he was bent upon that! 'Of course, you understand I'm not *questioning* your decision. I'm only pointing out. . . . You like me to do that.'

'I like everybody to do it. I thought we'd been fairly clear on politics.'

'Yes, yes. Fairly strong. But too reasonable. Too much simple exposition, as if people could *think*. They can't. They can feel; but only to the beat of drums; the sobs of women and children. Anything sensible's outside their octave. And we haven't *exploited* them. We should get a lot more attention if we shouted.'

'Hm.' William remained static. 'Everybody's shouting nowadays. An old actor could make a whisper heard. You'd shout for the Militants?'

'Oh, I grant they're a bore. But they're *news*. They've grasped the fact that you move crowds by feelings; and that's something that *we* ought to remember, too. *Large* crowds. By the way, Firth's in a mess over the Militants. He just lies low and says nuffin. They interrupt his meetings. I think *we,* at any rate, ought to back 'em. With paradox. For the wrong reasons. Madly. It makes excitement, don't you see. Liveliness. Of course, I don't believe in 'em. I don't believe in women at all. Nor does he. I don't know whether you do or not.'

So excited was Milton that his voice squeaked. But William remained calm. Without removing his pipe from between his teeth he said:

'I believe in them all right. I was borne by one of them. I married another.'

'Yes, but as a Social Force. As the Equals of Men. All rot. I say nothing about them as bedfellows and domestic aids. But are you going to have them marching in here like Cromwell's Ironsides——'

As if in ridicule of his over-pictorial description, the door at that moment was timidly and cautiously opened, and Dick Firth's secretary, Miss Neilson, put her dark head round it. Miss Neilson was no Suffragette; but she had lately cut her hair quite short, with the result that she looked impressively emancipated. Milton, checked in full tide, laughed maliciously and stopped speaking. Even William smiled.

'Come along, Miss Neilson,' he said. 'Don't mind Milton. He was blaspheming.'

Miss Neilson came forward, casting a very glum glance at Milton, and another glance, almost as glum, at William's pipe. She said, with assumed indifference:

'He's always blaspheming. It makes him feel manly.'

'Go on, Doris; and Mr Harvest's a chimney!' jeered Milton.

'I will not *have* you calling me "Doris"!' cried Miss Neilson, excitedly. She stamped. 'I shall complain to Mr Firth. I never gave you leave to do so.'

'No; but you let Firth do it,' murmured Milton, in a voice inaudible to William.

Miss Neilson flushed a swarthy red. Tears started to her eyes. She turned in vehement temper.

'How dare you, Mr Milton! It's utterly untrue. I shall speak to Mr Firth as soon as he comes.'

'And yet you *won't,* you know,' he whispered. 'You daren't.'

From close quarters they exchanged looks of menace in which Milton's had the cruel advantage of persistency. Then, at a word and a nod from William, Milton withdrew—still maliciously smiling; while William, seeking to placate the frantically distressed Miss Neilson, set down his pipe, and rose. Poor thing, she was quivering, he could see, with anger, and was upon the verge of noisy weeping. Her face twitched. She could not keep still. He felt great pity for her softness, that sensitive emotional flaccidity which was due in part to unsatisfied instinct and in part to inferior breeding. Against such a new-type young man as Milton, who felt respect for nobody and who presumed upon his own unproved distinction, she had no defence.

'I don't know what that boy said, Miss Neilson, for I didn't hear it; but he's a cheeky cub, and you mustn't let him upset you,' William remarked, with kind intention. Her short hair, the rather masculine dress, the flabby self-control accompanied by a curious air of very faint virginal mustiness, all struck him afresh and disagreeably. Excitement did not suit her. It brought her almost to the level of those dirty-fingered slatterns whom he had seen in cheap restaurants blubbering possessively to seedy men with bad teeth. It set his fastidiousness on edge.

But Miss Neilson was unconscious of the impression she created. She was suffering.

'He's worse than cheeky, Mr Harvest,' she chokingly cried, biting her lip to keep back a flood of weeping. 'It's not only the familiarity. It's the insults. You didn't hear what he said. No, and I'm glad you didn't. . . .' She tried to retrieve a slipping composure. 'It was something *horrible*. Just like he always is. Oh, he's a beast, a nasty beast. . . .'

She drew a sobbing breath.

'And the way he goes behind everybody's back to Mr Firth. It's no business of mine, Mr Harvest; but I think *you* ought to know that, as well as anybody else. He's always in and out with him, pestering, whispering, criticising.' As her words evoked memories she impotently jabbed the air before her with large white clenched hands. 'He's not a gentleman. He's not *nice*. Ever since he came, he's made mischief. He's had his knife into different people. Mr Bryant would have gone if it hadn't been for you finding him that job. Mr Firth never did like him, and he was only too ready to listen weakly to Mr Milton. And now it's me. Always me. He's on to me all the time, trying to find a way round behind me and get me out, just because he knows Mr Firth thinks rather a lot of me and tells me his private business. But I can't stand it much longer. I shall have a row. For if there's a thing I hate it's lies and treachery, Mr Harvest——'

William heard and comprehended all—even her powerlessness to find any alternative to 'standing' it. He was moved to yet greater pity. But he said, smiling:

'I always thought it was Mr Milton's fun.'

'Fun! That?' Miss Neilson's voice shook in agony. She pointed at the closed door as if it barely hid Milton. 'He's made with self-seeking. Yes, and because he's wormed his way into Mr Firth's good graces—as easy as you please—he thinks he can treat us all with impudence. He's a *horrid* man. Everybody would tell you the same, only they don't like to worry you, Mr Harvest. Everybody.'

She was clearly overwrought; but her good faith could not be doubted. 'Everybody.' There was more here than met the eye. William's interest quickened.

'Hullo,' he said. 'This is new to me.' His words were unheard.

'That about your smoking,' continued Miss Neilson. 'I happened to say, months ago, before I began to watch my tongue, that I'd come up here and found you smoking——'

'Like a chimney,' smiled William, through whose mind ran the thought: 'Poor dear, she'll *never* learn to watch her tongue!' 'Well?'

'I may have used those words. I don't remember. If I did, it wasn't unkind. . . . But you saw how he brought it up. He made it sound spiteful. It was to work mischief. Oh, Mr Harvest, don't trust him. There's none so high he wouldn't pull them down.'

None so high! William recognised hysteria. But he knew that more lay behind the warning than idle suspicion of Milton's good faith. It was true that he had saved Bryant; and he remembered how Dick Firth had introduced Milton nine or ten months earlier as a bright young friend who might be useful. A friend in a business. Often enough a cuckoo in the nest. Milton had grasped things quickly, and his power with Firth had certainly increased. Well? The implications were plain. The young man was ambitious. He might aspire to a career greater even than Firth's. But what if an editorship were a rung in the ascent?

Ridiculous! Not so ridiculous. William would not allow Miss Neilson either to frighten him or to carry away any repeatable declaration. He believed her to be indiscreet. But some thought was desirable. Therefore, without snubbing, he must end this scene.

'I wonder what you came to see me about?' he gently said.

Miss Neilson was recalled with a start to her errand. She stared. She blanched.

'Oh, Mr Harvest!' she gasped, twisting her hands. 'And I've left her down there all this time. It's that Mrs Perse. She came to see Mr Firth; and I saw her—to say he's away. He's often away, now, to her. And then, as we were talking, she said she thought she'd like to see you; and I felt it would look better if I came myself. You know how it is with these people. Especially as——'

She was flurried. She disliked Mrs Perse. She had all along suspected her relationship with Dick Firth. She was uneasy in her company, and conscious of social inferiority as well as resentful of the fact that only a near-lady would make her aware of it. And yet she had been gratified by Mrs Perse's manner.

William gazed inscrutably at Miss Neilson. Then it was not only Milton's rudeness that had agitated her.

'All right,' he said. 'Send Mrs Perse up. Miss Jenkins is downstairs. She can bring her.'

'Thank you, Mr Harvest.' Miss Neilson went to the door. She there turned with a sharp glance. 'Oh,' she said; 'do you want Miss Jenkins here, Mr Harvest?'

It was involuntary; not an impertinence. William laughed.

'Do you think I'm afraid?' he demanded.

There came, surprisingly, a laugh from Miss Neilson. She was immediately happier.

'I just wondered,' she thought aloud, still busy with an impression. 'Because, a little while ago, Mr Firth took to having *me* there when she came.'

What a world! William said:

'I'm as brave as a lion.'

'Yes,' answered Miss Neilson, unconvinced. She seemed about to make some other communication, hesitated, thought better of it, and disappeared.

II

Now Miss Jenkins, William's secretary, was very different from her colleague. She was a red-haired gamine, very freckled, impudent, as sharp as a cat, a rapid worker, and one whose adoration of William contained no trace of unhealthy fervour. She was loyal to the bone; and while she could not write a grammatical sentence she was in almost every other respect invaluable to him. Young, frisky, and wise, she saw and heard all and kept her mouth tight shut. William admired her. And he relishingly noticed with what sportive satisfaction she led the unavailingly patronising Mrs Perse to his room.

The lady, who sought to establish an understanding—not amorous, but familiar—with every man she met, strolled forward with a calm nod to her host. They had met before. She then gave a bright and knowing eye to Adela Jenkins's progress to her desk. Miss Jenkins plumped herself down for a long stay.

'Good morning. I don't bite,' said Mrs Perse to William, indicating the girl.

'Nor do I,' confessed William, pleasantly. 'It's a beastly habit. Won't you sit down? I expect you'll smoke.' He offered her a cigarette.

'Thanks.' She sat back with her legs crossed. Oh, Granny! what red lips you've got! thought Miss Jenkins. And skinny legs, too! She could see such things without moving; for she had cultivated the gift. Mrs Perse's black eyebrows almost met as she quizzed William. It was always the man who interested her. And men, in her eyes, always liked to be seen as tigers. 'You've never been to see me.'

'This paper's the apple of my eye,' said William.

'Yes, but you don't sleep with it, I suppose. You go out in the evenings.'

'In the evenings I go home to my wife.'

'Oh.' It was a rather long-drawn 'Oh', and was uttered in a curious smoke-dried voice. The cigarette was already at the corner of her mouth, waggling as she spoke. 'Domesticated. Well, I'm sorry. I should like to have been better acquainted with you. I say, the stuff I sent in last week hasn't appeared. D'you know why?'

'You probably sent it as usual to Mr Firth,' answered William, sitting back in his turn.

'Hm. That's what I wanted to know.' She gave a grunting, familiar laugh. 'Why's he sat on it?' Then, confident in the power of direct attack: 'How much do you really know?'

'On this, my mind's a blank,' said William.

'Hm. Rubbish. You weren't born yesterday, I imagine. Are you afraid to tell me before the child?' Her eyes said: 'Get rid of her'; but William ignored their message.

'If I'd sat on it I'd have told you,' he assured her.

'I believe you would.' Mrs Perse lowered her voice to a hoarse murmur. 'Then it's he, eh? I wouldn't believe it. What's he after? Can you tell me anything?' At his shaken head the anxiety behind her bluff manner became visible. 'You're not in his confidence? Funny, I thought I was.' She smoked in silence for a moment; and William saw the lissomeness depart for an instant from her body.

How carefully it had been preserved there: when it went one saw that she was old. But she was desperately discouraged. There was a tremor in her voice as she said: 'Does that mean I'm finished here? For God's sake, man, tell me what you know.'

'I know nothing. I guess a little,' said William, with sympathy. 'Whatever I've had of yours has come through Mr Firth. Some of it I've used, some not.'

'You've always used the worst,' she flashed.

'The paper's built on that basis,' he said. 'But you understand I've only used what I wanted of what I've received. Mr Firth——'

'Well, he's the boss, isn't he?'

'The editor's the boss, here.'

'You're not a friend of mine, then. Hence the girl. I understand. But I don't understand why Dick's turned unpleasant. He's slippery.'

'He may be tired.'

'Of me? Of course.' She was haggard. 'Oh, that was long ago. I take a utilitarian view. You see, I'm thinking of bread-and-butter now. It used to be easier. But one by one—— Damn!' She bit her lips. 'D'you say that he'd avoid an old friend?'

'No.'

She brightened.

'You mean that? Yes, I see you do. Look here, if I send to you direct, will you use . . . what you like? I mean, because he's—well, *that's* what I can't understand. There's a woman, of course. It's always a woman, with Dick. But why against me?'

'Whatever you send I'll consider,' William promised. 'You can rely on that.'

'Mr Harvest——'

There was an extraordinary triangular interchange, as the result of which, with no word spoken, Miss Jenkins slipped from the room. Mrs Perse sat perfectly still in her chair. At last she said:

'Have you got a heart?'

'I can't afford too large a heart, Mrs Perse.'

She showed some yellow teeth in a sardonic smile.

'You don't wear it on your sleeve,' she said. 'But you've got a lucky face, as the gipsies say. Look here, I'm absolutely at the end of my tether. I've written to him, and he hasn't answered; rung him up and he's always out. It's clear he's keeping out of the way; although that big-bottomed woman swears he hasn't been to the office. Three or four years ago—nineteen seven, eight—I was making a good living. People were kind; I went where I liked. But the old ones die, and the young ones follow new roads. Good luck to them. And since this new king, who's respectable, came to the throne nobody's wanted my stuff about the old lot. They're *démodés;* and I don't know the new ones and can't get to know them. I've had to fudge. You know that, damn you!'

'We all have our ears to the ground,' said William. He was sorry for this woman. Under the bravado, which might have concealed design, was an honest heart.

'Your instinct's devilish, I can tell you. Well, I've been a good friend to Dick. When he had his trouble with that German girl— the one he was in love with—Manning—he was nearly off his head. He was hunting for her everywhere; and then he broke up completely. You remember? I was sorry for him. I did my best for him. I let other people go a bit. It was a mistake, because you can never get back. Now I'm paying the price. Yes, but what am I to do? I'm absolutely broke; I'm behind with the payments on my husband; I've got no relations or friends—even old Teddy Boonge is dead; never left me a farthing. And Dick's dropped me. I'm at my wits' end, Mr Harvest.'

William had the power—it is invaluable—of being able to absorb shocks without showing a wound. He had heard a name, had remembered a period, a night. His body was tingling. But Mrs Perse did not suspect that she had revealed anything to him but her own trouble. He said merely, after a pause which was not long enough to seem strained:

'Have you quarrelled?'

She shook her head.

'Not a word. He doesn't quarrel. He goes.'

'Or others go,' commented William. Of course his thoughts were immediately back among the happenings of that rainy, windy night, when Minna had stood before him in a sodden coat, and with her hair blown—the night upon which he had fallen in love with her. With what clearness it returned! How he remembered the jump of his heart, and the touch of the wet coat, and the sight of Minna's wide, secret-brimming eyes, which she had turned perpetually from him. She had trembled with fear, with terror. It was of Dick. Incredible! Of Dick . . . Nothing, with men and women, was incredible. Nothing. And then Dick's illness—oh, there had been genuine passion. How far? Good God! For a moment he hated Dick! Nevertheless he could say quietly: 'Well, my impression is that he's not ungenerous. If there's no row, I think something can be done. I'll speak to him.'

'God bless you,' muttered Mrs Perse. She could say no more, and she kept her head lowered. After a minute she stood up, once again mistress of herself. 'Thanks,' she said, in the old, leisurely, hoarse voice. Then: 'I suppose you couldn't—— No, of course not. Of course you couldn't——'

'I think I could,' said William, his hand to his sovereign-case.

She drew a quick breath. The voice was like a rasping file. She did not look up.

'I've had no breakfast. My God, you're a good man. . . . Why don't women of my sort get hold of men like you? I suppose because you know too much.'

William smiled again as she gripped his hand.

'Because you don't really want us,' he said. 'When the devil was sick——'

'God! Nobody would take *you* for a fool.'

Mrs Perse stared, laughed her smoky laugh and departed. And when Miss Jenkins came back into the room an instant afterwards she found William standing with his hand to his cheek, lost in thought. He had forgotten Mrs Perse. He was thinking of Minna and of Dick, of the mystery, of the incredible association between them. So absorbed was he in his difficult effort to penetrate two secret hearts that he did not see Miss Jenkins or hear her, in passing, utter a post-mortem comment upon Mrs Perse and the wages of sin; and Miss Jenkins was disconcerted by a first suspicion that the visitor, after all, had made a conquest.

III

Dick Firth himself paid William a visit that afternoon. Because a journalist must flog his wits though they are half-dead, William was busy upon his weekly notes surveying the condition of England, when he heard a soft voice say 'Hello,' and looked up to find Dick smiling mischievously from the door. Dick had evidently just arrived, and he was a little breathless from a rapid ascent of the stairs.

'How are you?' he whispered. 'I . . . I thought I'd peep in. I knew I should find you busy, as usual; and you are. What industry! A-and to such good purpose! Everybody praises your notes to me, and says what an able fellow you are. I say, you'll be glad to know that John Burns is bringing in a Bill for your down-and-outs this Autumn. I heard it today. It's another victory for you.'

'Ah,' grumbled William, self-righteously. 'Now young Milton's just been scorning me for that very thing.'

'I *know*,' smiled Dick. 'I . . . I've just told him. He's *very* sick about it.'

'So he ought to be. But whether he ought to go to you like this I'm not so sure,' said William, fixing Dick with an eye in which reproof was mingled with kindness. 'In fact I think it's a bit thick.'

'Oh, Harvest!' protested Dick. He crept noiselessly forward and sank gracefully into the visitor's armchair. William saw his long lashes quivering as they always did when he was arch and in good-humour. 'It's not done—as I'm sure you know—with any evil intent. Far from it. I . . .. I mean, I shouldn't tolerate . . . Oh, but I see you're joking. You needn't trouble, at any time, to do anything else. Between ourselves, I . . . I think young Milton's a perfect jackass. But he's useful. You find him useful, don't you? I think he's very useful. No brains, but a kind of quickness. He amuses me, too. . . .' Reminiscently, and with a good deal of malice, Dick laughed under his breath. He was now quite fat in the face, and his body had thickened; but his face was still white, his chin and nose were as sharp as ever, and he continued to look very alert. The eyes were those of a well-fed, intelligent man, such as one sees in the West End of every big city. They slightly protruded. 'I say, did . . . did you see a visitor for me this morning?'

'I did. I saw Mrs Perse,' said William, meaningly. 'You've heard of that.'

Dick demurely answered:

'Sooner or later I hear of everything. It's so useful. Is she very angry?'

'She's starving.'

'No! Oh, no!' Dick's face expressed great shockedness. 'Oh, Harvest, why didn't you tell me?' He rose from the chair, and walked about the room a little. Long, stealthy steps; and the fingers of both hands at his lips. 'See, I didn't pass on to you what she sent me last week, did I? Well, it was so poor. *So* poor. I . . . I put it straight into the waste-paper basket. I must have put her letter with it. She's finished, of course, poor soul. Can't adapt herself. She's too old. But starving. You don't mean that literally? Oh, dear! Oh, dear! I . . . I really don't know what to do about everybody. Why can't they die when one's tired of them? Yes, I know that's why respectable men murder their wives; but all the same this continued life, accumulating until it becomes a public nuisance, is . . . is very inconvenient. It clogs one's actions so. Don't you agree? So much lumber as one collects through life— human lumber. But then I don't believe you've got any troubles at all, Harvest. Have you? I'm full of them.'

He grimaced. When he did that, he looked very droll and charming.

'Perhaps you invite rather more than I do,' suggested William, drily.

'I do, don't I.' Dick fell into unexpected reverie, but only for a moment, at the end of which, flinging himself down again in the chair, he gave a great smiling sigh. 'You know this *is* a blessed room, Harvest. When I come up and see you my troubles fly away. Why is it? Something in you, of course. It's . . . it's an extraordinary thing, but you produce an *effect,* my dear fellow. A spiritual effect. Somebody once described something like it as "a cool hand laid upon the soul". D'you like that phrase?'

'No,' said William, bluntly. 'It's awful.'

'Ah, it's my baroque taste again, I suppose. Deplorable. But I don't think anything ever worries you. It's very remarkable. I . . . I must admit I've never known any man I liked as much as you. But then I don't as a rule feel at my best with men. Another mystery. And you're so wise, too. You give good, disinterested advice. It's invaluable. Sometimes I take it. The truth is, I've come to you this afternoon for some important advice.'

'And you've been kissing the blarney stone en route,' observed William.

'Oh, no! Not the blarney stone. A pretty girl, I grant. Oh, but whether I'm wise to do that is another matter, isn't it. I can't defend myself. I . . . I know I'm incorrigible. Yes, but what on earth shall I do with Agatha Perse? She was very good to me at a particularly bad time. I'd had the biggest blow I've ever had. *The* biggest. I thought I never should get over it. I was suddenly let down by the person I loved best in the world. Let down. It was unpardonable. It doesn't bear thinking of, even now.' Indeed, Dick's expression had quite changed; and William could have sworn that his face had grown thinner and very pale. You may be sure that William had been observing very closely, and listening hard. He next heard Dick say: 'Harvest, you're what I call a decent fellow. You know the world; but you don't allow it to influence your own actions. I assume—I've never met your wife; but—I assume that you're happily married. Children?'

'Two,' answered William.

'And I've never known it. I suppose that you don't speak to me about your affairs. Why should you? I haven't your patience. I remember that your wife was ill. Is she better?'

'Long ago. She's subject to heavy colds.'

'Colds, eh? I don't like colds. Be careful, Harvest. But I'm sure you are. You're happy. I wish to heaven *I* was. . . . Harvest, how much sympathy have you got with . . . with those who break the rules?' With his head down he watched William, intent to discover the smallest involuntary movement of distaste.

'What rules?' asked William, careful to betray no such movement.

'Oh, one's conscious that there *are* rules——' cried Dick, almost petulantly. 'The rules that practically all the plays on the stage are written about. The man and the woman; the man and two women. Does it matter how many women?'

Now this was a matter which William was in no state to discuss calmly that day. He was on edge concerning Dick's relations with one woman only. So he improvised a reply to the question. He said:

'Well, my impression is that you aren't too tolerant of smokers and drinkers.'

'No, I'm not. I see what you mean.' Dick's face fell. 'You think I'm asking for special dispensation. I am. Do you put tobacco and drink in the same category as women? I don't. I *hate* smokers and drinkers.'

'You think they're unadventurous, perhaps?'

'Oh,' cried Dick, reviving. 'I think they haven't got past the bottle and comforter stage. I think them infantile. No; it's the *moral* question that troubles me. One's conscious of English puritanism everywhere. Rigidity. No allowance made. But you know, Harvest, I've been in search of my ideal all my life. All my life. You won't think I'm boasting, when I say that nothing disgusts me more than the average sensual man. He's a mere repellent amorist. I loathe him. I admit that sometimes I've sunk rather low; but I've . . . I've always tried very hard to do the right thing. Always. It's been very unfortunate, in one way; my wife, a charming girl, an only child, with a little money, is simply not able to live up to my rise in the world. For I *have* risen, you know, Harvest. She won't make any attempt to keep pace with me—politics, ideas, society, all blanks to her. Three children, and servant troubles; lace curtains, afternoon calls; a matinée and a day's shopping now and then in the West End . . . that *is* my wife. You can see my difficulty. I'm handicapped. With a different woman, with my ideal, I should have been a puritan myself. I *am* a puritan.'

'I take it that the blow you spoke of,' said William, slowly, with his heart beating faster; 'that it was from a woman.'

'From a woman,' answered Dick Firth. 'All my troubles have been caused by women.'

'Such as Mrs Perse?' William suggested.

'Oh, Harvest, not! Dreary in the extreme! That façade is nothing. She's dull. All those stale anecdotes. One gets so tired of the merely adroit. One longs for innocence. The woman I wanted was very different. Beautiful. Virginal. Exquisite. I could have taught her—oh, dear me, I could have made her happy. Taught her to love.'

'Is that all?' interjected William, under his breath, scornfully. The imagining was intolerable.

Neither spoke for a moment.

'I forgive nothing,' continued Dick at last, his face livid, but his voice still caressing. 'It was an offence to my pride. It broke my heart.' The tone changed. With choking savagery, he cried: 'I wish she may rot in Hell. . . .' He beat the arms of the chair with his hands. But a moment afterwards he had recovered self-possession. 'However,' he said, 'Agatha Perse was good to me, I admit. At a time when I was . . . not myself. I think I ought to do something for her. Some allowance, do you think?'

William was as pale as he. As agitated. As vehement in self-control.

'How about seeing her?' he asked, unsteadily.

Dick grimaced, pouting and cocking his head upon one side.

'That would harden my heart. I know myself.'

'Well, then, don't see her. Translate the debt into cash. She's in real need.'

'Really? What, clothes, food?'

'What she wears, no food, and nothing to pay her husband's fees.'

'Good heavens, what a fool to marry a drunkard! There must be something wrong with a woman like that, mustn't there! She's coarse. I don't like coarse women. They should be kept for bruisers. But I'll do as you say. Harvest . . .' He had become very gentle and humble and contrite. 'Harvest, you don't think I'm an utter rotter, do you?'

There was something very pathetic indeed in his appeal. William, who was suffering, said deliberately:

'Speaking as I find, I should say that you were extraordinarily generous. You've been that to me.'

'But then I like you so much. And you've helped me. . . . Look at the paper!' Dick sighed again; and again grimaced. 'I . . . I owe you a lot, personally and publicly. But I *have* been decent, haven't I. . . . I mean, I've let you have your way, and . . . You understand me. I don't pretend to be better than I am. I know I'm sometimes . . . Well, poor human nature. If we were all Utopians it would be a dull, dull, unexciting world. But now the advice. I won't forget Agatha. This is something bigger: bigger, at least, in its possible consequences. So you must be very careful. What do you think—casting your mind back, as they say—what's your opinion of Bob Whistler?'

It was the last name that William expected to hear. And he knew that Dick took pleasure in his surprise; for Dick enjoyed giving surprises.

'How very strange!' cried William. 'I had a letter from him this morning.'

'Good old Bob! You keep up with him, then. He's back in Moreton, isn't he. How's he doing there?'

William smiled. These were the two who, long ago, had torn his face against Daddy Griffin's wall, and tossed his cap into Daddy's garden. But for them he would never have known Daddy; he might never have left Moreton. He might be working still in the 'Gazette' office, an underling bewailing his stars. Well, there was melancholy in the recollection, together with surprise and pleasure. He must answer Firth. . . .

'He's never quite out of trouble. I doubt if he ever will be. He complains now of competition—unfair competition. He's being undersold; and he's again rather short of capital.'

'Capital! He's not thinking of applying to me, is he? That would be ludicrous. I . . . I forgave him a lot when he closed down the Seahampton shop. I let him off half what he owed me. He wasn't grateful. He's an ungracious fellow. I'm half a mind . . . Yes, but I've got a reason. . . . Didn't you let him take over your house—Daddy's house that was? I suppose he didn't thank you for that. Did he?'

William did not tell Dick that Bob's letter had arrived unstamped, and that it contained complaints of a leakage from the roof a well as of unfair competition. Bob paid no rent. Dick went on:

'I know Bob. I . . . I've known him ever since he cribbed my . . . my French at school. And I cribbed his sums. I . . . I never was any good at sums. He was excellent. But he can't get them right now he's a man, can he! Yes, I . . . I feel very dubious. But I was wondering . . . He *does* know the grocery business, I suppose? Well? In all its branches? I want a little practical help.'

'Yes, I think he knows. I don't think he's interested in *retail* trade.'

Dick slapped the arms of his chair again.

'My dear Harvest, he's got big ideas, and no character. He can't think. Do you suppose he's honest? You do? And a worker? No, he's not. Can't be. But he does understand about purchases and markets? I may say that I . . . I need a man of his experience. In what *might* be a very big thing.' Dick's smile deepened with malice until he looked in William's eyes a fascinating and enigmatic figure. From behind the mask of that smile followed the inquiry: 'What's his wife like? I . . . I only saw her when she was ugly with child.'

William cautiously said:

'She's more intelligent than he is.'

'Yet she married him!' Dick gave a little laugh—high in his head. 'For his *beaux yeux?*'

William had no bitterness; but his reply was unkind.

'Perhaps a misunderstanding.'

'I always suspected that. His build's deceptive. But there was also the shop. French practicality. Nobody knew his mother was a financier. Is the wife happy? Are they happy together?'

'In a discontented way, I think.'

'I'm a good mind to go and see him. I . . . I wonder how he'd treat me. He's the sort of fellow you can't help; and yet I *could* . . .' Dick pulled himself out of the chair. 'Well, I . . . I must tear myself away. Quite a long talk. You're good for me. Better than anybody. As secret as a well.' He permitted himself a considerable sidelong glance at William. 'God bless you, Harvest. I . . . I'll arrange something for Agatha.'

He was at the door when William said:

'I told her she could send stuff in to me. I don't know if it would help; but I think I could put her on to some other work.'

Dick hesitated.

'You're too kind, Harvest,' he said. 'Young Milton hates her. He swears she'll ruin the paper.'

'I shall give young Milton a kick in the breeches,' remarked William.

Dick laughed again.

'I . . . I'll tell him that,' he cried. 'It all helps friendly relations. And do as you like. Goodbye, my dear fellow.'

IV

William Harvest left his office that evening unaware that Miss Adela Jenkins blew a kiss to his retreating figure. This she did with the utmost grace, for she was a charming girl; and with a good heart, because she was well pleased with William. And since she was going to a dance that night with the young man of her fancy, and since she was alone in the room, she swirled her skirts about her in a few blithe steps of the fandango. She thought: 'Dear little man! He must have known I wanted to leave early!'

Miss Jenkins did William too much honour. He had not given a thought to her wishes. On the contrary, so full was his mind of other engrossing matters, he had half-forgotten her existence. In the course of that day he had learned almost the whole story of Dick and Minna—the whole of it as far as it could be told by anybody but Minna herself; and therefore, to him, less than half the truth. He had learned how alarmingly great was Milton's power with Dick, but not the reason of it. He had confirmed his belief that Dick's weakness was women. He knew that Dick, having confided in him, might thereafter suspect and dislike him; but did not fear such a consequence. He had seen the hearts of Mrs Perse and Miss Neilson. And, as his imagination was actively trying to reach the truth of Minna's relationship with Dick, the other discoveries came and went in his consciousness as do goldfish in a pond. He felt very tired indeed; more tired than a young man of his age should feel at the end of a day's work.

Extremely moody, although none would have supposed it from his demeanour, he determined to remain alone as long as possible; and as he walked through Bloomsbury and Camden Town he used his eyes and head to record in spite of every preoccupation all those emblems and portents and instances from which mundane philosophers draw inexhaustible nourishment. That pair, for example, by a shop-front in Long Acre; the young man lolling against the building with a cigarette between his lips, his cap on the back of his head, and a look of lofty boredom upon his face, while a girl, standing a yard away, wooed him. Eventually the girl would cuff the young man, who would pursue her; and the game would take its appointed course. That glimpse of Bow Street, and the blue lamp and a single policeman to present the symbol of order in a great city. Or of Covent Garden Opera House immediately opposite, where the best, but not the finest, auditorium in the world was set amid the cabbage stumps and other refuse of one of England's three most famous markets. Was there not something appallingly national in its situation?

William passed. In Endell Street the outwardly inconspicuous public bath, with its hint of England's still rudimentary interest in social hygiene; St. Giles's, where the bloods of a hundred years ago were bled; the Bloomsbury squares, the British Museum, the great school, the hospital—all typical; Euston, from which the railway lines began to spread northward over the whole country; the first poor small houses behind Euston, and dirty children playing after dark in the gutters, while their mothers loitered near in the doorways and shouted friendly gibes at passers; Richard Cobden and his statue at Mornington Crescent . . . these were the tangibles from which innumerable intangibles arose as unmistakably as the odours of each separate district.

Shabby little shops; the tipsters' boasts of the previous day's odds; the dim lights within the houses, where the rites of English privacy were being performed; busy scenes upon the kerb, the dreariness of the public houses where men stood to drink and chat together in momentary heart and amity . . . The shabby, the shoddy, and the disheartened gave their colour to this district; and at the same time, though shabbiness advanced and the town grew darker with smoke and speed and the mechanical devices of industrialism, the Englishness from which he and these others drew their common goodwill was unextinguished. William did not sentimentalise the English or their country. He wished them, often enough, changed out of recognition, and salved from their inevitable squalor. But if the editor of a paper called 'England' be not aware of his countrymen's ways and qualities, from their own level and with their own peculiar half self-contemptuous arrogance, he will, you must agree, fail in his aim.

William's dream, then, was of a free and happy England; and his aim was to speak for and to that England persuasively, frankly, so that England should listen to his words and find in them the expression of its own otherwise inarticulate thoughts. He loved his country. He loved life. He loved his paper, which he took seriously. He did not exaggerate his own importance, and neither flattered for sale nor fulminated for effect. But he had made it an unusually truthful paper; and although he did not guess the extent of his influence he was becoming gradually aware of widely-felt respect. It was very sweet. He wanted neither fame nor wealth; but when, sometimes, he had a glimpse of what reward a man may gain by gifted honesty he was moved to considerable thankfulness.

No thought of reward touched him upon this evening. He passed and saw; and below reflection his more secret thoughts made haste in forming and re-forming the kaleidoscope of his preoccupations. No plan; all confusion. A wish for the happiness of all. Acceptance of his own conflicting loves and pities for those most dear to him, but no belief that these were anything but well-guarded property. No active fear for the material future; but a sense that tactics might have to be devised against Milton; even against Milton's protector. And, deeper yet, engrossing and agitating his inmost consciousness, the frightful picture of Dick and Minna.

Dick and Minna: he could not free himself from them. They were there as he had seen or understood them at essential times, Dick smiling; Minna—he could believe it—drawn irresistibly by a magnetism which William could not deny; the two naturally approaching one another as man and woman, she (as Dick had boasted) innocent, virginal, but as desirous of happy mating as any other good woman. And then Minna as she had been upon that windy night. Hatless, dishevelled, terrified . . . What had happened? Why? What had saved her? How had she known what direction to take for sanctuary? So absorbed, a man would travel sightless through a thousand such dingy streets.

William had walked up Highgate Hill from the busy corner of Junction Road, past the Whittington Stone and St. Joseph's Retreat; and he had just turned from the village towards home when he heard a step behind him. 'Mr Harvest!' said a voice. Though it was dark, William recognised against the glittering lamps of a cable car the young doctor who attended his children.

'Hullo,' he cried, stopping; sure of nothing more than a familiar face. 'Good evening. Are you coming my way?'

Doctor Redding, an ex-Rugby footballer and an excellent fellow, took his arm and walked alongside. Being very tall, he had to stoop a little in order to talk to William.

'I've been there, thanks. Roland's rather feverish—nothing to worry about; but Mrs Harvest thought she'd like me to look at him. Well to be on the safe side. I caught sight of you just now, and thought I'd like a word——'

That was ominous. Roland? Rosie? William, suddenly chilled, passed at once to his mother. She was not yet old; but she was fragile, and it might be——

'Some trouble?' he quickly asked. 'My mother?'

'Oh, no; *she's* as right as rain,' cried the doctor, in that hearty voice which, intending reassurance, deepens fear. He was young and muscular and outspoken; not yet the suave medicine man who hides his thoughts and his ignorance behind an encouraging mask; and he had a heavy tongue. 'No, I just wondered . . . Well, naturally the last thing I want to do is to cause alarm, and I said nothing at all while I was there. Nothing, you understand.' That was very firm: man to man: on oath. But the voice, falling again, grew confidential. 'But, seeing you, I wondered whether . . .'

'For God's sake!' exclaimed William. 'Nothing could be as bad as this.'

The doctor was humble. Here was a man more subtle than himself, and a hundred times quicker in reaching truth.

'I'm sorry,' he apologised. 'I'm clumsy. What I'm driving at is that I thought you might persuade Mrs Harvest to let me have a look at her.'

'My wife? Look?' William's tone was sharper still. He was wide-awake—alert—alarmed. 'What d'you mean?'

From far away came a hesitant growl.

'I don't expect there's anything at all——'

'Well, you *are* a hand!' protested William. 'You're terrifying me.'

Firm fingers closed about his arm, squeezing with unintentional force.

'Mr Harvest, I know I'm a bad hand. It's because I like you all so much. I don't want to be alarming. And—well, there's no need, either. But when I was looking at the boy this afternoon, I suddenly thought he was getting a number of these feverish colds. Like Mrs Harvest——'

William felt his heart freeze.

'What are you afraid of?' he demanded, stopping dead. Already deeply troubled, and exhausted by his walk, he groped for an instant. Perception came to him. Roland! Kitty! 'Oh, my God, I don't think I can bear you to tell me.' He could say no more. Releasing himself with a brusque gesture from the doctor's friendly grasp, he turned away into the darkness.

CHAPTER XVIII

Secrets

WILLIAM HARVEST, a passenger to Moreton in March, knew as soon as he saw the pale grassland about the town that his happy memory of it, radiant, flecked by moving shadows and stirred by wandering breezes from the south-west, was not to be flouted. Roofs glistened in the sun; the blue sky was sweet with small piles of brilliantly white cumulus cloud; and when at last the train had freed him the old lazy air of the place was pure holiday, as quaint and strangely coloured as a picture by Peter Brueghel. He joyously stretched his limbs, breathing in draughts of the perfumed air. His eyes sparkled. Before him the length and breadth of the High Street lay unspoiled as it had done for a hundred and fifty years.

William saw and did not see the hollowed paving-stones, a crumbling wall, the lack of a coat of paint upon a familiar door, the humdrum shabbiness of the shop-windows. He was here upon a pilgrimage, to see Doctor Hodge and Bob Whistler and the dwellers in his legacy-cottages; and with the day so fine, and his paper on sale that morning, he could rejoice with the birds that everything moved with the Spring. That dead fly among the cobbler's stock, for example, seemed to him to be no ordinary fly, but a fragment of last year's history. The broken bar in the drain was just as he remembered it to have been three years earlier. The very curtains at the window from which as a child he had looked out upon the whole world were a royal and ancient purple which, although they affronted the eye, awoke the soul. You see that William was a journalist, or romantic historian of his hour. For a few moments he could cheat himself into belief that the town's living death was the peace of an earthly Paradise.

The mood survived until he reached Doctor Hodge's door, when it was dispersed by the odour of carbolic. He turned upon the doctor's step, saw the town lying dead about him, and rang the bell, caught unexpectedly by a perception that visions were not proof against disinfectant.

'Ay, you're amused,' muttered the doctor's sardonic voice, as he opened the door. 'Ye laugh.' That lean face had grown leaner; those grim eyes still glowed with the secret humour of the Scot, which may represent anything from tolerance to Olympian scorn. 'If one took this wurruld seriously one would cut a throat. Somebody else's for choice. One's own in the last resort.'

'I came for cheer, doctor,' answered William, passing the threshold. 'I find you pessimistic.'

'Humour me,' said the doctor. 'I'll no bore ye long. Come in.' They entered his study, a bare, cosy room containing an armchair or two upholstered in leather, a large desk, one or two Arundel prints, and a set of neat pigeonholes. It was easy for William, as he heard the old clock faintly ticking above the fire, to remember that in times past this had been the consulting room; but he had no qualms, for Doctor Hodge had sold his practice, and now advised for their own good only the oldest and poorest in the town. 'I've seen the best of my wurruld,' continued the doctor. 'And this poor place is derelict, stranded after the passing of prosperity. You, coming from the home of prosperity, can do nothing for it.'

However true and moving such words might be, they had lost their virtue for William. And since the immediate mattered more to him than the abstract he observed with concern that the doctor was, physically, much feebler than he had been at their last meeting. The hand resting upon his arm was that of an octogenarian, aiming at impressive tenacity, but using the arm, for all that, as a support. Death was in the air. William's smile grew darker. He looked aside at Doctor Hodge with a veiling of the eyes similar to that which Hodge himself had employed a hundred times in the course of his life. Nevertheless, he answered the previous speech.

'Preserve it,' he suggested.

The doctor shook his head.

'As a specimen,' he observed, 'it's not a patch on Pompeii. It will not survive. I wonder what England will be like in a hundred years, when London covers the whole of the South. I sit here and wonder.' He sat opposite to William, having poured out two glasses of sherry. 'Are you old enough to live in the past, William? You're not. You like the present. You're all for it."

'The future!' toasted William. How thin, he thought, the doctor's hands were becoming! The cheeks were sunken. His figure was growing gaunt. He was wasting.

'You're welcome to it,' said the old man, running his tongue over his lips after sipping the wine. Did William realise that this was damned good sherry? He did not. The fellow was no drinker; he had no palate!

'I never see,' added William, thoughtfully, 'what opposition there need be. The past, the present, the future, all good things, brother. Why must one cling only to one of them? But what a grimace that is, doctor!'

'I was thinking, William,' observed the doctor, in retort, 'that you have no taste and no principles. Mentally, a rolling stone. Where are you now?' He was highly quizzical.

'In the midst of life,' said William, smiling. 'Gulliver in Brobdingnag.'

'Or Lilliput,' grunted the doctor. 'That's what it looks like to me.'

'Oh, no. From close at hand, things seem very large. More important than they are. You don't realise the benefit of living here——'

'In the tomb.'

'With everything in focus. I envy you, doctor. In London we have no time to think. No air to breathe. We live on predigested food, snuffle vitiated air, gobble our opinions from the daily paper, forget what we thought yesterday, grow neurotic——'

'Ye look it,' grimly said Doctor Hodge. 'And as to yourself, William. Are you going to visit your friend Whistler? He's a discontented, disjaskit fellow.. So's his wife, by the look of her. My,

William, but you were awful fond of her, I think. She'd have done better to have you than yon fellow. Character for character; man for man. At the *lowest*. I doubt she gets little satisfaction from him, the hulk.'

'You underrate him,' observed William, calmly. He admitted nothing. 'You don't like him; so you belittle him. Even slander. It's a common habit.'

With dry melancholy, Doctor Hodge accepted the rebuke. He grunted.

'Uh-hm. Uh-hm. There's occasionally something in what you say. Not much. He wouldn't be greatly missed by the wurruld. As for the wee gurrul, she's a miserable slip of a thing. Frightened of her own shadow.'

William saw that the doctor gave himself a hitch in his chair. It showed that he was determined to sit upright. Like William's mother, who was also determined to sit upright. In both, the fear of being considered old was pathetically at work; and perhaps the fear of admitting age even to themselves. But in neither was the clinging to life a selfishness. It was due to pride, and a dread of any stooping on the part of those they loved.

The doctor continued:

'That child doesn't play with the common children, and daren't try to play with anybody else for fear she gets a snub. Who's to blame? The father or the mother? She's frightened of her surly father, nervous of her nervy mother; a hotchpotch of nerves and fears. I feel angry whenever I see her go shrinking by. . . . Angry to see what people can do for their children by not loving them. D'ye see, William? There are some will tell you a babe's a sacred spirit, and abortion a deadly sin. D'ye know what an auld gardener once said to his mistress? He was a sensitive man, and she asked him if he objected to drowning kittens. He said "No, ma'am. Not once I know it's got to be done. For they're better dead than as they'd be in most homes." Eh, William? Is not the same true of children? I'd have drowned thousands, if I'd had my way. How many people know how to bring up a child? How many stupid fools of mothers and fathers take the smallest interest in their brats?'

He had grown earnest. Upon his face was an expression of disgust.

'Not guilty!' cried William. 'Or guilty! as the case may be. Our children are tyrants.'

'Oho, you!' said the doctor, interrupting what might have been a proud and tiresome recital. 'You're soft. You think they're miracles. *I'm* thinking of a hundred or so pairs of fornicators in this town who ought never to have had children at all. Not the poor. The substantial folk with banking accounts and self-complacency. They bully and check and cheat their children and send them to boarding schools to be rid of them. By Jove, I'd sterilise such people. I'd doctor them, as they call it. The thought that they bring lumps of vital flesh into the world, and have them stuffed with the multiplication tables, and feed and clothe them until they're old enough to continue breeding on the same dreary system, horrifies me. D'ye not see them stretching boredom into infinity?'

'Well, we're not quarrelling,' answered William, who saw the faint flush of anger in the doctor's cheeks. 'I'd hang them all.'

'Oh, we'll never quarrel, you and I,' said Doctor Hodge. 'I'm just an older fool than you are; that's all. And that reminds me. That auld creature you have down at the Crossgate in one of those swell cottages . . . She's asking for ye.'

'Which old creature?' demanded William. 'Mrs Pink? Sarah? Flora?'

'Ho-ho, Mrs Pink! Mrs Pink's an auld fraud. Living rent free. She has a hundred and fifty pounds tied up in a stocking. And a hulking son in Chicago who sends her something every month. She cheats you nicely. No, it was Sarah I meant; she that used to be Griffin's maid. She thinks she's dying. Well, maybe she's dying; they incline to do that when they've had enough of life. I'd have thought the mother would go first; but she'll likely live for ever.'

William could tell that the doctor was glad, now that he was old, to have an audience for his monologue. It was a remote, teasing, meditative mind; not very alert, but shrewd and well-docketed. There were thousands such in England, probably in every country, primed with a certain wisdom. . . . As newspaper-readers (for so William considered them) they could be stirred by candour, but they were too little sanguine to be an active force in the world. All negative. Was anything to be done with them?

'What are you thinking of, William?'

William started. How far away he had been!

'Of the old,' he answered; the softened kindness of his heart showing in his expression. He saw the doctor smile gravely, quizzingly, but with affectionate understanding.

'You should think of yourself, sometimes.'

'I do that, too.' But the words were questioningly spoken. What had the old man meant?

'Well, don't forget old Flora, either. Sarah, I mean. I've never known her speak three words at a time; but she says she wants to *talk* to you. My word, that'll be a performance! I say, William; it's just struck me. You do a fair proportion of listening: does it mean anything to you?'

'What did it mean to you,' laughed William; 'when your patients talked?'

The doctor smiled his grim smile. A few subdued grunts of laughter slightly shook him.

'You mean you're one of these mind-healers, do you?' he cried. 'It's the new fad, William. But they never tell you the truth. Ah, they're all yarners. Like me. Only what I tell you is true enough.'

'But then it's about other people,' answered William. 'Children, and suchlike.'

'How far is anything one says *not* about one's self?' asked Doctor Hodge. His old eyes slowly blinked. 'And what could I tell you, except that people would say I'd been a failure because I've led a happy, useful life? . . . I don't care what they say of me. Do you?'

'Half-a-dozen people,' replied William. 'You among them.'

The doctor sighed with gratification.

'For all that,' he said; 'you'll get no "story"—isn't that what you call it?—out of me. I'll take it to the grave, so that nobody will know there never *was* a story.'

'You mean a sentimental story,' prompted William, teasing him.

'I could never abide the thought of being tied to one woman all

my life long, William. You'll say I'm an immoral fellow; but the
truth is I like to be alone. It's a rare quality, or defect. And you'll
get your stories out of the people who have slipped about from
woman to woman, or from failure to failure, or from one folly to
another. They've got plenty to tell; and will spare you little of
it.'

'Perfectly true, doctor,' agreed William. 'I could prove every
word of that.'

'Don't I know it! However, I don't envy you the other tales
you'll hear today. They won't be over-pretty, I daresay.'

He pursed his lips, nodding gloomily; and William was amused
at his pessimism. But he spoke, as it proved, more prophetically
than, in his half-serious humour, he had meant to do.

II

William, leaving the doctor, came out into the High Street to
find that the sky, as if in sympathy with his own mood, had become
overcast. How different the town looked now! As dull and shabby
as the doctor's picture of it. He would hear no good news from
Robert.

The Whistlers lived in Daddy's old house, which William had
handed over to them in what he felt to be an adjustment of
Daddy's unpaid debt to Julie. It had been ruined, as to externals,
by its conversion into a shop, and was an unsightly hybrid such as
he never saw without shame. However, once the grisly threshold
had been crossed the worst was over. A wall had been knocked
down, a counter had been put in, and Bob, waiting in the half-
light for customers who did not enter, was delighted to welcome
a friend. Within the dark, heavily-racked and many-scented recesses
of what had been the small sitting-room behind Daddy's study
they sat and talked together in confidence for half-an-hour; and
William, resting upon a chair, felt his eardrums tickle and vibrate
with the hoarse murmurs of Robert's post-prandially spirit-laden
voice. Just so do boys sit close in tent or earthy nook and pretend
to be men, sharing secrets and now and again swearing; and this

private corner was like a smuggler's cave, enchanting with make-believe until its reality became appalling. William's heart rose again. He liked Robert. Robert was honest, he thought.

Robert was honest. From William he would have concealed only the truth that he concealed from himself. But William knew more of Robert than Robert guessed, and could so clearly read a history in half a sentence that he went far behind Robert's knowledges into essential character. Moreover, in speech Robert was much less cheerless than he had been in writing, where a lack of skill restricted him to bare and misleading statements. The leaky roof of which he had complained was mended; trade had improved; some shares which had slumped were recovering; and life was rosier. What had chiefly depressed him was something not touched upon in his letter; and in order to explain it he dropped his voice and whispered directly into William's ear.

'They say,' he began, 'that it's a sign of weakness to tell another man your private troubles. But whether it is or isn't you know how I've always felt about you, Harvest. Safe. Whatever your limitations in other ways, I feel you understand. The majority don't. They couldn't. Too damned self-complacent. But you're different; and, by Jove, it's a relief to be able to let your tongue wag. Bottled up inside, these things churn and churn about. Well, I always say they curdle. You know? No, I know you don't; you don't have any troubles. Everything's plain sailing with you. And you don't seem to get any older. Whereas, with me . . . You ought to see my grey hairs. It's worry. . . .

'Well, my worry's Julie,' declared Robert, bluntly. 'Of course, not what people would expect when I say a thing like that. But until you're married to a person—twenty-four hours a day, eh?— you can't . . . Now *I* understand her perfectly. Perfectly. She's got great qualities. I should be the last person . . . Yes, but listen to this. I don't think I've ever told you. Stop me if I have. When the old girl died, and we gave up the place at Seahampton and came here—by Jove, what a relief it was, too!—Julie made me settle two thousand pounds on her. She'd been frightened, you see. Well, I don't grumble. I myself thought it was wise. You never know, and I'd had a fright, too, thanks to that damned swine Dick Firth. . . .

I handed it over. She has the interest on it for herself and the kid and insurances and so on. Yes; but as it happens I *need* that money. I haven't been lucky this Winter, and some of the shares I've got can't be sold until they rise a bit. They've gone to pieces. Perfectly sound, of course; but only realisable at a big loss . . .

'I've asked her to lend me some of hers—she could easily have done it through the Bank. But will she? She'd sooner see me put up the shutters. My God, Harvest; you should have heard her! You'd have thought money was everything. You'd have thought I was a scoundrel. I'm not afraid of her—that goes without saying —but it upset me. She can be very unreasonable and in that French way of hers very excited. Well, as you know, I'm not one to complain—in fact I never do—but I do think that when your husband's financial business calls for a little sacrifice, you should . . . Don't you think so? I mean, we're both in it together. But try to point that out! It's impossible. She's like a tigress.'

Robert's bulk at least was visible to the listener, and his signs and the cracking of the chair upon which he sat showed that even in the recollection of his failure he was exasperated. William smiled in the darkness, picturing that scene of cross-purposes, the reasonable and the unreasonable in conflict. But he did not say anything.

'With her,' Robert resumed, 'money's a god. Oh, it's something sacred. Kindred, morals, everything you can think of, is less important that the sanctity of her two thousand pounds of capital. It means safety, she says. Safety! A love of money like that is something I *cannot* understand. You see, she doesn't realise that my speculation's been all in her interest. I mean, the old girl didn't leave as much as we expected—she'd made away with some of it, I'll swear—and most of it went—extraordinary how it did go— in getting away from Seahampton and paying off that damned swindler Dick Firth and setting up here——'

'Just a minute,' interrupted William. 'You didn't have to pay him every penny, did you?'

'Every penny, and more!' cried Bob. 'That I *owed* him. Of course, he wanted more than he got. He always would do. But I made him a fair offer; and in the end he was forced to take more or less what I'd offered in the first place. He showed himself in his true colours, by the way.'

Not quite the same story, thought William, as the one told by Dick. It wouldn't be. He had a momentary vision of Dick's face. How funny to see those two together! He said:

'You wouldn't have any more to do with him?'

'Hell!' Robert swore under his breath. 'Little rotter! He's rotten, d'you see! His one idea's to get rich, go crooked, and grind the poor.'

'You being the poor.'

'Oh, not only the poor. They're everywhere; and Dick Firth's after them. He's mean and greedy. With him, money's the be-all and end-all. Personally, I wouldn't have any more to do with him——'

'Even if he offered to make you rich?'

'Eh?' Robert was taken aback. William heard him swallow. Almost bullyingly, he continued: 'I'd shove his offer down his throat, the little brute; and my fist after it. I've got a long score to settle with him. But I've been caught every time. He'd get round the Angel Gabriel. I don't know why; for he blinks and yaps and stutters like a curate at a tea-fight. Damn him! He won't do it again. . . . However, where was I? Oh, yes, money. Well, there wasn't much left when Julie had had her two thousand and that swine his ill-gotten gains; and I was feeling poor again. I'd learnt my lesson about stock at Seahampton. I knew I mustn't over-spend. And yet I knew that if we were ever to escape from this infernal rut I must use my knowledge of the markets (because I've got a real flair that way, you know) to turn the little balance over. Over and over, quickly. Naturally, when you do that with a small capital you're hampered. You miss the big coups. You have to take risks. And I admit I've gambled a bit. Unless you gamble you won't get more than three per cent; and for me that's no good at all. Not a scrap. So I've gambled. I'm down on balance—that I admit. Temporarily. But Julie, though she often throws in my teeth the fact that I'm still a retail grocer, doesn't appreciate the chances. She wants to eat her cake and have it. My God, she's unreasonable. Like all her sex!'

Much more followed in the same vein; for Robert had a long tongue and he was full of his own concerns. William, satisfied that Dick would make an easy reconquest of his old friend, now heard the hoarseness of that urgent whisper through a multitude of other messages producing the effect of a dream. Robert had spoken of Julie; and this place was full of memories of Julie. She seemed to be everywhere; that slim mystery of his boyhood, with its tantalising promise of ecstasy. Her preference for Robert had been the first—the only—great blow of his life. The one shattering disillusion, incalculable in its spiritual effects. Remembering it, William found his first long talk with Robert so vividly present that he could hear the very words uttered then as they strode along the deserted lanes. His stupefaction! His incredulity! His despair! And Minna's voice in the scented darkness . . .

Over Robert's shoulder William could just see a peep of light through a dirty window; and he knew the window overlooked Daddy's old garden, where he had heard that old man's confidences —as today he had heard those of Doctor Hodge—just before Julie had dismissed him. A century ago! The memory was very remote and very clear, like the sight of something a mile away through strong field-glasses. He stirred and yawned, stiff with long sitting, and weary of listening. Where was Julie? What was the truth about the child? To Bob she was no more than 'the kid'. Poor little devil! William's mind turned unexpectedly to Roly and Rosie, the happy pair at Highgate; and as he thought of them he very nearly laughed aloud, so light was his heart with love.

'If you can tell me how a man can get rich without speculating——' Robert was doggedly saying. But he broke off. An elderly woman had come into the shop; and with an excuse he went to attend to her.

William, left alone, saw a financial paper upon the shelf a yard away, and smiled grimly to himself at the mental picture of Robert thumbing through the share lists and picking out winners. Then he went to the window which he had noticed, and with his handkerchief rubbed a clear place in it. But what he saw gave him no pleasure; for the garden was untended. Bushes grew rankly; the roughly-scythed grass was coarse stubble; all was ugly and derelict.

Sighing, therefore, at the ruin of Daddy's pride, and at recollection of that long strand of convolvulus which he had once dug from the earth, William was about to turn away from the picture when a touch upon the elbow caused him to swing round. Scent, olive cheeks, slimness, secrecy; Julie was there.

'William,' she said, in that caressing voice of old, which held the enchantment of music. 'You are here, then, buried in this sepulchre. And serious. Perhaps that is because you are remembering . . . happy days?'

Her hand remained affectionately upon his arm. Her face was upon a level with his own. Her eyes, half-closed, were looking into his as if she felt sure of reading all that he thought. She was thinner; the expression upon her lips, although it still mocked, was one of melancholy discontent. She seemed to ask a hundred questions, pressing her fingers upon his arm in the half-light, so close that her breast almost touched him.

'I'm sure *all* your days are happy,' said William, in smiling greeting.

'You think so?' asked Julie. He saw the familiar, one-time irresistible, ironic movement of the shoulders. But a change. A grievous change. Did she reproach his indifference? 'Do you deny me, also, memory of the past?'

'Who could do that?' he quickly responded. 'I only wish it to be always pleasant.'

'Pleasant,' she repeated, under her breath.

'Is it not?' asked William.

She expressively grimaced.

'Pleasant. Unpleasant. What English words! Once you would have denied me nothing at all. Even happiness. Do you remember?' He heard in her tone the faintest murmur of mocking laughter; but he did not think the mockery was of himself.

'I remember many happy days,' he said, with cool frankness.

'No others?' That was arch. It was an appeal.

'Some unhappy ones, too. But those swim together a little.'

'Do they?' asked Julie. 'I am to blame for them all.'

'Then they're forgotten.'

She stood silent, regarding him gravely. He thought she added, in a whisper, and in French: 'That disappoints me'; but he could not be sure. The touch was no longer upon his elbow. She was, without having moved, farther from him. But she continued to give him her eyes, as if stealthily; as if, at a word or at a raised arm, she would gladly come nearer, right into his heart.

An instant later, at a sound indicating Robert's return, she had drawn right away; but the glance, the smile, the silence had all held unmistakable meaning.

III

He was thankful, soon, to leave them both; and as he hastened across the open space in front of the church, disturbed by old emotions and deeply troubled by that message, he shivered. So Julie, in the manner of her sex, had repented. If she had again to choose she would choose differently. She was ready to choose again. But it was too late.

And since a man's disagreeable thoughts breed fast William did not stop at this conclusion regarding Julie. He jumped instead to the night of his return to Balham after Daddy's death, and that supper by the dying embers, and Kitty in his arms—then, as so often since, her own tender, loving, gentle self; the heart without cruelty or chicane or bewildering incomprehensibility. It had been such ease to his tortured mind. Not an ecstasy. He had injured Kitty. For all his effort of loyalty, in marrying her while his pulse yet quickened for Julie, and because she confessed her own love, he had injured her. But for God's sake how could the most desperately honest man alive pass among others as sensitive and irrational as himself without inflicting incalculable injuries? He had done what he could. 'The coward does it with a kiss.'

William saw himself a coward, who kissed to be kind, and, being but kind, betrayed. Still bitterly arraigning himself, and in his agitation walking very rapidly, he came to the Crossgate, that small group of hovels bequeathed to him by Daddy Griffin. The cottages were as lovely to the eye as they had been, in the hour of acquisition, abominable to the mind. But they continued to give him a qualm, all the greater this afternoon, when in a mood of unusually destructive self-criticism he was ready to see his every act as a compromise with honour. And yet, short of gift, which had threatened to be a doubtful benefit to the old workers whose homes he had saved, he could not see any practical course open to one as comparatively poor as himself. One or two of the tenants, indeed, went so far as to feel grateful to him for what they considered mercy.

He came to the Crossgate by way of a riverside path, and saw that the long gardens in front of his property were full of colour. There were many wallflowers, straggling and sweet-scented and richly-hued, and among the wallflowers arose the speary foliage and brilliant yellow trumpets of innumerable daffodils. Beside the paths and among the worn stones polyanthus and primroses and scillas continued vividly to bloom; and in several of the casement windows stood old coloured pots containing indoor-grown tulips and hyacinths. A canary sang in a cage which had been hooked against a sunny wall. And from the doorway of the cottage at the end of the row, which had the shiniest windows and the trimmest curtains to be seen that day in Moreton, he saw a little old woman peeping. It was Flora, Sarah's mother.

Flora bobbed back in an instant; and he was kept waiting at the door when he had tapped. But not for long. The shrunken old thing, peering up and around the opening door, was all silvery white, her hair rather like those shreds of tissue paper with which chocolate boxes are sometimes stuffed out, her face bleached, her eyes pale with age. She looked very clean indeed, and although— because she had so few teeth—she did not part her lips William knew from the spreading wrinkles upon her cheeks that she smiled. She squeaked when she spoke.

'Well, Mrs Bright,' cried William, forgetting his woes. 'Here I am. And how are you? And how's the invalid?'

'Says she's going, sir,' squeaked Flora.

'Nonsense! A great strong thing like that!'

'So I tell her, sir. And young, too. Not sixty. Come in, sir. Talk to her. Wake her up. Will you stay to tea? There's . . .' She trembled with glee. 'I've got you some plum jam!'

From that triumphant hiss William received his cue. He cried:

'Plum jam! By Jove! I can't resist that'; and stepped into the poorly-furnished little room. But although it was shabby, the ceiling low, and the floor of bricks, all here was newly scoured, a testimony to the cleanliness of the two occupants; and the same was true of the sunless little bedroom into which he was straight away shown. There, in the smallest of small beds, lay Sarah; the coverlet being so flat that if her face had not been visible upon the pillow William would have supposed the bed to be empty.

'Here's Mr Harvest, Sally!' squeaked Mrs Bright. 'You'll have some tea, Sally?'

The weary head upon the pillow rolled slightly to and fro, to indicate a refusal; and a feeble croak of 'Shut door' made Flora cluck her tongue with an old woman's impatience as she struggled back into the living-room. Only when she had gone did Sarah greet William with a dumb regard. The ordeal was to begin.

'Anything I can do?' he asked, sitting down beside the bed, and suppressing a cowardly wish to be elsewhere at this moment. 'Doctor Hodge told me you wanted . . . to have a talk with me.' He smiled as that silent head shook, this time not sideways but as if in assent; and prepared to hear something of which he could not guess the nature. Sarah's hair was still dark; but there was little of it, and a few strands upon the pillow looked like pieces of grey wool. Never beautiful, the face William saw might now have been roughly carved in wood by an unskilled artist. It had not a good feature; for the nose was mis-shapen and the mouth was but a bitter opening above a sharp and crooked chin. Poor creature, the one sign she gave of happiness was that her eyes glowed devouringly at her present visitor with, in the heart of the glow, a suppliant admiration. 'He doesn't seem to think you're awfully ill.'

'Doesn't know,' murmured Sarah.

'They never do. They guess. Invent. Waggle their heads, and give you a bottle of nasty stuff which you don't take. It's not medicine you want, is it? But help? A friend?'

'Want to see you,' said Sarah.

'As a tonic!' laughed William. 'I shall tell my wife you said that.' Sarah might have smiled: he could not be sure. But a moment later one of her hands appeared from under the bedclothes, thin

and rather gnarled; and when she opened it William saw clutched
in the palm a small cheap gold brooch of which the design, in red
stones, represented two hearts joined by a filigree of winding
initials. He recognised it. He had seen that brooch before. He had
seen it pinned to Sarah's bodice. Yes, but when? By artificial light.
In the light of a candle. Ah! Ah! On that day, surely, when he
and Mr Merrow knelt together in the dark hall, and Sarah . . . She
was speaking. He listened. It was necessary to listen intently; for
the voice was low and gasping. Why, the poor woman could hardly
breathe!

'I've told mother . . . give you this. . . .' There was another,
longer pause. 'When I go.'

'Go!' cried William, dissembling his certainty that she was in
truth dying. 'But you mustn't *go*, Sarah. What would Flora do
without you? Eh? She needs you to look after her.'

Again the shaken head. The grey strands upon the pillow
twitched. The thin lips were twisted as if she were going to cry.
The eyelids dropped wearily and were raised again. She was tired
of life.

'Want to tell you,' said Sarah. She struggled for breath. 'Now.'

William, aware that she was in mortal combat with a secret, but
still not appreciating how much she was in torment over it, looked
at her with kind, smiling eyes.

'What?' he asked, coaxingly.

It took her a little while to begin. The speechlessness of a lifetime was not easily overcome; and every word was racked out of
her.

'Used to work for Whistlers.' With a feeble movement of the
gnarled hand, which had closed once more upon the brooch, Sarah
indicated herself. 'Jack Whistler . . . She was a brute to him.'

The grocer's shop; a thin man in a white apron, who once drove
a little boy from his doorway, through which the little boy saw
just those enchantments amid which he had sat today with Bob
and stood . . . with Julie.

'Robert's father, this is?' prompted William. 'I remember him.'

'He got fond of me. Gave me this.'

'Ah!' William cried. He drew his breath deep. The hearts; the intertwined letters. What was she telling him? 'He gave me this.' The treasure; a possession so valuable to her that as she lay dying she fondled it with passion. The great, he knew, had no monopoly of love; but this pathetic, terrible adoration——

'Want *you* to have it,' said Sarah, closing her eyes again. 'You're good.'

'Me? Thank you,' William answered, soberly; 'that's awfully kind, and a great compliment.' But he was preoccupied with frightful guesses at the meanings behind her difficult tale.

'Not now. I want it till I go,' said Sarah. And again: 'Till I go.' She seemed to smile.

'A long time,' he told her.

'No.'

'Tell me about it.'

'He had it made. All he ever gave me; though he'd have given me all he had.'

'I'm sure he would.'

'She was always creeping. Prying. She found it in my room.'

She! That stout woman in black silk; seen last when her natural pallor had grown ghastly in death.

'Did she know he'd given it?' whispered William. Creeping! Prying! The picture made him shudder.

'Got our initials.'

The brooch was brought again into view, and as she held it in one hand Sarah traced with the forefinger of the other hand the lines of the interlaced letters J and S. William heard the hiss of her sobbing breath.

'Yes,' he said. 'I see. It's beautiful.'

'She'd found us out. Must have seen us or heard us. We were like mice. Then killed him.' Sarah's voice grew much clearer. 'I know.'

'Good God!' cried William, sitting violently back in his chair. To hear such a thing spoken in such a murmur! Had he heard aright? 'Killed him'?

'On his way to me. In the dark. Easy, from behind.'

'He stumbled.' William was incredulous.

'He'd wakened her. She followed. I heard her say something.'

'What!'

'I was waiting for him. Upstairs in the dark. Heard the fall. I ran down. She didn't know. Heard her say: "Lie there, you blasted adulterer." He'd gone.'

'He was dead then?'

'Then or later. While I went for the doctor she was up in my room. Stole my brooch.'

'Sarah! That's impossible. With him lying dead!'

'I know. It was gone. She had it.'

'But said nothing. And you said nothing.'

'What was the good? My word against hers. His name ruined.'

William trembled with horror as he imagined that night scene. The two women; the body; the darkness; a frantic search. What madness! And as one picture led to another he recalled the evening when to his knowledge a second stumble had led to a second death, and when he in turn had knelt beside a silent body. What if that, too——

'Listen, Sarah,' he cried, in extreme agitation. 'I *must* ask you. That day we found Mrs Whistler——'

Sarah did not hear him. She was intent upon her story. She was staring now, and could have heard nothing.

'I went away. Ill. Fever. I wasn't always like I am now. Stayed in Birmingham six years. Thought about it all the time. Worried. Wanted it. At last I crept back here. . . . Nobody recognised. She never saw me. I worked—you know I did—for Mr Griffin. After he was dead I got it back. Went to her rooms. I'd tried often——'

William, pierced to the heart, repeated:

'Went to her rooms. Yes, but you were wearing it. You were wearing it that evening. Sarah, you knew she was dead! Sarah!'

Sarah turned her face from him. Her lips were twisted in a strange smile, and the hand clasping the brooch was pressed to her throat. William's blood ran cold.

IV

While William was in Moreton, all the other members of his family stayed at home in the little house at Highgate, where the

Spring day was equally fresh, and where the shadows were as soft and brown as they could be in any corner of England. And as Mrs Harvest watched over the children in the garden, where Roland, in imitation of his father, did some majestic digging as soon as his morning at school was over, and Rosie, in imitation of Roland, covered herself adorably with the moist earth, Kitty and Minna worked together within doors.

Kitty was ironing; Minna was making a dress for Kitty. And the window leading to the garden was open, so that they could hear the children's voices and the extremely merry singing of a thrush in the apple tree next door; and everything was so peaceful that they were both very nearly as happy as they were ever likely to be. They loved one another and talked or were silent without constraint as they worked. It was when the ironing was done that Kitty came to stand beside Minna, looking down at the frock with great satisfaction.

This brought the two young women into active contrast, Kitty so small and fair and fluffy-haired, although she was much less plump than she had been; and Minna, bending over her work, and then giving it a proud pat, and looking up at her friend with laughter, to share in the pleased observation of an ingenious and rather beautiful piece of embroidery. The dress was of a greyish-blue silk, which would have suited Minna as well as Kitty, or perhaps better than Kitty. Her flaxen hair, as Kitty saw it against the material, was much brighter than Kitty's, and she was fairer. Her hands were very white, and it was a perception of this fact which led Kitty to put her own darker and rougher hand upon a level with Minna's for purposes of comparison.

'Different, isn't it!' exclaimed Kitty.

Minna spread her fingers.

'Mine's bigger,' she said; so that Kitty, withdrawing the hand, used it to give her friend's shoulder a light push.

'So's Christmas,' she answered, rather carelessly and unintelligibly. 'Oh, well, I suppose I've got to get tea. Nothing but meals in this house. Meals and washing children and getting up in the morning.'

'And going out in the evening and eating grand dinners at

clubs,' rebuked Minna, lifting the dress slightly to point the rebuke. 'And wearing grand robes made by awful slaves.'

'Pooh!' cried Kitty. 'Who wants to go to old clubs and old dinners? See a lot of old quizzes and make a lot of conversation about things I don't understand.' She became a little moody as she spoke, infected by the view she was expressing. 'I only go because if I don't Will has to say a lot of lies about my being ill or a devoted mother or despising intellectual society or something.'

'Is that what he says?' demanded Minna, with a frown. 'Because if it is I don't think it's very nice of him.'

Kitty turned that off.

'Oh, I don't know what he says. What d'you suppose it is? Something silly, I expect. I often wonder what they think of me. Will says all the wives at these things are awful, anyway. He doesn't see why I shouldn't go. Or for that matter why I should.'

There was silence, in which both thought of William.

'He's a curmudgeon,' at last said Minna.

'He's a rake,' responded Kitty.

'He wants to do everything himself,' said Minna.

'He's always trying to make me make up my own mind,' retorted Kitty. 'And I haven't got a mind. He ought never to have married me.'

'It was the best thing he ever did for himself,' said Minna.

'He ought to have married *you*,' said Kitty.

Minna, with a stirring of the heart, bent over the blue dress.

'He could have done so,' she answered, in a low voice.

There passed between them such an intense flash of understanding at this speech that neither could say anything further for a moment. Minna made no attempt to use her needle; she could not see it. She had told Kitty one of her two secrets. And Kitty, standing very still at a little distance, was looking down at the floor, equally blind; having received confirmation of something which she felt she had known all along.

At last Kitty said:

'It's funny I'm not jealous of you, isn't it.'

'I'm not in love with him now,' Minna replied.

At that, Kitty turned her head and glanced sidelong at Minna.

She was smiling. She did not believe what Minna said. But, lest constraint should arise between them she added, in a moment:

'Lucky for me.'

She had gone to the door, and was upon her way out of the room, when another thought struck her. With a hand still upon the knob, and her forehead pressed against the edge of the door, she cried:

'You can't ask; and you can't take. You let me take him.'

'Is that what you did?' asked Minna, with a sudden turn of spirit.

Kitty pulled the door to behind her with a sharp bang; while Minna, setting aside the blue dress with a gesture of impatience, jumped to her feet and prepared to follow her friend. Nothing was clear to her except that Kitty had flashed a lamp of intuition into a dark place. But she was not unhappy. Why was she not unhappy?

v

Left to herself after Minna had gone home, for Mrs Harvest was in her own room, and the children had been put to bed, Kitty with interest remembered that brief conversation. She had been reading a newspaper, and had put it down in order to assure herself of the time. Seven o'clock; William would not be back from Moreton until nine. The sun had set; the shadows were creeping upon her; but she was in a thoughtful mood and was not yet ready to light the gas.

What Minna had said had been already known to her. More. More than Minna had said. Minna thought herself safe in saying it; but Minna was an innocent. Beside her, Kitty felt like an old, hard, experienced woman.

She felt so old and ripe and assured that she began to hum; but the humming died, and she made up the fire with a fierce poker. Then, as she saw the flames leap, and sat down again in her low chair to enjoy the dusk, little amusing fancies swept through her mind and she resumed her humming, which was like a little girl's. That old rug was beginning to wear; it had never been a good bargain. Mustn't let Will know, for she'd been so sure of it. He hadn't.

Old cleversticks! . . . You couldn't keep anything nice with children about. They kicked and battered. Wouldn't be without them,
though. Nor would Will. He was a child himself.

Laughing, Kitty knew that she wanted to hug William as much
as she wanted to hug Roly. She loved them both as the hungry
love pie. Roly was asleep; but before sleeping he had wanted to
say good night to Will, and it had been all she could do to get
him to sing his song, which was 'Yip-i-addy', and take his medicine.
. . . Medicine; Kitty's heart sank at that word. . . . Doctor Redding didn't *know*. William didn't know. And she knew only
enough to be alarmed. Little things one noticed; a catching in the
throat, sometimes a weakness or a loss of breath; enough to be
frightening, though it might be nothing at all. . . .

Nothing at all . . . A shiver. Stop that! . . .

Minna was simple. She was lovely, and didn't, somehow, *trade*
on it. As good as gold. Straight. A bit serious . . . 'No, I'm not
jealous,' said Kitty. She felt satisfied of that. Absolutely satisfied.
Nearly five minutes later she added: 'If they were different, I should
be.'

Different. Kitty moved restlessly. She was thinking of herself,
and when she did that she was never happy; for she knew little
of her own virtues. William did not tell her about them. He and
she didn't talk about themselves. He was never cross with her—
always kind. He was fond of her all right. As she wished. Perfectly as she wished. Though she might scoff at him, she adored
him. If he'd ever been able to feel as she felt. 'I should have gone
off my head with joy.' It wasn't possible. 'I'm not afraid,' Kitty
thought. 'I shouldn't ever be. And yet I wouldn't let them . . . as
some fools do . . .'

Although she had glimpsed the risk which she was unprepared
to take with her husband and her friend what she was thinking
did not quite complete itself; for at that moment she heard the
click of the front gate as it swung to. It was now almost dark. She
could not see who had thrust the gate open. But somebody was
there, at the door; she heard a step and a rustling. Was it a boy
with a telegram? William?

Matches were at hand; and as a knocking sounded Kitty went

towards the front door with nonchalance, carrying her box of matches and lighting the hall gas as she passed it. Pop! And then a hoarse roar as flame ran up the incandescent mantle. Silly thing! The wind from the door got into the pipe and made it noisy. As for the gas, it gave no proper light and cast a bilious glow over everything. She was not at all nervous, and indeed as she opened the door was still half-immersed in thought of William and Minna, and her confidence in them both.

'Good evening,' said a voice. An unfamiliar, but light and agreeable voice. The stranger tipped his hat. 'Is Mr Harvest home yet?'

'Not yet,' Kitty said. 'What did you want?'

'I . . . I hoped he would be back. I . . . I wanted to see him rather urgently.'

Kitty violently started, and from the sudden chill of her body knew that the shock had caused her to break into dreadful perspiration. She shivered until her teeth began to chatter. She knew that voice. It came from the forgotten past. For a moment she could not speak; but at last:

'He's not here,' she said. Her throat was dry. 'He won't be here for another two hours.'

There seemed to be a great pause, in which the gas roared and a cold wind shook the house and whirled under Kitty's arms. But at the end of it the stranger addressed her again.

'Excuse me, are you Mrs Harvest?'

Kitty knew the light was behind her. She could see him now; fatter, but the same. Of course she had been prepared for that, from seeing his photographs in the papers. He wouldn't remember her. Yes, he'd remember her. At once. With those eyes of his, that looked through you.

'I'm Mr Firth. I . . . I wonder . . . I've come specially. . . .'

Stubbornly, although she felt that he must hear her chattering teeth, Kitty insisted:

'You can't see him tonight. He's at Moreton.'

'I . . . I know. He was going to . . . That's why I . . . I wanted . . . I wonder if I could leave him a . . . a note?'

She had struggled vainly. She knew that—why?—he was determined to see her face, and that whatever the cost to herself she must do nothing that would harm William. But she was in despair. Trembling, she stood back to allow his entry.

It was all he had wanted—to see her face under the light. But she had changed. He was only curious. Curious to see William's wife. He didn't recognise her. Conversationally, apologetically, as he polished the soles of his shoes upon the doormat, he explained:

'You see, I . . . I shan't be at the office tomorrow. I'm going to Moreton myself. I . . . I've been sent for. My father's ill. You don't know him, of course, Mrs Harvest. Your husband was going to see Mr Whistler today——'

'Can he telephone to you tonight?' asked Kitty, shutting the front door, and standing with her back to it. Dick kept peering at her. She saw the glint of his eyes.

'I . . . I hoped to see him. It's so much . . . You know?'

Yes, he was smiling now. His teeth caught the light; little fox-like teeth, sharp-pointed . . . They frightened her. And then she saw that he expected her to show him into the fire-lit room.

'Would you like to wait?' Kitty asked. If she lighted the gas, and left him, turning away very quickly, he might not be able to see her. Ah, but if William came home, and this man stayed! He'd recognise her then, without doubt! She could not risk it. Unaware that she was doing it, she moved within the beam of the light. And at once she heard his breath sharply drawn.

'Good heavens! Haven't I . . . Haven't I . . .' Dick was staring at her like a cat. He was like a sleek, stealthy cat. Green-eyed, with claws. She could detect the sudden tautness of his body, as if he prepared to spring. 'Excuse me, you're so extraordinarily like somebody I used to know. Somebody I . . . I was very fond of. . . .'

'I don't know you,' cried Kitty. Too quickly. Too breathlessly. She knew that the moment she had spoken. He knew it. He was sure, now. Fool! Oh, fool! A terrible dizziness mounted to her head.

'Kitty!' cried Dick, in a loud whisper. 'Kitty! After all these years!'

But thank God William's mother, hearing voices, and knowing that Kitty might be in need of some help in dealing with a stranger

—for even an old woman is a witness and a reinforcement—came just then down the stairs, her skirt swishing and her hand in the tenacity of cautious progress grinding upon the balusters. 'Thank God! Thank God!' thought Kitty. He might stare, and smile, and try to get her alone—to talk and wheedle—but now the ordeal must end for this time. For this time.

She had known that one day it would happen. Known, yet prayed. She was almost fainting; but the knowledge that Mrs Harvest was there gave her new strength.

'It's funny you should think you know me,' said Kitty, stiff-lipped. She was able to smile now. 'Of course I know *you*. Mother, this is Mr Firth. My *husband's* mother, Mr Firth.'

Mrs Harvest was at her side, grey and gentle, but very fearless; and the three of them stood together in the dark hall, very near to one another, their hearts beating fast, and no speech coming from any of them. It was Mrs Harvest who then, having no present trouble, but only an instant intuition that Kitty had appealed to her, dealt with the stranger.

'How d'you do, Mr Firth,' she said. 'I'm sorry my son is from home. He's gone to Moreton to see friends. We weren't expecting you. The evening's been so light that you've found us, I'm afraid, in the gloaming. But perhaps you'd be so kind as to set light to the gas in the sitting-room. I think we mustn't offer you a glass of sherry?'

'Oh, no, no!' protested Dick. 'I . . . I . . . The light, certainly.' He had lost his confidence at the coming of a third person. Though still quickly glancing from one to the other, he began to fumble in his pockets. 'Will you allow me? I haven't any matches. I . . . I don't carry them. The truth is, I don't . . . I didn't wish to inflict myself upon you. All I . . . I wished . . .'

Mrs Harvest, inspired, turned to Kitty.

'The children are both asking for you, dear,' she said.

Kitty had escaped. She ran upstairs to the first floor; and only when she had reached the children's bedroom did she so tremble that her legs would no longer bear her. She sat down beside Rosie's little bed, clutching the iron bars of it, her strength gone. He'd recognised her. He could not force her to do anything, for his power had gone. But in some way, maliciously, malignantly, in his own time, he would tell William. Her happiness would be destroyed. William's happiness would be destroyed. Such hatred of her betrayer rose tempestuously in Kitty's breast that she could have killed him.

CHAPTER XIX

Roland Harvest

W<small>ILLIAM</small> <small>LOOKED</small> <small>DOWN</small> at his son. The little face upon the pillow was deeply flushed, and he could hear the boy's breathing, very quick and rather difficult. It didn't sound too good. Kitty, after making the discovery, had half re-drawn the blind, to prevent the sunshine from tormenting young Roly, and had then summoned William. She had now telephoned to the doctor; while William, after his bath, and still in his dressing-gown, had been unable to keep away from Roly's bedside. He was alarmed.

Of course he knew that some children were liable to feverish colds and that they threw them off, growing fine and strong and eventually casting their parents aside as a butterfly its chrysalis. Roly was different. They had been friends from the beginning-when Roly had smiled first of all at William; and every month had made them better acquainted. Better acquainted, and more closely identified; for while Mrs Harvest had seen in Roly the re-creation of William's father, and Kitty no re-creation, but William's son, William, less superficially, had seen the child as himself. This boy was no blank page, but an intricate sum, a personality, possessed of a will as strong as his own and as yet free from all that sense of responsibility which in the honest adult shackles, though it does not necessarily impair, the will. Good boy; he loved him. Roly, in return, loved William.

Yet he lay now, ever restless, with his heavy lids closed. The sound of his breathing disquieted them. The small round face, still snub-nosed, but otherwise so like and unlike William's, was as red as the sun through fog, and looked slightly swollen; and as William stood there he saw the little hands come again and again from under the bedclothes in a ceaseless effort for freedom and unfevered calm. At last, laden with fear, he turned away, to shave and dress before the doctor reached the house; and as he shaved he heard Kitty's light step re-entering the room he had just left. He listened for a moment, razor in hand, the foamy lather curdling upon his cheeks. Poor kid, she was frightened. With reason. Roly was very ill; and the thought that in spite of all their care he might die was so overwhelming that William, when it grew insistent, as it did now, felt that he must suffocate.

In a little while, knowing that Kitty was still there, he tip-toed back into the next room, and so to the bedside, where she stood with all her love for Roly concentrated in silence. Now and again she, as William had done, would gently draw the little tossing arm once more within the bedclothes; and when William stood beside her she swayed towards him for protection. With William's arm about her, and her hand upon his, they continued to watch the boy until the doctor came.

The doctor, their friend, was as silent as they. He could be extraordinarily quiet, in spite of his big-boned strength; and whatever he did he did with such sure-handedness that one forgot his bulk in confidence of his quality. He took Roly's wrist, uttered no word as he released it, idly touched the boy's forehead and looked into his throat, and finally applied the ends of his stethoscope to the narrow little chest within the dwarf pyjama jacket. Roly's eyes did not open; he slept on. And the doctor's grave glance thereafter at William was indication enough of his thoughts.

'Ah, well,' said Doctor Redding, with medical briskness; 'he's got a temperature. Keep him warm. He'll have to have some poultices on that chest of his. You can manage them, can't you, Mrs Harvest?'

Kitty again took William's hand. He could feel her fingers pressing his with bruising force.

'He's very . . . ill, isn't he?' she asked, thickly.

'Not too good,' answered the doctor, frankly. 'He's got a pretty thorough chill, somehow. However, I'd sooner trust him in your hands, Mrs Harvest, than most others I know of. We'll get him all right again.'

'Shall we?' she pressed.

'Oh, we mustn't suppose anything else. Come, you've had him ill before!' He added a few instructions, the object of some of which, William felt sure, was not to allay Kitty's fears but to give her something to do which would take her out of the room and keep her busy; and when Kitty had released William's hand, and when he and William were alone, he did not at once speak, but stood thinking, his head down and his eyes averted.

'It's pretty bad, I gather,' William said. His lips were rather stiff, and he could not pronounce the words very clearly; but he knew that he was dealing with a situation that called for every alertness.

The doctor came nearer, and dropped his voice.

'One of the lungs,' he said. 'You'll be staying here, will you?'

William was rigid. It was as bad as he had dreaded; worse than he had believed.

'As long as you want me. Are you alarmed?'

'It's your moral support. Nothing to beat it in this house. Well, I'm anxious, of course. I'm always a bit nervous of his stamina under severe strain, such as this. However, if I say that, you won't take it too seriously——'

'I shall take it just as you tell me to,' said William. 'And do whatever I can.'

'Good man. I'll come back in half-an-hour. Look after your wife.' Still thoughtful, he went to the washhand basin; and at last with a smile left the house.

That was why, upon this morning, William did not go to the office. It was Thursday; press day; the first time William had ever been forced to allow his paper to be sent to the machines without his own supervision.

II

The next day, Roly seemed a little easier. His temperature was slightly down, and the nursing had had its effect. By the Sunday he was decidedly better, and William spent a good deal of time in amusing him in various ways. Doctor Redding called several times each day, growing less constrained at each visit; until on Sunday evening he was seen to smile and went so far as to crack an antediluvian joke as he was leaving. It made them laugh with relief. Minna had been there throughout the weekend, to relieve Kitty and add her own energy to the general stock. And Rosie also proved a tower of strength; for she was in high spirits, very pretty, not once naughty, and in radiant health. On the Monday morning it was thought by Doctor Redding that William could safely go to his office, with the understanding that if any change for the worse occurred in the patient's condition he should be summoned instantly by telephone.

Only when he reached the office did William find time to examine the latest issue of his paper. And, having glanced casually through it without, in his preoccupied state, noticing anything amiss, he was about to turn to other matters when—just too late to prevent him from launching the copy to a side table—he caught a few words at the bottom of a page. '. . . under its new direction, the company . . . investors . . .' The effect of these words, which in effect were advice to readers of 'England' to buy certain shares in an unknown company, upon him was such as to send him at a bound to the table, from which he hastily raised the paper, found the page, read the whole paragraph, looked through all the pages with scrupulous care, and at last went to the office telephone which stood upon his desk.

'Ask Mr Milton to come to me at once, please!' he cried. His face had whitened. He was very angry.

It had been a rule without exceptions in this office that the editorial columns should never contain puffs of goods advertised or of companies in which Dick Firth was or might be financially interested. There was a similar rule by which certain notorious quack medicines were excluded from the advertisement pages. Both rules had been broken during the one important day of William's absence in which the paper went to press; and Milton, as sub-editor, was the person directly responsible. When he came, therefore, with an assumed air of languor which did not conceal his preparedness for trouble, William merely beckoned with one finger and, with Milton standing at his side, indicated the two paragraphs and the full page advertisement. He then looked up at Milton, saw that he had coloured faintly, and waited.

'Well?' he asked.

'Something wrong?' returned Milton, languidly.

'As you know,' said William. 'Any excuse?'

He saw the twist of Milton's lips, first in anger at this method of calling his bluff and then in the assumed disdain which served Milton as a common weapon. He could not doubt that the advertisement had been accepted and the paragraphs written and printed with a definite purpose. What purpose? Was it an attack upon himself? If so, was it with Dick Firth's consent? At his behest? Milton drawled:

'Well, as far as the advertisement was concerned, Meadows was a page short. Crapps had cancelled in a hurry. This came in at the last minute, at full price, on condition that we gave them editorial comment. I had to decide in a hurry. And as to Firth's grocery company——'

'You know perfectly well these other people have tried that on before——'

'I didn't know.'

'And been refused. Of course you knew.'

Milton sneered.

'What's the sense of refusing money?' he cried. 'The stuff's not poisonous.'

'It's fraudulent,' said William. 'And the grocery company?'

'That's Firth's own. He gave me the instructions.'

William looked at the young man with contempt.

'Did you protest?' he demanded. 'Say anything?'

'No. Why should I?'

'He told you to put it in? Did he insist? You must have known that if I'd been here I'd have kept them all out.'

Milton shrugged. William could see the perspiration about his eyes.

'You *weren't* here,' said Milton, with muffled insolence.

William threw down the paper and rose to his feet, taking a few steps across the room, and saying as he went:

'You know why. You know my boy was and is desperately ill. And you were in charge. At any minute you could have telephoned to me. You didn't telephone. You took an advertisement that we've declined again and again. You broke our rule, and puffed a quack medicine. And you encouraged a lot of poor flats to put money in a company of Firth's when you know I've refused from the start to have the paper used as a prospectus. You did it deliberately. Why?'

Milton moved in discomfort. His assurance had greatly diminished.

'Well, I don't know what one does when Firth——'

'You know perfectly well,' William told him in a low voice. 'Why didn't you do it?'

'Well, if you want to know,' cried Milton, in anger, 'I think they're damned silly rules. They aren't practised by any other paper.'

'They're practised here.'

Milton tried to stare William down; but he could not do it.

'I tell you I had to decide in a hurry. And I'm not a prig!' he shouted.

'All right,' said William. 'I can see what you are.' It was dismissal.

For an instant Milton held his ground. But he could not deal with somebody who was unimpressed by his manner; and like a sulky schoolboy he turned away, trying to make his retreat less than abject. Outside the door fury seized him. But William, his eyes still seeing that retreating figure, was troubled by other thoughts. Obviously Milton would not have acted thus if he had not felt secure. There were eight months to go on his own contract. What was in the wind?

III

Dick Firth returned from lunch that day in great good-humour. He came smiling through the outer office with an expression of gratified mischief, and as he hung up his hat he showed in the careless gesture the gaiety of one savouring victory. But even in victory he kept his own counsel, and beyond observing the fact that he smiled and minced in passing her the girl at the desk knew nothing of the plans dancing in Dick's mind or of the malicious pleasantries lurking at the tip of his little pointed tongue. She was afraid of Dick, and thought him horrid; whereas in his own eyes Dick was one of the most simple-hearted and kindly persons in the universe.

But other people *were* such poor fish! It was easy to read their minds and bait the hook and play them accordingly. A fisher of souls! Money, flattery, threat, cajolery: by means of them one could get what one wanted. If one knew what it was. If one wanted it enough. When he had shut the door of his room, and was alone, Dick did more than smile; he shook with silent laughter. For he had been giving lunch that day to Robert and Julie Whistler, and he was happy about it. About them.

Standing in his room, and smoothing his hair with both hands, Dick dropped a hand with one of his quick gestures, and shook it before him, open, with the palm uppermost. The movement might have indicated that one or both of his late guests loved money, or that he held one or both of them in the hollow of his hand. But whatever he may have believed about that he had no doubt of his own superior quickness of manœuvre.

'All right,' he whispered to himself, smiling again. 'All right.'

. . . She was handsome. In the thirties they often bloomed anew. Discontented. Yes, and handsome. Oho, you saw by the way she looked back at you . . . Vain as a peacock. Peahen? Perhaps they weren't . . . Poor solemn Robert! Slow—— 'Yes?' The last was a call; for somebody was at the door of his room.

It was Milton; sleek and black as a seal. 'Can you spare a minute?'

'Oh, Milton, yes. Come in. You . . . you look troubled. Trials and troubles too great to be borne——'

'Trials *indeed*. Harvest's back,' grumbled Milton. They spoke together as two men with a secret understanding.

'Splendid!' cried Dick. 'How's his boy? I must see him.'

Milton still grumbled.

'I didn't ask. He's up in arms, the damned prig.'

'Ah, Milton! You're wrong.' Dick shook his head, still smiling at his secret treasures. 'You're stupid and shallow. I've warned you of it. I must do it again, I see. Harvest's twenty times abler than you'll ever be.'

'Oh, my God!' groaned Milton. 'You too! I don't know what you see in the fellow. He's a crank. He's keeping you from making twenty thousand a year out of the paper. And you think he's a paragon.'

'I *know* he's a paragon, Milton. He made the paper. But for him it wouldn't exist. If he wants to be a little strict about advertisers and suchlike, let him.'

'I could double the sale,' cried Milton. 'Treble it. Quadruple it. I could make it the most popular paper in England——'

'There are so many of them! Full of lies.'

'I could put big money in your pocket; float your companies; dictate your policies——'

Dick sighed drolly.

'To be candid, Milton, I have *no* policies.'

'But you want power.'

'He's given me reputation. The reputation of an honest man. His own honesty! I get the credit for all his scruples. And the rest I can do for myself, Milton.'

'My God!' muttered Milton. 'I tell you the fellow's insufferable.'

Dick shook again with silent laughter. He was extraordinarily pleased with everything that day.

'But then he's been making you feel small, I'm sure. It's a way virtue has. It's never pleasant.'

Milton did not disguise his sulky annoyance. He growled:

'Talking as if I was an office boy——'

'As you are, my dear Milton; as you are! Didn't I tell you Harvest was able? He's quiet: it misleads you. He's modest: it's perplexing. To you, especially. But you *will* think you're Napoleon, when you're not. Harvest, quiet as he is, can make rings round you. Beautiful rings while you flounder within like a naughty child. He's only got one fault——'

'He's a prig.'

'He's evidently made you feel *very* small, Milton. I don't remember ever seeing you so disconcerted. Well, I'll make peace between you. I'll go and commune with him. I . . . I'm in the mood for it.'

Dick cheerfully brushed Milton aside as he went to the door. He looked at Milton with great malice. A small man; useful, free from

excessive scruple, well-informed upon many matters; but funda-
mentally stupid. You take a stupid fellow; you varnish him with
education; you polish his wits until they seem almost bright with
reflected light; and you use him as a subordinate. But the stupider
he is, the readier he is to despise others. On the whole Dick did
not like Milton. He only found him useful.

'Milton, thou should'st be living at this hour!' He would make
a mess of 'England'. He'd evidently annoyed Harvest. Harvest
mustn't be annoyed. Too valuable. Too likeable. If only he had a
little more humour! But what a prime joke—what an inexhaustible
secret joke!—that he should have married little Kitty Dooms!
Artful little piece! She must have played her cards well. Oh, why?
The fellow was as simple as a bumpkin; and she was pretty and
easy. Easy. That took Dick back twenty years. Had she 'told'?
Not his name, he'd swear! She'd been terrified. Why? Ah, well,
poor little thing . . .

Running quickly up to William's fine big room, Dick took
pleasure in his own lightness of step and his freedom from breath-
lessness. The result of a blameless life! No alcohol, no nicotine!
Forty-one years old; and his heart as sound as a bell! Not only—
might he say?—his heart! One or two disappointments, one of
them bitter; but otherwise . . . He reached William's room.

IV

For a moment, William was unaware that he was under observation. He had put his annoyance away long since, and was dictating
answers to some of the letters which had accumulated in his absence. Dick had a good view of him from the doorway, and was
amused at the sight of editor and little stenographer with flying
pencil. A skinny little girl with freckles and ginger hair. She left
him cold. Probably did the same by Harvest. You couldn't imagine
Harvest choosing a secretary for her looks. Or this child setting a
man's heart in a flame.

'Good afternoon, Harvest,' laughed Dick. 'Here I am, you see.'
The little ginger girl started. After getting speechless permission,

she jumped up and made her way past Dick, going out of the room as if he were not there. Like a walking machine, and as attractive, he thought. Some temper, though; and so, not without appeal to the senses. He and William exchanged smiles.

'Brusque,' said Dick.

'The modern absence of ceremony,' answered William. Both laughed slightly.

'But I . . . I say, I wanted to see you. I've seen Whistler. It's . . . it's all right. He's amazingly easy to handle, you know. Amazingly. Same old Bob. His wife was there. D'you like her? I like her. She's . . . she's got more brains than he. Quite a lot, I shouldn't wonder. Tied down there. She'll shine in London, eh? Already thinking in terms of a salon. A second Madame Récamier. Oh, but my dear fellow——'

'I wanted to see you, too,' said William, with a direct but not unpleasant glance. Dick did not pretend to misunderstand. He said at once:

'About that fool Milton. Fearful idiot. I . . . I say, what's he been doing? Very bad, is it?'

Dick was all solicitousness. He came and sat upon the arm of the visitor's chair, and had something, sitting there, of the appearance of Puck; for he looked as if his solicitousness had a core of mockery. And William, for answer, threw over a note from their common friend, J. B.

Dear W.:

What on earth are you doing? Are you away? Two pars this week that blot your copybook. Ring me up. But first box D. F.'s ears.

J. B.

Dick handed back the note very thoughtfully. It was a reproach to himself. Why did these fellows maintain such a strict watch over the columns of a paper? Couldn't they allow a man a little latitude? Was it so very wrong to tell people to buy a particular thing, even if one knew that it wasn't quite all that was claimed for it? Was one never to use one's own paper as a means of distribution? They didn't appreciate the difficulties of doing as many different things at once as he did.

'Hm,' he said; his smile gone. His tone was dry. He was not pleased. 'Very kind of him.' Then: 'I say, Harvest, how's your boy? I was so sorry——'

As if in answer to his question, the telephone bell rang; and William answered. Dick listened. He saw William's face whiten; he heard a voice that, even by telephone, and at the distance of a yard from the receiver, could not be mistaken. First he sat upright; then he stiffened. He knew that voice. It was Minna's. He would have known it anywhere and at any time, known it and been moved by it—as now—to the bitterest emotion. He had loved Minna. He now hated her. He did not hear the words she used; but only, from William:

'I'll come at once. This moment, Minna.'

William's hands were trembling as he clumsily replaced the receiver; and in some way he stumbled up from his place at the desk and as one walking in sleep groped by its edge to the open floor. With difficulty he recalled the fact that he had been engaged in conversation.

'I'm sorry, Firth,' he hoarsely said. 'I must go. My boy's very ill.'

No more. Dick had not moved. He continued to sit staring at the telephone. He did not look at William; for his mind was upon the voice he had heard, the name William had pronounced, and so by way of a memory of past humiliation to assurance that William knew everything. This fellow knew Minna. Moreton, of course, was the link. Neither had mentioned it. Both in the plot. That night, long ago, Harvest in the cottage up the hill. No wonder his frantic search had been vain. He'd never dreamed! By God, she'd made him ridiculous. Killed him. This fellow had known all along. He'd hidden her. He'd come back to the office, knowing, sniggering. . . . Through all those bitter weeks when he'd been nearly out of his mind, seeking her, frantic with the sense of loss, this fellow had known where she was and kept the knowledge to himself. Blast him! Anger flew to fury, and fury to madness. All reason was extinguished, and only a desire for vengeance burned hotly within as if it must blind him, dry his blood, consume his being.

He could have killed Harvest, now. Killed him. No; he'd ruin him. . . .

William, becoming gradually aware through his anguish that Dick was staring at him, stared in return, and saw Dick's face as a livid mask of hatred. But he could not as yet understand what had happened, for his thoughts were fixed upon the bedside five miles away, where Kitty and Minna were watching a small life flicker as it died. He said, in a tone of apology:

'My boy's dying, Firth. You'll excuse me. You understand why I must go at once.'

Dick stood up, facing William. His teeth were snarlingly bared. He had not heard what William said; for he in turn thought only of a night four years earlier.

'*I* know you, Harvest,' he stammered. 'By God, I know you now!'

'What?' William was arrested. 'You heard me receive a message. I must go.' He turned away and went to the hook upon which his coat and hat were hanging. As he struggled into the coat he saw Dick still staring fixedly at him. Odd: why was that? What had happened? He could not think. He did not imagine that he had spoken Minna's name or that Dick had recognised her voice.

'You and J. B.,' cried Dick savagely. 'A pair.'

'J. B.?' William was bewildered. 'This is my boy, Roland, I tell you——'

Dick checked him.

'What went into the paper went in by my instructions.'

William stopped at the door.

'I can't stay to speak of it,' he said. 'I've already talked to Milton. If he does a thing like that again, he'll have to go. But I shan't give him another chance of doing it.' He met Dick's glare of hatred with a glance as abrupt and as unshakeable.

'You don't understand,' retorted Dick. 'What he did was by my leave. By my order.'

William, his hand upon the doorknob, looked wearily at his employer.

'I don't believe you,' he said. And added: 'As long as I'm editor of this paper I decide what goes into it. That's our understanding.'

CHAPTER XX

The Ebb

WILLIAM THREW DOWN his pen, and listened. A street organ stood below, rattling out a song of the hour; and the sound of it lifted his heart. Some might curse the street organ, or mechanical music, or popular music, vulgarity, happiness, and expectation: he did not. He enjoyed all these things, especially the rakish zest with which the organ dashed into a tune. And as the sun was shining upon this July day, and the sky was blue, William was tempted. He thought how delightful it would be to let his pen lie, run down-stairs to Kitty, and invite her to go for a stroll past the Highgate Ponds to Hampstead Heath, and watch the children and sportive old men with boats and kites, and forget all that he had to do that day. . . .

But he disobeyed the impulse. Instead, after lighting his pipe, he resumed his seat and struggled to go on with his work. What an idiot!

The house in Highgate would have seemed to a casual observer unchanged a year after Roly's death; but it was desperately changed. Mrs Harvest continued to read the newspapers and to compose very libellous letters to their editors about the conduct of various men and women; Kitty continued to cook and iron and look after Rosie as if Rosie had never had an elder brother whom she had devotedly loved; Maggie, the daily maid, who went home after she had eaten a substantial lunch, still sang as she swept and washed up, although perhaps she did it in a lower tone than of old; and Minna, more and more absenting herself as the calls upon her time increased, often came to the house in the summer evenings and lent her aid. Only William, in his attic, knew that although they spoke seldom of Roly his death had struck a blow at their joy; only William, in his attic, looked to the future with a full measure of foreboding. It resembled a blank wall.

Upon this July day in 1914 he had felt, until that piano-organ pounced right into the middle of its tune and showed him the errors of lethargy, like a puny dreamer called upon to play substitute for Atlas. It is a mood common to unwilling workers upon July—and other—days; but perhaps in this instance William was more to be excused than most. For a year's experience had shown him that his old friend Dick Firth had a long and crooked arm. A damned mischievous arm that could have been seen, with the aid of passion, as an instrument of unkind Fate. And William had suffered severely from the activity of this arm. From its activity, that is, and the less deliberate disturbances to which its stirrings had given rise.

He had not expected, when Dick's apparently fantastic change of mood had been translated into a cheque for eight months' salary and commission, that another editorship would immediately be offered to him. The one he had enjoyed had come by chance, and it was withdrawn by chance. It was unnecessary to wail at injustice. But something else was more disquieting, a suspicion that wherever he went a false story of the circumstances had preceded him. What story it was, William could not discover. He was only aware of it as a retreating haze that re-formed behind him. And in the agony following Roly's death, when for all his outward calm he had been secretly consumed by a fever of uneasiness, he had been driven almost mad by the sense of unseizable opposition. The work he could get was small and ill-paid. Although still, apparently, popular with his fellow-journalists, he noticed how cautious they were, how deprecating, how hurried. Men, he found, instinctively avoid the unfortunate, and without ill-will unconsciously conspire against them. They feared the loss of their own jobs. They feared the inconvenience of any application from another.

But William was not without resource. Through his old friend J. B., who was safely in an editorial chair from which none could turn him, he syndicated a weekly article on current affairs to a few provincial papers. He reviewed some books. He wrote odd articles here and there. And he kept in touch, as well as he could, both with the political world, which he found increasingly sensitive with intrigue, and with Fleet Street. He did not hide, or sulk, or take men into corners for the purpose of complaining. He did not throw in his towel, as is done in the ring; but did his best to bear himself cheerfully and to keep a stout heart. Kitty and his mother never guessed how low his spirit sometimes sank; for their trust in him was unshakeable. And, in side remarks, sometimes in set explanation, he heard a great deal which he had not known before about Dick and his doings and his methods and their effects upon ever-widening circles of human beings. It proved instructive. If it had been less disturbing it would have been amusing. William had been charmed by Dick. Even now, when the explanation of Dick's conduct was clear to him, he could forgive the change of mood.

Nevertheless, William was in the doldrums, and he knew it. That was why, today, he longed to be out of doors and carefree in the sunshine. That was why he welcomed the piano-organ. That was why, when he saw the tanned, broken-nosed organ-player, who grinned below his old Panama hat and seemed to embody the triumph of vagabondage, he opened the attic-window and flung the man twopence. Easy work, turning a handle. A free choice of roads. Liberty . . . Afterwards, hearing the chinkle of the coppers as they struck the road, William imagined Kitty looking out of the ground floor window and then aloft, towards the reckless donor. She would be astounded. To give valuable pennies to organ-grinders was an act outside Kitty's sympathy. Organ-grinders did not work. They did not deserve help, but idled and drank and created useless noise. They were as idle as writers. All writers, that is, except William; for in Kitty's eyes William could do no wrong and was less a writer than an angel in coat and trousers.

II

By afternoon, although the sun grew more resplendent, William thought no more of it. He was upon his way to town, and he strode down the embanked footpath of Highgate Hill, under the arching trees, with such a load of thought upon his mind that he passed Minna without seeing her Only by running after him did she make her presence known; and then, in the instant of sweet, breathless greeting, they were simultaneously reminded of something which had happened long since, upon just such a Summer's day, in the garden at Royals.

'By Jove!' cried William. 'This is like the afternoon when you pushed me into the stream. Remember? A hundred years ago.'

'I'm more careful now,' Minna said. 'I didn't push you this time. Oh, dear, doesn't it seem a long time ago!' She was radiant; and in spite of a severe blue serge costume and a business-like black straw hat of the period which shaded her eyes, she resembled the child he recalled, for the little run had brought fresh colour to her cheeks. 'However, we mustn't talk like greybeards! Old as we are.'

'I was never younger!' protested William. 'Brisk, bright, brotherly.'

'Too brotherly by half,' said Minna. 'Ungallant, in fact. However, we shan't be together for long; because I'm going to my job.'

'Job!' teased William. He said, seriously: 'Which of your innumerable jobs is this?'

He could so easily have put his arms around her, as at Royals, that abstention hardly dimmed his present joy. A quickened pulse, a new sense of vitality, transformed him; while Minna's laughing confidence, which was once again cloudless as it had been in childhood, made her irresistible. He drew his breath, observing her. No treachery to Kitty was in their undeclared love; and yet, as their glances now encountered, each with marvelling terror read the ineffable answer to a wordless question. Upon Highgate Hill, where the footpath is high above the roadway, and under the shadow of trees in summer leaf, there was no longer disguise or uncertainty between them.

Only a moment passed.

'I'm going,' Minna continued; but the words she used were not meant to be heard, 'to help teach some very nice but not very sensible girls how to look after the sick. You mayn't know it; but I'm now an expert in First Aid. If you were to fall down at this moment, and break your arm—which, except professionally, I hope you won't do—I should be almost able to put you together again. It's a useful kind of knowledge.'

'Most useful,' agreed William. 'And if we were wrecked on a desert island it might be invaluable.'

'There's hardly any likelihood of that,' observed Minna, cheekily. Though what delight to be wrecked, alone, with William! 'I could nurse you in other ailments, too.' He said, still in lazy recollection: 'We were often wrecked at Royals.'

The tears leapt to Minna's eyes. She thought aloud.

'Beautiful Royals! It would break my heart to go there again.' Their steps had slackened.

'Oh, no,' said William. 'You'd cry; but you'd be very happy.'

'I shouldn't cry at all; but I should remember my own idiocies. I should think of mother. I should think of . . .'

He did not hear her say 'you'. He thought she would suffer only the pangs of revived childish glee and distress. How little William understood her! Miracle of sympathy though he was, he could never imagine himself as she saw him. They walked in silence. As they reached the dismal bottom of the hill, William asked:

'Is this job of yours in Upper Holloway?'

She, interrupted in reverie, answered:

'It is. Down a road, and down another road. In a musty little hall . . .'

'Golly! On such a day!' he groaned. 'What perversity!'

They had reached their point of parting. And then, not dreaming that he would misunderstand, Minna said something which had been in her mind before they met.

'William,' she began, impulsively. 'If you were to hear from somebody—you're not likely to, but you might—that a thoroughly efficient woman is wanted as companion-secretary-nurse to an old lady, I'm after *that* job, too. I feel I'm ready to tackle something new.'

William, thunderstruck, looked quickly into her face.

'Surely you've got your hands full as it is?'

'My hands, Will,' answered Minna, turning to him. 'But not my head.' Their glances met, long and candidly. Both trembled.

'I shall come a little way farther with you,' he said, in a cool voice. 'Because I don't want you to go away; and I don't think there's any need for you to go.'

'I'm *not* going away,' answered Minna, in the same cool voice. 'There's no need whatever to go away. But I want a job.' She had not resisted his determination to walk farther with her, and they were now moving down past the shops of which both were unaware. Reflected in the plate glass windows they were seen to be in deadly earnest; although to passers-by they might have been two friends chatting. 'A job that'll fill my time.'

'Your life.'

'No.'

'A job that will take you away,' he explained. 'For good.'

'A job that will leave me free to see you as often as ever,' she insisted.

William stopped. His air was one of breathless relief. She saw that he was white.

'Oh, if you say *that!*' he cried. 'You frightened me.'

Minna, inexpressibly moved, took his arm and pressed it to her side. Her lips would not frame the words she wanted them to speak. But she was celestially happy. At last:

'You weren't frightened,' she said, teasingly, caressingly. 'You've never been frightened . . . for me.' How natural it was to touch him once more as she had done without fear in childhood, to walk thus, linked and in a single rhythm! She was astonished at the sweetness of this moment.

'Well,' answered William, smiling, but with a darkness of trouble. 'Perhaps I've come to rely on you more than I used. Or to realise it.'

'As everybody—including me—relies on *you!*' she answered. They had stopped walking. She could look at him from under her hat, and saw that he was puzzled by her remark, and indifferent to it. 'I don't want that sort of reliance.'

'You won't get it,' said William, coolly.

His face was so close that Minna kissed his cheek and pushed him away.

'Be off!' she cried; and left him.

III

On his way home, William walked down the Strand as far as Charing Cross; and was tempted to stand for a few minutes, watching the pigeons in Trafalgar Square, and the falling spray from the fountains. Then, as the shadows grew longer, he strolled towards a bus-stop, and was diverted by the sight of a tall man, top-hatted and frock-coated, who stood with a cigar in the corner of his mouth surveying the front of the National Gallery. Prosperity glowed and glittered upon this man. Though he was still young there was a portliness in his figure and a grandeur in his carriage that made William think of Porthos in middle-age. Having smiled at the figure, he was surprised to find that he had been looking at Robert Whistler; and at the same moment Robert caught sight of him.

Robert did not delay to spring forward and shake William warmly by the hand.

'Come and have a drink!' he demanded.

'No!' cried William. 'I'm on my way home; and my wife's a martinet.'

'Poor old chap!' Robert lifted his head in commiseration.

'But you look very prosperous, Whistler!' said William. 'Anybody could see you owned the Mint.'

'That's the idea,' agreed Robert. 'Well, have a cigar, then.' He produced a big case. 'I don't mind telling you that I'm now able to gratify my taste for good cigars. And what's more, I put 'em down to expenses, my boy. What d'you think of that!'

'Very corrupt,' declared William, taking a cigar.

'Corrupt be blowed!' Robert smacked him upon the shoulder. 'All the same, I've learnt a thing or two in the last year, Harvest. I mean, about corruption.'

'The slippery slope,' suggested William.

'Well.' Robert eyed him over the tip of the cigar with eyes which perhaps were more bulbous than of yore. His face, ruddier than it had been—but perhaps it was only a post-luncheon colour—was slightly swollen; not bloated. He was mysterious. 'Well, there's more things in heaven and earth than are dreamt of in *your* philosophy, my boy.'

'One half the world doesn't know how the other half lives,' retorted William.

'I believe you!' agreed Robert. 'But I've been a bit lucky, you know. A bit lucky. I've become involved in big business. The sort of thing I've always——'

'The sort of thing you're cut out for!' said William, suavely.

Robert gave him an expressive glance.

'That little swine, Dick Firth, again,' he explained, in a dropped voice. 'It's thanks to him.'

'Oh, Whistler! Oh, the descent!' cried William. 'And you said you'd ram it down his throat!'

Robert, pursing his lips, hid a smile.

'I told you he'd always been able to get round me,' he answered. 'But this time he'd got something to *give*. That is, he wanted a man with my experience at his finger-tips. He'd got hold of something good; but he needed an expert. I'm the expert. Well, he had to make it worth my while. So I'm in on the ground floor; we've got a chain operating through the best part of the south coast—none of your Seahamptons and Moretons!—and making a decided profit. I tell you, it's been an education to me; an education. I'm making a couple of thousand a year now; I've got a manager in at Moreton, and I mean to take that place into a new chain we're forming; and before you've had time to turn round half-a-dozen times I shall be making ten or twenty thousand a year.'

'Good!' cried William. 'Excellent. So you think better of Firth now.'

'I think I've *got* the better of him,' was the reply.

William grinned. With all his liking for Robert he could not believe that.

'You might watch your agreements,' he said, mildly.

Robert started, puffed two or three agitated and extravagant clouds of smoke from his cigar, and asked:

'Anything the matter with yours?'

'It came to an end,' William said. 'No complaints.'

'He doesn't talk about you. I tried to get him to. The fact is, old chap, I tried to do you a good turn. He shut up. Shut me up, too. Did you have a row?'

'A little misunderstanding,' William answered. 'It doesn't matter. How does Julie like the *beau monde?*'

Robert raised his rubicund face to heaven. He extended the cigar-laden hand.

'Eats it,' he expressively declared. 'She's a different woman. Dances, goes everywhere. . . .' His laugh was cosy and gratified. 'Come and see us, Harvest; will you? Look here, I'll give you my card.' He fumbled. 'I don't want you to suppose that in the days of my prosperity I discard my old friends.'

They exchanged cards. They shook hands.

'I forgot to ask what *you* were doing, Harvest,' cried Robert, as they were parting.

'I'm collecting the wealth of the Indies,' laughed William. But he did not stay to explain to Robert the extraordinary subtlety of this remark. On the contrary, he ran for his omnibus and in triumph caught it.

IV

This encounter was not the end of William's day; for when he reached home he found Kitty sitting by herself indoors, while his mother and Rosie still pottered in the garden. Something in Kitty's pose startled him, for it was both tired and dispirited; and as she smiled at his entry he for the first time noticed a new shadowy thinness in her cheek. She was unwell.

Now William knew that his first act must not involve any comment upon this discovery; but he made up his mind that the heat of that July day had tried Kitty and that she needed a change. To prepare for the suggestion of a holiday, he spoke of the meeting with Robert Whistler, and gave an exaggerated account of the worldly prosperity indicated by Robert's clothing. He imitated the complacency of Robert's manner. He produced Robert's card, which gave a very curly address in Kensington as Robert's abode. And when Kitty did not smile at his story he knew that her spirits were very low indeed.

But he was unprepared for her reply to his effort. She said:
'I hate them all.'

'You don't hate Robert?' asked William. 'He's an awfully decent chap. He's been unlucky.'

'He's been lucky in his dealings with you,' said Kitty. 'Living rent free at Moreton. Is he going to pay some rent now?' She leant up and caught William by the arm, and he sat down upon the arm of the chair, so that she could nestle her head against him.

'You're tired,' he told her. 'How about putting that child to bed and asking mother if she'd mind being left while we go to a theatre?' The head resting at his waist was waggled in refusal. 'Well, a holiday, then? Take ma and Rosie to the seaside?' Again that refusal.

'Got the hump,' Kitty confided, in a very low voice. 'Had it for months.' She caught his hand and put it to her cheek. 'All my own fault.'

'Me?' William asked. The head was violently shaken. He stooped, and drew her closer. 'What then?'

There was a long silence. William, who knew so much, who guessed so much, who loved her and would have borne her every burden, heard a heavy sigh, and felt a sudden jerk of her body as it was shaken by a sob. He, too, sighed.

'It is Roly?' he whispered. 'My dearest, it was terrible for all of us; for you most of all. But——'

'It was my fault,' she whispered back, her face pressed against him.

He caught his breath. It was monstrous that she should think such a thing.

'Good heavens, no. You did everything——'

The little voice persisted:

'Me. It's in me. My father, my uncle; both died of consump—— The illness——'

'Good God! Good God!' cried William, stabbed to the heart with self-reproach. He would have leapt to his feet in desperation if every duty had not kept him at her side. 'Kitty, dearest; have I let you bear this awful thing for a year without knowing anything about it?' He was terribly moved, taken completely by surprise. 'Oh, it's unforgivable! Of course that's not true.'

'It is!'

'No, no, no! Dearest, you don't know what you're talking about. I swear to you——'

'It's true,' she groaned. 'Oh, and I watch Rosie all the time—watch, watch, watch!—all the time!' A great sob choked her. Breathlessly, she struggled against the passionate grief which threatened to rob her of all self-control. 'It drives me silly. It's awful. And I haven't been able to tell you. Or anybody. Bottling it up. It drives me *mad*——'

And with that, gasping 'Oh, I'm punished! I'm punished!' she began to cry as if her heart must break; while William, holding her to his breast, his cheek gently against her soft hair, his hand gripped by hers, listened, murmuring consolation and waiting in misery until the sobbing should die. His heart was like lead. As he sat there in the quiet room, and the last rays of evening sunlight cast ever wilder hues upon wall and garden, he thought of all the wrong things he had done in his life, the mistakes he had made, the pain he had felt and caused to those whom he loved; and as he contrasted his strength to bear ill with that of the poor child in his arms, whose only faults had arisen from the impulse of a warm and eager heart, and who had suffered and must still suffer through the rest of her shortening life from sorrow which he could not hope to avert, he felt his strength ebbing. Only the knowledge that he must not fail those who depended upon him kept William silent and resolute. Otherwise he must have yielded to despair.

PART V

The Man Who Went To Market

CHAPTER XXI

Shadows Before

THE LIGHTS OF LONDON were up again. Windows were no longer shrouded. People walked with freer steps in the West End; and it was believed that the world had been made safe from threat for all time. But the Winter evenings fell early; and upon windless nights Julie Whistler, like other women, still looked towards the sky, eastwards, with a sinking of the stomach. She dreamed, as other women did, of great fleets of hostile aeroplanes, flying high, which in contempt of Peace were to destroy the city as its caution was trustfully relaxed.

You would not have realised Julie's trepidation if, early in 1919, you had seen her languidly stepping, fur-coated, from a famous Piccadilly shop into the waiting limousine. You would have thought, perhaps, that she was bored and preoccupied, pale and rather beautiful; but you would not have been able to guess what lay behind the languor and the preoccupation. What did lie behind? Was it nothing?

Once Julie had been wrapped about with a rug, and once, in the gathering darkness, she felt the swimming of people and vehicles about her as the car threaded a way westward, she let her head rest against cushions and wearily closed her eyes. The darkness was full of horrors—sparks of fire from headlights crossing and impending, glittering streaks from shop-windows, and a sense of chaos. She opened her eyes again as she was flashed down the hill towards Hyde Park Corner, and in relief at the cessation of War she welcomed the lines of distant street-lamps as if they had been stars in a windswept sky; but she was now very tired, and she yielded herself to drowsiness with extreme pleasure. Parkins, the chauffeur, had confident leather-gloved hands upon the steering-wheel; a memory of his peaked cap and square shoulders and set jaw gave her reassurance. But she no longer felt proud of the limousine and its appointments, as she had once done. They were a part of the familiar bore of life.

Julie had been shopping. With money to spend—and save—she could still relish the satisfaction of being married to a rich man. She had gone from one department of Hortons' to another, buying here a vanity bag for herself and a cheap necklace for Rachel, there a rug for the side of her bed; adding to her store of gloves and shoes, and remembering that Rachel had asked if she, too, could have some new stockings and a pair of thick shoes to replace some which she had ruined by foolishly drying them at a too-hot fire after a soaking. Rachel! Such an expense! So pale! So thin and without style! Julie bit her lip as she thought impatiently of her daughter.

Rachel, at a daily school, would soon be fourteen. No companion. No chic. Stupid. There was no comfort to be found there. But perhaps in two or three years she would improve. The school was a good one—expensive. They would teach her something there. Julie stirred impatiently, not at first understanding that the car had stopped outside her house; but when Parkins opened the door she threw the rug aside and went indoors without a word to him or to the maid, going straight into the drawing-room, where a fire burned and subdued lights heightened the silence and the curtains had been drawn. Silence. Silence. This room at least satisfied her. It was all in cream and black, very spacious, with yellow and copper-coloured chrysanthemums in great vases; and African iris at the two ends of the mantelpiece. A large gilt-framed mirror in the satin-cream wall opposite showed Julie her own figure.

Ah! The cold made her ugly. She swung round to observe the fall of the coat, which was of nutria; but she would not approach the mirror more closely, because she did not wish to see how grey the frosty air had turned her cheeks. Slowly she drew off her gloves and tried to warm the hands with the long fingers, and looked about the room as if its emptiness was a commentary upon her life. Then, still wearily, she turned again and went upstairs to her bedroom. Every day the same. The War, the War . . . it had ruined the world. There remained only this new life of income and expenditure; to which she had looked forward and upon which she now turned so melancholy an eye. 'Mrs Robert Whistler'—nobody recognised the name. 'My husband': something in the City. 'My friends': where were they?

She had no friends. Robert's business colleagues brought their wives. All dowdy, provincial women who tried to pretend that they were ladies. They had no breeding. They spoke of how much things cost, of what they had bought—always stingily and stupidly —at sales, of servants as if such creatures were as new to them as in their well-trained aloofness they were to Julie, of husbands as 'Mister' This and That, of books and plays that were 'rather rather', of what the doctor said—'And *doctor* . . .'—of aristocratic peccadilloes with the furtive sniggerings of envious kitchenmaids. . . . And Julie, so polite, so strange in manner, so 'French' at a time when the French were unpopular with the English, after a War in which they had fought side by side, but so desperately bored at having to entertain such women while their men-folk dawdled over cigars and drinks that made them greasily merry about nothing at all . . . She was disgusted. Were *these* business men? Little shrewd eyes, no manners; inclined to suppose that because she was French she was hot stuff. . . . 'La Vie Parisienne', the Folies Bergères, gay Paree . . . Oh, they revolted her! They made her feel sick with boredom.

So much for this life. Julie felt an aristocrat among the bourgeoisie. She flung down her fur coat so that it trailed from the arm of a chair to the floor: the maid would pick it up. That was a gesture of sufficient meaning. A fur coat which had cost two hundred pounds: what of that? She could afford to buy another. Gay Paree and 'La Vie Parisienne' and the Folies Bergères: who cared if such people estimated the only civilised nation in the world by such standards? Hot stuff: where, among these pig-eyed mediocrities with greedy hands and swollen bellies, was there one who could fire *her*?

II

At the other end of the town, in a building with many lighted windows, clerks stood or squatted at their high desks and stenographers tapped endlessly in the production of commercial cliché. Telephones buzzed and office boys with waste-paper baskets full of mail clattered down stone staircases to the street, bumping into each other and scampering to pour their burdens into letter-boxes. Horse-drawn vans loitered in narrow streets and stopped everything that travelled faster than themselves; and later sparrows pecked their food before it should be sluiced away for ever by the evening scavengers. The sky, like yellowish-grey smoke above the City's lights, seemed to rest upon the very roofs of the taller buildings; but upon the ground so many men and women poured hither and thither that from above they made there a continuous troubled movement akin to that of swarming bees.

In the entrance to the building of which we spoke, which had a dank and dungeony air, and where grimy light bulbs dimmed everything to gloom, a commissionaire guarded an antediluvian lift. He had medals across his breast, and he had lost a hand; and his face, tanned and drawn by War-time experience, had not yet recovered in Peace its old complaisant stupidity. He sat upon a stool, looking at newcomers with the apathy of one half-killed by mud and horror, and scowling at the cheery boys who charged down the stairs; and his eyes from time to time vacantly regarded the wall upon which were painted in black the names of all firms having offices in this building. But to the commissionaire all such offices were but quarters occupied by brass hats, bits of boys, and immense bevies of girls the like of whom he had never in his life seen before.

These girls arrived in the morning in bunches, and crowded merrily into the lift, while he pulled on the steel rope and bore them skywards. They screamed at him as he passed their floors. They gushed out upon the landing. Took no notice of him except as the lift-man. And he, half-dead, with shrapnel still in his body, and bad dreams disturbing his rest every night, could not yet deal calmly with such indifference or consider it anything but an indignity. Had he lost his hand to give jobs to such as these? They were impudent, cheeky, sure of themselves—boys in skirts. They were—Nicodemus Trott did not know that he was stealing a phrase from Pooh-Bah—they were not young ladies; they were young persons. And the sooner they were packed off back to their homes, to make room for the returning boys, the better. Crowds of girls in his lift! Like rabbits. What had *they* done in the Great War, daddy? They'd swarmed out of school and pinched the men's jobs. . . . Girls . . . Kids of things . . . Not ladies . . .

Upstairs, in a big office, where a dozen or more of these kids of things worked, there was intense clatter. All the typewriters in the place were going at high speed, and the girls were working under big lights that threw deep shadows upon their neat costumes. And at the extreme end of the office there was a massive door at which nobody thought of looking. It was a large door. Behind it was a large room. And in the large room, at a large desk, was a large man. He was reclining in his chair and reading a paper; and the paper was called 'England'. But it was nothing like the 'England' that William had edited. It was very much smarter; it contained pages of snappy paragraphs headed 'We Hear That——' and 'We Want to Know' and 'You Have Money to Invest' and 'Proposals I Have Refused' and 'How to Attract the Other Sex'. It contained advertisements headed 'Girls! Here's Your Chance!' and 'She Married the Boss!' and 'Feeling Slack? Snooker's Wine Will Tone You Up' and 'Don't Be Nervy and Depressed; Take Pip-Pop and Kick over the Traces'. And the centre opening, at which the large man was glancing with a kind of eager distaste, was no longer a Harvestian one-syllabled essay on first principles, but was headed 'This Week's Society Secret History'. Across the cover were printed the words: 'Guaranteed Circulation 800,000 Copies Weekly. Help Us to Make it a Million!' Milton had fulfilled his promise.

But the large man was not quite pleased with what he read. Although he was avid, he held the paper at arms' length and wrinkled his nose; and finally he tossed 'England' aside with a single contemptuous hand, so that it fell in a flurry right into his waste-paper basket. 'Disgusting,' said the large man. 'And they *sell* it!' He then looked at his gold watch, rose to his feet and revealed what a big fellow he was, and stretched himself. His name was Robert Whistler. All the girls in the outer office called him 'Sir'. He had grown rather stout in the last five years, stout and a little florid; but he had not lost his figure, for during the whole War, however busy he had been in supplying the country with foodstuffs, he had acted as a Special Constable and at nights had patrolled the streets of London, and upon fine mornings he had made a point of walking a part of the way to the office, through Rotten Row and Piccadiliy, down to Charing Cross. He had also, unknown to Julie, joined a golf-club and another, social, club which had a squash rackets court; and although at squash he was hopelessly slow he had kept the worst of his weight down by means of golfing weekends and this strenuous exercise whenever could spare an hour in the afternoon.

Nevertheless he was stouter. His body had settled into its final proportions. He was forty-six, and he knew it. Indeed, the doctor had warned him against alcohol, too many cigars, and excessive strenuousness at squash. 'All these things,' said this Wimpole Street fellow, in his best man-of-the-world style, 'in reason. But don't overdo it, Mr Whistle.' 'Whistler,' Robert said. But the doctor had made the same mistake at parting—'Whistle.' Robert was used to envelopes addressed 'Whistling', 'Whustler', 'Whesselt', and 'Whinstler'; but he thought a doctor ought to know more about the City than that. 'Whistler. Whistler.' He made a point, now, of having his name printed at the head of his notepaper. 'From Robert Whistler.' But partly that was in imitation of Dick Firth, who since his knighthood in 1917 had always used notepaper headed 'Sir Furness Firth'. Robert still called him 'Dick.' Made a point of it. A *point*, God damn it.

After a few moments Robert looked again at his watch. Now that the War was over he could take things a little more easily. Improve his golf. Might even get a little place in the country for weekends. Quiet. Keep Julie amused. She was fidgety; 'nerves'; aftermath of the War. He could probably manage an afternoon in mid-week. He could leave the office details to subordinates. Phew! What a lot of details there were! A busy man these days. And that reminded him: he pressed a button and removed one of two telephone instruments which stood upon his large desk.

'Miss Neilson? Good afternoon. Mr Whistler speaking.'

'Good afternoon, Mr Whistler. Sir Furness is here. Do you want to come over?'

Robert grunted.

'All right,' he said. But when he had clashed down the telephone he did not immediately rise. She was too damned peremptory. Funny how women grabbed their privileges. Julie was the same: anybody would think it was she who made the money. And Miss Neilson, since Dick's knighthood, behaved as if she'd been given the Garter, at least. 'Yes, Sir Furness,' 'No, Sir Furness,' 'Sir Furness says——' Damn it, she was like a syphon, hissing away with self-importance. . . . Miss Neilson! Well, he would have to go across and see Dick. Dick's temper hadn't improved: or was it only to Bob that he was sharp? Bob wasn't going to stand any damned self-importance from anybody, be she Miss Neilson—who was a very decent woman, except when Dick was about—*or* be he Dick Firth. 'Sir Furness.' 'Dick, I tell you!' muttered Robert, rising from his chair. Eh? He was still light on his feet. Not sluggish. Alert as a young man; but finding it just a little difficult to digest. . . . 'I shall call him "Dick". I've done it all my life.'

III

Dick Firth had always been quick in his movements; but he was now quicker. The plumpness had gone from his face. He was as thin and sharp-featured as an ascetic. His eyes had sunken a little in his head, and as he was always using them upon figures and people they had sometimes an uncanny stare. You could tell that his nerves were beginning to retaliate for overwork by causing him sleeplessness, irritability, and sometimes a hardly perceptible tic. He carried a great many things in his head, made rapid decisions, snapped out instructions, and was short in his manner to those who perhaps felt themselves superior to that kind of treatment.

When Miss Neilson told him that Bob Whistler had come across the landing from the office of the Southern Counties Supplies Company to the R.F.F. Holdings Association (the Association being in a large degree proprietors of the Supplies Company), he was engaged upon the telephone. Miss Neilson saw his impatience, the quick drift of his glance from herself to the door, to his desk, the ceiling, and back to herself—much worse than of old; and when she noiselessly with her lips indicated 'Mr Whistler' he jerked his neck within a chafing collar. A bad sign. He raised a nervous hand, bidding her wait, and continued his exasperated conversation.

'No, she'll have to go. What? It's absurd. Well, I shall be home in half-an-hour. I'll see her. But it's a thing you ought to be able to manage yourself. Eh? I don't see why not. A child like that. What? Oh, very well, my dear; but there's no question about her going. It's been decided and she must do it. She ought to be catching the—what? What? Perfectly ridiculous. All right.'

Looking at Miss Neilson, Dick saw—in this moment of anger with his eldest daughter—how ugly she was beginning to get. Not only slipping downhill with that ease which her former flaccidity had promised, but becoming unsavoury. Silly woman; with younger women coming on, and a higher standard of training being attained . . . To let herself go! What she wanted was beauty treatment. What did she do with the six hundred a year he paid her? A nest egg? More probably keeping some dirty accompanist with greasy long hair and hands like mutton fat. God! The imagination of their amours was disgusting!

'What does he want?' Dick demanded, leaving his wife still talking over a dead wire. 'I don't want to see him. There's nothing to see him about, is there?'

'Only about what Mr Penter said, Sir Furness,' answered Miss Neilson.

'That can wait. It's three weeks to the meeting. I . . . I'm not in the mood today for that fat-faced jelly. The smell of brandy and cigars would make me sick, I think.'

'It's not very noticeable this afternoon, Sir Furness,' she pleaded, liquid-eyed. Though peremptory with others she was only so as Dick's representative. To Dick she was a slave. There was ecstasy in her abasement. Living as she did largely in the treacherous shallows of subjectivity, she could not realise that her spreading figure, being visible, displeased him, and that he cruelly saw the limits of her mind. In her heart, innocently, she was a sweet servant, ageless—or at any rate still young—and eternal. She thought longingly of him as she played voluptuous pieces for the 'cello in her studio in Fulham; and her accompanist was a crippled young woman more feverishly intense than herself, who clawed at the keys as fighting cocks claw their rivals, and who cried, not as Miss Neilson did, from melancholy alone, but from excitement.

'If I . . . I rush past him, d'you think I'll escape it?' demanded Dick, with his malicious smile. He jumped up and switched his overcoat from its peg. Then his hat. He said: 'Be ready to fling open the door, Miss Neilson; and good day to you. Good day!' He flew through the doorway.

There in his path was Robert, moodily striding up and down Miss Neilson's room, which was sandwiched between Dick's and the outer office.

'Hullo, hullo!' cried Dick. 'Sorry I can't stop. I'll see you next week, Whistler. Good day. Good day.' Like a gust of wind he had passed, slamming the door to the outer office and dashing through to the staircase without a pause. Robert, astounded and humiliated, felt quite disconsolate, especially as he read in Miss Neilson's face something like sympathy for his plight. He turned upon her.

'I thought you said he wanted to see me!'

Her breath caught.

'No, Mr Whistler. I said, did you want to come over. I didn't ring you——'

He cleared his throat. The blood rose to his cheeks.

'Extraordinary!' he exclaimed; and in his turn, although more massively, he strode away, savagely muttering at such treatment of a Director by one whom he had—so many years ago—thrown down in the playground at Moreton. 'Whippersnapper!' Robert said. 'And yet he's got the bloody sauce to treat me as if I was . . .' He did not complete the sentence. He went in fury back to his own office and kicked the waste-paper basket across the room so that 'England' whirled into the far corner like the seed-pod of a sycamore. 'Damn the fellow! As if I was . . .' Robert could not by any means discover a simile. He never would do so. For the little voice that ruined his life whispered at this moment, far down in the recesses of consciousness: 'You *are,* you know. You *are.* *Whatever* it is.'

The clerks did not understand why every door of the R.F.F. Holding Association and every door of the Southern Counties Supplies Company was sealed that day at Robert's passing with a crash resembling thunder.

IV

Meanwhile Dick Firth had already covered the length of Fenchurch Street. In five minutes he was speeding westward in a Central London electric train; and within a quarter of an hour he had reached his own splendid home in Mayfair. There, amid the majestic silences, he was confronted by a dilemma. His daughter Bianca, upon whom no threat, no cajolery, and no entreaty ever worked the smallest change, had that day refused to return to school. Her sisters had gone a day previously to another school; she, remaining, had at the last minute put her foot down. She knew enough, she said; and they had better realise it. Now Bianca, like himself, was a Firth. What she said, she meant. And, mother having failed, it was necessary for father to conquer that stubborn will.

Dick had first of all to find the rebel, which he did behind the locked door of her bedroom.

'I'm not going back to school,' declared a muffled voice from within. 'And it's no use your trying to make me go. I'll starve myself to death.'

'I . . . I shouldn't do that,' said Dick. 'It's disagreeable.' He was calm.

He had been calm, a few moments earlier, in his wife's boudoir. It had been Eileen who had been fretful, though not, he thought, deeply dejected. Eileen, milk-like, looking extremely pretty for her years in a light green dress which made insipidity a virtue, and peeping at him with suppressed excitement as though she secretly exulted in this challenge to his power; Dick sarcastic, smiling, blaming her for having allowed Bianca too much latitude . . . The boudoir a nest of pale grey which struck his soul with boredom by every resemblance to their first bedroom at Ealing . . . And upstairs a defiant daughter, a pretty problem. He would rather have faced a meeting of unruly shareholders.

However, there lay his battleground and the foe; and it was to Bianca's bedroom that Dick mounted. He was almost amused to see her school box, ready packed, upon the landing; not at all amused, but interested, to see how the luxury of the lower floors ended with the stairs, leaving the children's rooms conventual.

'The door's barricaded,' remarked Bianca, from her concealment.

'But mayn't we . . . mayn't we discuss the matter, my dear Bianca?' asked Dick, mildly. 'I . . . I feel we should understand each other so much better vis-à-vis.'

'You think you'll frighten me,' said that determined voice. 'Well, you won't.'

'The last thing I want to do,' remarked Dick, in a tone that had served him well upon the platform, when soothing an alarmed company. 'I . . . I only want to understand. If possible, to persuade . . . After all, you're a very little girl.'

To his cajolery she answered with the defiance which had served her since the morning.

'I'm not going back to school. I've had enough of it. I've made up my mind.'

Dick knew that he could have her door smashed and her person chastised. She was his child, and even in 1920 a parent could not be expected to submit to a fourteen-year-old girl. But that was not his present difficulty. He guessed that if left alone for a few hours she would emerge, famishing and humbled. She had no food, no money, nowhere to go. He did not want her humbled. He wanted to conquer her, so that she would not again resist his will; but he wanted also to leave her undefeated. How was that to be done? His mind schemed. He was pleased with his daughter. At last:

'Of course, my dear, that's nonsense,' said Dick, with great gentleness. He tried: 'You'd be . . . letting me down.'

'I don't care.'

'At the moment, no. In a month, yes.'

'Mother's tried all that on me.'

Dick smiled. He understood. This particular road was closed; he must try another.

'I don't want my daughter to be a laughing-stock,' he suggested.

'She won't be.' It was as dry as anything he could have said himself. His brows shot up. Decidedly, he had not appreciated Bianca enough hitherto.

'I'm afraid she will, you know,' he urged. 'But we won't discuss it. Naturally *you* don't want to be ridiculous.' A slight pause. In the matter of what modern criticasters of the theatre call 'timing' he had long been expert. Just quickly enough, he resumed: 'I shall have to try and invent an excuse. Say you're ill. Perhaps say you've come out in mysterious spots.'

There was a gasp from the other side of the door.

'I haven't!' cried Bianca, in a fury.

'That, of course, I can't be sure of,' said Dick. 'I . . . I haven't seen you.'

'I *haven't!*' insisted the voice. 'Oh, I *haven't!*' It was agonised.

'Especially on the nose,' said Dick, with relish. 'I . . . I feel sure the nose.' There was desperate silence. 'So we're keeping you in your room for a time. On . . . on bread and water.'

'That wouldn't be true,' cried Bianca.

'Naturally they wouldn't want a spotty-faced girl to go back to school until she was cured. Such a bad advertisement, don't you think?' Dick listened. Although there was no reply he was satisfied with his daughter's progress from defiance to distress. 'Yes, I'll go and write that now to Miss Pevensey——'

'You're not to!' shouted Bianca. 'Father!'

'She might otherwise think something serious had happened to you . . . *en route*. Goodbye, my dear, for the present.'

He walked across to the head of the stairs; and his feet made a perceptible noise upon the thinly-carpeted boards. As protests followed him he lost himself in reflection. What a barracks this place was, once one had gone beyond the more visible floors. The façade. The stucco. What with Victorian builders and suburban women . . . Economising! Dick felt no impatience with Bianca, interest in whom had just been born; only with his wife, interest in whom had died within a month of their wedding.

He could no longer hear the agitated calls from behind. Evidently Bianca was thinking hard. Yes, his guess had been a good, as well as a simple one. Fourteen, precocious, vain. Some of her mother's conventionality. From this age onward appearance counted above

. . . Hey! Was there a *boy* at the bottom of this? Dick whistled. A boy! Fourteen! Gosh! Early enough, no doubt; but these girls' schools were hotbeds. He struck one hand upon the stair-rail at his discovery. Pimples: what a lucky stroke! His eyes were so closed in merriment that for a minute he could not see to go down the stairs.

Now to verisimilitude; always, for a financier and man of affairs, an adjunct of the greatest importance. On the stage of life one could not make a scrap of paper answer for a treaty. . . . Dick went to his own room, called the study, where most of the really hard work of his money-making days was done. The door ajar, for interruption; a sheet of notepaper; his fountain pen. 'Dear Miss Pevensey, I am so very sorry that my daughter is prevented for a few days from . . .' Was that a noise overhead?

His thoughts troubled him. Yes, but at Bianca's age a strong attachment might be deucedly inconvenient. What boy was this? There had been parties. Plenty of them, here and elsewhere. Thinking of her as an uninteresting child, he hadn't taken any notice. But Eileen should have done so. Good heavens, what had she been thinking about! At fourteen, a boy. There would be trouble. . . . 'T-t t-t, these modern children!' Eh? There *was* a noise overhead! A piece of furniture was being stealthily moved. To continue the letter: 'She has obviously been eating the wrong kind of food at some of the children's Christmas parties; for she has broken out into a most disfiguring rash——'

'Father!' A swirl of young skirts; an agonised cry. Bianca was in the room, at his side. She had taken one glance at his property letter, snatched it, crumpled it. Then, with danger-pink cheeks, she was standing before him, a slim child normally as fair as her mother, rather sandy, with Dick's eyes and some of her mother's milk-white pallor. Fourteen, but with little breasts, as Dick's swift eye recognised at once, already threatening an early maturity. Oh, no wonder his ruse had succeeded! She was in a flurry of youthful panic, her lips parted and her ears flushed with shame. 'Father! It's beastly of you! Beastly! And it's not *true*. Oh, it's beastly of you!' She was crying with anger and perturbation.

'Oh,' said Dick, with elaborate surprise. 'You've emerged! I

thought . . . Well! So you don't like . . . Ah! I see I . . . I was
mistaken about those . . . those *spots*.'

He looked at his daughter with that inquisitive, all-knowing
smile which he had so often used in dealing with older persons of
her sex, and in which admiration had its flattering place. Without
doubt there was a boy. You could tell by the confusion. By Jove,
the child was almost pretty! She had spirit and secrecy. She could
move. Yes, but secrecy; look at the use of those tear-bestrewn
eyelashes. Danger! Poor child! . . . With a sudden impulse of protective kindness, Dick put out his hand and took Bianca's little
rough paw, reading yet another message in her shiver of resistance.
The brown arm, the white throat, the veiled glance—not of fear,
but of surreptitious curiosity, of suspicion! What a mixture of
muscle and sweetness, of tomboy and virgin! His daughter! What
immature mystery! It was fascinating! Dick fell paternally in love
with the child.

'Come, my pet,' he coaxingy murmured. He half-rose. His eyes
glowed as if with mystical illumination. 'We must have a talk.
You and I, d'you see? As . . . man to man.' He laughed a very
little, under his breath. 'You shall tell me all there is to know
about . . . everything. Eh?'

Bianca looked and pulled away from her father. Dick, the muscles
of his wrist and arm like steel, drew her closer, closer, in spite of
resistance, until, breathing hard, she was at his side. The resemblance between the two faces would then have startled an observer;
for although it was Dick who smiled, while his daughter remained
stubbornly serious, there was in the expression of each a demure
uncommunicativeness that argued secret purposes.

v

It was to Moreton that William had returned after his War
service; for it was there, in Daddy's old house (relinquished by
Robert now that his chain had recaptured his father's old shop),
that Kitty and Rosie and Mrs Harvest had spent the four years of

qualified misery. And it was in Moreton that William remained, three weeks after his demobilisation, on the day when Julie rode in her car and Robert was snubbed and Dick discovered charm in his eldest daughter.

William's women-folk had no car; they walked. William had no need to discover the charm of his daughter, for snapshots of her had been in his pocket-book during many months and she had re-approved him from the moment of his return home. And William, though since his emancipation from the military machine never snubbed, had less to expect from life than either of his fellow-townsmen. He was out of the Army; he was very poor; he was almost wholly unemployed. And he had come back to begin his career anew.

First of all, the problem of a job seemed insoluble. Wherever he went he found that those who had been free to stay at home had entrenched themselves. His applications were made and noted; his prospects were poor. Nobody wanted a man of forty-one whose experience of public affairs had lapsed for four years. Would they ever again want such a man? Was he finished? William had no influential friends; he had not thriftily gathered them in his days of plenty, and he was too proud to beg. Nevertheless he saw clearly enough that the alternatives were poverty or attack. What if attack failed?

As an opportunity for planning the attack, William had spent this day at work in Daddy's old garden, which was a wilderness. With a saw, an axe, and a pair of sécateurs he had been pruning trees to good effect; and as darkness fell he wearily threw his tools into a barrow and trundled everything back to the house, where light shone and fires glowed as if plenty abounded. Winter was the king of seasons! This was home! Tired and glowing with exercise in the cold air, William had recovered his spirits. He marched into the house whistling. They heard him everywhere.

Kitty, indeed, put a head out from the kitchen, where she was busy.

'Goodness!' cried she. 'Thought it was a regiment!'

'It's the Tea Brigade,' retorted William. 'An army of wolves.'

She drew him into the kitchen.

'Sniff,' she said. 'There's a cake and jam tarts in the oven; and I've made girdle-cakes, too. Where's my medal?'

'You're an angel, Kitty; and I'm nothing but an animal!' cried William, sitting upon the kitchen table. 'The medal's of gold.'

'Cake'll be another two or three minutes. Then we'll have tea,' said Kitty, perching herself beside him. 'Only good thing in this barracks—the oven.'

William understood that to her house was a prison.

'You hate it?' he asked. Kitty vigorously nodded. 'But you've been better here, haven't you?'

'Since you came home,' she said.

'Not before that?'

'Oh, not bad. Don't think I'm grumbling.' Her hand was tucked within his arm. 'Your mother thinks it's lovely. It'll be different now you're here. Everything different.'

William, having had his own impressions, wondered if it would. He asked:

'Is there anywhere you'd *like* to live?'

Kitty sighed. She thought: 'Watching the dead town from a mouldering house full of bogeys.' Loneliness. Worse than loneliness, fear. Others growing rich while Will served for his pay. The cheatery and villainy . . . All those other men—millions of them dead; buried in the mud. She dreamed of them; and awoke, sweating, to the frightful knowledge of illness, of coming death. And now what?

'I'm restless,' she said, with only half-intentional evasiveness. 'I feel I ought to have some more good news. That's greedy, I know——'

'So soon again?' asked William. 'It *is* greedy.' He pointed his disengaged arm towards the oven, the scent from which had subtly changed in that last instant. Kitty slipped from the table; and the fine odour of a cake perfectly cooked burst upon the kitchen.

'Done!' cried Kitty. Her pensiveness was gone, and in its place came the generalship of the housewife. 'Now tea. Take the tray. Call mother: she's making sure Rosie washes herself. That child takes a *pride* in being dirty. And see to the fire. Oh, if Minna was only back again, too, I shouldn't be greedy!'

They were in the drawing-room which Julie had once decorated; and although the wallpaper was soiled and peeling, and the furniture shabby, a fire glowed, the gas shone brightly, and as the curtains were drawn to shut out the afternoon darkness all was as cosy as could be. Old Mrs Harvest—now really upon the verge of elderliness, and to William's eye tragically aged by the War—sat stiffly at the table; Rosie, aged seven, beamed with polished cleanliness across at her; William fenced with one of his daughter's arithmetical catches, of which she had three or four, all of them guaranteed to discomfit ingenuous elders; and Kitty poured out the tea. She had a cushion upon her chair, to raise the level at which she sat.

And then, as they prepared to feast upon everything except the new cake, the old bell on the stairs began to waggle and at last emitted a feeble peal. Somebody was at the front door.

'Who is it!' challenged Rosie. 'Who d'you *want* it to be, daddy?' She was arch. 'Hey?' Her eyes sparkled; her polished cheeks shone like a pair of glazed cherries. She slipped off her chair. She ran helter-skelter to the door.

'I'd better go,' said William, starting up. But Rosie was already clattering without.

'She knows something, the tinker!' exclaimed Kitty, tea-strainer in hand. All weariness had fallen from her. She listened with curiosity.

As he ascended the stairs William heard Rosie's excited voice and laughter at the front door, and felt his heart miss a beat. Nobody but Minna could so move the kiddy! When the door slammed, and the little chattering voice continued, he went no farther, but stood in half-darkness upon the stairs, awkwardly, full of embarrassment, feeling that his sluggish legs would no longer bear his heavy body. They trembled. He had heard Minna's voice.

How strange that he should be so affected! He had not seen her, of course, all the time he had been away; but they had corresponded, and he had thought himself disciplined for life. Yet now, when they were to meet, he could not mount the stairs, but remained with a hand upon the rail, looking towards the faint light above. She was coming. He had been unprepared. Half-blind in the darkness, he groped his way at last back to the drawing-room, with raised finger bidding the others to listen for descending steps.

VI

So they waited, as Rosie jumped the stairs—hop, hop, one at a time—in her glee; and Kitty and Mrs Harvest rose, while William, behind the door, holding it open, heard again the sound of that remembered voice. He could tell that Minna was laughing; but Rosie was the more voluble, and was crowding and stammering her words in unwonted excitement. A moment later she was in the room, the old Minna, radiant, with outstretched hands for her friends, going in triumph towards them. William had stepped back; and he, unseen, knowing that when Kitty's voice wholly failed, as it did now, she was painfully moved, observed also how, after embracing Minna, she continued to cling to her as she had done to himself three weeks earlier. The dependence, the trust, the affection, all, unmarred, were as of old.

And yet, being given time in this way for a single comprehensive glance at Minna, William's first disastrous impression was of a stranger. He was bitterly disappointed. The light shone down upon her face, and revealed it as thinner, older, with sharper cheekbones and a colder smile. Not hers the unsteady voice. Not to her eyes did the tears leap. She was calm. She was kind and direct as of old, but harder. Hastily to say that in four years of nursing she had looked upon death and terrible disfigurement and the monstrous evils of war was not enough. The change lay deeper.

When that prolonged greeting was at last ended, Minna turned to look for William; and his feeling changed once more. She seemed to measure him, looking earnestly, not coolly, into his eyes. She was still his friend; but as for their former unreserve, he knew that it had gone. She had endured so much in those four years, and experience had so greatly matured her character, that as he stood before her, under that scrutiny, William felt himself grow smaller. Small, small; a very little man; a failure . . . She had learned to know better men than he. Oh, it was salutary. It was overwhelming.

'William's fainted standing!' laughed Kitty, careless in her glee.

'He's struck dumb!' declared Minna, becoming suddenly as nonsensically radiant. 'He doesn't recognise me. Don't you remember, William, that once, long ago, you knew somebody named Minna. . . .' She mocked him.

'I was in a dream,' said William, rousing himself with an effort from doubt. 'I almost said "Isn't life wonderful!" But I didn't say it, and shan't, because it's only too true. Well, Minna, how are you?'

Her hand, cool and steady, remained in his. They had not kissed. Their glances again met. Gone were the smiling, unfathomable depths he remembered, in which love and candour played together; and in their place was a reserve equal to his own. Equal to his own; it was something William did not realise. Then they were two very odd people, shaking hands, both—were both equal also in disappointment?

'All sit down!' cried Kitty, with brisk mastership of the scene. 'Silly to stand gaping. I shall have to make fresh tea. Oh, how happy I am!' She hurried from the room. They heard her singing in the kitchen; and hearing that joyous sound, William again looked at Minna, to find that she had not withdrawn her eyes but still regarded him with the same listening seriousness as before. His heart sank lower and lower.

CHAPTER XXII

Ways of Love

THE SAME listening seriousness. What had she any reason to expect in him that she did not find? William gave it up. He could not see himself, and he was in a false position; and like others in false positions he suffered from restricted outlook. Moreover, in order to understand, he would have had to know far more than he would ever learn about Minna's recent life.

She had been for four years at work in military hospitals. Where other persons of her age and sex had known five or six or twenty men she had closely encountered hundreds. Some of these, grateful or adventurous, coarse or tender, had fallen in love with her or had tried to make love to her; the majority, in need of sympathy and realising her gift for it, had confided in terms which would have been impossible to men less stricken by the twin fears of life and death. Thus, for the first time, her real contact with the world had exceeded William's; and the consequences were momentous.

What they were, William did not immediately learn; for Minna departed again next day and left him guessing. Thereafter her visits, paid in a small car which she drove herself, were brief. She stayed an hour, resumed her seat in the car, and disappeared; leaving them all confounded by a consciousness of provincial stagnation. Eyes were rubbed in Daddy's house, and smiles exchanged; the smiles rather rueful.

The Harvests, unfortunately, could not at present leave Moreton. The late Winter was wet, and Kitty was so hoarse and sometimes so alarmingly flushed and languid that removal was out of the question. Furthermore, Mrs Harvest clung to the town; and as

William did not get a job they were better off there than they would have been elsewhere. William, true to recent military cliché, launched an offensive upon the contemporary Press; but his offensive, like many another, petered out for want of encouragement, and left him no farther advanced than before. Money was short; hopefulness, when in his heart hope was dying, proved a laboured affair; and in Minna's absence he had no secret-sharer. Isolated, he was driven to the taking of long walks about the district, in which he magnified fifty-fold every unpleasant truth about himself and wore out much shoe leather to little purpose. If he had not been born cheerful, William must have cut his throat.

Kitty, he could not doubt, was growing weaker. There were still days when she looked extraordinarily young and blithe, but they were succeeded by darker days when he knew she was so much afraid that his strength alone supported her. Kitty would take his hand, and hold it tightly, half-smiling or wholly serious, sometimes at last raising the hand to her cheek and holding it there until with a murmur or exclamation of tenderness she moved away at a restless thought of Rosie or, more slowly and unwillingly, upon some household duty. Upon such days William would not leave her. But later, when the grievous moods passed, he was waylaid by other fears, not base but urgent, lest his own continued professional failure or some mishap to Rosie, or some suspicion of his love for herself, might carry poison to her happiness. He loved tenderly, protectively; she was not his star. Because of this knowledge William felt sometimes that he must be in Hell.

One morning in the very early Spring, when he was digging in a far corner of the garden, while a thrush sang overhead and robins looked boldly up from their perches at his very feet, William heard Kitty's voice calling. He answered, and turned, still in his old Army jacket, to scrape caking earth from his shoes upon the top edge of the spade, and to see her coming towards him from the house. The day was clear, but rather cold; and Kitty had pulled on one of William's overcoats, to guard herself from the chill air. Her fluffy hair was being blown by the breeze, and as if she guessed that she was bringing good news she smiled broadly, as Rosie would have done. But William did not know, until she produced it from the coat-pocket, that she carried a letter which had come by the second post; and by that time Kitty had taken a seat upon the handle of his stout barrow.

A single glance at the letter was enough. The sun seemed to both of them to burst from behind a curtain of cloud. And at William's shout of joy Kitty jumped quickly up, took his arm, and with her cheek against his shoulder read the first good news they had had since his return home.

DEAR MR HARVEST, [said the letter].

When next you are in London, will you call and see me? Let me know when you are coming. I hear you are demobilised and applying for work: well, I too am demobbed, and I feel sure we can do business together. You don't know me, but you have met my brother, Bernard Mather. He, at any rate, knows you, and says you are just the man for my particular job. As for me, I have long been your admirer, and if you are able and willing to help, as I hope you will be, I shall be in luck.

Yours sincerely,
T. F. MATHER

William, holding the letter in one hand, saw it shake slightly. He gave it to Kitty, so that she might read it again; and he knew that he must be trembling with relief. In an instant several hundredweights of anxiety had been lifted from his shoulders; and as more and more of the possibilities revealed by the letter opened themselves to his imagination he grew so exultant that he could not keep still, but walked about near by until Kitty looked up.

'Here!' she cried. 'Come here and stand still. D'you know him?'

William, stopping in his stroll, folded his arms. He was transfigured.

'I know *all* about him,' said he, triumphantly. '*All.*'

'Then let's hear some of it!' she begged. 'Or else I shall go dotty.'

They sat side by side upon the barrow's edge while William unfolded the tale.

'Bernard Mather,' he explained, 'is or was a young barrister. I say "was" because he's older now than when I last saw him.'

'Extraordinary!' interjected Kitty, in high spirits. 'Of course, everybody else has stayed where they were.'

'He began,' said William, as if ignoring her impudence; 'he began to make a name before the War, not by defending pickpockets or manslaughterers, but in cases of company law, and so on. And he's evidently by some miracle come through the War—he went into something naval, I believe—so he'll probably finish making his name very quickly. You'll hear of him. He's got brains. Very few barristers have brains. Those who have, pop to the top like corks.'

'Let's hear the news first,' suggested Kitty. 'What you think of barristers can wait. Old Bernard Shaw!' She had no outward reverence for William's opinions.

'Very well,' agreed William, promptly. 'I met Bernard Shaw—I mean, Bernard Mather—one night at the Press Club, and he made a speech. Legal Night. A good speech. And I had to propose something or other. Another good speech. Afterwards he came reverently up to me—you know how these poor wretches do——'

'You're excited!' Kitty punched William. 'Get on!'

'That's all about Bernard Mather,' said he. 'We had a chat. Very pleasant. I should say he's about the same age as I am. We meant to see more of each other. I read reports of his cases; probably he read some of my articles. As I've told you before, *in this life nothing is wasted.*'

'Pooh! Your tongue works overtime.' William's sententiousness never reached Kitty. She was concerned only with the practical. 'And do you suppose he's told his brother all that? Is his brother rich?'

'His brother is rich. His brother is a gentleman. He also wants very much to improve the world.'

Kitty wrinkled her nose. She had always disliked the word 'improve'; and being so much of an anti-prig she risked obscurantism.

'I s'pose that means he's Temp'rance,' she said. 'Oatmeal, cocoa, poitry; and he'll lose his money.'

'Not Temperance or poitry. League of Nations and National Purity.'

'Sell all thou hast, and rob the poor.'

'Factory Acts, Pensions for Mothers, Minimum Wage Agreements, Compulsory Arbitration, revise the Commercial Laws, abolish the Peers——'

'And ruin the country,' said Kitty. 'Oo, he sounds horrible. What did we fight for?'

'Well, unless we fought for those things it must have been for the honour of Little Belgium. At any rate, T. F. Mather was said to be going to start a great new paper when the War began. Better than "England". Better informed than anything I could have done. He must have revived the idea now. He probably wants me to——'

'Edit it!' exclaimed Kitty, clapping her hands. 'Now I see why you've lost your head!'

'No, not edit it. He'll do that himself,' said William. But as her face fell he added: 'To write for it at an immense salary.'

'Hope it's immense!' cried Kitty, captivated by the notion. She whistled to herself—not very well—with ambition. 'Thousands a year.'

'Pooh!' was what William said. 'We shouldn't know how to spend thousands.'

'Try me!' exclaimed Kitty. 'I'd get rid of this old place, and go and live at Brighton, or somewhere lively; and have furs and a motor-car; and sweep out of shops with my nose in the air, without buying anything. You know, like a lady. And I'd get you some new clothes, instead of darning the things until I'm ashamed to look a needle in the eye. And have caviare sandwiches and smoked trout and port——'

'Oh, God!' William groaned. 'I was afraid you'd come to port in the end.'

'That's what you *do* do, if you're lucky. I suppose it's low?'

'It's sweet. Modern Women buy it in buffets so as to see rainbows.'

Kitty did not mind his teasing. She said:

'Bernard Mather's a friend of Minna's. She told me so.'

'What!' To William the fact was a blow. Did he owe this new chance to Minna? The letter fell from his hand. The first lustre of his joy was dimmed. 'She told you? About *this!*' He picked the letter up.

'No, silly!' cried Kitty. 'She knew nothing about this. But she knew Bernard Mather at her aunt's. Don't you remember? Then she nursed him. I think he's sweet on her.'

'Well, you couldn't wonder at it,' answered William, coolly, stuffing the letter into his pocket. He had recovered from his fit of vanity. 'On the whole.'

'Yes; but she belongs to us,' Kitty said. She turned her eyes full upon William as she spoke. But what was in her mind he did not know; for the glance was clear and thoughtful, and full of love.

'She *did.*' William uttered his doubt aloud. 'She doesn't any longer. That I'm sure of.' He rose from his place beside Kitty, and stood there fretting. But when Kitty sneezed he took her arm and ran her indoors at high speed; they never ended the discussion of Minna. Nor did William learn the meaning of Kitty's glance. She would not, in any case, have told him.

II

A little after this, Robert Whistler had a shock. He went home one afternoon immediately after lunch, feeling bilious; and he found nobody there but the servants. He had not expected to see his daughter, Rachel, because Rachel went to a day school. Julie, however, was also absent. He grumbled his way about the house, looking for her, and at last came to rest, for some reason, in the dining-room, which was heated by a gas-fire. Perhaps one reason for his choice of the dining-room was the fact that a tantalus was to be found there, to which he had a key. Robert, feeling bilious, was visited by a belief that he had caught an internal chill, for which brandy would be a cure; and after he had drunk a very moderate half-tumblerful of raw spirit he sat over the fire, with a rug round him, thinking of his trials.

He had an inconsiderate wife: that was one thing. She was selfish to the core. His house was a most uncomfortable house: that was another thing. There was not a room in it which at this chilly season of the year held even moderate warmth. No wonder Americans found English homes ice-wells and death-traps. He saw a number of Americans, now; and all of them preferred to dine at one of the big hotels, rather than in an English home. They were wise. He'd had this chill hanging over him for days. It was due to an underheated house. You'd have thought Julie, being from the South, would have felt it. Well, as a matter of fact, she did. . . .

Business thoughts supervened; thoughts of Dick Firth and a number of subordinates whose manner, it seemed to Robert, was less respectful to himself than it should have been. He did not move, and he did not sleep; but gradually, what with the gas-fire and his rug and the brandy, he fell into a pleasant warmth, in which life was less troublesome and in which other men became less objectionable. Oh, life wasn't too bad at all. Those who fussed and worried got nowhere. The great thing was to keep a level keel, plenty of exercise, moderation in all things, and not to be put on. 'Oh, but I'm a good-natured fellow,' thought Robert. 'Many a man would go storming about the house if he came home ill and found his wife gadding. I don't. Let her go out, if she wants to. I should be the last person. The *last* person . . .'

He was thinking this, and noticing how the dusk had gathered, so that the room was beginning to shimmer into greyness, lighted only by the red glow of the gas-fire, when he heard the front door opened and shut. In another moment—there was no sound—the dining-room door was stealthily opened, and Rachel came upon tip-toe into the room. She was a little lanky for her years, and her feet were long and conspicuously at right angles to her legs. Dark hair hung in plaits over her shoulders, and she still wore the ribboned felt hat of her High School. Robert, amused to think that she had not seen him, watched her tip-toe to the sideboard, open a door, fumble for a moment, and produce the big silver cigarette box which Julie had bought to celebrate the end of the War. He saw her abstract two or three cigarettes from this box, and although he did not think very quickly he was so much impressed by the secretness of Rachel's movements that he guessed something to be afoot.

'Here, what are you doing there!' he shouted, half-angry and half-amused.

With a squeal, Rachel dropped the cigarette box. Its contents were scattered. Her cheeks went as grey as putty. Two large globes stared from above them. Breathlessly, she put her hands behind her back in terror, and stood as if she could not move. She did not answer him.

Robert had a strange consciousness of power, which pleased him.

'Come here,' he said, more quietly. Rachel did not stir. She merely stared at him in affright. 'Well,' thought Robert; 'that's all very well, but I'm not a bear, am I? Not a brute, am I?' He continued: 'Didn't you hear me? What are you frightened of? I'm not going to hurt you.' There was no answer; and when he rose to his feet, flinging aside the rug, Rachel shrank back against the sideboard, cowering as if she were in fear of a blow. 'Look here,' said Robert, disturbed by these signs of distrust; 'you're not afraid of me, are you?' At her painfully nodded head he was shocked. 'Eh? Good God!' he muttered. 'Afraid? Why? I don't see why you should be. I've never . . . You've got a tongue, haven't you?'

'Yes,' he heard. Oh, a tiny voice.

'Well, then, tell me what you were doing. D'you smoke?' He had a vague feeling that this was a situation to be handled with care. It could be left to him—safely. 'You're not old enough to smoke, are you? See, how old *are* you? I know you're a big girl; but not that age. It . . . it . . . ah . . . Well, I was going to say it would stop your growing; but I don't know that you'd mind that. It's a dirty habit, you know. Don't you know that?'

'You do it,' came a murmur.

'Ah, well, that's different. I'm a man, you see. Men have got a lot of dirty habits.' Robert felt that he was getting on very nicely with this conversation. Friendly, not at all strict, just the right note of knowing better than she did; but making, of course, no claims. Nowadays it didn't do to make claims. 'You don't want to copy men, you know.'

Rachel stared at him in doubt, skinny and timid and half-wild, like a small savage or a young animal in a trap. Then, finding his mood not vindictive, she stooped suddenly, still facing Robert, and picked up the cigarette box, into which she began to scramble the fallen cigarettes. In doing this she saw and hid the fact that in its fall the box had been badly dented; but Robert was as much aware of the dent as she.

'I don't know what your mother will say when she sees what you've done to that box,' he said, with judicial lightness. 'I rather think there'll be a spot of trouble about it.'

'I'm not frightened of mother,' flashed Rachel. She had shaken the cigarettes into regularity, and, still with her face towards Robert, was stepping backwards to the door.

'You're not. But you are of me.' He added, when there was no answer: 'You look silly, backing to the door like that. Here, don't go. It's not often I see you. I almost forget what you're like. Come and talk to me. I'm not well. Aren't you sorry? You're not? You're an unnatural girl, then. Here, d'you like money? Let's see if I've got a shilling or two to spare for my daughter—— Good God!' She had gone. With one swift dash she had reached the door and darted through it, leaving Robert alone.

That was such a shock to him that tears started to his eyes. Had he deserved it? He'd never meant to frighten her—now or at any other time. She'd gone. Rather than be with him any longer, even with the reward of a tip, she had run away. That wasn't right. Painfully unhappy, Robert went back to his chair and mechanically wrapped the rug about his knees. He'd have to speak to Julie about this. It had been a great blow. For a long time he sat there considering it; and at last, with the back of his hand, wiped away some moisture from his cheeks. How lonely he felt!

III

Robert would have been even more unhappy if he had known where Julie was at that moment. She was within a mile of home, and alone in a strange room which Robert had never entered. There, with curtains drawn, and the room illumined only by a small electric table-lamp and by a bright coal fire, she stood tapping

an impatient foot. She listened, consulted a clock which stood upon
the mantelpiece, and at last threw herself down moodily into an
armchair near the fire. As she did this it became evident that the
outer garment she wore was a silken dressing-gown.

The room was not a large one, and it was beautifully warm,
which pleased Julie, who believed that she suffered at home from
low temperatures imposed by her husband's love of the cold. The
carpet was very thick and soft, and there was a large soft rug
before the fire. And the room, which by its silence seemed to lie a
hundred miles from the risk of interruption, looked as if it were
well-used, for there were shelves full of brightly-bound books, and
the pictures, though they were small, were all very highly-coloured,
catching and reflecting gleams from both lamp and fire. But Julie,
absorbed in the act of intense listening, no longer noticed what
decoration was about her. She knew that nothing would happen
in her heart until she heard a key in the door below, the door in the
cul-de-sac by which all comers to this flat must enter, the door
which shut the outer world from uneasy lovers within. Uneasy
because furtive: what was love?

For Julie, love was agitation; never tranquillity. It had become
something to which one was driven by the body's urgencies, and
not by any ecstasy of gift. She was restless, filled with suspicion.
She hardly dared to look far within, because to have done so would
have been to discover self-accusation, the last and least endurable
secret of unhappiness. Her mind busied itself, rather, with reflections upon her own hardships, upon the extent to which she had
been defrauded by Robert, and then starved of love, and teased
by placatory gifts from a husband who could give her no contentment. If scrambling poverty had yielded now to a sort of plenty,
the plenty was a stingy allowance of material good things which
left her spirit unsatisfied. She had no friends. Those whom she
would have welcomed fought shy of her; the rest she despised. She
was married to a stupid, shrewd fool. She had missed happiness.
Now, in these secret meetings with Dick Firth, whose fever-
creating charm was that his fidelity could not be trusted, she was
irritable through lost self-respect. She was angry, she was sad, she
was humiliated.

But when at length the sound of that key reached her ears Julie felt her heart spring into life. She felt herself stifling through excitement. And as Dick's steps upon the stair quickened, and he swept into the room, she stood again, meaning to be distant with him, although she knew that while at first her body stiffened in resistance she would shortly yield under those eager, purposeful, confident kisses and be as before the victim of her own hunger for passion. His pale cheeks were cold from the outer air. She saw his long light eyelashes and the little sharp smile. And since resentment of his power to agitate her was at the root of unhappiness in these meetings it caused her to turn away from him even as she failed to deny his ever-expert caress.

'My God,' Dick said, breathlessly, accounting for Julie's reluctance. 'I'm later than I realised. I . . . I was kept. A bore stood up and addressed the meeting. I could have shot him where he stood. Oh, but you're beautiful this afternoon: beautiful——'

'You forgot me,' Julie said, sombre-eyed, keeping him away. Dick, challenged, smiled with a joyous malignance that stirred her blood. He declared:

'Never. I flew. I always fly to you. I . . . I'm like a bird.'

Too quick. Too ready. He lied. She was blacker than ever in spirit; although at his hand's touch she shivered again.

'Yes, you are in a hurry,' Julie said, repelling the hand.

'I'm on fire!' Dick cried. 'You mustn't be so cruel. So cruel.'

'You are never on fire, my friend,' Julie told him, sadly. 'You kiss, you calculate.'

'I love,' he interrupted, embracing her.

Yes, he was in a hurry. She caught his glance at the clock in that very instant of protestation. In a hurry to be gone from her; while she, a beggar, had waited for him. Had waited, and was now, in the confusion of defence, a suppliant. She could not resist. She could not quarrel. His arms were about her; thin, tenacious arms that she could have burst asunder if her desire for him had been less hungry. His eyes hypnotised her. His hands, his bitter, burning lips, were irresistible. This was the love she craved. At last, recklessly and with ardour, she responded to its pertinacity.

IV

'I've been writing to "The Times", William,' said Mrs Harvest.

'You couldn't be better employed, mother,' answered William.

'But of course I shan't send the letter,' said Mrs Harvest.

'You'd be departing from custom if you did,' answered William.

'It's about the Tory party,' said Mrs Harvest. 'They're such humbugs, William. They do all the things that the other parties have intended to do.'

'Being barren, they can do nothing else,' William assured her. 'Their position is negative; they're the political limpets.'

'That's *just* what I've said!' cried Mrs Harvest, triumphantly. 'But I've used the word "barnacles". I don't know what a barnacle is, or if it's a binnacle I mean; but I've used it as belonging to the Ship of State.'

'Barnacle is the word; and it's a kind of inedible shell fish,' said William, laughing slightly. 'But I wonder whether the Ship of State isn't rather a cliché, mother.'

'Well, I shan't send the letter, of course, William.'

'One day you *will* send one; and it'll be printed; and you'll get a dozen angry rejoinders through the post that will make your blood boil. Because—I don't know why it is—large numbers of people resent criticism of the Tory party. As well as all the other things you attack in your letters, mother.'

'Not *attack,* darling,' objected Mrs Harvest, who believed herself to be merely stating facts.

'You probably don't realise how ferocious you are—on paper.'

'Oh, William! "Ferocious"!' Mrs Harvest was delighted with the word.

She and William were sitting together by the fire, and Kitty was upstairs putting Rosie to bed. She was doing this because Mrs Harvest had been a little tired, and also because Rosie had shown an inclination to worry her Grannie. They had a peep of gas, but the light in the room was of a pleasant dimness to encourage confidences.

'Ferocious is the word, mother,' insisted William. 'On paper. Not, of course, in reality. In reality, you're what I should call peaceable.'

Mrs Harvest did not answer. It was several minutes before she spoke again, and then it was to say, unexpectedly:

'Do you really like my water-colours, William? I can just see them on the other wall. I don't like them much, myself. They're colourless. I've always kept them, though; for association's sake. I've been thinking a lot, lately, about your father, Will. He'd have been sixty-eight this month, if he'd lived.'

William stretched his legs, leaning well back in the armchair and bracing himself against a possible call for aid.

'Does it make you miserable?' he asked, cautiously.

But he saw the small elderly head shaken. Mrs Harvest said:

'Oh, no. In a way, you've taken his place. Not really. Nobody could do that. But you're more *immediate,* naturally. I've had a lot of time to think about you both; and I can't help feeling there's a sort of irony in the fact of our all living in this house.'

'An irony.' William's brows were raised. 'Well, that's one word for it.'

'Is it a cliché?' asked Mrs Harvest, innocently. 'You don't really know the truth about his death, do you.'

William's brows were still raised. He felt that he must be dreaming. He let several seconds go by before he answered that question.

'Short of asking *you,*' he said; 'I've done all I could to find out. I've read the report of the inquest. I've talked to Doctor Hodge.'

'Ah, yes; he didn't know.' Mrs Harvest spoke with eager impatience. 'And the inquest—I don't think inquests always quite discover the truth. Do you, William?'

William said:

'I never do know the truth, mother. I'm a sceptic.'

'You're a very good boy,' his mother declared, warmly. 'And always have been. You know Mr Griffin was your grandfather, don't you?'

There was dead silence.

'So *that's* it!' murmured William, at last. He was completely

taken aback. But Mrs Harvest, who had not been surprised, continued to speak quietly and reflectively.

'Horrid old man,' she said. 'But I oughtn't to say so, as he's dead.
And yet at one time I hated him. Later, I came to despise him;
and then to feel sorry for him. I was dreadfully tempted when he
wanted to pay for your education. D'you remember? You wouldn't
have it. You were funny; but very nice. Very firm. And though I
kept quiet I was boiling inside; because I knew Mr Griffin had
been the cause of your father's death. . . .' She gave William time
to absorb that; and then, speaking familiar memory, said: 'You
see, old Mr Harvest suddenly found out, long after his wife's
death, that Mr Griffin was James's father. It drove him quite mad—
he never was very sensible—and he got a gun and went out one
day intending to shoot Mr Griffin. I don't know how James knew;
but he went after and caught him as he took aim, and ran to try
and get the gun away——'

'Daddy was there, then?' demanded William. 'He knew?'

'He was only a few yards away, shouting and caught in a hedge.'

'And father?'

'Mr Harvest fired straight into James's body. He fell down, and
some people must have heard the shot—I suppose; for I never
could understand . . . Mr Griffin didn't wait, but crept away, so
as not to be found near—such a coward, he was—and the other
poor old man, seeing what he'd done, went quite mad and ran
away, too. He hid. When they found him he was raving, and they
put him into an asylum, where he died. They brought James home
to me, dying. That was awful. He could hardly speak. . . .'

There was considerable silence in the room. Mrs Harvest did
not cry; she was not the sort of woman to cry. She clasped her
hands tightly together, and sat quite still, perhaps rather paler than
usual. After a time William, who had also suffered as a consequence of the recital, put a question.

'He told you what had happened. And why. Did he tell you to
say nothing?'

William could see an assenting movement of the head.

'He told me to say nothing. I never have said anything, till now.

I hesitated whether to tell you at all. It's all—no, it's *not* all nasty, because James acted very fearlessly, as he always did. And in thinking about it I made up my mind to tell you before . . . It's strange how your use of the word "ferocious" made me do it now. Does it —will it—worry you, dear?'

William uttered a sound like the end of a deep sigh.

'It will worry me less than the other fear I had,' he said.

She caught her breath.

'What: that he had . . . killed himself? They tried to suggest it. I didn't know you knew that. . . . But "fear", William: you don't mean that you . . . Oh, William!' She half-rose from her chair. 'William!'

'It's all right, mother,' said William. 'I've never thought of it. I've only wondered if, at some time, there was a danger of something cracking——'

'Don't talk rubbish, Will!' The old lady's tone had grown sharp, '*You'll* never take the easy way.'

William smiled in the half-light.

'Is it so easy?' he asked.

'Oh, yes; to those who don't want to struggle any longer.'

'I see.'

'You're past the worst.'

'I wonder if I am.'

'I'm proud of you *all*,' said Mrs Harvest. 'Very proud indeed.'

William did not ask what she meant by 'all'. It was a little dangerous. Instead, he put another question.

'Daddy,' said he. 'How much did *he* know?'

'He knew nothing,' replied Mrs Harvest, with what seemed like malicious satisfaction. 'Nobody ever told him anything. *Anything.*'

They sat together without further speech, until Kitty came back into the room, singing.

v

It was quite by chance that they had gone to Royals; but the house was empty and the Spring day was fine and very warm, and as Minna had a reason for revisiting her old home William accompanied her. This was the longest stay she had made with the Harvests. It was a Sunday, and the shops in the town were shut, and sedate couples and small bands of young men were walking along the road which led past Royals and onward towards the south and, eventually, the sea. Such a fine afternoon had tempted many out of doors who would ordinarily have stayed within and spent the day in dozing or singing hymns or spelling out the sensations of a Sunday newspaper.

William and Minna, outpacing everybody else upon the road, had made the journey for the most part in silence, she busy with plans (it seemed) and he more reflective. Both in reality were thinking of each other and were aware in their different ways of all that was formidable in the other. William, glancing, saw Minna wearing the blue costume which she had now permanently adopted, and with her sharpened face apparently set in resolve—all, to him, was symbolic of friendly estrangement; Minna, not needing even to glance, saw William stern, brown, far away from herself, but none the less as the man inevitably of her heart. They turned in at that familiar gate as they had done many times before; and the house, haunted by ghosts, was under their eyes. Its black, diamond-paned windows chilled them both, as did the overgrown laurels and morose firs which darkened the moss-littered gravel pathway.

'No. It won't do,' Minna said, with her new decidedness. 'Hopeless. Let's go and look, for old times' sake, at the garden.' They skirted the house, to be confronted by a dreary tangle of weeds. 'Why, how small it is!' she cried, in distress. 'It's shrunk, William! It's tiny!'

William, standing beside her upon the stones behind the house, looked towards the little wood, and to the stream and the rough grass which had served long ago as the scene of such unnumbered games. He saw it as less changed than she; but he too was oppressed by a sense of persistent decay.

'Well,' he said, smiling grimly. 'It's shrunk. And we've grown gigantic and seen larger worlds. But don't forget that if you put London children in an acre of grass it will seem to them as immense as it did to us.'

'To us,' echoed Minna. 'But we were two. Put twenty down here; and where's the room for them?'

'Even so,' William reminded her. 'They'd have more space than they've ever known before. And there are the adjoining fields.' He pointed to these, which spread greenly in the sunshine; but——

'We can't get the fields,' said Minna, abruptly. 'The farmer wants them for grazing. Let's look at the house.'

Her plan had been to open in London a clinic for very poor children, and to use Royals, with its supposedly limitless garden, as a Summer-time country home for her patients. She felt that she was now committed to nursing as an occupation, and the Mathers and others were behind a larger scheme for good works. It would be those others who would finally decide what should be done, and Minna knew it; but she had been eager to make her own contribution. Royals, vacated at the beginning of Winter by its recent chilblain-tormented tenants, had not been re-let; it was her property; she would never live there again. And she had thought that if it seemed suitable she could transfer the place by deed to her committee and be quit of it. Hence bitter disappointment now. In silence she and William unlocked the door and went into the house, where shadows and echoes of the past were all about them.

Here William had come upon his first visit more than thirty years earlier; here Minna had been born. Her mother had been used to sit there, by the open fireplace, where logs hissed; and by this door Minna had stood upon the evening when William after walking fruitlessly with Robert Whistler had shown that the secrets of his heart were secrets indeed. Here she and William had been together when a telegram summoned her to one scene of distress; yonder were the stairs down which she had hurried, sobbing, to William's arms after the death of her mother. She and William. She and William. Their steps clattered as they crossed the tiled floor. Without speaking, they mounted the stairs, heavy-hearted.

Minna's first visit was made to her own old room, where the sight of the patchy tiles about the fireplace made her lips tremble. Poor little idiot, she had worked so hard and unskilfully; and had been so proud of her performance, and so ashamed of it! What waste! The tiles were ugly. They were awry. Some had disappeared, and others were broken. . . . Waste, waste heart, waste energy; so young and engrossed and trusting, and so silly with inexperience and romanticism . . . No wonder William had not loved the swelling heart that lay behind such fatuous self-importance. She had changed too late. . . .

William was at the window through which she had heard birds singing as the Springtime day began. He was looking out of it, his back to Minna, his hands in his pockets, his shoulders as deceptively sturdy-seeming as they had always been; but beyond knowing that he surveyed the garden from a new altitude she could not guess his thoughts. Or he hers.

'Let's go away from here,' Minna said. Her throat felt full and swollen. She did not dare to look back at William as he followed; but entered her mother's bedroom and came quickly away again. All the other rooms upon that ample first floor were dark with oaken beams and the discolouration of the uneven walls and the dust upon every window-pane; and the longer they stayed the clearer it became that whatever use this old house might have it was not, as Minna had hoped it would be, a fit place for her purpose. She grew very depressed. At last: 'I wish we hadn't come,' she said, irritably. 'It's no good, and it makes me feel wretched.'

'I don't think it's any good,' William responded. 'But it's beautiful, all the same. I'm glad you did come.'

She impatiently retorted:

'You say "beautiful". It seems to me hopelessly dreary.'

That was not what she wanted to say. It was nothing like what she wanted to say.

'You're disappointed,' William told her, as if he understood. 'And it's too full of contrasts for you.'

'Contrasts between what I am and what I was? Or what I might be?' Minna asked, in scorn. 'Because personally I've been thinking what a sickening child I must have been. Sentimental. Idiotic. It makes me angry—humiliates me.'

William seemed to be smiling at her. His lips were parted. She did not look higher than his lips.

'Thirty-two years since I first came here,' he said. And then he laughed at a vivid memory of that evening—of Dick Firth's historic plunge into the pool, of the little white figure in the dusk. 'You don't remember that.'

Minna shook her head. She hardly attended.

'Well, I must stop being sentimental,' she answered, continuing her own thoughts. 'There's no time for that now. Work's the first thing, and the last.' How firm she sounded! Then, less firmly: 'William, I *must* go back once more to my little room. I can't leave it. Wait here.' She, too, laughed slightly; but she went back, none the less, to the room, thinking: 'Once sentimental, always sentimental! That's what I shall be to the end of my days. And he knows it.'

It was possible to see, at a tear in the later wallpaper, a scrap of the paper she had known. She could remember where her bookshelves had stood; and the oaken floor still, she thought, bore faint traces of the movement of her little bed. She heard William leave her and go down to the big dining-room; and she listened to his steps below. How often she must have done that in the past, when he came while she was changing her dress or moping or writing her little verses. She had hastened at the sound of such steps. She did not hasten now. She dared not hasten.

But at length Minna went downstairs again, to find William standing in the doorway and still looking out at the garden in which they had played. He half-turned as she reached him, and said:

'When I said "contrasts" I was thinking of size, and memory; but really what I had in mind was something I can't give a name to. It's every comparison. What one believed to be true; what one now disbelieves. What one hoped; what one now despairs of——'

'Despairs of,' ruefully echoed Minna.

'The contrast's always a kind of pickle. Mixed emotions, they call it.'

'But always unsatisfactory,' added Minna, sharply.

'By no means!' cried William, with spirit. 'That's the superficial mistake. This garden was immense to you and it was so. You've gone on enlarging it to keep proportion with your expanding world. Now you blame yourself for ever having thought it fine.'

'Not the garden. Myself,' Minna rejoined.

'Well, you were. You are. Your old feeling was never wasted. It was like the sun and wind to you—to the essential you. When you stuck those little tiles, for example——'

'Tiles?' said Minna, wonderingly. Her cheeks grew warm. Under her breath, she murmured: 'It's devilish.' As ever, he had read her mind.

'In your bedroom. You're ashamed of them now. You have been for years. I know it. But at the time—by Jove, what a joy they were to you! What a pride!'

'And you laughed at them,' said Minna, in reproach.

'If I did'—he had forgotten it—'I was a fool.'

'You were never that.'

'Always,' cried William, in fierce despair. 'Always. Oh, if you knew the shame I feel now at what I've said and done to wound you——'

'To wound me?' exclaimed Minna, amazed. 'To console. To support . . . Oh, God, Will, stop! You're making me cry!' She turned away, biting her lips. But William, standing there by the door, did not move. He said:

'Idiot vanity. Blindly committing myself to folly, and pretending to be wise. What a farce! Well, I know it now. I see the weakness. I see the stupidity. But I can't cure it. Everything I've ever done.'

'Every *good* thing!' she cried. 'The thousands!'

'No good thing.' He walked to and fro in agitation. 'Never any good thing. Cowardice the whole way. Cowardice cockered into idleness, into kindness—good God! into a pretence of generosity. The kind, protective elder brother. Well, you endured it like an angel——'

'An angel!' Crying, Minna laughed aloud. 'An angel, and I listen to you! Why, you silly! When I've adored you all my life, and been abject before you——'

'No longer,' William asserted, in a quiet voice of certainty. 'That's over. Finished.'

'It's different.'

'It's finished.'

Minna for a moment made no reply. She stood looking at him as he paced the room. She at last knew her power.

'If you mean that you're in love with me,' she said, coolly; 'why don't you say so? I've loved you all my life; and I shall love you till I die. There won't ever be anybody else. There *couldn't* be. William!' She held out her arms to him.

CHAPTER XXIII

Every Man for Himself

THREE YEARS LATER; and Summer-time. The scene again London, and again the heart of the City; but where that dingy building with many windows stood in the year when lights went up again in Europe is another building, much larger than the old and to uncritical eyes very solid and very splendid. Upon entering it one is no longer in a dark hall dominated by the gloomy, War-haunted commissionaire, with mouldering lift and dirty stone stairs leading to a warren of chilly rooms and cupboards. Instead, behind giant doors modelled upon those of Florentine bankers, and inner doors only a little less substantial, lies a spacious office with high lamp-studded ceiling and vast expanses of cream-painted walls. The new counters and desks are of mahogany. Even the waiting-room is as big as a parlour; and in it, for the use of callers, are mirrors, ashtrays, writing-materials, many periodicals, and one or two books of reference. These last are chained by the covers to their shelves; but few callers know that, and they make wonderful furnishing.

The place, they say, looks like a bank in Utopia. It is, in fact, the sumptuous registered office of the R.F.F. Holdings Association, in whose balance sheets it figures at a valuation of nearly two hundred thousand pounds; and upon upper floors of the building a bewildering number of other companies occupy themselves with the intricacies of bookkeeping and correspondence. Not a lump of sugar or a grain of tea or a bean of coffee is ever seen here; not a scrap of timber or a bar of iron or a pot of paint; not a cake of soap or a pint of oil or a single biscuit. But the books and order forms and invoices stored in room after room of this massy building are full of dealings in such things. One company sells them to another, having first bought them from a third by which they have been made or grown or imported. One group of ledgers deals with this, another with that, and twenty more with other matters; and yet all are involved in the same congeries of organizations; for in wholesale business there is a never-ending transfer of money and goods from this pocket to that, as if consummate conjuring tricks and acrobatic performances of the mind and heart and purse were the very object of existence. Over all its subsidiary companies, the R.F.F. Holdings Association exercises an unseen control. These are all, in one sense, and whatever the names upon the doors, its offices. Sir Furness Firth is rarely to be seen in any of them. He, however, is the earthly God at whose instigation the businesses work. He is the penny that sets the machine in motion.

Sir Furness himself may be anywhere in England or upon the Continent of Europe; yet the companies continue. He does much of his essential business at home, or at a club, or over dinner at some house which is not his own. He has been photographed in Winter at Monte Carlo, where he never gambles, and in the Summer at Trouville, where he likes to see smart women. He visits America, where, since the War, all the money in the world seems to have collected. He gives largely to charities. He makes speeches at dinners given in aid of good objects. He has moved, socially, right outside Kensington and the intellectual order; and his name figures occasionally in lists of those who have been entertained in company with peers, ambassadors, and Cabinet Ministers. And in spite of these grandeurs Sir Furness, upon waking up in the morning, continues to think of himself as Dick Firth, the clever boy of Moreton, the idealist, the lover of beauty in women, the surprised recipient of unexpected gifts at the hands of Fortune. He does not drink; he does not smoke; his favourite reading, apart from the Prayer Book, many phrases in which electrify audiences by their power and unfamiliarity, is, as it always had been, Donne's 'Poems' and the 'Decameron' of Boccaccio. Silken underclothing, his own valet, a secretary at home as well as secretaries at his various offices, and a rise in the expensiveness rather than the intrinsic quality of his women friends, are the luxuries Dick allows himself. But if he had not these luxuries he might wonder what advantages he gained from life; for his days and nights are crowded with innumerable cares.

The ordinary bull-necked man who trudges to work in the morning for a weekly wage has only one fear—unemployment. His responsibilities are featherweights. When Dick said, as he was saying upon this Summer afternoon to a young woman who wished him to finance her in a theatrical production, that his shoulders were bowed under the burden of a thousand commitments, he spoke the truth. He had many fears. And the young woman, in Dick's eyes, was not attractive.

'My dear Sylvia,' Dick was saying. 'If you think that five . . . five thousand pounds will put this play on, and keep it on, you're mistaken. It won't.'

The young lady, who had asked him to tea at her flat, and who was a clever actress but in dealing with financiers a dolt of the first order, presumed upon their acquaintance. She said:

'I know that, you silly. But don't you see I want to be able to say you're *ready* to put it up.'

'Why?' asked Dick, at his tartest. He was only half-attending to her; for he was bored. His gaze passed from the actress, who was small and ugly and of a complexion which suggested that iron ran in her veins; and roved to a door which stood ajar. Through the open space he glimpsed or imagined untidiness. It was insufferable to him. There was poverty in this room itself: well, she had not pretended otherwise. 'Poor but honest,' she had said; 'talented' was implied. A sloven, and avaricious. He did not know why he had come here. He was tired.

'Well, but Di-ick,' she drawled; 'if I can *say* that, I can get another three, and another two, and a one. I *know* I can. And of course I'm positive the play will be a wow——'

Her tone was false. Dick knew that she thought she was managing him. He would snub her for that, the fool.

'No,' he said, sharply. 'I've got no money.'

'Hoh!' she laughed, incredulous. 'You've got no money! Why, everybody knows you're one of the richest men in London.'

'Does everybody know that? Then there's been a leakage somewhere.'

'And it's only five thousand pounds. To you, it's a fleabite.'

Dick rose. He said:

'Five thousand pounds is no fleabite to anybody, my dear. And it's not as though I was in love with you.' Poor homely fool, he must undeceive her! He saw that she flinched.

'Nobody asked you, sir,' she hastily retorted.

'Except for money,' said Dick. She had the grace to flush. He went on: 'In any case, I . . . I don't care for the play. It's immoral.'

Sylvia's mouth opened. Such a large, ugly mouth; like a cavern full of good teeth. Her one chance of success was in intellectual drama. Yes, good teeth. Tolerable eyes. Nothing else he cared for. Nothing worth five thousand pounds. His cruel eyes strayed over her.

'But Di-ick! Charmian says it's a *sweet* play. And everybody knows *her* judgment's superb.'

He stammered:

'Mine's better, and I . . . I disagree. It's about people who ignore the decalogue; horrid people. Quite horrid. I couldn't take my daughter to it. Wouldn't let her take *me*. No, I shan't give you a penny. Or lend, or invest. I want money for myself and my shareholders. I . . . I'm a trustee for *them*. I can't spare another ounce of energy for anything. And now I'm going.' He turned to his hat, which lay with a pair of new gloves upon a chair by the door.

'But Dick!' She tried to dissuade him. 'You don't *understand*.' Seeing that he was bent upon leaving her, she grew a little angry. Her tone changed to one of savage impatience. 'It's so jolly hard to get money, to get *anything* done. . . .' Her lips quivered. 'It's the chance of a lifetime; theatre, play, everything——'

'Except my money,' smiled Dick, showing his teeth. 'Goodbye, my dear.' He took her hand. If she had been pretty . . . No! Even then, he'd had enough. 'Goodbye. I hate sinners. I . . . I hate the theatre——'

'You did it for Sophia Western!' shouted Sylvia, as a last shot. He was unperturbed: he had been expecting that, and the occurrence of what he expected was always amusing. Raising a finger to his lips, he murmured:

'Sh! Hush! Protect my reputation! Goodbye.'

Dick was outside the flat and in the street. He did not see a man who stood a little way away and who looked sidelong at him; but with a faintly malicious smile walked in haste from this would-be star. Sophia Western was an episode . . . forgotten, lovely, mercurial: finished as soon as he found that she drank to assure vivacity. How he hated cadgers! Cadge, cadge. Worse than sinners. 'I'm tired, tired, tired!' Wherever he looked, somebody was lying in wait, to cadge. This legend of his wealth! 'Oh, I'm sick of women,' thought Dick, in passing disgust. 'If they weren't necessary to me, I should . . . One's never done with them.'

Unconscious that the man at the street-corner followed, he traversed Orchard Street, stopping in doubt as he came to the thicker traffic. He was near home; but at home Eileen would be waiting, and he dreaded the milky boredom of that encounter. In Kensington, Julie . . . How weary he was of Julie: so much melodrama! Her wrongs; good heavens! Her egoism. As soon a harlot. No doubt life with Robert was hell; but the greedy passion of her response to him was unpleasing. It was nothing but passion. And then Robert's fat face and the stink of cigars . . . After lunch, faugh! A bore in brandy! If one could export him! America? What a poor figure he'd cut there! But Robert's company was the only one that showed a profit again this year. . . . The only one. They had all supposed the profits of the War years would continue. It had seemed reasonable, with more men home and a general resumption of trade. In fact Dick had expected a boom, and spent accordingly. Instead, the War once over, everything had slumped and was still slumping. It was costly to borrow; he had only managed to pay dividends in the last two years by bringing in reserves and resorting to one or two not unfamiliar devices. The reserves wouldn't last indefinitely. What then? Penter, his accountant, was producing columns of figures as long as a dining-table at full stretch. And the damned figures wouldn't stay where they belonged. In Dick's dreams they moved across, like the pointing hand upon an oculist's sight-testing card, into the Liabilities; and sometimes in daylight, too, they had to be forcibly included among Assets.

'I'm tired,' thought Dick Firth, walking in Hyde Park with the sunlight hot upon him. 'I shall have a holiday.'

He'd give Eileen the slip. She could take the younger girls to Ilfracombe, as arranged—splashing like curds in the blue sea— while he ran Bianca over to Paris. Paris would be crowded. Damn! Everywhere. Fun for Bianca, though. Yes, but what to do about Robert Whistler? And his dame! By Jove, there would be scenes. . . . Get rid of both. How? Dick, with an uncomfortable feeling that somebody was following him, sauntered towards Hyde Park Corner, looking over his shoulder every now and again from nervous habit, but not, of course, seeing anybody. He did not notice the flower-beds, which were brilliant, or the men or the children whom he passed; but sometimes, abstractedly, he glanced at a young woman—the knee, the waist, the neck, at last the eyes. One or two people recognised him, and pointed him out to their companions. Dick was indifferent.

He and Bianca would go to the Crillon. Queer little thing; she hadn't any interest in frocks or sweets, but she had excellent taste. She knew what suited her, and took it. As he did. She was quite a credit. Oh, but as hard as concrete . . . the naughty child!

In Knightsbridge Dick saw a man selling newspapers and journals; and upon an impulse he bought a copy of 'The Candid Friend', Mather's weekly paper, for which William Harvest wrote the chief article on current events. It was the sort of thing William had written for 'England', but in keeping with the character of the paper was more sharply critical in tone. Dick read it every week. He no longer read 'England', which he had sold to a new company, called 'England Publications, Limited'. And his feeling for the Mather brothers as that of a deep-seated sneer. But he read their paper. Still carrying the copy he had bought, he was continuing to stroll westwards when he remembered that Penter, the accountant, would probably be waiting for him at home. Damn Penter! He cannoned into a man who had been walking behind him, and set off at a brisk pace for the house in Mayfair.

'Damn!' said Dick, aloud. '*I'm* not an accountant. I detest money.'

He was troubled.

II

The meeting with Penter was as unpleasant as he had feared. Penter, who looked like a gentleman-farmer, with trim moustache and prominent smiling eyes, had a mind like an adding-machine. Figures and golf were his only recreations. He was sitting in Dick's study, and was so perfectly happy in checking his own elaborate columns that Dick felt like a nervous man who interrupts a rat at breakfast in his larder.

'Damn you, Penter,' said he, fidgetily. 'You're never welcome. You're like a toothache. You're like a cloud in a clear sky. I . . . I hate you.'

Penter struggled to his feet.

'I'm sorry to hear you say that, Sir Furness', he jovially objected. 'Of course I'm well used to your——'

'Yes, well, cut that out, Penter,' snapped Dick. 'What's the trouble now? We're ruined, are we?'

Penter gave his employer a queer look as he sat down again. For answer, he tendered what seemed to be an endless chart. If unfolded to its full length it would have covered nearly the whole of the desk by which they now sat, and indeed, as Dick flaccidly grasped the chart with distaste some of it flapped down in disorder.

'Not quite that, Sir Furness,' Penter slowly added. 'Still——'

Dick threw down the chart, which sprawled upon the desk. He impatiently cried:

'I can't understand these figures. They might be Arabic. What do they tell me?'

The notion of a famous man of affairs being unable to understand figures made John Penter smile. To himself, who had no head for business, they were as clear as the multiplication table. Nevertheless he explained. He and Dick put their heads together over the great chart. Penter lowered his voice. He stretched a forefinger, first to this point and then to the other. He produced other papers from his case which showed the figures in more complete detail. He was still demonstrating these figures when the dressing

'It *must* be, sir,' observed Penter, sipping again. 'I know that by the taste.' Even he, it appeared, was not wholly a stranger to innuendo.

Something happened in Miss Neilson's mind. It came like a wave of certainty, and she fell out of her prolonged calf-love for Dick Firth. At one moment she had been as ecstatically servile as ever, and at the next she—— 'For God's sake, woman! Surely even *you* can see——' was what he contemptuously exclaimed—felt that she had given him the best of her life for nothing. 'Even *you*.' Because she had reminded him that balances could not be got out specially, as he wanted them, without high-pressure overtime. And 'Woman'! That was unpardonable. As recently as a year ago she might have found excuses for Dick: now such a sense of injury possessed her that love at once soured. 'Woman'! That was what he thought her. He found her old, and a mere female bundle.

Of course, she cried that night, and did not sleep; and all the next day she was listless. Then she began to feel afraid, for she had seen something of Dick's impatient methods. Old, highly-paid, despised; she was in danger of being discharged. Only two thousand pounds saved. Terror swept through her. At her age another job . . . Oh, she'd get another job. It might even become necessary to do so. 'I'm not *quite* a fool,' thought Miss Neilson. 'And I know the R.F.F. Holdings must be . . .' The word she sought was 'shaky'. Calmly, she reflected: 'His nerves are on edge.' But that did not soften her resentment.

When, therefore, Robert Whistler complained shortly afterwards that Dick was treating him as an office boy, Miss Neilson did not attempt contradiction. She sat at her desk regarding Robert and feeling rather sorry for him. Her eyes were consciously half-closed: when she looked like that she felt wise and Scotland Yardy, and her lips stiffened into a faint smile at the sense that she knew so much. 'I know so much about everybody's business,' she thought. 'They don't know I know. Even the *things* I know haven't struck them.' She saw Robert stride about the room in dejection, putting a face on things; a great clumsy man, a big boy, as if he had never quite grown up. . . .

'Mr Whistler,' said Miss Neilson. 'I'm . . . taking a liberty; but I really don't *think* you're being treated fairly.'

'Eh? I'm sure I'm not,' growled Robert, pausing. 'Why, what d'you mean?'

She looked meaningly at him; the soft eyes purposely hardened to seem keen.

'Well, after all, yours is the only company that's showing a profit.'

Robert angrily exclaimed:

'I know that. It's the only one that's properly managed.'

There was a little pause. A three bar interval. Miss Neilson said:

'He wants to transfer you.' Oh, it was treachery! She felt hot as she pronounced the words.

'What's that?' shouted Robert, in a fury. 'He can't!' His eyes seemed ready to start from his high-coloured face. 'He can't *do* it!'

Miss Neilson did not reply. She looked at the wall to the right of Robert, where there was a small drawing of Brahms, showing a little man with a big hairy head. One had only to think of Brahms, she felt, to realise how simple Mr Whistler was; and how much she herself knew that was quite beyond Mr Whistler's grasp. Brahms was so deep, so German; and Mr Whistler was so English and boyish and . . . well, if you *must* know, stupid. She was sorry for Robert.

He, for his part, went to the door, opened it, looked outside in order to make sure that nobody listened, and in a lowered tone demanded:

'What d'you mean, Miss Neilson? As man to man.'

Stung into emotion, with the tears leaping to her eyes, Miss Neilson began to speak. She had not intended to say as much; but when once she unlocked her tongue it could not be checked. Robert came nearer; they were close enough to each other to exchange hardly articulated speech; and as Miss Neilson divulged her thoughts Robert heard alarming confirmation of a thousand nocturnally-active fears. He lost colour and his heart fell. Not only did Miss Neilson explain that his contract had recently been called

for, and that Sir Furness had afterwards seemed very pleased with
what he had read in it, but she told him of similar happenings in
the past over other contracts, of Mr Harvest's abrupt departure
from 'England', of how Sir Furness took sudden whims—'I never
know when it'll be *me*, Mr Whistler'—and unaccountable dislikes——

'He doesn't like me,' murmured Robert, in extreme candour.
'You know that. I know that. Well, he's afraid of me. I know too
much.'

'Tell him so,' eagerly whispered Miss Neilson. Her fists clenched
and jerked. 'Stand up to him.'

'By God, I will!' swore Robert, under his breath. He thought for
an instant. 'Of course, *I'm* not afraid of *him*.'

'Oh, no,' agreed Miss Neilson. She laughed nervously. 'Nobody
would ever——'

'If he tries any funny business——'

'It's as well to be armed, isn't it, Mr Whistler.'

Robert presently went away, to arm himself. He was desperately
worried. What did the blasted woman mean about his contract?
His contract: why, it had been vetted, hadn't it? Water-tight? Yes,
but nobody knew better than Robert that his position was difficult. In the game of counters that they played in this great building it looked good upon paper. He managed his own company,
but his place on the board of that company was subject to Dick's
whim, and his contract as manager was only yearly. He held shares;
but he had no voting power. He sometimes boomed at the meetings, and received thanks there, but at almost a moment's notice
he could be deposed in favour of another puppet. Oh, God! this
fellow had them all on strings! He himself danced to the crack
of a whip.

Exaggerated consciousness of all this made him, when he saw
Dick, rather too truculent to his old friend.

IV

Julie thought quickly. She had run up to her room, leaving
Robert downstairs, frighteningly sober after telling the story of his

quarrel with Dick three hours earlier. Some immediate action was needed if the quarrel were not to become an enmity. Otherwise everything—happiness, prosperity, hope—would be irretrievably wrecked. Happiness! The mockery! One resisted an impalpable force. One fought in darkness. But Robert, it was clear, had been deliberately provoked. Then goaded. Then humiliated. Why? Julie shrugged. That was Dick's way. What had happened was what she had long feared.

'Ah, my friend!' she thought, with bitter admiration of her lover. The French boast that they see what is, and not what they wish. He had tired of her. Therefore he quarrelled with her husband. 'Ah, my friend; you are so clever! And so easy to read, because so callous!'

If she were to telephone to his house, his butler would deny that he was there. The stone-faced lying of servants. He would avoid their place of rendezvous. Heartless! Incalculable and heartless! He turned the page. He never looked back at a beloved picture. But he would still do for her what he would not do for Robert. Yes? Julie's breath failed her. Perhaps not even that.

Presently, nevertheless, she was at the telephone. The whirr of the bell continued in her ears; but there was no other sound. Damn the telephone! Damn it, for remaining silent when all depended upon Dick's voice. But if he spoke? To see him—*that* was her one thought. With another man, yes; but with him, so smiling, so evasive, there was no hope. A dozen remembered indications of weariness darted into Julie's mind, rising into a column of threat. She flung down the receiver. In ten minutes she was again at the door of the room in which Robert sat. She barely showed herself, wrapped in a long black cloak and wearing a hat which covered her eyes.

'I have to go out,' she said. 'Immediately.'

He sat by the unlighted gas fire, his head sunk in his shoulders; and Julie could see that he was very pale. She knew that ever since she had left him he had been seeing deeper and deeper into the consequences of his quarrel. Deeper and deeper, until he came to the end, which was nothing. His hand, as he raised it, trembled.

'Where are you going?' Robert asked, in a baffled voice. He stared stupidly at her, his mouth open. But although he seemed dazed he had not, as she at first suspected, been drinking in her absence. The shock had been too sharp for that. 'It's late, isn't it?' He expected no answer. Fretfully, he continued: 'You seem to have been an awful time. Now you want to go out. What's the sense of that? Can't you sit down? I need company. This damned thing's upset me.'

Julie made an assenting noise. She was not unkind, or contemptuous.

'It is because of that I must go,' she answered.

'What?' He had become more alert. Sharper still: 'What?'

'One must *act,* my dear Robert.'

He was listening. He leant back, sitting rigidly upright; and his hands were both upon the arms of the chair.

'But *you* can't do anything—— What can *you* do?'

'It remains to be seen.' Julie was already turning away; and Robert could see nothing under the brim of her hat but shadow and a white sharpness which was her chin. 'Perhaps.'

'Julie!' He struggled to his feet, and became impressive. 'You're not thinking of seeing that swine. I won't have it. Good God, d'you think I've got no pride?' He strode across the room as she withdrew from it, and they were simultaneously in the hall. He tried to catch her arm; but she shrank away as softly as a cat. 'Julie! Listen!' She was a stranger. In that mood he could do nothing with her, but was afraid of her. His voice echoed and sounded false, as if he were only pretending to protest. But he was not pretending. He was only still stupefied by what he had seen of the future. He choked: 'Eating dirt. My God, you wouldn't——'

'I would eat offal, my dear.'

'But it's my affair!' cried Robert.

Julie was at last scornful. She cried, using English as an unfamiliar language:

'You've messed it up, my dear Robert. Now it is mine.'

'I won't have my wife——'

She was gone. Robert reached the door as it slammed; and although he fumbled to open it again his fingers were clammy and clumsy, and he was late. In the windy darkness of a night of cloud he could not see any movement. And so at last, after turning and calling and striding a little distance, he stumbled back into the house and to his seat in the armchair, sitting like an old man and staring before him in exhaustion. All the strength had gone from his body and brain, which always failed him under great tension.

'She's gone.' His wife. It would be useless. Of course she thought —a woman—Dick's a man: I can . . . Rubbish! It wasn't in her power. No, the trouble was the same as before: Dick had always tricked him. Not straight. Never straight. Long ago, Robert had learned that. He'd been a fool to trust him. He'd given good service, as Dick would find out presently, when it was too late. The folly! But for himself much worse. God, he was frightened! Julie was frightened. She couldn't keep quiet; couldn't *endure*. Not English.

Why had she gone? And here? What to do? She didn't know the fellow. What? Didn't know him. In that case, why go? Eh? . . . Damned mysterious. Damned . . . In that cloak; like a conspirator. That black cloak.

Through the dull churning of thought came an unexpected sharpness. What!

'That's funny!' said Robert, aloud. There was a long pause, while he thought: 'That cloak. I've seen it before. When she's slipped out. At night. Eh? When was that?' A fog crept down upon him again. He rubbed his head. 'Stupid I feel! I remember something . . . But I can't remember what it was.'

He racked his memory. Long ago. Not so long. She'd hurried in. He rose and began to pace the room. She'd seemed upset. He hadn't known her. Why the cloak? She goes now . . . Backwards and forwards he went, his hands clasped behind his bulky body, his heavy shoulders bent, thinking, remembering, trying to pierce the fog. . . .

Meanwhile Julie had seen a taxicab and chartered it. She had reached the secret place of rendezvous in which she and Dick had in the last year spent stolen hours. Darkness. A little dust upon the mahogany table at which they had sometimes eaten. What else had she expected? While Robert strode moodily—now fast, now slow—about the room at home, Julie, upon whom his thoughts were set, went quickly here and there in the flat, drawing the flowered curtains in order to shut in the light and the shadows, and in time flicking her fingers to rid them of greasy London dust. Dick did not mean to come here tonight. No message. She would never see him again. It was unbearable. She wept.

In another turn of mood Julie thought again of money. Money —it was a terrible preoccupation of hers. Apart from her own thrifty savings, she and Robert had nothing but a few of his fantastic investments—three or four thousand pounds, it might be— she could not tell. There was her own hoarded money. It was a little more than Robert's, perhaps. Enough to avert starvation, she hoped. Three, four, five pounds a week, it might be. But she was as frightened now, with that, as she had been when they had nothing at all. More frightened than she had been; for it is worse to return to poverty than it is to hope for release from it. There was no security anywhere. As for love . . .

As for love, what did life hold? With a sigh that tore her heart she felt that she could no longer bear that stifling atmosphere of expectant silence. She resumed the cloak which she had cast aside, and with a bleak glance about the room extinguished the light and went hastily down the stairs. She had formed a resolve. It was so strong and sudden and irresistible that she had attention for nothing else, and did not notice how loudly she slammed the street door and how the noise echoed. She knew what to do. She was going to Dick's home. She was going to see Dick's wife.

v

What struck Eileen, as she first entered the room in which Julie waited for her, was that her visitor was theatrical. Insatiable. One of those *women*. Julie had thrown aside her cloak, for the evening was warm; but she was dressed with a chic to which Eileen had never aspired. It would not have suited her own mind, and she did not care for the sort of mind that found it appropriate. Boldly cut, the dress was of a rich crimson from which Julie's creamy shoulders wonderfully rose, and as Julie moved forward there was such a suggestion of lithe movement within the dress that a first shocked consciousness thrust the word 'naked' into Eileen's thoughts. Naked, assured, unscrupulous, embarrassing. That impression, accordingly, was not good.

What struck Julie, at sight of Eileen, was that this was Dick's chosen and discarded bedfellow. Her impulse was one of impatience. She thought: 'Bread and butter.' Extreme fairness, a small nose which had once appeared fine and was now insipidly obstinate, thin lips, a meagre body, scant hair of weary gold, a tasteless pale green dress, eyes intimidatingly set and hueless, and a manner which would have been *grande dame* if that had been allowed by Eileen's physique. A heart afflicted with lassitude, a nature timid and . . . was it implacable? Julie chilled as she observed. But her own manner, which at the moment was directed towards pathetic dignity, did not alter. Her lips drooped; her chin was a little raised in entreaty. She was not acting, but feeling.

Both women moved forward, Eileen with a grimacing half-smile and raised shoulders and eyebrows of one who cannot account for the interview, Julie with an impulsiveness which gave fervour to her handshake. She was oppressed by a sense that their positions should have been reversed: it was cruel of Fate to make her the suppliant. How differently she would have received. With what grandeur of comprehension. But need was too urgent to allow of finesse. She must at once, abandoning pride, plead for Robert.

'Madame,' said Julie, her voice rich. 'How strange it must seem to you that I should come now, at this hour! I beg you to forgive me!' Oh, those pale eyes, and the little white false teeth! They froze her. And, when Eileen spoke, her polite, repressive voice:

'Not at all. I . . . We've never met before.'

Julie agreed:

'Never before.'

With childish dignity Eileen said:

'I see very few people. My own interests, you know.'

'I, too, madame,' said Julie. 'I have been very lonely.'

'Oh, one's not *lonely*.' What a fragile little voice! Like the voice of a doll. A cold, timid, implacable doll. Every sentence a question.

Julie was disconcerted afresh. 'I never feel lonely. On the contrary, there's so much——'

'Excuse me. I shouldn't have troubled you. But I am in great distress——'

'Actressy!' thought Eileen, disconcerted in turn by the interruption. Those big, ruthless eyes made one shiver a little. French. Dick had said so. They were so unscrupulous. Not really nice. What did she want? But one must be courteous.

'I'm so sorry. Won't you sit down?'

'Oh, heaven!' thought Julie, with difficulty restraining visible appeal to the Almighty. She sat down. How impossible *not* to sit with an air, even though her heart sank lower and lower. To a Frenchwoman one could have said all in a moment, confident of understanding; but to this frozen-hearted creature——

'It is your husband and my husband!' she cried, when she was seated.

'Oh!' That was breathless. Eileen had taken fright. 'Oh, I never interfere in business——'

'Or in anything else!' thought Julie. Save as ice interferes with the temperature of room or wine. Only to chill, to oppose! To nullify! Poor negative, poor nothing!

'This is not business,' she pleaded. 'It is a quarrel. It is the happiness of us all. It is two silly men who, for pride and anger, may harm each other——'

'I'm very sorry, Mrs Whistler.' Eileen trembled slightly; for she was socially alarmed at the—to her—theatrical fervour of Julie's speech. It had no quietness; it was managing. She did not trust this woman, or like her. She had never liked the husband, a great blusterer. . . .

'At least hear me,' begged Julie. 'I know you have a daughter . . . daughters?'

'Three,' corrected Eileen, not softening, but caught.

'I—only one. That is a grief to me. My husband . . . However, you will appreciate . . . It is shocking to me to think that these friends—they are old friends, you know, madame——'

'But Mrs Whistler. I don't see that I can do anything. Perhaps if you saw my husband? He's not here just now. He's very busy.'

Hard eyes; defensiveness; pride in her husband; resentment that he should be elsewhere . . . That was what Julie thought; but she had no time to observe. She must hasten.

'It was because he was not here that I asked for you. But I thought—you will agree—how much wiser we women are than men. . . .' Julie checked herself; her breath was sobbing.

'Are we?' asked that little voice.

'Oh, God!' Impossible to restrain the cry. 'Mrs Firth, I implore you. Your husband has great power. *You* have great power. Let me tell you what has happened——'

'I'm afraid——'

'My husband has given years of his life. His ambition. His service. He has made his company a success. The only successful——'

'I know nothing——'

'But, madame, I tell you. Your husband, who has been good to us in the past, has indicated to mine that certain purchases must be made from other companies in the group. Very large—enormous. He has declined—in the interest of his company—to make them. His agreement has been terminated. He has been offered —in contempt—the management of one of the failures. He has protested——'

'Mrs Whistler!' cried Eileen, repelling Julie's too vigorous hand, which would have rested upon her arm. 'This *is* business, you know; and I *told* you——'

'Wait!' commanded Julie. 'That is the beginning only. My husband speaks without thought. He says what comes to his tongue. He angers yours; they quarrel; they part. Do you understand what I mean? They are both sorry; but being men—stupid, prideful—they cannot say "Let us forget, forgive." They part; they refer their quarrel to lawyers; they are in train to fight. That is suicidal. It is fantastic. Madame, it is masculine. But you and I have not such pride. We are women, loyal to our sex and to reason. Besides, through the greatness and weakness of our sex, we are forced always to forgive——'

Eileen Firth was standing erect, so straight, and with such a curious, stiff smile upon her little mouth, that Julie stopped.

'Not always. I agree that we forgive a good deal, Mrs Whistler,' said Eileen. 'But not everything. I'm not sure that we ought to.'

'In this case,' cried Julie, vehemently. 'Do you not sympathise with me?'

Eileen was silent. She did; she didn't. On the whole, no. She didn't want—it was impossible—to take upon herself the burden that was asked. When——

'I sympathise with you,' she said, coldly. As if she said: 'I detest you.' It was terrible. That little bleat, to which the vindictive was as natural as the inane. Still Julie would not yield.

'And you will help?' she begged. She saw the resolutely shaken head.

'I can't do that.'

'My God! Nor try?'

'You don't understand my position.'

With anger in her heart Julie stood back from that woman of ice. To strike at her, to spit at her . . . To stare reproachfully and with incredulity.

'You have so much power,' she said, in scorn.

Eileen would have answered, bitterly, 'None.' But she could not do so. She had too much pride to say: 'I am a nonentity. My husband despises me—as you do. He would ignore my appeal. He would smile. Frown. Go. And, as far as hate can live in such as I, I hate him for that and the heaped indignities of a lifetime.' She said, instead, in a tone that sounded flippant:

'In business, men seem to do very strange things.'

Julie drew her breath.

'They fail,' she cried. 'They go bankrupt.' It was a threat. 'Do you realise that without my husband yours may be ruined?'

She never forgot the extraordinary light that crossed the white face before her. Having no clue to it, she yet saw evil emotion touch and pass those hueless eyes and that thin little mouth. Hardness other than her own, and such as this, was alarming.

'You don't in the least frighten me, Mrs Whistler. I still think it's a matter for our . . . our husbands.'

'Whatever the consequences?'

'Whatever the consequences.'

'Without an effort?'

'You must excuse me.'

They paused long, and looked almost sightlessly at one another, seeing only hostility and all that each most detested in character. Julie, oppressed by despair, deeply sighed.

'Then I, too, have failed,' she mournfully said. 'I have no hope.' Her head was bowed. She turned for her cloak; and even Eileen could see that under the darkness of her skin she had grown pallid.

But Eileen did not answer. She waited to see the fatal movement with which the cloak was swept about that crimson figure, and then she rang the bell. The door opened. Julie, without a glance, left her; and Eileen, alone in the big drawing-room, which was so filled with half-hearted luxury that it was like a frosted Christmas card, was trembling from head to foot, not with fear or sorrow, but with excitement in which dislike, relief, hatred, and triumph were all involved. She looked calm; but she could have screamed and pounded the soft cushions of her divan and in frenzy kicked the senseless body of the woman who had left her. Hatred. Hatred. That, she knew, was what she most strongly felt. She had no doubt at all that she had seen and by this refusal scathingly humiliated one who had been her rival.

CHAPTER XXIV

Writings on the Wall

WILLIAM LOOKED DOWN at the bed where Kitty lay, and seated himself at last in the chair beside it. The afternoon was sunless, and although the curtains had been drawn as widely apart as possible the room was dusky with shadows. He had thought Kitty sleeping; not realising that she never slept when he was near, but lovingly watched him in secret, drawing strength from the act. Her hand, now so wasted, was drawn painfully from under the clothes and put into his own. The two hands, clasped, rested upon the coverlet.

Poor child; hers was as white and soft as a feather. And she did not at first speak to him, but turned her head and lay smiling, her eyes dark and tender. Out of doors a small rising wind very occasionally shook the casement, as if signalling for it to be opened; within all was warm, and as yet the curtains hardly stirred. It was quiet, too; for although this was no longer Moreton the house in which the Harvests lived stood upon high ground well back from the sea at Brighton, and for all they knew of it the brilliance of the King's Road might have been twenty miles distant. Firelight flickered upon a large wardrobe and a washstand bearing various bottles and jars; but otherwise all was grey. Presently the fingers within William's clasp moved.

'What time is it?' whispered Kitty. She no longer had any voice.

'Four o'clock,' William whispered in reply, stooping nearer as he did so. He added: 'Soon be dark now. And teatime.'

She thought for a while. The movement of her lashes showed him that her eyes moved quickly. Then she asked:

'Done your work? Been out?' Yes; no. 'Soon be time for you to go.'

'Not yet. I can go later.' They still whispered.

'Have you seen Minna?'

'Not yet. I'll go when she comes.'

Another pause.

'You should take her with you.'

William shook his head, but made no audible reply to this. He could not have explained, without giving it too much positiveness, that he read her meaning perfectly. It was better, therefore, to say nothing. Much was unspoken between them; upon her side because although she felt deeply she had no language with which to express her feeling, and upon his because he thought they understood each other very well without the unravellings to which more explicit moderns are prone.

In a moment Kitty's fragile fingers tightened again—a very faint pressure.

'Nobody there, is there?' she asked, turning her head. Nobody was there in the twilight but themselves. 'I've been thinking.'

'I must get you some books.'

'No, really. I've got plenty of time for thinking, I mean, lying here.' It seemed to amuse her to say this, as if she were pretending to have had an idle day in bed. 'I've been thinking about you.' William, it may be, shrank slightly, for Kitty, quickly glancing, added: 'And me, of course. Us. Old stagers.' She returned to her reverie. After a time she added: 'Going back to Balham . . . and that. Doesn't seem to be me at all; running up and down stairs. D'you remember? Remember breakfast? I used to hide your long envelopes—silly of me; but I didn't want the others to know.' She laughed quietly. 'I never thought . . .' The hoarse little whisper faded. She drew his hand to her cheek. Her mouth was contorted as she strugged against tears.

William stared down at his knees. She had never thought they would be married. But they had been married, and happy together; and now she was dying.

'You never thought of that!' he teased.

'Wanted it. What hopes! Say the fairy tales aren't true!'

'Oh, they're true enough.'

If Kitty could remember, so could William. But his memories

of those days, unlike hers, were dark. They were of unhappy doings; doings serious in effect upon his character, in that in them
he had known defeat. She guessed nothing of his broken pride; for
only to Minna had William ever spoken harshly of himself. Kitty
did not understand that in thinking of such days he was troubled
by a nightmare sense of failure in essential things. But instead of
grizzling he archly pinched her fingers.

'Like yesterday,' Kitty said, blissfully. 'You fast asleep. Old ruffle-
head. You *do* go to sleep, you know. It's like a baby—off! Funny,
isn't it! William, if you'd known—*you* know, if you could have
seen—what would happen to us, would you——' She was breathless.

'This moment!' declared William, smiling.

Her relief was ecstasy.

'You wouldn't! Would you, really?' She watched him anew in
love and pity. Then grimaced a little. 'I don't think you would.'

'Across my heart,' he said.

'Hm.' Kitty was delighted. 'I wonder. *I* should. But that's different. What a lucky girl I've been!'

'A mascot,' teased William.

'No, in myself. Best husband in the world; two lovely children;
Minna . . .'

'What else?' asked William, finding her silent.

'I shan't tell you. It all comes back to the first.'

'Which was the first?'

'H.U.S.B. . . . William'—her tone changed; she delayed; her
face grew pinched—'I always *wanted* to be the first to die.'

'What!' William almost stood upright with the shock of
her revealed knowledge. 'My dearest, you mustn't . . . You
mustn't——'

Kitty did not laugh. She smiled.

'But you knew,' she said, with great simplicity. 'You knew. It
isn't anything. It isn't . . . anything. . . .' She was crying, for all
her courage. 'I wanted . . . to live till we were both old; but I
can't. I'm so tired. I can't——'

William's arms were about her shoulders, and he was whispering in her ear the tendernesses of despair. And in turn, her cheek
pressed to his, her arms were round his neck, very soft and gentle.

He could feel the tears upon his face, and the sobs shaking her body, but he could not hear what she lovingly stammered. Only when she coughed did his alarm outsoar his other distress.

'Look, you mustn't talk,' he protested. 'That bloody cough. Lie down again.' The cough had ceased; it had made no more sound than the rustling of dry leaves. 'Lie down and I'll talk to you.' She shook her head. 'If you don't, I shall get into a row with nurse, and she's a termagant——'

'An angel!' she insisted. 'Let me lie down. But I want to talk. Something I want to say.'

'Hurry up, then,' said William.

'It's nothing.' She took his hand again. 'It's only . . . It's only . . .' Although she smiled, the tears ran down her cheeks in two little streams. 'I can't say it,' she whispered. 'Isn't it funny. It makes me cry.'

'I'll say it for you,' William offered. But Kitty shook her head.

'Nobody could say it for me,' she answered. 'Nobody on earth. It's only . . . It's only . . .' With all her feeble strength she persisted: '. . . that I love you so! . . .' And with that she burst into an agony of sobbing, clinging to him as if she could not bear ever again to be taken from his protection.

II

And while Kitty and William sat together in that little bedroom, as near as they had ever been to common emotion, other events were taking place in London which had their powerful effect upon the lives of some who were known to them. What was greyness in Brighton was in London premature night, with the reflections of street lamps and shop-windows spreading ever wider upon the wet roadways and being caught in the falling rain as it drenched unhappy passers. And in an office high up in an old building in Lincoln's Inn Dick Firth was deeply engaged with an elderly man in discussing papers which lay before them upon a desk.

The solicitor rose from his chair at the very moment when Kitty's fingers lay within William's. He moved over to the fireplace and stood there. He was a portly, bald man with golden-rimmed spectacles; and his face, as is proper in a good father and ardent gardener, was benevolent. But he had thought so much upon what are known as the finer points of the Law that his grey eyes, behind the spectacles, were like shifting flints.

'Settle,' he remarked. Of all the salient words in the English language it was the one he most often pronounced; for in Law it is the word of economy. 'Settle,' he added.

'He won't,' said Dick Firth.

The solicitor's hand went to his chin.

'It oughtn't to have come to that,' said he. 'But I still say "settle". You see, Sir Furness, you can only suffer a certain amount of publicity that will do you no good.'

Dick smiled.

'It's not as simple, Mr Fotheringdew, as that,' he observed. The carefree expression upon his face was little guide to the conflict within. 'I . . . I acted on your advice throughout. I put the contract to you; I offered him an alternative job; I . . . I then offered him a lump sum. He was obstinate. I . . . I'm sorry to say he brought private pressure to bear on me. His wife went to *my* wife. It was disagreeable. Finally, there was . . . was the anonymous letter.'

'The anonymous letter!' cried the solicitor. 'Really, Sir Furness! That doesn't seem to have been . . . Have I heard of that? If there were any suggestion of blackmail——'

'Of course, the whole thing's blackmail!' declared Dick. He lay back in his chair, looking about the box and file and paper crowded room, and between the solicitor's legs at the fire. 'Hasn't that been clear all along?'

'What did the anonymous letter say?' inquired Mr Fotheringdew, non-committally.

'The anonymous letter, which was typed, on a sheet of plain paper, said that the writer had certain private information about me which would be put at the disposal of the appropriate parties. It mentioned what that information was. It warned me to be very careful what I . . . I was doing.'

'And the writer suggested a reward?' inquired the solicitor, benevolently.

'N . . . not at all,' replied Dick, with considerable blandness.

'But you've had anonymous letters before, Sir Furness?'

'One or two. From discharged servants. Common form. I've handed them to the police. This one's different.'

'What makes you attach importance to this one?'

Dick peeped at Mr Fotheringdew.

'Oh,' he said. 'It covers some ground. It's quite . . . a nasty anonymous letter.'

'I see,' remarked the solicitor. He looked down from a height upon the seated figure of his client, and was conscious of admiration for the little man. But what a life he must have led! Ageing now, of course, and much more nervous in the last few months. No doubt there were difficulties: so much was clear. And as to his private life Mr Fotheringdew had heard a few stories to which he had given only so much attention as was unavoidable. 'Good ground; but no blackmail. Threat?'

'W . . . warning,' replied Dick, flicking his gloves upon his knee. Kitty was in William's arms. Dick had forgotten all about her. He had forgotten most of them; but not Minna.

'Yes, but of what?' asked the legal-minded Mr Fotheringdew.

'The wages of sin,' answered Dick, lightly. 'I . . . I gathered that was the intention. At . . . at any rate, Whistler won't settle. We must go on, whatever Counsel says. In Law, he admits we're all right——'

'Oh, yes; it's the jury he's afraid of, Sir Furness. The British jury's a curious thing; it doesn't think; it feels. It may feel you've stood harshly on the letter. In any case, all this . . . He's a quarrelsome fellow.'

'My dear Mr Fotheringdew, he's my oldest friend. I . . . I could tell you things about him—which I won't do—that go back to Standard One. We were in it together.'

'Hm,' said the portly gentleman by the fireplace. 'Settle.'

Dick threw his gloves sharply to the floor, picked them up, and stood.

'Dammit,' he cried. 'D'you think I . . . I don't agree with you? But I tell you he *won't*. We must fight and kill.' He went to the door, and with no more than a nod of farewell slammed it after him as he went. In a room in Brighton Kitty had begun to cough as Minna arrived; and blood stained the coverlet of her bed.

III

In Court, experienced Counsel can tell—or think they can tell— by many indications how a case is going. It rarely goes as they expect it to do, for any hearing is like the first performance of a play. A line that seemed good at rehearsal is missed by the audience; another, as the result of some turn or chance association, is instantly successful. Atmosphere helps; the manner of a witness; the impatience of a judge; the private conviction of a member of the jury. And, in the presentation of a case, Counsel's secret is the secret of omission. An able man will suppress a thousand details which it is better for the jury not to know, and will keep them suppressed.

The jury in this case of Whistler versus Firth for slander (the wrongful dismissal was ingeniously subordinated to the question of what Dick Firth had said of Robert to others) sat morosely in their box. They were listening: therefore they frowned in the effort to concentrate. The Judge sat with his mind and fingers busy taking notes. He was small and spare, sharp-nosed and red-cheeked. He spoke quickly, rather like a governess, and dominated the Court. Solicitors and witnesses were gathered closely together in the pews under the Judge's eye, and if they had business together they tiptoed and whispered out of respect for him. Dick Firth, at one side of the Court, took in the whole scene, every roving turn of the sharp-faced Judge's eye, the glances exchanged between Counsel, the fumbling among papers, the odd contrast between the usher's flowing gown and his trim poll. He had a clear view of Robert's Counsel, a large man with an ugly voice and a sneering face. He could no longer see Robert, who sat flushed and sweating at the other side of the Court. They had met and avoided each other in the stone corridor without, during the conclusion of an earlier case, and both had been conscious of enmity.

And yet, sitting there, Dick could not fail to reflect upon the absurdity of the whole business. He had actively befriended Robert; at last he had found it intolerable to bear with him any longer; that was all. Quite clear. On his side a complete readiness to make the going easy. With what total loss of dignity Robert had countered! Instead of realising, with gratitude, what Dick had done for him—lifting him from debt and retail business to prosperity— he had turned blusteringly nasty. Barked. Threatened. That was ridiculous. Ridiculous, and might be serious. Dick felt slightly uneasy. He believed himself to have read aright the messages almost imperceptibly interchanged between Mr Fotheringdew and Mr Pooch, his Counsel. Meeting failure half-way. The sponges already in their hands. Tails down. Corners of mouths down. A flurried obsequiousness to the Judge. A fussing with papers. Apparently demoralised. Ought to have had a better man. The other fellow was cool and confident; while Pooch sweated. Yet Pooch was the best possible man, Fotheringdew said. Well, in that case it was an inferior profession; for in Dick's eyes the proceedings, and in particular his own Counsel's share in them, were largely childish.

That red-faced, blue-chinned, sharp-nosed man on the bench, for example, had ridiculous power. He interrupted what was being said, demanded books, raised his eyebrows scornfully as he wrote, and looked with chilly scepticism at whatever was brought to his attention. A legalistic mind. Not an able man, Dick understood. Hen-pecked, a sufferer from indigestion, an ambitious golfer whom nobody could teach. When, in reply to questions, Dick had named the judge appointed to hear the case, one or two knowledgeable associates had shrugged their shoulders. They had said: 'Hm. Dull. A stickler. Not a success at the Bar, and can't stand corn. I wish you'd had So-and-so.' As a verdict it might be customary, for all vain men seek to impress the world by decrying others; but it was inauspicious. Well, he'd had no choice; that was a part of the System. Who distributed the cases among the judges? Was it the Lord Chief?

Drone, drone, drone. The opposing Counsel, an unpleasant fellow, made his case sound a good one. He had a voice like a rasp. A face like an artful priest. Yes, but there was more in the affair than that. If you dealt with the immediate facts only, and showed one side black and the other white, of course you made a good case. But it wasn't only a case; it was a lifetime. Back at school; that bloody night when Bob had chased him—there was nearly murder done then! All forgiven. Bear that in mind: it was a question of perspective. And the money: look at the *money* he'd found for Bob! You couldn't bring all that to light in Court, with question and answer. Ten minutes' confidential chat with the Judge, and the result wouldn't be in question. But if a witness were to try and tell the whole truth he'd be cowed with 'Answer the question!' . . . The many-sided truth! . . .

Julie! At the thought of Julie, who sat beside Robert dressed in black, Dick's eyebrows lifted high, and he whistled under his breath. What a bitch! He'd had to send her a message explaining that in England blackmail could be punished with a life sentence. That—except for the anonymous letter—had stopped her. She'd had a hand in the anonymous letter. Several people; but she especially. Never cared for her. All deceptive. You expected her to be tantalising, difficult, knowing; and she was as dull as uninspired flesh could be. A bolster. Nothing in it, for him. But for her, after Bob, perhaps, anything . . . The reproachful heaviness . . . My God, it had been a mistake all through. One learned too late. And then was tender-hearted. Damn women! Even Eileen, that morning, had pestered him beyond bearing. She'd clung to him; he'd had to push her away. But the fall had been artificial, he'd swear. Really! Good God, the thought of him as a wife-beater . . . It was monstrous!

Well, it was evident that Fotheringdew expected a verdict for the other side. Dick judged that he already heard in his own mind Counsel's plea in mitigation of damages: they would never dare to defend as they should do. Convention. You'd think Bob was a paragon of virtue. What did it matter to the Judge and jury that he stunk of brandy and cigars every afternoon until a fellow felt he must retch? By God, the Law stood in need of a few reforms. If Dick had still owned 'England' he might have done some useful agitation. Damn Harvest! He'd liked Harvest, who'd let him down.

The one man! The one man! Dick was conscious of discomfort.

The reverie into which he had been lulled by a rasping recital of familiar facts, and the blurring of the jurymen's faces, was disturbed by a general rustling in Court. People were moving about; members of the jury were staring here and there; the usher was speaking to somebody; a figure was detaching itself from the general backness of coats and gowns. It was Bob. With a curious stilled malice Dick watched that bulk, that throat-clearing self-conscious stiffness, and the sweep of frock-coat tails as Bob climbed into the witness box. His eyes narrowed. His tongue gently moistened the edge of his upper lip. Bob was red, sweating, awkward. Forced to stoop in order to rest his hands wide apart upon the edge of the box; when he was cramped, or wished to turn his head, he stood upright with the air of a cripple who had lost his crutches. Bob was pretending to be at ease. What a farce! The same old clumsy Bob, that a man felt sorry for. A born inferior. Well, he was thinner than he had been; the fright had done him good. Stopped the brandy, perhaps; until the case was lost! His voice boomed: it sounded better in Court than Dick had expected. He was answering as if he believed himself. They knew all about that. Well, he *must* believe himself. Of course, he was being led gently through his evidence: the fun would begin when he was cross-examined. Expectation of that caused Dick's smile to deepen; there was at the back of his throat the tiniest suppressed laugh in the world. Hysteria! Yes, he could feel his heart thumping. . . .

Good God! A white, dreadful alternation of heat and chill ran like a squirt of water behind Dick's waist. By the afternoon he himself might be in the box!

Even as he caught his breath, he received a nudge from somebody beside him, and while Robert's voice resonantly floated towards the jury he ceased to follow it. A note had been thrust into his hand, written in pencil, from Counsel. It ran: 'Have you got that anonymous letter with you?'

This made Dick shiver afresh. He trembled excessively. Why, that letter: his first impulse had been to destroy it. He turned a severe look upon the man; but the Court dominated him as it seemed to dominate everybody else. In a cathedral, awe; in a court, fear. All were like flies at the end of Summer, cowed and lethargic. Their stomachs rumbled with fear! His own likewise. He could not resist. He felt in his pocket, and from his note-case produced the anonymous letter. His hands shook. There was perspiration around his eyes. At the beginning of the day he had been completely free from nerves; but in this atmosphere of solemnity, it was impossible to keep still. He was used to moving quickly. He was used to making his own decisions. He had enjoyed power. The Court stopped that. His own Counsel—what were they doing? Counsel and Mr Fotheringdew had their heads together. . . . Fools! Improvisators! They should have had their case ready a month ago. They had done. Now they were in a panic. As bad as all that? God damn his leaden stomach!

There was quite suddenly an altercation. The Judge had a paper in his hand; Robert was looking at him; both Counsel were upon their feet. 'Me lud . . . me lud . . .' 'Mister Pooch . . .' 'Yes, me lud. No, me lud. As your ludship pleases.' Shaken heads; glum looks; meaning glances at the jurymen, one of whom was whispering to another . . . Mr Pooch and Mr Fotheringdew conferred together. Mr Pooch—thin as a pole, bitterly sallow and thin-lipped —fingered the collar of his gown and spoke earnestly. He emphasised something with his clenched fist: 'taking it out of the odds and ends' after reproof from the Judge. The bad fellow! The Judge, meanwhile, continued to make some complaint of which Dick, having missed the occasion, did not grasp the meaning. His mouth hardly opened; across that blue chin a harsh slit appeared, like a tear in a rubber ball. Wah-wah-wah. What was the old tough worrying about, anyhow?

A few moments later Mr Fotheringdew slipped from his place, touching Dick's arm as he passed in signal that he should follow. They were just outside the swing doors of the Court, to whisper in that silent corridor where every sound roused ghostly echoes in the November dankness. Mr Fotheringdew, treating Dick as a nobody (for to these men Sir Furness Firth, whatever his record of greatness and public service, was but a piece of meat in the legal sausage-mill), said: 'Sure he wrote that? It's what you think, isn't it? Pooch is very keen on it. Recognise the typewriter? Pooch says I've got to find the machine and the writer in the luncheon interval. I'm sending a message at once to my managing clerk. At a shot, eh?'

'But I . . . I can't stoop——' whispered Dick.

He was peremptorily interrupted.

'You've got to win this case. Make no mistake about that.' Now that he was in the Law Courts, and reinforced by Counsel, Mr Fotheringdew was a tyrant. 'Any suggestions as to the possible typist? Think, man!'

Dick thought. The corridor was as draughty as an old house: that must be why he was shivering. He took several rapid steps up and down, his mind seeking. Bob: a typewriter at home: he was still at the office when the letter . . . The office! 'My God, I can't think. I can't think.' At last:

'Damn it; you can't possibly use that letter! It would ruin me.'

Mr Fotheringdew caught his elbow in authoritative explanation.

'Pooch knows what he can do. He wins cases. He won't read it all, if he can help it. Pass to the Judge. To the jury. Show it to Whistler. Ask if he recognises. Ask if he wrote. Come, Sir Furness, who'd have typed it for him? The need's urgent. . . .'

The need! Then he had not misread their glum interchange. The Judge was hostile. It was thought that he might be very sharp. Pooch had seen him like this before; and it always meant mischief. But the jury? Mr Fotheringdew could assure Sir Furness that the jury . . . In any case the need was urgent.

Urgent. Urgent. Dick had thought of all this before; but for his own purposes. He had seen strange hands at work in the affair. Was that loss of nerve? Difficult to distinguish between prescience and funk. Was this the ebb tide at last? He hesitated. In a moment, having satisfied Mr Fotheringdew, he was thankful to creep back to his place in Court.

Robert was finishing with his Counsel. It became clear that lunch would be taken immediately. Mr Fothingdew dismissed Dick, who passed from the echoes into the bewildering thunder of the Strand as a monk might pass from the cloister to pandemonium. Dick felt small. He felt trepidant. He felt ignominious. A bad state of mind.

He was back in Court before the Judge. Almost before anybody else. And as he stood within the doors Mr Pooch also entered. He nodded to Dick, but did not smile. His ascetic features were lengthened into dismalness. He looked like a mute.

'How . . . how d'you think——' began Dick, his eyes and his brain playing all round this fellow whose mind went plonk-plonk along straight lines until it could get no farther. Lightning about a tram. Simultaneously:

'Have you got that——' began Mr Pooch, peremptorily. He might have been repelling a beggar.

Both stopped. And in that very instant Mr Fotheringdew appeared beside them like a large genie. He was transformed; no longer discreetly ambiguous, but jubilant. His ruddy face glowed. He smiled. He might have been one of the brothers Cheeryble.

'Got her!' he whispered. 'And the typewriter. Absolute triumph.'

With hissing exclamations, all three were again outside the Court, in a thrill of excitement.

'But how——' began Dick. He was ignored. He could not hear a word of the hurried explanation. But Mr Pooch whispered in Mr Fotheringdew's ear.

'When I've been cross-examining ten minutes,' he said, 'bring in the machine. Not by this door; by the other one—the one facing the witness box. Have it put on the table in front of me. Ceremonially. Five minutes later, bring the girl in. Same door. Full view of the witness. Give her a seat behind me. That's all.' He hurried into Court.

The case was no longer a controversy to be decided in Law. It had become a pitting of wit against stupidity. In a flash, Dick realised that he had underrated Mr Pooch. He was no tram, but a rat-catcher! And Dick, hastening back to his place, saw everything with a different kind of excitement, as one who from the wings watches a play in which, though he is still to appear in the last act, everything depends upon what happens now. He saw Robert back in the box—rather pale with dread of his cross-examiner, and swallowing often and quickly as he sought to be brave and alert for questions which might be nothing but traps. Yes, they might be nothing but traps! They *would* be nothing but traps. These devils, how great an advantage they had! Stoats! Watching, steely-eyed, Dick felt a kind of malignant pity for Bob.

Mr Pooch began with great courtesy. He suggested various points upon which the witness might have been mistaken. He led Robert to confirm dates and phrases, interviews and interpretations. Always gently, not raising his voice, which was very different from the rasp of his opponent, and bringing to his long face a smile which Dick had not seen there before. An unearthly smile, like that of a man who hears and is transported by the first movement of Mozart's Jupiter Symphony. It fascinated the jurymen, who all watched Mr Pooch as if spellbound. And so, very gradually, Counsel reached Robert's opinion of Dick, which proved—in Court—to be surprisingly favourable. With qualifications. He had been well-coached. And at last, as Dick, with difficulty restraining himself, bit his lip and drove his thumbnails into the tips of his middle and fore-fingers, they came to the anonymous letter.

At once there was rasping protest. Both Counsel stood, Mr Pooch negligently smiling, and his enemy gesticulating with what seemed to Dick to be well-simulated fury. The Judge interposed. He asked, glanced, shook his head, and snapped first at one and then at the other. The jury stared. Backwards and forwards went the argument, while Dick, without mercy, watched Robert. He knew, and Bob knew, what that letter contained. Oh, yes, Bob knew. He denied it; but he knew every word of it as well as Dick did. As well as he had once known the Lord's Prayer. Dick saw Robert stand erect—you would have thought him Sidney Carton!—as he swore entire ignorance of the letter. Against his will he admired a man who could lie with such conviction. Perfect conviction. Scorn. Injury. And then a drop of the jaw. Other eyes, besides Robert's, strayed to the door through which a young man at this moment carried a typewriter; but Dick's eyes never left Bob's uneasy face.

'You did not write this letter?' questioned Mr Pooch.

withdrew his gaze from Robert it fell upon the woman who had been brought to a seat immediately behind Mr Pooch. It was Miss Neilson.

V

All was over. Mr Pooch, and the English Law's horror of libel, had triumphed. Dick, carried to ecstasy by his escape, saw the case collapse, saw Robert, entirely cowed, drawn away by such poor companions as he had into the remoteness of hiding, while he, a free man, his good name vindicated, could pass at once back into the society of his coevals. For a time after the delivery of the verdict he had sat lost in a dream. Well, that was that. That was that, he thought, over and over again, a little bewildered. He had won the case. His luck had held. Luck? Nonsense! . . .

When the Court emptied he smilingly approached Mr Pooch, who with many papers bundled under his arm, and his wig tilted, stood in consultation with Mr Fotheringdew. Mr Pooch did not see his client. He was speaking in a low voice; and Dick heard only the word 'write' or 'bite', which was several times repeated. Mr Pooch cared nothing for clients whose cases he had won or lost for them. He was already, with resumed dismalness, preparing to engage in fresh triumphs for new clients. His smile had been packed away for use upon another jury. His mind had left its straight lines. At last he used the word 'golf' and looked at his watch.

Then it was that, having remembered why he had been in this Court upon this day, Mr Pooch saw Dick and received the appropriate congratulations. He merely nodded, stared down at his late client, shook hands in farewell with Dick and Mr Fotheringdew, and disappeared. It seemed that Mr Fotheringdew was also in a hurry to leave. Everybody else in the Court had disappeared, and as the lights were put out it looked dingily forlorn. The stone passages into which they drifted were empty. As Dick reached the great Entrance the few policemen who stood there saw only a slim figure which passed them, looking uncontrollably behind him into that cavernous vista as if he feared some unimaginable attack.

Once in the roaring, crowded Strand, where all the vehicles were lighted, and where office lights bewildered him, Dick felt suddenly very sick and faint, as if he had not eaten all day. He had been rapidly consuming his nervous strength, and the case had caused him appalling strain. Never mind, he had won it. He had come in triumph from the ordeal. . . . Had he won it? That had been a lifetime ago. The Court, the Judge, Robert's collapse: all were like a dream. And triumph? He was alone. He felt peculiarly alone at this moment, for the coolness of Mr Pooch, the glassy benevolent haste of Mr Fotheringdew, had had a strange effect upon his smiling spirit. He thought: 'I'm tired. I . . . I'm too sensitive.' And then his heart stood still; because he saw a newspaper placard: 'FIRTH CASE WHISTLER IN THE BOX.' Damnation! Damnation! And, while he still stared, a newspaper van swept up to the kerb, and upon it was another bill: 'FIRTH CASE RESULT.' Firth case! Firth case! His lips were trembling; a cold sweat burst from his body. He saw a million pairs of eyes fixed upon that heading in the paper, here and everywhere in England.

They wouldn't print the letter. The thought, in one respect reassuring, caused him to grimace in a nervous smile. No paper would print the libellous letter. Fear of the Law, fear that they would lose advertising revenue from his companies, would be a guarantee of that. He was safe. But Pooch had been chilly. Fotheringdew had looked down his nose. Other people? Dick caught himself fingering his lips. How lonely he felt. He bought a paper, and his penny slipped to the pavement from a shaky hand. This wouldn't do. It wouldn't *do*. He must pull himself together.

What was Bob doing? Drinking, he'd be bound. Drinking and stinking of drink.

'Taxi! Taxi!' cried Dick, without knowing what he did. He climbed into the taxi, dropping his paper; and when the paperman picked it up and thrust it back into his hand Dick saw a look in his eyes which told him that the man thought him drunk. Thank God it was dark! He couldn't read the paper, but lay back in the cab and closed his eyes. He felt ill. His heart was much too noisy, and was irregular. It fluttered. He remembered how the heart of a hedge warbler had trembled against his fingers many

many years ago, an instant before the bird died of fear. Not afraid! Not afraid!

Home; that was where he must go. He had told the man to drive him there. All this terrible anxiety about the businesses had kept him upon the stretch for the last year. If once he lost his nerve they would go. A hideous mess. Hideous. Bob had been the only competent man he'd had. He ought to have stuck to Bob. It was an appalling mistake to quarrel with such a man. Losing grip. Losing touch. Nerve. 'Yes, but I'm flesh and blood. I'm human. I couldn't *stand* him. Detestable. Or Julie.' But he was the competent man: 'Fool that I've been!' Well, things were difficult.

What a word! Things were *damned bad*. They were not absolutely fatal. He had carried through a wangle that would give him another year. Say six months. No throwing in the sponge. Yes, but it would be wise to give an eye to the possible worst. He had done all he could do. He had long ago settled sixty thousand pounds on Eileen absolutely. They wouldn't be able to touch that. Nobody—except Eileen—could touch it. Nor the Trust for the kids, he thought. Another ten thousand. Well, on the interest of sixty thousand he could manage very well, whatever happened. Three thousand a year . . .

'I don't drink. I don't smoke. But I'll have to get myself over-hauled.'

The taxi swept through the streets once the Piccadilly traffic was passed; and it took Dick a moment to realise that he had reached home. He sat staring before him. Yes, that letter had won the day. A disgraceful letter. Not a word of truth, of course; but 'the greater the truth, the greater the libel'. Who really *had* written it? Bob was the only one who knew the early stuff; the Neilson touch was plain here and there. Harvest? No, he didn't think Harvest had any hand in it. If he had, it would have been better written. The fools! He was well rid of them. He'd show them all. . . . Dick beat his knee with the folded newspaper. He was well rid of such rats. Well rid. Well rid. But he was very tired; and at last was glad to accept the driver's help as he descended before the

door of his own house. Decent fellow. Give him half-a-crown. . . .
Very kind. 'Good night.'

Then indoors, and his hat and coat deftly taken from him
as if he visited the White Cat. He would have something to eat and
drink in his study before doing anything else. Already, being safely
indoors, where it was natural to him to be alone, he felt a little
better, and his mind began to fly as usual, remembering Miss
Neilson's appearance—crying, of course—and Robert's face and a
thousand details which he had not known himself to have observed. But when he thought of a resumption of business details
on the morrow he realised how the case had taken all his thoughts
for weeks past, in some way supplying him with an anodyne for
graver, very urgent, but for one moment less insistent, problems.

He began to walk about the study as soon as he reached it,
thankful at last to have the free use of his limbs and the possibility
of movement. Only when the butler brought a tray did he go to
the desk upon which it was set, and seat himself in the swivel chair
there. Even then he was half-lost in a dream, so that he was
hardly conscious of being alone again; and it was not until his
eyes fell that he remembered where he was, or what he had been
intending to do. A small pile of letters lay upon the desk, and as
Dick ate he carelessly glanced at the envelopes one by one, tossing
the letters aside, unopened, after a light scrutiny of handwritings.
But as he did this he caught sight at last of one which had not
come through the post. His own envelope. A familiar look. Eileen's
handwriting.

Eileen's handwriting? Dick sat upright. Why, what on earth——
The letter was no letter. It said only:

DEAR DICK:

*I have taken the two younger girls. You will be hearing from the
solicitor at once. We have had you watched for some time, and* . . .

Dick could read no more. His eyes became sightless. He beat
his hands against the desk, bruising them terribly, as he sprang
to his feet. Eileen! Watched! Divorce! Good God, he was beaten,
after all!

CHAPTER XXV

Sequels

THEN, WITHOUT WARNING, the articles began to appear. They were in Mather's paper, 'The Candid Friend', and the first of them was as shattering as a bomb. Within an hour of its appearance Dick's accountant, Penter, came rushing to him in panic. He stammered something incoherent; and Dick, taking the paper from Penter's shaking hand, felt an extraordinary whirr of pain in his heart. His eyes skimmed the lines, filled with tears, and were again keen.

We have lately seen in the Court . . . no comment upon the result of that remarkable case; but . . . public interest . . . Sir Furness Firth, whose name is associated . . . Large sums of money invested in these companies, often in small amounts; and it . . . Are they in fact soundly run? We believe they are not. We believe that they represent, on the contrary, a disgraceful succession of frauds upon the investing public. It will be our business in this and the two following issues of 'The Candid Friend' to narrate the history of these companies; to show how Sir Furness Firth by the questionable magic of book-keeping alone has managed for the past several years to pay dividends which have not been earned; to prove by references to prospectuses, balance-sheets, and other documents in our possession, as to the authenticity of which there can be no doubt, that Sir Furness Firth has wilfully . . .

Let us be specific. We assert that Sir Furness Firth, who by the terms of his contracts is entitled to draw in addition to his Directors' Fees (amounting to £8,500 per annum) further bonus payments whenever the dividends payable by his companies shall exceed six per cent per annum . . . These bonus payments (amounting in all to £22,000 per annum) he has drawn for the past seven years, although we shall prove that with one exception the com-

*panies nominally under his control have in the past four years
earned no profits whatsoever, but instead have sustained losses the
severity of which no adroit accountancy can conceal. . . .*

*We challenge Sir Furness Firth or any other person to disprove
our statements. We are prepared . . .*

'They must be stopped!' howled Penter.

Stopped! When the only reply to such articles—as Dick's racing
heart suggested—was instant flight. He let the paper fall. Impossible
to keep still. God, he couldn't breathe. Stifling. With his hands
jabbed deep in his trousers pockets he took some quick steps about
the room. Who was behind this? An enemy; a group of
enemies . . .

'How?' snapped Dick. 'Don't be a fool!'

'It's all very well for you,' Penter stammered. His tongue was
loose; and he was ready to babble all his panic thoughts. 'You've
got resources——'

'What do you mean?' demanded Dick. 'I've got no resources.
Everything I've got——'

'You don't understand,' said Penter. 'It's the end. The *end*, Sir
Furness!' He had become flabby. The geniality and polish of his
manner were gone. He was the colour of putty; his eyes protruded.
'They know everything.'

'Rubbish!' But Dick felt like a dying man. First Robert; then
Eileen; now this. All completely unexpected. A dreadful series of
fatalities. He picked the paper up again, and the type danced; he
was forced to turn away his eyes. Penter was right; they knew
everything. Otherwise they never would have dared the challenge in
these bold terms. As if they said: 'We've got you, Dick Firth! Sue
us! Sue us! Watch the result!'

No bluff there. Well, they had determined to ruin him, and
they would do it. Strange that once one missed step with prosperity one fell into the abyss. These people had waited for the
lost step. All enemies. Out of Dick's recollection came seven
people, every one of them to be feared. First, a tall, ascetic man
with a resolute jaw—T. F. Mather, the owner and editor of this
paper. Rigid; high-principled; ruthless. Second, a slighter man

with a small moustache and a misleading simper, a man whom he had met and despised and reluctantly admired in the past, a barrister, the friend of Minna Manning, dangerous—Bernard Mather. Fiendishly clever in the Law; unremittingly an enemy. Why hadn't he made him a friend? Third, Will Harvest, with whom, though in burning anger, and not in contempt, he had years ago quarrelled. Not an enemy; a cool joker, disinterested, righteous; a friend. A man to trust. Alienated by jealousy, by hatred. One liked; one hated. Well, Dick hated Minna. She was the fourth of them. There were, besides, Bob, Julie, Doris Neilson. Those seven. A conspiracy, damnable and overwhelming.

A sudden thought came: would Harvest, in spite of everything, show greatness and help him? If they would stop the articles . . . Something could be saved. Time gained. But as he thought of William hope faded. Not he! A good man, without greatness. He'd probably written the article himself! Useless. Dick was forced to sit down. His legs were like lead.

What was he to do? Show nothing, at all events. He had his pride.

'I . . . I'm afraid you've lost your nerve, Penter,' he drily and maliciously said, grinning. Damn! He was afraid. Say he sued, which he couldn't do. Say the Public Prosecutor . . . That was the terror in his veins! He couldn't run away. The very money which he had settled upon Eileen in case of emergency—but not *this* emergency!—was beyond his reach. Eileen! Could he cajole her? No longer. She was divorcing him; she kept the money; a wonderful bargain! Who was the fool?

'I'm terrified, Sir Furness,' Penter shakily whispered. 'My wife and kiddies. Madge just going to boarding-school. All that . . .' He was white-lipped. 'It might mean five years,' he said. 'Oh, my God, Sir Furness! It would kill me.'

Good God! They were already estimating terms of imprisonment! In that case, for himself, seven or fourteen years. He'd be an old man.

'Don't be a fool!' Dick uttered the rebuke spitefully, and with one white finger indicated the door. 'Leave the paper. I'll see Mr Fotheringdew.'

But when he was alone he put his hands to his mouth, for his lips felt as if they sagged, leaving his teeth bare. He was trembling very much. No money, because of Eileen. He had lived well up to his income, and his income had never been as large as was supposed. Certainly not thirty thousand a year. Far less. Not as clever as they took him for . . . Too damned honest.

He muttered:

'I'm not dishonest. Never. Never. Things have gone wrong.'

But although he said the words as if to a confessor he did not think them. He was thinking:

The row with Bob. The break with Julie. Those were what had led to this. He had been too busy to guard against betrayal. Too busy, or too stupid. What a fool!

II

Mr Fotheringdew was hushed. He, too, had seen the article; he, too, had recognised the challenge. The word 'settle' no longer occurred to him; for it seemed to Mr Fotheringdew that he could read the writing on the wall. He was not unfriendly. He had never invested in Dick's companies. On the contrary, Dick had employed him for years, and the account had been a good one. Had been. As he glimpsed the future, Mr Fotheringdew's jaw dropped a little.

Dick, sitting in Mr Fotheringdew's office, and from time to time looking out at the bare and delicate boughs of the trees in Lincoln's Inn Fields, read doom in his solicitor's gravity.

'I . . . I think we must issue a writ,' he said, aften ten minutes' discussion.

'I'd like Counsel's opinion,' replied Mr Fotheringdew. 'The Law of Libel is very tricky——'

'You're right,' Dick quickly agreed. 'It . . . it is. The damages would be heavy——'

'The damages,' breathed Mr Fotheringdew. 'Yes.' Such a curious 'yes.'

They exchanged a glance that was full of measuring gravity.

'Who will you get?' asked Dick.

She was dressed, as her mother had often been, in a green frock which drew attention to the dead whiteness of her arms and neck and face; and the frock was cut so suggestively low that if the wearer had not been his daughter Dick would satirically have lifted his Victorian brows. Upon her it evoked in him an extraordinary sympathy. He longed to put his arms in consolation about those sharp little shoulders, to draw her close. Pitiably brave and hopeless little creature! His daughter. He had pride in her. Pride and pity. Pride and pity and love. Bianca's lips were as thin as his own, and her eyes as bright. But she was not as tall as Dick, and the slightness of her figure made her look very small indeed. Piquante; a little hard; not beautiful.

For a moment they did nothing but stare. Then Bianca, in a thick dry smoke-ridden voice which was then the fashion, said:

'I say, seen "The Candid Friend"?'

'What do your friends say to *that?*' asked Dick, searching her expression, but standing quite still by his desk. Poor child! The modern hardness, which he did not like; but underneath it a raw sensitiveness as of old. She was the same rebel who had been reduced in the past by his invention of pimples.

'The cuts very rapid,' Bianca drawled. 'Except Toby Lemon. He offered me a flat.'

'A flat?' Dick did not at first accept the implication. 'Good heavens. The swine.'

'Oh, no. Only opportunist. Wanted to be helpful, and cash in.' Her voice was thicker than usual. The words were slurred. 'As a matter of fact I've just slung him out. You probably heard the door go.'

Dick was horrified.

'You'll have to go to your mother,' he said. 'She's got all the money there is.'

Bianca shook her head.

'No . . . fear.' She spared him the adjective. 'But is what they say true?'

'No!' declared Dick, slowly. Ah! he saw the old estimating glance from below those long fair eyelashes. He did not realise that he saw it by means of the parent glance. Less stoutly, he continued:

'No; not all of it. Nevertheless——' She understood; and at once said:

'I suppose if I try and get a job——'

Well, Dick saw at once that his old power was now a liability. 'Daughter of Firth . . .' His silence led Bianca to give an imitation cynical laugh which jarred his nerves. She was as hard as stone.

'I'm sorry, dear,' he said, under his breath. 'I've let you in for that. Fortunately, your mother's got plenty of money—for *you*.'

Bianca again shook her head, this time grimacing as at a nasty smell.

'Not if she'd got a million,' she said. 'I'd rather take Tony Lemon's flat.'

Dick, infuriated, took a couple of vehement steps towards her, and Bianca evaded him with a movement so practiced that he knew what her experience of men had been. She was quite assured. She was looking, hard-eyed, and with a faint smile, as if she coolly classed him among other men. His daughter! That was like poison. Was she impure? He had imagined an impossible relationship between them.

'Stop that!' said Dick.

'*You* won't do it,' answered Bianca. 'I can look after myself, thanks.'

'That's what all half-baked sophisticates think. You can't do it.'

She laughed a second time. But all she drily said was:

'We grow up early, nowadays.'

'No earlier than of old, my dear,' replied Dick, thinking of his own boyhood. 'You make more fuss about it.'

'Oh, but it was you who made the fuss,' objected Bianca. 'The Victorian father.'

He had recovered.

'I expect it was. I . . . I'm troubled about you. I . . . I'm thinking entirely of you. You shall have everything I can save from this affair. But, naturally, I don't know how things will go.'

'It's new to think of *you* making a fool of yourself,' observed Bianca.

'We all do it,' retorted Dick. 'Sooner or later.'

She shrugged those meagre, dazzling shoulders.

'Yes, but you can't wonder at the loss of respect.'

'Loss of respect?' He was surprised. 'Whose, of whom?'

'Well, d'you suppose I——'

'Oh, I see.' To his daughter's impertinence Dick opposed his own coldness. 'But then the family relation's based on *love,* isn't it?'

Bianca repeated that drawling laugh which was so expressive of post-War uneasiness masquerading as knowledge of evil.

'I *don't* think,' she said, briefly. 'Our family?' Then, turning away, she added: 'Why, did you imagine . . . Ha, ha!' From the door, in a nasal voice of assumed detachment: 'I hope I've never deceived you to *that* extent, papa dear. No, I think you're interesting. I know you've been over a lot of grass. But I'm not a fool. Besides—well, I won't say that. I take it that you're not going to South America in a false wig?'

Dick moistened his lips.

'Only if you can touch your mother's heart for me,' he said, quickly. It was an inspiration.

'Don't count on it,' drawled Bianca. 'She hasn't got one. Nor have I. Good night.'

At one moment the white back was turned to him; at the next Dick was alone. Only then, released from the hypnotic effect of his daughter's presence, did he realise that in part her thick speech and unpleasant manner had been due to the fact that she was half-drunk.

IV

Dick's first impression as he came up the white-tiled passage to the Old Bailey dock was that the Court was large and that he himself was insignificant. Subsequently he knew that there were only two people in it who mattered in the least, himself and the Judge. He detested the Judge, because of his long ant-eater's nose and aged severity to all supposed evildoers; but he had seen him before, years ago in the House, more recently at public dinners and elsewhere, and he knew by gossip all about his unhealthy private life. It seemed to Dick to be appalling that a man with the reputed character of this Judge should by the mere act of dressing

up be in a position to treat him as if he had done something
wrong. . . .

'I've done nothing wrong,' Dick thought to himself. 'Nothing
whatsoever wrong.'

As he watched the unfolding of the case against him, which was
purely financial, he could clearly see the face of every person who
had business in the Court, from Bianca, who sat near Mr Fotheringdew, to Bernard Mather, who in wig and gown was really
farther away, but seemed menacingly omnipresent, so that he was
always in Dick's eye. According to his degree of consciousness, for
the strain had affected him greatly, Dick came and went among
the crowds and faces like the voice of a speaker in the Albert Hall,
alternately clear and dim as the result of acoustical vagary. But
what troubled him most of all, more than his leaden stomach and
dry mouth and trembling hands, was the question of the Judge's
fitness to administer justice. He could not do it. The mere assumption of a wig did not change a man's character, did it? A wig, a
gown. Bow to the wig, you fool; not to the man under it! What a
farce it was!

You could protest against a juryman. Not against a Judge, even if
his nose hung over the end of the bench and his ears stood in-
visibly up through holes in his wig! Dick knew that he could not
shout aloud: 'I decline to submit my case to this man!' It was
an instance of the wrongs under which he had suffered all his life.
'I do not accept the jurisdiction of this Court! You can't touch
me! I'm Richard Firth. I've always done as I liked; I shall continue
to do as I like.' Without moving his lips, but expressly framing
the protest, Dick glanced aside at his companions in the dock,
two warders whose grey, beefy faces made him think of over-
cooked Sunday dinners long ago in Moreton. The sound of the
organ was in his ears as an accompaniment; but that was because
all meals had waited until his father's return from church.

The weather throughout the trial was very warm; and one day,
when thousands of tedious figures were being put in and chewed
and digested and forgotten, Dick for about an hour lost all awareness of the case. The Court became a mist in which the dimmest of
dim shadows moved and gesticulated. He forgot the long-nosed

Judge, who was so old that his body had wasted and he seemed to crackle like a sheet of parchment; he forgot Counsel, warders, and the generally assembled people who had come to hear his arraignment. In imagination he sat before a real Judge, one who cared nothing for trivial minutiæ, but wholly for what Dick described as spiritual balance. This was a Judge to whom he could trust his life. He felt at ease before him, stretching his legs, smiling, talking with that buoyancy which he had often felt upon the platform. And he was saying:

'In certain things I've been unlucky. Lucky in others. You understand, I only want to be fair, to others as well as . . . I should describe myself as impulsive. Yes, that's the word. I've been guided by very strong principles. For example, so good to others. Always that, first of all. A man I used to know—Harvest, his name was—once said to me: "Speaking as I find, I should say that you were extraordinarily generous. Extraordinarily." Well, I think I can honestly say that I haven't been a selfish man. Not selfish. Strong affections; perhaps a little too strong, at times. But there it is; I certainly have . . . But I've never treated them other than decently. Eileen: never humiliated her, though I had every excuse to do so. A small nature, very suburban, furtive, vindictive . . . The insipidity of her! Inconceivable to anybody who hasn't experienced . . . But I needn't explain to *you*. Women *are* insipid; one's always disappointed in them. However, I never thought she'd have the venom to divorce me. That came as a decided shock. And it arose from the curious accident that I happened to push her away from me—a thing I'd never done before in my life. One of the absurdities of the English Divorce Law. Well, I attribute a lot of my troubles to a sort of domestic paralysis. It's a principle with me not to blame others for my own . . . but . . .

'I must admit I've been unlucky with friends. Unlucky. I don't mean rats, the sort of people who fly at the first breath of trouble. Plenty of them. Some in the public gallery, damn them! But friends. I haven't made them. The sort of companions with whom one intimately discusses life, the men who are always *there,* if you know what I mean. Behind you. For times of trouble. I haven't got them. I'm a lonely man. I've been too busy, and—well, somehow events haven't shaped like that at all. Continuous public work, politics, big business don't leave one much time. Besides, I've preferred to be alone. . . . I had a great disappointment once, God, and that was a woman, too. I suppose I was infatuated with her. It happens. And, as so many other people have done, she repaid love with treachery. She left me in the lurch. Ran away. If I'd had her beside me—of course the situation was difficult. I know that. It called for sacrifice on her part, and she was like a worldly judge, a stickler for the letter. She should have been greater. On my side, the difficulty was that the good name of a public man . . . My good name was essential to *both* of us. Both. She didn't understand that. . . .

'And so you see I've been unlucky. Born poor; the rise due entirely to character and parts; a little money here and there . . . I'm not complaining. My friends have been inconstant; they've played for their own hands, which is a habit I despise. I loathe it. And I except Harvest. Yes, Harvest was a loss. If I'd had Harvest and Minna—my God, what a difference to my life! . . . I should like very much to know if Kitty ever told Harvest. That was a most extraordinary thing. . . . Oh, women have meant a great deal to me. I grew tired of them, of course; but, really, what hypocrites those people are who want to make out that I was fickle. Not fickle; always constant to the *ideal*. I've been very attractive to women; less so to men. . . .

'Minna ran away. What, then; is there something repulsive in me? Honestly, candidly, I don't think there's anything anybody could object to. I know that at times I've been a little quick-tempered; and it's been said that I was unreliable. That was never true. Questions of policy. Politics. You know how it is, when . . .'

The mist cleared. Sir Harold Bingleton was still pounding away, and the jury yawning. Dick yawned, too, a little, slightly bewildered by his dream. He must have fallen asleep. . . .

He did not object to the warders, who were respectful to the last, and to whom he in turn was invariably polite. He did not object to the well-brushed jury, who looked typically bourgeois and bored. But he greatly disliked the small, avid audience in the public gallery, every member of which stared at him as if at a corpse or a cockfight, the devil! He disliked Sir Harold Bingleton, the Attorney-General, because Sir Harold, laboriously courteous otherwise, had said at one desperate point that Dick was not, in certain replies, doing himself justice. And his dislike of Mr Pooch surpassed all these other dislikes (but not his detestation of the Judge). What Mr Pooch was after, Dick could not imagine. Note after note, scribbled and despatched as inspirations and frantic explanations occurred to Dick, had been ignored. Every strong argument had been withheld; every weak one flirted with and set aside as if its worthlessness had all the time been recognised. Infuriating incompetence sat upon the fellow's brow. But hope died hard in Dick's mind.

It mingled there with indignation during the Judge's summing up. Dick watched that long nose, with the trembling and snuffing end, as if he would put a spell upon it. A nose like that passed over a sheet of paper as one of these new fangled suction sweepers might do. It was the veritable nose of Slawkenbergius. It trailed a fact as dogs trail a hare. It offended Dick more than any other feature could have done. He saw the Judge's shifty eyes glancing a little at himself and at the jury and at various odd spots about the Court. He saw the Judge's quivering hand rise up (as a match to the bowl of a churchwarden pipe) to dash away a dribble which as if upon some endless aqueduct of antiquity had crept resolutely to the end of the nose and twinkled there. And he felt sardonic superiority to everybody in the Court. They, pedestrian mediocrities, might collect facts; they might in obedience to the Law for groundlings sentence him; they would never be, as he was, Richard Firth, himself, an original, spirit-fixed man, incorrigible because incorruptible, and unpunishable because he lived alone in a state of superior virtue. Slaves to a system. Lickspittles. Groundlings. Fact-nibblers. He was above them all. . . .

They had brought him back into Court, and the verdict had sent its pain to his vitals, so that he felt them turn in one instant to water. Then Slawkenbergius spoke. Dick stared at him with a smile of contempt. Slawkenbergius! The man who, it was said, preferred boys to women; and thereby was less than man. Slawkenbergius was prating. Myah, myah, myah! The bore! Dick shook a reproving head at him; almost smiled. . . .

Five years, they said. Hell! It was worse than death. No sun, no wind, no life, no women. No women! Thank God he'd always been fastidious. It was going to be Hell. But Penter was all right; Dick was glad of that.

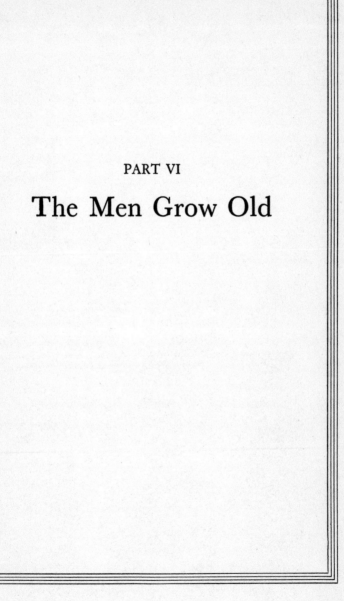

PART VI

The Men Grow Old

CHAPTER XXVI

What They Thought of Themselves

WILLIAM HARVEST entered the house in which he and Minna, their two sons, Mrs Harvest, and the now grown-up Rosie lived. It was in a curious short, wide turning off one of the roads running down towards the sea at Brighton; it was Georgian in date; it had only three neighbours (for the turning was a *cul-de-sac*); and once in every two years it needed to be painted from top to bottom. William had been in London all day; but when he went there he always caught the five o'clock return train from Victoria, which makes the journey in sixty minutes; and it was a little more than a quarter-past six as he hung up his hat in the warm hall. This was Thursday evening. He was finished with London for four days.

William was sixty, and he looked fifty-three. The passing of the years had greyed his hair and deepened the two lines from his nose to the corners of his mouth, but to those who loved him he was just what he had been as a boy and young man. A stranger might have passed him unnoticing, for William had no physical foibles, and he moved and dressed inconspicuously. But little boys and girls at Minna's convalescent home for children liked him at once, cats marked his legs as excellent rubbing-places and his hands as reliable strokers and ticklers, and as he walked along the Brighton Front dogs, who quickly read a heart, often inconveniently brought sticks or balls to be thrown in sport. Being by good fortune a happy man, he inspired others with confidence.

But if William was happy he was not self-satisfied. He entered the house on this particular January evening with an expression that was far from complacent, and when he found that his wife was still out—as he thought—he rather restlessly made his way to her small sitting-room and stood over a jig-saw puzzle which one or other of the children had begun to arrange upon a folding-table. He had, in the years of their happy marriage, learned so to depend upon Minna that it was as if his life had been completed. The work which filled his days in London produced a sufficient income for the modest needs of the household; what work he did outside 'The Candid Friend' was easy and congenial; and as far as his own future was concerned he had no qualms. He grew old gracefully. Indeed, he felt younger than he had ever done.

While William regarded the jig-saw puzzle, every piece of which looked as if it could not possibly have any relation to the other pieces, he heard the door behind him open; and he was joined by Minna. She, too, had matured without ageing. Nobody would have supposed that she had passed fifty. Her step was quick and her manner, although it was that of a sensitive and intelligent woman, escaped the false brightness to which so many of those who have the management of children are reduced by the nature of their occupation. This was as much because she was happy at home as because her former impulsiveness had yielded to the years. She smiled at the sight of William's intentness upon the jig-saw, and slipped her arm within his, just touching his shoulder with her cheek.

'The futility of this jig-saw,' murmured William, in her ear.

'The futility of everything,' she teased. 'You've come home a moralist.'

William looked into Minna's laughing face; there was no grey in her hair, and no loss of clearness in her eyes. He smiled quietly.

'It's a frightful opening,' he remarked. 'Do you expect me to draw a moral and say that life's a jig-saw? I won't do it. All the same, it's shocking to think what a lot of rubbish goes on in the world. I'm guilty of some of it, I suppose.' He clucked his tongue. 'I was just wondering if *this* piece goes *there*.' He picked up a piece of the jig-saw and fitted it into its proper place.

'Symbolic act,' sighed Minna.

William kissed her.

'Acceptance,' he answered. 'Not symbolic. Characteristic. Sometimes people use words without distinguishing between them. Character, personality, temperament; symbolic, typical——'

'Shut up!' cried Minna. 'Let's go out. There's just time before supper. Would you like to?'

They were out of doors within five minutes, and fighting with a stiff breeze. It was a clear, cold evening, starry and without moon; and the brilliant lights were doubly fine in the crisp air. But very few pedestrians were about at this hour, for a little determination was necessary to continue progress, and the wind was searching. The two walked arm in arm, not upon the promenade, but somewhat under the lee of tall buildings. White crests covered the visible sea; the sound of breakers and running shingle was carried to their ears; when Minna moistened her upper lip she tasted salt upon the tip of her tongue. The night was one for exultation.

'I thought we wouldn't go on the promenade,' she said, 'in case we met the Bing Boys.'

'Firth and Whistler? We shouldn't meet them. In any case they wouldn't recognise you.'

'Hm,' observed Minna. 'I wish they didn't live here.'

William laughed.

'I'm sorry for them,' he said.

'You're sorry for everybody except yourself,' answered Minna. She saw him smile; but he said nothing in reply. So she added: 'I'm sorry for them, too; but not with your sickening amiability.'

'I'll tell you what's the matter with me,' shouted William, against the wind. 'I'm futile.'

'Modest!' she cried. 'You could make mincement of both of them. Lazy.'

They argued no more about that. It did no good. But Minna had her own opinion. She had learned much about the psychology of men during the War, and much about the psychology of children since. If she had been able to think of William with detachment she might have made learned remarks about his 'case' which would have been almost certainly untrue. But she could not think of William with detachment. She loved him. Furthermore, being sure that he loved her, and depended upon her, she knew such triumph that in spite of her fifty-two years she gave a little skip.

'I've had a good day,' said she. 'Have you?'

'I've had a good *life*,' declared William. 'Today's only a day.'

'That jig-saw's working like a maggot in your brain,' said Minna.

The wind blew; the stars shone; the big lamps stretching ahead of them glistened brightly. Today had been a good day; all their days were good days; the sum of good days was happiness. But whether they were happy because they were fools, or because they shut their minds to the future, or because they loved each other, or because their digestions were good, or because they had enough money to buy food for themselves and to pay for the rearing of their children, or because they did not suffer from that envious discontent which in modern times is a recurrent source of self-righteous misery, it would be difficult to say. Perhaps love had most to do with it. Or modesty. Or goodwill. One must cultivate one's garden.

II

Robert Whistler, leaving Julie and their daughter still at tea, left home by the side door and began to battle with the wind. It was the evening after that walk and talk in which Will and Minna had engaged; and the wind was perhaps a little higher than it had been. Robert was glad to escape, and Julie was not sorry to see him go. Robert felt his dependent position very much; he had been humiliated, now, for ten years; and he felt in his bones that he was finished. Grumblingly so.

'I'm not well,' he thought, as he struggled to the sea. 'I'm not the man I was. On the dole.' That was his bitter way of phrasing it. 'Sick and tired of these rows. A French tart. That's all she is. All she ever was. I'm not well. I'm frightened about it. Not frightened; uneasy . . . Damned impudence to talk to me. Women are all alike. If you're on the up and up they insist on sharing—their rights. Think they've earned it. Some way. It's past me. But . . . damned French tart. If I'd got some money. If I'd got some money. Oh, it's humiliating. . . .'

He had reached the promenade, and he was forced to stand for a few moments looking out at the snowy sea. Clouds hung over it and made a terrible darkness at a mile's distance. His heart was beating. There was a twinge of pain in his stomach. It came of late more frequently. When that twinge came he was always alarmed. You didn't know what it was; and you were . . . call it nervous . . . of finding out. A black, searing twinge—at its worst. It made him feel sick, and sweat. They told you to see a doctor; but it wasn't so easy. Hold out as long as possible. 'I've been healthy all my life. Never anything . . .' Ah, but what he suspected . . . It was only indigestion. Nervous indigestion. Julie was indifferent.

Robert had lived down the shame of seeing Julie cited in the Firth case. In a sort of way he—not welcomed, not condoned; but . . . It blackened his view of Dick Firth. It gave him a release from Julie's sour-eyed reproaches. He'd felt it very much at the time. There had been a frightful row. He'd shouted. No good shouting. But it had brought the truth from her; the truth that she'd wanted Harvest all the time. Harvest, the half-sized simpleton; and he'd never guessed it. Perhaps she had lied to wound him? Black-hearted woman! She'd ruined his life. God! The twinge was repeated. It shook him. He felt he was being disembowelled. There must be something *there*. He must take another purge tonight. He couldn't stand this. He must walk.

So Robert walked, breathing hard, with wind driving him along and causing him to bend his great body backwards from the waist. That was better. He felt a different man.

Away from them both. On the dole. She'd got plenty. She was as stingy as a miser. French. Stingy. She made a bit out of the hat shop. Yes, and there was always enough for food and clothing for *them*. . . . Not for him. No clothes for him unless it was for a job, or a special occasion. No employment; his savings practically swallowed up by the case. And that swine Dick, whom he'd probably see again this evening. Well, he'd let him see he wasn't afraid. Despised the fellow. Why did she have to come *here* to set up her shop? Ridiculous!

The sea was rough; breakers booming. Before he got back the rain would probably be sheeting. Wind, rain, cold; and he felt ill. Nobody about. If he were to be taken ill, nobody would see him on a night like this. Found on a seat. Robert Whistler! What a life he'd had! Oh, God! The pain was back. It was wrenching his inside as if they'd discovered a new torture and were experimenting on him with it. Frightful, ghastly agony made it impossible for him to stand erect. He bent double, and staggered to the broad railing at the edge of the promenade. He could breathe only with extreme difficulty. The pain tore at his vitals. Not knowing what he was doing, Robert turned away from the sea and moved hastily to a seat which had protective glass windscreens; and in this partial shelter he crouched panting and sweating as fresh and ever-new gripings seized him. He was blind to the night. He thought only that he must be dying. A great groan passed his lips.

It was so violent that, as William Harvest crossed the King's Road from his home, he heard it through the strong bluster of the wind. Otherwise it is possible that he might not have seen Robert, but would have turned east or west, unconscious of the plight of his old fellow-townsman. But having heard this terrible cry, William was driven by very humanity to seek its cause. It was in this way that he found Robert half-unconscious upon the sheltered seat, and stopped, and addressed him. There was no reply beyond a further groan, and Robert's head sank lower and lower.

William would long ago have been Robert's good friend in need; and at their first encounter in Brighton he had advanced towards him with outstretched hand. But Robert had two grievances, first that he had failed, and second that Julie had made him believe that she had had William for a lover—perhaps, so wild is the suspicion of man, that William might after all be the father of Rachel—and Robert, seeing the friendly hand, had turned aside his head and stridden onward as if William had been a foe. The movement was involuntary; but having been made, it was not to be recalled. Thus it was that they had met and passed daily for so many years without speech. Now, however, Robert could not repel the aid of a well-wisher; and William, who might have left him in the belief that Robert was drunk, would not do so, but laid a hand upon the fallen shoulder.

'What is it?' William asked. 'Whistler! Are you ill?'

He could tell that Robert had not heard him. No such groan could come from one who was not in the greatest of physical pain. William case a glance around him; he could see nobody near.

Those black clouds had come closer. They hung over the sea and blotted it out. They rolled low over the land, ready at once to pour their contents in a deluge upon the town. No mere walkers were abroad here in the moment's blackness before storm. He and Robert were alone.

Something must instantly be done. The man might be dying. There would be a cab somewhere near if only he could find it; and with the aid of the driver——

Light steps came pattering by. A shadow was abreast of William. He caught sight of a ghostly figure, as black as the night, as unsubstantial——

'Firth!' he cried. 'Firth! Come here!'

The light figure did not stop. Dick Firth did not respond to cries for help. He did not . . . There was but one man in the world who could have persuaded him, as he did at this moment, to turn back, to come close, to survey the unconscious mass which lay like a bundle in the sheltered seat.

'This chap's dying, Firth,' cried William. 'Will you get a cab.'

'I . . . I don't think I will, my dear Harvest,' answered Dick. The old quiet, rather sneering voice. The old scepticism. They had not spoken for more than twenty years, and yet William felt a slight trembling of excitement run through his veins at the knowledge that men do not change. Dick said: 'Knowing what I do of our . . . our friend, I should say that he's probably drunk. A-and a sousing in that case will be ex-exceedingly salutary.'

'No, it's more than drunkenness,' insisted William. 'Besides, look at him. Sniff. I don't insist that you should come with us.'

'Oh, but I should like to do that—with you, Harvest,' sighed Dick. 'A-at any time. With the good Robert, no.' He paused. As invited, he sniffed. 'Yes, I think he's ill. I'll get that cab.'

He went. And as he went the clouds opened. Swift speary rain of an icy coldness drenched them all. William saw Dick begin to run. He ran through the rain with incredible speed, and was immediately lost in the darkness. And as William turned up the collar of Robert's coat, and, in a vague belief that this might avail, freed Robert's neck from the strangling grip of his tall white collar, his hands were wet as they would have been if he had dipped them in

the sea. A storm, with much more to come. What must be done?
He would take Robert to his own house close by; Sweet, a surgeon,
lived next door, and Will knew him to be able; and Minna was the
best nurse in the world.

A moment afterwards the cab was there, and Dick was back at
his side, accompanied by the driver. Between them, struggling
desperately, they dragged Robert to the road and into the cab; and
to William's surprise Dick took his place within, along with them,
as if, after these long years, his heart would not allow him to lose
the chance of renewed friendship. So much was true. In this way
the three men came to William's home.

III

Through a haze of sickness Robert recovered consciousness.
Shadows were still in his mind, lurking there like the continuing
vapour of the anæsthetic; and he cautiously groped his way back
into life as if he went upon tip-toe into a house of the dead. High
above he saw a distant white ceiling. The net curtains were like
criss-crossed wires, and a cause of alarm to one whose nightmares
were always of prison and confinement. Plain walls, a burning fire;
somewhere in his middle an endless smart. His slow hand fumbled
about his waist, which he could not reach. But that did not matter,
for he sank into sleep again and knew nothing more. Later—hours
later—he opened his eyes again; to see a white-clad figure.

'I must get up,' thought Robert, with a silent groan. 'Lying here.'

He did not move. Out of the misty brightness came a strange
face, the face of a woman.

'I don't know you,' remarked Robert, with a heavy tongue. The
tongue felt as if it were bruised and coated. They had shoved
something in his mouth, to keep the tongue still.

'P'raps not,' answered the nurse. 'But you soon will do. You're
doing very nicely.'

She raised his head and rearranged the pillows beneath it. Robert
stared at her. He felt that he might be sick at any moment.

'I'm not well, you know,' he felt it necessary to tell her. 'I feel awful.'

'You feel much better,' replied the nurse briskly. 'And you'll soon feel like a king.'

'Hm,' grunted Robert. He could not understand what she said. Something about a king. After a moment, still feeling a way through the baffling softness of his mind, he thickly demanded: 'What's the matter with me?'

'Well,' said the nurse. 'You've had your nasty murderous little appendix out.'

'Oh,' grumbled Robert. Appendix. He could not imagine what that was. It was a word he knew; but he could attach no meaning to it. Then: 'Where am I?'

'Well,' said the nurse, who was a youngish woman with a rosy, nun-like face, who prefaced most of her brisk remarks with this word, 'you're in a room in Mr Harvest's house. What's called the schoolroom.'

'Who's Mr Harvest? The schoolroom?' muttered Robert. His head fell sideways upon the pillow. He felt that he could not go on talking, like this. He did not want to talk. He needed rest. But this damned bright woman in the stiff white coif would insist . . . Who's Mr Harvest? Round and round groped his thoughts. He wondered if he had died. He felt very weak, as if the bed were a cloud. But that smarting in his belly . . . He again tried to reach the place, only to meet bandages once more.

Harvest. How that name kept on returning! Harvest. He had once known . . . He had known a man . . . There was something about Julie which he couldn't . . . Harvest . . . The main street at Moreton flickered before his eyes, in sunshine. Daddy Griffin's house. The passage beside it, along which the boys had run from school. He had pushed young Harvest's face against the wall, while Dick threw the kid's cap high over Daddy's wall. . . . Dick. Julie said she'd wanted Harvest. Is the kid mine? Can't trust anybody. . . . I will not have anything to do with it, Dick; and you know it. The ramp . . . It's a bloody ramp. Write him a letter; not my own name. But show I know what his game is. Frighten him. Did I write? I can't remember. Harvest in Trafalgar Square . . . Oh! Oh! I can't bear this pain. It makes me shriek. He heard his own groans. There were faces about him; unrecognisable faces. Then the dream of his mother; and coming in at night to find his father lying dead. She'd taken away his little boat that he'd been carving. It's not as if I get anything out of it! . . .

'It's not as if I get anything out of it!' gasped Robert.

The voice answering him was not that of the nurse. It was a man's voice.

'You'll get more now, my boy,' said the voice. 'Like a giant refreshed.'

Robert opened his eyes, and saw a man with grey hair and a broad mouth and very clear eyes standing by the bed and looking down at him. He thought it was another ghost.

'Harvest!' he exclaimed. The nurse's words came back at him like the slow cotton-wool effect of gun-smoke against a blue sky. In Mr Harvest's house. 'How on earth do you come to be here? What am I doing here?'

'I found you on the front; and Dick Firth and I brought you here. You had to have an operation; and now you'll live to be a hundred.'

A hundred. I found you . . .

'Dick Firth!' Robert's tongue seized upon that name before his mind had grasped it. 'He's a swine. I won't owe . . . I don't owe him . . .'

'He's been very decent. He helped you in; he brought the surgeon from next door; he's only just gone home; and he's coming back this evening, to see how you are. He got so soaked that we had to rig him out in some clothes, I can tell you.'

Robert could not take in what had been said to him.

'I can't understand it,' he muttered. 'You've always been a decent chap, Harvest. I've always felt you . . . No offence, of course; but not that you'd ever get anywhere . . . Julie thought that, too. You know what I mean—— Not get anywhere because—nothing the matter, but not much there, if you know what I mean. . . .'

'Oh, I've been lucky,' said William, smiling down at the stammerer.

'It's what I've *never* been,' Robert slowly answered. 'I've had everything against me all my life. However much I've tried—and I'm not a fool, you know, Harvest; I've got a good headpiece. I see things very clearly. . . .'

'You'll see things ten times as clearly when you wake up again,' William assured him. 'We've got Julie downstairs.'

A shock ran through Robert's body.

'I don't want to see her,' he urgently whispered. 'What's she doing?'

'Talking to my wife.'

Talking. Talking. That was a thing Robert knew he had never been good at. That fellow Harvest had made them laugh. Talking to a strange foreign girl. What was that? French, wasn't it?

'She's nothing but a French tart,' muttered Robert.

'You should look after her better,' said William. 'And you will do, too.'

The two of them exchanged a long glance, which was broken by the dropping of Robert's eyelids.

IV

Julie was saying to Minna:

'Me? I have had to do everything. To push my husband along is like trying to drive a pig to market. He will not go. It has been the same all our lives. He has been no good to me. You would not understand that, Mrs Harvest. Your life has been an easy one, as I can see from your expression. But with me it has been different. I am of the French *noblesse,* impoverished, but eternally proud. I was forced, as perhaps you recall, to take refuge, after many hardships, with that miser, Mr Griffin, in Moreton; where I worked my hands to the bone, never once thinking of myself, but only of that old man who lived on and on and on and on. . . .

'Mon dieu! How he lived! From day to day, and month to month. And then he died. But he had left me nothing. Not one penny. After all my years of work for him. I married Robert—not from love, but in despair, Mrs Harvest; for you will understand that my situation was precarious. But alas! I found that Robert's mother, from whom he inherits that characteristic, was of implacable enmity towards me. She was no woman, but a monster. She thought of nothing but money, money, money! It is the same with Robert; but though he thinks of it all the time it does not come to him. We were immediately in great difficulties, from which that awful man, Firth, seemed at first to extricate us. It was useless. I did all I could; I sacrificed myself again and again; but all was to no purpose. We were ruined. Mrs Harvest, we have *kept on* being ruined. Whenever Robert undertook anything, either he misman-aged it or he was cheated of his just rewards; and all the time he grew stupider and stupider, and . . . Mrs Harvest, he began heavily to drink. . . . What I have had to endure! It passes belief.

'Now I make and take all the money. I have my own shop, where I sell dresses and hats, and where if at any time . . . But you must not imagine . . . I go to Paris, leaving my daughter at home; and she, although she is, like her father, stupid, manages while I bring the new styles back and copy them and—on the whole, in spite of the struggle with this terrible poverty and this useless man who is unable to get work . . . Yes, Mrs Harvest; he is now unable to get work. After the great crash of his company of which you may recall something he was for two or three years able to work; but he was drinking so much that he always lost his positions. Out again. In again. Out again . . . And so at last I was forced to take command. I said: "This is what *I* shall do. *I* will manage a business." And so it has been, Mrs Harvest, while he——'

Julie shrugged and spread her hands. Minna, who had been up all night, yawned with fatigue, but did not flinch from the narra-tive, in which she found considerable interest. She said:

'It was very brave of you to take that decision.'

'Oh, yes,' sighed Julie, the corners of her lips down, and her nose finely drawn. 'I do not lack courage. It has been necessary to me.'

The nurse at that moment entered the room in which they were, to say that Robert had awakened and that he was comfortable. Mr Harvest was with him at the moment, she said.

'Thank you, nurse. You see? All will be well.' Minna turned smilingly to Julie. 'I'm sure of that.'

Julie rose. Minna saw in the morning light of this winter day the same woman whom she had seen all those years ago, as a girl, in the

High Street at Moreton. Her slimness had become a carefully regulated absence of flesh; but the face, from which the enchanting bloom alone had disappeared, was the same as it had been at that first meeting. It had then lacked animation when she spoke to Minna, but as soon as William responded it had risen to dangerous charm. How fast Minna's heart had beaten that day with jealousy! He had loved her. Young, engrossed, trembling love; not the passionate trust which had made their own marriage perfect. Minna, proudly, was no longer jealous, and would not be again.

'I may come back?' Julie asked, pleadingly.

'Whenever you like. Or would you prefer to stay now, and see your husband?' There was a brusquely shaken head. 'Come at any time. I may not be here in the mornings, because I spend a good deal of time at a Convalescent Home for Children——'

Julie leapt at that. Her eyes darkened and shone. She said:

'You have no children of your own?'

'I have two,' answered Minna, smiling again. 'With Rosie, three.'

She saw the curious expression pass again, with new meaning, over Julie's face. It was as if the thought came: 'They might have been mine!' Minna read it with all the cruelty of a candid mind. Julie breathlessly said:

'You have been happy, yes? You have never been unhappy?'

'Not since I was married.'

Julie sighed. Almost with unction, she whispered:

'Is it so indiscreet to say that William once loved me? Has he told you this?'

'I knew it many years ago, Mrs Whistler. I'm very grateful to you for not taking him.' 'Oh!' thought Minna. 'What a cat I am! And yet I didn't mean it so. Did she? I think not.'

'But he married,' continued Julie in the same maliciously confidential manner which did such injustice to her motive.

'He married one who was my friend. He was devoted to her until she died.'

'And you have *power* over him?'

'I never wished it. But he relies on me; and that makes me very proud.'

Minna saw the face before her grow haggard. She could tell now that it was a face of constantly varying expression, and thus, for a lover, full of beauties. But she had no fear. She had understood the truth of these statements and inquiries. They held no malice; only a kind of desperate curiosity which betrayed the stricken self-confidence of the disappointed woman before her.

Still with the unintentional patronage of an egoist, Julie exclaimed:

'You do not realise it, Mrs Harvest; but you are a very fortunate woman.'

'On the contrary, Mrs Whistler, I realise it very well,' answered Minna, laughing. 'And I always have done so. That's a part of the fortune, you know.'

'But *how* fortunate,' whispered Julie, not appreciating Minna's good fortune, and thinking only of her own lack of it.

'With incredulity,' insisted Minna. Her smile had faded. She looked with pity at Julie, and as she held the hand of her visitor she saw Julie's teeth bite the thin nether lip. Then she saw the dark head turned away, felt her hand convulsively pressed, and could not move quickly enough to overtake Robert's wife before she had opened the front door for herself. There was a parting glimpse only of tear-filled eyes, and then with bowed head Julie turned the corner and was lost to sight.

Having closed the door with caution, Minna went thoughtfully back to the room in which they had talked, and, without very clearly knowing what she did, poked the fire. She sat down again by herself, yawning. It had been a difficult emergency and a trying night, in which the experience gained in War-time had been called peremptorily and with excellent results into play. The surgeon, she knew, had done his work well, although he had turned a sour face upon Robert's flabbiness; and the surgeon had been pleased with her. Pleased with William, too. Most of all pleased with himself. A nasty job, but a job to his taste. They had telephoned for another nurse, and telephoned for Julie; while Dick and William, after much waiting and drying of clothes, had finally talked together by this very fire.

What the children would say at the seizure of their schoolroom, Minna did not know. She hoped they would be reasonable. Hoped:

didn't expect it. She would have to summon William to hypnotise them with his goodwill. He managed them better than she. Managed! Bamboozled, poor mites!

That poor woman! How envious. An incessant comparison of fortunes. 'It is not in our stars, but in ourselves.' For Julie, that would be blasphemy. But Minna . . .

William had come into the room now; and Minna knew that it would not do to let him suppose that she had been depressed by what had happened. Rear-guard explanations were no part of this household's solvent for happiness.

'Oh, you're alone,' William said. He strolled over to the fireplace; and Minna, without moving, looked up in middle-aged candour. 'I think Whistler will do. Sweet's been again. I thought you'd keep her.'

'She's coming back,' Minna explained. 'She preferred to go. She's unhappy, and she's got a shop of some sort.'

'Poor soul,' said William.

'Both,' answered Minna, in a disturbed voice. 'Both.'

'Oh, yes; he's just as poor. But *he* can be helped. Can she?'

Minna looked up at William. Could he remember, as clearly as she did, the first meeting with Julie? Did he not know that once, long ago, just as he had done, she had been made to suffer by his infatuation with Julie? That Julie still thought possessively of him? That somehow, in all her dreams, Julie believed that she would have been happy if only she had married him; and that Julie, imagining herself unchanged, had . . . Well, it was another link between them.

'I think if she can come here, and be made to forget herself——'

'She'll never forget herself,' William interrupted, with unexpected but characteristic perception. 'And neither will he. Do you know that as soon as he was conscious he had the cheek to tell me I was lucky?'

Minna laughed heartily, at memory, at William. She said, with an assumption of gravity:

'And are you?'

'That's another matter. What I object to is that he suggests I don't deserve my luck.'

'It's what you say yourself.'

'I know. I don't. But it rankles when somebody else says it.'

Minna dismissed Robert, who to her was just a man with a loud voice.

'He doesn't matter, anyhow.'

William did not contradict her. Instead, he went on:

'Firth's different. Even in anger, far or near, Firth's never under-rated me.'

Minna looked at him, smiling. But a kind of horror was mixed with her amusement at these signs in her husband of undiminished vanity. Firth. Dick Firth. Everybody had been in the house this night. Everybody. Where the carcase is, there the crows will gather. But was William the carcase? The lodestone, rather?

'But then Firth is a clever man,' she felt compelled to answer. 'A rogue; but he has taste.'

Something in William's loving glance, which was so cordial and protective and quizzical, caused Minna to jump to her feet and take two steps forward. His arms were about her, and they stood breast to breast, her hands lightly about his shoulders, and their eyes meeting very directly. Both were without disguise.

'How much do you know?' asked she. William thought for a moment.

'Everything,' he frankly but a little complacently answered.

Minna started.

'Liar,' she said. But she knew it was true. Then: 'How long?'

'Always,' answered William. They stood cheek to cheek.

'If I didn't love you I should be afraid of you,' Minna ruminated.

'In a burst of confidence,' responded William, 'I may say the same of you.'

With brimming eyes they both laughed in a sort of ecstasy of comprehension. Minna could feel the jerking of William's body. After a moment she demurely said:

'Julie thought *I* was lucky, too.'

It had its effect. William, with excellent mimicry, answered:

'Really. Did you deny it?'

'Only partially—William!'

Two middle-aged people, on a cold November morning, after a

night in which neither of them had slept. Their children, mercifully dozing in the rooms above, if they could have observed the scene would have found such sentiment entirely disgusting, and would have said so. But fortunately sentiment comes with age, and in age and solitude it may perhaps be excusable. Not that the Harvests would in any case have cared what their children said.

THE END